D1739860

TALES
OF THE FIVE TOWNS
BY ARNOLD BENNETT

THE GRIM SMILE OF THE
FIVE TOWNS
BY ARNOLD BENNETT

THE MATADOR
OF THE FIVE TOWNS
AND OTHER STORIES
BY ARNOLD BENNETT

Cover Illustration: © Timothy Large | Dreamstime.com

ISBN-13: 978-1477684160
ISBN-10: 1477684166
© verneysbooks 2012

**For
Tom Wordley**

TALES OF THE FIVE TOWNS

BY
ARNOLD BENNETT

CONTENTS

PART I
AT HOME
HIS WORSHIP THE GOOSEDRIVER
THE ELIXIR OF YOUTH
MARY WITH THE HIGH HAND
THE DOG
A FEUD
PHANTOM
TIDDY-FOL-LOL
THE IDIOT

PART II
ABROAD
THE HUNGARIAN RHAPSODY
THE SISTERS QITA
NOCTURNE AT THE MAJESTIC
CLARICE OF THE AUTUMN CONCERTS
A LETTER HOME

PART I
AT HOME

HIS WORSHIP THE GOOSEDRIVER

I

It was an amiable but deceitful afternoon in the third week of December. Snow fell heavily in the windows of confectioners' shops, and Father Christmas smiled in Keats's Bazaar the fawning smile of a myth who knows himself to be exploded; but beyond these and similar efforts to remedy the forgetfulness of a careless climate, there was no sign anywhere in the Five Towns, and especially in Bursley, of the immediate approach of the season of peace, goodwill, and gluttony on earth.

At the Tiger, next door to Keats's in the market-place, Mr. Josiah Topham Curtenty had put down his glass (the port was kept specially for him), and told his boon companion, Mr. Gordon, that he must be going. These two men had one powerful sentiment in common: they loved the same woman. Mr. Curtenty, aged twenty-six in heart, thirty-six in mind, and forty-six in looks, was fifty-six only in years. He was a rich man; he had made money as an earthenware manufacturer in the good old times before Satan was ingenious enough to invent German competition, American tariffs, and the price of coal; he was still making money with the aid of his son Harry, who now managed the works, but he never admitted that he was making it. No one has yet succeeded, and no one ever will succeed, in catching an earthenware manufacturer in the act of making money; he may confess with a sigh that he has performed the feat in the past, he may give utterance to a vague, preposterous hope that he will perform it again in the remote future, but as for surprising him in the very act, you would as easily surprise a hen laying an egg. Nowadays Mr. Curtenty, commercially secure, spent most of his energy in helping to shape and control the high destinies of the town. He was Deputy-Mayor, and Chairman of the General Purposes Committee of the Town Council; he was also a Guardian of the Poor, a Justice of the Peace, President of the Society for the Prosecution of Felons, a sidesman, an Oddfellow, and several other things that meant dining, shrewdness, and good-nature. He was a short, stiff, stout, red-faced man, jolly with the jollity that springs from a kind heart, a humorous disposition, a perfect digestion, and the respectful deference of one's bank-manager. Without being a member of the Browning Society, he held firmly to the belief that all's right with the world.

Mr. Gordon, who has but a sorry part in the drama, was a younger, quieter, less forceful person, rather shy; a municipal mediocrity, perhaps a little inflated that day by reason of his having been elected to the Chairmanship of the Gas and Lighting Committee.

Both men had sat on their committees at the Town Hall across the way that deceitful afternoon, and we see them now, after refreshment well earned and consumed, about to separate and sink into private life. But as they came out into the portico of the Tiger, the famous Calypso-like barmaid of the Tiger a hovering enchantment in the background, it occurred that a flock of geese were meditating, as geese will, in the middle of the road. The gooseherd, a shabby middle-aged man, looked as though he had recently lost the Battle of Marathon, and was asking himself whether the path of his retreat might not lie through the bar-parlour of the Tiger.

'Business pretty good?' Mr. Curtenty inquired of him cheerfully.

In the Five Towns business takes the place of weather as a topic of salutation.

'Business!' echoed the gooseherd.

In that one unassisted noun, scorning the aid of verb, adjective, or adverb, the gooseherd, by a masterpiece of profound and subtle emphasis, contrived to express the fact that he existed in a world of dead illusions, that he had become a convert to Schopenhauer, and that Mr. Curtenty's inapposite geniality was a final grievance to him.

'There ain't no business!' he added.

'Ah!' returned Mr. Curtenty, thoughtful: such an assertion of the entire absence of business was a reflection upon the town.

'Sithee!' said the gooseherd in ruthless accents, 'I druv these 'ere geese into this 'ere town this morning.' (Here he exaggerated the number of miles traversed.) 'Twelve geese and two gander—a Brent and a Barnacle. And how many is there now? How many?'

'Fourteen,' said Mr. Gordon, having counted; and Mr. Curtenty gazed at him in reproach, for that he, a Town Councillor, had thus mathematically demonstrated the commercial decadence of Bursley.

'Market overstocked, eh?' Mr. Curtenty suggested, throwing a side-glance at Callear the poulterer's close by, which was crammed with everything that flew, swam, or waddled.

'Call this a market?' said the gooseherd. 'I'st tak' my lot over to Hanbridge, wheer there *is* a bit doing, by all accounts.'

Now, Mr. Curtenty had not the least intention of buying those geese, but nothing could be better calculated to straighten the back of a Bursley man than a reference to the mercantile activity of Hanbridge, that Chicago of the Five Towns.

'How much for the lot?' he inquired.

In that moment he reflected upon his reputation; he knew that he was a cure, a card, a character; he knew that everyone would think it just like Jos Curtenty, the renowned Deputy-Mayor of Bursley, to stand on the steps of the Tiger and pretend to chaffer with a gooseherd for a flock of geese. His imagination caught the sound of an oft-repeated inquiry, 'Did ye hear about old Jos's latest—trying to buy them there geese?' and the appreciative laughter that would follow.

The gooseherd faced him in silence.

'Well,' said Mr. Curtenty again, his eyes twinkling, 'how much for the lot?'

The gooseherd gloomily and suspiciously named a sum.

Mr. Curtenty named a sum startlingly less, ending in sixpence.

'I'll tak' it,' said the gooseherd, in a tone that closed on the bargain like a vice.

The Deputy-Mayor perceived himself the owner of twelve geese and two ganders—one Brent, one Barnacle. It was a shock, but he sustained it. Involuntarily he looked at Mr. Gordon.

'How are you going to get 'em home, Curtenty?' asked Gordon, with coarse sarcasm; 'drive 'em?'

Nettled, Mr. Curtenty retorted:

'Now, then, Gas Gordon!'

The barmaid laughed aloud at this sobriquet, which that same evening was all over the town, and which has stuck ever since to the Chairman of the Gas and Lighting Committee. Mr. Gordon wished, and has never ceased to wish, either that he had been elected to some other committee, or that his name had begun with some other letter.

11

The gooseherd received the purchase-money like an affront, but when Mr. Curtenty, full of private mirth, said, 'Chuck us your stick in,' he give him the stick, and smiled under reservation. Jos Curtenty had no use for the geese; he could conceive no purpose which they might be made to serve, no smallest corner for them in his universe. Nevertheless, since he had rashly stumbled into a ditch, he determined to emerge from it grandly, impressively, magnificently. He instantaneously formed a plan by which he would snatch victory out of defeat. He would take Gordon's suggestion, and himself drive the geese up to his residence in Hillport, that lofty and aristocratic suburb. It would be an immense, an unparalleled farce; a wonder, a topic for years, the crown of his reputation as a card.

He announced his intention with that misleading sobriety and ordinariness of tone which it has been the foible of many great humorists to assume. Mr. Gordon lifted his head several times very quickly, as if to say, 'What next?' and then actually departed, which was a clear proof that the man had no imagination and no soul.

The gooseherd winked.

'You be rightly called "Curtenty," mester,' said he, and passed into the Tiger.

'That's the best joke I ever heard,' Jos said to himself 'I wonder whether he saw it.'

Then the procession of the geese and the Deputy-Mayor commenced. Now, it is not to be assumed that Mr. Curtenty was necessarily bound to look foolish in the driving of geese. He was no nincompoop. On the contrary, he was one of those men who, bringing common-sense and presence of mind to every action of their lives, do nothing badly, and always escape the ridiculous. He marshalled his geese with notable gumption, adopted towards them exactly the correct stress of persuasion, and presently he smiled to see them preceding him in the direction of Hillport. He looked neither to right nor left, but simply at his geese, and thus the quidnuncs of the market-place and the supporters of shop-fronts were unable to catch his eye. He tried to feel like a gooseherd; and such was his histrionic quality, his instinct for the dramatic, he *was* a gooseherd, despite his blue Melton overcoat, his hard felt hat with the flattened top, and that opulent-curving collar which was the secret despair of the young dandies of Hillport. He had the most natural air in the world. The geese were the victims of this imaginative effort of Mr. Curtenty's. They took him seriously as a gooseherd. These fourteen intelligences, each with an object in life, each bent on self-aggrandisement and the satisfaction of desires, began to follow the line of least resistance in regard to the superior intelligence unseen but felt behind them, feigning, as geese will, that it suited them so to submit, and that in reality they were still quite independent. But in the peculiar eye of the Barnacle gander, who was leading, an observer with sufficient fancy might have deciphered a mild revolt against this triumph of the absurd, the accidental, and the futile; a passive yet Promethean spiritual defiance of the supreme powers.

Mr. Curtenty got his fourteen intelligences safely across the top of St. Luke's Square, and gently urged them into the steep defile of Oldcastle Street. By this time rumour had passed in front of him and run off down side-streets like water let into an irrigation system. At every corner was a knot of people, at most windows a face. And the Deputy-Mayor never spoke nor smiled. The farce was enormous; the memory of it would survive revolutions and religions.

Halfway down Oldcastle Street the first disaster happened. Electric tramways had not then knitted the Five Towns in a network of steel; but the last word of civilization and refinement was about to be uttered, and a gang of men were making patterns with wires on the skyscape of Oldcastle Street. One of the wires, slipping from its temporary gripper, swirled with an extraordinary sound into the roadway, and writhed there in spirals. Several of Mr. Curtenty's geese were knocked down, and rose obviously annoyed; but the Barnacle gander fell with a clinging circle of wire round his muscular, glossy neck, and did not rise again. It was a violent, mysterious, agonizing, and sudden death for him, and must have confirmed his theories about the arbitrariness of things. The thirteen passed pitilessly on. Mr. Curtenty freed the gander from the coiling wire, and picked it up, but, finding it far too heavy to carry, he handed it to a Corporation road-sweeper.

'I'll send for it,' he said; 'wait here.'

These were the only words uttered by him during a memorable journey.

The second disaster was that the deceitful afternoon turned to rain—cold, cruel rain, persistent rain, full of sinister significance. Mr. Curtenty ruefully raised the velvet of his Melton. As he did so a brougham rolled into Oldcastle Street, a little in front of him, from the direction of St. Peter's Church, and vanished towards Hillport.

He knew the carriage; he had bought it and paid for it. Deep, far down, in his mind stirred the thought:

'I'm just the least bit glad she didn't see me.'

He had the suspicion, which recurs even to optimists, that happiness is after all a chimera.

The third disaster was that the sun set and darkness descended. Mr. Curtenty had, unfortunately, not reckoned with this diurnal phenomenon; he had not thought upon the undesirability of being under compulsion to drive geese by the sole illumination of gas-lamps lighted by Corporation gas.

After this disasters multiplied. Dark and the rain had transformed the farce into something else. It was five-thirty when at last he reached The Firs, and the garden of The Firs was filled with lamentable complainings of a remnant of geese. His man Pond met him with a stable-lantern.

'Damp, sir,' said Pond.

'Oh, nowt to speak of,' said Mr. Curtenty, and, taking off his hat, he shot the fluid contents of the brim into Pond's face. It was his way of dotting the 'i' of irony. 'Missis come in?'

'Yes, sir; I have but just rubbed the horse down.'

So far no reference to the surrounding geese, all forlorn in the heavy winter rain.

'I've gotten a two-three geese and one gander here for Christmas,' said Mr. Curtenty after a pause. To inferiors he always used the dialect.

'Yes, sir.'

'Turn 'em into th' orchard, as you call it.'

'Yes, sir.'

'They aren't all here. Thou mun put th' horse in the trap and fetch the rest thysen.'

'Yes, sir.'

'One's dead. A roadman's takkin' care on it in Oldcastle Street. He'll wait for thee. Give him sixpence.'

'Yes, sir.'

'There's another got into th' cut [canal].'

'Yes, sir.'

'There's another strayed on the railway-line—happen it's run over by this.'

'Yes, sir.'

'And one's making the best of her way to Oldcastle. I couldna coax her in here.'

'Yes, sir.'

'Collect 'em.'

'Yes, sir.'

Mr. Curtenty walked away towards the house.

'Mester!' Pond called after him, flashing the lantern.

'Well, lad?'

'There's no gander i' this lot.'

'Hast forgotten to count thysen?' Mr. Curtenty answered blithely from the shelter of the side-door.

But within himself he was a little crest-fallen to think that the surviving gander should have escaped his vigilance, even in the darkness. He had set out to drive the geese home, and he had driven them home, most of them. He had kept his temper, his dignity, his cheerfulness. He had got a bargain in geese. So much was indisputable ground for satisfaction. And yet the feeling of an anticlimax would not be dismissed. Upon the whole, his transit lacked glory. It had begun in splendour, but it had ended in discomfort and almost ignominy. Nevertheless, Mr. Curtenty's unconquerable soul asserted itself in a quite genuine and tuneful whistle as he entered the house.

The fate of the Brent gander was never ascertained.

II

The dining-room of The Firs was a spacious and inviting refectory, which owed nothing of its charm to William Morris, Regent Street, or the Arts and Crafts Society. Its triple aim, was richness, solidity, and comfort, but especially comfort; and this aim was achieved in new oak furniture of immovable firmness, in a Turkey carpet which swallowed up the feet like a feather bed, and in large oil-paintings, whose darkly-glinting frames were a guarantee of their excellence. On a winter's night, as now, the room was at its richest, solidest, most comfortable. The blue plush curtains were drawn on their stout brass rods across door and French window. Finest selected silkstone fizzed and flamed in a patent grate which had the extraordinary gift of radiating heat into the apartment instead of up the chimney. The shaded Welsbach lights of the chandelier cast a dazzling luminance on the tea-table of snow and silver, while leaving the pictures in a gloom so discreet that not Ruskin himself could have decided whether these were by Whistler or Peter Paul Rubens. On either side of the marble mantelpiece were two easy-chairs of an immense, incredible capacity, chairs of crimson plush for Titans, chairs softer than moss, more pliant than a loving heart, more enveloping than a caress. In one of these chairs, that to the left of the fireplace, Mr. Curtenty was accustomed to snore every Saturday and Sunday afternoon, and almost every evening. The other was usually empty, but to-night it was occupied by Mrs. Curtenty, the jewel of the casket. In the presence of her husband she always used a small rocking-chair of ebonized cane.

To glance at this short, slight, yet plump little creature as she reclined crosswise in the vast chair, leaving great spaces of the seat unfilled, was to think rapturously to one's self: *This is a woman*. Her fluffy head was such a dot against the back of the chair, the curve of her chubby ringed hand above the head was so adorable, her black eyes were so provocative, her slippered feet so wee—yes, and there was something so mysteriously thrilling about the fall of her skirt that you knew instantly her name was Clara, her temper both fiery and obstinate, and her personality distracting. You knew that she was one of those women of frail physique who can endure fatigues that would destroy a camel; one of those dæmonic women capable of doing without sleep for ten nights in order to nurse you; capable of dying and seeing you die rather than give way about the tint of a necktie; capable of laughter and tears simultaneously; capable of never being in the wrong except for the idle whim of so being. She had a big mouth and very wide nostrils, and her years were thirty-five. It was no matter; it would have been no matter had she been a hundred and thirty-five. In short....

Clara Curtenty wore tight-fitting black silk, with a long gold chain that descended from her neck nearly to her waist, and was looped up in the middle to an old-fashioned gold brooch. She was in mourning for a distant relative. Black pre-eminently suited her. Consequently her distant relatives died at frequent intervals.

The basalt clock on the mantelpiece trembled and burst into the song of six. Clara Curtenty rose swiftly from the easy-chair, and took her seat in front of the tea-tray. Almost at the same moment a neat black-and-white parlourmaid brought in teapot, copper kettle, and a silver-covered dish containing hot pikelets; then departed. Clara was alone again; not the same Clara now, but a personage demure, prim, precise, frightfully upright of back—a sort of impregnable stronghold—without doubt a Deputy-Mayoress.

At five past six Josiah Curtenty entered the room, radiant from a hot bath, and happy in dry clothes—a fine, if mature, figure of a man. His presence filled the whole room.

'Well, my chuck!' he said, and kissed her on the cheek.

She gazed at him with a look that might mean anything. Did she raise her cheek to his greeting, or was it fancy that she had endured, rather than accepted, his kiss? He was scarcely sure. And if she had endured instead of accepting the kiss, was her mood to be attributed to his lateness for tea, or to the fact that she was aware of the episode of the geese? He could not divine.

'Pikelets! Good!' he exclaimed, taking the cover off the dish.

This strong, successful, and dominant man adored his wife, and went in fear of her. She was his first love, but his second spouse. They had been married ten years. In those ten years they had quarrelled only five times, and she had changed the very colour of his life. Till his second marriage he had boasted that he belonged to the people and retained the habits of the people. Clara, though she also belonged to the people, very soon altered all that. Clara had a passion for the genteel. Like many warm-hearted, honest, clever, and otherwise sensible persons, Clara was a snob, but a charming little snob. She ordered him to forget that he belonged to the people. She refused to listen when he talked in the dialect. She made him dress with opulence, and even with tidiness; she made him buy a fashionable house and fill it with fine furniture; she made him buy a brougham in which her gentility could pay calls and do shopping (she shopped in Oldcastle, where a decrepit aristocracy of tradesmen sneered at Hanbridge's lack of style); she had her 'day'; she taught the servants to enter the reception-rooms without knocking; she took tea in bed in the morning, and tea in the afternoon in the drawing-room. She would have instituted dinner at seven, but she was a wise woman, and realized that too much tyranny often means revolution and the crumbling of-thrones; therefore the ancient plebeian custom of high tea at six was allowed to persist and continue.

She it was who had compelled Josiah (or bewitched, beguiled, coaxed and wheedled him), after a public refusal, to accept the unusual post of Deputy-Mayor. In two years' time he might count on being Mayor. Why, then, should Clara have been so anxious for this secondary dignity? Because, in that year of royal festival, Bursley, in common with many other boroughs, had had a fancy to choose a Mayor out of the House of Lords. The Earl of Chell, a magnate of the county, had consented to wear the mayoral chain and dispense the mayoral hospitalities on condition that he was provided with a deputy for daily use.

It was the idea of herself being deputy to the lovely, meddlesome, and arrogant Countess of Chell that had appealed to Clara.

The deputy of a Countess at length spoke.

'Will Harry be late at the works again to-night?' she asked in her colder, small-talk manner, which committed her to nothing, as Josiah well knew.

Her way of saying that word 'Harry' was inimitably significant. She gave it an air. She liked Harry, and she liked Harry's name, because it had a Kensingtonian sound. Harry, so accomplished in business, was also a dandy, and he was a dog. 'My stepson'—she loved to introduce him, so tall, manly, distinguished, and dandiacal. Harry, enriched by his own mother, belonged to a London club; he ran down to Llandudno for week-ends; and it was reported that he had been behind the scenes at the Alhambra. Clara felt for the word 'Harry' the unreasoning affection which most women lavish on 'George.'

'Like as not,' said Josiah. 'I haven't been to the works this afternoon.'

Another silence fell, and then Josiah, feeling himself unable to bear any further suspense as to his wife's real mood and temper, suddenly determined to tell her all about the geese, and know the worst. And precisely at the instant that he opened his mouth, the maid opened the door and announced:

'Mr. Duncalf wishes to see you at once, sir. He won't keep you a minute.'

'Ask him in here, Mary,' said the Deputy-Mayoress sweetly; 'and bring another cup and saucer.'

Mr. Duncalf was the Town Clerk of Bursley: legal, portly, dry, and a little shy.

'I won't stop, Curtenty. How d'ye do, Mrs. Curtenty? No, thanks, really——' But she, smiling, exquisitely gracious, flattered and smoothed him into a chair.

'Any interesting news, Mr. Duncalf?' she said, and added: 'But we're glad that *anything* should have brought you in.'

'Well,' said Duncalf, 'I've just had a letter by the afternoon post from Lord Chell.'

'Oh, the Earl! Indeed; how very interesting.'

'What's he after?' inquired Josiah cautiously.

'He says he's just been appointed Governor of East Australia—announcement 'll be in to-morrow's papers—and so he must regretfully resign the mayoralty. Says he'll pay the fine, but of course we shall have to remit that by special resolution of the Council.'

'Well, I'm damned!' Josiah exclaimed.

'Topham!' Mrs. Curtenty remonstrated, but with a delightful acquitting dimple. She never would call him Josiah, much less Jos. Topham came more easily to her lips, and sometimes Top.

'Your husband,' said Mr. Duncalf impressively to Clara, 'will, of course, have to step into the Mayor's shoes, and you'll have to fill the place of the Countess.' He paused, and added: 'And very well you'll do it, too—very well. Nobody better.'

The Town Clerk frankly admired Clara.

'Mr. Duncalf—Mr. Duncalf!' She raised a finger at him. 'You are the most shameless flatterer in the town.'

The flatterer was flattered. Having delivered the weighty news, he had leisure to savour his own importance as the bearer of it. He drank a cup of tea. Josiah was thoughtful, but Clara brimmed over with a fascinating loquacity. Then Mr. Duncalf said that he must really be going, and, having arranged with the Mayor-elect to call a special meeting of the Council at once, he did go, all the while wishing he had the enterprise to stay.

Josiah accompanied him to the front-door. The sky had now cleared.

'Thank ye for calling,' said the host.

'Oh, that's all right. Good-night, Curtenty. Got that goose out of the canal?'

So the story was all abroad!

Josiah returned to the dining-room, imperceptibly smiling. At the door the sight of his wife halted him. The face of that precious and adorable woman flamed out lightning and all menace and offence. Her louring eyes showed what a triumph of dissimulation she must have achieved in the presence of Mr. Duncalf, but now she could speak her mind.

19

'Yes, Topham!' she exploded, as though finishing an harangue. 'And on this day of all days you choose to drive geese in the public road behind my carriage!'

Jos was stupefied, annihilated.

'Did you see me, then, Clarry?'

He vainly tried to carry it off.

'Did I see you? Of course I saw you!'

She withered him up with the hot wind of scorn.

'Well,' he said foolishly, 'how was I to know that the Earl would resign just to-day?'

'How were you to———?'

Harry came in for his tea. He glanced from one to the other, discreet, silent. On the way home he had heard the tale of the geese in seven different forms. The Deputy-Mayor, so soon to be Mayor, walked out of the room.

'Pond has just come back, father,' said Harry; 'I drove up the hill with him.'

And as Josiah hesitated a moment in the hall, he heard Clara exclaim, 'Oh, Harry!'

'Damn!' he murmured.

III

The *Signal* of the following day contained the announcement which Mr. Duncalf had forecast; it also stated, on authority, that Mr. Josiah Curtenty would wear the mayoral chain of Bursley immediately, and added as its own private opinion that, in default of the Right Honourable the Earl of Chell and his Countess, no better 'civic heads' could have been found than Mr. Curtenty and his charming wife. So far the tone of the *Signal* was unimpeachable. But underneath all this was a sub-title, 'Amusing Exploit of the Mayor-elect,' followed by an amusing description of the procession of the geese, a description which concluded by referring to Mr. Curtenty as His Worship the Goosedriver.

Hanbridge, Knype, Longshaw, and Turnhill laughed heartily, and perhaps a little viciously, at this paragraph, but Bursley was annoyed by it. In print the affair did not look at all well. Bursley prided itself on possessing a unique dignity as the 'Mother of the Five Towns,' and to be presided over by a goosedriver, however humorous and hospitable he might be, did not consort with that dignity. A certain Mayor of Longshaw, years before, had driven a sow to market, and derived a tremendous advertisement therefrom, but Bursley had no wish to rival Longshaw in any particular. Bursley regarded Longshaw as the Inferno of the Five Towns. In Bursley you were bidden to go to Longshaw as you were bidden to go to ... Certain acute people in Hillport saw nothing but a paralyzing insult in the opinion of the *Signal* (first and foremost a Hanbridge organ), that Bursley could find no better civic head than Josiah Curtenty. At least three Aldermen and seven Councillors privately, and in the Tiger, disagreed with any such view of Bursley's capacity to find heads.

And underneath all this brooding dissatisfaction lurked the thought, as the alligator lurks in a muddy river, that 'the Earl wouldn't like it'—meaning the geese episode. It was generally felt that the Earl had been badly treated by Jos Curtenty. The town could not explain its sentiments—could not argue about them. They were not, in fact, capable of logical justification; but they were there, they violently existed. It would have been useless to point out that if the inimitable Jos had not been called to the mayoralty the episode of the geese would have passed as a gorgeous joke; that everyone had been vastly amused by it until that desolating issue of the *Signal* announced the Earl's retirement; that Jos Curtenty could not possibly have foreseen what was about to happen; and that, anyhow, goosedriving was less a crime than a social solecism, and less a social solecism than a brilliant eccentricity. Bursley was hurt, and logic is no balm for wounds.

Some may ask: If Bursley was offended, why did it not mark its sense of Josiah's failure to read the future by electing another Mayor? The answer is, that while all were agreed that his antic was inexcusable, all were equally agreed to pretend that it was a mere trifle of no importance; you cannot deprive a man of his prescriptive right for a mere trifle of no importance. Besides, nobody could be so foolish as to imagine that goosedriving, though reprehensible in a Mayor about to succeed an Earl, is an act of which official notice can be taken.

The most curious thing in the whole imbroglio is that Josiah Curtenty secretly agreed with his wife and the town. He wasashamed, overset. His procession of geese appeared to him in an entirely new light, and he had the strength of mind to admit to himself, 'I've made a fool of myself.'

Harry went to London for a week, and Josiah, under plea of his son's absence, spent eight hours a day at the works. The brougham remained in the coach-house.

The Town Council duly met in special conclave, and Josiah Topham Curtenty became Mayor of Bursley.

Shortly after Christmas it was announced that the Mayor and Mayoress had decided to give a New Year's treat to four hundred poor old people in the St. Luke's covered market. It was also spread about that this treat would eclipse and extinguish all previous treats of a similar nature, and that it might be accepted as some slight foretaste of the hospitality which the Mayor and Mayoress would dispense in that memorable year of royal festival. The treat was to occur on January 9, the Mayoress's birthday.

On January 7 Josiah happened to go home early. He was proceeding into the drawing-room without enthusiasm to greet his wife, when he heard voices within; and one voice was the voice of Gas Gordon.

Jos stood still. It has been mentioned that Gordon and the Mayor were in love with the same woman. The Mayor had easily captured her under the very guns of his not formidable rival, and he had always thereafter felt a kind of benevolent, good-humoured, contemptuous pity for Gordon—Gordon, whose life was a tragic blank; Gordon, who lived, a melancholy and defeated bachelor, with his mother and two unmarried sisters older than himself. That Gordon still worshipped at the shrine did not disturb him; on the contrary, it pleased him. Poor Gordon!

'But, really, Mrs. Curtenty,' Gordon was saying—'really, you know I—that—is—really—'

'To please me!' Mrs. Curtenty entreated, with a seductive charm that Jos felt even outside the door.

Then there was a pause.

'Very well,' said Gordon.

Mr. Curtenty tiptoed away and back into the street. He walked in the dark nearly to Oldcastle, and returned about six o'clock. But Clara said no word of Gordon's visit. She had scarcely spoken to Topham for three weeks.

The next morning, as Harry was departing to the works, Mrs. Curtenty followed the handsome youth into the hall.

'Harry,' she whispered, 'bring me two ten-pound notes this afternoon, will you, and say nothing to your father.'

IV

Gas Gordon was to be on the platform at the poor people's treat. As he walked down Trafalgar Road his eye caught a still-exposed fragment of a decayed bill on a hoarding. It referred to a meeting of the local branch of the Anti-Gambling League a year ago in the lecture-hall of the Wesleyan Chapel, and it said that Councillor Gordon would occupy the chair on that occasion. Mechanically Councillor Gordon stopped and tore the fragment away from the hoarding.

The treat, which took the form of a dinner, was an unqualified success; it surpassed all expectations. Even the diners themselves were satisfied—a rare thing at such affairs. Goose was a prominent item in the menu. After the repast the replete guests were entertained from the platform, the Mayor being, of course, in the chair. Harry sang 'In Old Madrid,' accompanied by his stepmother, with faultless expression. Mr. Duncalf astonished everybody with the famous North-Country recitation, 'The Patent Hair-brushing Mashane.' There were also a banjo solo, a skirt dance of discretion, and a campanological turn. At last, towards ten o'clock, Mr. Gordon, who had hitherto done nothing, rose in his place, amid good-natured cries of 'Gas!'

'I feel sure you will all agree with me,' he began, 'that this evening would not be complete without a vote of thanks—a very hearty vote of thanks—to our excellent host and chairman.'

Ear-splitting applause.

'I've got a little story to tell you,' he continued—'a story that up to this moment has been a close secret between his Worship the Mayor and myself.' His Worship looked up sharply at the speaker. 'You've heard about some geese, I reckon. (*Laughter.*) Well, you've not heard all, but I'm going to tell you. I can't keep it to myself any longer. You think his Worship drove those geese—I hope they're digesting well (*loud laughter*)—just for fun. He didn't. I was with him when he bought them, and I happened to say that goosedriving was a very difficult accomplishment.'

'Depends on the geese!' shouted a voice.

'Yes, it does,' Mr. Gordon admitted. 'Well, his Worship contradicted me, and we had a bit of an argument. I don't bet, as you know—at least, not often—but I don't mind confessing that I offered to bet him a sovereign he couldn't drive his geese half a mile. "Look here, Gordon," he said to me: "there's a lot of distress in the town just now—trade bad, and so on, and so on. I'll lay you a level ten pounds I drive these geese to Hillport myself, the loser to give the money to charity." "Done," I said. "Don't say anything about it," he says. "I won't," I says—but I am doing. (*Applause.*) I feel it my duty to say something about it. (*More applause.*) Well, I lost, as you all know. He drove 'em to Hillport. ('*Good old Jos!*') That's not all. The Mayor insisted on putting his own ten pounds to mine and making it twenty. Here are the two identical notes, his and mine.' Mr. Gordon waved the identical notes amid an uproar. 'We've decided that everyone who has dined here to-night shall receive a brand-new shilling. I see Mr. Septimus Lovatt from the bank there with a bag. He will attend to you as you go out. (*Wild outbreak and tumult of rapturous applause.*) And now three cheers for your Mayor—and Mayoress!'

It was colossal, the enthusiasm.

'*And* for Gas Gordon!' called several voices.

The cheers rose again in surging waves.

Everyone remarked that the Mayor, usually so imperturbable, was quite overcome—seemed as if he didn't know where to look.

Afterwards, as the occupants of the platform descended, Mr. Gordon glanced into the eyes of Mrs. Curtenty, and found there his exceeding reward. The mediocrity had blossomed out that evening into something new and strange. Liar, deliberate liar and self-accused gambler as he was, he felt that he had lived during that speech; he felt that it was the supreme moment of his life.

'What a perfectly wonderful man your husband is!' said Mrs. Duncalf to Mrs. Curtenty.

Clara turned to her husband with a sublime gesture of satisfaction. In the brougham, going home, she bewitched him with wifely endearments. She could afford to do so. The stigma of the geese episode was erased.

But the barmaid of the Tiger, as she let down her bright hair that night in the attic of the Tiger, said to herself, 'Well, of all the——' Just that.

THE ELIXIR OF YOUTH

It was Monday afternoon of Bursley Wakes—not our modern rectified festival, but the wild and naïve orgy of seventy years ago, the days of bear-baiting and of bull-baiting, from which latter phrase, they say, the town derives its name. In those times there was a town-bull, a sort of civic beast; and a certain notorious character kept a bear in his pantry. The 'beating' (baiting) occurred usually on Sunday mornings at six o'clock, with formidable hungry dogs; and little boys used to look forward eagerly to the day when they would be old enough to be permitted to attend. On Sunday afternoons colliers and potters, gathered round the jawbone of a whale which then stood as a natural curiosity on the waste space near the corn-mill, would discuss the fray, and make bets for next Sunday, while the exhausted dogs licked their wounds, or died. During the Wakes week bull and bear were baited at frequent intervals, according to popular demand, for thousands of sportsmen from neighbouring villages seized the opportunity of the fair to witness the fine beatings for which Bursley was famous throughout the country of the Five Towns. In that week the Wakes took possession of the town, which yielded itself with savage abandonment to all the frenzies of license. The public-houses remained continuously open night and day, and the barmen and barmaids never went to bed; every inn engaged special 'talent' in order to attract custom, and for a hundred hours the whole thronged town drank, drank, until the supply of coin of George IV., converging gradually into the coffers of a few persons, ceased to circulate. Towards the end of the Wakes, by way of a last ecstasy, the cockfighters would carry their birds, which had already fought and been called off, perhaps, half a dozen times, to the town-field (where the discreet 40 per cent. brewery now stands), and there match them to a finish. It was a spacious age.

On this Monday afternoon in June the less fervid activities of the Wakes were proceeding as usual in the market-place, overshadowed by the Town Hall—not the present stone structure with its gold angel, but a brick edifice built on an ashlar basement. Hobby-horses and revolving swing-boats, propelled, with admirable economy to the proprietors, by privileged boys who took their pay in an occasional ride, competed successfully with the skeleton man, the fat or bearded woman, and Aunt Sally. The long toy-tents, artfully

roofed with a tinted cloth which permitted only a soft, mellow light to illuminate the wares displayed, were crowded with jostling youth and full of the sound of whistles, 'squarkers,' and various pipes; and multitudes surrounded the gingerbread, nut, and savoury stalls which lined both sides of the roadway as far as Duck Bank. In front of the numerous boxing-booths experts of the 'fancy,' obviously out of condition, offered to fight all comers, and were not seldom well thrashed by impetuous champions of local fame. There were no photographic studios and no cocoanut-shies, for these things had not been thought of; and to us moderns the fair, despite its uncontrolled exuberance of revelry, would have seemed strangely quiet, since neither steam-organ nor hooter nor hurdy-gurdy was there to overwhelm the ear with crashing waves of gigantic sound. But if the special phenomena of a later day were missing from the carnival, others, as astonishing to us as the steam-organ would have been to those uncouth roisterers, were certainly present. Chief, perhaps, among these was the man who retailed the elixir of youth, the veritable *eau de jouvence*, to credulous drinkers at sixpence a bottle. This magician, whose dark mysterious face and glittering eyes indicated a strain of Romany blood, and whose accent proved that he had at any rate lived much in Yorkshire, had a small booth opposite the watch-house under the Town Hall. On a banner suspended in front of it was painted the legend:
THE INCA OF PERU'S
ELIXER OF YOUTH
SOLD HERE.
ETERNAL YOUTH FOR ALL.
DRINK THIS AND YOU WILL NEVER GROW OLD
AS SUPPLIED TO THE NOBILITY& GENTRY
SIXPENCE PER BOT.
WALK IN, WALK IN, &
CONSULT THE INCA OF PERU.

The Inca of Peru, dressed in black velveteens, with a brilliant scarf round his neck, stood at the door of his tent, holding an empty glass in one jewelled hand, and with the other twirling a long and silken moustache. Handsome, graceful, and thoroughly inured to the public gaze, he fronted a small circle of gapers like an actor adroit to make the best of himself, and his tongue wagged fast enough to wag a man's leg off. At a casual glance he might have been taken for thirty, but his age was fifty and more—if you could catch him in the morning before he had put the paint on.

'Ladies and gentlemen of Bursley, this enlightened and beautiful town which I am now visiting for the first time,' he began in a hard, metallic voice, employing again with the glib accuracy of a machine the exact phrases which he had been using all day, 'look at me— look well at me. How old do you think I am? How old do I seem? Twenty, my dear, do you say?' and he turned with practised insolence to a pot-girl in a red shawl who could not have uttered an audible word to save her soul, but who blushed and giggled with pleasure at this mark of attention. 'Ah! you flatter, fair maiden! I look more than twenty, but I think I may say that I do not look thirty. Does any lady or gentleman think I look thirty? No! As a matter of fact, I was twenty-nine years of age when, in South America, while exploring the ruins of the most ancient civilization of the world—of the world, ladies and gentlemen—I made my wonderful discovery, the Elixir of Youth!'

'What art blethering at, Licksy?' a drunken man called from the back of the crowd, and the nickname stuck to the great discoverer during the rest of the Wakes.

'That, ladies and gentlemen,' the Inca of Peru continued unperturbed, 'was—seventy-two years ago. I am now a hundred and one years old precisely, and as fresh as a kitten, all along of my marvellous elixir. Far older, for instance, than this good dame here.'

He pointed to an aged and wrinkled woman, in blue cotton and a white mutch, who was placidly smoking a short cutty. This creature, bowed and satiate with monotonous years, took the pipe from her indrawn lips, and asked in a weary, trembling falsetto:

'How many wives hast had?'

'Seventane,' the Inca retorted quickly, dropping at once into broad dialect, 'and now lone and lookin' to wed again. Wilt have me?'

'Nay,' replied the crone. 'I've buried four mysen, and no man o' mine shall bury me.'

There was a burst of laughter, amid which the Inca, taking the crowd archly into his confidence, remarked:

'I've never administered my elixir to any of my wives, ladies and gentlemen. You may blame me, but I freely confess the fact;' and he winked.

'Licksy! Licksy!' the drunken man idiotically chanted.

'And now,' the Inca proceeded, coming at length to the practical part of his ovation, 'see here!' With the rapidity of a conjurer he whipped from his pocket a small bottle, and held it up before the increasing audience. It contained a reddish fluid, which shone bright and rich in the sunlight. 'See here!' he cried magnificently, but he was destined to interruption.

A sudden cry arose of 'Black Jack! Black Jack! 'Tis him! He's caught!' And the Inca's crowd, together with all the other crowds filling the market-place, surged off eastward in a dense, struggling mass.

The cynosure of every eye was a springless clay-cart, which was being slowly driven past the newly-erected 'big house' of Enoch Wood, Esquire, towards the Town Hall. In this, cart were two constables, with their painted staves drawn, and between the constables sat a man securely chained—Black Jack of Moorthorne, the mining village which lies over the ridge a mile or so east of Bursley. The captive was a ferocious and splendid young Hercules, tall, with enormous limbs and hands and heavy black brows. He was dressed in his soiled working attire of a collier, the trousers strapped under the knees, and his feet shod in vast clogs. With open throat, small head, great jaws, and bold beady eyes, he looked what he was, the superb brute—the brute reckless of all save the instant satisfaction of his desires. He came of a family of colliers, the most debased class in a lawless district. Jack's father had been a colliery-serf, legally enslaved to his colliery, legally liable to be sold with the colliery as a chattel, and legally bound to bring up all his sons as colliers, until the Act of George III. put an end to this incredible survival from the customs of the Dark Ages. Black Jack was now a hero to the crowd, and knew it, for those vast clogs had kicked a woman to death on the previous day. She was a Moorthorne woman, not his wife, but his sweetheart, older than he; people said that she nagged him, and that he was tired of her. The murderer had hidden for a night, and then, defiantly, surrendered to the watch, and the watch were taking him to the watch-house in the ashlar basement of the Town Hall. The feeble horse between the shafts of the cart moved with difficulty through the press, and often the coloured staves of the constables came down thwack on the heads of heedless youth. At length the cart reached the space between the watch-house and the tent of the Inca of Peru, where it stopped while the constables unlocked a massive door; the prisoner remained proudly in the cart, accepting, with obvious delight, the tribute of cheers and jeers, hoots and shouts, from five thousand mouths.

The Inca of Peru stood at the door of his tent and surveyed Black Jack, who was not more than a few feet away from him.

'Have a glass of my elixir,' he said to the death-dealer; 'no one in this town needs it more than thee, by all accounts. Have a glass, and live for ever. Only sixpence.'

The man in the cart laughed aloud.

'I've nowt on me—not a farden,' he answered, in a strong grating voice.

At that moment a girl, half hidden by the cart, sprang forward, offering something in her outstretched palm to the Inca; but he, misunderstanding her intention, merely glanced with passing interest at her face, and returned his gaze to the prisoner.

'I'll give thee a glass, lad,' he said quickly, 'and then thou canst defy Jack Ketch.'

The crowd yelled with excitement, and the murderer held forth his great hand for the potion. Using every art to enhance the effect of this dramatic advertisement, the Inca of Peru raised his bottle on high, and said in a loud, impressive tone:

'This precious liquid has the property, possessed by no other liquid on earth, of frothing twice. I shall pour it into the glass, and it will froth. Black Jack will drink it, and after he has drunk it will froth again. Observe!'

He uncorked the bottle and filled the glass with the reddish fluid, which after a few seconds duly effervesced, to the vague wonder of the populace. The Inca held the glass till the froth had subsided, and then solemnly gave it to Black Jack.

'Drink!' commanded the Inca.

Black Jack took the draught at a gulp, and instantly flung the glass at the Inca's face. It missed him, however. There were signs of a fracas, but the door of the watch-house swung opportunely open, and Jack was dragged from the cart and hustled within. The crowd, with a crowd's fickleness, turned to other affairs.

That evening the ingenious Inca of Peru did good trade for several hours, but towards eleven o'clock the attraction of the public-houses and of a grand special combined bull and bear beating by moonlight in the large yard of the Cock Inn drew away the circle of his customers until there was none left. He retired inside the tent with several pounds in his pocket and a god's consciousness of having made immortal many of the sons and daughters of Adam.

As he was counting out his gains on the tub of eternal youth by the flicker of a dip, someone lifted the flap of the booth and stealthily entered. He sprang up, fearing robbery with violence, which was sufficiently common during the Wakes; but it was only the young girl who had stood behind the cart when he offered to Black Jack his priceless boon. The Inca had noticed her with increasing interest several times during the evening as she loitered restless near the door of the watch-house.

'What do you want?' he asked her, with the ingratiating affability of the rake who foresees everything.

'Give me a drink.'

'A drink of what, my dear?'

'Licksy.'

He raised the dip, and by its light examined her face. It was a kind of face which carries no provocative signal for nine men out of ten, but which will haunt the tenth: a child's face with a passionate woman's eyes burning and dying in it—black hair, black eyes, thin pale cheeks, equine nostrils, red lips, small ears, and the smallest chin conceivable. He smiled at her, pleased.

'Can you pay for it?' he said pleasantly.

The girl evidently belonged to the poorest class. Her shaggy, uncovered head, lean frame, torn gown, and bare feet, all spoke of hardship and neglect.

'I've a silver groat,' she answered, and closed her small fist tighter.

'A silver groat!' he exclaimed, rather astonished. 'Where did you get that from?'

'He give it me for a-fairing yesterday.'

'Who?'

'Him yonder'—she jerked her head back to indicate the watch-house—'Black Jack.'

'What for?'

'He kissed me,' she said boldly; 'I'm his sweetheart.'

'Eh!' The Inca paused a moment, startled. 'But he killed his sweetheart yesterday.'

'What! Meg!' the girl exclaimed with deep scorn. 'Her weren't his true sweetheart. Her druv him to it. Serve her well right! Owd Meg!'

'How old are you, my dear?'

'Don't know. But feyther said last Wakes I was fourtane. I mun keep young for Jack. He wunna have me if I'm owd.'

'But he'll be hanged, they say.'

She gave a short, satisfied laugh.

'Not now he's drunk Licksy—hangman won't get him. I heard a man say Jack 'd get off wi' twenty year for manslaughter, most like.'

'And you'll wait twenty years for him?'

'Yes,' she said; 'I'll meet him at prison gates. But I mun be young. Give me a drink o' Licksy.'

He drew the red draught in silence, and after it had effervesced offered it to her.

"Tis raight?' she questioned, taking the glass.

The Inca nodded, and, lifting the vessel, she opened her eager lips and became immortal. It was the first time in her life that she had drunk out of a glass, and it would be the last.

Struck dumb by the trusting joy in those profound eyes, the Inca took the empty glass from her trembling hand. Frail organism and prey of love! Passion had surprised her too young. Noon had come before the flower could open. She went out of the tent.

'Wench!' the Inca called after her, 'thy groat!'

She paid him and stood aimless for a second, and then started to cross the roadway. Simultaneously there was a rush and a roar from the Cock yard close by. The raging bull, dragging its ropes, and followed by a crowd of alarmed pursuers, dashed out. The girl was plain in the moonlight. Many others were abroad, but the bull seemed to see nothing but her, and, lowering his huge head, he charged with shut eyes and flung her over the Inca's booth.

'Thou's gotten thy wish: thou'rt young for ever!' the Inca of Peru, made a poet for an instant by this disaster, murmured to himself as he bent with the curious crowd over the corpse.

Black Jack was hanged.

Many years after all this Bursley built itself a new Town Hall (with a spire, and a gold angel on the top in the act of crowning the bailiwick with a gold crown), and began to think about getting up in the world.

31

MARY WITH THE HIGH HAND

In the front-bedroom of Edward Beechinor's small house in Trafalgar Road the two primary social forces of action and reaction—those forces which under a thousand names and disguises have alternately ruled the world since the invention of politics—were pitted against each other in a struggle rendered futile by the equality of the combatants. Edward Beechinor had his money, his superior age, and the possible advantage of being a dying man; Mark Beechinor had his youth and his devotion to an ideal. Near the window, aloof and apart, stood the strange, silent girl whose aroused individuality was to intervene with such effectiveness on behalf of one of the antagonists. It was early dusk on an autumn day.

'Tell me what it is you want, Edward,' said Mark quietly. 'Let us come to the point.'

'Ay,' said the sufferer, lifting his pale hand from the counterpane, 'I'll tell thee.'

He moistened his lips as if in preparation, and pushed back a tuft of sparse gray hair, damp with sweat.

The physical and moral contrast between these two brothers was complete. Edward was forty-nine, a small, thin, stunted man, with a look of narrow cunning, of petty shrewdness working without imagination. He had been clerk to Lawyer Ford for thirty-five years, and had also furtively practised for himself. During this period his mode of life had never varied, save once, and that only a year ago. At the age of fourteen he sat in a grimy room with an old man on one side of him, a copying-press on the other, and a law-stationer's almanac in front, and he earned half a crown a week. At the age of forty-eight he still sat in the same grimy room (of which the ceiling had meanwhile been whitened three times), with the same copying-press and the almanac of the same law-stationers, and he earned thirty shillings a week. But now he, Edward Beechinor, was the old man, and the indispensable lad of fourteen, who had once been himself, was another lad, perhaps thirtieth of the dynasty of office-boys. Throughout this interminable and sterile desert of time he had drawn the same deeds, issued the same writs, written the same letters, kept the same accounts, lied the same lies, and thought the same thoughts. He had learnt nothing except craft, and forgotten nothing except happiness. He had never married, never loved, never been a rake, nor deviated from respectability. He was a success because he had conceived an object, and by sheer persistence attained it. In the eyes of Bursley people he was a very decent fellow, a steady fellow, a confirmed bachelor, a close un, a knowing customer, a curmudgeon, an excellent clerk, a narrow-minded ass, a good Wesleyan, a thrifty individual, and an intelligent burgess—according to the point of view. The lifelong operation of rigorous habit had sunk him into a groove as deep as the canon of some American river. His ideas on every subject were eternally and immutably fixed, and, without being altogether aware of it, he was part of the solid foundation of England's greatness. In 1892, when the whole of the Five Towns was agitated by the great probate case of Wilbraham *v.* Wilbraham, in which Mr. Ford acted for the defendants, Beechinor, then aged forty-eight, was torn from his stool and sent out to Rio de Janeiro as part of a commission to take the evidence of an important witness who had declined all offers to come home.

The old clerk was full of pride and self-importance at being thus selected, but secretly he shrank from the journey, the mere idea of which filled him with vague apprehension and alarm. His nature had lost all its adaptability; he trembled like a young girl at the prospect of new experiences. On the return voyage the vessel was quarantined at Liverpool for a fortnight, and Beechinor had an attack of low fever. Eight months afterwards he was ill again. Beechinor went to bed for the last time, cursing Providence, Wilbraham *v.* Wilbraham, and Rio.

Mark Beechinor was thirty, just nineteen years younger than his brother. Tall, uncouth, big-boned, he had a rather ferocious and forbidding aspect; yet all women seemed to like him, despite the fact that he seldom could open his mouth to them. There must have been
something in his wild and liquid dark eyes which mutely appealed for their protective sympathy, something about him of shy and wistful romance that atoned for the huge awkwardness of this taciturn elephant. Mark was at present the manager of a small china manufactory at Longshaw, the farthest of the Five Towns in Staffordshire, and five miles from Bursley. He was an exceptionally clever potter, but he never made money. He had the dreamy temperament of the inventor. He was a man of ideas, the kind of man who is capable of forgetting that he has not had his dinner, and

who can live apparently content amid the grossest domestic neglect. He had once spoilt a hundred and fifty pounds' worth of ware by firing it in a new kiln of his own contrivance; it cost him three years of atrocious parsimony to pay for the ware and the building of the kiln. He was impulsively and recklessly charitable, and his Saturday afternoons and Sundays were chiefly devoted to the passionate propagandism of the theories of liberty, equality, and fraternity.

'Is it true as thou'rt for marrying Sammy Mellor's daughter over at Hanbridge?' Edward Beechinor asked, in the feeble, tremulous voice of one agonized by continual pain.

Among relatives and acquaintances he commonly spoke the Five Towns dialect, reserving the other English for official use.

Mark stood at the foot of the bed, leaning with his elbows on the brass rail. Like most men, he always felt extremely nervous and foolish in a sick-room, and the delicacy of this question, so bluntly put, added to his embarrassment. He looked round timidly in the direction of the girl at the window; her back was towards him.

'It's possible,' he replied. 'I haven't asked her yet.'

'Her'll have no money?'

'No.'

'Thou'lt want some brass to set up with. Look thee here, Mark: I made my will seven years ago i' thy favour.'

'Thank ye,' said Mark gratefully.

'But that,' the dying man continued with a frown—'that was afore thou'dst taken up with these socialistic doctrines o' thine. I've heard as thou'rt going to be th' secretary o' the Hanbridge Labour Church, as they call it.'

Hanbridge is the metropolis of the Five Towns, and its Labour Church is the most audacious and influential of all the local activities, half secret, but relentlessly determined, whose aim is to establish the new democratic heaven and the new democratic earth by means of a gradual and bloodless revolution. Edward Beechinor uttered its abhorred name with a bitter and scornful hatred characteristic of the Toryism of a man who, having climbed high up out of the crowd, fiercely resents any widening or smoothing of the difficult path which he himself has conquered.

'They've asked me to take the post,' Mark answered.

'What's the wages?' the older man asked, with exasperated sarcasm.

'Nothing.'

'Mark, lad,' the other said, softening, 'I'm worth seven hundred pounds and this freehold house. What dost think o' that?'

Even in that moment, with the world and its riches slipping away from his dying grasp, the contemplation of this great achievement of thrift filled Edward Beechinor with a sublime satisfaction. That sum of seven hundred pounds, which many men would dissipate in a single night, and forget the next morning that they had done so, seemed vast and almost incredible to him.

'I know you've always been very careful,' said Mark politely.

'Give up this old Labour Church'—again old Beechinor laid a withering emphasis on the phrase—'give up this Labour Church, and its all thine—house and all.'

Mark shook his head.

'Think twice,' the sick man ordered angrily. 'I tell thee thou'rt standing to lose every shilling.'

'I must manage without it, then.'

A silence fell.

Each brother was absolutely immovable in his decision, and the other knew it. Edward might have said: 'I am a dying man: give up this thing to oblige me.' And Mark could have pleaded: 'At such a moment I would do anything to oblige you—except this, and this I really can't do. Forgive me.' Such amenities would possibly have eased the cord which was about to snap; but the idea of regarding Edward's condition as a factor in the case did not suggest itself favourably to the grim Beechinor stock, so stern, harsh, and rude. The sick man wiped from his sunken features the sweat which continually gathered there. Then he turned upon his side with a grunt.

'Thou must fetch th' lawyer,' he said at length, 'for I'll cut thee off.'

It was a strange request—like ordering a condemned man to go out and search for his executioner; but Mark answered with perfect naturalness:

'Yes. Mr. Ford, I suppose?'

'Ford? No! Dost think I want *him* meddling i' my affairs? Go to young Baines up th' road. Tell him to come at once. He's sure to be at home, as it's Saturday night.'

'Very well.'

Mark turned to leave the room.

'And, young un, I've done with thee. Never pass my door again till thou know'st I'm i' my coffin. Understand?'

Mark hesitated a moment, and then went out, quietly closing the door. No sooner had he done so than the girl, hitherto so passive at the window, flew after him.

There are some women whose calm, enigmatic faces seem always to suggest the infinite. It is given to few to know them, so rare as they are, and their lives usually so withdrawn; but sometimes they pass in the street, or sit like sphinxes in the church or the theatre, and then the memory of their features, persistently recurring, troubles us for days. They are peculiar to no class, these women: you may find them in a print gown or in diamonds. Often they have thin, rather long lips and deep rounded chins; but it is the fine upward curve of the nostrils and the fall of the eyelids which most surely mark them. Their glances and their faint smiles are beneficent, yet with a subtle shade of half-malicious superiority. When they look at you from under those apparently fatigued eyelids, you feel that they have an inward and concealed existence far beyond the ordinary—that they are aware of many things which you can never know. It is as though their souls, during former incarnations, had trafficked with the secret forces of nature, and so acquired a mysterious and nameless quality above all the transient attributes of beauty, wit, and talent. They exist: that is enough; that is their genius. Whether they control, or are at the mercy of, those secret forces; whether they have in fact learnt, but may not speak, the true answer to the eternal Why; whether they are not perhaps a riddle even to their own simple selves: these are points which can never be decided.

Everyone who knew Mary Beechinor, in her cousin's home, or at chapel, or on Titus Price's earthenware manufactory, where she worked, said or thought that 'there was something about her ...' and left the phrase unachieved. She was twenty-five, and she had lived under the same roof with Edward Beechinor for seven years, since the sudden death of her parents. The arrangement then made was that Edward should keep her, while she conducted his household. She had insisted on permission to follow her own occupation, and in order that she might be at liberty to do so she personally paid eighteenpence a week to a little girl who came in to perform sundry necessary duties every day at noon. Mary Beechinor was a paintress by trade. As a class the paintresses of the Five Towns are somewhat similar to the more famous mill-girls of Lancashire and Yorkshire—fiercely independent by reason of good wages earned, loving finery and brilliant colours, loud-tongued and aggressive, perhaps, and for the rest neither more nor less kindly, passionate, faithful, than any other Saxon women anywhere. The paintresses, however, have some slight advantage over the mill-girls in the outward reticences of demeanour, due no doubt to the fact that their ancient craft demands a higher skill, and is pursued under more humane and tranquil conditions. Mary Beechinor worked in the 'band-and-line' department of the painting-shop at Price's. You may have observed the geometrical exactitude of the broad and thin coloured lines round the edges of a common cup and saucer, and speculated upon the means by which it was arrived at. A girl drew those lines, a girl with a hand as sure as Giotto's, and no better tools than a couple of brushes and a small revolving table called a whirler. Forty-eight hours a week Mary Beechinor sat before her whirler. Actuating the treadle, she placed a piece of ware on the flying disc, and with a single unerring flip of the finger pushed it precisely to the centre; then she held the full brush firmly against the ware, and in three seconds the band encircled it truly; another brush taken up, and the line below the band also stood complete. And this process was repeated, with miraculous swiftness, hour after hour, week after week, year after year. Mary could decorate over thirty dozen cups and saucers in a day, at three halfpence the dozen. 'Doesn't she ever do anything else?' some visitor might curiously inquire, whom Titus Price was showing over his ramshackle manufactory. 'No, always the same thing,' Titus would answer, made proud for the moment of this phenomenon of stupendous monotony. 'I wonder how she can stand it—she has a refined face,' the visitor might remark; and Mary Beechinor was left alone again. The idea that her work was monotonous probably never occurred to the girl. It was her work—as natural as sleep, or the knitting which she always did in the dinner-hour. The calm and silent regularity of it had become part of her, deepening her original quiescence, and setting its seal upon her inmost spirit. She was not in the fellowship of the other girls in the painting-shop. She seldom joined their more boisterous diversions, nor talked their talk, and she never manoeuvred for their men. But they liked her, and their attitude showed a certain respect, forced from them by they knew not what. The powers in the office spoke of Mary Beechinor as 'a very superior girl.'

She ran downstairs after Mark, and he waited in the narrow hall, where there was scarcely room for two people to pass. Mark looked at her inquiringly. Rather thin, and by no means tall, she seemed the merest morsel by his side. She was wearing her second-best crimson merino frock, partly to receive the doctor and partly because it was Saturday night; over this a plain bibless apron. Her cold gray eyes faintly sparkled in anger above the cheeks white with watching, and the dropped corners of her mouth showed a contemptuous indignation. Mary Beechinor was ominously roused from the accustomed calm of years. Yet Mark at first had no suspicion that she was disturbed. To him that pale and inviolate face, even while it cast a spell over him, gave no sign of the fires within.

She took him by the coat-sleeve and silently directed him into the gloomy little parlour crowded with mahogany and horsehair furniture, white antimacassars, wax flowers under glass, and ponderous gilt-clasped Bibles.

'It's a cruel shame!' she whispered, as though afraid of being overheard by the dying man upstairs.

'Do you think I ought to have given way?' he questioned, reddening.

'You mistake me,' she said quickly; and with a sudden movement she went up to him and put her hand on his shoulder. The caress, so innocent, unpremeditated, and instinctive, ran through him like a voltaic shock. These two were almost strangers; they had scarcely met till within the past week, Mark being seldom in Bursley. 'You mistake me—it is a shame of *him!* I'm fearfully angry.'

'Angry?' he repeated, astonished.

'Yes, angry.' She walked to the window, and, twitching at the blind-cord, gazed into the dim street. It was beginning to grow dark. 'Shall you fetch the lawyer? I shouldn't if I were you. I won't.'

'I must fetch him,' Mark said.

She turned round and admired him. 'What *will* he do with his precious money?' she murmured.

'Leave it to you, probably.'

'Not he. I wouldn't touch it—not now; it's yours by rights. Perhaps you don't know that when I came here it was distinctly understood I wasn't to expect anything under his will. Besides, I have my own money ... Oh dear! If he wasn't in such pain, wouldn't I talk to him—for the first and last time in my life!'

'You must please not say a word to him. I don't really want the money.'

'But you ought to have it. If he takes it away from you he's *unjust*.'

'What did the doctor say this afternoon?' asked Mark, wishing to change the subject.

'He said the crisis would come on Monday, and when it did Edward would be dead all in a minute. He said it would be just like taking prussic acid.'

'Not earlier than Monday?'

'He said he thought Monday.'

'Of course I shall take no notice of what Edward said to me—I shall call to-morrow morning—and stay. Perhaps he won't mind seeing me. And then you can tell me what happens to-night.'

'I'm sure I shall send that lawyer man about his business,' she threatened.

'Look here,' said Mark timorously as he was leaving the house, 'I've told you I don't want the money—I would give it away to some charity; but do you think I ought to pretend to yield, just to humour him, and let him die quiet and peaceful? I shouldn't like him to die hating——'

'Never—never!' she exclaimed.

'What have you and Mark been talking about?' asked Edward Beechinor apprehensively as Mary re-entered the bedroom.

'Nothing,' she replied with a grave and soothing kindliness of tone.

'Because, miss, if you think——'

'You must have your medicine now, Edward.'

But before giving the patient his medicine she peeped through the curtain and watched Mark's figure till it disappeared up the hill towards Bleakridge. He, on his part, walked with her image always in front of him. He thought hers was the strongest, most righteous soul he had ever encountered; it seemed as if she had a perfect passion for truth and justice. And a week ago he had deemed her a capable girl, certainly—but lackadaisical!

The clock had struck ten before Mr. Baines, the solicitor, knocked at the door. Mary hesitated, and then took him upstairs in silence while he suavely explained to her why he had been unable to come earlier. This lawyer was a young Scotsman who had descended upon the town from nowhere, bought a small decayed practice, and within two years had transformed it into a large and flourishing business by one of those feats of energy, audacity, and tact, combined, of which some Scotsmen seem to possess the secret.

'Here is Mr. Baines, Edward,' Mary said quietly; and then, having rearranged the sick man's pillow, she vanished out of the room and went into the kitchen.

The gas-jet there showed only a point of blue, but she did not turn it up. Dragging an old oak rush-seated rocking-chair near to the range, where a scrap of fire still glowed, she rocked herself gently in the darkness.

After about half an hour Mr. Baines's voice sounded at the head of the stairs:

'Miss Beechinor, will ye kindly step up? We shall want some asseestance.'

She obeyed, but not instantly.

In the bedroom Mr. Baines, a fountain-pen between his fine white teeth, was putting some coal on the fire. He stood up as she entered.

'Mr. Beechinor is about to make a new will,' he said, without removing the pen from his mouth, 'and ye will kindly witness it.'

The small room appeared to be full of Baines—he was so large and fleshy and assertive. The furniture, even the chest of drawers, was dwarfed into toy-furniture, and Beechinor, slight and shrunken-up, seemed like a cadaverous manikin in the bed.

'Now, Mr. Beechinor.' Dusting his hands, the lawyer took a newly-written document from the dressing-table, and, spreading it on the lid of a cardboard box, held it before the dying man. 'Here's the pen. There! I'll help ye to hold it.'

Beechinor clutched the pen. His wrinkled and yellow face, flushed in irregular patches as though the cheeks had been badly rouged, was covered with perspiration, and each difficult movement, even to the slightest lifting of the head, showed extreme exhaustion. He cast at Mary a long sinister glance of mistrust and apprehension.

'What is there in this will?'

Mr. Baines looked sharply up at the girl, who now stood at the side of the bed opposite him. Mechanically she smoothed the tumbled bed-clothes.

'That's nowt to do wi' thee, lass,' said Beechinor resentfully.

'It isn't necessary that a witness to a will should be aware of its contents,' said Baines. 'In fact, it's quite unusual.'

'I sign nothing in the dark,' she said, smiling. Through their half-closed lids her eyes glimmered at Baines.

'Ha! Legal caution acquired from your cousin, I presume.' Baines smiled at her. 'But let me assure ye, Miss Beechinor, this is a mere matter of form. A will must be signed in the presence of two witnesses, both present at the same time; and there's only yeself and me for it.'

Mary looked at the dying man, whose features were writhed in pain, and shook her head.

'Tell her,' he murmured with bitter despair, and sank down into the pillows, dropping the fountain-pen, which had left a stain of ink on the sheet before Baines could pick it up.

'Well, then, Miss Beechinor, if ye must know,' Baines began with sarcasm, 'the will is as follows: The testator—that's Mr. Beechinor—leaves twenty guineas to his brother Mark to show that he bears him no ill-will and forgives him. The rest of his estate is to be realized, and the proceeds given to the North Staffordshire Infirmary, to found a bed, which is to be called the Beechinor bed. If there is any surplus, it is to go to the Law Clerks' Provident Society. That is all.'

'I shall have nothing to do with it,' Mary said coldly.

'Young lady, we don't want ye to have anything to do with it. We only desire ye to witness the signature.'

'I won't witness the signature, and I won't see it signed.'

'Damn thee, Mary! thou'rt a wicked wench,' Beechinor whispered in hoarse, feeble tones. He saw himself robbed of the legitimate fruit of all those interminable years of toilsome thrift. This girl by a trick would prevent him from disposing of his own. He, Edward Beechinor, shrewd and wealthy, was being treated like a child. He was too weak to rave, but from his aggrieved and furious heart he piled silent curses on her. 'Go, fetch another witness,' he added to the lawyer.

'Wait a moment,' said Baines. 'Miss Beechinor, do ye mean to say that ye will cross the solemn wish of a dying man?'

'I mean to say I won't help a dying man to commit a crime.'

'A crime?'

'Yes,' she answered, 'a crime. Seven years ago Mr. Beechinor willed everything to his brother Mark, and Mark ought to have everything. Mark is his only brother—his only relation except me. And Edward knows it isn't me wants any of his money. North Staffordshire Infirmary indeed! It's a crime!... What business have*you*,' she went on to Edward Beechinor, 'to punish Mark just because his politics aren't——'

'That's beside the point,' the lawyer interrupted. 'A testator has a perfect right to leave his property as he chooses, without giving reasons. Now, Miss Beechinor, I must ask ye to be judeecious.'

Mary shut her lips.

'Her'll never do it. I tell thee, fetch another witness.'

The old man sprang up in a sort of frenzy as he uttered the words, and then fell back in a brief swoon.

Mary wiped his brow, and pushed away the wet and matted hair. Presently he opened his eyes, moaning. Mr. Baines folded up the will, put it in his pocket, and left the room with quick steps. Mary heard him open the front-door and then return to the foot of the stairs.

'Miss Beechinor,' he called, 'I'll speak with ye a moment.'

She went down.

'Do you mind coming into the kitchen?' she said, preceding him and turning up the gas; 'there's no light in the front-room.'

He leaned up against the high mantelpiece; his frock-coat hung to the level of the oven-knob. She had one hand on the white deal table. Between them a tortoiseshell cat purred on the red-tiled floor.

'Ye're doing a verra serious thing, Miss Beechinor. As Mr. Beechinor's solicitor, I should just like to be acquaint with the real reasons for this conduct.'

'I've told you.' She had a slightly quizzical look.

'Now, as to Mark,' the lawyer continued blandly, 'Mr. Beechinor explained the whole circumstances to me. Mark as good as defied his brother.'

'That's nothing to do with it.'

'By the way, it appears that Mark is practically engaged to be married. May I ask if the lady is yeself?'

She hesitated.

'If so,' he proceeded, 'I may tell ye informally that I admire the pluck of ye. But, nevertheless, that will has got to be executed.'

'The young lady is a Miss Mellor of Hanbridge.'

'I'm going to fetch my clerk,' he said shortly. 'I can see ye're an obstinate and unfathomable woman. I'll be back in half an hour.'

When he had departed she bolted the front-door top and bottom, and went upstairs to the dying man.

Nearly an hour elapsed before she heard a knock. Mr. Baines had had to arouse his clerk from sleep. Instead of going down to the front-door, Mary threw up the bedroom window and looked out. It was a mild but starless night. Trafalgar Road was silent save for the steam-car, which, with its load of revellers returning from Hanbridge—that centre of gaiety—slipped rumbling down the hill towards Bursley.

'What do you want—disturbing a respectable house at this time of night?' she called in a loud whisper when the car had passed. 'The door's bolted, and I can't come down. You must come in the morning.'

'Miss Beechinor, ye will let us in—I charge ye.'

'It's useless, Mr. Baines.'

'I'll break the door down. I'm a strong man, and a determined. Ye are carrying things too far.'

In another moment the two men heard the creak of the bolts. Mary stood before them, vaguely discernible, but a forbidding figure.

'If you must—come upstairs,' she said coldly.

'Stay here in the passage, Arthur,' said Mr. Baines; 'I'll call ye when I want ye;' and he followed Mary up the stairs.

Edward Beechinor lay on his back, and his sunken eyes stared glassily at the ceiling. The skin of his emaciated face, stretched tightly over the protruding bones, had lost all its crimson, and was green, white, yellow. The mouth was wide open. His drawn features wore a terribly sardonic look—a purely physical effect of the disease; but it seemed to the two spectators that this mean and disappointed slave of a miserly habit had by one superb imaginative effort realized the full vanity of all human wishes and pretensions.

'Ye can go; I shan't want ye,' said Mr. Baines, returning to the clerk.

The lawyer never spoke of that night's business. Why should he? To what end? Mark Beechinor, under the old will, inherited the seven hundred pounds and the house. Miss Mellor of Hanbridge is still Miss Mellor, her hand not having been formally sought. But Mark, secretary of the Labour Church, is married. Miss Mellor, with a quite pardonable air of tolerant superiority, refers to his wife as 'a strange, timid little creature—she couldn't say Bo to a goose.'

43

THE DOG

This is a scandalous story. It scandalized the best people in Bursley; some of them would wish it forgotten. But since I have begun to tell it I may as well finish. Moreover, like most tales whispered behind fans and across club-tables, it carries a high and valuable moral. The moral—I will let you have it at once—is that those who love in glass houses should pull down the blinds.

I

He had got his collar on safely; it bore his name—Ellis Carter. Strange name for a dog, perhaps; and perhaps it was even more strange that his collar should be white. But such dogs are not common dogs. He tied his necktie exquisitely; caressed his hair again with two brushes; curved his young moustache, and then assumed his waistcoat and his coat; the trousers had naturally preceded the collar. He beheld the suit in the glass, and saw that it was good. And it was not built in London, either. There are tailors in Bursley. And in particular there is the dog's tailor. Ask the dog's tailor, as the dog once did, whether he can really do as well as London, and he will smile on you with gentle pity; he will not stoop to utter the obvious Yes. He may casually inform you that, if he is not in London himself, the explanation is that he has reasons for preferring Bursley. He is the social equal of all his clients. He belongs to the dogs' club. He knows, and everybody knows, that he is a first-class tailor with a first-class connection, and no dog would dare to condescend to him. He is a great creative artist; the dogs who wear his clothes may be said to interpret his creations. Now, Ellis was a great interpretative artist, and the tailor recognised the fact. When the tailor met Ellis on Duck Bank greatly wearing a new suit, the scene was impressive. It was as though Elgar had stopped to hear Paderewski play 'Pomp and Circumstance' on the piano.

Ellis descended from his bedroom into the hall, took his straw hat, chose a stick, and went out into the portico of the new large house on the Hawkins, near Oldcastle. In the neighbourhood of the Five Towns no road is more august, more correct, more detached, more umbrageous, than the Hawkins. M.P.'s live there. It is the link between the aristocratic and antique aloofness of Oldcastle and the solid commercial prosperity of the Five Towns. Ellis adorned the portico. Young (a bare twenty-two), fair, handsome, smiling, graceful, well-built, perfectly groomed, he was an admirable and a characteristic specimen of the race of dogs which, with the modern growth of luxury and the Luxurious Spirit, has become so marked a phenomenon in the social development of the once barbarous Five Towns.

When old Jack Carter (reputed to be the best turner that Bursley ever produced) started a little potbank near St. Peter's Church in 1861—he was then forty, and had saved two hundred pounds—he little dreamt that the supreme and final result after forty years would be the dog. But so it was. Old Jack Carter had a son John Carter, who married at twenty-five and lived at first on twenty-five shillings a week, and enthusiastically continued the erection of the fortune which old Jack had begun. At thirty-three, after old Jack's death, John became a Town Councillor. At thirty-six he became Mayor and the father of Ellis, and the recipient of a silver cradle. Ellis was his wife's maiden name. At forty-two he built the finest earthenware manufactory in Bursley, down by the canal-side at Shawport. At fifty-two he had been everything that a man can be in the Five Towns—from County Councillor to President of the Society for the Prosecution of Felons. Then Ellis left school and came to the works to carry on the tradition, and his father suddenly discovered him. The truth was that John Carter had been so laudably busy with the affairs of his town and county that he had nearly forgotten his family. Ellis, in the process of achieving doghood, soon taught his father a thing or two. And John learnt. John could manage a public meeting, but he could not manage Ellis. Besides, there was plenty of money; and Ellis was so ingratiating, and had curly hair that somehow won sympathy. And, after all, Ellis was not such a duffer as all that at the works. John knew other people's sons who were worse. And Ellis could keep order in the paintresses' 'shops' as order had never been kept there before.

John sometimes wondered what old Jack would have said about Ellis and his friends, those handsome dogs, those fine dandies, who taught to the Five Towns the virtue of grace and of style and of dash, who went up to London—some of them even went to Paris—and brought back civilization to the Five Towns, who removed from the Five Towns the reproach of being uncouth and behind the times. Was the outcome of two generations of unremitting toil merely

45

Ellis? (Ellis had several pretty sisters, but they did not count.) John could only guess at what old Jack's attitude might have been towards Ellis—Ellis, who had his shirts made to measure. He knew exactly what was Ellis's attitude towards the ideals of old Jack, old Jack the class-leader, who wore clogs till he was thirty, and dined in his shirt-sleeves at one o'clock to the end of his life.

Ellis quitted the portico, ran down the winding garden-path, and jumped neatly and fearlessly on to an electric tramcar as it passed at the rate of fifteen miles an hour. The car was going to Hanbridge, and it was crowded with the joy of life; Ellis had to stand on the step. This was the Saturday before the first Monday in August, and therefore the formal opening of Knype Wakes, the most carnivalesque of all the carnivals which enliven the four seasons in the Five Towns. It is still called Knype Wakes, because once Knype overshadowed Hanbridge in importance; but its headquarters are now quite properly at Hanbridge, the hub, the centre, the Paris of the Five Towns—Hanbridge, the county borough of sixty odd thousand inhabitants. It is the festival of the masses that old Jack sprang from, and every genteel person who can leaves the Five Towns for the seaside at the end of July. Nevertheless, the district is never more crammed than at Knype Wakes. And, of course, genteel persons, whom circumstances have forced to remain in the Five Towns, sally out in the evening to 'do' the Wakes in a spirit of tolerant condescension. Ellis was in this case. His parents and sisters were at Llandudno, and he had been left in charge of the works and of the new house. He was always free; he could always pity the bondage of his sisters; but now he was more free than ever—he was absolutely free. Imagine the delicious feeling that surged in his heart as he prepared to plunge himself doggishly into the wild ocean of the Wakes. By the way, in that heart was the image of a girl.

II

He stepped off the car on the outskirts of Hanbridge, and strolled gently and spectacularly into the joyous town. The streets became more and more crowded and noisy as he approached the market-place, and in Crown Square tramcars from the four quarters of the earth discharged tramloads of humanity at the rate of two a minute, and then glided off again empty in search of more humanity. The lower portion of Crown Square was devoted to tramlines; in the upper portion the Wakes began, and spread into the market-place, and thence by many tentacles into all manner of streets.

No Wakes is better than Knype Wakes; that is to say, no Wakes is more ear-splitting, more terrific, more dizzying, or more impassable. When you go to Knype Wakes you get stuck in the midst of an enormous crowd, and you see roundabouts, swings, switchbacks, myrioramas, atrocity booths, quack dentists, shooting-galleries, cocoanut-shies, and bazaars, all around you. Every establishment is jewelled, gilded, and electrically lighted; every establishment has an orchestra, most often played by steam and conducted by a stoker; every establishment has a steam—whistle, which shrieks at the beginning and at the end of each round or performance. You stand fixed in the multitude listening to a thousand orchestras and whistles, with the roar of machinery and the merry din of car-bells, and the popping of rifles for a background of noise. Your eyes are charmed by the whirling of a million lights and the mad whirling of millions of beautiful girls and happy youths under the lights. For the roundabouts rule the scene; the roundabouts take the money. The supreme desire of the revellers is to describe circles, either on horseback or in yachts, either simple circles or complex circles, either up and down or straight along, but always circles. And it is as though inventors had sat up at nights puzzling their brains how best to make revellers seasick while keeping them equidistant from a steam-orchestra.... Then the crowd solidly lurches, and you find yourself up against a dentist, or a firm of wrestlers, or a roundabout, or an ice-cream refectory, and you take what comes. You have begun to 'do' the Wakes. The splendid insanity seizes you. The lights, the colours, the explosions, the shrieks, the feathered hats, the pretty faces as they fly past, the gilding, the statuary, the August night, and the mingling of a thousand melodies in a counterpoint beyond the dreams of Wagner—these things have stirred the sap of life in you, have shown you how fine it is to be alive, and, careless and free, have caught up your spirit into a heaven from which you scornfully survey the year of daily toil between one Wakes and another as the eagle scornfully surveys the potato-field. Your nostrils dilate—nay, matters reach such a pass that, even if you are genteel, you forget to condescend.

III

After Ellis had had the correct drink in the private bar up the passage at the Turk's Head, and after he had plunged into the crowd and got lost in it, and submitted good-humouredly to the frequent ordeal of the penny squirt as administered by adorable creatures in bright skirts, he found himself cast up by the human ocean on the macadam shore near a shooting-gallery. This was no ordinary shooting-gallery. It was one of Jenkins's affairs (Jenkins of Manchester), and on either side of it Jenkins's Venetian gondalas and Jenkins's Mexican mustangs were whizzing round two of Jenkins's orchestras at twopence a time, and taking thirty-two pounds an hour. This gallery was very different from the old galleries, in which you leaned against a brass bar and shot up a kind of a drain. This gallery was a large and brilliant room, with the front-wall taken out. It was hung with mirrors and cretonnes, it was richly carpeted, and, of course, it was lighted by electricity. Carved and gilded tables bore a whole armoury of weapons. You shot at tobacco-pipes, twisting and stationary, at balls poised on jets of water, and at proper targets. In the corners of the saloon, near the open, were large crimson plush lounges, on which you lounged after the fatigue of shooting.

A pink-clad girl, young and radiant, had the concern in charge.

She was speeding a party of bankrupt shooters, when she caught sight of Ellis. Ellis answered her smile, and strolled up to the booth with a countenance that might have meant anything. You can never tell what a dog is thinking.

"'Ello!' said the girl prettily (or, rather, she shouted prettily, having to compete with the two orchestras). 'You here again?'

The truth was that Ellis had been there on the previous night, when the Wakes was only half opened, and he had come again to-night expressly in order to see her; but he would not have admitted, even to himself, that he had come expressly in order to see her; in his mind it was just a chance that he might see her. She was a jolly girl. (We are gradually approaching the scandalous part.)

'What a jolly frock!' he said, when he had shot five celluloid balls in succession off a jet of water.

Smiling, she mechanically took a ball out of the basket and let it roll down the conduit to the fountain.

'Do you think so?' she replied, smoothing the fluffy muslin apron with her small hands, black from contact with the guns. 'That one I wore last night was my second-best. I only wear this on Saturdays and Mondays.'

He nodded like a connoisseur. The sixth ball had sprung up to the top of the jet. He removed it with the certainty of a King's Prize winner, and she complimented him.

'Ah!' he said, 'you should have seen me before I took to smoking and drinking!'

She laughed freely. She was always showing her fine teeth. And she had such a frank, jolly countenance, not exactly pretty—better than pretty. She was a little short and a little plump, and she wore a necklace round her neck, a ring on her dainty, dirty finger, and a watch-bracelet on her wrist.

'Why!' she exclaimed. 'How old are you?'

'How old are *you*?' he retorted.

Dogs do not give things away like that.

'I'm nineteen,' she said submissively. 'At least, I shall be come Martinmas.'

And she yawned.

'Well,' he said, 'a little girl like you ought to be in bed.'

'Sunday to-morrow,' she observed.

'Aren't you glad you're English?' he remarked. 'If you were in Paris you'd have to work Sundays too.'

'Not me!' she said. 'Who told you that? Have you been to Paris?'

'No,' he admitted cautiously; 'but a friend of mine has, and he told me. He came back only last week, and he says they keep open Sundays, and all night sometimes. Sunday is the great day over there.'

'Well,' said the girl kindly, 'don't you believe it. The police wouldn't allow it. I know what the police are.'

More shooters entered the saloon. Ellis had finished his dozen; he sank into a lounge, and elegantly lighted a cigarette, and watched her serve the other marksmen. She was decidedly charming, and so jolly—with him. He noticed with satisfaction that with the other marksmen she showed a certain high reserve.

They did not stay long, and when they were gone she came across to the lounge and gazed at him provocatively.

'Dashed if she hasn't taken a fancy to me!'

The thought ran through him like lightning.

49

'Well?' she said.

'What do you do with yourself Sundays?' he asked her.

'Oh, sleep.'

'All day?'

'All morning.'

'What do you do in the afternoon?'

'Oh, nothing.'

She laughed gaily.

'Come out with me, eh?'

'To-morrow? Oh, I should LOVE TO!' she cried.

Her voice expanded into large capitals because by a singular chance both the neighbouring orchestras stopped momentarily together, and thus gave her shout a fair field. The effect was startling. It startled Ellis. He had not for an instant expected that she would consent. Never, dog though he was, had he armed a girl out on any afternoon, to say nothing of Sunday afternoon, and Knype's Wakes Sunday at that! He had talked about girls at the club. He understood the theory. But the practice——

The foundation of England's greatness is that Englishmen hate to look fools. The fear of being taken for a ninny will spur an Englishman to the most surprising deeds of courage. Ellis said 'Good!' with apparent enthusiasm, and arranged to be waiting for her at half-past two at the Turk's Head. Then he left the saloon and struck out anew into the ocean. He wanted to think it over.

Once, painful to relate, he had thoughts of failing to keep the appointment. However, she was so jolly and frank. And what a fancy she must have taken to him! No, he would see it through.

IV

If anybody had prophesied to Ellis that he would be driving out a Wakes girl in a dogcart that Sunday afternoon he would have laughed at the prophet; but so it occurred. He arrived at the Turk's Head at two twenty-five. She was there before him, dressed all in blue, except the white shoes and stockings, weighing herself on the machine in the yard. She showed her teeth, told him she weighed nine stone one, and abruptly asked him if he could drive. He said he could. She clapped her hands and sprang off the machine. Her father had bought a new mare the day before, and it was in the Turk's Head stable, and the yardman said it wanted exercise, and there was a dogcart and harness idling about, and, in short, Ellis should drive her to Sneyd Park, which she had long desired to see.

Ellis wished to ask questions, but the moment did not seem auspicious.

In a few minutes the new mare, a high and somewhat frisky bay, with big shoulders, was in the shafts of a high, green dogcart. When asked if he could drive, Ellis ought to have answered: 'That depends—on the horse.' Many men can tool a fifteen-year-old screw down a country lane who would hesitate to get up behind a five-year-old animal (in need of exercise) for a spin down Broad Street, Hanbridge, on Knype Wakes Sunday. Ellis could drive; he could just drive. His father had always steadfastly refused to keep horses, but the fathers of other dogs were more progressive, and Ellis had had opportunities. He knew how to take the reins, and get up, and give the office; indeed, he had read a handbook on the subject. So he rook the reins and got up, and the Wakes girl got up.

He chirruped. The mare merely backed.

'Give 'er 'er mouth,' said the yardman disgustedly.

'Oh!' said Ellis, and slackened the reins, and the mare pawed forward.

Then he had to turn her in the yard, and get her and the dogcart down the passage. He doubted whether he should do it, for the passage seemed a size too small. However, he did it, or the mare did it, and the entire organism swerved across a portion of the footpath into Broad Street.

For quite a quarter of a mile down Broad Street Ellis blushed, and kept his gaze between the mare's ears. However, the mare went beautifully. You could have driven her with a silken thread, so it seemed. And then the dog, growing accustomed to his prominence up there on the dogcart, began to be a bit doggy. He knew the little thing's age and weight, but, really, when you take a girl out for a Sunday spin you want more information about her than that. Her asked her name, and her name was Jenkins—Ada. She was the great Jenkins's daughter.

('Oh,' thought Ellis, 'the deuce you are!')

'Father's gone to Manchester for the day, and aunt's looking after me,' said Ada.

'Do they know you've come out—like this?'

'Not much!' She laughed deliciously. 'How lovely it is!'

At Knype they drew up before the Five Towns Hotel and descended. The Five Towns Hotel is the greatest hotel in North Staffordshire. It has two hundred rooms. It would not entirely disgrace Northumberland Avenue. In the Five Towns it is august, imposing, and unique. They had a lemonade there, and proceeded. A clock struck; it was a near thing. No more refreshments now until they had passed the three-mile limit!

Yes! Not two hundred yards further on she spied an ice-cream shop in Fleet Road, and Ellis learnt that she adored ice-cream. The mare waited patiently outside in the thronged street.

After that the pilgrimage to Sneyd was punctuated with ice-creams. At the Stag at Sneyd (where, among ninety-and-nine dogcarts, Ellis's dogcart was the brightest green of them all) Ada had another lemonade, and Ellis had something else. They saw the Park, and Ada giggled charmingly her appreciation of its beauty. The conversation throughout consisted chiefly of Ada's teeth. Ellis said he would return by a different route, and he managed to get lost. How anyone driving to Hanbridge from Sneyd could arrive at the mining village of Silverton is a mystery. But Ellis arrived there, and he ultimately came out at Hillport, the aristocratic suburb of Bursley, where he had always lived till the last year. He feared recognition there, and his fear was justified. Some silly ass, a schoolmate, cried, 'Go it!' as the machine bowled along, and the mischief was that the mare, startled, went it. She went it down the curving hill, and the vehicle after her, like a kettle tied to a dog's tail.

Ellis winked stoutly at Ada when they reached the bottom, and gave the mare a piece of his mind, to which she objected. As they crossed the railway-bridge a goods-train ran underneath and puffed smoke into the mare's eyes. She set her ears back.

'Would you!' cried Ellis authoritatively, and touched her with the whip (he had forgotten the handbook).

He scarcely touched her, but you never know where you are with any horse. That mare, which had been a mirror of all the virtues all the afternoon, was off like a rocket. She overtook an electric car as if it had been standing still. Ellis sawed her mouth; he might as well have sawed the funnel of a locomotive. He had meant to turn off and traverse Bursley by secluded streets, but he perceived that safety lay solely in letting her go straight ahead up the very steep slope of Oldcastle Street into the middle of the town. It would be an amazing mare that galloped to the top of Oldcastle Street! She galloped nearly to the top, and then Ellis began to get hold of her a bit.

'Don't be afraid,' he said masculinely to Ada.

And, conscious of victory, he jerked the mare to the left to avoid an approaching car....

The next instant they were anchored against the roots of a lamp-post. When Ellis saw the upper half of the lamp-post bent down at right angles, and pieces of glass covering the pavement, he could not believe that he and his dogcart had done that, especially as neither the mare, nor the dogcart, nor its freight, was damaged. The machine was merely jammed, and the mare, satisfied, stood quiet, breathing rapidly.

But Ada Jenkins was crying.

And the car stopped a moment to observe. And then a number of chapel-goers on their way to the Sytch Chapel, which the Carter family still faithfully attended, joined the scene; and then a policeman.

Ellis sat like a stuck pig in the dogcart. He knew that speech was demanded of him, but he did not know where to begin.

The worst thing of all was the lamp-post, bent, moveless, unnatural, atrociously comic, accusing him.

The affair was over the town in a minute; the next morning it reached Llandudno. Ellis Carter had been out on the spree with *a Wakes girl* in a dogcart on Sunday afternoon, and had got into such a condition that he had driven into a lamp-post at the top of Oldcastle Street just as people were going into chapel.

The lamp-post remained bent for three days—a fearful warning to all dogs that doggishness has limits.

If it had not been a dogcart, and such a high, green dogcart; if it had been, say, a brougham, or even a cab! If it had not been Sunday! And, granting Sunday, if it had not been just as people were going into chapel! If he had not chosen that particular lamp-post, visible both from the market-place and St. Luke's Square! If he had only contrived to destroy a less obtrusive lamp-post in some unfrequented street! And if it had not been a Wakes girl—if the reprobate had only selected for his guilty amours an actress from one of the touring companies, or even a star from the Hanbridge Empire—yea, or even a local barmaid! But *a Wakes girl!*

Ellis himself saw the enormity of his transgression. He lay awake astounded by his own doggishness.

And yet he had seldom felt less doggy than during that trip. It seemed to him that doggishness was not the glorious thing he had thought. However, he cut a heroic figure at the dogs' club. Every admiring face said: 'Well, you *have* been going the pace! We always knew you were a hot un, but, really——'

V

On the following Friday evening, when Ellis jumped off the car opposite his home on the Hawkins, he saw in the road, halted, a train of vast and queer-shaped waggons in charge of two traction-engines. They were painted on all sides with the great name of Jenkins. They contained Jenkins's roundabouts and shooting-saloons, on their way to rouse the joy of life in other towns. And he perceived in front of the portico the high, green dogcart and the lamp-post-destroying mare.

He went in. The family had come home that afternoon. Sundry of his sisters greeted him with silent horror on their faces in the hall. In the breakfast-room, which gave off the drawing-room, was his mother in the attitude of an intent listener. She spoke no word.

And Ellis listened, too.

'Yes,' a very powerful and raucous voice was saying in the drawing-room, 'I reckoned I'd call and tell ye myself, Mister Carter, what I thought on it. My gell, a motherless gell, but brought up respectable; sixth standard at Whalley Range Board School; and her aunt a strict God-fearing woman! And here your son comes along and gets hold of the girl while her aunt's at the special service for Wakes folks in Bethesda Chapel, and runs off with her in my dogcart with one of my hosses, and raises a scandal all o'er the Five Towns. God bless my soul, mister! I tell'n ye I hardly liked to open o' Monday afternoon, I was that ashamed! And I packed Ada off to Manchester. It seems to me that if the upper classes, as they call 'em—the immoral classes *I* call 'em—'ud look after themselves a bit instead o' looking after other people so much, things might be a bit better, Mister Carter. I dare say you think it's nothing as your son should go about ruining the reputation of any decent, respectable girl as he happens to fancy, Mister Carter; but this is what I say. I say——'

54

Mr. Carter was understood to assert, in his most pacific and pained public-meeting voice, that he regretted, infinitely regretted——

Mrs. Carter, weeping, ran out of the breakfast-room.

And soon afterwards the traction-engines rumbled off, and the high, green dogcart followed them.

Ellis sat spell-bound.

He heard the parlourmaid go into the drawing-room and announce, 'Tea is ready, sir!' and then his father's dry cough.

And then the parlourmaid came into the breakfast-room: 'Tea is ready, Mr. Ellis!'

Oh, the meal!

A FEUD

When Clive Timmis paused at the side-door of Ezra Brunt's great shop in Machin Street, and the door was opened to him by Ezra Brunt's daughter before he had had time to pull the bell, not only all Machin Street knew it within the hour, but also most persons of consequence left in Hanbridge on a Thursday afternoon—Thursday being early-closing day. For Hanbridge, though it counts sixty thousand inhabitants, and is the chief of the Five Towns—that vast, huddled congeries of boroughs devoted to the manufacture of earthenware—is a place where the art of attending to other people's business still flourishes in rustic perfection.

Ezra Brunt's drapery establishment was the foremost retail house, in any branch of trade, of the Five Towns. It had no rival nearer than Manchester, thirty-six miles off; and even Manchester could exhibit nothing conspicuously superior to it. The most acutely critical shoppers of the Five Towns—women who were in the habit of going to London every year for the January sales—spoke of Brunt's as a 'right-down good shop.' And the husbands of these ladies, manufacturers who employed from two hundred to a thousand men, regarded Ezra Brunt as a commercial magnate of equal importance with themselves. Brunt, who had served his apprenticeship at Birmingham, started business in Machin Street in 1862, when Hanbridge was half its present size and all the best shops of the district were in Oldcastle, an ancient burg contiguous with, but holding itself proudly aloof from, the industrial Five Towns. He paid eighty pounds a year rent, and lived over the shop, and in the summer quarter his gas bill was always under a sovereign. For ten years success tarried, but in 1872 his daughter Eva was born and his wife died, and from that moment the sun of his prosperity climbed higher and higher into heaven. He had been profoundly attached to his wife, and, having lost her he abandoned himself to the mercantile struggle with that morose and terrible ferocity which was the root of his character. Of rude, gaunt aspect, gruffly taciturn by nature, and variable in temper, he yet had the precious instinct for soothing customers. To this day he can surpass his own shop-walkers in the admirable and tender solicitude with which, forsaking dialect, he drops into a lady's ear his famous stereotyped phrase: 'Are you receiving proper attention, madam?' From the first he eschewed the facile trickeries and ostentations which allure the populace. He sought a high-class trade, and by waiting he found it. He would never advertise on hoardings; for many years he had no signboard over his shop-front; and whereas the name of 'Bostocks,' the huge cheap drapers lower down Machin Street, on the opposite side, attacks you at every railway-station and in every tramcar, the name of 'E. Brunt' is to be seen only in a modest regular advertisement on the front page of the *Staffordshire Signal*. Repose, reticence, respectability—it was these attributes which he decided his shop should possess, and by means of which he succeeded. To enter Brunt's, with its silently swinging doors, its broad, easy staircases, its long floors covered with warm, red linoleum, its partitioned walls, its smooth mahogany counters, its unobtrusive mirrors, its rows of youths and virgins in black, and its pervading atmosphere of quietude and discretion, was like entering a temple before the act of oblation has commenced. You were conscious of some supreme administrative influence everywhere imposing itself. That influence was Ezra Brunt. And yet the man differed utterly from the thing he had created. His was one of those dark and passionate souls which smoulder in this harsh Midland district as slag-heaps smoulder on the pit-banks, revealing their strange fires only in the darkness.

In 1899 Brunt's establishment occupied four shops, Nos. 52, 56, 58, and 60, in Machin Street. He had bought the freeholds at a price which timid people regarded as exorbitant, but the solicitors of Hanbridge secretly applauded his enterprise and shrewdness in anticipating the enormous rise in ground-values which has now been in rapid, steady progress there for more than a decade. He had thrown the interiors together and rebuilt the frontages in handsome freestone. He had also purchased several shops opposite, and rumour said that it was his intention to offer these latter to the Town Council at a low figure if the Council would cut a new street leading from his premises to the Market Square. Such a scheme would have met with general approval. But there was one serious hiatus in the plans of Ezra Brunt—to wit, No. 54, Machin Street. No. 54, separating 52 and 56, was a chemist's shop, shabby but sedate as to appearance, owned and occupied by George Christopher Timmis, a mild and venerable citizen, and a local preacher in the Wesleyan Methodist Connexion. For nearly thirty years Brunt had coveted Mr. Timmis's shop; more than twenty years have elapsed since he first opened negotiations for it. Mr. Timmis was by no means eager to sell—indeed, his attitude was distinctly a repellent one—but a bargain would undoubtedly have been concluded had not a report reached the ears of Mr. Timmis to the effect that Ezra Brunt had remarked at the Turk's Head that 'th' old leech was only sticking out for every brass farthing he could get.' The report was untrue, but Mr. Timmis believed it, and from that moment Ezra Brunt's chances of obtaining the chemist's shop vanished completely. His lawyer expended diplomacy in vain, raising the offer week by week till the incredible sum of three thousand pounds was reached. Then Ezra Brunt himself saw Mr. Timmis, and without a word of prelude said:

'Will ye take three thousand guineas for this bit o' property?'

'Not thirty thousand guineas,' said Mr. Timmis quietly; the stern pride of the benevolent old local preacher had been aroused.

'Then be damned to you!' said Ezra Brunt, who had never been known to swear before.

Thenceforth a feud existed, not less bitter because it was a feud in which nothing was said and nothing done—a silent and implacable mutual resistance. The sole outward sign of it was the dirty and stumpy brown-brick shop-front of Mr. Timmis, squeezed in between those massive luxurious façades of stone which Ezra Brunt soon afterwards erected. The pharmaceutical business of Mr. Timmis was not a very large one, and, fiscally, Ezra Brunt could have swallowed him at a meal and suffered no inconvenience; but in that the aged chemist had lived on just half his small income for some fifty years past, his position was impregnable. Hanbridge smiled cynically at this *impasse* produced by an idle word, and, recognising the equality of the antagonists, leaned neither to one side nor to the other. At intervals, however, the legend of the feud was embroidered with new and effective detail in the mouth of some inventive gossip, and by degrees it took high place among those piquant social histories which illustrate the real life of a town, and which parents recount to their children with such zest in moods of reminiscence.

When George Christopher Timmis buried his wife, Ezra Brunt, as a near neighbour, was asked to the funeral. 'The cortège will move at 1.30,' ran the printed invitation, and at 1.15 Brunt's carriage was decorously in place behind the hearse and the two mourning-coaches. The demeanour of the chemist and the draper towards each other was a sublime answer to the demands of the occasion; some people even said that the breach had been healed, but these were not of the discerning.

The most active person at the funeral was the chemist's only nephew, Clive Timmis, partner in a small but prosperous firm of majolica manufacturers at Bursley. Clive, who was seldom seen in Hanbridge, made a favourable impression on everyone by his pleasing, unaffected manner and his air of discretion and success. He was a bachelor of thirty-two, and lived in lodgings at Bursley. On the return of the funeral-party from the cemetery, Clive Timmis found Brunt's daughter Eva in his uncle's house. Uninvited, she had left her place in the private room at her father's shop in order to assist Timmis's servant Sarah in the preparation of that solid and solemn repast which must inevitably follow every proper interment in the Five Towns. Without false modesty, she introduced herself to one or two of the men who had surprised her at her work, and then quietly departed just as they were sitting down to table and Sarah had brought in the hot tea-cakes. Clive Timmis saw her only for a moment, but from that moment she was his one thought. During the evening, which he spent alone with his uncle, he behaved in every particular as a nephew should, yet he was acting a part; his real self roved after Ezra Brunt's daughter, wherever she might be. Clive had never fallen in love, though several times in his life he had tried hard to do so. He had long wished to marry—wished ardently; he had even got into the way of regarding every woman he met—and he met many—in the light of a possible partner. 'Can it be *she*? he had asked himself a thousand times, and then answered half sadly, 'No.' Not one woman had touched his imagination, coincided with his dream. It is strange that after seeing Eva Brunt he forgot thus to interrogate himself. For a fortnight, while he went his ways as usual, her image occupied his heart, throwing that once orderly chamber into the wildest confusion; and he let it remain, dimly aware of some delicious danger. He inspected the image every night before he slept, and every morning when he awoke, and made no effort to define its distracting charm; he knew only that Eva Brunt was absolutely and in every detail unlike all other women. On the second Sunday he murmured during the sermon: 'But I only saw her for a minute.' A few days afterwards he took the tram to Hanbridge.

'Uncle,' he said, 'how should you like me to come and live here with you? I've been thinking things out a bit, and I thought perhaps you'd like it. I expect you must feel rather lonely now.'

The neat, fragrant shop was empty, and the two men stood behind the big glass-fronted case of Burroughs and Wellcome's preparations. Clive's venerable uncle happened to be looking into a drawer marked 'Gentianæ Rad. Pulv.' He closed the drawer with slow hesitation, and then, stroking his long white beard, replied in that deliberate voice which seemed always to tremble with religious fervour:

'The hand of the Lord is in this thing, Clive. I have wished that you might come to live here with me. But I was afraid it would be too far from the works.'

'Pooh! that's nothing,' said Clive.

As he lingered at the shop door for the Bursley car to pass the end of Machin Street, Eva Brunt went by. He raised his hat with diffidence, and she smiled. It was a marvellous chance. His heart leapt into a throb which was half agony and half delight.

'I am in love,' he said gravely.

He had just discovered the fact, and the discovery filled him with exquisite apprehension.

If he had waited till the age of thirty-two for that springtime of the soul which we call love, Clive had not waited for nothing. Eva was a woman to enravish the heart of a man whose imagination could pierce the agitating secrets immured in that calm and silent bosom. Slender and scarcely tall, she belonged to the order of spare, slight-made women, who hide within their slim frames an endowment of profound passion far exceeding that of their more voluptuously-formed sisters, who never coarsen into stoutness, and who at forty are as disturbing as at twenty. At this date Eva was twenty-six. She had a rather small, white face, which was a mask to the casual observer, and the very mirror of her feelings to anyone with eyes to read its signs.

'I tell you what you are like,' said Clive to her once: 'you are like a fine racehorse, always on the quiver.'

Yet many people considered her cold and impassive. Her walk and bearing showed a sensitive independence, and when she spoke it was usually in tones of command. The girls in the shop, where she was a power second only to Ezra Brunt, were a little afraid of her, chiefly because she poured terrible scorn on their small affectations, jealousies, and vendettas. But they liked her because, in their own phrase, 'there was no nonsense about' this redoubtable woman. She hated shams and make-believes with a bitter and ruthless hatred.

60

She was the heiress to at least five thousand a year, and knew it well, but she never encouraged her father to complicate their simple mode of life with the pomps of wealth. They lived in a house with a large garden at Pireford, which is on the summit of the steep ridge between the Five Towns and Oldcastle, and they kept two servants and a coachman, who was also gardener. Eva paid the servants good wages, and took care to get good value therefor.

'It's not often I have any bother with my servants,' she would say, 'for they know that if there is any trouble I would just as soon clear them out and put on an apron and do the work myself.'

She was an accomplished house-mistress, and could bake her own bread: in towns not one woman in a thousand can bake. With the coachman she had little to do, for she could not rid herself of a sentimental objection to the carriage—it savoured of 'airs'; when she used it she used it as she might use a tramcar. It was her custom, every day except Saturday, to walk to the shop about eleven o'clock, after her house had been set in order. She had been thoroughly trained in the business, and had spent a year at a first-rate shop in High Street, Kensington. Millinery was her speciality, and she still watched over that department with a particular attention; but for some time past she had risen beyond the limitations of departments, and assisted her father in the general management of the vast concern. In commercial aptitude she resembled the typical Frenchwoman.

Although he was her father, Ezra Brunt had the wit to recognise her talents, and he always listened to her suggestions, which, however, sometimes startled him. One of them was that he should import into the Five Towns a modiste from Paris, offering a salary of two hundred a year. The old provincial stood aghast. He had the idea that all Parisian women were stage-dancers. And to pay four pounds a week to a female!

Nevertheless, Mademoiselle Bertot—styled in the shop 'Madame'—now presides over Ezra Brunt's dressmakers, draws her four pounds a week (of which she saves two), and by mere nationality has given a unique distinction and success to her branch of the business.

Eva occupied a small room opening off the principal showroom, and during hours of work she issued thence but seldom. Only customers of the highest importance might speak with her. She was a power felt rather than seen. Employés who knocked at her door always did so with a certain awe of what awaited them on the other side, and a consciousness that the moment was unsuitable for levity. 'If you please, Miss Eva——'. Here she gave audience to the 'buyers' and window-dressers, listened to complaints and excuses, and occasionally had a secret orgy of afternoon tea with one or two of her friends. None but these few girls—mostly younger than herself, and remarkable only in that their dislike of the snobbery of the Five Towns, though less fiercely displayed, agreed with her own—really knew Eva. To them alone did she unveil herself, and by them she was idolized.

'She is simply splendid when you know her—such a jolly girl!' they would say to other people; but other people, especially other women, could not believe it. They fearfully respected her because she was very well dressed and had quantities of money. But they called her 'a curious creature'; it was inconceivable to them that she should choose to work in a shop; and her tongue had a causticity which was sometimes exceedingly disconcerting and mortifying. As for men, she was shy of them, and, moreover, she loathed the elaborate and insincere ritual of deference which the average man practises towards women unrelated to him, particularly when they are young and rich. Her father she adored, without knowing it; for he often angered her, and humiliated her in private. As for the rest, she was, after all, only six-and-twenty.

'If you don't mind, I should like to walk along with you,' Clive Timmis said to her one Sunday evening in the porch of the Bethesda Chapel.

'I shall be glad,' she answered at once; 'father isn't here, and I'm all alone.'

Ezra Brunt was indeed seldom there, counting in the matter of attendance at chapel among what were called 'the weaker brethren.'

'I am going over to Oldcastle,' Clive explained calmly.

So began the formal courtship—more than a month after Clive had settled in Machin Street, for he was far too discreet to engender by precipitancy any suspicion in the haunts of scandal that his true reason for establishing himself in his uncle's household was a certain rich young woman who was to be found every day next door. Guided as much by instinct as by tact, Clive approached Eva with an almost savage simplicity and naturalness of manner, ignoring not only her father's wealth, but all the feigned punctilio of a wooer. His face said: 'Let there be no beating about the bush—I like you.' Hers answered: 'Good! we will see.'

From the first he pleased her, and not least in treating her exactly as she would have wished to be treated—namely, as a quite plain person of that part of the middle class which is neither upper nor lower. Few men in the Five Towns would have been capable of forgetting Ezra Brunt's income in talking to Ezra Brunt's daughter. Fortunately, Timmis had a proud, confident spirit—the spirit of one who, unaided, has wrested success from the world's deathlike clutch. Had Eva the reversion of fifty thousand a year instead of five, he, Clive, was still a prosperous plain man, well able to support a wife in the position to which God had called him.

Their walks together grew more and more frequent, and they became intimate, exchanging ideas and rejoicing openly at the similarity of those ideas. Although there was no concealment in these encounters, still, there was a circumspection which resembled the clandestine. By a silent understanding Clive did not enter the house at Pireford; to have done so would have excited remark, for this house, unlike some, had never been the rendezvous of young men; much less, therefore, did he invade the shop. No! The chief part of their love-making (for such it was, though the term would have roused Eva's contemptuous anger) occurred in the streets; in this they did but follow the traditions of their class. Thus, the idyll, so matter-of-fact upon the surface, but within which glowed secret and adorable fires, progressed towards its culmination. Eva, the artless fool—oh, how simple are the wisest at times!—thought that the affair was hid from the shop. But was it possible? Was it possible that in those tiny bedrooms on the third floor, where the heavy evening hours were ever lightened with breathless interminable recitals of what some 'he' had said and some 'she' had replied, such an enthralling episode should escape discovery? The dormitories knew of Eva's 'attachment' before Eva herself. Yet none knew how it was known. The whisper arose like Venus from a sea of trivial gossip, miraculously, exquisitely. On the night when the first rumour of it traversed the passages there was scarcely any sleep at Brunt's, while Eva up at Pireford slumbered as a young girl.

On the Thursday afternoon with which we began, Brunt's was deserted save for the housekeeper and Eva, who was writing letters in her room.

'I saw you from my window, coming up the street,' she said to Clive, 'and so I ran down to open the door. Will you come into father's room? He is in Manchester for the day, buying.

'I knew that,' said Timmis.

'How did you know?' She observed that his manner was somewhat nervous and constrained.

'You yourself told me last night—don't you remember?'

'So I did.'

'That's why I sent the note round this morning to say I'd call this afternoon. You got it, I suppose?'

She nodded thoughtfully.

'Well, what is this business you want to talk about?'

It was spoken with a brave carelessness, but he caught the tremor in her voice, and saw her little hand shake as it lay on the table amid her father's papers. Without knowing why he should do so, he stepped hastily forward and seized that hand. Her emotion unmanned him. He thought he was going to cry; he could not account for himself.

'Eva,' he said thickly, 'you know what the business is; you know, don't you?'

She smiled. That smile, the softness of her hand, the sparkle in her eye, the heave of her small bosom ... it was the divinest miracle! Clive, manufacturer of majolica, went hot and then cold, and then his wits were suddenly his own again.

'That's all right,' he murmured, and sighed, and placed on Eva's lips the first kiss that had ever lain there.

'Dear boy,' she said later, 'you should have come up to Pireford, not here, and when father was there.'

'Should I?' he answered happily. 'It just occurred to me all of a sudden this morning that you would be here, and that I couldn't wait.'

'You will come up to-night and see father?'

'I had meant to.'

'You had better go home now.'

'Had I?'

She nodded, putting her lips tightly together—a trick of hers.

'Come up about half-past eight.'

'Good! I will let myself out.'

He left her, and she gazed dreamily at the window, which looked on to a whitewashed yard. The next moment someone else entered the room with heavy footsteps. She turned round a little startled.

It was her father.

64

'Why! You *are* back early, father! How——' She stopped. Something in the old man's glance gave her a premonition of disaster. To this day she does not know what accident brought him from Manchester two hours sooner than usual, and to Machin Street instead of Pireford.

'Has young Timmis been here?' he inquired curtly.

'Yes.'

'Ha!' with subdued, sinister satisfaction, 'I saw him going out. He didna see me.' Ezra Brunt deposited his hat and sat down.

Intimate with all her father's various moods, she saw instantly and with terrible certainty that a series of chances had fatally combined themselves against her. If only she had not happened to tell Clive that her father would be at Manchester this day! If only her father had adhered to his customary hour of return! If only Clive had had the sense to make his proposal openly at Pireford some evening! If only he had left a little earlier! If only her father had not caught him going out by the side-door on a Thursday afternoon when the place was empty! Here, she guessed, was the suggestion of furtiveness which had raised her father's unreasoning anger, often fierce, and always incalculable.

'Clive Timmis has asked me to marry him, father.'

'Has he!'

'Surely you must have known, father, that he and I were seeing each other a great deal.'

'Not from your lips, my girl.'

'Well, father——' Again she stopped, this strong and capable woman, gifted with a fine brain to organize and a powerful will to command. She quailed, robbed of speech, before the causeless, vindictive, and infantile wrath of an old man who happened to be in a bad temper. She actually felt like a naughty schoolgirl before him. Such is the tremendous influence of lifelong habit, the irresistible power of the *patria potestas* when it has never been relaxed. Ezra Brunt saw in front of him only a cowering child. 'Clive is coming up to see you to-night,' she went on timidly, clearing her throat.

'Humph! Is he?'

The rosy and tender dream of five minutes ago lay in fragments at Eva's feet. She brooded with stricken apprehension upon the forms of obstruction which his despotism might choose.

The next morning Clive and his uncle breakfasted together as usual in the parlour behind, the chemist's shop.

'Uncle,' said Clive brusquely, when the meal was nearly finished, 'I'd better tell you that I've proposed to Eva Brunt.'

Old George Timmis lowered the *Manchester Guardian* and gazed at Clive over his steel-rimmed spectacles.

'She is a good girl,' he remarked; 'she will make you a good wife. Have you spoken to her father?'

'That's the point. I saw him last night, and I'll tell you what he said. These were his words: "You can marry my daughter, Mr. Timmis, when your uncle agrees to part with his shop!"'

'That I shall never do, nephew,' said the aged patriarch quietly and deliberately.

'Of course you won't, uncle. I shouldn't think of suggesting it. I'm merely telling you what he said.' Clive laughed harshly. 'Why,' he added, 'the man must be mad!'

'What did the young woman say to that?' his uncle inquired.

Clive frowned.

'I didn't see her last night,' he said. 'I didn't ask to see her. I was too angry.'

Just then the post arrived, and there was a letter for Clive, which he read and put carefully in his waistcoat pocket.

'Eva writes asking me to go to Pireford to-night,' he said, after a pause. 'I'll soon settle it, depend on that. If Ezra Brunt refuses his consent, so much the worse for him. I wonder whether he actually imagines that a grown man and a grown woman are to be.... Ah well, I can't talk about it! It's too silly. I'll be off to the works.'

When Clive reached Pireford that night, Eva herself opened the door to him. She was wearing a gray frock, and over it a large white apron, perfectly plain.

'My girls are both out to-night,' she said, 'and I was making some puffs for the sewing-meeting tea. Come into the breakfast-room.... This way,' she added, guiding him. He had entered the house on the previous night for the first time. She spoke hurriedly, and, instead of stopping in the breakfast-room, wandered uncertainly through it into the greenhouse, to which it gave access by means of a French window. In the dark, confined space, amid the close-packed blossoms, they stood together. She bent down to smell at a musk-plant. He took her hand and drew her soft and yielding form towards him and kissed her warm face.

'Oh, Clive!' she said. 'Whatever are we to do?'

'Do?' he replied, enchanted by her instinctive feminine surrender and reliance upon him, which seemed the more precious in that creature so proud and reserved to all others. 'Do! Where is your father?'

'Reading the *Signal* in the dining-room.'

Every business man in the Five Towns reads the *Staffordshire Signal* from beginning to end every night.

'I will see him. Of course he is your father; but I will just tell him—as decently as I can—that neither you nor I will stand this nonsense.'

'You mustn't—you mustn't see him.'

'Why not?'

'It will only lead to unpleasantness.'

'That can't be helped.'

'He never, never changes when once he has *said* a thing. I know him.'

Clive was arrested by something in her tone, something new to him, that in its poignant finality seemed to have caught up and expressed in a single instant that bitterness of a lifetime's renunciation which falls to the lot of most women.

'Will you come outside?' he asked in a different voice.

Without replying, she led the way down the long garden, which ended in an ivy-grown brick wall and a panorama of the immense valley of industries below. It was a warm, cloudy evening. The last silver tinge of an August twilight lay on the shoulder of the hill to the left. There was no moon, but the splendid watch-fires of labour flamed from ore-heap and furnace across the whole expanse, performing their nightly miracle of beauty. Trains crept with noiseless mystery along the middle distance, under their canopies of yellow steam. Further off the far-extending streets of Hanbridge made a map of starry lines on the blackness. To the south-east stared the cold, blue electric lights of Knype railway-station. All was silent, save for a distant thunderous roar, the giant breathing of the forge at Cauldon Bar Ironworks.

Eva leaned both elbows on the wall and looked forth.

'Do you mean to say,' said Clive, 'that Mr. Brunt will actually stick by what he has said?'

'Like grim death,' said Eva.

'But what's his idea?'

67

'Oh! how can I tell you?' she burst out passionately.

'Perhaps I did wrong. Perhaps I ought to have warned him earlier—said to him, "Father, Clive Timmis is courting me!" Ugh! He cannot bear to be surprised about anything. But yet he must have known.... It was all an accident, Clive—all an accident. He saw you leaving the shop yesterday. He would say he*caught* you leaving the shop—*sneaking* off like——'

'But, Eva——'

'I know—I know! Don't tell me! But it was that, I am sure. He would resent the mere look of things, and then he would think and think, and the notion of your uncle's shop would occur to him again, after all these years. I can see his thoughts as plain ... My dear, if he had not seen you at Machin Street yesterday, or if you had seen him and spoken to him, all might have gone right. He would have objected, but he would have given way in a day or two. Now he will never give way! I asked you just now what was to be done, but I knew all the time that there was nothing.'

'There is one thing to be done, Eva, and the sooner the better.'

'Do you mean that old Mr. Timmis must give up his shop to my father? Never! never!'

'I mean,' said Clive quietly, 'that we must marry without your father's consent.'

She shook her head slowly and sadly, relapsing into calmness.

'You shake your head, Eva, but it must be so.'

'I can't, my dear.'

'Do you mean to say that you will allow your father's childish whim—for it's nothing else; he can't find any objection to me as a husband for you, and he knows it—that you will allow his childish whim to spoil your life and mine? Remember, you are twenty-six and I am thirty-two.'

'I can't do it! I daren't! I'm mad with myself for feeling like this, but I daren't! And even if I dared I wouldn't. Clive, you don't know! You can't tell how it is!'

Her sorrowful, pathetic firmness daunted him. She was now composed, mistress again of herself, and her moral force dominated him.

'Then, you and I are to be unhappy all our lives, Eva?'

The soft influences of the night seemed to direct her voice as, after a long pause, she uttered the words: 'No one is ever quite unhappy in all this world.' There was another pause, as she gazed steadily down into the wonderful valley. 'We must wait.'

'Wait!' echoed Clive with angry grimness. 'He will live for twenty years!'

'No one is ever quite unhappy in all this world,' she repeated dreamily, as one might turn over a treasure in order to examine it.

Now for the epilogue to the feud. Two years passed, and it happened that there was to be a Revival at the Bethesda Chapel. One morning the superintendent minister and the revivalist called on Ezra Brunt at his shop. When informed of their presence, the great draper had an impulse of anger, for, like many stouter chapel-goers than himself, he would scarcely tolerate the intrusion of religion into commerce. However, the visit had an air of ceremony, and he could not decline to see these ambassadors of heaven in his private room. The revivalist, a cheery, shrewd man, whose powers of organization were obvious, and who seemed to put organization before everything else, pleased Ezra Brunt at once.

'We want a specially good congregation at the opening meeting to-night,' said the revivalist. 'Now, the basis of a good congregation must necessarily be the regular pillars of the church, and therefore we are making a few calls this morning to insure the presence of our chief men—the men of influence and position. You will come, Mr. Brunt, and you will let it be known among your employés that they will please you by coming too?'

Ezra Brunt was by no means a regular pillar of the Bethesda, but he had a vague sensation of flattery, and he consented; indeed, there was no alternative.

The first hymn was being sung when he reached the chapel. To his surprise, he found the place crowded in every part. A man whom he did not know led him to a wooden form which had been put in the space between the front pews and the Communion-rail. He felt strange there, and uneasy, apprehensive.

The usual discreet somnolence of the chapel had been disturbed as by some indecorous but formidable awakener; the air was electric; anything might occur. Ezra was astounded by the mere volume of the singing; never had he heard such singing. At the end of the hymn the congregation sat down, hiding their faces in expectation. The revivalist stood erect and terrible in the pulpit, no longer a shrewd, cheery man of the world, but the very mouthpiece of the wrath and mercy of God. Ezra's self-importance dwindled before that gaze, till, from a renowned magnate of the Five Towns, he became an item in the multitude of suppliants. He profoundly wished he had never come.

'Remember the hymn,' said the revivalist, with austere emphasis:

"'My   richest   gain   I   count   but   loss,
And pour contempt on all my pride.'"

The admirable histrionic art with which he intensified the consonants in the last line produced a tremendous effect. Not for nothing was this man cerebrated throughout Methodism as a saver of souls. When, after a pause, he raised his hand and ejaculated, 'Let us pray,' sobs could be heard throughout the chapel. The Revival had begun.

At the end of a quarter of an hour Ezra Brunt would have given fifty pounds to be outside, but he could not stir; he was magnetized. Soon the revivalist came down from the pulpit and stood within the Communion-rail, whence he addressed the nearmost part of the people in low, soothing tones of persuasion. Apparently he ignored Ezra Brunt, but the man was convicted of sin, and felt himself melting like an icicle in front of a fire. He recalled the days of his youth, the piety of his father and mother, and the long traditions of a stern Dissenting family. He had backslidden, slackened in the use of the means of grace, run after the things of this world. It is true that none of his chiefest iniquities presented themselves to him; he was quite unconscious of them even then; but the lesser ones were more than sufficient to overwhelm him. Class-leaders were now reasoning with stricken sinners, and Ezra, who could not take his eyes off the revivalist, heard the footsteps of those who were going to the 'inquiry-room' for more private counsel. In vain he argued that he was about to be ridiculous; that the idea of him, Ezra Brunt, a professed Wesleyan for half a century, being publicly 'saved' at the age of fifty-seven was not to be entertained; that the town would talk; that his business might suffer if for any reason he should be morally bound to apply to it too strictly the principles of the New Testament. He was under the spell. The tears coursed down his long cheeks, and he forgot to care, but sat entranced by the revivalist's marvellous voice. Suddenly, with an awful sob, he bent and hid his face in his hands. The spectacle of the old, proud man helpless in the grasp of profound emotion was a sight to rend the heart-strings.

'Brother, be of good cheer,' said a tremulous and benign voice above him. 'The love of God compasseth all things. Only believe.'

He looked up and saw the venerable face and long white beard of George Christopher Timmis.

Ezra Brunt shrank away, embittered and ashamed.

'I cannot,' he murmured with difficulty.

'The love of God is all-powerful.'

'Will it make you part with that bit o' property, think you?' said Ezra Brunt, with a kind of despairing ferocity.

'Brother,' replied the aged servant of God, unmoved, 'if my shop is in truth a stumbling-block in this solemn hour, you shall have it.'

Ezra Brunt was staggered.

'I believe! I believe!' he cried.

'Praise God!' said the chemist, with majestic joy.

Three months afterwards Eva Brunt and Clive Timmis were married. It is characteristic of the fine sentimentality which underlies the surface harshness of the inhabitants of the Five Towns that, though No. 54 Machin Street was duly transferred to Ezra Brunt, the chemist retiring from business, he has never rebuilt it to accord with the rest of his premises. In all its shabbiness it stands between the other big dazzling shops as a reminding monument.

PHANTOM

I

The heart of the Five Towns—that undulating patch of England covered with mean streets, and dominated by tall smoking chimneys, whence are derived your cups and saucers and plates, some of your coal, and a portion of your iron—is Hanbridge, a borough larger and busier than its four sisters, and even more grimy and commonplace than they. And the heart of Hanbridge is probably the offices of the Five Towns Banking Company, where the last trace of magic and romance is beaten out of human existence, and the meaning of life is expressed in balances, deposits, percentages, and overdrafts—especially overdrafts. In a fine suite of rooms on the first floor of the bank building resides Mr. Lionel Woolley, the manager, with his wife May and their children.

Yet Mr. Woolley was once brought into contact with the things which cannot be defined and assessed; once he stood face to face with some strange visible resultant of those secret forces that lie beyond the human ken. And, moreover, the adventure affected the whole of his domestic life. The wonder and the pathos of the story lie in the fact that Nature, prodigal though she is known to be, should have wasted the rare and beautiful visitation on just Mr. Woolley. Mr. Woolley was bathed in romance of the most singular kind, and the precious fluid ran off him like water off a duck's back.

II

Ten years ago on a Thursday afternoon in July, Lionel Woolley, as he walked up through the new park at Bursley to his celibate rooms in Park Terrace, was making addition sums out of various items connected with the institution of marriage. Bursley is next door to Hanbridge, and Lionel happened then to be cashier of the Bursley branch of the bank. He had in mind two possible wives, each of whom possessed advantages which appealed to him, and he was unable to decide between them by any mathematical process. Suddenly, from a glazed shelter near the empty bandstand, there emerged in front of him one of the delectable creatures who had excited his fancy. May Lawton was twenty-eight, an orphan, and a schoolmistress. She, too, had celibate rooms in Park Terrace, and it was owing to this coincidence that Lionel had made her acquaintance six months previously. She was not pretty, but she was tall, straight, well dressed, well educated, and not lacking in experience; and she had a little money of her own.

'Well, Mr. Woolley,' she said easily, stopping for him as she raised her sunshade, 'how satisfied you look!'

'It's the sight of you,' he replied, without a moment's hesitation.

He had a fine assured way with women (he need not have envied a curate accustomed to sewing meetings), and May Lawton belonged to the type of girl whose demeanour always challenges the masculine in a man. Gazing at her, Lionel was swiftly conscious of several things: the piquancy of her snub nose, the brightness of her smile, at once defiant and wistful, the lingering softness of her gloved hand, and the extraordinary charm of her sunshade, which matched her dress and formed a sort of canopy and frame for that intelligent, tantalizing face. He remembered that of late he and she had grown very intimate; and it came upon him with a shock, as though he had just opened a telegram which said so, that May, and not the other girl, was his destined mate. And he thought of her fortune, tiny but nevertheless useful, and how clever she was, and how inexplicably different from the rest of her sex, and how she would adorn his house, and set him off, and help him in his career. He heard himself saying negligently to friends: 'My wife speaks French like a native. Of course, my wife has travelled a great deal. My wife has thoroughly studied the management of children. Now, my wife does understand the art of dress. I put my wife's bit of money into so-and-so.' In short, Lionel was as near being in love as his character permitted.

And while he walked by May's side past the bowling-greens at the summit of the hill, she lightly quizzing the raw newness of the park and its appurtenances, he wondered, he honestly wondered, that he could ever have hesitated between May Lawton and the other. Her superiority was too obvious; she was a woman of the world! She.... In a flash he knew that he would propose to her that very afternoon. And when he had suggested a stroll towards Moorthorne, and she had deliciously agreed, he was conscious of a tumultuous uplifting and splendid carelessness of spirits. 'Imagine me bringing it to a climax to-day,' he reflected, profoundly pleased with himself. 'Ah well, it will be settled once for all!' He admired his own decision; he was quite struck by it. 'I shall call her May before I leave her,' he thought, gazing at her, and discovering how well the name suited her, with its significances of alertness, geniality, and half-mocking coyness.

'So school is closed,' he said, and added humorously: '"Broken up" is the technical term, I believe.'

'Yes,' she answered, 'and I had walked out into the park to meditate seriously upon the question of my holiday.'

She caught his eye in a net of bright glances, and romance was in the air. They had crossed a couple of smoke-soiled fields, and struck into the old Hanbridge road just below the abandoned toll-house with its broad eaves.

'And whither do your meditations point?' he demanded playfully.

'My meditations point to Switzerland,' she said. 'I have friends in Lausanne.'

The reference to foreign climes impressed him.

'Would that I could go to Switzerland too!' he exclaimed; and privately: 'Now for it! I'm about to begin.'

'Why?' she questioned, with elaborate simplicity.

At the moment, as they were passing the toll-house, the other girl appeared surprisingly from round the corner of the toll-house, where the lane from Toft End joins the highroad. This second creature was smaller than Miss Lawton, less assertive, less intelligent, perhaps, but much more beautiful.

Everyone halted and everyone blushed.

'May!' the interrupter at length stammered.

'May!' responded Miss Lawton lamely.

The other girl was named May too—May Deane, child of the well-known majolica manufacturer, who lived with his sons and daughter in a solitary and ancient house at Toft End.

Lionel Woolley said nothing until they had all shaken hands—his famous way with women seemed to have deserted him—and then he actually stated that he had forgotten an appointment, and must depart. He had gone before the girls could move.

When they were alone, the two Mays fronted each other, confused, hostile, almost homicidal.

'I hope I didn't spoil a *tête-à-tête,*'said May Deane, stiffly and sharply, in a manner quite foreign to her soft and yielding nature.

The schoolmistress, abandoning herself to an inexplicable but overwhelming impulse, took breath for a proud lie.

'No,' she answered; 'but if you had come three minutes earlier——'

She smiled calmly.

'Oh!' murmured May Deane, after a pause.

III

That evening May Deane returned home at half-past nine. She had been with her two brothers to a lawn-tennis party at Hillport, and she told her father, who was reading the *Staffordshire Signal* in his accustomed solitude, that the boys were staying later for cards, but that she had declined to stay because she felt tired. She kissed the old widower good-night, and said that she should go to bed at once. But before retiring she visited the housekeeper in the kitchen in order to discuss certain household matters: Jim's early breakfast, the proper method of washing Herbert's new flannels (Herbert would be very angry if they were shrunk), and the dog-biscuits for Carlo. These questions settled, she went to her room, drew the blind, lighted some candles, and sat down near the window.

She was twenty-two, and she had about her that strange and charming nunlike mystery which often comes to a woman who lives alone and unguessed-at among male relatives. Her room was her bower. No one, save the servants and herself, ever entered it. Mr. Deane and Jim and Bertie might glance carelessly through the open door in passing along the corridor, but had they chanced in idle curiosity to enter, the room would have struck them as unfamiliar, and they might perhaps have exclaimed with momentary interest, 'So this is May's room!' And some hint that May was more than a daughter and sister—a woman, withdrawn, secret, disturbing, living her own inner life side by side with the household life—might have penetrated their obtuse paternal and fraternal masculinity. Her beautiful face (the nose and mouth were perfect, and at either extremity of the upper lip grew a soft down), her dark hair, her quiet voice and her gentle acquiescence (diversified by occasional outbursts of sarcasm), appealed to them and won them; but they accepted her as something of course, as something which went without saying. They adored her, and did not know that they adored her.

May took off her hat, stuck the pins into it again, and threw it on the bed, whose white and green counterpane hung down nearly to

75

the floor on either side. Then she lay back in the chair, and, pulling away the blind, glanced through the window; the moon, rather dim behind the furnace lights of Red Cow Ironworks, was rising over Moorthorne. May dropped the blind with a wearied gesture, and turned within the room, examining its contents as if she had not seen them before: the wardrobe, the chest of drawers, which was also a dressing-table, the washstand, the dwarf book-case with its store of Edna Lyalls, Elizabeth Gaskells, Thackerays, Charlotte Yonges, Charlotte Brontës, a Thomas Hardy or so, and some old school-books. She looked at the pictures, including a sampler worked by a deceased aunt, at the loud-ticking Swiss clock on the mantelpiece, at the higgledy-piggledy photographs there, at the new Axminster carpet, the piece of linoleum in front of the washstand, and the bad joining of the wallpaper to the left of the door. She missed none of the details which she knew so well, with such long monotonous intimacy, and sighed.

Then she got up from the chair, and, opening a small drawer in the chest of drawers, put her hand familiarly to the back and drew forth a photograph. She carried the photograph to the light of the candles on the mantelpiece, and gazed at it attentively, puckering her brows. It was a portrait of Lionel Woolley. Heaven knows by what subterfuge or lucky accident she had obtained it, for Lionel certainly had not given it to her. She loved Lionel. She had loved him for five years, with a love silent, blind, intense, irrational, and too elemental to be concealed. Everyone knew of May's passion. Many women admired her taste; a few were shocked and puzzled by it. All the men of her acquaintance either pitied or despised her for it. Her father said nothing. Her brothers were less cautious, and summed up their opinion of Lionel in the curt, scornful assertion that he showed a tendency to cheat at tennis. But May would never hear ill of him; he was a god to her, and she could not hide her worship. For more than a year, until lately, she had been almost sure of him, and then came a faint vague rumour concerning Lionel and May Lawton, a rumour which she had refused to take seriously. The encounter of that afternoon, and Miss Lawton's triumphant remark, had dazed her. For seven hours she had existed in a kind of semi-conscious delirium, in which she could perceive nothing but the fatal fact, emerging more clearly every moment from the welter of her thoughts, that she had lost Lionel. Lionel had proposed to May Lawton, and been accepted, just before she surprised them together;

and Lionel, with a man's excusable cowardice, had left his betrothed to announce the engagement.

She tore up the photograph, put the fragments in the grate, and set a light to them.

Her father's step sounded on the stairs; he hesitated, and knocked sharply at her door.

'What's burning, May?'

'It's all right, father,' she answered calmly, 'I'm only burning some papers in the fire-grate.'

'Well, see you don't burn the house down.'

He passed on.

Then she found a sheet of notepaper, and wrote on it in pencil, using the mantelpiece for a desk: 'Dear home. Good-night, good-bye.' She cogitated, and wrote further: 'Forgive me.—MAY.'

She put the message in an envelope, and wrote on the envelope 'Jim,' and placed it prominently in front of the clock. But after she had looked at it for a minute, she wrote 'Father' above Jim, and then 'Herbert' below.

There were noises in the hall; the boys had returned earlier than she expected. As they went along the corridor and caught a glimpse of her light under the door, Jim cried gaily: 'Now then, out with that light! A little thing like you ought to be asleep hours since.'

She listened for the bang of their door, and then, very hurriedly, she removed her pink frock and put on an old black one, which was rather tight in the waist. And she donned her hat, securing it carefully with both pins, extinguished the candles, and crept quietly downstairs, and so by the back-door into the garden. Carlo, the retriever, came halfway out of his kennel and greeted her in the moonlight with a yawn. She patted his head and ran stealthily up the garden, through the gate, and up the waste green land towards the crown of the hill.

IV

The top of Toft End is the highest land in the Five Towns, and from it may be clearly seen all the lurid evidences of manufacture which sweep across the borders of the sky on north, east, west, and south. North-eastwards lie the moorlands, and far off Manifold, the 'metropolis of the moorlands,' as it is called. On this night the furnaces of Red Cow Ironworks, in the hollow to the east, were in full blast; their fluctuating yellow light illuminated queerly the grass of the fields above Deane's house, and the regular roar of their breathing reached that solitary spot like the distant rumour of some leviathan beast angrily fuming. Further away to the south-west the Cauldon Bar Ironworks reproduced the same phenomena, and round the whole horizon, near and far, except to the north-east, the lesser fires of labour leapt and flickered and glinted in their mists of smoke, burning ceaselessly, as they burned every night and every day at all seasons of all years. The town of Bursley slept in the deep valley to the west, and vast Hanbridge in the shallower depression to the south, like two sleepers accustomed to rest quietly amid great disturbances; the beacons of their Town Halls and churches kept watch, and the whole scene was dominated by the placidity of the moon, which had now risen clear of the Red Cow furnace clouds, and was passing upwards through tracts of stars.

Into this scene, climbing up from the direction of Manifold, came Lionel Woolley, nearly at midnight, having walked some eighteen miles in a vain effort to re-establish his self-satisfaction by a process of reasoning and ingenious excuses. Lionel felt that in the brief episode of the afternoon he had scarcely behaved with dignity. In other words, he was fully and painfully aware that he must have looked a fool, a coward, an ass, a contemptible and pitiful person, in the eyes of at least one girl, if not of two. He did not like this—no man would have liked it; and to Lionel the memory of an undignified act was acute torture. Why had he bidden the girls adieu and departed? Why had he, in fact, run away? What precisely would May Lawton think of him? How could he explain his conduct to her—and to himself? And had that worshipping, affectionate thing, May Deane, taken note of his confusion—of the confusion of him who was never confused, who was equal to every occasion and every emergency? These were some of the questions which harried him and declined to be settled. He had walked to Manifold, and had tea at the Roebuck, and walked back, and still the questions were harrying; and as he came over the hill by the field-path, and descried the lone house of the Deanes in the light of the Red Cow furnaces and of the moon, the worship of May Deane seemed suddenly very precious to him, and he could not bear to think that any stupidity of his should have impaired it.

Then he saw May Deane walking slowly across the field, close to an abandoned pit-shaft, whose low protecting circular wall of brick

78

was crumbling to ruin on the side nearest to him.

She stopped, appeared to gaze at him intently, turned, and began to approach him. And he too, moved by a mysterious impulse which he did not pause to examine, swerved, and quickened his step in order to lessen the distance between them. He did not at first even feel surprise that she should be wandering solitary on the hill at that hour. Presently she stood still, while he continued to move forward. It was as if she drew him; and soon, in the pale moonlight and the wavering light of the furnaces, he could decipher all the details of her face, and he saw that she was smiling fondly, invitingly, admiringly, lustrously, with the old undiminished worship and affection. And he perceived a dark discoloration on her right cheek, as though she had suffered a blow, but this mark did not long occupy his mind. He thought suddenly of the strong probability that her father would leave a nice little bit of money to each of his three children; and he thought of her beauty, and of her timid fragility in the tight black dress, and of her immense and unquestioning love for him, which would survive all accidents and mishaps. He seemed to sink luxuriously into this grand passion of hers (which he deemed quite natural and proper) as into a soft feather-bed. To live secure in an atmosphere of exhaustless worship; to keep a fount of balm and admiration for ever in the house, a bubbling spring of passionate appreciation which would be continually available for the refreshment of his self-esteem! To be always sure of an obedience blind and willing, a subservience which no tyranny and no harshness and no whim would rouse into revolt; to sit on a throne with so much beauty kneeling at his feet!

And the possession of her beauty would be a source of legitimate pride to him. People would often refer to the beautiful Mrs. Woolley.

He felt that in sending May Deane to interrupt his highly emotional conversation with May Lawton Providence had watched over him and done him a good turn. May Lawton had advantages, and striking advantages, but he could not be sure of her. The suspicion that if she married him she would marry him for her own ends caused him a secret disquiet, and he feared that one day, perhaps one morning at breakfast, she might take it into her intelligent head to mock him, to exercise upon him her gift of irony, and to intimate to him that if he fancied she was his slave he was deceived. That she sincerely admired him he never for an instant doubted. But——

And, moreover, the unfortunate episode of the afternoon might have cooled her ardour to freezing-point.

He stood now in front of his worshipper, and the notion crossed his mind that in after-years he could say to his friends: 'I proposed to my wife at midnight under the moon. Not many men have done that.'

'Good-evening,' he ventured to the girl; and he added with bravado: 'We've met before to-day, haven't we?'

She made no reply, but her smile was more affectionate, more inviting, than ever.

'I'm glad of this opportunity—very glad,' he proceeded. 'I've been wanting to ... You must know, my dear girl, how I feel....'

She gave a gesture, charming in its sweet humility, as if to say: 'Who am I that I should dare——'

And then he proposed to her, asked her to share his life, and all that sort of thing; and when he had finished he thought, 'It's done now, anyway.'

Strange to relate, she offered no immediate reply, but she bent a little towards him with shining, happy eyes. He had an impulse to seize her in his arms and kiss her, but prudence suggested that he should defer the rite. She turned and began to walk slowly and meditatively towards the pit-shaft. He followed almost at her side, but a foot or so behind, waiting for her to speak. And as he waited, expectant, he looked at her profile and reflected how well the name May suited her, with its significances of shyness and dreamy hope, and hidden fire and the modesty of spring.

And while he was thus savouring her face, and they were still ten yards from the pit-shaft, she suddenly disappeared from his vision, as it were by a conjuring trick. He had a horrible sensation in his spinal column. He was not the man to mistrust the evidence of his senses, and he knew, therefore, that he had been proposing to a phantom.

V

The next morning—early, because of Jim's early breakfast—when May Deane's disappearance became known to the members of the household, Jim had the idea of utilizing Carlo in the search for her. The retriever went straight, without a fault, to the pit-shaft, and May was discovered alive and unscathed, save for a contusion of the face and a sprain in the wrist.

Her suicidal plunge had been arrested, at only a few feet from the top of the shaft, by a cross-stay of timber, upon which she lay prone. There was no reason why the affair should be made public, and it was not. It was suppressed into one of those secrets which embed themselves in the history of families, and after two or three generations blossom into romantic legends full of appropriate circumstantial detail.

Lionel Woolley spent a woeful night at his rooms. He did not know what to do, and on the following day May Lawton encountered him again, and proved by her demeanour that the episode of the previous afternoon had caused no estrangement. Lionel vacillated. The sway of the schoolmistress was almost restored, and it would have been restored fully had he not been preoccupied by a feverish curiosity—the curiosity to know whether or not May Deane was dead. He felt that she must indeed be dead, and he lived through the day expectant of the news of her sudden decease. Towards night his state of mind was such that he was obliged to call at the Deanes'. May heard him, and insisted on seeing him; more, she insisted on seeing him alone in the breakfast-room, where she reclined, interestingly white, on the sofa. Her father and brothers objected strongly to the interview, but they yielded, afraid that a refusal might induce hysteria and worse things.

And when Lionel Woolley came into the room, May, steeped in felicity, related to him the story of her impulsive crime.

'I was so happy,' she said, 'when I knew that Miss Lawton had deceived me.' And before he could inquire what she meant, she continued rapidly: 'I must have been unconscious, but I felt you were there, and something of me went out towards you. And oh! the answer to your question—I heard your question; the real *me* heard it, but that *something* could not speak.'

'My question?'

'You asked a question, didn't you?' she faltered, sitting up.

He hesitated, and then surrendered himself to her immense love and sank into it, and forgot May Lawton.

'Yes,' he said.

'The answer is yes. Oh, you must have known the answer would be yes! You did know, didn't you?'

He nodded grandly.

She sighed with delicious and overwhelming joy.

In the ecstasy of the achievement of her desire the girl gave little thought to the psychic aspect of the possibly unique wooing.

As for Lionel, he refused to dwell on it even in thought. And so that strange, magic, yearning effluence of a soul into a visible projection and shape was ignored, slurred over, and, after ten years of domesticity in the bank premises, is gradually being forgotten.

He is a man of business, and she, with her fading beauty, her ardent, continuous worship of the idol, her half-dozen small children, the eldest of whom is only eight, and the white window-curtains to change every week because of the smuts—do you suppose she has time or inclination to ponder upon the theory of the subliminal consciousness and kindred mysteries?

TIDDY-FOL-LOL

It was the dinner-hour, and a group of ragged and clay-soiled apprentice boys were making a great noise in the yard of Henry Mynors and Co.'s small, compact earthenware manufactory up at Toft End. Toft End caps the ridge to the east of Bursley; and Bursley, which has been the home of the potter for ten centuries, is the most ancient of the Five Towns in Staffordshire. The boys, dressed for the most part in shirt, trousers, and boots, all equally ragged and insecure, were playing at prison-bars.

Soon the game ended abruptly in a clamorous dispute upon a point of law, and it was not recommenced. The dispute dying a natural death, the tireless energies of the boys needed a fresh outlet. Inspired by a common instinct, they began at once to bait one of their number, a slight youngster of twelve years, much better clothed than the rest, who had adventurously strolled in from a neighbouring manufactory. This child answered their jibes in an amiable, silly, drawling tone which seemed to justify the epithet 'Loony,' frequently applied to him. Now and then he stammered; and then companions laughed loud, and he with them. It was known that several years ago he had fallen down a flight of stone steps, alighting on the back of his head, and that ever since he had been deaf of one ear and under some trifling mental derangement. His sublime calmness under their jests baffled them until the terrible figure of Mr. Machin, the engine-man, standing at the door of the slip-house, caught their attention and suggested a plan full of joyous possibilities. They gathered round the lad, and, talking in subdued murmurs, unanimously urged him with many persuasions to a certain course of action. He declined the scheme, and declined again. Suddenly a boy shouted:

'Thee dars' na'!'

'I dare,' was the drawled, smiling answer.

'I tell thee thee dars' na'!'

'I tell thee I dare.' And thereupon he slowly but resolutely set out for the slip-house door and Mr. Machin.

Eli Machin was beyond doubt the most considerable employé on Clarke's 'bank' (manufactory). Even Henry Clarke approached him with a subtly-indicated deference, and whenever Silas Emery, the immensely rich and miserly sleeping partner in the firm, came up to visit the works, these two old men chatted as old friends. In a modern earthenware manufactory the engine-room is the source of all activity, for, owing to the inventive genius of a famous and venerable son of the Five Towns, steam now presides at nearly every stage in the long process of turning earth into ware. It moves the pug-mill, the jollies, and the marvellous batting machines, dries the unfired clay, heats the printers' stoves, and warms the offices where the 'jacket-men' dwell. Coal is a tremendous item in the cost of production, and a competent, economical engine-man can be sure of good wages and a choice of berths; he is desired like a good domestic servant. Eli Machin was the prince of engine-men. His engine never went wrong, his coal bills were never extravagant, and (supreme virtue!) he was never absent on Mondays. From his post in the slip-house he watched over the whole works like a father, stern, gruff, forbidding, but to be trusted absolutely. He was sixty years old, and had been 'putting by' for nearly half a century. He lived in a tiny villa-cottage with his bed-ridden, cheerful wife, and lent small sums on mortgage of approved freeholds at 5 per cent.—no more and no less. Secure behind this rampart of saved money, he was the equal of the King on the throne. Not a magnate in all the Five Towns who would dare to be condescending to Eli Machin. He had been a sidesman at the old church. A trades-union had once asked him to become a working-man candidate for the Bursley Town Council, but he had refused because he did not care for the possibility of losing caste by being concerned in a strike. His personal respectability was entirely unsullied, and he worshipped this abstract quality as he worshipped God.

There was only one blot—but how foul!—on Eli Machin's career, and that had been dropped by his daughter Miriam, when, defying his authority, she married a scene-shifter at Hanbridge Theatre. The atrocious idea of being connected with the theatre had rendered him speechless for a time. He could but endure it in the most awful silence that ever hid passionate feeling. Then one day he had burst out, 'The wench is no better than a tiddy-fol-lol!' Only this solitary phrase—nothing else.

What a tiddy-fol-lol was no one quite knew; but the word, getting about, stuck to him, and for some weeks boys used to shout it after him in the streets, until he caught one of them, and in thirty seconds put an end to the practice. Thenceforth Miriam, with all hers, was dead to him. When her husband expired of consumption, Eli Machin saw the avenging arm of the Lord in action; and when her boy grew to be a source of painful anxiety to her, he said to himself that the wrath of Heaven was not yet cooled towards this impious daughter. The passage of fifteen years had apparently in no way softened his resentment.

The challenged lad in Mynors' yard slowly approached the slip-house door, and halted before Eli Machin, grinning.

'Well, young un,' the old man said absently, 'what dost want?'

'Tiddy-fol-lol, grandfeyther,' the child drawled in his silly, irritating voice, and added: 'They said I darena say it to ye.'

Without and instant's hesitation Eli Machin raised his still powerful arm, and, catching the boy under the ear, knocked him down. The other boys yelled with unaffected pleasure and ran away.

'Get up, and be off wi' ye. Ye dunna belong to this bank,' said Eli Machin in cold anger to the lad. But the lad did not stir; the lad's eyes were closed, and he lay white on the stones.

Eli Machin bent down, and peered through his spectacles at the prone form upon which the mid-day sun was beating.

'It's Miriam's boy!' he ejaculated under his breath, and looked round as if in inquiry—the yard was empty. Then with quick decision he picked up this limp and inconvenient parcel of humanity and hastened—ran—with it out of the yard into the road.

Down the road he ran, turned to the left into Clowes Street, and stopped before a row of small brown cottages. At the open door of one of these cottages a woman sat sewing. She was rather stout and full-bosomed, with a fair, fresh face, full of sense and peace; she looked under thirty, but was older.

'Here's thy Tommy, Miriam,' said Eli Machin shortly. 'He give me some of his sauce, and I doubt I've done him an injury.'

The woman dropped her sewing.

'Eh, dear!' she cried, 'is that lad o' mine in mischief again? I do hope he's no limb brokken.'

'It in'na that,' said the old man, 'but he's dazed-like. Better lay him on th' squab.'

She calmly took Tommy and placed him gently down on the check-covered sofa under the window. 'Come in, father, do.'

The man obeyed, astonished at the entire friendliness of this daughter, whom, though he had frequently seen her, he had never spoken to for more than ten years. Her manner, at once filial and quite natural, perfectly ignored the long breach, and disclosed no trace of animosity.

Father and daughter examined the unconscious child. Pale, pulseless, cold, he lay on the sofa like a corpse except for the short, faint breaths which he drew through his blue lips.

'I doubt I've killed him,' said Eli.

'Nay, nay, father!' And her face actually smiled. This supremacy of the soul against years of continued misfortune lifted her high above him, and he suddenly felt himself an inferior creature.

'I'll go for th' doctor,' he said.

'Nay! I shall need ye.' And she put her head out of the window. 'Mrs. Walley, will ye let your Lucy run quick for th' club doctor? my Tommy's hurt.'

The whole street awoke instantly from its nap, and in a few moments every door was occupied. Miriam closed her own door softly, as though she might wake the boy, and spoke in whispers to people through the window, finally telling them to go away. When the doctor came, half an hour afterwards, she had done all that she knew for Tommy, without the slightest apparent result.

'What is it?' asked the doctor curtly, as he lifted the child's thin and lifeless hand.

Eli Machin explained that he had boxed the boy's ear.

'Tommy was impudent to his grandfather,' Miriam added hastily.

'Which ear?' the doctor inquired. It was the left. He gazed into it, and then raised the boy's right leg and arm. 'There is no paralysis,' he said. Then he felt the heart, and then took out his stethoscope and applied it, listening intently.

'Canst hear owt?' the old man said.

'I cannot,' he answered.

'Don't say that, doctor—don't say that! said Miriam, with an accent of appeal.

'In these cases it is almost impossible to tell whether the patient is alive or dead. We must wait. Mrs. Baddeley, make a mustard plaster for his feet, and we will put another over the heart.' And so they waited one hour, while the clock ticked and the mustard plasters gradually cooled. Then Tommy's lips parted.

After another half-hour the doctor said:

'I must go now; I will come again at six. Do nothing but apply fresh plasters. Be sure to keep his neck free. He is breathing, but I may as well be plain with you—there is a great risk of your child dying in this condition.'

Neighbours were again at the window, and Miriam drew the blind, waving them away. At six o'clock the doctor reappeared. 'There is no change,' he remarked. 'I will call in before I go to bed.'

When he lifted the latch for the third time, at ten o'clock, Eli Machin and Miriam still sat by the sofa, and Tommy still lay thereon, moveless, a terrible enigma. But the glass lamp was lighted on the mantelpiece, and Miriam's sewing, by which she earned a livelihood, had been hidden out of sight.

'There is no change,' said the doctor. 'You can do nothing except hope.'

'And pray,' the calm mother added.

Eli neither stirred nor spoke. For nine hours he had absolutely forgotten his engine. He knew the boy would die.

The clock struck eleven, twelve, one, two, three, each time fretting the nerves of the old man like a rasp. It was the hour of summer dawn. A cold gray light fell unkindly across the small figure on the sofa.

'Open th' door a bit, father,' said Miriam. 'This parlour's gettin' close; th' lad canna breathe.'

'Nay, lass,' Eli sighed, as he stumbled obediently to the door. 'The lad'll breathe no more. I've killed him i' my anger.' He frowned heavily, as though someone was annoying him.

'Hist!' she exclaimed, when, after extinguishing the lamp, she returned to her boy's side. 'He's reddened—he's reddened! Look thee at his cheeks, father!' She seized the child's inert hands and rubbed them between her own. The blood was now plain in Tommy's face. His legs faintly twitched. His breathing was slower. Miriam moved the coverlet and put her head upon his heart. 'It's beating loud, father,' she cried. 'Bless God!'

Eli stared at the child with the fixity of a statue. Then Tommy opened his eyes for an instant. The old man groaned. Tommy looked vacantly round, closed his eyes again, and was unmistakably asleep. He slept for one minute, and then waked. Eli involuntarily put a hand on the sofa. Tommy gazed at him, and, with the most heavenly innocent smile of recognition, lightly touched his grandfather's hand. Then he turned over on his right side. In the anguish of sudden joy Eli gave a deep, piteous sob. That smile burnt into him like a coal of fire.

'Now for the beef-tea,' said Miriam, crying.

'Beef-tea?' the boy repeated after her, mildly questioning.

'Yes, my poppet,' she answered; and then aside, 'Father, he can hear i' his left ear. Did ye notice it?'

'It's a miracle—a miracle of God!' said Eli.

In a few hours Tommy was as well as ever—indeed, better; not only was his hearing fully restored, but he had ceased to stammer, and the thin, almost imperceptible cloud upon his intellect was dissipated. The doctor expressed but little surprise at these phenomena, and, in fact, stated that similar things had occurred often before, and were duly written down in the books of medicine. But Eli Machin's firm, instinctive faith that Providence had intervened will never be shaken.

Miriam and Tommy now live in the villa-cottage with the old people.

THE IDIOT

William Froyle, ostler at the Queen's Arms at Moorthorne, took the letter, and, with a curt nod which stifled the loquacity of the village postman, went at once from the yard into the coach-house. He had recognised the hand-writing on the envelope, and the recognition of it gave form and quick life to all the vague suspicions that had troubled him some months before, and again during the last few days. He felt suddenly the near approach of a frightful calamity which had long been stealing towards him.

A wire-sheathed lantern, set on a rough oaken table, cast a wavering light round the coach-house, and dimly showed the inner stable. Within the latter could just be distinguished the mottled-gray flanks of a fat cob which dragged its chain occasionally, making the large slow movements of a horse comfortably lodged in its stall. The pleasant odour of animals and hay filled the wide spaces of the shed, and through the half-open door came a fresh thin mist rising from the rain-soaked yard in the November evening.

Froyle sat down on the oaken table, his legs dangling, and looked again at the envelope before opening it. He was a man about thirty years of age, with a serious and thoughtful, rather heavy countenance. He had a long light moustache, and his skin was a fresh, rosy salmon colour; his straw-tinted hair was cut very short, except over the forehead, where it grew full and bushy. Dressed in his rough stable corduroys, his forearms bare and white, he had all the appearance of the sturdy Englishman, the sort of Englishman that crosses the world in order to find vent for his taciturn energy on virgin soils. From the whole village he commanded and received respect. He was known for a scholar, and it was his scholarship which had obtained for him the proud position of secretary to the provident society styled the Queen's Arms Slate Club. His respectability and his learning combined had enabled him to win with dignity the hand of Susie Trimmer, the grocer's daughter, to whom he had been engaged about a year. The village could not make up its mind concerning that match; without doubt it was a social victory for Froyle, but everyone wondered that so sedate and sagacious a man should have seen in Susie a suitable mate.

He tore open the envelope with his huge forefinger, and, bending down towards the lantern, began to read the letter. It ran:

89

'OLDCASTLE STREET,
'BURSLEY.
'DEAR WILL,

'I asked father to tell you, but he would not. He said I must write. Dear Will, I hope you will never see me again. As you will see by the above address, I am now at Aunt Penrose's at Bursley. She is awful angry, but I was obliged to leave the village because of my shame. I have been a wicked girl. It was in July. You know the man, because you asked me about him one Sunday night. He is no good. He is a villain. Please forget all about me. I want to go to London. So many people know me here, and what with people coming in from the village, too. Please forgive me.

'S. TRIMMER.'

After reading the letter a second time, Froyle folded it up and put it in his pocket. Beyond a slight unaccustomed pallor of the red cheeks, he showed no sign of emotion. Before the arrival of the postman he had been cleaning his master's bicycle, which stood against the table. To this he returned. Kneeling down in some fresh straw, he used his dusters slowly and patiently—rubbing, then stopping to examine the result, and then rubbing again. When the machine was polished to his satisfaction, he wheeled it carefully into the stable, where it occupied a stall next to that of the cob. As he passed back again, the animal leisurely turned its head and gazed at Froyle with its large liquid eyes. He slapped the immense flank. Content, the animal returned to its feed, and the weighted chain ran down with a rattle.

The fortnightly meeting of the Slate Club was to take place at eight o'clock that evening. Froyle had employed part of the afternoon in making ready his books for the event, to him always so solemn and ceremonious; and the affairs of the club were now prominent in his mind. He was sorry that it would be impossible for him to attend the meeting; fortunately, all the usual preliminaries were complete.

He took a piece of notepaper from a little hanging cupboard, and, sprawling across the table, began to write under the lantern. The pencil seemed a tiny toy in his thick roughened fingers:

'*To Mr. Andrew McCall, Chairman Queen's Arms Slate Club.*

'DEAR SIR,

'I regret to inform you that I shall not be at the meeting to-night. You will find the' books in order....'

Here he stopped, biting the end of the pencil in thought. He put down the pencil and stepped hastily out of the stable, across the yard, and into the hotel. In the large room, the room where cyclists sometimes took tea and cold meat during the summer season, the long deal table and the double line of oaken chairs stood ready for the meeting. A fire burnt warmly in the big grate, and the hanging lamp had been lighted. On the wall was a large card containing the rules of the club, which had been written out in a fair hand by the schoolmaster. It was to this card that Froyle went. Passing his thumb down the card, he paused at Rule VII.:

'Each member shall, on the death of another member, pay 1s. for benefit of widow or nominee of deceased, same to be paid within one month after notice given.'

'Or nominee—nominee,' he murmured reflectively, staring at the card. He mechanically noticed, what he had noticed often before with disdain, that the chairman had signed the rules without the use of capitals.

He went back to the dusk of the coach-house to finish his letter, still murmuring the word 'nominee,' of whose meaning he was not quite sure:

'I request that the money due to me from the Slate Club on my death shall be paid to my nominee, Miss Susan Trimmer, now staying with her aunt, Mrs. Penrose, at Bursley.

'Yours respectfully,

'WILLIAM FROYLE.'

After further consideration he added:

'P.S.—My annual salary of sixpence per member would be due at the end of December. If so be the members would pay that, or part of it, should they consider the same due, to Susan Trimmer as well, I should be thankful.—Yours resp, W.F.'

He put the letter in an envelope, and, taking it to the large room, laid it carefully at the end of the table opposite the chairman's seat. Once more he returned to the coach-house. From the hanging cupboard he now produced a piece of rope. Standing on the table he could just reach, by leaning forward, a hook in the ceiling, that was sometimes used for the slinging of bicycles. With difficulty he made the rope fast to the hook. Putting a noose on the other end, he tightened it round his neck. He looked up at the ceiling and down at the floor in order to judge whether the rope was short enough.

'Good-bye, Susan, and everyone,' he whispered, and then stepped off the table.

The tense rope swung him by his neck halfway across the coach-house. He swung twice to and fro, but as he passed under the hook for the fifth time his toes touched the floor. The rope had stretched. In another second he was standing firm on the floor, purple and panting, but ignominiously alive.

'Good-even to you, Mr. Froyle. Be you committing suicide?' The tones were drawling, uncertain, mildly astonished.

He turned round hastily, his hands busy with the rope, and saw in the doorway the figure of Daft Jimmy, the Moorthorne idiot.

He hesitated before speaking, but he was not confused. No one could have been confused before Daft Jimmy. Neither man nor woman in the village considered his presence more than that of a cat.

'Yes, I am,' he said.

The middle-aged idiot regarded him with a vague, interested smile, and came into the coach-house.

'You'n gotten the rope too long, Mr. Froyle. Let me help you.'

Froyle calmly assented. He stood on the table, and the two rearranged the noose and made it secure. As they did so the idiot gossiped:

'I was going to Bursley to-night to buy me a pair o' boots, and when I was at top o' th' hill I remembered as I'd forgotten the measure o' my feet. So I ran back again for it. Then I saw the light in here, and I stepped up to bid ye good-evening.'

Someone had told him the ancient story of the fool and his boots, and, with the pride of an idiot in his idiocy, he had determined that it should be related of himself.

Froyle was silent.

The idiot laughed with a dry cackle.

'Now you go,' said Froyle, when the rope was fixed.

'Let me see ye do it,' the idiot pleaded with pathetic eyes.

'No; out you get!'

Protesting, the idiot went forth, and his irregular clumsy footsteps sounded on the pebble-paved yard. When the noise of them ceased in the soft roadway, Froyle jumped off the table again. Gradually his body, like a stopping pendulum, came to rest under the hook, and hung twitching, with strange disconnected movements. The horse in the stable, hearing unaccustomed noises, rattled his chain and stamped about in the straw of his box.

Furtive steps came down the yard again, and Daft Jimmy peeped into the coach-house.

'He done it! he done it!' the idiot cried gleefully. 'Damned if he hasna'.' He slapped his leg and almost danced. The body still twitched occasionally. 'He done it!'

'Done what, Daft Jimmy? You're making a fine noise there! Done what?'

The idiot ran out of the stable. At the side-entrance to the hotel stood the barmaid, the outline of her fine figure distinct against the light from within.

The idiot continued to laugh.

'Done what?' the girl repeated, calling out across the dark yard in clear, pleasant tones of amused inquiry. 'Done what?'

'What's that to you, Miss Tucker?'

'Now, none of your sauce, Daft Jimmy! Is Willie Froyle in there?'

The idiot roared with laughter.

'Yes, he is, miss.'

'Well, tell him his master wants him. I don't want to cross this mucky, messy yard.'

'Yes, miss.'

The girl closed the door.

The idiot went into the coach-house, and, slapping William's body in a friendly way so that it trembled on the rope, he spluttered out between his laughs:

'Master wants ye, Mr. Froyle.'

Then he walked out into the village street, and stood looking up the muddy road, still laughing quietly. It was quite dark, but the moon aloft in the clear sky showed the highway with its shining ruts leading in a straight line over the hill to Bursley.

'Them shoes!' the idiot ejaculated suddenly. 'Well, I be an idiot, and that's true! They can take the measure from my feet, and I never thought on it till this minute!'

Laughing again, he set off at a run up the hill.

PART II
ABROAD

THE HUNGARIAN RHAPSODY

I

After a honeymoon of five weeks in the shining cities of the Mediterranean and in Paris, they re-entered the British Empire by the august portals of the Chatham and Dover Railway. They stood impatiently waiting, part of a well-dressed, querulous crowd, while a few officials performed their daily task of improvising a Custom-house for registered luggage on a narrow platform of Victoria Station. John, Mr. Norris's man, who had met them, attended behind. Suddenly, with a characteristic movement, the husband lifted his head, and then looked down at his wife.

'I say, May!'

'Well?'

She knew that he was about to propose some swift alteration of their plans, but she smiled upwards out of her furs at his grave face, and the tone of her voice granted all requests in advance.

'I think I'd better go to the office,' he said.

'Now?'

She smiled again, inviting him to do exactly what he chose. She was already familiar with his restiveness under enforced delays and inaction, and his unfortunate capacity for being actively bored by trifles which did not interest him aroused in her a sort of maternal sympathy.

'Yes,' he answered. 'I can be there and back in an hour or less. You titivate yourself, and we'll dine at the Savoy, or anywhere you please. We'll keep the ball rolling to-night. Yes,' he repeated, as if to convince himself that he was not a deserter, 'I really must call in at the office. You and John can see to the luggage, can't you?'

'Of course,' she replied, with calm good-nature, and also with perfect self-confidence. 'But give me the keys of the trunks, and don't be late, Ted.'

'Oh, I shan't be late,' he said.

Their fingers touched as she took the keys. He went away enraptured anew by her delightful acquiescences, her unique smile, her common-sense, her mature charm, and the astonishing elegance of her person. The honeymoon was over—and with what finished discretion, combining the innocent girl with the woman of the world, she had lived through the honeymoon!—another life, more delicious, was commencing.

'What a wife!' he thought triumphantly. 'She does understand a man! And fancy leaving any ordinary bride to look after luggage!'

Nevertheless, once in his offices at Winchester House, he managed to forget her, and to forget time, for nearly an hour and a half. When at last he came to himself from the enchantment of affairs, he jumped into a hansom, and told the driver to drive fast to Knightsbridge. He was ardent to see her again. In the dark seclusion of the cab he speculated upon her toilette, the colour of her shoes. He thought of the last five weeks, of the next five years. Dwelling on their mutual love and esteem, their health, their self-knowledge and experience and cheerfulness, her sense and grace, his talent for getting money first and keeping it afterwards, he foresaw nothing but happiness for them. Children? H'm! Possibly....

At Piccadilly Circus it began to rain—cold, heavy March rain.

'Window down, sir?' asked the voice of the cabman.

'Yes,' he ordered sardonically. 'Better be suffocated than drowned.'

'You're right, sir,' said the voice.

Soon, through the streaming glass, which made every gas-jet into a shooting pillar of flame, Norris discerned vaguely the vast bulk of Hyde Park Mansions. 'Good!' he muttered, and at that very moment he was shot through the window into the thin, light-reflecting mire of the street. Enormous and strange beasts menaced him with pitiless hoofs. Millions of people crowded about him. In response to a question that seemed to float slowly towards him, he tried to give his address. He realized, by a considerable feat of intellect, that the horse must have fallen down; and then, with a dim notion that nothing mattered, he went to sleep.

II

In the boudoir of the magnificent flat on the first floor, shielded from the noise and the inclemency of the world by four silk-hung walls and a double window, and surrounded by all the multitudinous and costly luxury that a stockbroker with brains and taste can obtain for the wife of his love, May was leisurely finishing her toilette. And every detail in the long, elaborate process was accomplished with a passionate intention to bewitch the man at Winchester House.

These two had first met seven years before, when May, the daughter of a successful wholesale draper at Hanbridge, in the Five Towns district of Staffordshire, was aged twenty-two. Mr. Scarratt went to Manchester each Tuesday to buy, and about once a month he took May with him. One day, when they were lunching at the Exchange Restaurant, a young man came up whom her father introduced as Mr. Edward Norris, his stockbroker. Mr. Norris, whose years were thirty, glanced keenly at May, and accepted Mr. Scarratt's invitation to join them. Ever afterwards May vividly remembered the wonderful sensation, joyous yet disconcerting, which she then experienced—the sensation of having captivated her father's handsome and correct stockbroker. The three talked horses with a certain freedom, and since May was accustomed to drive the Scarratt dogcart, so famous in the Five Towns, she could bring her due share to the conversation. The meal over, Mr. Norris discussed business matters with his client, and then sedately departed, but not without the obviously sincere expression of a desire to meet Miss Scarratt again. The wholesale draper praised Edward's financial qualities behind his back, and wondered that a man of such aptitude should remain in Manchester while London existed. As for May, she decided that she would have a new frock before she came to Manchester in the following month.

She had a new frock, but not of the colour intended. By the following month her father was enclosed in a coffin, and it happened to his estate, as to the estates of many successful men who employ stockbrokers, that the liabilities far more than covered the assets. May and her mother were left without a penny. The mother did the right thing, and died—it was best. May went direct to Brunt's, the largest draper in the Five Towns, and asked for a place under 'Madame' in the dress-making department. Brunt's daughter, who was about to be married, gave her the place instantly. Three years later, when 'Madame' returned to Paris, May stepped into the French-woman's shoes.

On Sundays and on Thursday afternoons, and sometimes (but not too often) at the theatre, May was the finest walking advertisement that Brunt's ever had. Old Brunt would have proposed to her, it was rumoured, had he not been scared by her elegance. Sundry sons of prosperous manufacturers, unabashed by this elegance, did in fact secretly propose, but with what result was known only to themselves.

Later, as May waxed in importance at Brunt's, she was sent to Manchester to buy. She lunched at the Exchange Restaurant. The world and Manchester are very small. The first man she set eyes on was Edward Norris. Another week, Norris said to her with a thrill, and he would have been gone for ever to London. Chance is not to be flouted. The sequel was inevitable. They loved. And all the select private bars in Hanbridge tinkled to the news that May Scarratt had been and hooked a stockbroker!

When the toilette was done, and the maid gone, she wound a thin black scarf round her olive neck and shoulders, and sat down negligently on a Chippendale settee in the attitude of a portrait by Boldini; her little feet were tucked up sideways on the settee; the perforated lace ends of the scarf fell over her low corsage to the level of the seat. And she waited, still the bride. He was late, but she knew he would be late. Sure in the conviction that he was a strong man, a man of imagination and of deeds, she could easily excuse this failing in him, as she did that other habit of impulsive action in trifles. Nay, more, she found keen pleasure in excusing it. 'Dear thing!' she reflected, 'he forgets so.' Therefore she waited, content in enjoying the image in the glass of her dark face, her small plump person, and her Paris gown—that dream! She thought with assuaged grief of her father's tragedy; she would have liked him to see her now, the jewel in the case—her father and she had understood each other.

All around, and above and below, she felt, without hearing it, the activity of the opulent, complex life of the mansions. Her mind dwelt with satisfaction on long carpeted corridors noiselessly paraded by flunkeys, mahogany lifts continually ascending and descending like the angels of the ladder, the great entrance hall with its fire always burning and its doors always swinging, the*salle à manger* sown with rose-shaded candles, and all the splendid privacies rising stage upon stage to the attics, where the flunkeys philosophized together. She confessed the beauty and distinction achieved by this extravagant organization for gratifying earthly desires. Often, in the pinching days of her servitude, she had murmured against the injustice of things, and had called wealth a crime while poverty starved. But now she perceived that society was what it was inevitably, and could not be altered. She accepted it in profound peace of mind, gaily fraternal towards the fortunate, compassionate towards those in adversity.

In the next flat someone began to play very brilliantly a Hungarian Rhapsody of Liszt's. And even the faint sound of that riotous torrent of melody, so arrogantly gorgeous, intoxicated her soul. She shivered under the sudden vision of the splendid joy of being alive. And how she envied the player! French she had learned from 'Madame,' but she had no skill on the piano; it was her one regret.

She touched the bell.

'Has your master come in yet?' she inquired of the maid.

'No, madam, not yet.'

She knew he had not come in, but she could not resist the impulse to ask.

Ten minutes later, when the piano had ceased, she jumped up, and, creeping to the front-door of the flat, gazed foolishly across the corridor at the grille of the lift. She heard the lift in travail. It appeared and passed out of sight above. No, he had not come! Glancing aside, she saw the tall slender figure of a girl in a green tea-gown—a mere girl: it was the player of the Hungarian Rhapsody. And this girl, too, she thought, was expectant and disappointed! They shut their doors simultaneously, she and May, who also had her girlish moments. Then the rhapsody recommenced.

'Oh, madam!' screamed the maid, almost tumbling into the boudoir.

'What is it?' May demanded with false calm.

The maid lifted the corner of her black apron to her eyes, as though she had been a stage soubrette in trouble.

'The master, madam! He's fell out of his cab—just in front of the mansions—and they're bringing him in—such blood I never did see!'

The maid finished with hysterics.

III

'And them just off their honeymoon!'

The inconsolable tones of the lady's-maid came from the kitchen to the open door of the bedroom, where May was giving instructions to the elderly cook.

'Send that girl out of the flat this moment!' May said.

'Yes, ma'am.'

'Make the beef-tea in case it's wanted, and let me have some more warm water. There's John and the doctor!'

She started at a knock.

'No, it's only the postman, ma'am.'

Some letters danced on the hall floor and on her nerves.

'Oh dear!' May whispered. 'I thought it was the doctor at last.'

'John's bound to be back with one in a minute, ma'am. Do bear up,' urged the cook, hurrying to the kitchen.

She could have destroyed the woman for those last words.

With the proud certainty of being equal to the dreadful crisis, she turned abruptly into the bedroom, where her husband lay insensible on one of the new beds. Assisted by the policemen and the cook, she had done everything that could be done: cut away the coats and the waistcoat, removed the boots, straightened the limbs, washed the face and neck—especially the neck—which had to be sponged continually, and scattered messengers, including John, over the vicinity in search of medical aid. And now the policemen had gone, the general emotion on the staircase had subsided, the front-door of the flat was shut. The great ocean of the life of the mansions had closed smoothly upon her little episode. She was alone with the shattered organism.

She bent fondly over the bed, and her Paris frock, and the black scarf which she had not removed, touched its ruinous burden. Her right hand directed the sponge with ineffable tenderness, and then the long thin fingers tightened to a frenzied clutch to squeeze it over the basin. The whole of her being was absorbed in a deep passion of pity and an intolerable hunger for the doctor.

Through the wall came once more the faint sound of the Hungarian Rhapsody, astonishingly rapid and brilliant. She set her teeth to endure its unconscious message of the vast indifference of life to death.

The organism stirred, and May watched the deathly face for a sign. The eyes opened and stared at her in agonized bewilderment. The lips tried to speak, and failed.

'It's all right, darling,' she said softly. 'You're in your own bed. The doctor will be here directly. Drink this.'

She gave him some brandy-and-water, and they looked at each other. He was no longer Edward Norris, the finely regulated intelligence, the masterful volition, the conqueror of the world and of a woman; but merely the embodiment of a frightened, despairing, flickering, hysterical will-to-live, which glanced in terror at the corners of the room as though it saw fate there. And beneath her intense solicitude was the instinctive feeling, which hurt her, but which she could not dismiss, of her measureless, dominating superiority. With what glad relief would she have changed places with him!

'I'm dying, May,' he murmured at length, with a sigh. 'Why doesn't the doctor come?'

'He is coming,' she replied soothingly. 'You'll be better soon.'

But his effort in speaking obliged her to use the sponge again, and he saw it, and drew another sigh, more mortal than the first.

'Oh! I'm dying,' he repeated.

'Not you, Ted!' And her smile cost her an awful pang.

'I am. I know it.' This time he spoke with sad resignation. 'You must face it. And—listen.'

'What, dear?'

A physical sensation of sickness came over her. She could not disguise from herself the fact that he was dying. The warped and pallid face, the panic-struck eyes, the sweat, the wound in the neck, the damp hands nervously pulling the hem of the sheet—these indications were not to be gainsaid. The truth was too horrible to grasp; she wanted to put it away from her. 'This calamity cannot happen to me!' she thought urgently, and all the while she knew that it was happening to her.

He collected the feeble remnant of his powers by an immense effort, and began to speak, slowly and fragmentarily, and with such weakness that she could only catch his words by putting her ear to his mouth. The restless hands dropped the sheet and took the end of the black scarf.

'You'll be comfortable—for money,' he said. 'Will made.... It's not that. It's ... I must tell you. It's——'

'Yes?' she encouraged him. 'Tell me. I can hear.'

'It's about your father. I didn't treat him quite right ... once.... Week after I first met you, May.... No, not quite right. He was holding Hull and Barnsley shares ... you know, railway ... great gambling stock, then, Hull and Barn—Barnsley. Holding them on cover; for the rise.... They dropped too much—dropped to 23.... He couldn't hold any longer ... wired to me to sell and cut the loss. Understand?'

'Yes,' she said, trembling. 'I quite understand.'

'Well ... I wired back, "Sold at 23." ... But some mistake. Shares not sold. Clerk's mistake.... Clerk didn't sell.... Next day rise began.... I didn't wire him shares not sold. Somehow, I couldn't.... Put it off.... Rise went on.... I took over shares myself ... you see—myself.... Made nearly five thousand clear.... I wanted money then.... I think I would have told him, perhaps, later ... made it right ... but he died ... sudden ... I wasn't going to let his creditors have that five thou.... No, he'd meant to sell ... and, look here, May, if those shares had dropped lower ... 'stead of rising ... I should have had to stand the racket ... with your father, for my clerk's mistake.... See?... He'd meant to sell.... Hard lines on him, but he'd meant to sell.... He'd meant——'

'Don't say any more, dear.'

'Must explain this, May. Why didn't I give the money to you ... when he was dead?... Because I knew you'd only ... give it ... to creditors.... I knew you.... That's straight.... I've told you now.'

He lost consciousness again, but for an instant May did not notice it. She was crying, and her tears fell on his face.

Then came a doctor, a little dark man, who explained with calm politeness that he had been out when the messenger first arrived. He took off his coat, hung it up, opened his bag, and proceeded to a minute examination of the patient. His movements were so methodical, and he gave orders to May in a tone so quiet, casual, and ordinary, that she almost lost her sense of the reality of the scene.

'Yes, yes,' he said, from time to time, as if to himself; nothing else; not a single enlightening word to May.

'I'm dying,' moaned Edward, opening his eyes.

The doctor glanced round at May and winked. That wink, deliberate and humorous, was like an electric shock to her. She could actually feel her heart leap in her breast. If she had not been afraid of the doctor, she would have fainted.

'You all think you're dying,' the doctor remarked in a low, amused tone to the ceiling, as he wiped a pair of scissors, 'when you've been knocked silly, especially if there's a lot of blood about.'

The door opened.

'Here's John, ma'am,' said the cook, 'with two more doctors. What am I to do?'

May involuntarily turned towards the door.

'Don't you go, Mrs. Norris,' the little dark man commanded. 'I want you.' Then he carelessly scrutinized the elderly servant. 'Tell 'em they're too late,' he said. 'It's generally like that when there's an accident,' he continued after the housekeeper had gone. 'First you can't get a doctor anywhere, and then in half an hour or so we come in crowds. I've known seven doctors turn up one after another. But in that affair the man happened to have been killed outright.'

He smiled grimly. In a little while he was snapping his bag.

'I'll come in the morning, of course,' he said, as he wrote on a piece of paper. 'Have this made up, and give it him in the night if he is wakeful. Keep him warm. You might put a couple of hot-water bags, one on either side of him. You've got beef-tea made, you say? That's right. Let him have as much as he wants. Mr. Norris, you'll sleep like a top.'

'But, doctor,' May inquired the next morning in the hall, after Edward had smiled at a joke, and been informed that he must run down to Bournemouth in a week, 'have we nothing to fear?'

'I think not,' was the measured answer. 'These affairs nearly always seem much worse than they are. Of course, the immediate upset is tremendous—the disorganization, and all that sort of thing. But Nature's pretty wonderful. You'll find your husband will soon get over it. I should say he had a good constitution.'

'And there will be no permanent effects?'

'Yes,' said the doctor, with genial cynicism. 'There'll be one permanent effect. Nobody will ever persuade him to ride in a hansom again. If he can't find a four-wheeler, he'll walk in future.'

She returned to the bedroom. The man on the bed was Edward Norris once more, in control of himself, risen out of his humiliation. A feeling of thankfulness overwhelmed her for a moment, and she sat down.

'Well, May?' he murmured.

'Well, dear.'

They both realized that what they had been through was a common, daily street accident. The smile of each was self-conscious, apprehensive, insincere.

'Quite a concert going on next door,' he said with an affectation of lightness.

It was the Hungarian Rhapsody, impetuous and brilliant as ever. How she hated it now—this symbol of the hurried, unheeding, relentless, hollow gaiety of the world! Yet she longed for the magic fingers of the player, that she, too, might smother grief in such glittering veils!

IV

The marriage which had begun so dramatically fell into placid routine. Edward fulfilled the prophecy of the doctor. In a week they were able to go to Bournemouth for a few days, and in less than a fortnight he was at the office—the strong man again, confident and ambitious.

After days devoted to finance, he came home in the evenings high-spirited and determined to enjoy himself. His voice was firm and his eye steady when he spoke to his wife; there was no trace of self-consciousness in his demeanour. She admired the masculinity of the brain that could forget by an effort of will. She felt that he trusted her to forget also; that he relied on her common-sense, her characteristic sagacity, to extinguish for ever the memory of an awkward incident. He loved her. He was intensely proud of her. He treated her with every sort of generosity. And in return he expected her to behave like a man.

She loved him. She esteemed him as a wife should. She made a profession of wifehood. He gave his days to finance and his nights to diversion; but her vocation was always with her—she was never off duty. She aimed to please him to the uttermost in everything, to be in all respects the ideal helpmate of a husband who was at once strenuous, fastidious, and wealthy. Elegance and suavity were a religion with her. She was the delight of the eye and of the ear, the soother of groans, the refuge of distress, the uplifter of the heart.

She made new acquaintances for him, and cemented old friendships. Her manner towards his old friends enchanted him; but when they were gone she had a way of making him feel that she was only his. She thought that she was succeeding in her aim. She thought that all these sweet, endless labours—of traffic with dressmakers, milliners, coiffeurs, maids, cooks, and furnishers; of paying and receiving calls; of delicious surprise journeys to the City to bring home the breadwinner; of giving and accepting dinners; of sitting alert and appreciative in theatres and music-halls; of supping in golden restaurants; of being serious, cautionary, submissive, and seductive; of smiles, laughter, and kisses; and of continuous sympathetic responsiveness—she thought that all these labours had attained their object: Edward's complete serenity and satisfaction. She imagined that love and duty had combined successfully to deceive him on one solitary point. She was sure that he was deceived. But she was wrong.

One evening they were at the theatre alone together. It was a musical comedy, and they had a large stage-box. May sat a little behind. After having been darkened for a scenic conjuring trick, the stage was very suddenly thrown into brilliant light. Edward turned with equal suddenness to share his appreciation of the effect with his wife, and the light and his eye caught her unawares. She smiled instantly, but too late; he had seen the expression of her features. For a second she felt as if the whole fabric which she had been building for the last six months had crumbled; but this disturbing idea passed as she recovered herself.

'Let's go home, eh?' he said, at the end of the first act.

'Yes,' she agreed. 'It would be nice to be in early, wouldn't it?'

In the brougham they exchanged the amiable banalities of people who are thoroughly intimate. When they reached the flat, she poured out his whisky-and-potass, and sat on the arm of his particular arm-chair while he sipped it; then she whispered that she was going to bed.

'Wait a bit,' he said; 'I want to talk to you seriously.'

'Dear thing!' she murmured, stroking his coat.

She had not the slightest notion of his purpose.

'You've tried your best, May,' he said bluntly, 'but you've failed. I've suspected it for a long time.'

She flushed, and retired to a sofa, away from the orange electric lamp.

'What do you mean, Edward?' she asked.

'You know very well what I mean, my dear,' he replied. 'What I told you—that night! You've tried to forget it. You've tried to look at me as though you had forgotten it. But you can't do it. It's on your mind. I've noticed it again and again. I noticed it at the theatre to-night. So I said to myself, "I'll have it out with her." And I'm having it out.'

'My dear Ted, I assure you——'

'No, you don't,' he stopped her. 'I wish you did. Now you must just listen. I know exactly what sort of an idiot I was that night as well as you do. But I couldn't help it. I was a fool to tell you. Still, I thought I was dying. I simply had a babbling fit. People are like that. You thought I was dying, too, didn't you?'

'Yes,' she said quietly, 'for a minute or two.'

'Ah! It was that minute or two that did it. Well, I let it out, the rotten little secret. I admit it wasn't on the square, that bit of business. But, on the other hand, it wasn't anything really bad—like cruelty to animals or ruining a girl. Of course, the chap was your father, but, but——. Look here, May, you ought to be able to see that I was exactly the same man after I told you as I was before. You ought to be able to see that. My character wasn't wrecked because I happened to split on myself, like an ass, about that affair. Mind you, I don't blame you. You can't help your feelings. But do you suppose there's a single man on this blessed earth without a secret? I'm not going to grovel before gods or men. I'm not going to pretend I'm so frightfully sorry. I'm sorry in a way. But can't you see——'

'Don't say any more, Ted,' she begged him, fingering her sash. 'I know all that. I know it all, and everything else you can say. Oh, my darling boy! do you think I would look down on you ever so little because of—what you told me? Who am I? I wouldn't care twopence even if——'

'But it's between us all the same,' he broke in. 'You can't get over it.'

'Get over it!' she repeated lamely.

'Can you? Have you?' He pinned her to a direct answer.

She did not flinch.

'No,' she said.

'I thought you would have done,' he remarked, half to himself. 'I thought you would. I thought you were enough a woman of the world for that, May. It isn't as if the confounded thing had made any real difference to your father. The old man died, and——'

'Ted!' she exclaimed, 'I shall have to tell you, after all. It killed him.'

'What killed him? He died of gastritis.'

'He was ill with gastritis, but he died of suicide. It's easy for a gastritis patient to commit suicide. And father did.'

'Why?'

'Oh, ruin, despair! He'd been in difficulties for a long time. He said that selling those shares just one day too soon was the end of it. When he saw them going up day after day, it got on his mind. He said he knew he would never, never have any luck. And then ...'

'You kept it quiet.' He was walking about the room.

'Yes, that was pretty easy.'

'And did your mother know?'

He turned and looked at her.

'Yes, mother knew. It finished her. Oh, Ted!' she burst out, 'if you'd only telegraphed to him the next morning that the shares weren't sold, things might have been quite different.'

'You mean I killed your father—and your mother.'

'No, I don't,' she cried passionately. 'I tell you I don't. You didn't know. But I think of it all, sometimes. And that's why—that's why——'

She sat down again.

'By God, May,' he swore, 'I'm frightfully sorry!'

'I never meant to tell you,' she said, composing herself. 'But, there! things slip out. Good-night.'

She was gone, but in passing him she had timidly caressed his shoulder.

'It's all up,' he said to himself. 'This will always be between us. No one could expect her to forget it.'

V

Gradually her characteristic habits deserted her; she seemed to lose energy and a part of her interest in those things which had occupied her most. She changed her dress less frequently, ignoring dressmakers, and she showed no longer the ravishing elegance of the bride. She often lay in bed till noon, she who had always entered the dining-room at nine o'clock precisely to dispense his coffee and listen to his remarks on the contents of the newspaper. She said 'As you please' to the cook, and the meals began to lose their piquancy. She paid no calls, but some of her women friends continued, nevertheless, to visit her. Lastly, she took to sewing. The little dark doctor, who had become an acquaintance, smiled at her and told her to do no more than she felt disposed to do. She reclined on sofas in shaded rooms, and appeared to meditate. She was not depressed, but thoughtful. It was as though she had much to settle in her own mind. At intervals the faint sound of the Hungarian Rhapsody mingled with her reveries.

As for Edward, his behaviour was immaculate. During the day he made money furiously. In the evening he sat with his wife. They did not talk much, and he never questioned her. She developed a certain curious whimsicality now and then; but for him she could do no wrong.

The past was not mentioned. They both looked apprehensively towards the future, towards a crisis which they knew was inexorably approaching. They were afraid, while pretending to have no fear.

And one afternoon, precipitately, surprisingly, the crisis came.

'You are the father of a son—a very noisy son,' said the doctor, coming into the drawing-room where Edward had sat in torture for three hours.

'And May?'

'Oh, never fear: she's doing excellently.'

'Can I go and see her?' he asked, like a humble petitioner.

'Well—yes,' said the doctor, 'for one minute; not more.'

So he went into the bedroom as into a church, feeling a fool. The nurse, miraculously white and starched, stood like a sentinel at the foot of the bed of mystery.

'All serene, May?' he questioned. If he had attempted to say another word he would have cried.

The pale mother nodded with a fatigued smile, and by a scarcely perceptible gesture drew his attention to a bundle. From the next flat came a faint, familiar sound, insolently joyous.

'Yes,' he thought, 'but if they had both been lying dead here that tune would have been the same.'

Two months later he left the office early, telling his secretary that he had a headache. It was a mere fibbing excuse. He suffered from sudden fits of anxiety about his wife and child. When he reached the flat, he found no one at home but the cook.

'Where's your mistress?' he demanded.

'She's out in the park with baby and nurse, sir.'

'But it's going to rain,' he cried angrily. 'It is raining. They'll get wet through.'

He rushed into the corridor, and met the procession—May, the perambulator, and the nursemaid.

'Only fancy, Ted!' May exclaimed, 'the perambulator will go into the lift, after all. Aren't you glad?'

'Yes,' he said. 'But you're wet, surely?'

'Not a drop. We just got in in time.'

'Sure?'

'Quite.'

The tableau of May, elegant as ever, but her eyes brighter and her body more leniently curved, of the hooded perambulator, and of the fluffy-white nursemaid behind—it was too much for him. Touching clumsily the apron of the perambulator, the stockbroker turned into his doorway. Just then the girl from the next flat came out into the corridor, dressed for social rites of the afternoon. The perambulator was her excuse for stopping.

'What a pretty boy!' she exclaimed in ecstasy, trying to squeeze her picture hat under the hood of the perambulator.

'Do you really think so?' said the mother, enchanted.

'Of course! The darling! How I envy you!'

May wanted to reciprocate this politeness.

'I can't tell you,' she said, 'how I envy you your piano-playing. There's one piece——'

'Envy me! Why! It's only a pianola we've got!'

'Isn't he the picture of his granddad?' said May to Edward when they bent over the cot that night before retiring.

And as she said it there was such candour in her voice, such content in her smiling and courageous eyes, that Edward could not fail to comprehend her message to him. Down in some very secret part of his soul he felt for the first time the real force of the great explanatory truth that one generation succeeds another.

THE SISTERS QITA
The manuscript ran thus:

When I had finished my daily personal examination of the ropes and-trapezes, I hesitated a moment, and then climbed up again, to the roof, where the red and the blue long ropes were fastened. I took my sharp scissors from my chatelaine, and gently fretted the blue rope with one blade of the scissors until only a single strand was left intact. I gazed down at the vast floor a hundred feet below. The afternoon varieties were over, and a phrenologist was talking to a small crowd of gapers in a corner. The rest of the floor was pretty empty save for the chairs and the fancy stalls, and the fatigued stall-girls in their black dresses. I too, had once almost been a stall-girl at the Aquarium! I descended. Few observed me in my severe street dress. Our secretary, Charles, attended me on the stage.

'Everything right, Miss Paquita?' he said, handing me my hat and gloves, which I had given him, to hold.

I nodded. I could see that he thought I was in one of my stern, far-away moods.

'Miss Mariquita is waiting for you in the carriage,' he said.

We drove away in silence—I with my inborn melancholy too sad, Sally (Mariquita) too happy to speak. This daily afternoon drive was really part of our 'turn'! A team of four mules driven by a negro will make a sensation even in Regent Street. All London looked at us, and contrasted our impassive beauty—mine mature (too mature!) and dark, Sally's so blonde and youthful, our simple costumes, and the fact that we stayed at an exclusive Mayfair hotel, with the stupendous flourish of our turnout. The renowned Sisters Qita—Paquita and Mariquita Qita—and the renowned mules of the Sisters Qita! Two hundred pounds a week at the Aquarium! Twenty-five thousand francs for one month at the Casino de Paris! Twelve thousand five hundred dollars for a tour of fifty performances in the States! Fifteen hundred pesos a night and a special train *de luxe* in Argentina and Brazil! I could see the loungers and the drivers talking and pointing as usual. The gilded loungers in Verrey's café got up and watched us through the windows as we passed. This was fame. For nearly twenty years I had been intimate with fame, and with the envy of women and the foolish homage of men.

We saw dozens of omnibuses bearing the legend 'Qita.' Then we met one which said: 'Empire Theatre. Valdès, the matchless juggler,' and Sally smiled with pleasure.

'He's coming to see our turn to-night, after his,' she remarked, blushing.

'Valdès? Why?' I asked, without turning my head.

'He wants us to sup with him, to celebrate our engagement.'

'When do you mean to get married?' I asked her shortly. I felt quite calm.

'I guess you're a Tartar to-day,' said the pretty thing, with a touch of her American sauciness. 'We haven't studied it out yet. It was only yesterday afternoon he kissed me for the first time.' Then she bent towards me with her characteristic plaintive, wistful appeal. 'Say! You aren't vexed, Selina, are you, because of this? Of course, he wants me to tour with him after we're married, and do a double act. He's got lots of dandy ideas for a double act. But I won't, I won't, Selina, unless you say the word. Now, don't you go and be cross, Selina.'

I let myself expand generously.

'My darling girl!' I said, glancing at her kindly. 'You ought to know me better. Of course I'm not cross. And of course you must tour with Valdès. I shall be all right. How do you suppose I managed before I invented you?' I smiled like an indulgent mother.

'Oh! I didn't mean that,' she said. 'I know you're frightfully clever. I'm nothing——'

'I hope you'll be awfully happy,' I whispered, squeezing her hand. 'And don't forget that I introduced him to you—I knew him years before you did. I'm the cause of this bliss——Do you remember that cold morning in Berlin?'

'Oh! well, I should say!' she exclaimed in ecstasy.

When we reached our rooms in the hotel I kissed her warmly. Women do that sort of thing.

Then a card was brought to me. 'George Capey,' it said; and in pencil, 'Of the Five Towns.'

I shrugged my shoulders. Sally had gone to scribble a note to her Valdès. 'Show Mr. Capey in,' I said, and a natty young man entered, half nervousness, half audacity.

'How did you know I come from the Five Towns?' I questioned him.

'I am on the *Evening Mail*,' he said, 'where they know everything, madam.'

I was annoyed. 'Then they know, on the *Evening Mail* that Paquita Qita has never been interviewed, and never will be,' I said.

'Besides,' he went on, 'I come from the Five Towns myself.'

'Bursley?' I asked mechanically.

'Bursley,' he ejaculated; then added, 'you haven't been near old Bosley since——'

It was true.

'No,' I said hastily. 'It is many years since I have been in England, even. Do they know down there who Qita is?'

'Not they!' he replied.

I grew reflective. Stars such as I have no place of origin. We shoot up out of a void, and sink back into a void. I had forgotten Bursley and Bursley folk. Recollections rushed in upon me.... I felt beautifully sad. I drew off my gloves, and flung my hat on a chair with a movement that would have bewitched a man of the world, but Mr. George Capey was unimpressed. I laughed.

'What's the joke?' he inquired. I adored him for his Bursliness.

'I was just thinking, of fat Mrs. Cartledge, who used to keep that fishmonger's shop in Oldcastle Street, opposite Bates's. I wonder if she's still there?'

'She is,' he said. 'And fatter than ever! She's getting on in years now.'

I broke the rule of a lifetime, and let him interview me.

'Tell them I'm thirty-seven,' I said. 'Yes, I mean it. Tell them.'

And then for another tit-bit I explained to him how I had discovered Sally at Koster and Bial's, in New York, five years ago, and made her my sister for stage purposes because I was lonely, and liked her American simplicity and twang. He departed full of tea and satisfaction.

It was our last night at the Aquarium. The place was crammed. The houses where I performed were always crammed. Our turn was in three parts, and lasted half an hour. The first part was a skirt dance in full afternoon dress (*danse de modernité*, I called it); the second was a double horizontal bar act; the third was the famous act of the red and the blue ropes, in full evening dress. It was 10.45 when we climbed the silk ladders for the third part. High up in the roof, separated from each other by nearly the length of the great hall, Sally and I stood on two little platforms. I held the ends of the red and the blue ropes. I had to let the blue rope swing across the hall to her. She would seize it, and, clutching it, swoop like the ball of an enormous pendulum from her platform to mine. (But would she?) I should then swing on the red rope to the platform she had left.

Then the band would stop for the thrilling moment, and the lights would be lowered. Each lighting and holding a powerful electric hand-light—one red, one blue—we should signal the drummer and plunge simultaneously into space, flash past each other in mid-flight, exchanging lights as we passed (this was the trick), and soar to opposite platforms again, amid frenzied applause. There were no nets.

That was what ought to occur.

I stood bowing to the floor of tiny upturned heads, and jerking the ropes a little. Then I let Sally's rope go with a push, and it dropped away from me, and in a few seconds she had it safe in her strong hand. She was taller than me, with a fuller figure, yet she looked quite small on her distant platform. All the evening I had been thinking of fat old Mrs. Cartledge messing and slopping among cod and halibut on white tiles. I could not get Bursley and my silly infancy out of my head. I followed my feverish career from the age of fifteen, when that strange Something in me, which makes an artist, had first driven me forth to conquer two continents. I thought of all the golden loves I had scorned, and my own love, which had been ignored, unnoticed, but which still obstinately burned. I glanced downwards and descried Valdès precisely where Sally had said he would be. Valdès, what a fool you were! And I hated a fool. I am one of those who can love and hate, who can love and despise, who can love and loathe the same object in the same moment. Then I signalled to Sally to plunge, and my eyes filled with tears. For, you see, somehow, in some senseless sentimental way, the thought of fat Mrs. Cartledge and my silly infancy had forced me to send Sally the red rope, not the blue one. We exchanged ropes on alternate nights, but this was her night for the blue one.

She swung over, alighting accurately at my side with that exquisite outward curve of the spine which had originally attracted me to her.

'You sent me the red one,' she said to me, after she had acknowledged the applause.

'Yes,' I said. 'Never mind; stick to it now you've got it. Here's the red light. Have you seen Valdès?'

She nodded.

I took the blue light and clutched the blue rope. Instead of murder—suicide, since it must be one or the other. And why not? Indeed, I censured myself in that second for having meant to kill Sally. Not because I was ashamed of the sin, but because the revenge would have been so pitiful and weak. If Valdès the matchless was capable of passing me over and kneeling to the pretty thing——

I stood ready. The world was to lose that fineness, that distinction, that originality, that disturbing subtlety, which constituted Paquita Qita. I plunged.

... I was on the other platform. The rope had held, then: I remembered nothing of the flight except that I had passed near the upturned, pleasant face of Valdès.

The band stopped. The lights of the hall were lowered. All was dark. I switched on my dazzling blue light; Sally switched on her red one. I stood ready. The rope could not possibly endure a second strain. I waved to Sally and signalled to the conductor. The world was to lose Paquita. The drum began its formidable roll. Whirrr! I plunged, and saw the red star rushing towards me. I snatched it and soared upwards. The blue rope seemed to tremble. As I came near the platform at decreasing speed, it seemed to stretch like elastic. It broke! The platform jumped up suddenly over my head, but I caught at the silk ladder. I was saved! There was a fearful silence, and then the appalling shock of hysterical applause from seven thousand throats. I slid down the ladder, ran across the stage into my dressing-room for a cloak, out again into the street. In two days I was in Buda-Pesth.

NOCTURNE AT THE MAJESTIC

I

In the daily strenuous life of a great hotel there are periods during which its bewildering activities slacken, and the vast organism seems to be under the influence of an opiate. Such a period recurs after dinner when the guests are preoccupied by the mysterious processes of digestion in the drawing-rooms or smoking-rooms or in the stalls of a theatre. On the evening of this nocturne the well-known circular entrance-hall of the Majestic, with its tessellated pavement, its malachite pillars, its Persian rugs, its lounges, and its renowned stuffed bears at the foot of the grand stairway, was for the moment deserted, save by the head hall-porter and the head night-porter and the girl in the bureau. It was a quarter to nine, and the head hall-porter was abdicating his pagoda to the head night-porter, and telling him the necessary secrets of the day. These two lords, before whom the motley panorama of human existence was continually being enrolled, held a portentous confabulation night and morning. They had no illusions; they knew life. Shakespeare himself might have listened to them with advantage.

The girl in the bureau, like a beautiful and languishing animal in its cage, leaned against her window, and looked between two pillars at the magnificent lords. She was too far off to catch their talk, and, indeed, she watched them absently in a reverie induced by the sweet melancholy of the summer twilight, by the torpidity of the hour, and by the prospect of the next day, which was her day off. The liveried functionaries ignored her, probably scorned her as a mere pretty little morsel. Nevertheless, she was the centre of energy, not they. If money were payable, she was the person to receive it; if a customer wanted a room, she would choose it; and the lords had to call her 'miss.' The immense and splendid hotel pulsed round this simple heart hidden under a white blouse. Especially in summer, her presence and the presence of her companions in the bureau (but to-night she was alone) ministered to the satisfaction of male guests, whose cruel but profoundly human instincts found pleasure in the fact that, no matter when they came in from their wanderings, the pretty captives were always there in the bureau, smiling welcome, puzzling stupid little brains and puckering pale brows over enormous ledgers, twittering borrowed facetiousness from rosy mouths, and smoothing out seductive toilettes with long thin hands that were made for ring and bracelet and rudder-lines, and not a bit for the pen and the ruler.

The pretty little thing despised of the functionaries corresponded almost exactly in appearance to the typical bureau girl. She was moderately tall; she had a good slim figure, all pleasant curves, flaxen hair and plenty of it, and a dainty, rather expressionless face; the ears and mouth were very small, the eyes large and blue, the nose so-so, the cheeks and forehead of an equal ivory pallor, the chin trifling, with a crease under the lower lip and a rich convexity springing out from below the crease. The extremities of the full lips were nearly always drawn up in a smile, mechanical, but infallibly attractive. The hair was of an orthodox frizziness. You would have said she was a nice, kind, good-natured girl, flirtatious but correct, well adapted to adorn a dogcart on Sundays.

This was Nina, foolish Nina, aged twenty-one. In her reverie the entire Hôtel Majestic weighed on her; she had a more than adequate sense of her own solitary importance in the bureau, and stirring obscurely beneath that consciousness were the deep ineradicable longings of a poor pretty girl for heaps of money, endless luxury of finery and chocolates, and sentimental silken dalliance.

Suddenly a stranger entered the hall. His advent seemed to wake the place out of the trance into which it had fallen. The nocturne had begun. Nina straightened herself and intensified her eternal smile. The two porters became military, and smiled with a special and peculiar urbanity. Several lesser but still lordly functionaries appeared among the pillars; a page-boy emerged by magic from the region of the chimney-piece like Mephistopheles in Faust's study; and some guests of both sexes strolled chattering across the tessellated pavement as they passed from one wing of the hotel to the other.

'How do, Tom?' said the stranger, grasping the hand of the head hall-porter, and nodding to the head night-porter.

His voice showed that he was an American, and his demeanour that he was one of those experienced, wealthy, and kindly travellers who know the Christian names of all the hall-porters in the world, and have the trick of securing their intimacy and fealty. He wore a blue suit and a light gray wideawake, and his fine moustache was grizzled. In his left hand he carried a brown bag.

'Nicely, thank you, sir,' Tom replied. 'How are you, sir?'

'Oh, about six and six.'

Whereupon both porters laughed heartily.

Tom escorted him to the bureau, and tried to relieve him of his bag. Inferior lords escorted Tom.

'I guess I'll keep the grip,' said the stranger. 'Mr. Pank will be around with some more baggage pretty soon. We've expressed the rest on to the steamer. Well, my dear,' he went on, turning to Nina, 'you're a fresh face here.'

He looked her steadily in the eyes.

'Yes, I am,' she said, conquered instantly.

Radiant and triumphant, the man brought good-humour into every face, like some wonderful combination of the sun and the sea-breeze.

'Give me two bedrooms and a parlour, please,' he commanded.

'First floor?' asked Nina prettily.

'First floor! Well—I should say! *And* on the Strand, my dear.'

She bent over her ledgers, blushing.

'Send someone to the 'phone, Tom, and let 'em put me on to the Regency, will you?' said the stranger.

'Yes, sir. Samuels, go and ring up the Regency Theatre—quick!'

Swift departure of a lord.

'And ask Alphonse to come up to my bedroom in ten minutes from now,' the stranger proceeded to Tom. 'I shall want a dandy supper for fourteen at a quarter after eleven.'

'Yes, sir. No dinner, sir?'

'No; we dined on the Pullman. Well, my dear, figured it out yet?'

'Numbers 102, 120, and 107,' said Nina.

'Keys 102, 120, and 107,' said Tom.

Swift departure of another lord to the pagoda.

'How much?' demanded the stranger.

'The bedrooms are twenty-five shillings, and the sitting-room two guineas.'

'I guess Mr. Pank won't mind that. Hullo, Pank, you're here! I'm through. Your number's 102 or 120, which you fancy. Just going to the 'phone a minute, and then I'll join you upstairs.'

Mr. Pank was a younger man, possessing a thin, astute, intellectual face. He walked into the hall with noticeable deliberation. His travelling costume was faultless, but from beneath his straw hat his black hair sprouted in a somewhat peculiar fashion

116

over his broad forehead. He smiled lazily and shrewdly, and without a word disappeared into a lift. Two large portmanteaus accompanied him.

Presently the elder stranger could be heard battling with the obstinate idiosyncrasies of a London telephone.

'You haven't registered,' Nina called to him in her tremulous, delicate, captivating voice, as he came out of the telephone-box.

He advanced to sign, and, taking a pen and leaning on the front of the bureau, wrote in the visitor's book, in a careful, legible hand: 'Lionel Belmont, New York.' Having thus written, and still resting on the right elbow, he raised his right hand a little and waved the pen like a delicious menace at Nina.

'Mr. Pank hasn't registered, either,' he said slowly, with a charming affectation of solemnity, as though accusing Mr. Pank of some appalling crime.

Nina laughed timidly as she pushed his room-ticket across the page of the big book. She thought that Mr. Lionel Belmont was perfectly delightful.

'No,' he hasn't,' she said, trying also to be arch; 'but he must.'

At that moment she happened to glance at the right hand of Mr. Belmont. In the brilliance of the electric light she could see the fair skin of the wrist and forearm within the whiteness of his shirt-sleeve. She stared at what she saw, every muscle tense.

'I guess you can round up Mr. Pank yourself, my dear, later on,' said Lionel Belmont, and turned quickly away, intent on the next thing.

He did not notice that her large eyes had grown larger and her pale face paler. In another moment the hall was deserted again. Mr. Belmont had ascended in the lift, Tom had gone to his rest, and the head night-porter was concealed in the pagoda. Nina sank down limply on her stool, her nostrils twitching; she feared she was about to faint, but this final calamity did not occur. She had, nevertheless, experienced the greatest shock of her brief life, and the way of it was thus.

II

Nina Malpas was born amid the embers of one of those fiery conjugal dramas which occur with romantic frequency in the provincial towns of the northern Midlands, where industrial conditions are such as to foster an independent spirit among women of the lower class generally, and where by long tradition 'character' is allowed to exploit itself more freely than in the southern parts of our island. Lemuel Malpas was a dashing young commercial traveller, with what is known as 'an agreeable address,' in Bursley, one of the Five Towns, Staffordshire. On the strength of his dash he wooed and married the daughter of an hotel-keeper in the neighbouring town of Hanbridge. Six months after the wedding—in other words, at the most dangerous period of the connubial career— Mrs. Malpas's father died, and Mrs. Malpas became the absolute mistress of eight thousand pounds. Lemuel had carefully foreseen this windfall, and wished to use the money in enterprises of the earthenware trade. Mrs. Malpas, pretty and vivacious, with a self-conceit hardened by the adulation of saloon-bars, very decidedly thought otherwise. Her motto was, 'What's yours is mine, but what's mine's my own.' The difference was accentuated. Long mutual resistances were followed by reconciliations, which grew more and more transitory, and at length both recognised that the union, not founded on genuine affection, had been a mistake.

This name is pronounced with the accent on the first syllable in the Five Towns.

'Keep your d——d brass!' Lemuel exclaimed one morning, and he went off on a journey and forgot to come back. A curious letter dated from Liverpool wished his wife happiness, and informed her that, since she was well provided for, he had no scruples about leaving her. Mrs. Malpas was startled at first, but she soon perceived that what Lemuel had done was exactly what the brilliant and enterprising Lemuel might have been expected to do. She jerked up her doll's head, and ejaculated, 'So much the better!'

A few weeks later she sold the furniture and took rooms in Scarborough, where, amid pleasurable surroundings, she determined to lead the joyous life of a grass-widow, free of all cares. Then, to her astonishment and disgust, Nina was born. She had not bargained for Nina. She found herself in the tiresome position of a mother whose explanations of her child lack plausibility. One lodging-housekeeper to whom she hazarded the statement that Lemuel was in Australia had saucily replied: 'I thought maybe it was the North Pole he was gone to!'

This decided Mrs. Malpas. She returned suddenly to the Five Towns, where at least her reputation was secure. Only a week previously Lemuel had learnt indirectly that she had left their native district. He determined thenceforward to forget her completely. Mrs. Malpas's prettiness was of the fleeting sort. After Nina's birth she began to get stout and coarse, and the nostalgia of the saloon-bar, the coffee-room, and the sanded portico overtook her. The Tiger at Bursley was for sale, a respectable commercial hotel, the best in the town. She purchased it, wines, omnibus connection, and all, and developed into the typical landlady in black silk and gold rings.

In the Tiger Nina was brought up. She was a pretty child from her earliest years, and received the caresses of all as a matter of course. She went to a good school, studied the piano, and learnt dancing, and at sixteen did her hair up. She did as she was told without fuss, being apparently of a lethargic temperament; she had all the money and all the clothes that her heart could desire; she was happy, and in a quiet way she deemed herself a rather considerable item in the world. When she was eighteen her mother died miserably of cancer, and it was discovered that the liabilities of Mrs. Malpas's estate exceeded its assets—and the Tiger mortgaged up to its value! The creditors were not angry; they attributed the state of affairs to illness and the absence of male control, and good-humouredly accepted what they could get. None the less, Nina, the child of luxury and sloth, had to start life with several hundreds of pounds less than nothing. Of her father all trace had been long since lost. A place was found for her, and for over two years she saw the world from the office of a famous hotel in Doncaster. Her lethargy, and an invaluable gift of adapting herself to circumstances, saved her from any acute unhappiness in the Yorkshire town. Instinctively she ceased to remember the Tiger and past splendours. (Equally, if she had married a Duke instead of becoming a book-keeper, she would have ceased to remember the Tiger and past humility.) Then by good or ill fortune she had the offer of a situation at the Hôtel Majestic, Strand, London. The Majestic and the sights thereof woke up the sleeping soul.

Before her death Mrs. Malpas had told Nina many things about the vanished Lemuel; among others, the curious detail that he had two small moles—one hairless, the other hirsute—close together on the under side of his right wrist. Nina had seen precisely such marks of identification on the right wrist of Mr. Lionel Belmont.

She was convinced that Lionel Belmont was her father. There could not be two men in the world so stamped by nature. She perceived that in changing his name he had chosen Lionel because of its similarity to Lemuel. She felt certain, too, that she had noticed vestiges of the Five Towns accent beneath his Americanisms. But apart from these reasons, she knew by a superrational instinct that Lionel Belmont was her father; it was not the call of blood, but the positiveness of a woman asserting that a thing is so because she is sure it is so.

III

Nina was not of an imaginative disposition. The romance of this extraordinary encounter made no appeal to her. She was the sort of girl that constantly reads novelettes, and yet always, with fatigued scorn, refers to them as 'silly.' Stupid little Nina was intensely practical at heart, and it was the practical side of her father's reappearance that engaged her birdlike mind. She did not stop to reflect that truth is stranger than fiction. Her tiny heart was not agitated by any ecstatic ponderings upon the wonder and mystery of fate. She did not feel strangely drawn towards Lionel Belmont, nor did she feel that he supplied a something which had always been wanting to her.

On the other hand, her pride—and Nina was very proud—found much satisfaction in the fact that her father, having turned up, was so fine, handsome, dashing, good-humoured, and wealthy. It was well, and excellently well, and delicious, to have a father like that. The possession of such a father opened up vistas of a future so enticing and glorious that her present career became instantly loathsome to her.

It suddenly seemed impossible that she could have tolerated the existence of a hotel clerk for a single week. Her eyes were opened, and she saw, as many women have seen, that luxury was an absolute necessity to her. All her ideas soared with the magic swiftness of the bean-stalk. And at the same time she was terribly afraid, unaccountably afraid, to confront Mr. Belmont and tell him that she was his Nina; he was entirely unaware that he had a Nina.

'I'm your daughter! I know by your moles!'

She whispered the words in her tiny heart, and felt sure that she could never find courage to say them aloud to that great and important man. The announcement would be too monstrous, incredible, and absurd. People would laugh. He would laugh. And

120

Nina could stand anything better than being laughed at. Even supposing she proved to him his paternity—she thought of the horridness of going to lawyers' offices—he might decline to recognise her. Or he might throw her fifty pounds a year, as one throws sixpence to an importunate crossing-sweeper, to be rid of her. The United States existed in her mind chiefly as a country of highly-remarkable divorce laws, and she thought that Mr. Belmont might have married again. A fashionable and arrogant Mrs. Belmont, and a dazzling Miss Belmont, aged possibly eighteen, might arrive, both of them steeped in all conceivable luxury, at any moment. Where would Nina be then, with her two-and-eleven-pence-halfpenny blouse from Glave's?...

Mr. Belmont, accompanied by Alphonse, the head-waiter in the *salle à manger*, descended in the lift and crossed the hall to the portico, where he stood talking for a few seconds. Mr. Belmont turned, and, as he conversed with Alphonse, gazed absently in the direction of the bureau. He looked straight through the pretty captive. After all, despite his superficial heartiness, she could be nothing to him—so rich, assertive, and truly important. A hansom was called for him, and he departed; she observed that he was in evening dress now.

No! Her cause was just; but it was too startling—that was what was the matter with it.

Then she told herself she would write to Lionel Belmont. She would write a letter that night.

At nine-thirty she was off duty. She went upstairs to her perch in the roof, and sat on her bed for over two hours. Then she came down again to the bureau with some bluish note-paper and envelopes in her hand, and, in response to the surprised question of the pink-frocked colleague who had taken her place, she explained that she wanted to write a letter.

'You do look that bad, Miss Malpas,' said the other girl, who made a speciality of compassion.

'Do I?' said Nina.

'Yes, you do. What have you got *on, now*, my poor dear?'

'What's that to you? I'll thank you to mind your own business, Miss Bella Perkins.'

Usually Nina was not soon ruffled; but that night all her nerves were exasperated and exceedingly sensitive.

'Oh!' said the girl. 'What price the Duchess of Doncaster? And I was just going to wish you a nice day to-morrow for your holiday, too.'

Nina seated herself at the table to write the letter. An electric light burned directly over her frizzy head. She wrote a weak but legible and regular back-hand. She hated writing letters, partly because she was dubious about her spelling, and partly because of an obscure but irrepressible suspicion that her letters were of necessity silly. She pondered for a long time, and then wrote: 'Dear Mr. Belmont,—I venture——' She made a new start: 'Dear Sir,—I hope you will not think me——' And a third attempt: 'My dear Father——' No! it was preposterous. It could no more be written than it could be said.

The situation was too much for simple Nina.

Suddenly the grand circular hall of the Majestic was filled with a clamour at once charming and fantastic. There was chattering of musical, gay American voices, pattering of elegant feet on the tessellated pavement, the unique incomparable sound of the *frou-frou* of many frocks; and above all this the rich tones of Mr. Lionel Belmont. Nina looked up and saw her radiant father the centre of a group of girls all young, all beautiful, all stylish, all with picture hats, all self-possessed, all sparkling, doubtless the recipients of the dandy supper.

Oh, how insignificant and homicidal Nina felt!

'Thirteen of you!' exclaimed Lionel Belmont, pulling his superb moustache. 'Two to a hansom. I guess I'll want six and a half hansoms, boy.'

There was an explosion of delicious laughter, and the page-boy grinned, ran off, and began whistling in the portico like a vexed locomotive. The thirteen fair, shepherded by Lionel Belmont, passed out into the murmurous summer night of the Strand. Cab after cab drove up, and Nina saw that her father, after filling each cab, paid each cabman. In three minutes the dream-like scene was over. Mr. Belmont re-entered the hotel, winked humorously at the occupant of the pagoda, ignored the bureau, and departed to his rooms.

Nina ripped her inchoate letters into small pieces, and, with a tart good-night to Miss Bella Perkins, who was closing her ledgers, the hour being close upon twelve-thirty, she passed sedately, stiffly, as though in performance of some vestal's ritual, up the grand staircase. Turning to the right at the first landing, she traversed a long corridor which was no part of the route to her cubicle on the ninth floor. This corridor was lighted by glowing sparks, which hung on yellow cords from the central line of the ceiling; underfoot was a heavy but narrow crimson patterned carpet with a strip of polished oak parquet on either side of it. Exactly along the central line of the carpet Nina tripped, languorously, like an automaton, and exactly over her head glittered the line of electric sparks. The corridor and the journey seemed to be interminable, and Nina on some inscrutable and mystic errand. At length she moved aside from the religious line, went into a service cabinet, and emerged with a small bunch of pass-keys. No. 107 was Lionel Belmont's sitting-room; No. 102, his bedroom, was opposite to 107. No. 108, another sitting-room, was, as Nina knew, unoccupied. She noiselessly let herself into No. 108, closed the door, and stood still. After a minute she switched on the light. These two rooms, Nos. 108 and 107, had once communicated, but, as space grew precious with the growing success of the Majestic, they had been finally separated, and the door between them locked and masked by furniture. By reason of the door, Nina could hear Lionel Belmont moving to and fro in No. 107. She listened a long time. Then, involuntarily, she yawned with fatigue.

'How silly of me to be here!' she thought. 'What good will this do me?'

She extinguished the light and opened the door to leave. At the same instant the door of No. 107, three feet off, opened. She drew back with a start of horror. Suppose she had collided with her father on the landing! Timorously she peeped out, and saw Lionel Belmont, in his shirt-sleeves, disappear round the corner.

'He is going to talk with his friend Mr. Pank,' Nina thought, knowing that No. 120 lay at some little distance round that corner.

Mr. Belmont had left the door of No. 107 slightly ajar. An unseen and terrifying force compelled Nina to venture into the corridor, and then to push the door of No. 107 wide open. The same force, not at all herself, quite beyond herself, seemed to impel her by the shoulders into the room. As she stood unmistakably within her father's private sitting-room, scared, breathing rapidly, inquisitive, she said to herself:

'I shall hear him coming back, and I can run out before he turns the corner of the corridor.' And she kept her little pink ears alert.

She looked about the softly brilliant room, such an extravagant triumph of luxurious comfort as twenty years ago would have aroused comment even in Mayfair; but there were scores of similar rooms in the Majestic. No one thought twice of them. Her father's dress-coat was thrown arrogantly over a Louis Quatorze chair, and this careless flinging of the expensive shining coat across the gilded chair somehow gave Nina a more intimate appreciation of her father's grandeur and of the great and glorious life he led. She longed to recline indolently in a priceless tea-gown on the couch by the fireplace and issue orders.... She approached the writing-table, littered with papers, documents, in scores and hundreds. To the left was the brown bag. It was locked, and very heavy, she thought. To the right was a pile of telegrams. She picked up one, and read:

'*Pank, Grand Hotel, Birmingham. Why not burgle hotel? Simplest most effective plan and solves all difficulties.—* BELMONT.'

She read it twice, crunched it in her left hand, and picked up another one:

'*Pank, Adelphi Hotel, Liverpool. Your objection absurd. See safe in bureau at Majestic. Quite easy. Scene with girl second evening.—* BELMONT.'

The thing flashed blindingly upon her. Her father and Mr. Pank belonged to the swell mob of which she had heard and seen so much at Doncaster. She at once became the excessively knowing and suspicious hotel employé, to whom every stranger is a rogue until he has proved the contrary. Had she lived through three St. Leger weeks for nothing? At the hotel at Doncaster, what they didn't know about thieves and sharpers was not knowledge. The landlord kept a loaded revolver in his desk there during the week. And she herself had been provided with a whistle which she was to blow at the slightest sign of a row; she had blown it once, and seven policemen had appeared within thirty seconds. The landlord used to tell tales of masterly and huge scoundrelism that would make Charles Peace turn in his grave. And the landlord had ever insisted that no one, no one at all, could always distinguish with certainty between a real gent and a swell-mobsman.

So her father and Mr. Pank had deceived everyone in the hotel except herself, and they meant to rob the safe in the bureau to-morrow night. Of course Mr. Lionel Belmont was a villain, or he would not have deserted her poor dear mother; it was annoying, but indubitable.... Even now he was maturing his plans round the corner with that Mr. Pank.... Burglars always went about in shirt-sleeves.... The brown bag contained the tools....

The shock was frightful, disastrous, tragic; but it had solved the situation by destroying it. Practically, Nina no longer had a father. He had existed for about four hours as a magnificent reality, full of possibilities; he now ceased to be recognisable.

She was about to pick up a third telegram when a slight noise caused her to turn swiftly; she had forgotten to keep her little pink ears alert. Her father stood in the doorway. He was certainly the victim of some extraordinary emotion; his face worked; he seemed at a loss what to do or say; he seemed pained, confused, even astounded. Simple, foolish Nina had upset the balance of his equations.

Then he resumed his self-control and came forward into the room with a smile intended to be airy. Meanwhile Nina had not moved. One is inclined to pity the artless and defenceless girl in this midnight duel of wits with a shrewd, resourceful, and unscrupulous man of the world. But one's pity should not be lavished on an undeserving object. Though Nina trembled, she was mistress of herself. She knew just where she was, and just how to behave. She was as impregnable as Gibraltar.

'Well,' said Mr. Lionel Belmont, genially gazing at her pose, 'you do put snap into it, any way.'

'Into what?' she was about to inquire, but prudently she held her tongue. Drawing, herself up with the gesture of an offended and unapproachable queen, the little thing sailed past him, close past her own father, and so out of the room.

'Say!' she heard him remark: 'let's straighten this thing out, eh?'

But she heroically ignored him, thinking the while that, with all his sins, he was attractive enough. She still held the first telegram in her long, thin fingers.

So ended the nocturne.

IV

At five o'clock the next morning Nina's trifling nose was pressed against the windowpane of her cubicle. In the enormous slate roof of the Majestic are three rows of round windows, like port-holes. Out of the highest one, at the extremity of the left wing, Nina looked.

From thence she could see five other vast hotels, and the yard of Charing Cross Station, with three night-cabs drawn up to the kerb, and a red van of W.H. Smith and Son disappearing into the station. The Strand was quite empty. It was a strange world of sleep and grayness and disillusion. Within a couple of hundred yards or so of her thousands of people lay asleep, and they would all soon wake into the disillusion, and the Strand would wake, and the first omnibus of all the omnibuses would come along....

Never had simple Nina felt so sad and weary. She was determined to give up her father. She was bound to tell the manager of her discovery, for Nina was an honest servant, and she was piqued in her honesty. No one should know that Lionel Belmont was her father....

She saw before her the task of forgetting him and forgetting the rich dreams of which he had been the origin. She was once more a book-keeper with no prospects.

At eight she saw the manager in the managerial room. Mr. Reuben was a young Jew, aged about thirty-four, with a cold but indestructibly polite manner. He was a great man, and knew it; he had almost invented the Majestic.

She told him her news; it was impossible for foolish Nina to conceal her righteousness and her sense of her importance.

'Whom did you say, Miss Malpas?' asked Mr. Reuben.

'Mr. Lionel Belmont—at least, that's what he calls himself.'

'Calls himself, Miss Malpas?'

'Here's one of the telegrams.'

Mr. Reuben read it, looked at little Nina, and smiled; he never laughed.

'Is it possible, Miss Malpas,' said he, 'that you don't know who Mr. Belmont and Mr. Pank are?' And then, as she shook her head, he continued in his impassive, precise way: 'Mr. Belmont is one of the principal theatrical managers in the United States. Mr. Pank is one of the principal playwrights in the United States. Mr. Pank's melodrama 'Nebraska' is now being played at the Regency by Mr. Belmont's own American company. Another of Mr. Belmont's companies starts shortly for a tour in the provinces with the musical comedy 'The Dolmenico Doll.' I believe that Mr. Pank and Mr. Belmont are now writing a new melodrama, and as they have both been travelling, but not together, I expect that these telegrams relate to that melodrama. Did you suppose that safe-burglars wire their plans to each other like this?' He waved the telegram with a gesture of fatigue.

Silly, ruined Nina made no answer.

'Do you ever read the papers—the *Telegraph* or the *Mail*, Miss Malpas?'

'N-no, sir.'

'You ought to, then you wouldn't be so ignorant and silly. A hotel-clerk can't know too much. And, by-the-way, what were you doing in Mr. Belmont's room last night, when you found these wonderful telegrams?'

'I went there—I went there—to——'

'Don't cry, please, it won't help you. You must leave here to-day. You've been here three weeks, I think. I'll tell Mr. Smith to pay you your month's wages. You don't know enough for the Majestic, Miss Malpas. Or perhaps you know too much. I'm sorry. I had thought you would suit us. Keep straight, that's all I have to say to you. Go back to Doncaster, or wherever it is you came from. Leave before five o'clock. That will do.'

With a godlike air, Mr. Reuben swung round his office-chair and faced his desk. He tried not to perceive that there was a mysterious quality about this case which he had not quite understood. Nina tripped piteously out.

In the whole of London Nina had one acquaintance, and an hour or so later, after drinking some tea, she set forth to visit this acquaintance. The weight of her own foolishness, fatuity, silliness, and ignorance was heavy upon her. And, moreover, she had been told that Mr. Lionel Belmont had already departed back to America, his luggage being marked for the American Transport Line.

She was primly walking, the superlative of the miserable, past the façade of the hotel, when someone sprang out of a cab and spoke to her. And it was Mr. Lionel Belmont.

'Get right into this hansom, Miss Malpas,' he said kindly, 'and I guess we'll talk it out.'

'Talk what out?' she thought.

But she got in.

'Marble Arch, and go up Regent Street, and don't hurry,' said Mr. Belmont to the cabman.

'How did he know my name?' she asked herself.

'A hansom's the most private place in London,' he said after a pause.

It certainly did seem to her very cosy and private, and her nearness to one of the principal theatrical managers in America was almost startling. Her white frock, with the black velvet decorations, touched his gray suit.

'Now,' he said, 'I do wish you'd tell me why you were in my parlour last night. Honest.'

'What for?' she parried, to gain time.

Should she begin to disclose her identity?

'Because—well, because—oh, look here, my girl, I want to be on very peculiar terms with you. I want to straighten out everything. You'll be sort of struck, but I'll be bound to tell you I'm your father. Now, don't faint or anything.'

'Oh, I knew that!' she gasped. 'I saw the moles on your wrist when your were registering—mother told me about them. Oh, if I had only known you knew!'

They looked at one another.

'It was only the day before yesterday I found out I possessed such a thing as a daughter. I had a kind of fancy to go around to the old spot. This notion of me having a daughter struck me considerable, and I concluded to trace her and size her up at once.' Nina was bound to smile. 'So your poor mother's been dead three years?'

'Yes,' said Nina.

'Ah! don't let us talk about that. I feel I can't say just the right thing.... And so you knew me by those pips.' He pulled up his right sleeve. 'Was that why you came up to my parlour?'

Nina nodded, and Lionel Belmont sighed with relief.

'Why didn't you tell me at once, my dear, who you where?'

'I didn't dare,' she smiled; 'I was afraid. I thought you wouldn't——'

'Listen,' he said; 'I've wanted someone like you for years, years, and years. I've got no one to look after——'

'Then why didn't *you* tell *me* at once who you were?' she questioned with adorable pertness.

'Oh!' he laughed; 'how could I—plump like that? When I saw you first, in the bureau, the stricken image of your mother at your age, I was nearly down. But I came up all right, didn't I, my dear? I acted it out well, didn't I?'

The hansom was rolling through Hyde Park, and the sunshiny hour was eleven in June. Nina looked forth on the gay and brilliant scene: rhododendrons, duchesses, horses, dandies—the incomparable wealth and splendour of the capital. She took a long breath, and began to be happy for the rest of her life. She felt that, despite her plain frock, she was in this picture. Her father had told her that his income was rising on a hundred and fifty thousand dollars a year, and he would thank her to spend it. Her father had told her, when she had confessed the scene with Mr. Reuben and what led to it, that she had grit, and that the mistake was excusable, and that a girl as pretty as she was didn't want to be as fly as Mr. Reuben had said. Her father had told her that he was proud of her, and he had not been so rude as to laugh at her blunder.

She felt that she was about to enter upon the true and only vocation of a dainty little morsel—namely, to spend money earned by other people. She thought less homicidally now of the thirteen chorus-girls of the previous night.

'Say,' said her father, 'I sail this afternoon for New York, Nina.'

'They said you'd gone, at the hotel.'

'Only my baggage. The *Minnehaha* clears at five. I guess I want you to come along too. On the voyage we'll get acquainted, and tell each other things.'

'Suppose I say I won't?'

She spoke despotically, as the pampered darling should.

'Then I'll wait for the next boat. But it'll be awkward.'

'Then I'll come. But I've got no things.'

He pushed up the trap-door.

Driver, Bond Street. And get on to yourself, for goodness' sake! Hurry!'

'You told me not to hurry,' grumbled the cabby.

'And now I tell you to hustle. See?'

'Shall you want me to call myself Belmont?' Nina asked.

'I chose it because it was a fine ten-horse-power name twenty years ago,' said her father; and she murmured that she liked the name very much.

As Lionel Belmont the Magnificent paid the cabman, and Nina walked across the pavement into one of the most famous repositories of expensive frippery in the world, she thrilled with the profoundest pleasure her tiny soul was capable of. Foolish, simple Nina had achieved the *nec plus ultra* of her languorous dreams.

CLARICE OF THE AUTUMN CONCERTS

I

'What did you say your name was?' asked Otto, the famous concert manager.

'Clara Toft.'

'That won't do,' he said roughly.

'My real proper name is Clarice,' she added, blushing. 'But——'

'That's better, that's better.' His large, dark face smiled carelessly. 'Clarice—and stick an "e" on to Toft—Clarice Tofte. Looks like either French or German then. I'll send you the date. It'll be the second week in September. And you can come round to the theatre and try the piano—Bechstein.'

'And what do you think I had better play, Mr. Otto?'

'You must play what you have just played, of course. Tschaikowsky's all the rage just now. Your left hand's very weak, especially in the last movement. You've got to make more noise—at my concerts. And see here, Miss Toft, don't you go and make a fool of me. I believe you have a great future, and I'm backing my opinion. Don't you go and make a fool of me.'

'I shall play my very best,' she smiled nervously. 'I'm awfully obliged to you, Mr. Otto.'

'Well,' he said, 'you ought to be.'

At the age of fifteen her father, an earthenware manufacturer, and the flamboyant Alderman of Turnhill, in the Five Towns, had let her depart to London to the Royal College of Music. Thence, at nineteen, she had proceeded to the Conservatoire of Liége. At twenty-two she could play the great concert pieces—Liszt's 'Rhapsodies Hongroises,' Chopin's Ballade, Op. 47, Beethoven's Op. 111, etc.—in concert style, and she was the wonder of the Five Towns when she visited Turnhill. But in London she had obtained neither engagements nor pupils: she had never believed in herself. She knew of dozens of pianists whom she deemed more brilliant than little, pretty, modest Clara Toft; and after her father's death and the not surprising revelation of his true financial condition, she settled with her faded, captious mother in Turnhill as a teacher of the pianoforte, and did nicely.

Then, when she was twenty-six, and content in provincialism, she had met during an August holiday at Llandudno her old fellow pupil, Albert Barbellion, who was conducting the Pier concerts. Barbellion had asked her to play at a 'soirée musicale' which he gave one night in the ball-room of his hotel, and she had performed Tschaikowsky's immense and lurid Slavonic Sonata; and the unparalleled Otto, renowned throughout the British Empire for Otto's Bohemian Autumn Nightly Concerts at Covent Garden Theatre, had happened to hear her and that seldom played sonata for the first time. It was a wondrous chance. Otto's large, picturesque, extempore way of inviting her to appear at his promenade concerts reminded her of her father.

II

In the bleak three-cornered artists'-room she could faintly hear the descending impetuous velocities of the Ride of the Walkyries. She was waiting in her new yellow dress, waiting painfully. Otto rushed in, a glass in his hand.

'You all right?' he questioned sharply.

'Oh, yes,' she said, getting up from the cane-chair.

'Let me see you stand on one leg,' he said; and then, because she hesitated: 'Go on, quick! Stand on one leg. It's a good test.' So she stood on one leg, foolishly smiling. 'Here, drink this,' he ordered, and she had to drink brandy-and-soda out of the glass. 'You're better now,' he remarked; and decidedly, though her throat tingled and she coughed, she felt equal to anything at that moment.

A stout, middle-aged woman, in a rather shabby opera cloak, entered the room.

'Ah, Cornelia!' exclaimed Otto grandly.

'My dear Otto!' the woman responded, wrinkling her wonderfully enamelled cheeks.

'Miss Toft, let me introduce you to Madame Lopez.' He turned to the newcomer. 'Keep her calm for me, bright star, will you?'

Then Otto went, and Clarice was left alone with the world-famous operatic soprano, who was advertised to sing that night the Shadow Song from 'Dinorah.'

'Where did he pick you up, my dear?' the decayed diva inquired maternally.

Clarice briefly explained.

'You aren't paying him anything, are you?'

'Oh, no!' said Clarice, shocked. 'But I get no fee this time——'

'Of course not, my dear,' the Lopez cut her short. 'It's all right so long as you aren't paying him anything to let you go on. Now run along.'

Clarice's heart stopped. The call-boy, with his cockney twang, had pronounced her name.

She moved forward, and, by dint of following the call-boy, at length reached the stage. Applause—good-natured applause—seemed to roll towards her from the uttermost parts of the vast auditorium. She realized with a start that this applause was exclusively for her. She sat down to the piano, and there ensued a death-like silence—a silence broken only by the striking of matches and the tinkle of the embowered fountain in front of the stage. She had a consciousness, rather than a vision, of a floor of thousands of upturned faces below her, and tier upon tier of faces rising above her and receding to the illimitable dark distances of the gallery. She heard a door bang, and perceived that some members of the orchestra were creeping quietly out at the back. Then she plunged, dizzy, into the sonata, as into a heaving and profound sea. The huge concert piano resounded under the onslaught of her broad hands. When she had played ten bars she knew with an absolute conviction that she would do justice to her talent. She could see, as it were, the entire sonata stretched out in detail before her like a road over which she had to travel....

At the end of the first movement the clapping enheartened her; she smiled confidently at the conductor, who, unemployed during her number, sat on a chair under his desk. Before recommencing she gazed boldly at the house, and certain placards—'Smoking permitted,' 'Emergency exit,' 'Ices,' and 'Fancy Dress Balls'—were fixed for ever on the retina of her eye. At the end of the second movement there was more applause, and the conductor tapped appreciation with his stick against the pillar of his desk; the leader of the listless orchestra also tapped with his fiddle-bow and nodded. It seemed to her now that she more and more dominated the piano, and that she rendered the great finale with masterful and fierce assurance....

She was pleased with herself as she banged the last massive chord. And the applause, the clapping, the hammering of sticks, astounded her, staggered her. She might have died of happiness while she bowed and bowed again. She ran off the stage triumphant, and the applause seemed to assail her little figure from all quarters and overwhelm it. As she stood waiting, concealed behind a group of palms, it suddenly occurred to her that, after all, she had underestimated herself. She saw her rosy future as the spoiled darling of continental capitals. The hail of clapping persisted, and the apparition of Otto violently waved her to return to the stage. She returned, bowed her passionate exultation with burning face and trembling knees, and retired. The clapping continued. Yes, she would be compelled to grant an encore—to *grant* one. She would grant it like a honeyed but imperious queen.

Suddenly she heard the warning tap of the conductor's baton; the applause was hushed as though by a charm, and the orchestra broke into the overture to 'Zampa.' She could not understand, she could not think. As she tripped tragically to the artists'-room in her new yellow dress she said to herself that the conductor must have made some mistake, and that——

'Very nice, my dear,' said the Lopez kindly to her. 'You got quite a call—quite a call.'

She waited for Otto to come and talk to her.

At length the Lopez was summoned, and Clarice followed to listen to her. And when the Lopez had soared with strong practised flight through the brilliant intricacy of the Shadow Song, Clarice became aware what real applause sounded like from the stage. It shook the stage as the old favourite of two generations, wearing her set smile, waddled back to the debutante. Scores of voices hoarsely shouted 'Encore!' and 'Last Rose of Summer,' and with a proud sigh the Lopez went on again, bowing.

Clarice saw nothing more of Otto, who doubtless had other birds to snare. The next day only three daily papers mentioned the concert at all. In fact, Otto expected press notices but once a week. All three papers praised the matchless Lopez in her Shadow Song. One referred to Clarice as talented; another called her well-intentioned; the third merely said that she had played. The short dream of artistic ascendancy lay in fragments around her. She was a sensible girl, and stamped those iridescent fragments into dust.

III

The *Staffordshire Signal* contained the following advertisement: 'Miss Clara Toft, solo pianist, of the Otto Autumn Concerts, London, will resume lessons on the 1st proximo at Liszt House, Turnhill. Terms on application.' At thirty Clarice married James Sillitoe, the pianoforte dealer in Market Square, Turnhill, and captious old Mrs. Toft formed part of the new household. At thirty-four Clarice possessed a little girl and two little boys, twins. Sillitoe was a money-maker, and she no longer gave lessons.

Happy? Perhaps not unhappy.

A LETTER HOME
Written in 1893

I

Rain was falling—it had fallen steadily through the night—but the sky showed promise of fairer weather. As the first streaks of dawn appeared, the wind died away, and the young leaves on the trees were almost silent. The birds were insistently clamorous, vociferating times without number that it was a healthy spring morning and good to be alive.

A little, bedraggled crowd stood before the park gates, awaiting the hour named on the notice board when they would be admitted to such lodging and shelter as iron seats and overspreading branches might afford. A weary, patient-eyed, dogged crowd—a dozen men, a boy of thirteen, and a couple of women, both past middle age—which had been gathering slowly since five o'clock. The boy appeared to be the least uncomfortable. His feet were bare, but he had slept well in an area in Grosvenor Place, and was not very damp yet. The women had nodded on many doorsteps, and were soaked. They stood apart from the men, who seemed unconscious of their existence. The men were exactly such as one would have expected to find there—beery and restless as to the eyes, quaintly shod, and with nondescript greenish clothes which for the most part bore traces of the yoke of the sandwich board. Only one amongst them was different.

He was young, and his cap, and manner of wearing it, gave sign of the sea. His face showed the rough outlines of his history. Yet it was a transparently honest face, very pale, but still boyish and fresh enough to make one wonder by what rapid descent he had reached his present level. Perhaps the receding chin, the heavy, pouting lower lip, and the ceaselessly twitching mouth offered a key to the problem.

'Say, Darkey!' he said.

'Well?'

'How much longer?'

'Can't ye see the clock? It's staring ye in the face.'

'No. Something queer's come over my eyes.'

Darkey was a short, sturdy man, who kept his head down and his hands deep in his pockets. The raindrops clinging to the rim of an ancient hat fell every now and then into his gray beard, which presented a drowned appearance. He was a person of long and varied experiences; he knew that queer feeling in the eyes, and his heart softened.

'Come, lean against the pillar,' he said, 'if you don't want to tumble. Three of brandy's what you want. There's four minutes to wait yet.'

With body flattened to the masonry, legs apart, and head thrown back, Darkey's companion felt more secure, and his mercurial spirits began to revive. He took off his cap, and brushing back his light brown curly hair with the hand which held it, he looked down at Darkey through half-closed eyes, the play of his features divided between a smile and a yawn.

He had a lively sense of humour, and the irony of his situation was not lost on him. He took a grim, ferocious delight in calling up the might-have-beens and the 'fatuous ineffectual yesterdays' of life. There is a certain sardonic satisfaction to be gleaned from a frank recognition of the fact that you are the architect of your own misfortune. He felt that satisfaction, and laughed at Darkey, who was one of those who moan about 'ill-luck' and 'victims of circumstance.'

'No doubt,' he would say, 'you're a very deserving fellow, Darkey, who's been treated badly. I'm not.'

To have attained such wisdom at twenty-five is not to have lived altogether in vain.

A park-keeper presently arrived to unlock the gates, and the band of outcasts straggled indolently towards the nearest sheltered seats. Some went to sleep at once, in a sitting posture. Darkey produced a clay pipe, and, charging it with a few shreds of tobacco laboriously gathered from his waistcoat pocket, began to smoke. He was accustomed to this sort of thing, and with a pipe in his mouth could contrive to be moderately philosophical upon occasion. He looked curiously at his companion, who lay stretched at full length on another bench.

'I say, pal,' he remarked, 'I've known ye two days; ye've never told me yer name, and I don't ask ye to. But I see ye've not slep' in a park before.'

'You hit it, Darkey; but how?'

'Well, if the keeper catches ye lying down, he'll be on to ye. Lying down's not allowed.'

The man raised himself on his elbow.

'Really now,' he said; 'that's interesting. But I think I'll give the keeper the opportunity of moving me. Why, it's quite fine, the sun's coming out, and the sparrows are hopping round—cheeky little devils! I'm not sure that I don't feel jolly.'

'I wish I'd got the price of a pint about me,' sighed Darkey, and the other man dropped his head and appeared to sleep. Then Darkey dozed a little, and heard in his waking sleep the heavy, crunching tread of an approaching park-keeper; he started up to warn his companion, but thought better of it, and closed his eyes again.

'Now then, there,' the park-keeper shouted to the man with the sailor's cap, 'get up! This ain't a fourpenny doss, you know. No lying down.'

A rough shake accompanied the words, and the man sat up.

'All right, my friend.'

The keeper, who was a good-humoured man, passed on without further objurgation.

The face of the younger man had grown whiter.

'Look here, Darkey,' he said, 'I believe I'm done for.'

'Never say die.'

'No, just die without speaking.'

His head fell forward and his eyes closed.

'At any rate, this is better than some deaths I've seen,' he began again with a strange accession of liveliness. 'Darkey, did I tell you the story of the five Japanese girls?'

'What, in Suez Bay?' said Darkey, who had heard many sea-stories during the last two days, and recollected them but hazily.

'No, man. This was at Nagasaki. We were taking in a cargo of coal for Hong Kong. Hundreds of little Jap girls pass the coal from hand to hand over the ship's side in tiny baskets that hold about a plateful. In that way you can get three thousand tons aboard in two days.'

'Talking of platefuls reminds me of sausage and mash,' said Darkey.

'Don't interrupt. Well, five of these gay little dolls wanted to go to Hong Kong, and they arranged with the Chinese sailors to stow away; I believe their friends paid those cold-blooded fiends something to pass them down food on the voyage, and give them an airing at nights. We had a particularly lively trip, battened everything down tight, and scarcely uncovered till we got into port. Then I and another man found those five girls among the coal.'

'Dead, eh?'

'They'd simply torn themselves to pieces. Their bits of frock things were in strips, and they were scratched deep from top to toe. The Chinese had never troubled their heads about them at all, although they must have known it meant death. You may bet there was a row. The Japanese authorities make you search ship before sailing, now.'

'Well?'

'Well, I shan't die like that. That's all.'

He stretched himself out once more, and for ten minutes neither spoke. The park-keeper strolled up again.

'Get up, there!' he said shortly and gruffly.

'Up ye get, mate,' added Darkey, but the man on the bench did not stir. One look at his face sufficed to startle the keeper, and presently two policemen were wheeling an ambulance cart to the hospital. Darkey followed, gave such information as he could, and then went his own ways.

II

In the afternoon the patient regained full consciousness. His eyes wandered vacantly about the illimitable ward, with its rows of beds stretching away on either side of him. A woman with a white cap, a white apron, and white wristbands bent over him, and he felt something gratefully warm passing down his throat. For just one second he was happy. Then his memory returned, and the nurse saw that he was crying. When he caught the nurse's eye he ceased, and looked steadily at the distant ceiling.

'You're better?'

'Yes.'

He tried to speak boldly, decisively, nonchalantly. He was filled with a sense of physical shame, the shame which bodily helplessness always experiences in the presence of arrogant, patronizing health. He would have got up and walked briskly away if he could. He hated to be waited on, to be humoured, to be examined and theorized about. This woman would be wanting to feel his pulse. She should not; he would turn cantankerous. No doubt they had been saying to each other, 'And so young, too! How sad!' Confound them!

'Have you any friends that you would like to send for?'

'No, none.'

The girl—she was only a girl—looked at him, and there was that in her eye which overcame him.

'None at all?'

'Not that I want to see.'

'Are your parents alive?'

'My mother is, but she lives away in the Five Towns.'

'You've not seen her lately, perhaps?'

He did not reply, and the nurse spoke again, but her voice sounded indistinct and far off.

When he awoke it was night. At the other end of the ward was a long table covered with a white cloth, and on this table a lamp.

In the ring of light under the lamp was an open book, an inkstand and a pen. A nurse—not *his* nurse—was standing by the table, her fingers idly drumming the cloth, and near her a man in evening dress. Perhaps a doctor. They were conversing in low tones. In the middle of the ward was an open stove, and the restless flames were reflected in all the brass knobs of the bedsteads and in some shining metal balls which hung from an unlighted chandelier. His part of the ward was almost in darkness. A confused, subdued murmur of little coughs, breathings, rustlings, was continually audible, and sometimes it rose above the conversation at the table. He noticed all these things. He became conscious, too, of a strangely familiar smell. What was it? Ah, yes! Acetic acid; his mother used it for her rheumatics.

Suddenly, magically, a great longing came over him. He must see his mother, or his brothers, or his little sister—someone who knew him, someone who *belonged* to him. He could have cried out in his desire. This one thought consumed all his faculties. If his mother could but walk in just now through that doorway! If only old Spot even could amble up to him, tongue out and tail furiously wagging! He tried to sit up, and he could not move! Then despair settled on him, and weighed him down. He closed his eyes.

The doctor and the nurse came slowly up the ward, pausing here and there. They stopped before his bed, and he held his breath.

'Not roused up again, I suppose?'

'No.'

'H'm! He may flicker on for forty-eight hours. Not more.'

They went on, and with a sigh of relief he opened his eyes again. The doctor shook hands with the nurse, who returned to the table and sat down.

Death! The end of all this! Yes, it was coming. He felt it. His had been one of those wasted lives of which he used to read in books. How strange! Almost amusing! He was one of those sons who bring sorrow and shame into a family. Again, how strange! What a coincidence that he—just *he* and not the man in the next bed—should be one of those rare, legendary good-for-nothings who go recklessly to ruin. And yet, he was sure that he was not such a bad fellow after all. Only somehow he had been careless. Yes, careless; that was the word ... nothing worse.... As to death, he was indifferent. Remembering his father's death, he reflected that it was probably less disturbing to die one's self than to watch another pass.

He smelt the acetic acid once more, and his thoughts reverted to his mother. Poor mother! No, great mother! The grandeur of her life's struggle filled him with a sense of awe. Strange that until that moment he had never seen the heroic side of her humdrum, commonplace existence! He must write to her, now, at once, before it was too late. His letter would trouble her, add another wrinkle to her face, but he must write; she must know that he had been thinking of her.

'Nurse!' he cried out, in a thin, weak voice.

'Ssh!'

She was by his side directly, but not before he had lost consciousness again.

The following morning he managed with infinite labour to scrawl a few lines:

'DEAR MAMMA,

'You will be surprised but not glad to get this letter. I'm done for, and you will never see me again. I'm sorry for what I've done, and how I've treated you, but it's no use saying anything now. If Pater had only lived he might have kept me in order. But you were too kind, you know. You've had a hard struggle these last six years, and I hope Arthur and Dick will stand by you better than I did, now they are growing up. Give them my love, and kiss little Fannie for me.

'WILLIE.

'*Mrs. Hancock*——'

He got no further with the address.

By some turn of the wheel, Darkey gathered several shillings during the next day or two, and, feeling both elated and benevolent, he called one afternoon at the hospital, 'just to inquire like.' They told him the man was dead.

'By the way, he left a letter without an address. Mrs. Hancock—here it is.'

'That'll be his mother; he did tell me about her—lived at Knype, Staffordshire, he said. I'll see to it.'

They gave Darkey the letter.

'So his name's Hancock,' he soliloquized, when he got into the street. 'I knew a girl of that name—once. I'll go and have a pint of four-half.'

At nine o'clock that night Darkey was still consuming four-half, and relating certain adventures by sea which, he averred, had happened to himself. He was very drunk.

'Yes,' he said, 'and them five lil' gals was lying there without a stitch on 'em, dead as meat; 's true as I'm 'ere. I've seen a thing or two in my time, I can tell ye.'

'Talking about these Anarchists—' said a man who appeared anxious to change the subject.

'An—kists,' Darkey interrupted. 'I tell ye what I'd do with that muck.'

He stopped to light his pipe, looked in vain for a match, felt in his pockets, and pulled out a piece of paper—the letter.

'I tell you what I'd do. I'd—'

He slowly and meditatively tore the letter in two, dropped one piece on the floor, thrust the other into a convenient gas-jet, and applied it to the tobacco.

'I'd get 'em 'gether in a heap, and I'd—Damn this pipe!'

He picked up the other half of the letter, and relighted the pipe.

'After you, mate,' said a man sitting near, who was just biting the end from a cigar.

THE GRIM SMILE OF THE FIVE TOWNS

BY

ARNOLD BENNETT

CONTENTS

The Lion's Share
Baby's Bath
The Silent Brothers
The Nineteenth Hat
Vera's First Christmas Adventure
The Murder of the Mandarin
Vera's Second Christmas Adventure
The Burglary
News of the Engagement
Beginning the New Year
From One Generation to Another
The Death of Simon Fuge
In a New Bottle

THE LION'S SHARE

I

In the Five Towns the following history is related by those who know it as something side-splittingly funny—as one of the best jokes that ever occurred in a district devoted to jokes. And I, too, have hitherto regarded it as such. But upon my soul, now that I come to write it down, it strikes me as being, after all, a pretty grim tragedy. However, you shall judge, and laugh or cry as you please.

It began in the little house of Mrs Carpole, up at Bleakridge, on the hill between Bursley and Hanbridge. Mrs Carpole was the second Mrs Carpole, and her husband was dead. She had a stepson, Horace, and a son of her own, Sidney. Horace is the hero, or the villain, of the history. On the day when the unfortunate affair began he was nineteen years old, and a model youth. Not only was he getting on in business, not only did he give half his evenings to the study of the chemistry of pottery and the other half to various secretaryships in connection with the Wesleyan Methodist Chapel and Sunday-school, not only did he save money, not only was he a comfort to his stepmother and a sort of uncle to Sidney, not only was he an early riser, a total abstainer, a non-smoker, and a good listener; but, in addition to the practice of these manifold and rare virtues, he found time, even at that tender age, to pay his tailor's bill promptly and to fold his trousers in the same crease every night—so that he always looked neat and dignified. Strange to say, he made no friends. Perhaps he was just a thought too perfect for a district like the Five Towns; a sin or so might have endeared him to the entire neighbourhood. Perhaps his loneliness was due to his imperfect sense of humour, or perhaps to the dull, unsmiling heaviness of his somewhat flat features.

Sidney was quite a different story. Sidney, to use his mother's phrase, was a little jockey. His years were then eight. Fair-haired and blue-eyed, as most little jockeys are, he had a smile and a scowl that were equally effective in tyrannizing over both his mother and Horace, and he was beloved by everybody. Women turned to look at him in the street. Unhappily, his health was not good. He was afflicted by a slight deafness, which, however, the doctor said he would grow out of; the doctor predicted for him a lusty manhood. In the meantime, he caught every disease that happened to be about, and nearly died of each one. His latest acquisition had been scarlet fever. Now one afternoon, after he had 'peeled' and his room had been disinfected, and he was beginning to walk again, Horace came home and decided that Sidney should be brought downstairs for tea as a treat, to celebrate his convalescence, and that he, Horace, would carry him downstairs. Mrs Carpole was delighted with the idea, and Sidney also, except that Sidney did not want to be carried downstairs—he wanted to walk down.

'I think it will be better for him to walk, Horace dear,' said Mrs Carpole, in her thin, plaintive voice. 'He can, quite well. And you know how clumsy you are. Supposing you were to fall!'

Horace, nevertheless, in pursuance of his programme of being uncle to Sidney, was determined to carry Sidney. And carry Sidney he did, despite warnings and kickings. At least he carried him as far as the turn in the steep stairs, at which point he fell, just as his stepmother had feared, and Sidney with him. The half-brothers arrived on the ground floor in company, but Horace, with his eleven stone two, was on top, and the poor suffering little convalescent lay moveless and insensible.

It took the doctor forty minutes to bring him to, and all the time the odour of grilled herrings, which formed part of the uneaten tea, made itself felt through the house like a Satanic comment on the spectacle of human life. The scene was dreadful at first. The agony then passed. There were no bruises on the boy, not a mark, and in a couple of hours he seemed to be perfectly himself. Horace breathed again, and thanked Heaven it was no worse. His gratitude to Heaven was, however, slightly premature, for in the black middle of the night poor Sidney was seized with excruciating pains in the head, and the doctor lost four hours' sleep. These pains returned at intervals of a few days, and naturally the child's convalescence was retarded. Then Horace said that Airs Carpole should take Sidney to Buxton for a fortnight, and he paid all the expenses of the trip out of his savings. He was desolated, utterly stricken; he said he should never forgive himself. Sidney improved, slowly.

II

After several months, during which Horace had given up all his limited spare time to the superintendence of the child's first steps in knowledge, Sidney was judged to be sufficiently strong to go to school, and it was arranged that he should attend the Endowed School at the Wedgwood Institution. Horace accompanied him thither on the opening day of the term—it was an inclement morning in January—and left the young delicate sprig, apparently joyous and content, to the care of his masters and the mercy of his companions. But Sidney came home for dinner weeping—weeping in spite of his new mortar-board cap, his new satchel, his new box of compasses, and his new books. His mother kept him at home in the afternoon, and by the evening another of those terrible attacks had supervened. The doctor and Horace and Mrs Carpole once more lost much precious sleep. The mysterious malady continued. School was out of the question.

And when Sidney took the air, in charge of his mother, everybody stopped to sympathize with him and to stroke his curls and call him a poor dear, and also to commiserate Mrs Carpole. As for Horace, Bursley tried to feel sorry for Horace, but it only succeeded in showing Horace that it was hiding a sentiment of indignation against him. Each friendly face as it passed Horace in the street said, without words, 'There goes the youth who probably ruined his young stepbrother's life. And through sheer obstinacy too! He dropped the little darling in spite of warnings and protests, and then fell on the top of him. Of course, he didn't do it on purpose, but—'

The doctor mentioned Greatorex of Manchester, the celebrated brain specialist. And Horace took Sidney to Manchester. They had to wait an hour and a quarter to see Greatorex, his well-known consulting-rooms in John Dalton Street being crowded with imperfect brains; but their turn came at last, and they found themselves in Greatorex's presence. Greatorex was a fat man, with the voice of a thin man, who seemed to spend the whole of his career in the care of his fingernails.

'Well, my little fellow,' said Greatorex, 'don't cry.' (For Sidney was already crying.) And then to Horace, in a curt tone: 'What is it?'

And Horace was obliged to humiliate himself and relate the accident in detail, together with all that had subsequently happened.

'Yes, yes, yes, yes!' Greatorex would punctuate the recital, and when tired of 'yes' he would say 'Hum, hum, hum, hum!'

When he had said 'hum' seventy-two times he suddenly remarked that his fee was three guineas, and told Horace to strengthen Sidney all he could, not to work him too hard, and to bring him back in a year's time.

Horace paid the money, Greatorex emitted a final 'hum', and then the stepbrothers were whisked out by an expeditious footman. The experience cost Horace over four pounds and the loss of a day's time. And the worst was that Sidney had a violent attack that very night.

School being impossible for him, Sidney had intermittent instruction from professors of both sexes at home. But he learnt practically nothing except the banjo. Horace had to buy him a banjo: it cost the best part of a ten-pound note; still, Horace could do no less. Sidney's stature grew rapidly; his general health certainly improved, yet not completely; he always had a fragile, interesting air. Moreover, his deafness did not disappear: there were occasions when it was extremely pronounced. And he was never quite safe from these attacks in the head. He spent a month or six weeks each year in the expensive bracing atmosphere of some seaside resort, and altogether he was decidedly a heavy drain on Horace's resources. People were aware of this, and they said that Horace ought to be happy that he was in a position to spend money freely on his poor brother. Had not the doctor predicted, before the catastrophe due to Horace's culpable negligence, that Sidney would grow into a strong man, and that his deafness would leave him? The truth was, one never knew the end of those accidents in infancy! Further, was not Sidney's sad condition slowly killing his mother? It was whispered about that, since the disaster, Sidney had not been QUITE sound mentally. Was not the mere suspicion of this enough to kill any mother?

And, as a fact, Mrs Carpole did die. She died of quinsy, doubtless aggravated by Sidney's sad condition.

Not long afterwards Horace came into a small fortune from his maternal grandfather. But poor Sidney did not come into any fortune, and people somehow illogically inferred that Horace had not behaved quite nicely in coming into a fortune while his suffering invalid brother, whom he had so deeply harmed, came into nothing. Even Horace had compunctions due to the visitations of a similar idea. And with part of the fortune he bought a house with a large garden up at Toft End, the highest hill of the hilly Five Towns, so that Sidney might have the benefit of the air. He also engaged a housekeeper and servants. With the remainder of the fortune he obtained a partnership in the firm of earthenware manufacturers for whom he had been acting as highly-paid manager.

Sidney reached the age of eighteen, and was most effective to look upon, his bright hair being still curly, and his eyes a wondrous blue, and his form elegant; and the question of Sidney's future arose. His health was steadily on the up grade. The deafness had quite disappeared. He had inclinations towards art, and had already amused himself by painting some beautiful vases. So it was settled that he should enter Horace's works on the art side, with a view to becoming, ultimately, art director. Horace gave him three pounds a week, in order that he might feel perfectly independent, and, to the same end, Sidney paid Horace seven-and-sixpence a week for board and lodging. But the change of life upset the youth's health again. After only two visits to the works he had a grave recurrence of the head-attacks, and he was solemnly exhorted not to apply himself too closely to business. He therefore took several half-holidays a week, and sometimes a whole one. And even when he put in one of his full days he would arrive at the works three hours after Horace, and restore the balance by leaving an hour earlier. The entire town watched over him as a mother watches over a son. The notion that he was not QUITE right in the pate gradually died away, and everybody was thankful for that, though it was feared an untimely grave might be his portion.

III

She was a nice girl: the nicest girl that Horace had ever met with, because her charming niceness included a faculty of being really serious about serious things—and yet she could be deliciously gay. In short, she was a revelation to Horace. And her name was Ella, and she had come one year to spend some weeks with Mrs Penkethman, the widowed headmistress of the Wesleyan Day School, who was her cousin. Mrs Penkethman and Ella had been holidaying together in France; their arrival in Bursley naturally coincided with the reopening of the school in August for the autumn term.

Now at this period Horace was rather lonely in his large house and garden; for Sidney, in pursuit of health, had gone off on a six weeks' cruise round Holland, Finland, Norway, and Sweden, in one of those Atlantic liners which, translated like Enoch without dying, become in their old age 'steam-yachts', with fine names apt to lead to confusion with the private yacht of the Tsar of Russia. Horace had offered him the trip, and Horace was also paying his weekly salary as usual.

So Horace, who had always been friendly with Mrs Penkethman, grew now more than ever friendly with Mrs Penkethman. And Mrs Penkethman and Ella were inseparable. The few aristocrats left in Bursley in September remarked that Horace knew what he was about, as it was notorious that Ella had the most solid expectations. But as a matter of fact Horace did not know what he was about, and he never once thought of Ella's expectations. He was simply, as they say in Bursley, knocked silly by Ella. He honestly imagined her to be the wonderfullest woman on the earth's surface, with her dark eyes and her expressive sympathetic gestures, and her alterations of seriousness and gaiety. It astounded him that a girl of twenty-one could have thought so deeply upon life as she had. The inexplicable thing was that she looked up to HIM. She evidently admired HIM. He wanted to tell her that she was quite wrong about him, much too kind in her estimate of him—that really he was a very ordinary man indeed. But another instinct prevented him from thus undeceiving her.

And one Saturday afternoon, the season being late September, Horace actually got those two women up to tea in his house and garden. He had not dared to dream of such bliss. He had hesitated long before asking them to come, and in asking them he had blushed and stammered: the invitation had seemed to him to savour of audacity. But, bless you! they had accepted with apparent ecstasy. They gave him to think that they had genuinely wanted to come. And they came extra-specially dressed—visions, lilies of the field. And as the day was quite warm, tea was served in the garden, and everybody admired the view; and there was no restraint, no awkwardness. In particular Ella talked with an ease and a distinction that enchanted Horace, and almost made him talk with ease and distinction too. He said to himself that, seeing he had only known her a month, he was getting on amazingly. He said to himself that his good luck passed belief.

Then there was a sound of cab-wheels on the other side of the garden-wall, and presently Horace heard the housekeeper complimenting Sidney on his good looks, and Sidney asking the housekeeper to lend him three shillings to pay the cabman. The golden youth had returned without the slightest warning from his cruise. The tea trio, at the lower end of the garden, saw him standing in the porch, tanned, curly, graceful, and young. Horace half rose, and then sat down again. Ella stared hard.

'That must be your brother,' she said.

'Yes, that's Sid,' Horace answered; and then, calling out loudly: 'Come down here, Sid, and tell them to bring another cup and saucer.'

'Right you are, old man,' Sidney shouted. 'You see I'm back. What! Mrs Penkethman, is that you?' He came down the central path of the garden like a Narcissus.

'He DOES look delicate,' said Ella under her breath to Horace. Tears came to her eyes.

Naturally Ella knew all about Sidney. She enjoyed the entire confidence of Mrs Penkethman, and what Mrs Penkethman didn't know of the private history of the upper classes in Bursley did not amount to very much.

These were nearly the last words that Ella spoke to Horace that afternoon. The introduction was made, and Sidney slipped into the party as comfortably as he slipped into everything, like a candle slipping into a socket. But nevertheless Ella talked no more. She just stared at Sidney, and listened to him. Horace was proud that Sidney had made such an impression on her; he was glad that she showed no aversion to Sidney, because, in the event of Horace's marriage, where would Sidney live, if not with Horace and Horace's wife? Still, he could have wished that Ella would continue to display her conversational powers.

Presently, Sidney lighted a cigarette. He was of those young men whose delicate mouths seem to have been fashioned for the nice conduct of a cigarette. And he had a way of blowing out the smoke that secretly ravished every feminine beholder. Horace still held to his boyhood's principles; but he envied Sidney a little.

At the conclusion of the festivity these two women naturally could not be permitted to walk home alone. And, naturally, also, the four could not walk abreast on the narrow pavements. Horace went first with Mrs Penkethman. He was mad with anxiety to appropriate

Ella, but he dared not. It would not have been quite correct; it would have been, as they say in Bursley, too thick. Besides, there was the question of age. Horace was over thirty, and Mrs Penkethman was also—over thirty; whereas Sidney was twenty-one, and so was Ella. Hence Sidney walked behind with Ella, and the procession started in silence. Horace did not look round too often—that would not have been quite proper—but whenever he did look round the other couple had lagged farther and farther behind, and Ella seemed perfectly to have recovered her speech. At length he looked round, and lo! they had not turned the last corner; and they arrived at Mrs Penkethman's cottage at Hillport a quarter of an hour after their elders.

IV

The wedding cost Horace a large sum of money. You see, he could not do less than behave handsomely by the bride, owing to his notorious admiration for her; and of course the bridegroom needed setting up. Horace practically furnished their home for them out of his own pocket; it was not to be expected that Sidney should have resources. Further, Sidney as a single man, paying seven-and-six a week for board and lodging, could no doubt struggle along upon three pounds weekly. But Sidney as a husband, with the nicest girl in the world to take care of, and house-rent to pay, could not possibly perform the same feat. Although he did no more work at the manufactory—Horace could not have been so unbrotherly as to demand it—Horace paid him eight pounds a week instead of three.

And the affair cost Horace a good deal besides money. But what could Horace do? He decidedly would not have wished to wreck the happiness of two young and beautiful lives, even had he possessed the power to do so. And he did not possess the power. Those two did not consult Horace before falling in love. They merely fell in love, and there was an end of it—and an end of Horace too! Horace had to suffer. He did suffer.

Perhaps it was for his highest welfare that other matters came to monopolize his mind. One sorrow drives out another. If you sit on a pin you are apt to forget that you have the toothache. The earthenware manufactory was not going well. Plenty of business was being done, but not at the right prices. Crushed between the upper and nether millstones of the McKinley Tariff and German competition, Horace, in company with other manufacturers, was breathing out his life's blood in the shape of capital. The truth was that he had never had enough capital. He had heavily mortgaged the house at Toft End in order to purchase his partners' shares in the business and have the whole undertaking to himself, and he profoundly regretted it. He needed every penny that he could collect; the strictest economy was necessary if he meant to survive the struggle. And here he was paying eight pounds a week to a personage purely ornamental, after having squandered hundreds in rendering that personage comfortable! The situation was dreadful.

You may ask, Why did he not explain the situation to Sidney? Well, partly because he was too kind, and partly because he was too proud, and partly because Sidney would not have understood. Horace fought on, keeping up a position in the town and hoping that miracles would occur.

Then Ella's expectations were realized. Sidney and she had some twenty thousand pounds to play with. And they played the most agreeable games. But not in Bursley. No. They left Horace in Bursley and went to Llandudno for a spell. Horace envied them, but he saw them off at the station as an elder brother should, and tipped the porters.

Certainly he was relieved of the formality of paying eight pounds a week to his brother. But this did not help him much. The sad fact was that 'things' (by which is meant fate, circumstances, credit, and so on) had gone too far. It was no longer a question of eight pounds a week; it was a question of final ruin.

Surely he might have borrowed money from Sidney? Sidney had no money; the money was Ella's, and Horace could not have brought himself to borrow money from a woman—from Ella, from a heavenly creature who always had a soothing sympathetic word for him. That would have been to take advantage of Ella. No, if you suggest such a thing, you do not know Horace.

I stated in the beginning that he had no faults. He was therefore absolutely honest. And he called his creditors together while he could yet pay them twenty shillings in the pound. It was a noble act, rare enough in the Five Towns and in other parts of England. But he received no praise for it. He had only done what every man in his position ought to do. If Horace had failed for ten times the sum that his debts actually did amount to, and then paid two shillings in the pound instead of twenty, he would have made a stir in the world and been looked up to as no ordinary man of business.

Having settled his affairs in this humdrum, idiotic manner, Horace took a third-class return to Llandudno. Sidney and Ella were staying at the hydro with the strange Welsh name, and he found Sidney lolling on the sunshiny beach in front of the hydro discoursing on the banjo to himself. When asked where his wife was, Sidney replied that she was lying down, and was obliged to rest as much as possible.

Horace, ashamed to trouble this domestic idyl, related his misfortunes as airily as he could.

And Sidney said he was awfully sorry, and had no notion how matters stood, and could he do anything for Horace? If so, Horace might—

'No,' said Horace. 'I'm all right. I've very fortunately got an excellent place as manager in a big new manufactory in Germany.' (This is how we deal with German competition in the Five Towns.)

'Germany?' cried Sidney.

'Yes,' said Horace; 'and I start the day after tomorrow.'

'Well,' said Sidney, 'at any rate you'll stay the night.'

'Thanks,' said Horace, 'you're very kind. I will.'

So they went into the hydro together, Sidney caressing his wonderful new pearl-inlaid banjo; and Horace talked in low tones to Ella as she lay on the sofa. He convinced Ella that his departure to Germany was the one thing he had desired all his life, because it was not good that Ella should be startled, shocked, or grieved.

They dined well.

But in the night Sidney had a recurrence of his old illness—a bad attack; and Horace sat up through the dark hours, fetched the doctor, and bought things at the chemist's. Towards morning Sidney was better. And Horace, standing near the bed, gazed at his stepbrother and tried in his stupid way to read the secrets beneath that curly hair. But he had no success. He caught himself calculating how much Sidney had cost him, at periods of his career when he could ill spare money; and, having caught himself, he was angry with himself for such baseness. At eight o'clock he ventured to knock at Ella's door and explain to her that Sidney had not been quite well. She had passed a peaceful night, for he had, of course, refrained from disturbing her.

He was not quite sure whether Sidney had meant him to stay at the hydro as his guest, so he demanded a bill, paid it, said good-bye, and left for Bonn-on-the-Rhine. He was very exhausted and sleepy.

Happily the third-class carriages on the London & North-Western are pretty comfortable. Between Chester and Crewe he had quite a doze, and dreamed that he had married Ella after all, and that her twenty thousand pounds had put the earthenware business on a footing of magnificent and splendid security.

V

A few months later Horace's house and garden at Toft End were put up to auction by arrangement with his mortgagee and his trade-creditors. And Sidney was struck with the idea of buying the place. The impression was that it would go cheap. Sidney said it would be a pity to let the abode pass out of the family. Ella said that the idea of buying it was a charming one, because in the garden it was that she had first met her Sidney. So the place was duly bought, and Sidney and Ella went to live there.

Several years elapsed.

Then one day little Horace was informed that his uncle Horace, whom he had never seen, was coming to the house on a visit, and that he must be a good boy, and polite to his uncle, and all the usual sort of thing.

And in effect Horace the elder did arrive in the afternoon. He found no one to meet him at the station, or at the garden gate of the pleasaunce that had once been his, or even at the front door. A pert parlour-maid told him that her master and mistress were upstairs in the nursery, and that he was requested to go up. And he went up, and to be sure Sidney met him at the top of the stairs, banjo in hand, cigarette in mouth, smiling, easy and elegant as usual—not a trace of physical weakness in his face or form. And Horace was jocularly ushered into the nursery and introduced to his nephew. Ella had changed. She was no longer slim, and no longer gay and serious by turns. She narrowly missed being stout, and she was continuously gay, like Sidney. The child was also gay. Everybody was glad to see Horace, but nobody seemed deeply interested in Horace's affairs. As a fact he had done rather well in Germany, and had now come back to England in order to assume a working partnership in a small potting concern at Hanbridge. He was virtually beginning life afresh. But what concerned Sidney and Ella was themselves and their offspring. They talked incessantly about the infinitesimal details of their daily existence, and the alterations which they had

157

made, or meant to make, in the house and garden. And occasionally Sidney thrummed a tune on the banjo to amuse the infant. Horace had expected them to be curious about Germany and his life in Germany. But not a bit! He might have come in from the next street and left them only yesterday, for all the curiosity they exhibited.

'Shall we go down to the drawing-room and have tea, eh?' said Ella.

'Yes, let's go and kill the fatted calf,' said Sidney.

And strangely enough, inexplicably enough, Horace did feel like a prodigal.

Sidney went off with his precious banjo, and Ella picked up sundry belongings without which she never travelled about the house.

'You carry me down-stairs, unky?' the little nephew suggested, with an appealing glance at his new uncle. 'No,' said Horace, 'I'm dashed if I do!'

BABY'S BATH

I

Mrs Blackshaw had a baby. It would be an exaggeration to say that the baby interested the entire town, Bursley being an ancient, blase sort of borough of some thirty thousand inhabitants. Babies, in fact, arrived in Bursley at the rate of more than a thousand every year. Nevertheless, a few weeks after the advent of Mrs Blackshaw's baby, when the medical officer of health reported to the Town Council that the births for the month amounted to ninety-five, and that the birth-rate of Bursley compared favourably with the birth-rates of the sister towns, Hanbridge, Knype, Longshaw, and Turnhill—when the medical officer read these memorable words at the monthly meeting of the Council, and the Staffordshire Signal reported them, and Mrs Blackshaw perused them, a blush of pride spread over Mrs Blackshaw's face, and she picked up the baby's left foot and gave it a little peck of a kiss. She could not help feeling that the real solid foundation of that formidable and magnificent output of babies was her baby. She could not help feeling that she had done something for the town—had caught the public eye.

As for the baby, except that it was decidedly superior to the average infant in external appearance and pleasantness of disposition, it was, in all essential characteristics, a typical baby—that is to say, it was purely sensuous and it lived the life of the senses. It was utterly selfish. It never thought of anyone but itself. It honestly imagined itself to be the centre of the created universe. It was convinced that the rest of the universe had been brought into existence solely for the convenience and pleasure of it—the baby. When it wanted anything it made no secret of the fact, and it was always utterly unscrupulous in trying to get what it wanted. If it could have obtained the moon it would have upset all the astronomers of Europe and made Whitaker's Almanack unsalable without a pang. It had no god but its stomach. It never bothered its head about higher things. It was a bully and a coward, and it treated women as beings of a lower order than men. In a word, it was that ideal creature, sung of the poets, from which we gradually sink and fall away as we grow older.

At the age of six months it had quite a lot of hair, and a charming rosy expanse at the back of its neck, caused through lying on its back in contemplation of its own importance. It didn't know the date of the Battle of Hastings, but it knew with the certainty of absolute knowledge that it was master of the house, and that the activity of the house revolved round it.

Now, the baby loved its bath. In any case its bath would have been an affair of immense and intricate pomp; but the fact that it loved its bath raised the interest and significance of the bath to the nth power. The bath took place at five o'clock in the evening, and it is not too much to say that the idea of the bath was immanent in the very atmosphere of the house. When you have an appointment with the dentist at five o'clock in the afternoon the idea of the appointment is immanent in your mind from the first moment of your awakening. Conceive that an appointment with the dentist implies heavenly joy instead of infernal pain, and you will have a notion of the daily state of Mrs Blackshaw and Emmie (the nurse) with regard to the baby's bath.

Even at ten in the morning Emmie would be keeping an eye on the kitchen fire, lest the cook might let it out. And shortly after noon Mrs Blackshaw would be keeping an eye on the thermometer in the bedroom where the bath occurred. From four o'clock onwards the clocks in the house were spied on and overlooked like suspected persons; but they were used to that, because the baby had his sterilized milk every two hours. I have at length allowed you to penetrate the secret of his sex.

And so at five o'clock precisely the august and exciting ceremony began in the best bedroom. A bright fire was burning (the month being December), and the carefully-shaded electric lights were also burning. A large bath-towel was spread in a convenient place on the floor, and on the towel were two chairs facing each other, and a table. On one chair was the bath, and on the other was Mrs Blackshaw with her sleeves rolled up, and on Mrs Blackshaw was another towel, and on that towel was Roger (the baby). On the table were zinc ointment, vaseline, scentless eau de Cologne, Castile soap, and a powder-puff.

Emmie having pretty nearly filled the bath with a combination of hot and cold waters, dropped the floating thermometer into it, and then added more waters until the thermometer indicated the precise temperature proper for a baby's bath. But you are not to imagine that Mrs Blackshaw trusted a mere thermometer. No. She put her arm in the water up to the elbow. She reckoned the sensitive skin near the elbow was worth forty thermometers.

Emmie was chiefly an audience. Mrs Blackshaw had engaged her as a nurse, but she could have taught a nigger-boy to do all that she allowed the nurse to do. During the bath Mrs Blackshaw and Emmie hated and scorned each other, despite their joy. Emmie was twice Mrs Blackshaw's age, besides being twice her weight, and she knew twice as much about babies as Mrs Blackshaw did. However, Mrs Blackshaw had the terrific advantage of being the mother of that particular infant, and she could always end an argument when she chose, and in her own favour. It was unjust, and Emmie felt it to be unjust; but this is not a world of justice.

Roger, though not at all precocious, was perfectly aware of the carefully-concealed hostility between his mother and his nurse, and often, with his usual unscrupulousness, he used it for his own ends. He was sitting upon his mother's knees toying with the edge of the bath, already tasting its delights in advance. Mrs Blackshaw undressed the upper half of him, and then she laid him on the flat of his back and undressed the lower half of him, but keeping some wisp of a garment round his equatorial regions. And then she washed his face with a sponge and the Castile soap, very gently, but not half gently enough for Emmie, nor half gently enough for Roger, for Roger looked upon this part of the business as insulting and superfluous. He breathed hard and kicked his feet nearly off.

'Yes, it's dreadful having our face washed, isn't it?' said Mrs Blackshaw, with her sleeves up, and her hair by this time down. 'We don't like it, do we? Yes, yes.'

Emmie grunted, without a sound, and yet Mrs Blackshaw heard her, and finished that face quickly and turned to the hands.

'Potato-gardens every day,' she said. 'Evzy day-day. Enough of that, Colonel!' (For, after all, she had plenty of spirit.) 'Fat little creases! Fat little creases! There! He likes that! There! Feet! Feet! Feet and legs! Then our back. And then WHUP we shall go into the bath! That's it. Kick! Kick your mother!'

And she turned him over.

'Incredible bungler!' said the eyes of the nurse. 'Can't she turn him over neater than that?'

'Harridan!' said the eyes of Mrs Blackshaw. 'I wouldn't let you bath him for twenty thousand pounds!'

Roger continued to breathe hard, as if his mother were a horse and he were rubbing her down.

161

'Now! Zoop! Whup!' cried his mother, and having deprived him of his final rag, she picked him up and sat him in the bath, and he was divinely happy, and so were the women. He appeared a gross little animal in the bath, all the tints of his flesh shimmering under the electric light. His chest was superb, but the rolled and creased bigness of his inordinate stomach was simply appalling, not to mention his great thighs and calves. The truth was, he had grown so that if he had been only a little bit bigger, he would have burst the bath. He resembled an old man who had been steadily eating too much for about forty years.

His two womenfolk now candidly and openly worshipped him, forgetting sectarian differences.

And he splashed. Oh! he splashed. You see, he had learnt how to splash, and he had certainly got an inkling that to splash was wicked and messy. So he splashed—in his mother's face, in Emmie's face, in the fire. He pretty well splashed the fire out. Ten minutes before, the bedroom had been tidy, a thing of beauty. It was now naught but a wild welter of towels, socks, binders—peninsulas of clothes nearly surrounded by water.

Finally his mother seized him again, and, rearing his little legs up out of the water, immersed the whole of his inflated torso beneath the surface.

'Hallo!' she exclaimed. 'Did the water run over his mouf? Did it?'

'Angels and ministers of grace defend us! How clumsy she is!' commented the eyes of Emmie.

'There! I fink that's about long enough for this kind of wevver,' said the mother.

'I should think it was! There's almost a crust of ice on the water now!' the nurse refrained from saying.

And Roger, full of regrets, was wrenched out of the bath. He had ceased breathing hard while in the water, but he began again immediately he emerged.

'We don't like our face wiped, do we?' said his mother on his behalf. 'We want to go back into that bath. We like it. It's more fun than anything that happens all day long! Eh? That old dandruff's coming up in fine style. It's a-peeling off like anything.'

And all the while she wiped him, patted eau de Cologne into him with the flat of her hand, and rubbed zinc ointment into him, and massaged him, and powdered him, and turned him over and over and over, till he was thoroughly well basted and cooked. And he kept on breathing hard.

Then he sneezed, amid general horror!

'I told you so!' the nurse didn't say, and she rushed to the bed where all the idol's beautiful, clean, aired things were lying safe from splashings, and handed a flannel shirt, about two inches in length, to Mrs Blackshaw. And Mrs Blackshaw rolled the left sleeve of it into a wad and stuck it over his arm, and his poor little vaccination marks were hidden from view till next morning. Roger protested.

'We don't like clothes, do we?' said his mother. 'We want to tumble back into our tub. We aren't much for clothes anyway. We'se a little Hottentot, aren't we?'

And she gradually covered him with one garment or another until there was nothing left of him but his head and his hands and feet. And she sat him up on her knees, so as to fasten his things behind. And then it might have been observed that he was no longer breathing hard, but giving vent to a sound between a laugh and a cry, while sucking his thumb and gazing round the room.

'That's our little affected cry that we start for our milk, isn't it?' his mother explained to him.

And he agreed that it was.

And before Emmie could fly across the room for the bottle, all ready and waiting, his mouth, in the shape of a perfect rectangle, had monopolized five-sixths of his face, and he was scarlet and bellowing with impatience.

He took the bottle like a tiger his prey, and seized his mother's hand that held the bottle, and he furiously pumped the milk into that insatiable gulf of a stomach. But he found time to gaze about the room too. A tear stood in each roving eye, caused by the effort of feeding.

'Yes, that's it,' said his mother. 'Now look round and see what's happening. Curiosity! Well, if you WILL bob your head, I can't help it.'

'Of course you can!' the nurse didn't say.

Then he put his finger into his mouth side by side with the bottle, and gagged himself, and choked, and gave a terrible—excuse the word—hiccough. After which he seemed to lose interest in the milk, and the pumping operations slackened and then ceased.

'Goosey!' whispered his mother, 'getting seepy? Is the sandman throwing sand in your eyes? Old Sandman at it? Sh—' ... He had gone.

Emmie took him. The women spoke in whispers. And Mrs Blackshaw, after a day spent in being a mother, reconstituted herself a wife, and began to beautify herself for her husband.

II

Yes, there was a Mr Blackshaw, and with Mr Blackshaw the tragedy of the bath commences. Mr Blackshaw was a very important young man. Indeed, it is within the mark to say that, next to his son, he was the most important young man in Bursley. For Mr Blackshaw was the manager of the newly opened Municipal Electricity Works. And the Municipal Electricity had created more excitement and interest than anything since the 1887 Jubilee, when an ox was roasted whole in the market-place and turned bad in the process. Had Bursley been a Swiss village, or a French country town, or a hamlet in Arizona, it would have had its electricity fifteen years ago, but being only a progressive English Borough, with an annual value of a hundred and fifty thousand pounds, it struggled on with gas till well into the twentieth century. Its great neighbour Hanbridge had become acquainted with electricity in the nineteenth century.

All the principal streets and squares, and every decent shop that Hanbridge competition had left standing, and many private houses, now lighted themselves by electricity, and the result was splendid and glaring and coldly yellow. Mr. Blackshaw developed into the hero of the hour. People looked at him in the street as though he had been the discoverer and original maker of electricity. And if the manager of the gasworks had not already committed murder, it was because the manager of the gasworks had a right sense of what was due to his position as vicar's churchwarden at St Peter's Church.

But greatness has its penalties. And the chief penalty of Mr Blackshaw's greatness was that he could not see Roger have his nightly bath. It was impossible for Mr Blackshaw to quit his arduous and responsible post before seven o'clock in the evening. Later on, when things were going more smoothly, he might be able to get away; but then, later on, his son's bath would not be so amusing and agreeable as it then, by all reports, was. The baby was, of course,

164

bathed on Saturday nights, but Sunday afternoon and evening Mr Blackshaw was obliged to spend with his invalid mother at Longshaw. It was on the sole condition of his weekly presence thus in her house that she had consented not to live with the married pair. And so Mr Blackshaw could not witness Roger's bath. He adored Roger. He understood Roger. He weighed, nursed, and fed Roger. He was 'up' in all the newest theories of infant rearing. In short, Roger was his passion, and he knew everything of Roger except Roger's bath. And when his wife met him at the front door of a night at seven-thirty and launched instantly into a description of the wonders, delights, and excitations of Roger's latest bath, Mr Blackshaw was ready to tear his hair with disappointment and frustration.

'I suppose you couldn't put it off for a couple of hours one night, May?' he suggested at supper on the evening of the particular bath described above.

'Sidney!' protested Mrs Blackshaw, pained.

Mr Blackshaw felt that he had gone too far, and there was a silence.

'Well!' said Mr Blackshaw at length, 'I have just made up my mind. I'm going to see that Kid's bath, and, what's more, I'm going to see it tomorrow. I don't care what happens.'

'But how shall you manage to get away, darling?'

'You will telephone me about a quarter of an hour before you're ready to begin, and I'll pretend it's something very urgent, and scoot off.'

'Well, that will be lovely, darling!' said Mrs Blackshaw. 'I WOULD like you to see him in the bath, just once! He looks so—'

And so on.

The next day, Mr Blackshaw, that fearsome autocrat of the Municipal Electricity Works, was saying to himself all day that at five o'clock he was going to assist at the spectacle of his wonderful son's bath. The prospect inspired him. So much so that every hand on the place was doing its utmost in fear and trembling, and the whole affair was running with the precision and smoothness of a watch.

From four o'clock onwards, Mr Blackshaw, in the solemn, illuminated privacy of the managerial office, safe behind glass partitions, could no more contain his excitement. He hovered in front of the telephone, waiting for it to ring. Then, at a quarter to

165

five, just when he felt he couldn't stand it any longer, and was about to ring up his wife instead of waiting for her to ring him up, he saw a burly shadow behind the glass door, and gave a desolate sigh. That shadow could only be thrown by one person, and that person was his Worship the Mayor of Bursley. His Worship entered the private office with mayoral assurance, pulling in his wake a stout old lady whom he introduced as his aunt from Wolverhampton. And he calmly proposed that Mr Blackshaw should show the mayoral aunt over the new Electricity Works!

Mr Blackshaw was sick of showing people over the Works. Moreover, he naturally despised the Mayor. All permanent officials of municipalities thoroughly despise their mayors (up their sleeves). A mayor is here today and gone tomorrow, whereas a permanent official is permanent. A mayor knows nothing about anything except his chain and the rules of debate, and he is, further, a tedious and meddlesome person—in the opinion of permanent officials.

So Mr Blackshaw's fury at the inept appearance of the Mayor and the mayoral aunt at this critical juncture may be imagined. The worst of it was, he didn't know how to refuse the Mayor.

Then the telephone-bell rang.

'Excuse me,' said Mr Blackshaw, with admirably simulated politeness, going to the instrument. 'Are you there? Who is it?'

'It's me, darling,' came the thin voice of his wife far away at Bleakridge. 'The water's just getting hot. We're nearly ready. Can you come now?'

'By Jove! Wait a moment!' exclaimed Mr Blackshaw, and then turning to his visitors, 'Did you hear that?'

'No,' said the Mayor.

'All those three new dynamos that they've got at the Hanbridge Electricity Works have just broken down. I knew they would. I told them they would!'

'Dear, dear!' said the Mayor of Bursley, secretly delighted by this disaster to a disdainful rival. 'Why! They'll have the town in darkness. What are they going to do?'

'They want me to go over at once. But, of course, I can't. At least, I must give myself the pleasure of showing you and this lady over our Works, first.'

'Nothing of the kind, Mr Blackshaw!' said the Mayor. 'Go at once. Go at once. If Bursley can be of any assistance to Hanbridge

166

in such a crisis, I shall be only too pleased. We will come tomorrow, won't we, auntie?'

Mr Blackshaw addressed the telephone.

'The Mayor is here, with a lady, and I was just about to show them over the Works, but his Worship insists that I come at once.'

'Certainly,' the Mayor put in pompously.

'Wonders will never cease,' came the thin voice of Mrs Blackshaw through the telephone. 'It's very nice of the old thing! What's his lady friend like?'

'Not like anything. Unique!' replied Mr Blackshaw.

'Young?' came the voice.

'Dates from the thirties,' said Mr Blackshaw. 'I'm coming.' And rang off.

'I didn't know there was any electric machinery as old as that,' said the mayoral aunt.

'We'll just look about us a bit,' the Mayor remarked. 'Don't lose a moment, Mr Blackshaw.'

And Mr Blackshaw hurried off, wondering vaguely how he should explain the lie when it was found out, but not caring much. After all, he could easily ascribe the episode to the trick of some practical joker.

III

He arrived at his commodious and electrically lit residence in the very nick of time, and full to overflowing with innocent paternal glee. Was he not about to see Roger's tub? Roger was just ready to be carried upstairs as Mr Blackshaw's latchkey turned in the door.

'Wait a sec!' cried Mr Blackshaw to his wife, who had the child in her arms, 'I'll carry him up.'

And he threw away his hat, stick, and overcoat and grabbed ecstatically at the infant. And he had got perhaps halfway up the stairs, when lo! the electric light went out. Every electric light in the house went out.

'Great Scott!' breathed Mr Blackshaw, aghast.

He pulled aside the blind of the window at the turn of the stairs, and peered forth. The street was as black as your hat, or nearly so.

'Great Scott!' he repeated. 'May, get candles.'

Something had evidently gone wrong at the Works. Just his luck! He had quitted the Works for a quarter of an hour, and the current had failed!

Of course, the entire house was instantly in an uproar, turned upside down, startled out of its life. But a few candles soon calmed its transports. And at length Mr Blackshaw gained the bedroom in safety, with the offspring of his desires comfortable in a shawl.

'Give him to me,' said May shortly. 'I suppose you'll have to go back to the Works at once?'

Mr Blackshaw paused, and then nerved himself; but while he was pausing, May, glancing at the two feeble candles, remarked: 'It's very tiresome. I'm sure I shan't be able to see properly.'

'No!' almost shouted Mr Blackshaw. 'I'll watch this kid have his bath or I'll die for it! I don't care if all the Five Towns are in darkness. I don't care if the Mayor's aunt has got caught in a dynamo and is suffering horrible tortures. I've come to see this bath business, and dashed if I don't see it!'

'Well, don't stand between the bath and the fire, dearest,' said May coldly.

Meanwhile, Emmie, having pretty nearly filled the bath with a combination of hot and cold waters, dropped the floating thermometer into it, and then added more waters until the thermometer indicated the precise temperature proper for a baby's bath. But you are not to imagine that Mrs Blackshaw trusted a thermometer—

She did not, however, thrust her bared arm into the water this time. No! Roger, who never cried before his bath, was crying, was indubitably crying. And he cried louder and louder.

'Stand where he can't see you, dearest. He isn't used to you at bath-time,' said Mrs Blackshaw still coldly. 'Are you, my pet? There! There!'

Mr Blackshaw effaced himself, feeling a fool. But Roger continued to cry. He cried himself purple. He cried till the veins stood out on his forehead and his mouth was like a map of Australia. He cried himself into a monster of ugliness. Neither mother nor nurse could do anything with him at all.

'I think you've upset him, dearest,' said Mrs Blackshaw even more coldly. 'Hadn't you better go?'

'Well—' protested the father.

'I think you had better go,' said Mrs Blackshaw, adding no term of endearment, and visibly controlling herself with difficulty.

And Mr Blackshaw went. He had to go. He went out into the unelectric night. He headed for the Works, not because he cared twopence, at that moment, about the accident at the Works, whatever it was; but simply because the Works was the only place to go to. And even outside in the dark street he could hear the rousing accents of his progeny.

People were talking to each other as they groped about in the road, and either making jokes at the expense of the new Electricity Department, or frankly cursing it with true Five Towns directness of speech. And as Mr Blackshaw went down the hill into the town his heart was as black as the street itself with rage and disappointment. He had made his child cry!

Someone stopped him.

'Eh, Mester Blackshaw!' said a voice, and under the voice a hand struck a match to light a pipe. 'What's th' maning o' this eclipse as you'm treating us to?'

Mr Blackshaw looked right through the inquirer—a way he had when his brain was working hard. And he suddenly smiled by the light of the match.

'That child wasn't crying because I was there,' said Mr Blackshaw with solemn relief. 'Not at all! He was crying because he didn't understand the candles. He isn't used to candles, and they frightened him.'

And he began to hurry towards the Works.

At the same instant the electric light returned to Bursley. The current was resumed.

'That's better,' said Mr Blackshaw, sighing.

THE SILENT BROTHERS

I

John and Robert Hessian, brothers, bachelors, and dressed in mourning, sat together after supper in the parlour of their house at the bottom of Oldcastle Street, Bursley. Maggie, the middle-aged servant, was clearing the table.

'Leave the cloth and the coffee,' said John, the elder, 'Mr Liversage is coming in.'

'Yes, Mr John,' said Maggie.

'Slate, Maggie,' Robert ordered laconically, with a gesture towards the mantelpiece behind him.

'Yes, Mr Robert,' said Maggie.

She gave him a slate with slate-pencil attached, which hung on a nail near the mantlepiece.

Robert took the slate and wrote on it: 'What is Liversage coming about?'

And he pushed the slate across the table to John.

Whereupon John wrote on the slate: 'Don't know. He telephoned me he wanted to see us tonight.'

And he pushed back the slate to Robert.

This singular procedure was not in the least attributable to deafness on the part of the brothers; they were in the prime of life, aged forty-two and thirty-nine respectively, and in complete possession of all their faculties. It was due simply to the fact that they had quarrelled, and would not speak to each other. The history of their quarrel would be incredible were it not full of that ridiculous pathetic quality known as human nature, and did not similar things happen frequently in the manufacturing Midlands, where the general temperament is a fearful and strange compound of pride, obstinacy, unconquerableness, romance, and stupidity. Yes, stupidity.

No single word had passed between the brothers in that house for ten years. On the morning after the historical quarrel Robert had not replied when John spoke to him. 'Well,' said John's secret heart— and John's secret heart ought to have known better, as it was older than its brother heart—'I'll teach him a lesson. I won't speak until he does.' And Robert's secret heart had somehow divined this idiotic resolution, and had said: 'We shall see.' Maggie had been the first to notice the stubborn silence. Then their friends noticed it, especially Mr Liversage, the solicitor, their most intimate friend. But you are not to suppose that anybody protested very strongly. For John and Robert were not the kind of men with whom liberties may be taken; and, moreover, Bursley was slightly amused—at the beginning. It assumed the attitude of a disinterested spectator at a fight. It wondered who would win. Of course, it called both the brothers fools, yet in a tone somewhat sympathetic, because such a thing as had occurred to the Hessians might well occur to any man gifted with the true Bursley spirit. There is this to be said for a Bursley man: Having made his bed, he will lie on it, and he will not complain.

The Hessians suffered severely by their self-imposed dumbness, but they suffered like Stoics. Maggie also suffered, and Maggie would not stand it. Maggie it was who had invented the slate. Indeed, they had heard some plain truths from that stout, bustling woman. They had not yielded, but they had accepted the slate in order to minimize the inconvenience to Maggie, and afterwards they deigned to make use of it for their own purposes. As for friends— friends accustomed themselves to the status quo. There came a time when the spectacle of two men chattering to everybody else in a company, and not saying a word to each other, no longer appealed to Bursley's sense of humour. The silent scenes at which Maggie assisted every day did not, either, appeal to Maggie's sense of humour, because she had none. So the famous feud grew into a sort of elemental fact of Nature. It was tolerated as the weather is tolerated. The brothers acquired pride in it; even Bursley regarded it as an interesting municipal curiosity. The sole imperfection in a lovely and otherwise perfect quarrel was that John and Robert, being both employed at Roycroft's Majolica Manufactory, the one as works manager and the other as commercial traveller, were obliged to speak to each other occasionally in the way of business. Artistically, this was a pity, though they did speak very sternly and distantly. The partial truce necessitated by Roycroft's was confined strictly to Roycroft's. And when Robert was not on his journeys, these two tall, strong, dark, bearded men might often be seen of a night walking separately and doggedly down Oldcastle Street from the works, within five yards of each other.

And no one suggested the lunatic asylum. Such is the force of pride, of rank stupidity, and of habit.

The slate-scratching was scarcely over that evening when Mr Powell Liversage appeared. He was a golden-haired man, with a jolly face, lighter and shorter in structure than the two brothers. His friendship with them dated from school-days, and it had survived even the entrance of Liversage into a learned profession. Liversage, who, being a bachelor like the Hessians, had many unoccupied evenings, came to see the brothers regularly every Saturday night, and one or other of them dropped in upon him most Wednesdays; but this particular night was a Thursday.

'How do?' John greeted him succinctly between two puffs of a pipe.

'How do?' replied Liversage.

'How do, Pow?' Robert greeted him in turn, also between two puffs of a pipe.

And 'How do, little 'un?' replied Liversage.

A chair was indicated to him, and he sat down, and Robert poured out some coffee into a third cup which Maggie had brought. John pushed away the extra special of the Staffordshire Signal, which he had been reading.

'What's up these days?' John demanded.

'Well,' said Liversage, and both brothers noticed that he was rather ill at ease, instead of being humorous and lightly caustic as usual, 'the will's turned up.'

'The devil it has!' John exclaimed. 'When?'

'This afternoon.'

And then, as there was a pause, Liversage added: 'Yes, my sons, the will's turned up.'

'But where, you cuckoo, sitting there like that?' asked Robert. 'Where?'

'It was in that registered letter addressed to your sister that the Post Office people wouldn't hand over until we'd taken out letters of administration.'

'Well, I'm dashed!' muttered John. 'Who'd have thought of that? You've got the will, then?'

Liversage nodded.

The Hessians had an elder sister, Mrs Bott, widow of a colour merchant, and Mrs Bott had died suddenly three months ago, the night after a journey to Manchester. (Even at the funeral the brothers had scandalized the town by not speaking to each other.) Mrs Bott had wealth, wit, and wisdom, together with certain peculiarities, of which one was an excessive secrecy. It was known that she had made a will, because she had more than once notified the fact, in a tone suggestive of highly important issues, but the will had refused to be found. So Mr Liversage had been instructed to take out letters of administration of the estate, which, in the continued absence of the will, would be divided equally between the brothers. And twelve or thirteen thousand pounds may be compared to a financial beef-steak that cuts up very handsomely for two persons. The carving-knife was about to descend on its succulence, when, lo! the will!

'How came the will to be in the post?' asked Robert.

'The handwriting on the envelope was your sister's,' said Liversage. 'And the package was posted in Manchester. Very probably she had taken the will to Manchester to show it to a lawyer or something of that sort, and then she was afraid of losing it on the journey back, and so she sent it to herself by registered post. But before it arrived, of course, she was dead.'

'That wasn't a bad scheme of poor Mary Ann's!' John commented.

'It was just like her!' said Robert, speaking pointedly to Liversage. 'But what an odd thing!'

Now, both these men were, no doubt excusably, agonized by curiosity to learn the contents of the will. But would either of them be the first to express that curiosity? Never in this world! Not for the fortune itself! To do so would scarcely have been Bursleyish. It would certainly not have been Hessianlike. So Liversage was obliged at length to say—

'I reckon I'd better read you the will, eh?'

The brothers nodded.

'Mind you,' said Liversage, 'it's not my will. I've had nothing to do with it; so kindly keep your hair on. As a matter of fact, she must have drawn it up herself. It's not drawn properly at all, but it's witnessed all right, and it'll hold water, just as well as if the blooming Lord Chancellor had fixed it up for her in person.'

He produced the document and read, awkwardly and self-consciously—

'"This is my will. You are both of you extremely foolish, John and Robert, and I've often told you so. Nobody has ever understood, and nobody ever will understand, why you quarrelled like that over Annie Emery. You are punishing yourselves, but you are punishing her as well, and it isn't fair her waiting all these years. So I give all my estate, no matter what it is, to whichever of you marries Annie. And I hope this will teach you a lesson. You need it more than you need my money. But you must be married within a year of my death. And if the one that marries cares to give five thousand pounds or so to the other, of course there's nothing to prevent him. This is just a hint. And if you don't either of you marry Annie within a year, then I just leave everything I have to Miss Annie Emery (spinster), stationer and fancy-goods dealer, Duck Bank, Bursley. She deserves something for her disappointment, and she shall have it. Mr Liversage, solicitor, must kindly be my executor. And I commit my soul to God, hoping for a blessed resurrection. 20th January, 1896. Signed Mary Ann Bott, widow." As I told you, the witnessing is in order,' Liversage finished.

'Give it here,' said John shortly, and scanned the sheet of paper.

And Robert actually walked round the table and looked over his brother's shoulder—ample proof that he was terrifically moved.

'And do you mean to tell me that a will like that is good in law?' exclaimed John.

'Of course it's good in law!' Liversage replied. 'Legal phraseology is a useful thing, and it often saves trouble in the end; but it ain't indispensable, you know.'

'Humph!' was Robert's comment as he resumed his seat and relighted his pipe.

All three men were nervous. Each was afraid to speak, afraid even to meet the eyes of the other two. An unmajestic silence followed.

'Well, I'll be off, I think,' Liversage remarked at length with difficulty.

He rose.

'I say,' Robert stopped him. 'Better not say anything about this to Miss—to Annie, eh?'

'I will say nothing,' agreed Liversage (infamously and unprofessionally concealing the fact that he had already said something).

And he departed.

The brothers sat in flustered meditation over the past and the future.

Ten years before, Annie Emery had been an orphan of twenty-three, bravely starting in business for herself amid the plaudits of the admiring town; and John had fallen in love with her courage and her sense and her feminine charm. But alas, as Ovid points out, how difficult it is for a woman to please only one man! Robert also had fallen in love with Annie. Each brother had accused the other of underhand and unbrotherly practices in the pursuit of Annie. Each was profoundly hurt by the accusations, and each, in the immense fatuity of his pride, had privately sworn to prove his innocence by having nothing more to do with Annie. Such is life! Such is man! Such is the terrible egoism of man! And thus it was that, for the sake of wounded pride, John and Robert not only did not speak to one another for ten years, but they spoilt at least one of their lives; and they behaved ignobly to Annie, who would certainly have married either one or the other of them.

At two o'clock in the morning John pulled a coin out of his pocket and made the gesture of tossing.

'Who shall go first!' he explained.

Robert had a queer sensation in his spine as his elder brother spoke to him for the first time in ten years. He wanted to reply vocally. He had a most imperious desire to reply vocally. But he could not. Something stronger even than the desire prevented his tongue from moving.

John tossed the coin—it was a sovereign—and covered it with his hands.

'Tail!' Robert murmured, somewhat hoarsely.

But it was head.

Then they went to bed.

II

The side door of Miss Emery's shop was in Brick Passage, and not in the main street, so that a man, even a man of commanding stature and formidable appearance, might by insinuating himself into Brick Street, off King Street, and then taking the passage from the quieter end, arrive at it without attracting too much attention. This course was adopted by John Hessian. From the moment when he quitted his own house that Friday evening in June he had been subject to the delusion that the collective eye of Bursley was upon him. As a matter of fact, the collective eye of Bursley is much too large and important to occupy itself exclusively with a single individual. Bursley is not a village, and let no one think it. Nevertheless, John was subject to the delusion.

The shop was shut, as he knew it would be. But the curtained window of the parlour, between the side-door and the small shuttered side-window of the shop, gave a strange suggestion of interesting virgin spotless domesticity within. John cast a fearful eye on the main thoroughfare. Nobody seemed to be passing. The chapel-keeper of the Wesleyan Chapel on the opposite side of Trafalgar Road was refreshing the massive Corinthian portico of that fane, and paying no regard whatever to the temple of Eros which Miss Emery's shop had suddenly become.

So John knocked.

'I am a fool!' his thought ran as he knocked.

Because he did not know what he was about. He had won the toss, and with it the right to approach Annie Emery before his brother. But what then? Well, he did desire to marry her, quite as much for herself as for his sister's fortune. But what then? How was he going to explain the tepidity, the desertion, the long sin against love of ten years? In short, how was he going to explain the inexplicable? He could decidedly do nothing that evening except make a blundering ass of himself. And how soon would Robert have the right to come along and say HIS say? That point had not been settled. Points so extremely delicate cannot be settled on a slate, and he had not dared to broach it viva voce to his younger brother. He had been too afraid of a rebuff.

He then hoped that Annie's servant would tell him that Annie was out.

Annie, however, took him at a disadvantage by opening the door herself.

'Well, MR HESSIAN!' she exclaimed, her face bursting into a swift and welcoming smile.

'I was just passing,' the donkey in him blundered forth. 'And I thought—'

However, in fifteen seconds he was on the domestic side of the sitting-room window, and seated in the antimacassared armchair between the fire-place and the piano, and Annie had taken his hat and told him that her servant was out for the evening.

'But I'm disturbing your supper, Miss Emery,' he said. Flurried though he was, he could not fail to notice the white embroidered cloth spread diagonally on the table, and the cold meat and the pastry and the glittering cutlery and crystal thereon.

'Not at all,' she replied. 'You haven't had supper yet, I expect?'

'No,' he said, not thinking.

'It will be nice of you to help me to eat mine,' said she.

'Oh! But really—'

But she got plates and things out of the cupboard below the bookcase—and there he was! She would take no refusal. It was wondrous.

'I'm awfully glad I came now,' his thought ran; I'm managing it rather well.'

And—

'Poor Bob!'

His sole discomfort was that he could not invent a sufficiently ingenious explanation of his call. You can't tell a woman you've called to make love to her, and when your previous call happens to have been ten years ago, some kind of an explanation does seem to be demanded. Ultimately, as Annie was so very pleased to see him, so friendly, so feminine, so equal to the occasion, he decided to let his presence in her abode that night stand as one of those central facts in existence that need no explanation. And they went on talking and eating till the dusk deepened and Annie lit the gas and drew the blind.

He watched her on the sly as she moved about the room. He decided that she did not appear a day older. There was the same plump, erect figure, the same neatness, the same fair skin and fair hair, the same little nose, the same twinkle in the eye—only perhaps the twinkle in the eye was a trifle less cruel than it used to be. She was not a day older. (In this he was of course utterly mistaken; she was ten years older, she was thirty-three, with ten years of successful commercial experience behind her; she would never be twenty-three again. Still she was a most desirable woman, and a woman infinitely beyond his deserts.) Her air of general capability impressed him. And with that there was mingled a strange softness, a marvellous hint of a concealed wish to surrender.... Well, she made him feel big and masculine—in brief, a man.

He regretted the lost ten years. His present way of life seemed intolerable to him. The new heaven opened its gate and gave glimpses of paradise. After all, he felt himself well qualified for that paradise. He felt that he had all along been a woman's man, without knowing it.

'By Jove!' his thought ran. 'At this rate I might propose to her in a week or two.'

And again—

'Poor old Bobbie!'

A quarter of an hour later, in some miraculous manner, they were more intimate than they had ever been, much more intimate. He revised his estimate of the time that must elapse before he might propose to her. In another five minutes he was fighting hard against a mad impulse to propose to her on the spot. And then the fight was over, and he had lost. He proposed to her under the rose-coloured shade of the Welsbach light.

She drew away, as though shot.

And with the rapidity of lightning, in the silence which followed, he went back to his original criticism of himself, that he was a fool. Naturally she would request him to leave. She would accuse him of effrontery.

Her lips trembled. He prepared to rise.

'It's so sudden!' she said.

Bliss! Glory! Celestial joy! Her words were at least equivalent to an absolution of his effrontery! She would accept! She would accept! He jumped up and approached her. But she jumped up too and retreated. He was not to win his prize so easily.

'Please sit down,' she murmured. 'I must think it over,' she said, apparently mastering herself. 'Shall you be at chapel next Sunday morning?'

'Yes,' he answered.

'If I am there, and if I am wearing white roses in my hat, it will mean—' She dropped her eyes.

'Yes?' he queried.

And she nodded.

'And supposing you aren't there?'

'Then the Sunday after,' she said.

He thanked her in his Hessian style.

'I prefer that way of telling you,' she smiled demurely. 'It will avoid the necessity for another—so much—you understand?...'

'Quite so, quite so!' he agreed. 'I quite understand.'

'And if I DO see those roses,' he went on, 'I shall take upon myself to drop in for tea, may I?'

She paused.

'In any case, you mustn't speak to me coming out of chapel, PLEASE.'

As he walked home down Oldcastle Street he said to himself that the age of miracles was not past; also that, after all, he was not so old as the tale of his years would mathematically indicate.

III

Her absence from chapel on the next Sunday disagreed with him. However, Robert was away nearly all the week, and he had the house to himself to dream in. It frequently happened to him to pass by Miss Emery's shop, but he caught no glimpse of her, and though he really was in serious need of writing-paper and envelopes, he dared not enter. Robert returned on the Friday.

On the morning of the second Sunday, John got up early, in order to cope with a new necktie that he had purchased in Hanbridge. Nevertheless he found Robert afoot before him, and Robert, by some unlucky chance, was wearing not merely a new necktie, but a new suit of clothes. They breakfasted in their usual august silence, and John gathered from a remark of Robert's to Maggie when she brought in the boots that Robert meant to go to chapel. Now, Robert, being a commercial traveller and therefore a bit of a caution, did not attend chapel with any remarkable assiduity. And John, in the privacy of his own mind, blamed him for having been so clumsy as to choose that particular morning for breaking the habits of a lifetime. Still, the presence of Robert in the pew could not prejudicially affect John, and so there was no genuine cause for gloominess.

After a time it became apparent that each was waiting for the other to go. John began to get annoyed. At last he made the plunge and went. Turning his head halfway up Oldcastle Street, opposite the mansion which is called 'Miss Peel's', he perceived Robert fifty yards behind. It was a glorious June day.

He blushed as he entered chapel. If he was nervous, it may be accorded to him as excuse that the happiness of his life depended on what he should see within the next few minutes. However, he felt pretty sure, though it was exciting all the same.

To reach the Hessian pew he was obliged to pass Miss Emery's. And it was empty! Robert arrived.

The organist finished the voluntary. The leading tenor of the choir put up the number of the first hymn. The minister ascended the staircase of the great mahogany pulpit, and prayed silently, and

179

arranged his papers in the leaves of the hymn-book, and glanced about to see who was there and who was presumably still in bed, and coughed; and then Miss Annie Emery sailed in with that air of false calm which is worn by the experienced traveller who catches a train by the fifth of a second. The service commenced.

John looked.

She was wearing white roses. There could be no mistake as to that. There were about a hundred and fifty-five white roses in the garden of her hat.

What a thrill ran through John's heart! He had won Annie, and he had won the fortune. Yes, he would give Robert the odd five thousand pounds. His state of mind might even lead him to make it guineas. He heard not a word of the sermon, and throughout the service he rose up and sat down several instants after the rest of the congregation, because he was so absent-minded.

After service he waited for everybody else to leave, in order not to break his promise to the divine Annie. So did Robert. This ill-timed rudeness on Robert's part somewhat retarded the growth of a young desire in John's heart to make friends with poor Bob. Then he got up and left, and Robert followed.

They dined in silence, John deciding that he would begin his overtures of friendship after he had seen Annie, and could tell Robert that he was formally engaged. The brothers ate little. They both improved their minds during their repast—John with the Christian Commonwealth, and Robert with the Saturday cricket edition of the Signal (I regret it).

Then, after pipes, they both went out for a walk, naturally not in the same direction. The magnificence of the weather filled them both with the joy of life. As for John, he went out for a walk simply because he could not contain himself within the house. He could not wait immovable till four-thirty, the hour at which he meant to call on Annie for tea and the betrothal kiss. Therefore he ascended to Hillport and wandered as far as Oldcastle, all in a silk hat and a frock-coat.

It was precisely half-past four as he turned, unassumingly, from Brick Street into Brick Passage, and so approached the side door of Annie Emery's. And his astonishment and anger were immense when he saw Robert, likewise in silk hat and frock-coat, penetrating into Brick Passage from the other end.

They met, and their inflamed spirits collided.

180

'What's the meaning of this?' John demanded, furious; and, simultaneously, Robert demanded: 'What in Hades are YOU doing here?'

Only Sunday and the fine clothes and the proximity to Annie prevented actual warfare.

'I'm calling on Annie,' said John.

'So am I,' said Robert.

'Well, you're too late,' said John.

'Oh, I'm too late, am I?' said Robert, with a disdainful laugh. Thanks!'

'I tell you you're too late,' said John. 'You may as well know at once that I've proposed to Annie and she's accepted me.'

'I like that! I like that!' said Robert.

'Don't shout!' said John.

'I'm not shouting,' said Robert. 'But you may as well know that you're mistaken, my boy. It's me that's proposed to Annie and been accepted. You must be off your chump.'

'When did you propose to her?' said John.

'On Friday, if you must know,' said Robert.

'And she accepted you at once?' said John.

'No. She said that if she was wearing white roses in her hat this morning at chapel, that would mean she accepted,' said Robert.

'Liar!' said John.

'I suppose you'll admit she WAS wearing white roses in her hat?' said Robert, controlling himself.

'Liar!' said John, and continued breathless: 'That was what she said to ME. She must have told you that white roses meant a refusal.'

'Oh no, she didn't!' said Robert, quailing secretly, but keeping up a formidable show of courage. 'You're an old fool!' he added vindictively.

They were both breathing hard, and staring hard at each other.

'Come away,' said John. 'Come away! We can't talk here. She may look out of the window.'

So they went away. They walked very quickly home, and, once in the parlour, they began to have it out. And, before they had done, the reading of cricket news on Sunday was as nothing compared to the desecrating iniquity which they committed. The scene was not such as can be decently recounted. But about six o'clock Maggie entered, and, at considerable personal risk, brought them back to a

181

sense of what was due to their name, the town, and the day. She then stated that she would not remain in such a house, and she departed.

IV

'But whatever made you do it, dearest?'

These words were addressed to Annie Emery on the glorious summer evening which closed that glorious summer day, and they were addressed to her by no other person than Powell Liversage. The pair were in the garden of the house in Trafalgar Road occupied by Mr Liversage and his mother, and they looked westwards over the distant ridge of Hillport, where the moon was setting.

'Whatever made me do it!' repeated Annie, and the twinkle in her eye had that charming cruelty which John had missed. 'Did they not deserve it? Of course, I can talk to you now with perfect freedom, can't I? Well, what do you THINK of it? Here for ten years neither one nor the other does more than recognize me in the street, and then all of a sudden they come down on me like that—simply because there's a question of money. I couldn't have believed men could be so stupid—no, I really couldn't! They're friends of yours, Powell, I know, but—however, that's no matter. But it was too ridiculously easy to lead them on! They'd swallow any flattery. I just did it to see what they'd do, and I think I arranged it pretty well. I quite expected they would call about the same time, and then shouldn't I have given them my mind! Unfortunately they met outside, and got very hot—I saw them from the bedroom window— and went away.'

'You mustn't forget, my dear girl,' said Liversage, 'that it was you they quarrelled about. I don't want to defend 'em for a minute, but it wasn't altogether the money that sent them to you; it was more that the money gave them an excuse for coming!'

'It was a very bad excuse, then!' said Annie.

'Agreed!' Liversage murmured.

The moon was extremely lovely and romantic against the distant spire of Hillport Church, and its effect on the couple was just what might have been anticipated.

'Perhaps I'm sorry,' Annie admitted at length, with a charming grimace.

'Oh! I don't think there's anything to be SORRY about,' said Liversage. 'But of course they'll think I've had a hand in it. You see, I've never breathed a word to them about—about my feelings towards you.'

'No?'

'No. It would have been rather a delicate subject, you see, with them. And I'm sure they'll be staggered when they know that we got engaged last night. They'll certainly say I've—er—been after you for the—No, they won't. They're decent chaps, really; very decent.'

'Anyhow, you may be sure, dear,' said Annie stiffly, 'that *I* shan't rob them of their vile money! Nothing would induce me to touch it!'

'Of course not, dearest!' said Liversage—or, rather the finer part of him said it; the baser part somewhat regretted that vile twelve thousand or so. (I must be truthful.)

He took her hand again.

At the same moment old Mrs Liversage came hastening down the garden, and Liversage dropped the hand.

'Powell,' she said. 'Here's John Hessian, and he wants to see you!'

'The dickens!' exclaimed Liversage, glancing at Annie.

'I must go,' said Annie. 'I shall go by the fields. Good night, dear Mrs Liversage.'

'Wait ten seconds,' Liversage pleaded, 'and I'll be with you.' And he ran off.

John, haggard and undone, was awaiting him in the drawing-room.

'Pow,' said he, 'I've had a fearful row with Bob, and I can't possibly sleep in our house tonight. Don't talk to me. But let me have one of the beds in your spare room, will you? There's a good chap.'

'Why, of course, Johnnie,' said Liversage. 'Of course.'

'And I'll go right to bed now,' said John.

An hour later, after Powell Liversage had seen his affianced to her abode and returned home, and after his mother had gone to bed, there was a knock at the front door, and Liversage opened to Robert Hessian.

'Look here, Pow,' said Robert, whose condition was deplorable, 'I want to sleep here tonight. Do you mind? Fact is, I've had a devil of a shindy with Jack, and Maggie's run off, and, anyhow, I couldn't possibly stop in the same house with Jack tonight.'

'But what—?'

'See here,' said Robert. 'I can't talk. Just let me have a bed in your spare room. I'm sure you mother won't mind.'

'Why, certainly,' said Liversage.

He lit a candle, escorted Robert upstairs, opened the door of the spare room, gave the candle to Robert, pushed him in, said 'Good night,' and shut the door.

What a night!

THE NINETEENTH HAT

A dramatic moment was about to arrive in the joint career of Stephen Cheswardine and Vera his wife. The motor-car stood by the side of the pavement of the Strand, Torquay, that resort of southern wealth and fashion. The chauffeur, Felix, had gone into the automobile shop to procure petrol. Mr Cheswardine looking longer than ever in his long coat, was pacing the busy footpath. Mrs Cheswardine, her beauty obscured behind a flowing brown veil, was lolling in the tonneau, very pleased to be in the tonneau, very pleased to be observed by all Torquay in the tonneau, very satisfied with her husband, and with the Napier car, and especially with Felix, now buying petrol. Suddenly Mrs Cheswardine perceived that next door but one to the automobile shop was a milliner's. She sat up and gazed. According to a card in the window an 'after-season sale' was in progress that June day at the milliner's. There were two rows of hats in the window, each hat plainly ticketed. Mrs Cheswardine descended from the car, crossed the pavement, and gave to the window the whole of her attention.

She sniffed at most of the hats. But one of them, of green straw, with a large curving green wing on either side of the crown, and a few odd bits of fluffiness here and there, pleased her. It was Parisian. She had been to Paris—once. An 'after-season' sale at a little shop in Torquay would not, perhaps, seem the most likely place in the world to obtain a chic hat; it is, moreover, a notorious fact that really chic hats cannot be got for less than three pounds, and this hat was marked ten shillings. Nevertheless, hats are most mysterious things. Their quality of being chic is more often the fruit of chance than of design, particularly in England. You never know when nor where you may light on a good hat. Vera considered that she had lighted on one.

'They're probably duck's feathers dyed,' she said to herself. 'But it's a darling of a hat and it will suit me to a T.'

As for the price, when once you have taken the ticket off a hat the secret of its price is gone forever. Many a hat less smart than this hat has been marked in Bond Street at ten guineas instead of ten shillings. Hats are like oil-paintings—they are worth what people will give for them.

So Vera approached her husband, and said, with an enchanting, innocent smile—

'Lend me half-a-sovereign, will you, doggie?'

She called him doggie in those days because he was a sort of dog-man, a sort of St Bernard, shaggy and big, with faithful eyes; and he enjoyed being called doggie.

But on this occasion he was not to be bewitched by the enchanting innocence of the smile nor by the endearing epithet. He refused to relax his features.

'You aren't going to buy another hat, are you?' he asked sternly, challengingly.

The smile disappeared from her face, and she pulled her slim young self together.

'Yes,' she replied harshly.

The battle was definitely engaged. You may inquire why a man financially capable of hiring a 20-24 h.p. Napier car, with a French chauffeur named Felix, for a week or more, should grudge his wife ten shillings for a hat. Well, you are to comprehend that it was not a question of ten shillings, it was a question of principle. Vera already had eighteen hats, and it had been clearly understood between them that no more money should be spent on attire for quite a long time. Vera was entirely in the wrong. She knew it, and he knew it. But she wanted just that hat.

And they were on their honeymoon, you know: which enormously intensified the poignancy of the drama. They had been married only six days; in three days more they were to return to the Five Towns, where Stephen was solidly established as an earthenware manufacturer. You who have been through them are aware what ticklish things honeymoons are, and how much depends on the tactfulness of the more tactful of the two parties. Stephen, thirteen years older than Vera, was the more tactful of the two parties. He had married a beautiful and elegant woman, with vast unexploited capacities for love in her heart. But he had married a capricious woman, and he knew it. So far he had yielded to her caprices, as well became him; but in the depths of his masculine mind he had his own private notion as to the identity of the person who should ultimately be master in their house, and he had decided only the previous night that when the next moment for being firm arrived, firm he would be.

And now the moment was upon him. It was their eyes that fought, silently, bitterly. There is a great deal of bitterness in true love.

Stephen perceived the affair broadly, in all its aspects. He was older and much more experienced than Vera, and therefore he was responsible for the domestic peace, and for her happiness, and for his own, and for appearances, and for various other things. He perceived the moral degradation which would be involved in an open quarrel during the honeymoon. He perceived the difficulties of a battle in the street, in such a select and prim street as the Strand, Torquay, where the very backbone of England's respectability goes shopping. He perceived Vera's vast ignorance of life. He perceived her charm, and her naughtiness, and all her defects. And he perceived, further, that, this being the first conflict of their married existence, it was of the highest importance that he should emerge from it the victor. To allow Vera to triumph would gravely menace their future tranquillity and multiply the difficulties which her adorable capriciousness would surely cause. He could not afford to let her win. It was his duty, not merely to himself but to her, to conquer. But, on the other hand, he had never fully tested her powers of sheer obstinacy, her willingness to sacrifice everything for the satisfaction of a whim; and he feared these powers. He had a dim suspicion that Vera was one of that innumerable class of charming persons who are perfectly delicious and perfectly sweet so long as they have precisely their own way—and no longer.

Vera perceived only two things. She perceived the hat—although her back was turned towards it—and she perceived the half-sovereign—although it was hidden in Stephen's pocket.

'But, my dear,' Stephen protested, 'you know—'

'Will you lend me half-a-sovereign?' Vera repeated, in a glacial tone. The madness of a desired hat had seized her. She was a changed Vera. She was not a loving woman, not a duteous young wife, nor a reasoning creature. She was an embodied instinct for hats.

'It was most distinctly agreed,' Stephen murmured, restraining his anger.

Just then Felix came out of the shop, followed by a procession of three men bearing cans of petrol. If Stephen was Napoleon and Vera Wellington, Felix was the Blucher of this deplorable altercation. Impossible to have a row—yes, a row—with your wife in the

187

presence of your chauffeur, with his French ideas of chivalry.

'Will you lend me half-a-sovereign?' Vera reiterated, in the same glacial tone, not caring twopence for the presence of Felix.

And Stephen, by means of an interminable silver chain, drew his sovereign-case from the profundity of his hip-pocket; it was like drawing a bucket out of a well. And he gave Vera half-a-sovereign; and THAT was like knotting the rope for his own execution.

And while Felix and his three men poured gallons and gallons of petrol into a hole under the cushions of the tonneau, Stephen swallowed his wrath on the pavement, and Vera remained hidden in the shop. And the men were paid and went off, and Felix took his seat ready to start. And then Vera came out of the hat place, and the new green hat was on her head, and the old one in a bag in her pretty hands.

'What do you think of my new hat, Felix?' she smiled to the favoured chauffeur; 'I hope it pleases you.'

Felix said that it did.

In these days, chauffeurs are a great race and a privileged. They have usurped the position formerly held by military officers. Women fawn on them, take fancies to them, and spoil them. They can do no wrong in the eyes of the sex. Vera had taken a fancy to Felix. Perhaps it was because he had been in a cavalry regiment; perhaps it was merely the curve of his moustache. Who knows? And Felix treated her as only a Frenchman can treat a pretty woman, with a sort of daring humility, with worship—in short, with true Gallic appreciation. Vera much enjoyed Gallic appreciation. It ravished her to think that she was the light of poor Felix's existence, an unattainable star for him. Of course, Stephen didn't mind. That is to say, he didn't really mind.

The car rushed off in the direction of Exeter, homewards.

That day, by means of Felix's expert illegal driving, they got as far as Bath; and there were no breakdowns. The domestic atmosphere in the tonneau was slightly disturbed at the beginning of the run, but it soon improved. Indeed, after lunch Stephen grew positively bright and gay. At tea, which they took just outside Bristol, he actually went so far as to praise the hat. He said that it was a very becoming hat, and also that it was well worth the money. In a word, he signified to Vera that their first battle had been fought and that Vera had won, and that he meant to make the best of it and accept the situation.

Vera was naturally charmed, and when she was charmed she was charming. She said to herself that she had always known that she could manage a man. The recipe for managing a man was firmness coupled with charm. But there must be no half measures, no hesitations. She had conquered. She saw her future life stretching out before her like a beautiful vista. And Stephen was to be her slave, and she would have nothing to do but to give rein to her caprices, and charm Stephen when he happened to deserve it.

But the next morning the hat had vanished out of the bedroom of the exclusive hotel at Bath. Vera could not believe that it had vanished; but it had. It was not in the hat-box, nor on the couch, nor under the couch, nor perched on a knob of the bedstead, nor in any of the spots where it ought to have been. When she realized that as a fact it had vanished she was cross, and on inquiring from Stephen what trick he had played with her hat, she succeeded in conveying to Stephen that she was cross. Stephen was still in bed, comatose. The tone of his reply startled her.

'Look here, child,' he said, or rather snapped—he had never been snappish before—'since you took the confounded thing off last evening I haven't seen it and I haven't touched it, and I don't know where it is.'

'But you must—'

'I gave in to you about the hat,' Stephen continued to snap, 'though I knew I was a fool to do so, and I consider I behaved pretty pleasantly over it too. But I don't want any more scenes. If you've lost it, that's not my fault.'

Such speeches took Vera very much aback. And she, too, in her turn, now saw the dangers of a quarrel, and in this second altercation it was Stephen who won. He said he would not even mention the disappearance of the hat to the hotel manager. He was sure it must be in one of Vera's trunks. And in the end Vera performed that day's trip in another hat.

They reached the Five Towns much earlier than they had anticipated—before lunch on the ninth day, whereas the new servants in their new house at Bursley were only expecting them for dinner. So Stephen had the agreeable idea of stopping the car in front of the new Hotel Metropole at Hanbridge and lunching there. Precisely opposite this new and luxurious caravanserai (as they love to call it in the Five Towns) is the imposing garage and agency where Stephen had hired the Napier car. Felix said he would lunch hurriedly in order to transact certain business at the garage before taking them on to Bursley. After lunch, however, Vera caught him transacting business with a chambermaid in a corridor. Shocking though the revelation is, it needs to be said that Felix was kissing the chambermaid. The blow to Mrs Cheswardine was severe. She had imagined that Felix spent all his time in gazing up to her as an unattainable star.

She spoke to Stephen about it, in the accents of disillusion. 'What?' cried Stephen. 'Don't you know? They're engaged to be married. Her name is Mary Callear. She used to be parlourmaid at Uncle John's at Oldcastle. But hotels pay higher wages.'

Felix engaged to a parlourmaid! Felix, who had always seemed to Vera a gentleman in disguise! Yes, it was indeed a blow!

But balm awaited Vera at her new home in Bursley. A parcel, obviously containing a cardboard box, had arrived for Stephen. He opened it, and the lost hat was inside it. Stephen read a note, and explained that the hotel people at Bath had found it and forwarded it. He began to praise the hat anew. He made Vera put it on instantly, and seemed delighted. So much so that Vera went out to the porch to say good-bye to Felix in a most forgiving frame of mind. She forgave Felix for being engaged to the chambermaid.

And there was the chambermaid walking up the drive, quite calmly! Felix, also quite calmly, asked Vera to excuse him, and told the chambermaid to get into the car and sit beside him. He then informed Vera that he had to go with the car immediately to Oldcastle, and was taking Miss Callear with him for the run, this being Miss Callear's weekly afternoon off. Miss Callear had come to Bursley in the electric tram.

Vera shook with swift anger; not at Felix's information, but the patent fact that Mary Callear was wearing a hat which was the exact replica of the hat on Vera's own head. And Mary Callear was seated like a duchess in the car, while Vera stood on the gravel. And two of Vera's new servants were there to see that Vera was wearing a hat precisely equivalent to the hat of a chambermaid!

She went abruptly into the house and sought for Stephen—as with a sword. But Stephen was not discoverable. She ran to her elegant new bedroom and shut herself in. She understood the plot. She had plenty of wit. Stephen had concerted it with Felix. In spite of Stephen's allegations of innocence, the hat had been sent somewhere—probably to Brunt's at Hanbridge—to be copied at express speed, and Stephen had presented the copy to Felix, in order that Felix might present it to Mary Callear the chambermaid, and the meeting in the front garden had been deliberately arranged by that odious male, Stephen. Truly, she had not believed Stephen capable of such duplicity and cruelty.

She removed the hat, gazed at it, and then tore it to pieces and scattered the pieces on the carpet.

An hour later Stephen crept into the bedroom and beheld the fragments, and smiled.

'Stephen,' she exclaimed, 'you're a horrid, cruel brute.' 'I know I am,' said Stephen. 'You ought to have found that out long since.'

'I won't love you any more. It's all over,' she sobbed. But he just kissed her.

VERA'S FIRST CHRISTMAS ADVENTURE

I

Five days before Christmas, Cheswardine came home to his wife from a week's sojourn in London on business. Vera, in her quality of the best-dressed woman in Bursley, met him on the doorstep (or thereabouts) of their charming but childless home, attired in a teagown that would have ravished a far less impressionable male than her husband; while he, in his quality of a prosaic and flourishing earthenware manufacturer, pretended to take the teagown as a matter of course, and gave her the sober, solid kiss of a man who has been married six years and is getting used to it.

Still, the teagown had pleased him, and by certain secret symptoms Vera knew that it had pleased him. She hoped much from that teagown. She hoped that he had come home in a more pacific temper than he had shown when he left her, and that she would carry her point after all.

Now, naturally, when a husband in easy circumstances, the possessor of a pretty and pampered wife, spends a week in London and returns five days before Christmas, certain things are rightly and properly to be expected from him. It would need an astounding courage, an amazing lack of a sense of the amenity of conjugal existence in such a husband to enable him to disappoint such reasonable expectations. And Cheswardine, though capable of pulling the curb very tight on the caprices of his wife, was a highly decent fellow. He had no intention to disappoint; he knew his duty.

So that during afternoon tea with the teagown in a cosy corner of the great Chippendale drawing-room he began to unfasten a small wooden case which he had brought into the house in his own hand, opened it with considerable precaution, making a fine mess of packing-stuff on the carpet, and gradually drew to light a pair of vases of Venetian glass. He put them on the mantlepiece.

'There!' he said, proudly, and with a virtuous air.

They were obviously costly antique vases, exquisite in form, exquisite in the graduated tints of their pale blue and rose.

'Seventeenth century!' he said.

'They're very nice,' Vera agreed, with a show of enthusiasm. 'What are they for?'

'Your Christmas present,' Cheswardine explained, and added 'my dear!'

'Oh, Stephen!' she murmured.

A kiss on these occasions is only just, and Cheswardine had one.

'Duveens told me they were quite unique,' he said, modestly; 'and I believe 'em.'

You might imagine that a pair of Venetian vases of the seventeenth century, stated by Duveens to be unique, would have satisfied a woman who had a generous dress allowance and lacked absolutely nothing that was essential. But Vera was not satisfied. She was, on the contrary, profoundly disappointed. For the presence of those vases proved that she had not carried her point. They deprived her of hope. The unpleasantness before Cheswardine went to London had been more or less a propos of a Christmas present. Vera had seen in Bostock's vast emporium in the neighbouring town of Hanbridge, a music-stool in the style known as art nouveau, which had enslaved her fancy. She had taken her husband to see it, and it had not enslaved her husband's fancy in the slightest degree. It was made in light woods, and the woods were curved and twisted as though they had recently spent seven years in a purgatory for sinful trees. Here and there in the design onyx-stones had been set in the wood. The seat itself was beautifully soft. What captured Vera was chiefly the fact that it did not open at the top, as most elaborate music-stools do, but at either side. You pressed a button (onyx) and the panel fell down displaying your music in little compartments ready to hand; and the eastern moiety of the music-stool was for piano pieces, and the western moiety for songs. In short, it was the last word of music-stools; nothing could possibly be newer.

But Cheswardine did not like it, and did not conceal his opinion. He argued that it would not 'go' with the Chippendale furniture, and Vera said that all beautiful things 'went' together, and Cheswardine admitted that they did, rather dryly. You see, they took the matter seriously because the house was their hobby; they were always changing its interior, which was more than they could have done for a child, even if they had had one; and Cheswardine's finer and soberer taste was always fighting against Vera's predilection for the novel and the bizarre. Apart from clothes, Vera had not much more than the taste of a mouse.

They did not quarrel in Bostock's. Indeed, they did not quarrel anywhere; but after Vera had suggested that he might at any rate humour her by giving her the music-stool for a Christmas present (she seemed to think this would somehow help it to 'go' with the Chippendale), and Cheswardine had politely but firmly declined, there had been a certain coolness and quite six tears. Vera had caused it to be understood that even if Cheswardine was NOT interested in music, even if he did hate music and did call the Broadwood ebony grand ugly, that was no reason why she should be deprived of a pretty and original music-stool that would keep her music tidy and that would be HERS. As for it not going with the Chippendale, that was simply an excuse ... etc.

Hence it is not surprising that the Venetian vases of the seventeenth century left Vera cold, and that the domestic prospects for Christmas were a little cold.

However, Vera, with wifely and submissive tact made the best of things; and that evening she began to decorate the hall, dining-room, and drawing-room with holly and mistletoe. Before the pair retired to rest, the true Christmas feeling, slightly tinged with a tender melancholy, permeated the house, and the servants were growing excited in advance. The servants weren't going to have a dinner-party, with crackers and port and a table-centre unmatched in the Five Towns; the servants weren't going to invite their friends to an evening's jollity. The servants were merely going to work somewhat harder and have somewhat less sleep; but such is the magical effect of holly and mistletoe twined round picture-cords and hung under chandeliers that the excitement of the servants was entirely pleasurable.

And as Vera shut the bedroom door, she said, with a delightful, forgiving smile—-

'I saw a lovely cigar-cabinet at Bostock's yesterday.'

'Oh!' said Cheswardine, touched. He had no cigar-cabinet, and he wanted one, and Vera knew that he wanted one.

And Vera slept in the sweet consciousness of her thoughtful wifeliness.

The next morning, at breakfast, Cheswardine demanded—

'Getting pretty hard up, aren't you, Maria?'

He called her Maria when he wished to be arch.

Well,' she said, 'as a matter of fact, I am. What with the—'

And he gave her a five-pound note.

It happened so every year. He provided her with the money to buy him a Christmas present. But it is, I hope, unnecessary to say that the connection between her present to him and the money he furnished was never crudely mentioned.

She made an opportunity, before he left for the works, to praise the Venetian vases, and she insisted that he should wrap up well, because he was showing signs of one of his bad colds.

II

In the early afternoon she went to Bostock's emporium, at Hanbridge, to buy the cigar-cabinet and a few domestic trifles. Bostock's is a good shop. I do not say that it has the classic and serene dignity of Brunt's, over the way, where one orders one's dining-room suites and one's frocks for the January dances. But it is a good shop, and one of the chief glories of the Paris of the Five Towns. It has frontages in three streets, and it might be called the shop of the hundred windows. You can buy pretty nearly anything at Bostock's, from an art nouveau music-stool up to the highest cheese—for there is a provision department. (You can't get cheese at Brunt's.)

Vera made her uninteresting purchases first, in the basement, and then she went up-stairs to the special Christmas department, which certainly was wonderful: a blaze and splendour of electric light; a glitter of gilded iridescent toys and knick-knacks; a smiling, excited, pushing multitude of faces, young and old; and the cashiers in their cages gathering in money as fast as they could lay their tired hands on it! A joyous, brilliant scene, calculated to bring soft tears of satisfaction to the board of directors that presided over Bostock's. It was a record Christmas for Bostock's. The electric cars were thundering over the frozen streets of all the Five Towns to bring customers to Bostock's. Children dreamt of Bostock's. Fathers went to scoff and remained to pay. Brunt's was not exactly alarmed, for nothing could alarm Brunt's; but there was just a sort of suspicion of something in the air at Brunt's that did not make for odious self-conceit. People seemed to become intoxicated when they went into Bostock's, to close their heads in a frenzy of buying.

And there the art nouveau music-stool stood in the corner, where Vera had originally seen it! She approached it, not thinking of the terrible danger. The compartments for music lay invitingly open.

'Four pounds, nine and six, Mrs Cheswardine,' said a shop-walker, who knew her.

She stopped to finger it.

Well, of course everybody is acquainted with that peculiar ecstasy that undoubtedly does overtake you in good shops, sometimes, especially at Christmas. I prefer to call it ecstasy rather than intoxication, but I have heard it called even drunkenness. It is a magnificent and overwhelming experience, like a good wine. A blind instinct seizes your reason and throws her out of the window of your soul, and then assumes entire control of the volitional machinery. You listen to no arguments, you care for no consequences. You want a thing; you must have it; you do have it.

Vera was caught unawares by this magnificent and overwhelming experience, just as she stooped to finger the music-stool. A fig for the cigar-cabinet! A fig for her husband's objections! After all she was a grown-up woman (twenty-nine or thirty), and entitled to a certain freedom. She was not and would not be a slave. It would look perfect in the drawing-room.

'I'll take it,' she said.

'Yes, Mrs Cheswardine. A unique thing, quite unique. Penkethman!'

And Vera followed Penkethman to a cash desk and received half-a-guinea out of a five-pound note.

'I want it carefully packed,' said Vera.

'Yes, ma'am. It will be delivered in the morning.'

She was just beginning to realize that she had been under the sinister influence of the ecstasy, and that she had not bought the cigar-cabinet, and that she had practically no more money, and that Stephen's rule against credit was the strictest of all his rules, when she caught sight of Mr Charles Woodruff buying toys, doubtless for his nephews and nieces.

Mr Woodruff was the bachelor friend of the family. He had loved Vera before Stephen loved her, and he was still attached to her. Stephen and he were chums of the most advanced kind. Why! Stephen and Vera thought nothing of bickering in front of Mr Woodruff, who rated them both and sided with neither.

'Hello!' said Woodruff, flushing, and moving his long, clumsy limbs when she touched him on the shoulder. 'I'm just buying a few toys.'

She helped him to buy toys, and then he asked her to go and have tea with him at the newly-opened Sub Rosa Tea Rooms, in Machin Street. She agreed, and, in passing the music-stool, gave a small parcel which she was carrying to Penkethman, and told him he might as well put it in the music-stool. She was glad to have tea with Charlie Woodruff. It would distract her, prevent her from thinking. The ecstasy had almost died out, and she had a violent desire not to think.

III

A terrible blow fell upon her the next morning. Stephen had one of his bad colds, one of his worst. The mere cold she could have supported with fortitude, but he was forced to remain indoors, and his presence in the house she could not support with fortitude. The music-stool would be sure to arrive before lunch, and he would be there to see it arrive. The ecstasy had fully expired now, and she had more leisure to think than she wanted. She could not imagine what mad instinct had compelled her to buy the music-stool. (Once out of the shop these instincts always are difficult to imagine.) She knew that Stephen would be angry. He might perhaps go to the length of returning the music-stool whence it came. For, though she was a pretty and pampered woman, Stephen had a way, in the last resort, of being master of his own house. And she could not even placate him with the gift of a cigar-cabinet. She could not buy a five-guinea cigar-cabinet with ten and six. She had no other money in the world. She never had money, yet money was always running through her fingers. Stephen treated her generously, gave her an ample allowance, but he would under no circumstances permit credit, nor would he pay her allowance in advance. She had nothing to expect till the New Year.

She attended to his cold, and telephoned to the works for a clerk to come up, and she refrained from telling Stephen that he must have been very careless while in London, to catch a cold like that. Her self-denial in this respect surprised Stephen, but he put it down to the beneficent influence of Christmas and the Venetian vases.

Bostock's pair-horse van arrived before the garden gate earlier than her worse fears had anticipated, and Bostock's men were evidently in a tremendous hurry that morning. In quite an abnormally small number of seconds the wooden case containing the fragile music-stool was lying in the inner hall, waiting to be unpacked. Having signed the delivery-book Vera stood staring at the accusatory package. Stephen was lounging over the dining-room fire, perhaps dozing. She would have the thing swiftly transported up-stairs and hidden in an attic for a time.

But just then Stephen popped out of the dining-room. Stephen's masculine curiosity had been aroused by the advent of Bostock's van. He had observed the incoming of the package from the window, and he had ventured to the hall to inspect it. The event had roused him wonderfully from the heavy torpor which a cold induces. He wore a dressing-gown, the pockets of which bulged with handkerchiefs.

'You oughtn't to be out here, Stephen,' said his wife.

'Nonsense!' he said. 'Why, upon my soul, this steam heat is warmer than the dining-room fire.' Vera, silenced by the voice of truth, could not reply.

Stephen bent his great height to inspect the package. It was an appetizing Christmas package; straw escaped from between its ribs, and it had an air of being filled with something at once large and delicate.

'Oh!' observed Stephen, humorously. 'Ah! So this is it, is it? Ah! Oh! Very good!'

And he walked round it.

How on earth had he learnt that she had bought it? She had not mentioned the purchase to Mr Woodruff.

'Yes, Stephen,' she said timidly. 'That's it, and I hope—'

'It ought to hold a tidy few cigars, that ought,' remarked Stephen complacently.

He took it for the cigar-cabinet!

She paused, struck. She had to make up her mind in an instant.

'Oh yes,' she murmured.

'A thousand?'

'Yes, a thousand,' she said.

'I thought so,' murmured Stephen. 'I mustn't kiss you, because I've got a cold,' said he. 'But, all the same I'm awfully obliged, Vera. Suppose we have it opened now, eh? Then we could decide where it is to go, and I could put my cigars in it.'

'Oh no,' she protested. 'Oh no, Stephen! That's not fair! It mustn't be opened before Christmas morning.'

'But I gave you my vases yesterday.'

'That's different,' she said. 'Christmas is Christmas.' 'Oh, very well,' he yielded. 'That's all right, my dear.'

Then he began to sniff.

'There's a deuced odd smell from it,' he said.

'Perhaps it's the wood!' she faltered.

'I hope it isn't,' he said. 'I expect it's the straw. A deuced odd smell. We'll have the thing put in the side hall, next to the clock. It will be out of the way there. And I can come and gaze at it when I feel depressed. Eh, Maria?' He was undoubtedly charmed at the prospect of owning so large and precious a cigar-cabinet.

Considering that the parcel which she had given to Penkethman to put in the music-stool comprised a half-a-pound of Bostock's very ripest Gorgonzola cheese, bought at the cook's special request, the smell which proceeded from the mysterious inwards of the packing-case did not surprise Vera at all. But it disconcerted her none the less. And she wondered how she could get the cheese out.

For thirty hours the smell from the unopened packing-case waxed in vigour and strength. Stephen's cold grew worse and prevented him from appreciating its full beauty, but he savoured enough of it to induce him to compare it facetiously to the effluvium of a dead rat, and he said several times that Bostock's really ought to use better straw. He was frequently to be seen in the hall, gloating over his cigar-cabinet. Once he urged Vera to have it opened and so get rid of the straw, but she refused, and found the nerve to tell him that he was exaggerating the odour.

She was at a loss what to do. She could not get up in the middle of the night and unpack the package and hide its guilty secret. Indeed, to unpack the package would bring about her ruin instantly; for, the package unpacked, Stephen would naturally expect to see the cigar-cabinet. And so the hours crept on to Christmas and Vera's undoing. She gave herself a headache.

It was just thirty hours after the arrival of the package when Mr Woodruff dropped in for tea. Stephen was asleep in the dining-room, which apartment he particularly affected during his colds. Woodruff was shown into the drawing-room, where Vera was having her headache. Vera brightened. In fact, she suddenly grew very bright. And she gave Woodruff tea, and took some herself, and Woodruff passed an enjoyable twenty minutes.

The two Venetian vases were on the mantelpiece. Vera rose into ecstasies about them, and called upon Charlie Woodruff to rise too. He got up from his chair to examine the vases, which Vera had placed close together side by side at the corner of the mantelpiece nearest to him. Vera and Woodruff also stood close together side by side. And just as Woodruff was about to handle the vases, Vera knocked his arm; his arm collided with one vase; that vase collided with the next, and both fell to earth—to the hard, unfeeling, unyielding tiles of the hearth.

IV

They were smashed to atoms.

Vera screamed. She screamed twice, and ran out of the room.

'Stephen, Stephen!' she cried hysterically. 'Charlie has broken my vases, both of them. It IS too bad of him. He's really too clumsy!'

There was a terrific pother. Stephen wakened violently, and in a moment all three were staring ineffectually at the thousand crystal fragments on the hearth.

'But—' began Charlie Woodruff.

And that was all he did say.

He and Vera and Stephen had been friends since infancy, so she had the right not to conceal her feelings before him; Stephen had the same right. They both exercised it.

'But—' began Charlie again.

'Oh, never mind,' Stephen stopped him curtly. 'Accidents can't be helped.'

'I shall get another pair,' said Woodruff.

'No, you won't,' replied Stephen. 'You can't. There isn't another pair in the world. See?'

The two men simultaneously perceived that Vera was weeping. She was very pretty in tears, but that did not prevent the masculine world from feeling awkward and self-conscious. Charlie had notions about going out and burying himself.

'Come, Vera, come,' her husband enjoined, blowing his nose with unnecessary energy, bad as his cold was.

'I—I liked those vases more than anything you've—you've ever given me,' Vera blubbered, charmingly, patting her eyes.

Stephen glanced at Woodruff, as who should say: 'Well, my boy, you uncorked those tears, I'll leave you to deal with 'em. You see, I'm an invalid in a dressing-gown. I leave you.'

And went.

'No-but-look-here-I-say,' Charlie Woodruff expostulated to Vera when he was alone with her—he often started an expostulation with that singular phrase. 'I'm awfully sorry. I don't know how it

200

happened. You must let me give you something else.'

Vera shook her head.

'No,' she said. 'I wanted Stephen awfully to give me that music-stool that I told you about a fortnight ago. But he gave me the vases instead, and I liked them ever so much better.'

'I shall give you the music-stool. If you wanted it a fortnight ago, you want it now. It won't make up for the vases, of course, but—'

'No, no,' said Vera, positively.

'Why not?'

'I do not wish you to give me anything. It wouldn't be quite nice,' Vera insisted.

'But I give you something every Christmas.'

'Do you?' asked Vera, innocently.

'Yes, and you and Stephen give me something.'

'Besides, Stephen doesn't quite like the music-stool.'

'What's that got to do with it? You like it. I'm giving it to you, not to him. I shall go over to Bostock's tomorrow morning and get it.'

'I forbid you to.'

'I shall.'

Woodruff departed.

Within five minutes the Cheswardine coachman was driving off in the dogcart to Hanbridge, with the packing-case in the back of the cart, and a note. He brought back the cigar-cabinet. Stephen had not stirred from the dining-room, afraid to encounter a tearful wife. Presently his wife came into the dining-room bearing the vast load of the cigar-cabinet in her delicate arms.

'I thought it might amuse you to fill it with your cigars—just to pass the time,' she said.

Stephen's thought was: 'Well, women take the cake.' It was a thought that occurs frequently to the husbands of Veras.

There was ripe Gorgonzola at dinner. Stephen met it as one meets a person whom one fancies one has met somewhere but cannot remember where.

The next afternoon the music-stool came, for the second time, into the house. Charlie brought it in HIS dogcart. It was unpacked ostentatiously by the radiant Vera. What could Stephen say in depreciation of this gift from their oldest and best friend? As a fact he could and did say a great deal. But he said it when he happened to be all alone in the drawing-room, and had observed the appalling way in which the music-stool did not 'go' with the Chippendale.

'Look at the d—thing!' he exclaimed to himself. 'Look at it!'

However, the Christmas dinner-party was a brilliant success, and after it Vera sat on the art nouveau music-stool and twittered songs, and what with her being so attractive and birdlike, and what with the Christmas feeling in the air... well, Stephen resigned himself to the music-stool.

THE MURDER OF THE MANDARIN

I

'What's that you're saying about murder?' asked Mrs Cheswardine as she came into the large drawing-room, carrying the supper-tray.

'Put it down here,' said her husband, referring to the supper-tray, and pointing to a little table which stood two legs off and two legs on the hearth-rug.

'That apron suits you immensely,' murmured Woodruff, the friend of the family, as he stretched his long limbs into the fender towards the fire, farther even than the long limbs of Cheswardine. Each man occupied an easy-chair on either side of the hearth; each was very tall, and each was forty.

Mrs Cheswardine, with a whisk infinitely graceful, set the tray on the table, took a seat behind it on a chair that looked like a toddling grand-nephew of the arm-chairs, and nervously smoothed out the apron.

As a matter of fact, the apron did suit her immensely. It is astounding, delicious, adorable, the effect of a natty little domestic apron suddenly put on over an elaborate and costly frock, especially when you can hear the rustle of a silk petticoat beneath, and more especially when the apron is smoothed out by jewelled fingers. Every man knows this. Every woman knows it. Mrs Cheswardine knew it. In such matters Mrs Cheswardine knew exactly what she was about. She delighted, when her husband brought Woodruff in late of a night, as he frequently did after a turn at the club, to prepare with her own hands—the servants being in bed—a little snack of supper for them. Tomato sandwiches, for instance, miraculously thin, together with champagne or Bass. The men preferred Bass, naturally, but if Mrs Cheswardine had a fancy for a sip of champagne out of her husband's tumbler, Bass was not forthcoming.

Tonight it was champagne.

Woodruff opened it, as he always did, and involuntarily poured out a libation on the hearth, as he almost always did. Good-natured, ungainly, long-suffering men seldom achieve the art of opening champagne.

Mrs Cheswardine tapped her pink-slippered foot impatiently.

'You're all nerves tonight,' Woodruff laughed, 'and you've made me nervous,' And at length he got some of the champagne into a tumbler.

'No, I'm not,' Mrs Cheswardine contradicted him.

'Yes, you are, Vera,' Woodruff insisted calmly.

She smiled. The use of that elegant Christian name, with its faint suggestion of Russian archduchesses, had a strange effect on her, particularly from the lips of Woodruff. She was proud of it, and of her surname too—one of the oldest surnames in the Five Towns. The syllables of 'Vera' invariably soothed her, like a charm. Woodruff, and Cheswardine also, had called her Vera during the whole of her life; and she was thirty. They had all three lived in different houses at the top end of Trafalgar Road, Bursley. Woodruff fell in love with her first, when she was eighteen, but with no practical result. He was a brown-haired man, personable despite his ungainliness, but he failed to perceive that to worship from afar off is not the best way to capture a young woman with large eyes and an emotional disposition. Cheswardine, who had a black beard, simply came along and married the little thing. She fluttered down on to his shoulders like a pigeon. She adored him, feared him, cooed to him, worried him, and knew that there were depths of his mind which she would never plumb. Woodruff, after being best man, went on loving, meekly and yet philosophically, and found his chief joy in just these suppers. The arrangement suited Vera; and as for the husband and the hopeless admirer, they had always been fast friends.

'I asked you what you were saying about murder,' said Vera sharply, 'but it seems—'

'Oh! did you?' Woodruff apologized. 'I was saying that murder isn't such an impossible thing as it appears. Anyone might commit a murder.'

'Then you want to defend, Harrisford? Do you hear what he says, Stephen?'

The notorious and terrible Harrisford murders were agitating the Five Towns that November. People read, talked, and dreamt murder; for several weeks they took murder to all their meals.

'He doesn't want to defend Harrisford at all,' said Cheswardine, with a superior masculine air, 'and of course anyone might commit a murder. I might.'

'Stephen! How horrid you are!' 'You might, even!' said Woodruff, gazing at Vera.

'Charlie! Why, the blood alone—'

'There isn't always blood,' said the oracular husband.

'Listen here,' proceeded Woodruff, who read variously and enjoyed philosophical speculation. 'Supposing that by just taking thought, by just wishing it, an Englishman could kill a mandarin in China and make himself rich for life, without anybody knowing anything about it! How many mandarins do you suppose there would be left in China at the end of a week!'

'At the end of twenty-four hours, rather,' said Cheswardine grimly.

'Not one,' said Woodruff.

'But that's absurd,' Vera objected, disturbed. When these two men began their philosophical discussions they always succeeded in disturbing her. She hated to see life in a queer light. She hated to think.

'It isn't absurd,' Woodruff replied. 'It simply shows that what prevents wholesale murder is not the wickedness of it, but the fear of being found out, and the general mess, and seeing the corpse, and so on.'

Vera shuddered.

'And I'm not sure,' Woodruff proceeded, 'that murder is so very much more wicked than lots of other things.'

'Usury, for instance,' Cheswardine put in.

'Or bigamy,' said Woodruff.

'But an Englishman COULDN'T kill a mandarin in China by just wishing it,' said Vera, looking up.

'How do we know?' said Woodruff, in his patient voice. 'How do we know? You remember what I was telling you about thought-transference last week. It was in Borderland.'

Vera felt as if there was no more solid ground to stand on, and it angered her to be plunging about in a bog.

'I think it's simply silly,' she remarked. 'No, thanks.'

She said 'No, thanks' to her husband, when he tendered his glass.

He moved the glass still closer to her lips.

'I said "No, thanks,"' she repeated dryly.

'Just a mouthful,' he urged.

'I'm not thirsty.'

'Then you'd better go to bed,' said he.

205

He had a habit of sending her to bed abruptly. She did not dislike it. But she had various ways of going. Tonight it was the way of an archduchess.

II

Woodruff, in stating that Vera was all nerves that evening, was quite right. She was. And neither her husband nor Woodruff knew the reason.

The reason had to do most intimately with frocks.

Vera had been married ten years. But no one would have guessed it, to watch her girlish figure and her birdlike ways. You see, she was the only child in the house. She often bitterly regretted the absence of offspring to the name and honour of Cheswardine. She envied other wives their babies. She doted on babies. She said continually that in her deliberate opinion the proper mission of women was babies. She was the sort of woman that regards a cathedral as a place built especially to sit in and dream soft domestic dreams; the sort of woman that adores music simply because it makes her dream. And Vera's brown studies, which were frequent, consisted chiefly of babies. But as babies amused themselves by coming down the chimneys of all the other houses in Bursley, and avoiding her house, she sought comfort in frocks. She made the best of herself. And it was a good best. Her figure was as near perfect as a woman's can be, and then there were those fine emotional eyes, and that flutteringness of the pigeon, and an ever-changing charm of gesture. Vera had become the best-dressed woman in Bursley. And that is saying something. Her husband was wealthy, with an increasing income, though, of course, as an earthenware manufacturer, and the son and grandson of an earthenware manufacturer, he joined heartily in the general Five Towns lamentation that there was no longer any money to be made out of 'pots'. He liked to have a well-dressed woman about the house, and he allowed her an incredible allowance, the amount of which was breathed with awe among Vera's friends; a hundred a year, in fact. He paid it to her quarterly, by cheque. Such was his method.

Now a ball was to be given by the members of the Ladies' Hockey Club (or such of them as had not been maimed for life in the pursuit of this noble pastime) on the very night after the conversation about murder. Vera belonged to the Hockey Club (in a purely ornamental sense), and she had procured a frock for the ball which was calculated to crown her reputation as a mirror of elegance. The skirt had—but no (see the columns of the Staffordshire Signal for the 9th November, 1901). The mischief was that the gown lacked, for its final perfection, one particular thing, and that particular thing was separated from Vera by the glass front of Brunt's celebrated shop at Hanbridge. Vera could have managed without it. The gown would still have been brilliant without it. But Vera had seen it, and she WANTED it.

Its cost was a guinea. Well, you will say, what is a guinea to a dainty creature with a hundred a year? Let her go and buy the article. The point is that she couldn't, because she had only six and sevenpence left in the wide world. (And six weeks to Christmas!) She had squandered—oh, soul above money!—twenty-five pounds, and more than twenty-five pounds, since the 29th of September. Well, you will say, credit, in other words, tick? No, no, no! The giant Stephen absolutely and utterly forbade her to procure anything whatever on credit. She was afraid of him. She knew just how far she could go with Stephen. He was great and terrible. Well, you will say, why couldn't she blandish and cajole Stephen for a sovereign or so? Impossible! She had a hundred a year on the clear understanding that it was never exceeded nor anticipated. Well, you will discreetly hint, there are certain devices known to housewives.... Hush! Vera had already employed them. Six and sevenpence was not merely all that remained to her of her dress allowance; it was all that remained to her of her household allowance till the next Monday.

Hence her nerves.

There that poor unfortunate woman lay, with her unconscious tyrant of a husband snoring beside her, desolately wakeful under the night-light in the large, luxurious bedroom—three servants sleeping overhead, champagne in the cellar, furs in the wardrobe, valuable lace round her neck at that very instant, grand piano in the drawing-room, horses in the stable, stuffed bear in the hall—and her life was made a blank for want of fourteen and fivepence! And she had nobody to confide in. How true it is that the human soul is solitary, that content is the only true riches, and that to be happy we must be good!

It was at that juncture of despair that she thought of mandarins. Or rather—I may as well be frank—she had been thinking of mandarins all the time since retiring to rest. There MIGHT be something in Charlie's mandarin theory.... According to Charlie, so many queer, inexplicable things happened in the world. Occult—subliminal—astral—thoughtwaves. These expressions and many more occurred to her as she recollected Charlie's disconcerting conversations. There MIGHT.... One never knew.

Suddenly she thought of her husband's pockets, bulging with silver, with gold, and with bank-notes. Tantalizing vision! No! She could not steal. Besides, he might wake up.

And she returned to mandarins. She got herself into a very morbid and two-o'clock-in-the-morning state of mind. Suppose it was a dodge that DID work. (Of course, she was extremely superstitious; we all are.) She began to reflect seriously upon China. She remembered having heard that Chinese mandarins were very corrupt; that they ground the faces of the poor, and put innocent victims to the torture; in short, that they were sinful and horrid persons, scoundrels unfit for mercy. Then she pondered upon the remotest parts of China, regions where Europeans never could penetrate. No doubt there was some unimportant mandarin, somewhere in these regions, to whose district his death would be a decided blessing, to kill whom would indeed be an act of humanity. Probably a mandarin without wife or family; a bachelor mandarin whom no relative would regret; or, in the alternative, a mandarin with many wives, whose disgusting polygamy merited severe punishment! An old mandarin already pretty nearly dead; or, in the alternative, a young one just commencing a career of infamy!

'I'm awfully silly,' she whispered to herself. 'But still, if there SHOULD be anything in it. And I must, I must, I must have that thing for my dress!'

She looked again at the dim forms of her husband's clothes, pitched anyhow on an ottoman. No! She could not stoop to theft!

So she murdered a mandarin; lying in bed there; not any particular mandarin, a vague mandarin, the mandarin most convenient and suitable under all the circumstances. She deliberately wished him dead, on the off-chance of acquiring riches, or, more accurately, because she was short of fourteen and fivepence in order to look perfectly splendid at a ball.

In the morning when she woke up—her husband had already departed to the works—she thought how foolish she had been in the night. She did not feel sorry for having desired the death of a fellow-creature. Not at all. She felt sorry because she was convinced, in the cold light of day, that the charm would not work. Charlie's notions were really too ridiculous, too preposterous. No! She must reconcile herself to wearing a ball dress which was less than perfection, and all for the want of fourteen and fivepence. And she had more nerves than ever!

She had nerves to such an extent that when she went to unlock the drawer of her own private toilet-table, in which her prudent and fussy husband forced her to lock up her rings and brooches every night, she attacked the wrong drawer—an empty unfastened drawer that she never used. And lo! the empty drawer was not empty. There was a sovereign lying in it!

This gave her a start, connecting the discovery, as naturally at the first blush she did, with the mandarin.

Surely it couldn't be, after all.

Then she came to her senses. What absurdity! A coincidence, of course, nothing else? Besides, a mere sovereign! It wasn't enough. Charlie had said 'rich for life'. The sovereign must have lain there for months and months, forgotten.

However, it was none the less a sovereign. She picked it up, thanked Providence, ordered the dog-cart, and drove straight to Brunt's. The particular thing that she acquired was an exceedingly thin, slim, and fetching silver belt—a marvel for the money, and the ideal waist decoration for her wonderful white muslin gown. She bought it, and left the shop.

And as she came out of the shop, she saw a street urchin holding out the poster of the early edition of the Signal. And she read on the poster, in large letters: 'DEATH OF LI HUNG CHANG.' It is no exaggeration to say that she nearly fainted. Only by the exercise of that hard self-control, of which women alone are capable, did she refrain from tumbling against the blue-clad breast of Adams, the Cheswardine coachman.

She purchased the Signal with well-feigned calm, opened it and read: 'Stop-press news. Pekin. Li Hung Chang, the celebrated Chinese statesman, died at two o'clock this morning.—Reuter.'

III

Vera reclined on the sofa that afternoon, and the sofa was drawn round in front of the drawing-room fire. And she wore her fluffiest and languidest peignoir. And there was a perfume of eau de Cologne

209

in the apartment. Vera was having a headache; she was having it in her grand, her official manner. Stephen had had to lunch alone. He had been told that in all probability his suffering wife would not be well enough to go to the ball. Whereupon he had grunted. As a fact, Vera's headache was extremely real, and she was very upset indeed.

The death of Li Hung Chang was heavy on her soul. Occultism was justified of itself. The affair lay beyond coincidence. She had always KNOWN that there was something in occultism, supernaturalism, so-called superstitions, what not. But she had never expected to prove the faith that was in her by such a homicidal act on her own part. It was detestable of Charlie to have mentioned the thing at all. He had no right to play with fire. And as for her husband, words could give but the merest rough outline of her resentment against Stephen. A pretty state of things that a woman with a position such as she had to keep up should be reduced to six and sevenpence! Stephen, no doubt, expected her to visit the pawnshop. It would serve him right if she did so—and he met her coming out under the three brass balls! Did she not dress solely and wholly to please him? Not in the least to please herself! Personally she had a mind set on higher things, impossible aspirations. But he liked fine clothes. And it was her duty to satisfy him. She strove to satisfy him in all matters. She lived for him. She sacrificed herself to him completely. And what did she get in return? Nothing! Nothing! Nothing! All men were selfish. And women were their victims.... Stephen, with his silly bullying rules against credit and so forth.... The worst of men was that they had no sense.

She put a new dose of eau de Cologne on her forehead, and leaned on one elbow. On the mantelpiece lay the tissue parcel containing the slim silver belt, the price of Li's death. She wanted to stick it in the fire. And only the fact that it would not burn prevented her savagely doing so. There was something wrong, too, with the occultism. To receive a paltry sovereign for murdering the greatest statesman of the Eastern hemisphere was simply grotesque. Moreover, she had most distinctly not wanted to deprive China of a distinguished man. She had expressly stipulated for an inferior and insignificant mandarin, one that could be spared and that was unknown to Reuter. She supposed she ought to have looked up China at the Wedgwood Institution and selected a definite mandarin with a definite place of residence. But could she be expected to go about a murder deliberately like that?

With regard to the gross inadequacy of the fiscal return for her deed, perhaps that was her own fault. She had not wished for more. Her brain had been so occupied by the belt that she had wished only for the belt. But, perhaps, on the other hand, vast wealth was to come. Perhaps something might occur that very night. That would be better. Yet would it be better? However rich she might become, Stephen would cooly take charge of her riches, and dole them out to her, and make rules for her concerning them. And besides, Charlie would suspect her guilt. Charlie understood her, and perused her thoughts far better than Stephen did. She would never be able to conceal the truth from Charlie. The conversation, the death of Li within two hours, and then a sudden fortune accruing to her— Charlie would inevitably put two and two together and divine her shameful secret.

The outlook was thoroughly black anyway.

She then fell asleep.

When she awoke, some considerable time afterwards, Stephen was calling to her. It was his voice, indeed, that had aroused her. The room was dark.

'I say, Vera,' he demanded, in a low, slightly inimical tone, 'have you taken a sovereign out of the empty drawer in your toilet-table?'

'No,' she said quickly, without thinking.

'Ah!' he observed reflectively, 'I knew I was right.' He paused, and added, coldly, 'If you aren't better you ought to go to bed.'

Then he left her, shutting the door with a noise that showed a certain lack of sympathy with her headache.

She sprang up. Her first feeling was one of thankfulness that that brief interview had occurred in darkness. So Stephen was aware of the existence of the sovereign! The sovereign was not occult. Possibly he had put it there. And what did he know he was 'right' about?

She lighted the gas, and gazed at herself in the glass, realizing that she no longer had a headache, and endeavouring to arrange her ideas.

'What's this?' said another voice at the door. She glanced round hastily, guiltily. It was Charlie.

'Steve telephoned me you were too ill to go to the dance,' explained Charlie, 'so I thought I'd come and make inquiries. I quite expected to find you in bed with a nurse and a doctor or two at least. What is it?' He smiled.

'Nothing,' she replied. 'Only a headache. It's gone now.'

She stood against the mantelpiece, so that he should not see the white parcel.

'That's good,' said Charlie.

There was a pause.

'Strange, Li Hung Chang dying last night, just after we had been talking about killing mandarins,' she said. She could not keep off the subject. It attracted her like a snake, and she approached it in spite of the fact that she fervently wished not to approach it.

'Yes,' said Charlie. 'But Li wasn't a mandarin, you know. And he didn't die after we had been talking about mandarins. He died before.'

'Oh! I thought it said in the paper he died at two o'clock this morning.'

'Two a.m. in Pekin,' Charlie answered. 'You must remember that Pekin time is many hours earlier than our time. It lies so far eastward.'

'Oh!' she said again.

Stephen hurried in, with a worried air.

'Ah! It's you, Charlie!'

'She isn't absolutely dying, I find,' said Charlie, turning to Vera: 'You are going to the dance after all—aren't you?'

'I say, Vera,' Stephen interrupted, 'either you or I must have a scene with Martha. I've always suspected that confounded housemaid. So I put a marked sovereign in a drawer this morning, and it was gone at lunch-time. She'd better hook it instantly. Of course I shan't prosecute.'

'Martha!' cried Vera. 'Stephen, what on earth are you thinking of? I wish you would leave the servants to me. If you think you can manage this house in your spare time from the works, you are welcome to try. But don't blame me for the consequences.' Glances of triumph flashed in her eyes.

'But I tell you—'

'Nonsense,' said Vera. 'I took the sovereign. I saw it there and I took it, and just to punish you, I've spent it. It's not at all nice to lay traps for servants like that.'

'Then why did you tell me just now you hadn't taken it?' Stephen demanded crossly.

'I didn't feel well enough to argue with you then,' Vera replied.

'You've recovered precious quick,' retorted Stephen with grimness.

'Of course, if you want to make a scene before strangers,' Vera whimpered (poor Charlie a stranger!), 'I'll go to bed.'

Stephen knew when he was beaten.

She went to the Hockey dance, though. She and Stephen and Charlie and his young sister, aged seventeen, all descended together to the Town Hall in a brougham. The young girl admired Vera's belt excessively, and looked forward to the moment when she too should be a bewitching and captivating wife like Vera, in short, a woman of the world, worshipped by grave, bearded men. And both the men were under the spell of Vera's incurable charm, capricious, surprising, exasperating, indefinable, indispensable to their lives.

'Stupid superstitions!' reflected Vera. 'But of course I never believed it really.'

And she cast down her eyes to gloat over the belt.

VERA'S SECOND CHRISTMAS ADVENTURE

I

Curious and strange things had a way of happening to Vera—perhaps because she was an extremely feminine woman. But of all the curious and strange things that ever did happen to Vera, this was certainly the strangest and the most curious. It makes a somewhat exasperating narrative, because the affair ended—or, rather, Vera caused it to end—on a note of interrogation. The reader may, however, draw consolation from the fact that, if he is tormented by an unanswerable query, Vera herself was much more tormented by precisely the same query.

Two days before Christmas, at about three o'clock in the afternoon, just when it was getting dusk and the distant smokepall of the Five Towns was merging in the general greyness of the northern sky, Vera was sitting in the bow-window of the drawing-room of Stephen Cheswardine's newly-acquired house at Sneyd; Sneyd being the fashionable suburb of the Five Towns, graced by the near presence of a countess. And as the slim, thirty-year-old Vera sat there, moody (for reasons which will soon appear), in her charming teagown, her husband drove up to the door in the dogcart, and he was not alone. He had with him a man of vigorous and dashing appearance, fair, far from ugly, and with a masterful face, keen eyes, and most magnificent furs round about him. At sight of the visitor Vera's heart did not exactly jump, but it nearly jumped.

Presently, Stephen brought his acquaintance into the drawing-room.

"My wife," said Stephen, rubbing his hands. "Vera, this is Mr Bittenger, of New York. He will give us the pleasure of spending the night here."

And now Vera's little heart really did jump.

She behaved with the delicious wayward grace which she could always command when she chose to command it. No one would have guessed that she had not spoken to Stephen for a week.

'I'm most happy—most happy,' said Mr Bittenger, with a marked accent and a fine complimentary air. And obviously he was most happy. Vera had impressed him. There was nothing surprising in that. She was in the fullness of her powers in that direction.

It is at this point—at the point of the first jumping of Vera's heart—that the tale begins to be uncanny and disturbing. Thus runs the explanation.

During the year Stephen had gradually grown more and more preoccupied with the subject of his own health. The earthenware business was very good, although, of course, manufacturers were complaining just as usual. Trade, indeed, flourished to such an extent that Stephen had pronounced himself to be suffering from nervous strain and overwork. The symptoms of his malady were chiefly connected with the assimilation of food; to be brief, it was dyspepsia. And as Stephen had previously been one of those favoured people who can eat anything at any hour, and arise in the best of health the next day, Stephen was troubled. At last—about August, when he was obliged to give up wine—he had suddenly decided that the grimy air of the Five Towns was bad for him, and that the household should be removed to Sneyd. And removed to Sneyd it accordingly was. The new house was larger and more splendid even than the Cheswardine abode at Bursley. But Vera did not like the change. Vera preferred the town. Nevertheless, she could not openly demur, since Stephen's health was supposed to be at stake.

During the autumn she was tremendously bored at Sneyd. She had practically no audience for her pretty dresses, and her friends would not flock over from Bursley because of the difficulty of getting home at night. Then it was that Vera had the beautiful idea of spending Christmas in Switzerland. Someone had told her about a certain hotel called The Bear, where, on Christmas Day, never less than a hundred well-dressed and wealthy English people sat down to an orthodox Christmas dinner. The notion enchanted her. She decided, definitely, that she and Stephen should do their Christmassing at The Bear, wherever the Bear was. And as she was fully aware of the power of her capricious charm over Stephen, she regarded the excursion as arranged before she had broached it to him.

Stephen refused. He remarked bitterly that the very thought of a mince-tart made him ill; and that he hated 'abroad'.

Vera took her defeat badly.

She pouted. She sulked. She announced that, if she was not to be allowed to do her Christmassing at The Bear, she would not do it anywhere. She indicated that she meant to perish miserably of ennui in the besotted dullness of Sneyd, and that no Christmas-party of any kind should occur in HER house. She ceased to show interest in Stephen's health. She would not speak. In fact, she went too far. One day, in reply to her rude silence, Stephen said: 'Very well, child, if that's your game, I'll play it with you. Except when other people are present, not a word do I speak to you until you have first spoken to me.'

She knew he would abide by that. He was a monster. She hated him. She loathed him (so she said to herself).

That night, in the agony of her distress, she had dreamed a dream. She dreamed that a stranger came to the house. The details were vague, but the stranger had travelled many miles over water. She could not see him distinctly, but she knew that he was quite bald. In spite of his baldness he inspired her with sympathy. He understood her, praised her costumes, and treated a woman as a woman ought to be treated. Then, somehow or other, he was making love to her, the monster Stephen being absent. She was shocked by his making love to her, and she moved a little farther off him on the sofa (he had sat down by her on a vague sort of sofa in a vague sort of room); but still she was thrilled, and she could not feel as wicked as she felt she ought to feel. Then the dream became hazy; it became hazy at the interesting point of her answer to the love-making. A later stage was very clear. Something was afoot between the monster Stephen and the stranger in the dining-room, and she was locked out of the dining-room. It was Christmas night. She knocked frantically at the door, and at last forced it open, and Stephen was lying in the middle of the floor; the table had been pushed into a corner. 'I killed him quite by accident,' said the stranger affably. And then he seized her by the hand and ruthlessly dragged her away, away, away; and they travelled in trains and ships and trains, and they came to a very noisy, clanging sort of city—and Vera woke up. It had been a highly realistic dream, and it made a deep impression on Vera.

Can one wonder that Vera's heart, being a superstitious little heart, like all our hearts, should leap when the very next day Stephen turned up with a completely unexpected stranger from New York? Of course, dreams are nonsense! Of course! Still—

She did not know whether to rejoice or mourn over the fact that Mr Bittenger was not bald. He was decidedly unbald; he had a glorious shock of chestnut hair. That hair of his naturally destroyed any possible connection with the dream. None the less the coincidence was bizarre.

II

That evening, before dinner, Vera, busy in her chamber beautifying her charms for the ravishment of men from New York, waited with secret anxiety for the arrival of Stephen in his dressing-room. And whereas she usually closed the door between the bedroom and the dressing-room, on this occasion she carefully left it wide open. Stephen came at last. And she waited, listening to his movements in the dressing-room. Not a word! She made brusque movements in the bedroom to attract his attention; she even dropped a brush on the floor. Not a word! After a few moments, she actually ventured into the dressing-room. Stephen was wiping his face, and he glanced at her momentarily over the towel, which hid his nose and mouth. Not a word! And how hard was the monster's glance! She felt that Stephen was one of your absurd literal persons. He had said that he would not speak to her until she had first spoken to him—that was to say in private—public performances did not count. And he would stick to his text, no matter how deliciously she behaved.

She left the dressing-room in haste. Very well! Very well! If Stephen wished for war, he should have it. Her grievance against him grew into something immense. Before, it had been nothing but a kind of two-roomed cottage. She now erected it into a town hall, with imposing portals, and many windows and rich statuary, and suite after suite of enormous rooms, and marble staircases, and lifts that went up and down. She wished she had never married him. She wished that Mr Bittenger HAD been bald.

At dinner everything went with admirable smoothness. Mr Bittenger sat betwixt them. And utmost politeness reigned. In their quality of well-bred hosts, they both endeavoured to keep Mr Bittenger at his ease despite their desolating quarrel; and they entirely succeeded. As the champagne disappeared (and it was not Stephen that drank it), Mr Bittenger became more than at his ease. He was buyer for an important firm of earthenware dealers in New York (Vera had suspected as much—these hospitalities to American buyers are an essential part of business in the Five Towns), and he related very drolly the series of chances or mischances that had left

217

him stranded in England at that season so unseasonable for buying. Vera reflected upon the series of chances or mischances, and upon her dream of the man from over the long miles of water. Of course, dreams are nonsense.... But still—

The conversation passed to the topic of Stephen's health, as conversations in Stephen's house had a habit of doing. Mr Bittenger listened with grave interest.

'I know, I know!' said Mr Bittenger. 'I used to be exactly the same. I guess I understand how you feel—SOME! Don't I?'

'And you are cured?' Stephen demanded, eagerly, as he nibbled at dry toast.

'You bet I'm cured!' said Mr Bittenger.

'You must tell me about that,' said Stephen, and added, 'some time tonight.' He did not care to discuss the bewildering internal economy of the human frame at his dinner-table. There were details...and Mr Bittenger was in a mood that it was no exaggeration to describe as gay.

Shortly afterwards, there arose a discussion as to their respective ages. They coquetted for a few moments, as men invariably will, each diffident about giving away the secret, each asserting that the other was younger than himself.

'Well,' said Mr Bittenger to Vera, at length, 'what age should you give me?'

'I—I should give you five years less than Stephen,' Vera replied.

'And may I ask just how old you are?' Mr Bittenger put the question at close range to Stephen, and hit him full in the face with it.

'I'm forty,' said Stephen.

'So am I!' said Mr Bittenger.

'Well, you don't look it,' said Stephen.

'Sure!' Mr Bittenger admitted, pleased.

'My husband's hair is turning grey,' said Vera, 'while yours—'

'Turning grey!' exclaimed Mr Bittender. 'I wish mine was. I'd give five thousand dollars today if mine was.'

'But why—?' Vera smiled.

'Look here, my dear lady,' said Mr Bittenger, in a peculiar voice, putting down his glass.

And with a swift movement he lifted a wig of glorious chestnut hair from his head—just lifted it for an instant, and dropped it. The man was utterly and completely bald.

III

Vera did nothing foolish. She neither cried, screamed, turned deadly pale, clenched her fragile hands, bit her lips till the blood came, smashed a wine-glass, nor fell with a dull thud senseless to the floor. Nevertheless, she was extremely perturbed by this astounding revelation of Mr Bittenger's. Of course, dreams are nonsense. But still—The truth is, one tries to believe that dreams are nonsense, and up to a certain point one may succeed in believing. But it seemed to Vera that circumstances had passed that point. She could not but admit, also, that if the dream went on being fulfilled, within forty-eight hours Mr Bittenger would have made love to her, and would have killed her husband.

She was so incensed against Stephen that she really could not decide whether she wanted the dream to be fulfilled or not. No one would have imagined that that soft breast could conceal a homicidal thought. Yet so it was. That pretty and delightful woman, wandering about in the edifice of her terrific grievance against Stephen, could not say positively to herself that she would not care to have Stephen killed as a punishment for his sins.

After dinner, she found an excuse for retiring. She must think the puzzle out in solitude. Matters were really going too far. She allowed it to be understood that she was indisposed. Mr Bittenger was full of sorrow and sympathy. But did Stephen show the slightest concern? Stephen did not. She went upstairs, and she meditated, stretched on the sofa at the foot of the bed, a rug over her knees and the fire glinting on her face. Yes, it was her duty as a Christian, if not as an outraged wife, to warn Stephen that the shadow of death was creeping up behind him. He ought at least to be warned. But how could she warn him? Clearly she could not warn him in the presence of Mr Bittenger, the prospective murderer. She would, therefore, have to warn him when they were alone. And that meant that she would have to give way in the great conjugal sulking match. No, never! It was impossible that she should give way there! She frowned desperately at the leaping flames, and did ultimately decide that Stephen's death was preferable to her defeat in that contest. Of such is human nature.

After all, dreams were nonsense.

Surely Stephen would come upstairs to inquire about her health, her indisposition? But no! He came not. And, as he continued not to come, she went downstairs again and proclaimed that she was better.

And then she learned that she had been worrying herself to no purpose whatever. Mr Bittenger was leaving on the morrow, the morrow being Christmas Eve. Stephen would drive him to Bursley in the morning. He would go to the Five Towns Hotel to get his baggage, and catch the Liverpool express at noon. He had booked a passage on the Saxonia, which sailed at threethirty o'clock. Thus he would spend his Christmas at sea; and, spending his Christmas at sea, he could not possibly kill Stephen in the village of Sneyd on Christmas night.

Relief! And yet a certain vague regret in the superstitious little heart! The little heart went to bed again. And Stephen and the stranger stayed up talking very late—doubtless about the famous cure.

The leave-taking the next morning increased the vague regret. Mr Bittenger was the possessor of an attractive individuality, and Vera pondered upon its attractiveness far into the afternoon. How nicely Mr Bittenger had thanked her for her gracious hospitality—with what meaning he had charged the expression of his deep regret at leaving her!

After all, dreams WERE nonsense.

She was sitting in the bow-window of the drawing-room, precisely as she had been sitting twenty-four hours previously, when whom should she see, striding masculinely along the drive towards the house, but Mr Bittenger?

This time she was much more perturbed even than she had been by the revelation of Mr Bittenger's baldness.

After all—

She uprose, the blood having rushed to her head, and retreated she knew not whither, blindly, without a purpose. And found herself in a little morning-room which was scarcely ever used, at the end of the hall. She had not shut the door. And Mr Bittenger, having been admitted by a servant, caught sight of her, and breezily entered her retreat, clad in his magnificent furs.

And as he doffed the furs, he gaily told her what had happened. Owing to difficulties with the Cheswardine mare on the frosty, undulating road between Sneyd and Bursley, and owing to delays with his baggage at the Five Towns Hotel, he had just missed the Liverpool express, and, therefore, the steamer also. He had returned to Stephen's manufactory. Stephen had insisted that he should spend his Christmas with them. And, in brief, there he was. He had walked from Bursley. Stephen, kept by business, was coming later, and so was some of the baggage.

Mr Bittenger's face radiated joy. The loss of his twenty-guinea passage on the Saxonia did not appear to cause him the least regret.

And he sat down by the side of Vera.

And Vera suddenly noticed that they were on a sofa—the sofa of her dream—and she fancied she recognized the room.

'You know, my dear lady,' said Mr Bittenger, looking her straight in the eyes, 'I'm just GLAD I missed my steamer. It gives me a chance to spend a Christmas in England, and in your delightful society—your delightful society—' He gazed at her, without adding to the sentence.

If this was not love-making on a sofa, what could be?

Mr Bittenger had certainly missed the Liverpool express on purpose. Of that Vera was convinced. Or, if he had not missed it on purpose, he had missed it under the dictates of the mysterious power of the dream. Those people who chose to believe that dreams are nonsense were at liberty to do so.

IV

So that in spite of Vera's definite proclamation that there should be no Christmassing in her house that year, Christmassing there emphatically was. Impossible to deny anything to Mr Bittenger! Mr Bittenger wanted holly, the gardener supplied it. Mr Bittenger wanted mistletoe, a bunch of it was brought home by Stephen in the dogcart. Mr Bittenger could not conceive an English Christmas without turkey, mince-pies, plum-pudding, and all the usual indigestiveness. Vera, speaking in a voice which seemed somehow not to be hers, stated that these necessaries of Christmas life would be produced, and Stephen did not say that the very thought of a mince-tart made him ill. Even the English weather, which, it is notorious, has of late shown a sad disposition to imitate, and even to surpass, in mildness the weather of the Riviera at Christmas, decided to oblige Mr Bittenger. At nightfall on Christmas Eve it began to snow gently, but steadily—fine, frozen snow. And the waits, consisting of boys and girls from the Countess of Chell's celebrated institute close by, came and sang in the garden in the falling snow, by the light of a lantern. And Mr Bittenger's heart was as full as it could hold of English Christmas.

As for Vera's heart, it was full of she knew not what. Mr Bittenger's attitude towards her grew more and more chivalrous. He contrived to indicate that he regarded all the years he had spent before making the acquaintance of Vera as so many years absolutely wasted. And Stephen did not seem to care.

They retired to rest that evening up a staircase whose banisters the industrious hands of Mr Bittenger had entwined with holly and paper festoons, and bade each other a merry Christmas with immense fervour; but in the conjugal chamber Stephen maintained his policy of implacable silence. And, naturally, Vera maintained hers. Could it be expected of her that she should yield? The fault was all Stephen's. He ought to have taken her to The Bear, Switzerland. Then there would have been no dream, no Mr Bittenger, and no danger. But as things were, within twenty-four hours he would be a dead man.

And throughout Christmas Day Vera, beneath the gaiety with which she met the vivacious sallies of Mr Bittenger, waited in horrible suspense for the dream to fulfil itself. Stephen alone observed her agitated condition. Stephen said to himself: 'The quarrel is getting on her nerves. She'll yield before she's a day older. It will do her good. Then I'll make it up to her handsomely. But she must yield first.'

He little knew he was standing on the edge of the precipice of death.

The Christmas dinner succeeded admirably; and Stephen, in whom courage was seldom lacking, ate half a mince-pie. The day was almost over. No premature decease had so far occurred. And when both the men said that, if Vera permitted, they would come with her at once to the drawing-room and smoke there, Vera decided that after all dreams were nonsense. She entered the drawing-room first, and Mr Bittenger followed her, with Stephen behind; but just as Stephen was crossing the mat the gardener, holding a parcel in his hands and looking rather strange there in the hall, spoke to him. And Stephen stopped and called to Mr Bittenger. And the drawing-room door was closed upon Vera.

She waited, solitary, for an incredible space of time, and then, having heard unaccustomed and violent sounds in the distance, she could contain herself no longer, and she rang the bell.

'Louisa,' she demanded of the parlourmaid, 'where is your master?'

'Oh, ma'am,' replied Louisa, giggling—a little licence was surely permissible to the girl on Christmas night—'Oh, ma'am, there's such a to-do! Tinsley has just brought some boxing-gloves, and master and Mr Bittenger have got their coats off in the dining-room. And they've had the table pushed up by the door, and you never saw such a set-out in all your life ma'am.'

Vera dismissed Louisa.

There it was—the dream! They were going to box. Mr Bittenger was doubtless an expert, and she knew that Stephen was not. A chance blow by Mr Bittenger in some vital part, and Stephen would be lying stretched in eternal stillness in the middle of the dining-room floor where the table ought to be! The life of the monster was at stake! The life of the brute was in her hands! The dream was fulfilling itself to the point of tragedy!

She jumped up and rushed to the dining-room door. It would not open. Again, the dream!

'You can't come in,' cried Stephen, laughing. 'Wait a bit.'

She pushed against the door, working the handle.

She was about to insist upon the door being opened, when the idea of the danger of such a proceeding occurred to her. In the dream, when she got the door opened, her husband's death had already happened!

Frantically she ran to the kitchen.

'Louisa,' she ordered. 'Go into the garden and tap at the dining-room window, and tell your master that I must speak to him at once in the drawing-room.'

And in a pitiable state of excitation, she returned to the drawing-room.

After another interminable period of suspense, her ear caught the sound of the opening of doors, and then Stephen came into the drawing-room. A singular apparition! He was coatless, as Louisa had said, and the extremities of his long arms were bulged out with cream-coloured boxing-gloves.

She sprang at him and kissed him.

'Steve,' she said, 'are we friends?'

'I should think we were!' he replied, returning her kiss heartily. He had won.

'What are you doing?' she asked him.

'Bittenger and I are just going to have a real round with the gloves. It's part of his cure for my indigestion, you know. He says there's nothing like it. I've only just been able to get gloves. Tinsley brought them up just now. And so we sort of thought we'd like to have a go at once.'

'Why wouldn't you let me into the dining-room?'

'My child, the table was up against the door. And I fancied, perhaps, you wouldn't be exactly charmed, so I—'

'Stephen,' she said, in her most persuasive voice, 'will you do something to please me?'

'What is it?'

'Will you?'

A pause.

'Yes, certainly.'

'Don't box tonight.'

'Oh—well! What will Bittenger think?'

Another pause.

'Never mind! You don't want me to box, really?'

'I don't want you to box—not tonight.' 'Agreed, my chuck!' And he kissed her again. He could well afford to be magnanimous.

Mr Bittenger ploughed the seas alone to New York.

But supposing that Vera had not interfered, what would have happened? That is the unanswerable query which torments the superstitious little brain of Vera.

THE BURGLARY

I

Lady Dain said: 'Jee, if that portrait stays there much longer, you'll just have to take me off to Pirehill one of these fine mornings.'

Pirehill is the seat of the great local hospital; but it is also the seat of the great local lunatic asylum; and when the inhabitants of the Five Towns say merely 'Pirehill', they mean the asylum.

'I do declare I can't fancy my food now-a-days,' said Lady Dain, 'and it's all that portrait!' She stared plaintively up at the immense oil-painting which faced her as she sat at the breakfast-table in her spacious and opulent dining-room.

Sir Jehoshaphat made no remark.

Despite Lady Dain's animadversions upon it, despite the undoubted fact that it was generally disliked in the Five Towns, the portrait had cost a thousand pounds (some said guineas), and though not yet two years old it was probably worth at least fifteen hundred in the picture market. For it was a Cressage; and not only was it a Cressage—it was one of the finest Cressages in existence.

It marked the summit of Sir Jehoshaphat's career. Sir Jehoshaphat's career was, perhaps, the most successful and brilliant in the entire social history of the Five Towns. This famous man was the principal partner in Dain Brothers. His brother was dead, but two of Sir Jee's sons were in the firm. Dain Brothers were the largest manufacturers of cheap earthenware in the district, catering chiefly for the American and Colonial buyer. They had an extremely bad reputation for cutting prices. They were hated by every other firm in the Five Towns, and, to hear rival manufacturers talk, one would gather the impression that Sir Jee had acquired a tremendous fortune by systematically selling goods under cost. They were also hated by between eighteen and nineteen hundred employees. But such hatred, however virulent, had not marred the progress of Sir Jee's career.

He had meant to make a name and he had made it. The Five Towns might laugh at his vulgar snobbishness. The Five Towns might sneer at his calculated philanthropy. But he was, nevertheless, the best-known man in the Five Towns, and it was precisely his snobbishness and his philanthropy which had carried him to the top.

225

Moreover, he had been the first public man in the Five Towns to gain a knighthood. The Five Towns could not deny that it was very proud indeed of this knighthood. The means by which he had won this distinction were neither here nor there—he had won it. And was he not the father of his native borough? Had he not been three times mayor of his native borough? Was not the whole northern half of the county dotted and spangled by his benefactions, his institutions, his endowments?

And it could not be denied that he sometimes tickled the Five Towns as the Five Towns likes being tickled. There was, for example, the notorious Sneyd incident. Sneyd Hall, belonging to the Earl of Chell, lies a few miles south of the Five Towns, and from it the pretty Countess of Chell exercises that condescending meddlesomeness which so frequently exasperates the Five Towns. Sir Jee had got his title by the aid of the Countess-'Interfering Iris', as she is locally dubbed. Shortly afterwards he had contrived to quarrel with the Countess; and the quarrel was conducted by Sir Jee as a quarrel between equals, which delighted the district. Sir Jee's final word in it had been to buy a sizable tract of land near Sneyd village, just off the Sneyd estate, and to erect thereon a mansion quite as imposing as Sneyd Hall, and far more up to date, and to call the mansion Sneyd Castle. A mighty stroke! Iris was furious; the Earl speechless with fury. But they could do nothing. Naturally the Five Towns was tickled.

It was apropos of the house-warming of Sneyd Castle, also of the completion of his third mayoralty, and of the inauguration of the Dain Technical Institute, that the movement had been started (primarily by a few toadies) for tendering to Sir Jee a popular gift worthy to express the profound esteem in which he was officially held in the Five Towns. It having been generally felt that the gift should take the form of a portrait, a local dilettante had suggested Cressage, and when the Five Towns had inquired into Cressage and discovered that that genius from the United States was celebrated throughout the civilized world, and regarded as the equal of Velazquez (whoever Velazquez might be), and that he had painted half the aristocracy, and that his income was regal, the suggestion was accepted and Cressage was approached.

Cressage haughtily consented to paint Sir Jee's portrait on his usual conditions; namely, that the sitter should go to the little village in Bedfordshire where Cressage had his principal studio, and that the painting should be exhibited at the Royal Academy before being shown anywhere else. (Cressage was an R.A., but no one thought of putting R.A. after his name. He was so big, that instead of the Royal Academy conferring distinction on him, he conferred distinction on the Royal Academy.)

Sir Jee went to Bedfordshire and was rapidly painted, and he came back gloomy. The presentation committee went to Bedfordshire later to inspect the portrait, and they, too, came back gloomy.

Then the Academy Exhibition opened, and the portrait, showing Sir Jee in his robe and chain and in a chair, was instantly hailed as possibly the most glorious masterpiece of modern times. All the critics were of one accord. The committee and Sir Jee were reassured, but only partially, and Sir Jee rather less so than the committee. For there was something in the enthusiastic criticism which gravely disturbed him. An enlightened generation, thoroughly familiar with the dazzling yearly succession of Cressage's portraits, need not be told what this something was. One critic wrote that Cressage displayed even more than his 'customary astounding insight into character....' Another critic wrote that Cressage's observation was, as usual, 'calmly and coldly hostile'. Another referred to the 'typical provincial mayor, immortalized for the diversion of future ages.'

Inhabitants of the Five Towns went to London to see the work for which they had subscribed, and they saw a mean, little, old man, with thin lips and a straggling grey beard, and shifty eyes, and pushful snob written all over him; ridiculous in his gewgaws of office. When you looked at the picture close to, it was a meaningless mass of coloured smudges, but when you stood fifteen feet away from it the portrait was absolutely lifelike, amazing, miraculous. It was so wondrously lifelike that some of the inhabitants of the Five Towns burst out laughing. Many people felt sorry—not for Sir Jee—but for Lady Dain. Lady Dain was beloved and genuinely respected. She was a simple, homely, sincere woman, her one weakness being that she had never been able to see through Sir Jee.

Of course, at the presentation ceremony the portrait had been ecstatically referred to as a possession precious for ever, and the recipient and his wife pretended to be overflowing with pure joy in the ownership of it.

It had been hanging in the dining-room of Sneyd Castle about sixteen months, when Lady Dain told her husband that it would ultimately drive her into the lunatic asylum.

'Don't be silly, wife,' said Sir Jee. 'I wouldn't part with that portrait for ten times what it cost.'

This was, to speak bluntly, a downright lie. Sir Jee secretly hated the portrait more than anyone hated it. He would have been almost ready to burn down Sneyd Castle in order to get rid of the thing. But it happened that on the previous evening, in the conversation with the magistrates' clerk, his receptive brain had been visited by a less expensive scheme than burning down the castle.

Lady Dain sighed.

'Are you going to town early?' she inquired.

'Yes,' he replied. 'I'm on the rota today.'

He was chairman of the borough Bench of magistrates. As he drove into town he revolved his scheme and thought it wild and dangerous, but still feasible.

II

On the Bench that morning Sir Jee shocked Mr Sherratt, the magistrates' clerk, and he utterly disgusted Mr Bourne, superintendent of the borough police. (I do not intend to name the name of the borough—whether Bursley, Hanbridge, Knype, Longshaw, or Turnhill. The inhabitants of the Five Towns will know without being told; the rest of the world has no right to know.) There had recently occurred a somewhat thrilling series of burglaries in the district, and the burglars (a gang of them was presumed) had escaped the solicitous attentions of the police. But on the previous afternoon an underling of Mr Bourne's had caught a man who was generally believed to be wholly or partly responsible for the burglaries. The Five Towns breathed with relief and congratulated Mr Bourne; and Mr Bourne was well pleased with himself. The Staffordshire Signal headed the item of news, 'Smart Capture of a Supposed Burglar'. The supposed burglar gave his name as William Smith, and otherwise behaved in an extremely suspicious manner.

Now, Sir Jee, sitting as chief magistrate in the police-court, actually dismissed the charge against the man! Overruling his sole colleague on the Bench that morning, Alderman Easton, he

228

dismissed the charge against William Smith, holding that the evidence for the prosecution was insufficient to justify even a remand. No wonder that Mr Bourne was discouraged, not to say angry. No wonder that that pillar of the law, Mr Sherratt, was pained and shocked. At the conclusion of the case Sir Jehoshaphat said that he would be glad to speak with William Smith afterwards in the magistrates' room, indicating that he sympathized with William Smith, and wished to exercise upon William Smith his renowned philanthropy.

And so, at about noon, when the Court majestically rose, Sir Jee retired to the magistrates' room, where the humble Alderman Easton was discreet enough not to follow him, and awaited William Smith. And William Smith came, guided thither by a policeman, to whom, in parting from him, he made a rude, surreptitious gesture.

Sir Jee, seated in the arm-chair which dominates the other chairs round the elm table in the magistrates' room, emitted a preliminary cough.

'Smith,' he said sternly, leaning his elbows on the table, 'you were very fortunate this morning, you know.'

And he gazed at Smith.

Smith stood near the door, cap in hand. He did not resemble a burglar, who surely ought to be big, muscular, and masterful. He resembled an undersized clerk who has been out of work for a long time, but who has nevertheless found the means to eat and drink rather plenteously. He was clothed in a very shabby navy-blue suit, frayed at the wrists and ankles, and greasy in front. His linen collar was brown with dirt, his fingers were dirty, his hair was unkempt and long, and a young and lusty black beard was sprouting on his chin. His boots were not at all pleasant.

'Yes, governor,' Smith replied, lightly, with a Manchester accent. 'And what's YOUR game?'

Sir Jee was taken aback. He, the chairman of the borough Bench, and the leading philanthropist in the country, to be so spoken to! But what could he do? He himself had legally established Smith's innocence. Smith was as free as air, and had a perfect right to adopt any tone he chose to any man he chose. And Sir Jee desired a service from William Smith.

'I was hoping I might be of use to you,' said Sir Jehoshaphat diplomatically.

'Well,' said Smith, 'that's all right, that is. But none of your philanthropic dodges, you know. I don't want to lead a new life, and I don't want to turn over a new leaf, and I don't want a helpin' hand, nor none o' those things. And, what's more, I don't want a situation. I've got all the situation as I need. But I never refuse money, nor beer neither. Never did, and I'm forty years old next month.'

'I suppose burgling doesn't pay very well, does it?' Sir Jee boldly ventured.

William Smith laughed coarsely.

'It pays right enough,' said he. 'But I don't put my money on my back, governor, I put it into a bit of public-house property when I get the chance.'

'It may pay,' said Sir Jee. 'But it is wrong. It is very anti-social.'

'Is it, indeed?' Smith returned dryly. 'Anti-social, is it? Well, I've heard it called plenty o' things in my time, but never that. Now, I should have called it quite sociablelike, sort of making free with strangers, and so on. However,' he added, 'I come across a cove once as told me crime was nothing but a disease and ought to be treated as such. I asked him for a dozen o' port, but he never sent it.'

'Ever been caught before?' Sir Jee inquired.

'Not much!' Smith exclaimed. 'And this'll be a lesson to me, I can tell you. Now, what are you getting at, governor? Because my time's money, my time is.'

Sir Jee coughed once more.

'Sit down,' said Sir Jee.

And William Smith sat down opposite to him at the table, and put his shiny elbows on the table precisely in the manner of Sir Jee's elbows.

'Well?' he cheerfully encouraged Sir Jee.

'How would you like to commit a burglary that was not a crime?' said Sir Jee, his shifty eyes wandering around the room. 'A perfectly lawful burglary?'

'What ARE you getting at?' William Smith was genuinely astonished.

'At my residence, Sneyd Castle,' Sir Jee proceeded, 'there's a large portrait of myself in the dining-room that I want to have stolen. You understand?'

'Stolen?'

'Yes. I want to get rid of it. And I want—er—people to think that it has been stolen.'

'Well, why don't you stop up one night and steal it yourself, and then burn it?' William Smith suggested.

'That would be deceitful,' said Sir Jee, gravely. 'I could not tell my friends that the portrait had been stolen if it had not been stolen. The burglary must be entirely genuine.'

'What's the figure?' said Smith curtly.

'Figure?'

'What are you going to give me for the job?'

'GIVE you for doing the job?' Sir Jee repeated, his secret and ineradicable meanness aroused. 'GIVE you? Why, I'm giving you the opportunity to honestly steal a picture that's worth over a thousand pounds—I dare say it would be worth two thousand pounds in America—and you want to be paid into the bargain! Do you know, my man, that people come all the way from Manchester, and even London, to see that portrait?' He told Smith about the painting.

'Then why are you in such a stew to be rid of it?' queried the burglar.

'That's my affair,' said Sir Jee. 'I don't like it. Lady Dain doesn't like it. But it's a presentation portrait, and so I can't—you see, Mr Smith?'

'And how am I going to dispose of it when I've got it?' Smith demanded. 'You can't melt a portrait down as if it was silver. By what you say, governor, it's known all over the blessed world. Seems to me I might just as well try to sell the Nelson Column.'

'Oh, nonsense!' said Sir Jee. 'Nonsense. You'll sell it in America quite easily. It'll be a fortune to you. Keep it for a year first, and then send it to New York.'

William Smith shook his head and drummed his fingers on the table; and then quite suddenly he brightened and said—

'All right, governor. I'll take it on, just to oblige you.'

'When can you do it?' asked Sir Jee, hardly concealing his joy. 'Tonight?'

'No,' said Smith, mysteriously. 'I'm engaged tonight.'

'Well, tomorrow night?'

'Nor tomorrow. I'm engaged tomorrow too.'

'You seem to be very much engaged, my man,' Sir Jee observed.

'What do you expect?' Smith retorted. 'Business is business. I could do it the night after tomorrow.'

'But that's Christmas Eve,' Sir Jee protested.

'What if it is Christmas Eve?' said Smith coldly. 'Would you prefer Christmas Day? I'm engaged on Boxing Day AND the day after.'

'Not in the Five Towns, I trust?' Sir Jee remarked.

'No,' said Smith shortly. 'The Five Towns is about sucked dry.'

The affair was arranged for Christmas Eve.

'Now,' Sir Jee suggested, 'shall I draw you a plan of the castle, so that you can—'

William Smith's face expressed terrific scorn. 'Do you suppose,' he said, 'as I haven't had plans o' your castle ever since it was built? What do you take me for? I'm not a blooming excursionist, I'm not. I'm a business man—that's what I am.'

Sir Jee was snubbed, and he agreed submissively to all William Smith's arrangements for the innocent burglary. He perceived that in William Smith he had stumbled on a professional of the highest class, and this good fortune pleased him.

'There's only one thing that riles me,' said Smith, in parting, 'and that is that you'll go and say that after you'd done everything you could for me I went and burgled your castle. And you'll talk about the ingratitude of the lower classes. I know you, governor!'

III

On the afternoon of the 24th of December Sir Jehoshaphat drove home to Sneyd Castle from the principal of the three Dain manufactories, and found Lady Dain superintending the work of packing up trunks. He and she were to quit the castle that afternoon in order to spend Christmas on the other side of the Five Towns, under the roof of their eldest son, John, who had a new house, a new wife, and a new baby (male). John was a domineering person, and, being rather proud of his house and all that was his, he had obstinately decided to have his own Christmas at his own hearth. Grandpapa and Grandmamma, drawn by the irresistible attraction of that novelty, a grandson (though Mrs John HAD declined to have the little thing named Jehoshaphat), had yielded to John's solicitations, and the family gathering, for the first time in history, was not to occur round Sir Jee's mahogany.

Sir Jee, very characteristically, said nothing to Lady Dain immediately. He allowed her to proceed with the packing of the trunks, and then tea was served, and as the time was approaching for

232

the carriage to come round to take them to the station, at last he suddenly remarked—

'I shan't be able to go with you to John's this afternoon.'

'Oh, Jee!' she exclaimed. 'Really, you are tiresome. Why couldn't you tell me before?'

'I will come over tomorrow morning—perhaps in time for church,' he proceeded, ignoring her demand for an explanation.

He always did ignore her demand for an explanation. Indeed, she only asked for explanations in a mechanical and perfunctory manner—she had long since ceased to expect them. Sir Jee had been born like that—devious, mysterious, incalculable. And Lady Dain accepted him as he was. She was somewhat surprised, therefore, when he went on—

'I have some minutes of committee meetings that I really must go carefully through and send off tonight, and you know as well as I do that there'll be no chance of doing that at John's. I've telegraphed to John.'

He was obviously nervous and self-conscious.

'There's no food in the house,' sighed Lady Dain. 'And the servants are all going away except Callear, and HE can't cook your dinner tonight. I think I'd better stay myself and look after you.'

'You'll do no such thing,' said Sir Jee, decisively. 'As for my dinner, anything will do for that. The servants have been promised their holiday, to start from this evening, and they must have it. I can manage.'

Here spoke the philanthropist with his unshakable sense of justice.

So Lady Dain departed, anxious and worried, having previously arranged something cold for Sir Jee in the dining-room, and instructed Callear about boiling the water for Sir Jee's tea on Christmas morning. Callear was the under-coachman and a useful odd man. He it was who would drive Sir Jee to the station on Christmas morning, and then guard the castle and the stables thereof during the absence of the family and the other servants. Callear slept over the stables.

And after Sir Jee had consumed his cold repast in the dining-room the other servants went, and Sir Jee was alone in the castle, facing the portrait.

He had managed the affair fairly well, he thought. Indeed, he had a talent for chicane, and none knew it better than himself. It would have been dangerous if the servants had been left in the castle. They might have suffered from insomnia, and heard William Smith, and interfered with the operations of William Smith. On the other hand, Sir Jee had no intention whatever of leaving the castle uninhabited to the mercies of William Smith. He felt that he himself must be on the spot to see that everything went right and that nothing went wrong. Thus, the previously-arranged scheme for the servants' holiday fitted perfectly into his plans, and all that he had had to do was to refuse to leave the castle till the morrow. It was ideal.

Nevertheless, he was a little afraid of what he had done, and of what he was going to permit William Smith to do. It was certainly dangerous—certainly rather a wild scheme. However, the die was cast. And within twelve hours he would be relieved of the intolerable incubus of the portrait.

And when he thought of the humiliations which that portrait had caused him; when he remembered the remarks of his sons concerning it, especially John's remarks; when he recalled phrases about it in London newspapers, he squirmed, and told himself that no scheme for getting rid of it could be too wild and perilous. And, after all, the burglary dodge was the only dodge, absolutely the only conceivable practical method of disposing of the portrait—except burning down the castle. And surely it was preferable to a conflagration, to arson! Moreover, in case of fire at the castle some blundering fool would be sure to cry; 'The portrait! The portrait must be saved!' And the portrait would be saved.

He gazed at the repulsive, hateful thing. In the centre of the lower part of the massive gold frame was the legend: 'Presented to Sir Jehoshaphat Dain, Knight, as a mark of public esteem and gratitude,' etc. He wondered if William Smith would steal the frame. It was to be hoped that he would not steal the frame. In fact, William Smith would find it very difficult to steal that frame unless he had an accomplice or so.

'This is the last time I shall see YOU!' said Sir Jee to the portrait.

Then he unfastened the catch of one of the windows in the dining-room (as per contract with William Smith), turned out the electric light, and went to bed in the deserted castle.

He went to bed, but not to sleep. It was no part of Sir Jee's programme to sleep. He intended to listen, and he did listen.

And about two o'clock, precisely the hour which William Smith had indicated, he fancied he heard muffled and discreet noises. Then he was sure that he heard them. William Smith had kept his word. Then the noises ceased for a period, and then they recommenced. Sir Jee restrained his curiosity as long as he could, and when he could restrain it no more he rose and silently opened his bedroom window and put his head out into the nipping night air of Christmas. And by good fortune he saw the vast oblong of the picture, carefully enveloped in sheets, being passed by a couple of dark figures through the dining-room window to the garden outside. William Smith had a colleague, then, and he was taking the frame as well as the canvas. Sir Jee watched the men disappear down the avenue, and they did not reappear. Sir Jee returned to bed.

Yes, he felt himself equal to facing it out with his family and friends. He felt himself equal to pretending that he had no knowledge of the burglary.

Having slept a few hours, he got up early and, half-dressed, descended to the dining-room just to see what sort of a mess William Smith had made.

The canvas of the portrait lay flat on the hearthrug, with the following words written on it in chalk: 'This is no use to me.' It was the massive gold frame that had gone.

Further, as was later discovered, all the silver had gone. Not a spoon was left in the castle.

NEWS OF THE ENGAGEMENT

My mother never came to meet me at Bursley station when I arrived in the Five Towns from London; much less did she come as far as Knype station, which is the great traffic centre of the district, the point at which one changes from the express into the local train. She had always other things to do; she was 'preparing' for me. So I had the little journey from Knype to Bursley, and then the walk up Trafalgar Road, amid the familiar high chimneys and the smoke and the clayey mud and the football posts and the Midland accent, all by myself. And there was leisure to consider anew how I should break to my mother the tremendous news I had for her. I had been considering that question ever since getting into the train at Euston, where I had said goodbye to Agnes; but in the atmosphere of the Five Towns it seemed just slightly more difficult; though, of course, it wasn't difficult, really.

You see, I wrote to my mother regularly every week, telling her most of my doings. She knew all my friends by name. I dare say she formed in her mind notions of what sort of people they were. Thus I had frequently mentioned Agnes and her family in my letters. But you can't write even to your mother and say in cold blood: 'I think I am beginning to fall in love with Agnes,' 'I think Agnes likes me,' 'I am mad on her,' 'I feel certain she likes me,' 'I shall propose to her on such a day.' You can't do that. At least I couldn't. Hence it had come about that on the 20th of December I had proposed to Agnes and been accepted by Agnes, and my mother had no suspicion that my happiness was so near. And on the 22nd, by a previous and unalterable arrangement, I had come to spend Christmas with my mother.

I was the only son of a widow; I was all that my mother had. And lo! I had gone and engaged myself to a girl she had never seen, and I had kept her in the dark! She would certainly be extremely surprised, and she might be a little bit hurt—just at first. Anyhow, the situation was the least in the world delicate.

I walked up the whitened front steps of my mother's little house, just opposite where the electric cars stop, but before I could put my hand on the bell my little plump mother, in her black silk and her gold brooch and her auburn hair, opened to me, having doubtless watched me down the road from the bay-window, as usual, and she said, as usual kissing me—

'Well, Philip! How are you?'

And I said—

'Oh! I'm all right, mother. How are you?'

I perceived instantly that she was more excited than my arrival ordinarily made her. There were tears in her smiling eyes, and she was as nervous as a young girl. She did indeed look remarkably young for a woman of forty-five, with twenty-five years of widowhood and a brief but too tempestuous married life behind her.

The thought flashed across my mind: 'By some means or other she has got wind of my engagement. But how?'

But I said nothing. I, too, was naturally rather nervous. Mothers are kittle cattle.

'I'll tell her at supper,' I decided.

And she hovered round me, like a sea-gull round a steamer, as I went upstairs.

There was a ring at the door. She flew, instead of letting the servant go. It was a porter with my bag.

Just as I was coming down-stairs again there was another ring at the door. And my mother appeared magically out of the kitchen, but I was beforehand with her, and with a laugh I insisted on opening the front door myself this time. A young woman stood on the step.

'Please, Mrs Dawson wants to know if Mrs Durance can kindly lend her half-a-dozen knives and forks?'

'Eh, with pleasure,' said my mother, behind me. 'Just wait a minute, Lucy. Come inside on the mat.'

I followed my mother into the drawing-room, where she kept her silver in a cabinet.

'That's Mrs Dawson's new servant,' my mother whispered. 'But she needn't think I'm going to lend her my best, because I'm not.'

'I shouldn't, if I were you,' I supported her.

And she went out with some second-best in tissue paper, and beamed on Mrs Dawson's servant with an assumed benevolence.

'There!' she exclaimed. 'And the compliments of the season to your mistress, Lucy.'

After that my mother disappeared into the kitchen to worry an entirely capable servant. And I roamed about, feeling happily excited, examining the drawing-room, in which nothing was changed except the incandescent light and the picture postcards on the mantelpiece. Then I wandered into the dining-room, a small room at the back of the house, and here an immense surprise awaited me.

Supper was set for three!

'Well,' I reflected. 'Here's a nice state of affairs! Supper for three, and she hasn't breathed a word!'

My mother was so clever in social matters, and especially in the planning of delicious surprises, that I believed her capable even of miracles. In some way or other she must have discovered the state of my desires towards Agnes. She had written, or something. She and Agnes had been plotting together by letter to startle me, and perhaps telegraphing. Agnes had fibbed in telling me that she could not possibly come to Bursley for Christmas; she had delightfully fibbed. And my mother had got her concealed somewhere in the house, or was momentarily expecting her. That explained the tears, the nervousness, the rushes to the door.

I crept out of the dining-room, determined not to let my mother know that I had secretly viewed the supper-table. And as I was crossing the lobby to the drawing-room there was a third ring at the door, and a third time my mother rushed out of the kitchen.

'By Jove!' I thought. 'Suppose it's Agnes. What a scene!'

And trembling with expectation I opened the door. It was Mr Nixon.

Now, Mr Nixon was an old friend of the family's, a man of forty-nine or fifty, with a reputation for shrewdness and increasing wealth. He owned a hundred and seventy-five cottages in the town, having bought them gradually in half-dozens, and in rows; he collected the rents himself, and attended to the repairs himself, and was celebrated as a good landlord, and as being almost the only man in Bursley who had made cottage property pay. He lived alone in Commerce Street, and, though not talkative, was usually jolly, with one or two good stories tucked away in the corners of his memory. He was my mother's trustee, and had morally aided her in the troublous times before my father's early death.

'Well, young man,' cried he. 'So you're back in owd Bosley!' It amused him to speak the dialect a little occasionally.

And he brought his burly, powerful form into the lobby.

I greeted him as jovially as I could, and then he shook hands with my mother, neither of them speaking.

'Mr Nixon is come for supper, Philip,' said my mother.

238

I liked Mr Nixon, but I was not too well pleased by this information, for I wanted to talk confidentially to my mother. I had a task before me with my mother, and here Mr Nixon was plunging into the supper. I could not break it gently to my mother that I was engaged to a strange young woman in the presence of Mr Nixon. Mr Nixon had been in to supper several times during previous visits of mine, but never on the first night.

However, I had to make the best of it. And we sat down and began on the ham, the sausages, the eggs, the crumpets, the toast, the jams, the mince-tarts, the Stilton, and the celery. But we none of us ate very much, despite my little plump mother's protestations.

My suspicion was that perhaps something had gone slightly wrong with my mother's affairs, and that Mr Nixon was taking the first opportunity to explain things to me. But such a possibility did not interest me, for I could easily afford to keep my mother and a wife too. I was still preoccupied in my engagement—and surely there is nothing astonishing in that—and I began to compose the words in which, immediately on the departure of Mr Nixon after supper, I would tackle my mother on the subject.

When we had reached the Stilton and celery, I intimated that I must walk down to the post-office, as I had to dispatch a letter.

'Won't it do tomorrow, my pet?' asked my mother.

'It will not,' I said.

Imagine leaving Agnes two days without news of my safe arrival and without assurances of my love! I had started writing the letter in the train, near Willesden, and I finished it in the drawing-room.

'A lady in the case?' Mr Nixon called out gaily.

'Yes,' I replied with firmness.

I went forth, bought a picture postcard showing St Luke's Square, Bursley, most untruthfully picturesque, and posted the card and the letter to my darling Agnes. I hoped that Mr Nixon would have departed ere my return; he had made no reference at all during supper to my mother's affairs. But he had not departed. I found him solitary in the drawing-room, smoking a very fine cigar.

'Where's the mater?' I demanded.

'She's just gone out of the room,' he said. 'Come and sit down. Have a weed. I want a bit of a chat with you, Philip.'

I obeyed, taking one of the very fine cigars.

'Well, Uncle Nixon,' I encouraged him, wishing to get the chat over because my mind was full of Agnes. I sometimes called him uncle for fun.

'Well, my boy,' he began. 'It's no use me beating about the bush. What do you think of me as a stepfather?'

I was struck, as they say down there, all of a heap.

'What?' I stammered. 'You don't mean to say—you and mother—?'

He nodded.

'Yes, I do, lad. Yesterday she promised as she'd marry my unworthy self. It's been coming along for some time. But I don't expect she's given you any hint in her letters. In fact, I know she hasn't. It would have been rather difficult, wouldn't it? She couldn't well have written, "My dear Philip, an old friend, Mr Nixon, is falling in love with me and I believe I'm falling in love with him. One of these days he'll be proposing to me." She couldn't have written like that, could she?'

I laughed. I could not help it.

'Shake hands,' I said warmly. 'I'm delighted.'

And soon afterwards my mother sidled in, shyly.

'The lad's delighted, Sarah,' said Mr Nixon shortly.

I said nothing about my own engagement that night. I had never thought of my mother as a woman with a future, I had never realized that she was desirable, and that a man might desire her, and that her lonely existence in that house was not all that she had the right to demand from life. And I was ashamed of my characteristic filial selfish egoism. So I decided that I would not intrude my joys on hers until the next morning. We live and learn.

BEGINNING THE NEW YEAR

I

We are a stolid and a taciturn race, we of the Five Towns. It may be because we are geographically so self contained; or it may be because we work in clay and iron; or it may merely be because it is our nature to be stolid and taciturn. But stolid and taciturn we are; and some of the instances of our stolidity and our taciturnity are enough to astound. They do not, of course, astound us natives; we laugh at them, we think they are an immense joke, and what the outer world may think does not trouble our deep conceit of ourselves. I have often wondered what would be the effect, other than an effect of astonishment, on the outer world, of one of these narratives illustrating our Five Towns peculiarities of deportment. And I intend for the first time in history to make such a narrative public property. I have purposely not chosen an extreme example; just an average example. You will see how it strikes you.

Toby Hall, once a burgess of Turnhill, the northernmost and smallest of the Five Towns, was passing, last New Year's Eve, through the district by train on his way from Crewe to Derby. He lived at Derby, and he was returning from the funeral of a brother member of the Ancient Order of Foresters at Crewe. He got out of the train at Knype, the great railway centre of the Five Towns, to have a glass of beer in the second-class refreshment-room. It being New Year's Eve, the traffic was heavy and disorganized, especially in the refreshment-room, and when Toby Hall emerged on to the platform again the train was already on the move. Toby was neither young nor active. His years were fifty, and on account of the funeral he wore broadcloth and a silk hat, and his overcoat was new and encumbering. Impossible to take a flying leap into the train! He missed the train. And then he reflectively stroked his short grey beard (he had no moustache, and his upper lip was very long), and then he smoothed down his new overcoat over his rotund form.

'Young man,' he asked a porter. 'When's next train Derby way?'

'Ain't none afore tomorrow.'

Toby went and had another glass of beer.

'D—d if I don't go to Turnhill,' he said to himself, slowly and calmly, as he paid for the second glass of beer.

He crossed the station by the subway and waited for the loop-line train to Turnhill. He had not set foot in the Five Towns for three-and-twenty years, having indeed carefully and continuously avoided it, as a man will avoid the street where his creditor lives. But he discovered no change in Knype railway-station. And he had a sort of pleasure in the fact that he knew his way about it, knew where the loop-line trains started from and other interesting little details. Even the special form of the loop-line time-table, pasted here and there on the walls of the station, had not varied since his youth. (We return Radicals to Parliament, but we are proud of a railway which for fine old English conservatism brooks no rival.)

Toby gazed around, half challengingly and half nervously—it was conceivable that he might be recognized, or might recognize. But no! Not a soul in the vast, swaying, preoccupied, luggage-laden crowds gave him a glance. As for him, although he fully recognized nobody, yet nearly every face seemed to be half-familiar. He climbed into a second-class compartment when the train drew up, and ten other people, all with third-class tickets, followed his example; three persons were already seated therein. The compartment was illuminated by one lamp, and in the Bleakridge Tunnel this lamp expired. Everything reminded him of his youth.

In twenty minutes he was leaving Turnhill station and entering the town. It was about nine o'clock, and colder than winters of the period usually are. The first thing he saw was an electric tram, and the second thing he saw was another electric tram. In Toby's time there were no trams at Turnhill, and the then recently-introduced steam-trams between Bursley and Longshaw, long since superseded, were regarded as the final marvel of science as applied to traction. And now there were electric trams at Turnhill! The railway renewed his youth, but this darting electricity showed him how old he was. The Town Hall, which was brand-new when he left Turnhill, had the look of a mediaeval hotel de ville as he examined it in the glamour of the corporation's incandescent gas. And it was no more the sole impressive pile in the borough. The High Street and its precincts abounded in impressive piles. He did not know precisely what they were, but they had the appearance of being markets, libraries, baths, and similar haunts of luxury; one was a bank. He thought that Turnhill High Street compared very well with Derby. He would have preferred it to be less changed. If the High Street was thus changed, everything would be changed, including Child

Row. The sole phenomenon that recalled his youth (except the Town Hall) was the peculiar smell of oranges and apples floating out on the frosty air from holly-decorated greengrocers' shops.

He passed through the Market Square, noting that sinister freak, the Jubilee Tower, and came to Child Row. The first building on your right as you enter Child Row from the square is the Primitive Methodist Chapel. Yes, it was still there; Primitive Methodism had not failed in Turnhill because Toby Hall had deserted the cause three-and-twenty years ago! But something serious had happened to the structure. Gradually Toby realized that its old face had been taken out and a new one put in, the classic pillars had vanished, and a series of Gothic arches had been substituted by way of portico; a pretty idea, but not to Toby's liking. It was another change, another change! He crossed the street and proceeded downwards in the obscurity, and at length halted and peered with his little blue eyes at a small house (one of twins) on the other side from where he stood. That house, at any rate, was unchanged. It was a two-storeyed house, with a semicircular fanlight over a warped door of grained panelling. The blind of the window to the left of the door was irradiated from within, proving habitation.

'I wonder—' ran Toby's thought. And he unhesitatingly crossed the street again, towards it, feeling first for the depth of the kerbstone with his umbrella. He had a particular and special interest in that house (No. 11 it was—and is), for, four-and-twenty years ago he had married it.

II

Four-and-twenty years ago Toby Hall (I need not say that his proper Christian name was Tobias) had married Miss Priscilla Bratt, then a calm and self-reliant young woman of twenty-three, and Priscilla had the house, together with a certain income, under the will of her father. The marriage was not the result of burning passion on either side. It was a union of two respectabilities, and it might have succeeded as well as such unions generally do succeed, if Priscilla had not too frequently mentioned the fact that the house they lived in was hers. He knew that the house was hers. The whole world was perfectly aware of the ownership of the house, and her references to the matter amounted to a lack of tact. Several times Toby had indicated as much. But Priscilla took no heed. She had the

243

hide of an alligator herself (though a personable girl), and she assumed that her husband's hide was of similar stuff. This assumption was justifiable, except that in just one spot the skin of Toby was tender. He really did not care to be reminded that he was living under his wife's roof. The reiteration settled on his nerves like a malady. And before a year had elapsed Priscilla had contrived to remind him once too often. And one day he put some things in a carpet-bag, and a hat on his head, and made for the door. The house was antique, and the front-parlour gave directly on to the street.

'Where be going?' Priscilla asked him.

He hesitated a second, and said—

'Merica.'

And he was. In the Five Towns we are apt to end our marriages in that laconic manner. Toby did not complain too much; he simply and unaffectedly went. It might be imagined that the situation was a trying one for Priscilla. Not so! Priscilla had experienced marriage with Toby and had found it wanting. She was content to be relieved of Toby. She had her house and her money and her self-esteem, and also tranquillity. She accepted the solution, and devoted her days to the cleanliness of the house.

Toby drew all the money he had out of the Bursley and Turnhill Permanent Fifty Pounds Benefit Building Society (four shares, nearly paid up) and set sail—in the Adriatic, which was then the leading greyhound of the Atlantic—for New York. From New York he went to Trenton (New Jersey), which is the Five Towns of America. A man of his skill in handling clay on a wheel had no difficulty whatever in wresting a good livelihood from Trenton. When he had tarried there a year he caused a letter to be written to his wife informing her that he was dead. He wished to be quite free; and also (we have our feeling for justice) he wished his wife to be quite free. It did not occur to him that he had done anything extraordinary, either in deserting his wife or in forwarding false news of his death. He had done the simple thing, the casual thing, the blunt thing, the thing that necessitated the minimum of talking. He did not intend to return to England.

However, after a few years, he did return to England. The cause of his return is irrelevant to the history, but I may say that it sprang from a conflict between the Five Towns temperament and the Trenton Union of Earthenware Operatives. Such is the power of Unions in the United States that Toby, if he wished to remain under the Federal Flag, had either to yield or to starve. He would not yield. He changed his name and came to England; strolled calmly into the Crown Porcelain Works at Derby one day, and there recommenced his career as an artificer of earthenware. He did well. He could easily earn four pounds a week, and had no desires, save in the direction of fly-fishing—not an expensive diversion. He knew better than to marry. He existed quietly; and one year trod on the heels of another, and carried him from thirty to forty and forty to fifty, and no one found out his identity, though there are several direct trains daily between Derby and Knype.

And now, owing to the death of a friend and a glass of beer, he was in Child Row, crossing the street towards the house whose ownership had caused him to quit it.

He knocked on the door with the handle of his umbrella. There was no knocker; there never had been a knocker.

III

The door opened cautiously, as such doors in the Five Towns do, after a shooting of bolts and a loosing of chains; it opened to the extent of about nine inches, and Toby Hall saw the face of a middle-aged woman eyeing him.

'Is this Mrs Hall's?' he asked sternly.

'No. It ain't Mrs Hall's. It's Mrs Tansley's.'

'I thowt—'

The door opened a little wider.

'That's not you, Tobias?' said the woman unmoved.

'I reckon it is, though,' replied Toby, with a difficult smile.

'Bless us!' exclaimed the woman. The door oscillated slightly under her hand. 'Bless us!' she repeated. And then suddenly, 'You'd happen better come in, Tobias.'

'Aye!' said Tobias.

And he entered.

'Sit ye down, do,' said his wife. 'I thowt as you were dead. They wrote and told me so.'

'Aye!' said Tobias. 'But I am na'.'

He sat down in an arm-chair near the old-fashioned grate, with its hobs at either side. He was acquainted with that chair, and it had not appreciably altered since his departure. The lastingness of furniture under fair treatment is astonishing. This chair was uncomfortably in exactly the same spot where it had always been uncomfortable; and the same anti-macassar was draped over its uncompromising back. Toby put his hat on the table, and leaned his umbrella against the chimney-piece. His overcoat he retained. Same table; same chimney-piece; same clock and ornaments on the chimney-piece! But a different carpet on the floor, and different curtains before the window.

Priscilla bolted and chained the door, and then she too sat down. Her gown was black, with a small black silk apron. And she was stout, and she wore felt slippers and moved with the same gingerly care as Toby himself did. She looked fully her years. Her thin lips were firmer than ever. It was indeed Priscilla.

'Well, well!' she murmured.

But her capacity for wonder was nearly exhausted.

'Aye!' said Toby, with an air that was meant to be quasi-humorous. He warmed his hands at the fire, and then rubbed them over the front of his calves, leaning forward.

'So ye've come back?' said Priscilla.

'Aye!' concurred Toby.

There was a pause.

'Cold weather we're having,' he muttered.

'It's seasonable,' Priscilla pointed out.

Her glance rested on a sprig of holly that was tied under the gas-chandelier, unique relic of Christmas in the apartment.

Another pause. It would be hazardous to guess what their feelings were; perhaps their feelings were scarcely anything at all.

'And what be the news?' Toby inquired, with what passes in the Five Towns for geniality.

'News?' she repeated, as if not immediately grasping the significance of the question. 'I don't know as there's any news, nothing partic'ler, that is.'

Hung on the wall near the chimney-piece was a photograph of a girl. It was an excellent likeness to Priscilla, as she was in Toby's pre-Trenton days. How young and fresh the creature looked; so simple, so inexperienced! It startled Toby.

'I don't remember that,' he said.

'What?'

'That!' And he jerked his elbow towards the photograph.

'Oh! THAT! That's my daughter,' said Priscilla.

'Bless us!' said Toby in turn.

'I married Job Tansley,' Priscilla continued. 'He died four years ago last Knype Wakes Monday. HER'S married'—indicating the photograph—'her married young Gibson last September.'

'Well, well!' murmured Toby.

Another pause.

There was a shuffling on the pavement outside, and some children began to sing about shepherds and flocks.

'Oh, bother them childer,' said Priscilla. 'I must send 'em off.'

She got up.

'Here! Give 'em a penny,' Toby suggested, holding out a penny.

'Yes, and then they'll tell others, and I shan't have a moment's peace all night!' Priscilla grumbled.

However, she bestowed the penny, cutting the song off abruptly in the middle. And she bolted and chained the door and sat down again.

Another pause.

'Well, well!' said Priscilla.

'Aye!' Toby agreed. 'Good coal that!'

'Fourteen shilling a ton!'

Another pause, and a longer.

'Is Ned Walklate still at th' Rose and Crown?' Toby asked.

'For aught I know he is,' said Priscilla.

'I'll just step round there,' said Toby, picking up his hat and rising.

As he was manoeuvring the door-chain, Priscilla said—

'You're forgetting your umbrella, Tobias.'

'No,' he answered. 'I hanna' forgotten it. I'm coming back.'

Their eyes met, charged with meaning.

'That'll be all right,' she said. 'Well, well!'

'Aye!'

And he stepped round to Ned Walklate's.

FROM ONE GENERATION TO ANOTHER

I

It is the greatest mistake in the world to imagine that, because the Five Towns is an industrial district, devoted to the manufacture of cups and saucers, marbles and door-knobs, therefore there is no luxury in it.

A writer, not yet deceased, who spent two nights there, and wrote four hundred pages about it, has committed herself to the assertion that there are no private carriages in its streets—only perambulators and tramcars.

That writer's reputation is ruined in the Five Towns. For the Five Towns, although continually complaining of bad times, is immensely wealthy, as well as immensely poor—a country of contrasts, indeed—and private carriages, if they do not abound, exist at any rate in sufficient numbers.

Nay, more, automobiles of the most expensive French and English makes fly dashingly along its hilly roads and scatter in profusion the rich black mud thereof.

On a Saturday afternoon in last spring, such an automobile stood outside the garden entrance of Bleakridge House, just halfway between Hanbridge and Bursley. It belonged to young Harold Etches, of Etches, Limited, the great porcelain manufacturers.

It was a 20 h.p. Panhard, and was worth over a thousand pounds as it stood there, throbbing, and Harold was proud of it.

He was also proud of his young wife, Maud, who, clad in several hundred pounds' worth of furs, had taken her seat next to the steering-wheel, and was waiting for Harold to mount by her side. The united ages of this handsome and gay couple came to less than forty-five.

And they owned the motor-car, and Bleakridge House with its ten bedrooms, and another house at Llandudno, and a controlling interest in Etches, Limited, that brought them in seven or eight thousand a year. They were a pretty tidy example of what the Five Towns can do when it tries to be wealthy.

At that moment, when Harold was climbing into the car, a shabby old man who was walking down the road, followed by a boy carrying a carpet-bag, stopped suddenly and touched Harold on the shoulder.

'Bless us!' exclaimed the old man. And the boy and the carpet-bag halted behind him.

'What? Uncle Dan?' said Harold.

'Uncle Dan!' cried Maud, springing up with an enchanting smile. 'Why, it's ages since—'

'And what d'ye reckon ye'n gotten here?' demanded the old man.

'It's my new car,' Harold explained.

'And ca'st drive it, lad?' asked the old man.

'I should think I could!' said Harold confidently.

'H'm!' commented the old man, and then he shook hands, and thoroughly scrutinized Maud.

Now, this is the sort of thing that can only be seen and appreciated in a district like the Five Towns, where families spring into splendour out of nothing in the course of a couple of generations, and as often as not sink back again into nothing in the course of two generations more.

The Etches family is among the best known and the widest spread in the Five Towns. It originated in three brothers, of whom Daniel was the youngest. Daniel never married; the other two did. Daniel was not very fond of money; the other two were, and they founded the glorious firm of Etches. Harold was the grandson of one brother, and Maud was the Granddaughter of the other. Consequently, they both stood in the same relation to Dan, who was their great-uncle—addressed as uncle 'for short'.

There is a good deal of snobbery in the Five Towns, but it does not exist between relatives. The relatives in danger of suffering by it would never stand it. Besides, although Dan's income did not exceed two hundred a year, he was really richer than his grandnephew, since Dan lived on half his income, whereas Harold, aided by Maud, lived on all of his.

Consequently, despite the vast difference in their stations, clothes, and manners, Daniel and his young relatives met as equals. It would have been amusing to see anyone—even the Countess of Chell, who patronized the entire district—attempt to patronize Dan.

In his time he had been the greatest pigeon-fancier in the country.

'So you're paying a visit to Bursley, uncle?' said Maud.

'Aye!' Dan replied. 'I'm back i' owd Bosley. Sarah—my housekeeper, thou know'st—'

'Not dead?'

'No. Her inna' dead; but her sister's dead, and I've give her a week's play [holiday], and come away. Rat Edge'll see nowt o' me this side Easter.'

Rat Edge was the name of the village, five miles off, which Dan had honoured in his declining years.

'And where are you going to now?' asked Harold.

'I'm going to owd Sam Shawn's, by th' owd church, to beg a bed.'

'But you'll stop with us, of course?' said Harold.

'Nay, lad,' said Dan.

'Oh yes, uncle,' Maud insisted.

'Nay, lass,' said Dan.

'Indeed, you will, uncle,' said Maud positively. 'If you don't, I'll never speak to you again.'

She had a charming fire in her eyes, had Maud.

Daniel, the old bachelor, yielded at once, but in his own style.

'I'll try it for a night, lass,' said he.

Thus it occurred that the carpet-bag was carried into Bleakridge House, and that after some delay Harold and Maud carried off Uncle Dan with them in the car. He sat in the luxurious tonneau behind, and Maud had quitted her husband in order to join him. Possibly she liked the humorous wrinkles round his grey eyes. Or it may have been the eyes themselves. And yet Dan was nearer seventy than sixty.

The car passed everything on the road; it seemed to be overtaking electric trams all the time.

'So ye'n been married a year?' said Uncle Dan, smiling at Maud.

'Oh yes; a year and three days. We're quite used to it.'

'Us'n be in h-ll in a minute, wench!' exclaimed Dan, calmly changing the topic, as Harold swung the car within an inch of a brewer's dray, and skidded slightly in the process. No anti-skidding device would operate in that generous, oozy mud.

And, as a matter of fact, they were in Hanbridge the next minute—Hanbridge, the centre of the religions, the pleasures, and the vices of the Five Towns.

'Bless us!' said the old man. 'It's fifteen year and more since I were here.'

'Harold,' said Maud, 'let's stop at the Piccadilly Cafe and have some tea.'

'Cafe?' asked Dan. 'What be that?'

'It's a kind of a pub.' Harold threw the explanation over his shoulder as he brought the car up with swift dexterity in front of the Misses Callear's newly opened afternoon tea-rooms.

'Oh, well, if it's a pub,' said Uncle Dan, 'I dunna' object.'

He frankly admitted, on entering, that he had never before seen a pub full of little tables and white cloths, and flowers, and young women, and silver teapots, and cake-stands. And though he did pour his tea into his saucer, he was sufficiently at home there to address the younger Miss Callear as 'young woman', and to inform her that her beverage was lacking in Orange Pekoe. And the Misses Callear, who conferred a favour on their customers in serving them, didn't like it.

He became reminiscent.

'Aye!' he said, 'when I left th' Five Towns fifty-two years sin' to go weaving i' Derbyshire wi' my mother's brother, tay were ten shilling a pun'. Us had it when us were sick—which wasna' often. We worked too hard for be sick. Hafe past five i' th' morning till eight of a night, and then Saturday afternoon walk ten mile to Glossop with a week's work on ye' back, and home again wi' th' brass.

'They've lost th' habit of work now-a-days, seemingly,' he went on, as the car moved off once more, but slowly, because of the vast crowds emerging from the Knype football ground. 'It's football, Saturday; bands of a Sunday; football, Monday; ill i' bed and getting round, Tuesday; do a bit o' work Wednesday; football, Thursday; draw wages Friday night; and football, Saturday. And wages higher than ever. It's that as beats me—wages higher than ever—

'Ye canna' smoke with any comfort i' these cars,' he added, when Harold had got clear of the crowds and was letting out. He regretfully put his pipe in his pocket.

Harold skirted the whole length of the Five Towns from south to north, at an average rate of perhaps thirty miles an hour; and quite soon the party found itself on the outer side of Turnhill, and descending the terrible Clough Bank, three miles long, and of a steepness resembling the steepness of the side of a house.

The car had warmed to its business, and Harold took them down that declivity in a manner which startled even Maud, who long ago had resigned herself to the fact that she was tied for life to a young man for whom the word 'danger' had no meaning.

At the bottom they had a swerve skid; but as there was plenty of room for eccentricities, nothing happened except that the car tried to climb the hill again.

'Well, if I'd known,' observed Uncle Dan, 'if I'd guessed as you were reservin' this treat for th' owd uncle, I'd ha' walked.'

The Etches blood in him was pretty cool, but his nerve had had a shaking.

Then Harold could not restart the car. The engine had stopped of its own accord, and, though Harold lavished much physical force on the magic handle in front, nothing would budge. Maud and the old man got down, the latter with relief.

'Stuck, eh?' said Dan. 'No steam?'

'That's it!' Harold cried, slapping his leg. 'What an ass I am! She wants petrol, that's all. Maud, pass a couple of cans. They're under the seat there, behind. No; on the left, child.'

However, there was no petrol on the car.

'That's that cursed Durand' (Durand being the new chauffeur—French, to match the car). 'I told him not to forget. Last thing I said to the fool! Maud, I shall chuck that chap!'

'Can't we do anything?' asked Maud stiffly, putting her lips together.

'We can walk back to Turnhill and buy some petrol, some of us!' snapped Harold. 'That's what we can do!'

'Sithee,' said Uncle Dan. 'There's the Plume o' Feathers half-a-mile back. Th' landlord's a friend o' mine. I can borrow his mare and trap, and drive to Turnhill and fetch some o' thy petrol, as thou calls it.'

'It's awfully good of you, uncle.'

'Nay, lad, I'm doing it for please mysen. But Maud mun come wi' me. Give us th' money for th' petrol, as thou calls it.'

'Then I must stay here alone?' Harold complained.

'Seemingly,' the old man agreed.

After a few words on pigeons, and a glass of beer, Dan had no difficulty whatever in borrowing his friend's white mare and black trap. He himself helped in the harnessing. Just as he was driving triumphantly away, with that delicious vision Maud on his left hand and a stable-boy behind, he reined the mare in.

'Give us a couple o' penny smokes, matey,' he said to the landlord, and lit one.

The mare could go, and Dan could make her go, and she did go. And the whole turn-out looked extremely dashing when, ultimately, it dashed into the glare of the acetylene lamps which the deserted Harold had lighted on his car.

The red end of a penny smoke in the gloom of twilight looks exactly as well as the red end of an Havana. Moreover, the mare caracolled ornamentally in the rays of the acetylene, and the stable-boy had to skip down quick and hold her head.

'How much didst say this traction-engine had cost thee?' Dan asked, while Harold was pouring the indispensable fluid into the tank.

'Not far off twelve hundred,' answered Harold lightly. 'Keep that cigar away from here.'

'Fifteen pun' ud buy this mare,' Dan announced to the road.

'Now, all aboard!' Harold commanded at length. 'How much shall I give to the boy for the horse and trap, uncle?'

'Nothing,' said Dan. 'I havena' finished wi' that mare yet. Didst think I was going to trust mysen i' that thing o' yours again? I'll meet thee at Bleakridge, lad.'

'And I think I'll go with uncle too, Harold,' said Maud.

Whereupon they both got into the trap.

Harold stared at them, astounded.

'But I say—' he protested, beginning to be angry.

Uncle Dan drove away like the wind, and the stable-boy had all he could do to clamber up behind.

II

Now, at dinner-time that night, in the dining-room of the commodious and well-appointed mansion of the youngest and richest of the Etches, Uncle Dan stood waiting and waiting for his host and hostess to appear. He was wearing a Turkish tasselled smoking-cap to cover his baldness, and he had taken off his jacket and put on his light, loose overcoat instead of it, since that was a comfortable habit of his.

He sent one of the two parlourmaids upstairs for his carpet slippers out of the carpet-bag, and he passed part of the time in changing his boots for his slippers in front of the fire. Then at length, just as a maid was staggering out under the load of those enormous boots, Harold appeared, very correct, but alone.

'Awfully sorry to keep you waiting, uncle,' said Harold, 'but Maud isn't well. She isn't coming down tonight.'

'What's up wi' Maud?'

'Oh, goodness knows!' responded Harold gloomily. 'She's not well—that's all.'

'H'm!' said Dan. 'Well, let's peck a bit.'

So they sat down and began to peck a bit, aided by the two maids. Dan pecked with prodigious enthusiasm, but Harold was not in good pecking form. And as the dinner progressed, and Harold sent dish after dish up to his wife, and his wife returned dish after dish untouched, Harold's gloom communicated itself to the house in general.

One felt that if one had penetrated to the farthest corner of the farthest attic, a little parcel of spiritual gloom would have already arrived there. The sense of disaster was in the abode. The cook was prophesying like anything in the kitchen. Durand in the garage was meditating upon such of his master's pithy remarks as he had been able to understand.

When the dinner was over, and the coffee and liqueurs and cigars had been served, and the two maids had left the dining-room, Dan turned to his grandnephew and said—

'There's things as has changed since my time, lad, but human nature inna' one on em.'

'What do you mean, uncle?' Harold asked awkwardly, self-consciously.

'I mean as thou'rt a dashed foo'!'

'Why?'

'But thou'lt get better o' that,' said Dan.

Harold smiled sheepishly.

'I don't know what you're driving at, uncle,' said he.

'Yes, thou dost, lad. Thou'st been and quarrelled wi' Maud. And I say thou'rt a dashed foo'!'

'As a matter of fact—' Harold stammered.

'And ye've never quarrelled afore. This is th' fust time. And so thou'st under th' impression that th' world's come to an end. Well, th' fust quarrel were bound to come sooner or later.'

'It isn't really a quarrel—it's about nothing—'

'I know—I know,' Dan broke in. 'They always are. As for it not being a quarrel, lad, call it a picnic if thou'st a mind. But heir's sulking upstairs, and thou'rt sulking down here.'

'She was cross about the petrol,' said Harold, glad to relieve his mind. 'I hadn't a notion she was cross till I went up into the bedroom. Not a notion! I explained to her it wasn't my fault. I argued it out with her very calmly. I did my best to reason with her—'

'Listen here, young 'un,' Dan interrupted him. 'How old art?'

'Twenty-three.'

'Thou may'st live another fifty years. If thou'st a mind to spend 'em i' peace, thoud'st better give up reasoning wi' women. Give it up right now! It's worse nor drink, as a habit. Kiss 'em, cuddle 'em, beat 'em. But dunna' reason wi' 'em.'

'What should you have done in my place?' Harold asked.

'I should ha' told Maud her was quite right.'

'But she wasn't.'

'Then I should ha' winked at mysen i' th' glass,' continued Dan, 'and kissed her.'

'That's all very well—'

'Naturally,' said Dan, 'her wanted to show off that car i' front o' me. That was but natural. And her was vexed when it went wrong.'

'But I told her—I explained to her.'

'Her's a handsome little wench,' Dan proceeded. 'And a good heart. But thou'st got ten times her brains, lad, and thou ought'st to ha' given in.'

'But I can't always be—'

'It's allus them as gives in as has their own way. I remember her grandfather—he was th' eldest o' us—he quarrelled wi' his wife afore they'd been married a week, and she raced him all over th' town wi' a besom—'

'With a besom, uncle?' exclaimed Harold, shocked at these family disclosures.

'Wi' a besom,' said Dan. That come o' reasoning wi' a woman. It taught him a lesson, I can tell thee. And afterwards he always said as nowt was worth a quarrel—NOWT! And it isna'.'

'I don't think Maud will race me all over the town with a besom,' Harold remarked reflectively.

'There's worse things nor that,' said Dan. 'Look thee here, get out o' th' house for a' 'our. Go to th' Conservative Club, and then come back. Dost understand?'

'But what—'

'Hook it, lad!' said Dan curtly.

And just as Harold was leaving the room, like a school-boy, he called him in again.

'I havena' told thee, Harold, as I'm subject to attacks. I'm getting up in years. I go off like. It isna' fits, but I go off. And if it should happen while I'm here, dunna' be alarmed.'

'What are we to do?'

'Do nothing. I come round in a minute or two. Whatever ye do, dunna' give me brandy. It might kill me—so th' doctor says. I'm only telling thee in case.'

'Well, I hope you won't have an attack,' said Harold.

'It's a hundred to one I dunna',' said Dan.

And Harold departed.

Soon afterwards Uncle Dan wandered into a kitchen full of servants.

'Show me th' missis's bedroom, one on ye,' he said to the crowd.

And presently he was knocking at Maud's door.

'Maudie!'

'Who is it?' came a voice.

'It's thy owd uncle. Can'st spare a minute?'

Maud appeared at the door, smiling, and arrayed in a peignoir.

'HE'S gone out,' said Dan, implying scorn of the person who had gone out. 'Wilt come down-stairs?'

'Where's he gone to?' Maud demanded.

She didn't even pretend she was ill.

'Th' Club,' said Dan.

And in about a hundred seconds or so he had her in the drawing-room, and she was actually pouring out gin for him. She looked ravishing in that peignoir, especially as she was munching an apple, and balancing herself on the arm of a chair.

'So he's been quarrelling with ye, Maud?' Dan began.

'No; not quarrelling, uncle.'

'Well, call it what ye'n a mind,' said Dan. 'Call it a prayer-meeting. I didn't notice as ye came down for supper—dinner, as ye call it.'

'It was like this, uncle,' she said. 'Poor Harry was very angry with himself about that petrol. Of course, he wanted the car to go well while you were in it; and he came up-stairs and grumbled at me for leaving him all alone and driving home with you.'

'Oh, did he?' exclaimed Dan.

'Yes. I explained to him that of course I couldn't leave you all alone. Then he got hot. I kept quite calm. I reasoned it out with him as quietly as I could—'

'Maudie, Maudie,' protested the old man, 'thou'rt th' prettiest wench i' this town, though I AM thy great-uncle, and thou'st got plenty o' brains—a sight more than that husband o' thine.'

'Do you think so, uncle?'

'Aye, but thou hasna' made use o' 'em tonight. Thou'rt a foolish wench, wench. At thy time o' life, and after a year o' th' married state, thou ought'st to know better than reason wi' a man in a temper.'

'But, really, uncle, it was so absurd of Harold, wasn't it?'

'Aye!' said Dan. 'But why didst-na' give in and kiss him, and smack his face for him?'

'There was nothing to give in about, uncle.'

'There never is,' said Dan. 'There never is. That's the point. Still, thou'rt nigh crying, wench.'

'I'm not, uncle,' she contradicted, the tears falling on to the apple.

'And Harold's using bad language all up Trafalgar Road, I lay,' Dan added.

'It was all Harold's fault,' said Maud.

'Why, in course it were Harold's fault. But nowt's worth a quarrel, my dear—NOWT. I remember Harold's grandfeyther—he were th' second of us, your grandfeyther were the eldest, and I were the youngest—I remember Harold's grandfeyther chasing his wife all over th' town wi' a besom a week after they were married.'

'With a besom!' murmured Maud, pained and forgetting to cry. 'Harold's grandfather, not mine?'

'Wi' a besom,' Dan repeated, nodding. 'They never quarrelled again—ne'er again. Th' old woman allus said after that as quarrels were for fools. And her was right.'

'I don't see Harold chasing me across Bursley with a besom,' said Maud primly. 'But what you say is quite right, you dear old uncle. Men are queer—I mean husbands. You can't argue with them. You'd much better give in—'

'And have your own way after all.'

'And perhaps Harold was—'

Harold's step could be heard in the hall.

'Oh, dear!' cried Maud. 'What shall I do?'

'I'm not feeling very well,' whispered Uncle Dan weakly. 'I have these 'ere attacks sometimes. There's only one thing as'll do me any good—brandy.'

And his head fell over one side of the chair, and he looked precisely like a corpse.

'Maud, what are you doing?' almost shouted Harold, when he came into the room.

She was putting a liqueur-glass to Uncle Dan's lips.

'Oh, Harold,' she cried, 'uncle's had an attack of some sort. I'm giving him some brandy.'

'But you mustn't give him brandy,' said Harold authoritatively to her.

'But I MUST give him brandy,' said Maud. 'He told me that brandy was the only thing to save him.'

'Nonsense, child!' Harold persisted. 'Uncle told ME all about these attacks. They're perfectly harmless so long as he doesn't have brandy. The doctors have warned him that brandy will be fatal.'

'Harold, you are absolutely mistaken. Don't you understand that uncle has only this minute told me that he MUST have brandy?'

And she again approached the glass to the pale lips of the old man. His tasselled Turkish smoking-cap had fallen to the floor, and the hemisphere of his bald head glittered under the gas.

'Maud, I forbid you!' And Harold put a hand on the glass. 'It's a matter of life and death. You must have misunderstood uncle.'

'It was you who misunderstood uncle,' said Maud. 'Of course, if you mean to prevent me by brute force—'

They both paused and glanced at Daniel, and then at each other.

'Perhaps you are right, dearest,' said Harold, in a new tone.

'No, dearest,' said Maud, also in a new tone. 'I expect you are right. I must have misunderstood.'

'No, no, Maud. Give him the brandy by all means. I've no doubt you're right.'

'But if you think I'd better not give it him—'

'But I would prefer you to give it him, dearest. It isn't likely you would be mistaken in a thing like that.'

'I would prefer to be guided by you, dearest,' said Maud.

So they went on for several minutes, each giving way to the other in the most angelic manner.

'AND MEANTIME I'M SUPPOSED TO BE DYING, AM I?' roared Uncle Dan, suddenly sitting up. 'You'd let th' old uncle peg out while you practise his precepts! A nice pair you make! I thought for see which on ye' ud' give way to th' other, but I didna' anticipate as both on ye 'ud be ready to sacrifice my life for th' sake o' domestic peace.'

'But, uncle,' they both said later, amid the universal and yet rather shamefaced peace rejoicings, 'you said nothing was worth a quarrel.'

'And I was right,' answered Dan; 'I was right. Th' Divorce Court is full o' fools as have begun married life by trying to convince the other fool, instead o' humouring him—or her. Kiss us, Maud.'

THE DEATH OF SIMON FUGE

I

It was in the train that I learnt of his death. Although a very greedy eater of literature, I can only enjoy reading when I have little time for reading. Give me three hours of absolute leisure, with nothing to do but read, and I instantly become almost incapable of the act. So it is always on railway journeys, and so it was that evening. I was in the middle of Wordsworth's Excursion; I positively gloated over it, wondering why I should have allowed a mere rumour that it was dull to prevent me from consuming it earlier in my life. But do you suppose I could continue with Wordsworth in the train? I could not. I stared out of the windows; I calculated the speed of the train by my watch; I thought of my future and my past; I drew forth my hopes, examined them, polished them, and put them back again; I forgave myself for my sins; and I dreamed of the exciting conquest of a beautiful and brilliant woman that I should one day achieve. In short, I did everything that men habitually do under such circumstances. The Gazette was lying folded on the seat beside me: one of the two London evening papers that a man of taste may peruse without humiliating himself. How appetizing a morsel, this sheet new and smooth from the press, this sheet written by an ironic, understanding, small band of men for just a few thousand persons like me, ruthlessly scornful of the big circulations and the idols of the people! If the Gazette and its sole rival ceased to appear, I do believe that my existence and many similar existences would wear a different colour. Could one dine alone in Jermyn Street or Panton Street without this fine piquant evening commentary on the gross newspapers of the morning? (Now you perceive what sort of a man I am, and you guess, rightly, that my age is between thirty and forty.) But the train had stopped at Rugby and started again, and more than half of my journey was accomplished, ere at length I picked up the Gazette, and opened it with the false calm of a drunkard who has sworn that he will not wet his lips before a certain hour. For, well knowing from experience that I should suffer acute ennui in the train, I had, when buying the Gazette at Euston, taken oath that I would not even glance at it till after Rugby; it is always the final hour of these railway journeys that is the nethermost hell.

The second thing that I saw in the Gazette (the first was of course the 'Entremets' column of wit, humour, and parody, very uneven in its excellence) was the death of Simon Fuge. There was nearly a column about it, signed with initials, and the subheading of the article ran, 'Sudden death of a great painter'. That was characteristic of the Gazette. That Simon Fuge was indeed a great painter is now admitted by most dilettantes, though denied by a few. But to the great public he was not one of the few great names. To the great public he was just a medium name. Ten to one that in speaking of him to a plain person you would feel compelled to add: 'The painter, you know,' and the plain person would respond: 'Oh yes,' falsely pretending that he was perfectly familiar with the name. Simon Fuge had many friends on the press, and it was solely owing to the loyalty of these friends in the matter of obituary notices that the great public heard more of Simon Fuge in the week after his death than it had heard of him during the thirty-five years of his life. It may be asked: Why, if he had so many and such loyal friends on the press, these friends did not take measures to establish his reputation before he died? The answer is that editors will not allow journalists to praise a living artist much in excess of the esteem in which the public holds him; they are timid. But when a misunderstood artist is dead the editors will put no limit on laudation. I am not on the press, but it happens that I know the world.

Of all the obituary notices of Simon Fuge, the Gazette's was the first. Somehow the Gazette had obtained exclusive news of the little event, and some one high up on the Gazette's staff had a very exalted notion indeed of Fuge, and must have known him personally. Fuge received his deserts as a painter in that column of print. He was compared to Sorolla y Bastida for vitality; the morbidezza of his flesh-tints was stated to be unrivalled even by—I forget the name, painting is not my speciality. The writer blandly inquired why examples of Fuge's work were to be seen in the Luxembourg, at Vienna, at Florence, at Dresden; and not, for instance, at the Tate Gallery, or in the Chantrey collection. The writer also inquired, with equal blandness, why a painter who had been on the hanging committee of the Societe Nationale des Beaux Arts at Paris should not have been found worthy to be even an A.R.A. in London. In brief, old England 'caught it', as occurred somewhere or other most nights in the columns of the Gazette. Fuge also received his deserts as a man. And the Gazette did not conceal that he had not been a man after the heart of the British public. He had been too romantically and intensely alive for that. The writer gave a little penportrait of him. It was very good, recalling his tricks of manner, his unforgettable eyes, and his amazing skill in talking about himself and really interesting everybody in himself. There was a special reference to one of Fuge's most dramatic recitals—a narration of a night spent in a boat on Ham Lake with two beautiful girls, sisters, natives of the Five Towns, where Fuge was born. Said the obituarist: 'Those two wonderful creatures who played so large a part in Simon Fuge's life.'

This death was a shock to me. It took away my ennui for the rest of the journey. I too had known Simon Fuge. That is to say, I had met him once, at a soiree, and on that single occasion, as luck had it, he had favoured the company with the very narration to which the Gazette contributor referred. I remembered well the burning brilliance of his blue-black eyes, his touching assurance that all of us were necessarily interested in his adventures, and the extremely graphic and convincing way in which he reconstituted for us the nocturnal scene on Ham Lake—the two sisters, the boat, the rustle of trees, the lights on shore, and his own difficulty in managing the oars, one of which he lost for half-an-hour and found again. It was by such details as that about the oar that, with a tint of humour, he added realism to the romantic quality of his tales. He seemed to have no reticences concerning himself. Decidedly he allowed things to be understood...! Yes, his was a romantic figure, the figure of one to whom every day, and every hour of the day, was coloured by the violence of his passion for existence. His pictures had often an unearthly beauty, but for him they were nothing but faithful renderings of what he saw.

My mind dwelt on those two beautiful sisters. Those two beautiful sisters appealed to me more than anything else in the Gazette's obituary. Surely—Simon Fuge had obviously been a man whose emotional susceptibility and virile impulsiveness must have opened the door for him to multifarious amours—but surely he had not made himself indispensable to both sisters simultaneously. Surely even he had not so far forgotten that Ham Lake was in the middle of a country called England, and not the ornamental water in the Bois de Boulogne! And yet.... The delicious possibility of ineffable indiscretions on the part of Simon Fuge monopolized my mind till the train stopped at Knype, and I descended. Nevertheless, I think I am a serious and fairly insular Englishman. It is truly astonishing how a serious person can be obsessed by trifles that, to speak mildly, do not merit sustained attention.

I wondered where Ham Lake was. I knew merely that it lay somewhere in the environs of the Five Towns. What put fuel on the fire of my interest in the private affairs of the dead painter was the slightly curious coincidence that on the evening of the news of his death I should be travelling to the Five Towns—and for the first time in my life. Here I was at Knype, which, as I had gathered from Bradshaw, and from my acquaintance Brindley, was the traffic centre of the Five Towns.

II

My knowledge of industrial districts amounted to nothing. Born in Devonshire, educated at Cambridge, and fulfilling my destiny as curator of a certain department of antiquities at the British Museum, I had never been brought into contact with the vast constructive material activities of Lancashire, Yorkshire, and Staffordshire. I had but passed through them occasionally on my way to Scotland, scorning their necessary grime with the perhaps too facile disdain of the clean-faced southerner, who is apt to forget that coal cannot walk up unaided out of the mine, and that the basin in which he washes his beautiful purity can only be manufactured amid conditions highly repellent. Well, my impressions of the platform of Knype station were unfavourable. There was dirt in the air; I could feel it at once on my skin. And the scene was shabby, undignified, and rude. I use the word 'rude' in all its senses. What I saw was a pushing, exclamatory, ill-dressed, determined crowd, each member of which was bent on the realization of his own desires by the least ceremonious means. If an item of this throng wished to get past me, he made me instantly aware of his wish by abruptly changing my position in infinite space; it was not possible to misconstrue his meaning. So much crude force and naked will-to-live I had not before set eyes on. In truth, I felt myself to be a very brittle, delicate bit of intellectual machinery in the midst of all these physical manifestations. Yet I am a tallish man, and these potters appeared to me to be undersized, and somewhat thin too! But what elbows!

263

What glaring egoistic eyes! What terrible decisiveness in action!

'Now then, get in if ye're going!' said a red-haired porter to me curtly.

'I'm not going. I've just got out,' I replied.

'Well, then, why dunna' ye stand out o' th' wee and let them get in as wants to?'

Unable to offer a coherent answer to this crushing demand, I stood out of the way. In the light of further knowledge I now surmise that that porter was a very friendly and sociable porter. But at the moment I really believed that, taking me for the least admirable and necessary of God's creatures, he meant to convey his opinion to me for my own good. I glanced up at the lighted windows of the train, and saw the composed, careless faces of haughty persons who were going direct from London to Manchester, and to whom the Five Towns was nothing but a delay. I envied them. I wanted to return to the shelter of the train. When it left, I fancied that my last link with civilization was broken. Then another train puffed in, and it was simply taken by assault in a fraction of time, to an incomprehensible bawling of friendly sociable porters. Season-ticket holders at Finsbury Park think they know how to possess themselves of a train; they are deceived. So this is where Simon Fuge came from (I reflected)! The devil it is (I reflected)! I tried to conceive what the invaders of the train would exclaim if confronted by one of Simon Fuge's pictures. I could imagine only one word, and that a monosyllable, that would meet the case of their sentiments. And his dalliance, his tangential nocturnal deviations in gondolas with exquisite twin odalisques! There did not seem to be much room for amorous elegance in the lives of these invaders. And his death! What would they say of his death? Upon my soul, as I stood on that dirty platform, in a milieu of advertisements of soap, boots, and aperients, I began to believe that Simon Fuge never had lived, that he was a mere illusion of his friends and his small public. All that I saw around me was a violent negation of Simon Fuge, that entity of rare, fine, exotic sensibilities, that perfectly mad gourmet of sensations, that exotic seer of beauty.

I caught sight of my acquaintance and host, Mr Robert Brindley, coming towards me on the platform. Hitherto I had only met him in London, when, as chairman of the committee of management of the Wedgwood Institution and School of Art at Bursley, he had called on me at the British Museum for advice as to loan exhibits. He was then dressed like a self-respecting tourist. Now, although an architect by profession, he appeared to be anxious to be mistaken for a sporting squire. He wore very baggy knickerbockers, and leggings, and a cap. This raiment was apparently the agreed uniform of the easy classes in the Five Towns; for in the crowd I had noticed several such consciously superior figures among the artisans. Mr Brindley, like most of the people in the station, had a slightly pinched and chilled air, as though that morning he had by inadvertence omitted to don those garments which are not seen. He also, like most of the people there, but not to the same extent, had a somewhat suspicious and narrowly shrewd regard, as who should say: 'If any person thinks he can get the better of me by a trick, let him try—that's all.' But the moment his eye encountered mine, this expression vanished from his face, and he gave me a candid smile.

'I hope you're well,' he said gravely, squeezing my hand in a sort of vice that he carried at the end of his right arm.

I reassured him.

'Oh, I'm all right,' he said, in response to the expression of my hopes.

It was a relief to me to see him. He took charge of me. I felt, as it were, safe in his arms. I perceived that, unaided and unprotected, I should never have succeeded in reaching Bursley from Knype.

A whistle sounded.

'Better get in,' he suggested; and then in a tone of absolute command: 'Give me your bag.'

I obeyed. He opened the door of a first-class carriage.

'I'm travelling second,' I explained.

'Never mind. Get in.'

In his tones was a kindly exasperation.

I got in; he followed. The train moved.

'Ah!' breathed Mr Brindley, blowing out much air and falling like a sack of coal into a corner seat. He was a thin man, aged about thirty, with brown eyes, and a short blonde beard.

Conversation was at first difficult. Personally I am not a bubbling fount of gay nothings when I find myself alone with a comparative stranger. My drawbridge goes up as if by magic, my postern is closed, and I peer cautiously through the narrow slits of my turret to estimate the chances of peril. Nor was Mr Brindley offensively affable. However, we struggled into a kind of chatter. I had come to the Five Towns, on behalf of the British Museum, to inspect and appraise, with a view to purchase by the nation, some huge slip-decorated dishes, excessively curious according to photographs, which had been discovered in the cellars of the Conservative Club at Bursley. Having shared in the negotiations for my visit, Mr Brindley had invited me to spend the night at his house. We were able to talk about all this. And when we had talked about all this we were able to talk about the singular scenery of coal dust, potsherds, flame and steam, through which the train wound its way. It was squalid ugliness, but it was squalid ugliness on a scale so vast and overpowering that it became sublime. Great furnaces gleamed red in the twilight, and their fires were reflected in horrible black canals; processions of heavy vapour drifted in all directions across the sky, over what acres of mean and miserable brown architecture! The air was alive with the most extraordinary, weird, gigantic sounds. I do not think the Five Towns will ever be described: Dante lived too soon. As for the erratic and exquisite genius, Simon Fuge, and his odalisques reclining on silken cushions on the enchanted bosom of a lake—I could no longer conjure them up even faintly in my mind.

'I suppose you know Simon Fuge is dead?' I remarked, in a pause.

'No! Is he?' said Mr Brindley, with interest. 'Is it in the paper?'

He did not seem to be quite sure that it would be in the paper.

'Here it is,' said I, and I passed him the Gazette.

'Ha!' he exclaimed explosively. This 'Ha!' was entirely different from his 'Ah!' Something shot across his eyes, something incredibly rapid—too rapid for a wink; yet it could only be called a wink. It was the most subtle transmission of the beyond-speech that I have ever known any man accomplish, and it endeared Mr Brindley to me. But I knew not its significance.

'What do they think of Fuge down here?' I asked.

'I don't expect they think of him,' said my host.

He pulled a pouch and a packet of cigarette papers from his pocket.

'Have one of mine,' I suggested, hastily producing my case.

He did not even glance at its contents.

'No, thanks,' he said curtly.

I named my brand.

'My dear sir,' he said, with a return to his kindly exasperation, 'no cigarette that is not fresh made can be called a cigarette.' I stood corrected. 'You may pay as much as you like, but you can never buy cigarettes as good as I can make out of an ounce of fresh B.D.V. tobacco. Can you roll one?' I had to admit that I could not, I who in Bloomsbury was accepted as an authority on cigarettes as well as on porcelain. 'I'll roll you one, and you shall try it.'

He did so.

I gathered from his solemnity that cigarettes counted in the life of Mr Brindley. He could not take cigarettes other than seriously. The worst of it was that he was quite right. The cigarette which he constructed for me out of his wretched B.D.V. tobacco was adorable, and I have made my own cigarettes ever since. You will find B.D.V. tobacco all over the haunts frequented by us of the Museum now-a-days, solely owing to the expertise of Mr Brindley. A terribly capable and positive man! He KNEW, and he knew that he knew.

He said nothing further as to Simon Fuge. Apparently he had forgotten the decease.

'Do you often see the Gazette?' I asked, perhaps in the hope of attracting him back to Fuge.

'No,' he said; 'the musical criticism is too rotten.'

Involuntarily I bridled. It was startling, and it was not agreeable, to have one's favourite organ so abruptly condemned by a provincial architect in knickerbockers and a cap, in the midst of all that industrial ugliness. What could the Five Towns know about art? Yet here was this fellow condemning the Gazette on artistic grounds. I offered no defence, because he was right—again. But I did not like it.

'Do you ever see the Manchester Guardian?' he questioned, carrying the war into my camp.

'No,' I said.

'Pity!' he ejaculated.

'I've often heard that it's a very good paper,' I said politely.

'It isn't a very good paper,' he laid me low. 'It's the best paper in the world. Try it for a month—it gets to Euston at half-past eight—and then tell me what you think.'

I saw that I must pull myself together. I had glided into the Five Towns in a mood of gentle, wise condescension. I saw that it would be as well, for my own honour and safety, to put on another mood as quickly as possible, otherwise I might be left for dead on the field. Certainly the fellow was provincial, curt, even brutal in his despisal of diplomacy. Certainly he exaggerated the importance of cigarettes in the great secular scheme of evolution. But he was a man; he was a very tonic dose. I thought it would be safer to assume that he knew everything, and that the British Museum knew very little. Yet at the British Museum he had been quite different, quite deferential and rather timid. Still, I liked him. I liked his eyes.

The train stopped at an incredible station situated in the centre of a rolling desert whose surface consisted of broken pots and cinders. I expect no one to believe this.

'Here we are,' said he blithely. 'No, give me the bag. Porter!'

His summons to the solitary porter was like a clap of thunder.

III

He lived in a low, blackish-crimson heavy-browed house at the corner of a street along which electric cars were continually thundering. There was a thin cream of mud on the pavements and about two inches of mud in the roadway, rich, nourishing mud like Indian ink half-mixed. The prospect of carrying a pound or so of that unique mud into a civilized house affrighted me, but Mr Brindley opened his door with his latchkey and entered the abode as unconcernedly as if some fair repentent had cleansed his feet with her tresses.

'Don't worry too much about the dirt,' he said. 'You're in Bursley.'

The house seemed much larger inside than out. A gas-jet burnt in the hall, and sombre portieres gave large mysterious hints of rooms. I could hear, in the distance, the noise of frizzling over a fire, and of a child crying. Then a tall, straight, wellmade, energetic woman appeared like a conjuring trick from behind a portiere.

'How do you do, Mr Loring?' she greeted me, smiling. 'So glad to meet you.'

'My wife,' Mr Brindley explained gravely.

'Now, I may as well tell you now, Bob,' said she, still smiling at me. 'Bobbie's got a sore throat and it may be mumps; the chimney's been on fire and we're going to be summoned; and you owe me sixpence.'

'Why do I owe you sixpence?'

'Because Annie's had her baby and it's a girl.'

'That's all right. Supper ready?'

'Supper is waiting for you.'

She laughed. 'Whenever I have anything to tell my husband, I always tell him at ONCE!' she said. 'No matter who's there.' She pronounced 'once' with a wholehearted enthusiasm for its vowel sound that I have never heard equalled elsewhere, and also with a very magnified 'w' at the beginning of it. Often when I hear the word 'once' pronounced in less downright parts of the world, I remember how they pronounce it in the Five Towns, and there rises up before me a complete picture of the district, its atmosphere, its spirit.

Mr Brindley led me to a large bathroom that had a faint odour of warm linen. In addition to a lot of assorted white babyclothes there were millions of towels in that bathroom. He turned on a tap and the place was instantly full of steam from a jet of boiling water.

'Now, then,' he said, 'you can start.'

As he showed no intention of leaving me, I did start. 'Mind you don't scald yourself,' he warned me, 'that water's HOT.' While I was washing, he prepared to wash. I suddenly felt as if I had been intimate with him and his wife for about ten years.

'So this is Bursley!' I murmured, taking my mouth out of a towel.

'Bosley, we call it,' he said. 'Do you know the limerick—"There was a young woman of Bosley"?'

'No.'

He intoned the local limerick. It was excellently good; not meet for a mixed company, but a genuine delight to the true amateur. One good limerick deserves another. It happened that I knew a number of the unprinted Rossetti limericks, precious things, not at all easy to get at. I detailed them to Mr Brindley, and I do not exaggerate when I say that I impressed him. I recovered all the ground I had lost upon cigarettes and newspapers. He appreciated those limericks with a juster taste than I should have expected. So, afterwards, did his friends. My belief is that I am to this day known and revered in Bursley, not as Loring the porcelain expert from the British Museum, but as the man who first, as it were, brought the good news of the Rossetti limericks from Ghent to Aix.

'Now, Bob,' an amicable voice shrieked femininely up from the ground-floor, 'am I to send the soup to the bathroom or are you coming down?'

A limerick will make a man forget even his dinner.

Mr Brindley performed once more with his eyes that something that was, not a wink, but a wink unutterably refined and spiritualized. This time I comprehended its import. Its import was to the effect that women are women.

We descended, Mr Brindley still in his knickerbockers.

'This way,' he said, drawing aside a portiere. Mrs Brindley, as we entered the room, was trotting a male infant round and round a table charged with everything digestible and indigestible. She handed the child, who was in its nightdress, to a maid.

'Say good night to father.'

'Good ni', faver,' the interesting creature piped.

'By-bye, sonny,' said the father, stooping to tickle. 'I suppose,' he added, when maid and infant had gone, 'if one's going to have mumps, they may as well all have it together.'

'Oh, of course,' the mother agreed cheerfully. 'I shall stick them all into a room.'

'How many children have you?' I inquired with polite curiosity.

'Three,' she said; 'that's the eldest that you've seen.'

What chiefly struck me about Mrs Brindley was her serene air of capableness, of having a self-confidence which experience had richly justified. I could see that she must be an extremely sensible mother. And yet she had quite another aspect too—how shall I explain it?—as though she had only had children in her spare time.

We sat down. The room was lighted by four candles, on the table. I am rather short-sighted, and so I did not immediately notice that there were low book-cases all round the walls. Why the presence of these book-cases should have caused me a certain astonishment I do not know, but it did. I thought of Knype station, and the scenery, and then the other little station, and the desert of pots and cinders, and the mud in the road and on the pavement and in the hall, and the baby-linen in the bathroom, and three children all down with mumps, and Mr Brindley's cap and knickerbockers and cigarettes; and somehow the books—I soon saw there were at least a thousand of them, and not circulating-library books, either, but BOOKS— well, they administered a little shock to me.

To Mr Brindley's right hand was a bottle of Bass and a corkscrew.

'Beer!' he exclaimed, with solemn ecstasy, with an ecstasy gross and luscious. And, drawing the cork, he poured out a glass, with fine skill in the management of froth, and pushed it towards me.

'No, thanks,' I said.

'No beer!' he murmured, with benevolent, puzzled disdain. 'Whisky?'

'No, thanks,' I said. 'Water.'

'*I* know what Mr Loring would like,' said Mrs Brindley, jumping up. 'I KNOW what Mr Loring would like.' She opened a cupboard and came back to the table with a bottle, which she planted in front of me. 'Wouldn't you, Mr Loring?'

It was a bottle of mercurey, a wine which has given me many dreadful dawns, but which I have never known how to refuse.

'I should,' I admitted; 'but it's very bad for me.'

'Nonsense!' said she. She looked at her husband in triumph.

'Beer!' repeated Mr Brindley with undiminished ecstasy, and drank about two-thirds of a glass at one try. Then he wiped the froth from his moustache. 'Ah!' he breathed low and soft. 'Beer!'

They called the meal supper. The term is inadequate. No term that I can think of would be adequate. Of its kind the thing was perfect. Mrs Brindley knew that it was perfect. Mr Brindley also knew that it was perfect. There were prawns in aspic. I don't know why I should single out that dish, except that it seemed strange to me to have crossed the desert of pots and cinders in order to encounter prawns in aspic. Mr Brindley ate more cold roast beef than I had ever seen any man eat before, and more pickled walnuts. It is true that the cold roast beef transcended all the cold roast beef of my experience. Mrs Brindley regaled herself largely on trifle, which Mr Brindley would not approach, preferring a most glorious Stilton cheese. I lost touch, temporarily, with the intellectual life. It was Mr Brindley who recalled me to it.

'Jane,' he said. (This was at the beef and pickles stage.)

No answer.

'Jane!'

Mrs Brindley turned to me. 'My name is not Jane,' she said, laughing, and making a moue simultaneously. 'He only calls me that to annoy me. I told him I wouldn't answer to it, and I won't. He thinks I shall give in because we've got "company"! But I won't treat you as "company", Mr Loring, and I shall expect you to take my side. What dreadful weather we're having, aren't we?'

'Dreadful!' I joined in the game.

'Jane!'

'Did you have a comfortable journey down?'

'Yes, thank you.'

'Well, then, Mary!' Mr Brindley yielded.

'Thank you very much, Mr Loring, for your kind assistance,' said his wife. 'Yes, dearest?'

Mr Brindley glanced at me over his second glass of beer.

'If those confounded kids are going to have mumps,' he addressed his words apparently into the interior of the glass, 'it probably means the doctor, and the doctor means money, and I shan't be able to afford the Hortulus Animoe.'

I opened my ears.

'My husband goes stark staring mad sometimes,' said Mrs Brindley to me. 'It lasts for a week or so, and pretty nearly lands us in the workhouse. This time it's the Hortulus Animoe. Do you know what it is? I don't.'

'No,' I said, and the prestige of the British Museum trembled. Then I had a vague recollection. 'There's an illuminated manuscript of that name in the Imperial Library of Vienna, isn't there?'

'You've got it in one,' said Mr Brindley. 'Wife, pass those walnuts.'

'You aren't by any chance buying it?' I laughed.

'No,' he said. 'A Johnny at Utrecht is issuing a facsimile of it, with all the hundred odd miniatures in colour. It will be the finest thing in reproduction ever done. Only seventy-five copies for England.'

'How much?' I asked.

'Well,' said he, with a preliminary look at his wife,'thirty-three pounds.'

'Thirty-three POUNDS!' she screamed. 'You never told me.'

'My wife never will understand,' said Mr Brindley, 'that complete confidence between two human beings is impossible.'

'I shall go out as a milliner, that's all,' Mrs Brindley returned. 'Remember, the Dictionary of National Biography isn't paid for yet.'

'I'm glad I forgot that, otherwise I shouldn't have ordered the Hortulus.'

'You've not ORDERED it?'

'Yes, I have. It'll be here tomorrow—at least the first part will.'

Mrs Brindley affected to fall back dying in her chair.

'Quite mad!' she complained to me. 'Quite mad. It's a hopeless case.'

But obviously she was very proud of the incurable lunatic.

'But you're a book-collector!' I exclaimed, so struck by these feats of extravagance in a modest house that I did not conceal my amazement.

'Did you think I collected postage-stamps?' the husband retorted. 'No, I'm not a book-collector, but our doctor is. He has a few books, if you like. Still, I wouldn't swop him; he's much too fond of fashionable novels.'

'You know you're always up his place,' said the wife; 'and I wonder what I should do if it wasn't for the doctor's novels!' The doctor was evidently a favourite of hers.

'I'm not always up at his place,' the husband contradicted. 'You know perfectly well I never go there before midnight. And HE knows perfectly well that I only go because he has the best whisky in the town. By the way, I wonder whether he knows that Simon Fuge is dead. He's got one of his etchings. I'll go up.'

'Who's Simon Fuge?' asked Mrs Brindley.

'Don't you remember old Fuge that kept the Blue Bell at Cauldon?'

'What? Simple Simon?'

'Yes. Well, his son.'

'Oh! I remember. He ran away from home once, didn't he, and his mother had a port-wine stain on her left cheek? Oh, of course. I remember him perfectly. He came down to the Five Towns some years ago for his aunt's funeral. So he's dead. Who told you?'

'Mr Loring.'

'Did you know him?' she glanced at me.

'I scarcely knew him,' said I. 'I saw it in the paper.'

'What, the Signal?'

'The Signal's the local rag,' Mr Brindley interpolated. 'No. It's in the Gazette.'

'The Birmingham Gazette?'

'No, bright creature—the Gazette,' said Mr Brindley.

'Oh!' She seemed puzzled.

'Didn't you know he was a painter?' the husband condescendingly catechized.

'I knew he used to teach at the Hanbridge School of Art,' said Mrs Brindley stoutly. 'Mother wouldn't let me go there because of that. Then he got the sack.'

'Poor defenceless thing! How old were you?'

'Seventeen, I expect.'

'I'm much obliged to your mother.'

'Where did he die?' Mrs Brindley demanded.

'At San Remo,' I answered. 'Seems queer him dying at San Remo in September, doesn't it?'

'Why?'

'San Remo is a winter place. No one ever goes there before December.'

'Oh, is it?' the lady murmured negligently. 'Then that would be just like Simon Fuge. *I* was never afraid of him,' she added, in a defiant tone, and with a delicious inconsequence that choked her husband in the midst of a draught of beer.

'You can laugh,' she said sturdily.

At that moment there was heard a series of loud explosive sounds in the street. They continued for a few seconds apparently just outside the dining-room window. Then they stopped, and the noise of the bumping electric cars resumed its sway over the ear.

'That's Oliver!' said Mr Brindley, looking at his watch. 'He must have come from Manchester in an hour and a half. He's a terror.'

'Glass! Quick!' Mrs Brindley exclaimed. She sprang to the sideboard, and seized a tumbler, which Mr Brindley filled from a second bottle of Bass. When the door of the room opened she was standing close to it, laughing, with the full, frothing glass in her hand.

A tall, thin man, rather younger than Mr Brindley and his wife, entered. He wore a long dust-coat and leggings, and he carried a motorist's cap in a great hand. No one spoke; but little puffs of laughter escaped all Mrs Brindley's efforts to imprison her mirth. Then the visitor took the glass with a magnificent broad smile, and said, in a rich and heavy Midland voice—

'Here's to moy wife's husband!'

And drained the nectar.

'Feel better now, don't you?' Mrs Brindley inquired.

'Aye, Mrs Bob, I do!' was the reply. 'How do, Bob?'

'How do?' responded my host laconically. And then with gravity: 'Mr Loring—Mr Oliver Colclough—thinks he knows something about music.'

'Glad to meet you, sir,' said Mr Colclough, shaking hands with me. He had a most attractively candid smile, but he was so long and lanky that he seemed to pervade the room like an omnipresence.

274

'Sit down and have a bit of cheese, Oliver,' said Mrs Brindley, as she herself sat down.

'No, thanks, Mrs Bob. I must be getting towards home.'

He leaned on her chair.

'Trifle, then?'

'No, thanks.'

'Machine going all right?'

'Like oil. Never stopped th' engine once.'

'Did you get the Sinfonia Domestica, Ol?' Mr Brindley inquired.

'Didn't I say as I should get it, Bob?'

'You SAID you would.'

'Well, I've got it.'

'In Manchester?'

'Of course.'

Mr Brindley's face shone with desire and Mr Oliver Colclough's face shone with triumph.

'Where is it?'

'In the hall.'

'My hall?'

'Aye!'

'We'll play it, Ol.'

'No, really, Bob! I can't stop now. I promised the wife—'

'We'll PLAY it, Ol! You'd no business to make promises. Besides, suppose you'd had a puncture!'

'I expect you've heard Strauss's Sinfonia Domestica, Mr Loring, up in the village?' Mr Colclough addressed me. He had surrendered to the stronger will.

'In London?' I said. 'No. But I've heard of it.'

'Bob and I heard it in Manchester last week, and we thought it 'ud be a bit of a lark to buy the arrangement for pianoforte duet.'

'Come and listen to it,' said Mr Brindley. 'That is, if nobody wants any more beer.'

IV

The drawing-room was about twice as large as the dining-room, and it contained about four times as much furniture. Once again there were books all round the walls. A grand piano, covered with music, stood in a corner, and behind was a cabinet full of bound music.

Mr Brindley, seated on one corner of the bench in front of the piano, cut the leaves of the Sinfonia Domestica.

'It's the devil!' he observed.

'Aye, lad!' agreed Mr Colclough, standing over him. 'It's difficult.'

'Come on,' said Mr. Brindley, when he had finished cutting.

'Better take your dust-coat off, hadn't you?' Mrs Brindley suggested to the friend. She and I were side by side on a sofa at the other end of the room.

'I may as well,' Mr Colclough admitted, and threw the long garment on to a chair. 'Look here, Bob, my hands are stiff with steering.'

'Don't find fault with your tools,' said Mr Brindley; 'and sit down. No, my boy, I'm going to play the top part. Shove along.'

'I want to play the top part because it's easiest,' Mr Colclough grumbled.

'How often have I told you the top part is never easiest? Who do you suppose is going to keep this symphony together—you or me?'

'Sorry I spoke.'

They arranged themselves on the bench, and Mr Brindley turned up the lower corners of every alternate leaf of the music.

'Now,' said he. 'Ready?'

'Let her zip,' said Mr Colclough.

They began to play. And then the door opened, and a servant, whose white apron was starched as stiff as cardboard, came in carrying a tray of coffee and unholy liqueurs, which she deposited with a rattle on a small table near the hostess.

'Curse!' muttered Mr Brindley, and stopped.

'Life's very complex, ain't it, Bob?' Mr Colclough murmured.

'Aye, lad.' The host glanced round to make sure that the rattling servant had entirely gone. 'Now start again.'

'Wait a minute, wait a minute!' cried Mrs Brindley excitedly. 'I'm just pouring out Mr Loring's coffee. There!' As she handed me the cup she whispered, 'We daren't talk. It's more than our place is worth.'

The performance of the symphony proceeded. To me, who am not a performer, it sounded excessively brilliant and incomprehensible. Mr Colclough stretched his right hand to turn over the page, and fumbled it. Another stoppage.

'Damn you, Ol!' Mr Brindley exploded. 'I wish you wouldn't make yourself so confoundedly busy. Leave the turning to me. It takes a great artist to turn over, and you're only a blooming chauffeur. We'll begin again.'

'Sackcloth!' Mr Colclough whispered.

I could not estimate the length of the symphony; but my impression was one of extreme length. Halfway through it the players both took their coats off. There was no other surcease.

'What dost think of it, Bob?' asked Mr Colclough in the weird silence that reigned after they had finished. They were standing up and putting on their coats and wiping their faces.

'I think what I thought before,' said Mr Brindley. 'It's childish.'

'It isn't childish,' the other protested. 'It's ugly, but it isn't childish.'

'It's childishly clever,' Mr Brindley modified his description. He did not ask my opinion.

'Coffee's cold,' said Mrs Brindley.

'I don't want any coffee. Give me some Chartreuse, please. Have a drop o' green, Ol?'

'A split soda 'ud be more in my line. Besides, I'm just going to have my supper. Never mind, I'll have a drop, missis, and chance it. I've never tried Chartreuse as an appetizer.'

At this point commenced a sanguinary conflict of wills to settle whether or not I also should indulge in green Chartreuse. I was defeated. Besides the Chartreuse, I accepted a cigar. Never before or since have I been such a buck.

'I must hook it,' said Mr Colclough, picking up his dust-coat.

'Not yet you don't,' said Mr Brindley. 'I've got to get the taste of that infernal Strauss out of my mouth. We'll play the first movement of the G minor? La-la-la—la-la-la—la-la-la-ta.' He whistled a phrase.

Mr Colclough obediently sat down again to the piano.

The Mozart was like an idyll after a farcical melodrama. They played it with an astounding delicacy. Through the latter half of the movement I could hear Mr Brindley breathing regularly and heavily through his nose, exactly as though he were being hypnotized. I had a tickling sensation in the small of my back, a sure sign of emotion in me. The atmosphere was changed.

'What a heavenly thing!' I exclaimed enthusiastically, when they had finished.

Mr Brindley looked at me sharply, and just nodded in silence. Well, good night, Ol.'

'I say,' said Mr Colclough; 'if you've nothing doing later on, bring Mr Loring round to my place. Will you come, Mr Loring? Do! Us'll have a drink.'

These Five Towns people certainly had a simple, sincere way of offering hospitality that was quite irresistible. One could see that hospitality was among their chief and keenest pleasures.

We all went to the front door to see Mr Colclough depart homewards in his automobile. The two great acetylene head-lights sent long glaring shafts of light down the side street. Mr Colclough, throwing the score of the Sinfonia Domestica into the tonneau of the immense car, put on a pair of gloves and began to circulate round the machine, tapping here, screwing there, as chauffeurs will. Then he bent down in front to start the engine.

'By the way, Ol,' Mr Brindley shouted from the doorway, 'it seems Simon Fuge is dead.'

We could see the man's stooping form between the two head-lights. He turned his head towards the house.

'Who the dagger is Simon Fuge?' he inquired. 'There's about five thousand Fuges in th' Five Towns.'

'Oh! I thought you knew him.'

'I might, and I mightn't. It's not one o' them Fuge brothers saggar-makers at Longshaw, is it?'

'No, It's—'

Mr Colclough had succeeded in starting his engine, and the air was rent with gun-shots. He jumped lightly into the driver's seat.

'Well, see you later,' he cried, and was off, persuading the enormous beast under him to describe a semicircle in the narrow street backing, forcing forward, and backing again, to the accompaniment of the continuous fusillade. At length he got away, drew up within two feet of an electric tram that slid bumping down the main street, and vanished round the corner. A little ragged boy passed, crying, 'Signal, extra,' and Mr Brindley hailed him.

'What IS Mr Colclough?' I asked in the drawing-room.

'Manufacturer—sanitary ware,' said Mr Brindley. 'He's got one of the best businesses in Hanbridge. I wish I'd half his income. Never buys a book, you know.'

'He seems to play the piano very well.'

'Well, as to that, he doesn't what you may call PLAY, but he's the best sight-reader in this district, bar me. I never met his equal. When you come across any one who can read a thing like the Domestic Symphony right off and never miss his place, you might send me a telegram. Colclough's got a Steinway. Wish I had.'

Mrs Brindley had been looking through the Signal.

'I don't see anything about Simon Fuge here,' said she.

'Oh, nonsense!' said her husband. 'Buchanan's sure to have got something in about it. Let's look.'

He received the paper from his wife, but failed to discover in it a word concerning the death of Simon Fuge.

'Dashed if I don't ring Buchanan up and ask him what he means! Here's a paper with an absolute monopoly in the district, and brings in about five thousand a year clear to somebody, and it doesn't give the news! There never is anything but advertisements and sporting results in the blessed thing.'

He rushed to his telephone, which was in the hall. Or rather, he did not rush; he went extremely quickly, with aggressive footsteps that seemed to symbolize just retribution. We could hear him at the telephone.

'Hello! No. Yes. Is that you, Buchanan? Well, I want Mr Buchanan. Is that you, Buchanan? Yes, I'm all right. What in thunder do you mean by having nothing in tonight about Simon Fuge's death? Eh? Yes, the Gazette. Well, I suppose you aren't Scotch for nothing. Why the devil couldn't you stop in Scotland and edit papers there?' Then a laugh. 'I see. Yes. What did you think of those cigars? Oh! See you at the dinner. Ta-ta.' A final ring.

'The real truth is, he wanted some advice as to the tone of his obituary notice,' said Mr Brindley, coming back into the drawing-room. 'He's got it, seemingly. He says he's writing it now, for tomorrow. He didn't put in the mere news of the death, because it was exclusive to the Gazette, and he's been having some difficulty with the Gazette lately. As he says, tomorrow afternoon will be quite soon enough for the Five Towns. It isn't as if Simon Fuge was a cricket match. So now you see how the wheels go round, Mr Loring.'

He sat down to the piano and began to play softly the Castle motive from the Nibelung's Ring. He kept repeating it in different keys.

'What about the mumps, wife?' he asked Mrs Brindley, who had been out of the room and now returned.

'Oh! I don't think it is mumps,' she replied. 'They're all asleep.'

'Good!' he murmured, still playing the Castle motive.

'Talking of Simon Fuge,' I said determined to satisfy my curiosity, 'who WERE the two sisters?'

'What two sisters?'

'That he spent the night in the boat with, on Ilam Lake.'

'Was that in the Gazette? I didn't read all the article.'

He changed abruptly into the Sword motive, which he gave with a violent flourish, and then he left the piano. 'I do beg you not to wake my children,' said his wife.

'Your children must get used to my piano,' said he. 'Now, then, what about these two sisters?'

I pulled the Gazette from my pocket and handed it to him. He read aloud the passage describing the magic night on the lake.

'*I* don't know who they were,' he said. 'Probably something tasty from the Hanbridge Empire.'

We both observed a faint, amused smile on the face of Mrs Brindley, the smile of a woman who has suddenly discovered in her brain a piece of knowledge rare and piquant.

'I can guess who they were,' she said. 'In fact, I'm sure.'

'Who?'

'Annie Brett and—you know who.'

'What, down at the Tiger?'

'Certainly. Hush!' Mrs Brindley ran to the door and, opening it, listened. The faint, fretful cry of a child reached us. 'There! You've done it! I told you you would!'

She disappeared. Mr Brindley whistled.

'And who is Annie Brett?' I inquired.

'Look here,' said he, with a peculiar inflection. 'Would you like to see her?'

'I should,' I said with decision.

'Well, come on, then. We'll go down to the Tiger and have a drop of something.'

'And the other sister?' I asked.

'The other sister is Mrs Oliver Colclough,' he answered. 'Curious, ain't it?'

Again there was that swift, scarcely perceptible phenomenon in his eyes.

V

We stood at the corner of the side-street and the main road, and down the main road a vast, white rectangular cube of bright light came plunging—its head rising and dipping—at express speed, and with a formidable roar. Mr Brindley imperiously raised his stick; the extraordinary box of light stopped as if by a miracle, and we jumped into it, having splashed through mud, and it plunged off again—bump, bump, bump—into the town of Bursley. As Mr Brindley passed into the interior of the car, he said laconically to two men who were smoking on the platform—

'How do, Jim? How do, Jo?'

And they responded laconically—

'How do, Bob?'

'How do, Bob?'

We sat down. Mr Brindley pointed to the condition of the floor.

'Cheerful, isn't it?' he observed to me, shouting above the din of vibrating glass.

Our fellow-passengers were few and unromantic, perhaps half-a-dozen altogether on the long, shiny, yellow seats of the car, each apparently lost in gloomy reverie.

'It's the advertisements and notices in these cars that are the joy of the super-man like you and me,' shouted Mr Brindley. 'Look there, "Passengers are requested not to spit on the floor." Simply an encouragement to lie on the seats and spit on the ceiling, isn't it? "Wear only Noble's wonderful boots." Suppose we did! Unless they came well up above the waist we should be prosecuted. But there's no sense of humour in this district.'

Greengrocers' shops and public-houses were now flying past the windows of the car. It began to climb a hill, and then halted.

'Here we are!' ejaculated Mr Brindley.

And he was out of the car almost before I had risen.

We strolled along a quiet street, and came to a large building with many large lighted windows, evidently some result of public effort.

'What's that place?' I demanded.

'That's the Wedgwood Institution.'

'Oh! So that's the Wedgwood Institution, is it?'

'Yes. Commonly called the Wedgwood. Museum, reading-room, public library—dirtiest books in the world, I mean physically—art school, science school. I've never explained to you why I'm chairman of the Management Committee, have I? Well, it's because the Institution is meant to foster the arts, and I happen to know nothing about 'em. I needn't tell you that architecture, literature, and music are not arts within the meaning of the act. Not much! Like to come in and see the museum for a minute? You'll have to see it in your official capacity tomorrow.'

We crossed the road, and entered an imposing portico. Just as we did so a thick stream of slouching men began to descend the steps, like a waterfall of treacle. Mr Brindley they appeared to see, but evidently I made no impression on their retinas. They bore down the steps, hands deep in pockets, sweeping over me like Fate. Even when I bounced off one of them to a lower step, he showed by no sign that the fact of my existence had reached his consciousness—simply bore irresistibly downwards. The crowd was absolutely silent. At last I gained the entrance hall.

'It's closing-time for the reading room,' said Mr Brindley.

'I'm glad I survived it,' I said.

'The truth is,' said he, 'that people who can't look after themselves don't flourish in these latitudes. But you'll be acclimatized by tomorrow. See that?'

He pointed to an alabaster tablet on which was engraved a record of the historical certainty that Mr Gladstone opened the Institution in 1868, also an extract from the speech which he delivered on that occasion.

'What do you THINK of Gladstone down here?' I demanded.

'In my official capacity I think that these deathless words are the last utterance of wisdom on the subject of the influence of the liberal arts on life. And I should advise you, in your official capacity, to think the same, unless you happen to have a fancy for having your teeth knocked down your throat.'

'I see,' I said, not sure how to take him.

'Lest you should go away with the idea that you have been visiting a rude and barbaric people, I'd better explain that that was a joke. As a matter of fact, we're rather enlightened here. The only man who stands a chance of getting his teeth knocked down his throat here is the ingenious person who started the celebrated legend of the man-and-dog fight at Hanbridge. It's a long time ago, a very long time ago; but his grey hairs won't save him from horrible tortures if we catch him. We don't mind being called immoral, we're above a bit flattered when London newspapers come out with shocking details of debauchery in the Five Towns, but we pride ourselves on our manners. I say, Aked!' His voice rose commandingly, threateningly, to an old bent, spectacled man who was ascending a broad white staircase in front of us.

'Sir!' The man turned.

'Don't turn the lights out yet in the museum.'

'No, sir! Are you coming up?' The accents were slow and tremulous.

'Yes. I have a gentleman here from the British Museum who wants to look round.'

The oldish man came deliberately down the steps, and approached us. Then his gaze, beginning at my waist, gradually rose to my hat.

'From the British Museum?' he drawled. 'I'm sure I'm very glad to meet you, sir. I'm sure it's a very great honour.'

He held out a wrinkled hand, which I shook.

'Mr Aked,' said Mr Brindley, by way of introduction. 'Been caretaker here for pretty near forty years.'

'Ever since it opened, sir,' said Aked.

We went up the white stone stairway, rather a grandiose construction for a little industrial town. It divided itself into doubling curving flights at the first landing, and its walls were covered with pictures and designs. The museum itself, a series of three communicating rooms, was about as large as a pocket-handkerchief.

'Quite small,' I said.

I gave my impression candidly, because I had already judged Mr Brindley to be the rare and precious individual who is worthy of the high honour of frankness.

'Do you think so?' he demanded quickly. I had shocked him, that was clear. His tone was unmistakable; it indicated an instinctive, involuntary protest. But he recovered himself in a flash. 'That's jealousy,' he laughed. 'All you British Museum people are the same.' Then he added, with an unsuccessful attempt to convince me that he meant what he was saying: 'Of course it is small. It's nothing, simply nothing.'

Yes, I had unwittingly found the joint in the armour of this extraordinary Midland personage. With all his irony, with all his violent humour, with all his just and unprejudiced perceptions, he had a tenderness for the Institution of which he was the dictator. He loved it. He could laugh like a god at everything in the Five Towns except this one thing. He would try to force himself to regard even this with the same lofty detachment, but he could not do it naturally.

I stopped at a case of Wedgwood ware, marked 'Perkins Collection.'

'By Jove!' I exclaimed, pointing to a vase. 'What a body!'

He was enchanted by my enthusiasm.

'Funny you should have hit on that,' said he. 'Old Daddy Perkins always called it his ewe-lamb.'

Thus spoken, the name of the greatest authority on Wedgwood ware that Europe has ever known curiously impressed me.

'I suppose you knew him?' I questioned.

'Considering that I was one of the pall-bearers at his funeral, and caught the champion cold of my life!'

'What sort of a man was he?'

'Outside Wedgwood ware he wasn't any sort of a man. He was that scourge of society, a philanthropist,' said Mr Brindley. 'He was an upright citizen, and two thousand people followed him to his grave. I'm an upright citizen, but I have no hope that two thousand people will follow me to my grave.'

'You never know what may happen,' I observed, smiling.

'No.' He shook his head. 'If you undermine the moral character of your fellow-citizens by a long course of unbridled miscellaneous philanthropy, you can have a funeral procession as long as you like, at the rate of about forty shillings a foot. But you'll never touch the great heart of the enlightened public of these boroughs in any other way. Do you imagine anyone cared a twopenny damn for Perkins's Wedgwood ware?'

'It's like that everywhere,' I said.

'I suppose it is,' he assented unwillingly.

Who can tell what was passing in the breast of Mr Brindley? I could not. At least I could not tell with any precision. I could only gather, vaguely, that what he considered the wrong-headedness, the blindness, the lack of true perception, of his public was beginning to produce in his individuality a faint trace of permanent soreness. I regretted it. And I showed my sympathy with him by asking questions about the design and construction of the museum (a late addition to the Institution), of which I happened to know that he had been the architect.

He at once became interested and interesting. Although he perhaps insisted a little too much on the difficulties which occur when original talent encounters stupidity, he did, as he walked me up and down, contrive to convey to me a notion of the creative processes of the architect in a way that was in my experience entirely novel. He was impressing me anew, and I was wondering whether he was unique of his kind or whether there existed regiments of him in this strange parcel of England.

'Now, you see this girder,' he said, looking upwards.

That's surely something of Fuge's, isn't it?' I asked, indicating a small picture in a corner, after he had finished his explanation of the functions of the girder.

As on the walls of the staircase and corridors, so on the walls here, there were many paintings, drawings, and engravings. And of course the best were here in the museum. The least uninteresting items of the collection were, speaking generally, reproductions in monotint of celebrated works, and a few second—or third-rate loan pictures from South Kensington. Aside from such matters I had noticed nothing but the usual local trivialities, gifts from one citizen or another, travel-jottings of some art-master, careful daubs of apt students without a sense of humour. The aspect of the place was exactly the customary aspect of the small provincial museum, as I have seen it in half-a-hundred towns that are not among 'the great towns'. It had the terrible trite 'museum' aspect, the aspect that brings woe and desolation to the heart of the stoutest visitor, and which seems to form part of the purgatorio of Bank-holidays, wide mouths, and stiff clothes. The movement for opening museums on Sundays is the most natural movement that could be conceived. For if ever a resort was invented and fore-ordained to chime with the true spirit of the British sabbath, that resort is the average museum. I ought to know. I do know.

But there was the incomparable Wedgwood ware, and there was the little picture by Simon Fuge. I am not going to lose my sense of perspective concerning Simon Fuge. He was not the greatest painter that ever lived, or even of his time. He had, I am ready to believe, very grave limitations. But he was a painter by himself, as all fine painters are. He had his own vision. He was Unique. He was

285

exclusively preoccupied with the beauty and the romance of the authentic. The little picture showed all this. It was a painting, unfinished, of a girl standing at a door and evidently hesitating whether to open the door or not: a very young girl, very thin, with long legs in black stockings, and short, white, untidy frock; thin bare arms; the head thrown on one side, and the hands raised, and one foot raised, in a wonderful childish gesture—the gesture of an undecided fox-terrier. The face was an infant's face, utterly innocent; and yet Simon Fuge had somehow caught in that face a glimpse of all the future of the woman that the girl was to be, he had displayed with exquisite insolence the essential naughtiness of his vision of things. The thing was not much more than a sketch; it was a happy accident, perhaps, in some day's work of Simon Fuge's. But it was genius. When once you had yielded to it, there was no other picture in the room. It killed everything else. But, wherever it had found itself, nothing could have killed IT. Its success was undeniable, indestructible. And it glowed sombrely there on the wall, a few splashes of colour on a morsel of canvas, and it was Simon Fuge's unconscious, proud challenge to the Five Towns. It WAS Simon Fuge, at any rate all of Simon Fuge that was worth having, masterful, imperishable. And not merely was it his challenge, it was his scorn, his aristocratic disdain, his positive assurance that in the battle between them he had annihilated the Five Towns. It hung there in the very midst thereof, calmly and contemptuously waiting for the acknowledgement of his victory.

'Which?' said Mr Brindley.

That one.'

'Yes, I fancy it is,' he negligently agreed. 'Yes, it is.'

'It's not signed,' I remarked.

'It ought to be,' said Mr Brindley; then laughed, 'Too late now!'

'How did it get here?'

'Don't know. Oh! I think Mr Perkins won it in a raffle at a bazaar, and then hung it here. He did as he liked here, you know.'

I was just going to become vocal in its praise, when Mr Brindley said—

'That thing under it is a photograph of a drinking-cup for which one of our pupils won a national scholarship last year!'

Mr Aked appeared in the distance.

'I fancy the old boy wants to be off to bed,' Mr Brindley whispered kindly.

286

So we left the Wedgwood Institution. I began to talk to Mr Brindley about music. The barbaric attitude of the Five Towns towards great music was the theme of some very lively animadversions on his part.

VI

The Tiger was very conveniently close to the Wedgwood Institution. The Tiger had a 'yard', one of those long, shapeless expanses of the planet, partly paved with uneven cobbles and partly unsophisticated planet, without which no provincial hotel can call itself respectable. We came into it from the hinterland through a wooden doorway in a brick wall. Far off I could see one light burning. We were in the centre of Bursley, the gold angel of its Town Hall rose handsomely over the roof of the hotel in the diffused moonlight, but we might have been in the purlieus of some dubious establishment on the confines of a great seaport, where anything may happen. The yard was so deserted, so mysterious, so shut in, so silent, that, really, infamous characters ought to have rushed out at us from the obscurity of shadows, and felled us to the earth with no other attendant phenomenon than a low groan. There are places where one seems to feel how thin and brittle is the crust of law and order. Why one should be conscious of this in the precincts of such a house as the Tiger, which I was given to understand is as respectable as the parish church, I do not know. But I have experienced a similar feeling in the yards of other provincial hotels that were also as correct as parish churches. We passed a dim fly, with its shafts slanting forlornly to the ground, and a wheelbarrow. Both looked as though they had been abandoned for ever. Then we came to the lamp, which illuminated a door, and on the door was a notice: 'Private Bar. Billiards.'

I am not a frequenter of convivial haunts. I should not dare to penetrate alone into a private bar; when I do enter a private bar it is invariably under the august protection of an habitue, and it is invariably with the idea that at last I am going to see life. Often has this illusion been shattered, but each time it perfectly renewed itself. So I followed the bold Mr Brindley into the private bar of the Tiger.

It was a small and low room. I instinctively stooped, though there was no necessity for me to stoop. The bar had no peculiarity. It can be described in a breath: Three perpendicular planes. Back plane,

287

bottles arranged exactly like books on bookshelves; middle plane, the upper halves of two women dressed in tight black; front plane, a counter, dotted with glasses, and having strange areas of zinc. Reckon all that as the stage, and the rest of the room as auditorium. But the stage of a private bar is more mysterious than the stage of a theatre. You are closer to it, and yet it is far less approachable. The edge of the counter is more sacred than the footlights. Impossible to imagine yourself leaping over it. Impossible to imagine yourself in that cloistered place behind it. Impossible to imagine how the priestesses got themselves into that place, or that they ever leave it. They are always there; they are always the same. You may go into a theatre when it is empty and dark; but did you ever go into a private bar that was empty and dark? A private bar is as eternal as the hills, as changeless as the monomania of a madman, as mysterious as sorcery. Always the same order of bottles, the same tinkling, the same popping, the same time-tables, and the same realistic pictures of frothing champagne on the walls, the same advertisements on the same ash-trays on the counter, the same odour that wipes your face like a towel the instant you enter; and the same smiles, the same gestures, the same black fabric stretched to tension over the same impressive mammiferous phenomena of the same inexplicable creatures who apparently never eat and never sleep, imprisoned for life in the hallowed and mystic hollow between the bottles and the zinc.

In a tone almost inaudible in its discretion, Mr Brindley let fall to me as he went in—

This is she.'

She was not quite the ordinary barmaid. Nor, as I learnt afterwards, was she considered to be the ordinary barmaid. She was something midway in importance between the wife of the new proprietor and the younger woman who stood beside her in the cloister talking to a being that resembled a commercial traveller. It was the younger woman who was the ordinary barmaid; she had bright hair, and the bright vacant stupidity which, in my narrow experience, barmaids so often catch like an infectious disease from their clients. But Annie Brett was different. I can best explain how she impressed me by saying that she had the mien of a handsome married woman of forty with a coquettish and superficially emotional past, but also with a daughter who is just going into long skirts. I have known one or two such women. They have been beautiful; they are still handsome at a distance of twelve feet. They are rather effusive; they think they know life, when as a fact their instinctive repugnance for any form of truth has prevented them from acquiring even the rudiments of the knowledge of life. They are secretly preoccupied by the burning question of obesity. They flatter, and they will pay any price for flattery. They are never sincere, not even with themselves; they never, during the whole of their existence, utter a sincere word, even in anger they coldly exaggerate. They are always frothing at the mouth with ecstasy. They adore everything, including God; go to church carrying a prayer-book and hymn-book in separate volumes, and absolutely fawn on the daughter. They are stylish—and impenetrable. But there is something about them very wistful and tragic.

In another social stratum, Miss Annie Brett might have been such a woman. Without doubt nature had intended her for the role. She was just a little ample, with broad shoulders and a large head and a lot of dark chestnut hair; a large mouth, and large teeth. She had earrings, a brooch, and several rings; also a neat originality of cuffs that would not have been permitted to an ordinary barmaid. As for her face, there were crow's-feet, and a mole (which had selected with infinite skill a site on her chin), and a general degeneracy of complexion; but it was an effective face. The little thing of twenty-three or so by her side had all the cruel advantages of youth and was not ugly; but she was 'killed' by Annie Brett. Miss Brett had a maternal bust. Indeed, something of the maternal resided in all of her that was visible above the zinc. She must have been about forty; that is to say, apparently older than the late Simon Fuge. Nevertheless, I could conceive her, even now, speciously picturesque in a boat at midnight on a moonstruck water. Had she been on the stage she would have been looking forward to ingenue parts for another five years yet—such was her durable sort of effectiveness. Yes, she indubitably belonged to the ornamental half of the universe.

'So this is one of them!' I said to myself.

I tried to be philosophical; but at heart I was profoundly disappointed. I did not know what I had expected; but I had not expected THAT. I was well aware that a thing written always takes on a quality which does not justly appertain to it. I had not expected, therefore, to see an odalisque, a houri, an ideal toy or the remains of an ideal toy; I had not expected any kind of obvious brilliancy, nor a subtle charm that would haunt my memory for evermore. On the other hand, I had not expected the banal, the perfectly commonplace. And I think that Miss Annie Brett was the most banal person that it has pleased Fate to send into my life. I knew that instantly. She was a condemnation of Simon Fuge. SHE, one of the 'wonderful creatures who had played so large a part' in the career of Simon Fuge! Sapristi! Still, she WAS one of the wonderful creatures, etc. She HAD floated o'er the bosom of the lake with a great artist. She HAD received his homage. She HAD stirred his feelings. She HAD shared with him the magic of the night. I might decry her as I would; she had known how to cast a spell over him— she and the other one! Something there in her which had captured him and, seemingly, held him captive.

'Good-EVENING, Mr Brindley,' she expanded. 'You're quite a stranger.' And she embraced me also in the largeness of her welcome.

'It just happens,' said Mr Brindley, 'that I was here last night. But you weren't.'

'Were you now!' she exclaimed, as though learning a novel fact of the most passionate interest. The truth is, I had to leave the bar to Miss Slaney last night. Mrs Moorcroft was ill—and the baby only six weeks old, you know—and I wouldn't leave her. No, I wouldn't.'

It was plain that in Miss Annie Brett's opinion there was only one really capable intelligence in the Tiger. This glimpse of her capability, this out-leaping of the latent maternal in her, completely destroyed for the moment my vision of her afloat on the bosom of the lake.

'I see,' said Mr Brindley kindly. Then he turned to me with characteristic abruptness. 'Well, give it a name, Mr Loring.'

Such is my simplicity that I did not immediately comprehend his meaning. For a fraction of a second I thought of the baby. Then I perceived that he was merely employing one of the sacred phrases, sanctified by centuries of usage, of the private bar. I had already drunk mercurey, green Chartreuse, and coffee. I had a violent desire not to drink anything more. I knew my deplorable tomorrows. Still, I would have drunk hot milk, cold water, soda water, or tea. Why should I not have had what I did not object to having? Herein lies another mystery of the private bar. One could surely order tea or milk or soda water from a woman who left everything to tend a mother with a six-weeks-old baby! But no. One could not. As Miss

Annie Brett smiled at me pointedly, and rubbed her ringed hands, and kept on smiling with her terrific mechanical effusiveness, I lost all my self control; I would have resigned myself to a hundred horrible tomorrows under the omnipotent, inexplicable influence of the private bar. I ejaculated, as though to the manner born—

'Irish.'

It proved to have been rather clever of me, showing as it did a due regard for convention combined with a pretty idiosyncrasy. Mr Brindley was clearly taken aback. The idea struck him as a new one. He reflected, and then enthusiastically exclaimed—

'Dashed if I don't have Irish too!'

And Miss Brett, delighted by this unexpected note of Irish in the long, long symphony of Scotch, charged our glasses with gusto. I sipped, death in my heart, and rakishness in my face and gesture. Mr Brindley raised his glass respectfully to Miss Annie Brett, and I did the same. Those two were evidently good friends.

She led the conversation with hard, accustomed ease. When I say 'hard' I do not in the least mean unsympathetic. But her sympathetic quality was toughened by excessive usage, like the hand of a charwoman. She spoke of the vagaries of the Town Hall clock, the health of Mr Brindley's children, the price of coal, the incidence of the annual wakes, the bankruptcy of the draper next door, and her own sciatica, all in the same tone of metallic tender solicitude. Mr Brindley adopted an entirely serious attitude towards her. If I had met him there and nowhere else I should have taken him for a dignified mediocrity, little better than a fool, but with just enough discretion not to give himself away. I said nothing. I was shy. I always am shy in a bar. Out of her cold, cold roving eye Miss Brett watched me, trying to add me up and not succeeding. She must have perceived, however, that I was not like a fish in water.

There was a pause in the talk, due, I think, to Miss Annie Brett's preoccupation with what was going on between Miss Slaney, the ordinary barmaid, and her commercial traveller. The commercial traveller, if he was one, was reading something from a newspaper to Miss Slaney in an indistinct murmur, and with laughter in his voice.

'By the way,' said Mr Brindley, 'you used to know Simon Fuge, didn't you?'

'Old Simon Fuge!' said Miss Brett. 'Yes; after the brewery company took the Blue Bell at Cauldon over from him, I used to be there. He would come in sometimes. Such a nice queer old man!'

'I mean the son,' said Mr Brindley.

'Oh yes,' she answered. 'I knew young Mr Simon too.' A slight hesitation, and then: 'Of course!' Another hesitation. 'Why?'

'Nothing,' said Mr Brindley. 'Only he's dead.'

'You don't mean to say he's dead?' she exclaimed.

'Day before yesterday, in Italy,' said Mr Brindley ruthlessly.

Miss Annie Brett's manner certainly changed. It seemed almost to become natural and unecstatic.

'I suppose it will be in the papers?' she ventured.

'It's in the London paper.'

'Well I never!' she muttered.

'A long time, I should think, since he was in this part of the world,' said Mr Brindley. 'When did YOU last see him?'

He was exceedingly skilful, I considered.

She put the back of her hand over her mouth, and bending her head slightly and lowering her eyelids, gazed reflectively at the counter.

'It was once when a lot of us went to Ilam,' she answered quietly. 'The St Luke's lot, YOU know.'

'Oh!' cried Mr Brindley, apparently startled. 'The St Luke's lot?'

'Yes.'

'How came he to go with you?'

'He didn't go with us. He was there—stopping there, I suppose.'

'Why, I believe I remember hearing something about that,' said Mr Brindley cunningly. 'Didn't he take you out in a boat?'

A very faint dark crimson spread over the face of Miss Annie Brett. It could not be called a blush, but it was as like a blush as was possible to her. The phenomenon, as I could see from his eyes, gave Mr Brindley another shock.

'Yes,' she replied. 'Sally was there as well.'

Then a silence, during which the commercial traveller could be heard reading from the newspaper.

'When was that?' gently asked Mr Brindley.

'Don't ask ME when it was, Mr Brindley,' she answered nervously. 'It's ever so long ago. What did he die of?'

'Don't know.'

Miss Annie Brett opened her mouth to speak, and did not speak. There were tears in her reddened eyes. I felt very awkward, and I think that Mr Brindley also felt awkward. But I was glad. Those moist eyes caused me a thrill. There was after all some humanity in

Miss Annie Brett. Yes, she had after all floated on the bosom of the lake with Simon Fuge. The least romantic of persons, she had yet felt romance. If she had touched Simon Fuge, Simon Fuge had touched her. She had memories. Once she had lived. I pictured her younger. I sought in her face the soft remains of youthfulness. I invented languishing poses for her in the boat. My imagination was equal to the task of seeing her as Simon Fuge saw her. I did so see her. I recalled Simon Fuge's excited description of the long night in the boat, and I could reconstitute the night from end to end. And there the identical creature stood before me, the creature who had set fire to Simon Fuge, one of the 'wonderful creatures' of the Gazette, ageing, hardened, banal, but momentarily restored to the empire of romance by those unshed, glittering tears. As an experience it was worth having.

She could not speak, and we did not. I heard the commercial traveller reading: '"The motion was therefore carried by twenty-five votes to nineteen, and the Countess of Chell promised that the whole question of the employment of barmaids should be raised at the next meeting of the B.W.T.S." There! what do you think of that?'

Miss Annie Brett moved quickly towards the commercial traveller.

'Il tell you what *I* think of it,' she said, with ecstatic resentment. 'I think it's just shameful! Why should the Countess of Chell want to rob a lot of respectable young ladies of their living? I can tell you they're just as respectable as the Countess of Chell is—yes, and perhaps more, by all accounts. I think people do well to call her "Interfering Iris". When she's robbed them of their living, what does she expect them to do? Is she going to keep them? Then what does she expect them to do?'

The commercial traveller was inept enough to offer a jocular reply, and then he found himself involved in the morass of 'the whole question'. He, and we also, were obliged to hear in immense detail Miss Annie Brett's complete notions of the movement for the abolition of barmaids. The subject was heavy on her mind, and she lifted it off. Simon Fuge was relinquished; he dropped like a stone into the pool of forgetfulness. And yet, strange as it seems, she was assuredly not sincere in the expression of her views on the question of barmaids. She held no real views. She merely persuaded herself that she held them. When the commercial traveller, who was devoid of sense, pointed out that it was not proposed to rob anybody of a livelihood, and that existent barmaids would be permitted to continue to grace the counters of their adoption, she grew frostily vicious. The commercial traveller decided to retire and play billiards. Mr Brindley and I in our turn departed. I was extremely disappointed by this sequel.

'Ah!' breathed Mr Brindley when we were outside, in front of the Town Hall. 'She was quite right about that clock.'

After that we turned silently into a long illuminated street which rose gently. The boxes of light were flashing up and down it, but otherwise it seemed to be quite deserted. Mr Brindley filled a pipe and lit it as he walked. The way in which that man kept the match alight in a fresh breeze made me envious. I could conceive myself rivalling his exploits in cigarette-making, the purchase of rare books, the interpretation of music, even (for a wager) the drinking of beer, but I knew that I should never be able to keep a match alight in a breeze. He threw the match into the mud, and in the mud it continued miraculously to burn with a large flame, as though still under his magic dominion. There are some things that baffle the reasoning faculty. 'Well,' I said, 'she must have been a pretty woman once.'

'"Pretty," by God!' he replied, 'she was beautiful. She was considered the finest piece in Hanbridge at one time. And let me tell you we're supposed to have more than our share of good looks in the Five Towns.'

'What—the women, you mean?'

'Yes.'

'And she never married?'

'No.'

'Nor—anything?'

'Oh no,' he said carelessly.

'But you don't mean to tell me she's never—' I was just going to exclaim, but I did not, I said: 'And it's her sister who is Mrs Colclough?'

'Yes.' He seemed to be either meditative or disinclined to talk. However, my friends have sometimes hinted to me that when my curiosity is really aroused, I am capable of indiscretions.

'So one sister rattles about in an expensive motor-car, and the other serves behind a bar!' I observed.

He glanced at me.

'I expect it's a bit difficult for you to understand,' he answered; 'but you must remember you're in a democratic district. You told me once you knew Exeter. Well, this isn't a cathedral town. It's about a century in front of any cathedral town in the world. Why, my good sir, there's practically no such thing as class distinction here. Both my grandfathers were working potters. Colclough's father was a joiner who finished up as a builder. If Colclough makes money and chooses to go to Paris and get the best motor-car he can, why in Hades shouldn't his wife ride in it? If he is fond of music and can play like the devil, that isn't his sister-in-law's fault, is it? His wife was a dressmaker, at least she was a dressmaker's assistant. If she suits him, what's the matter?'

'But I never suggested—'

'Excuse me,' he stopped me, speaking with careful and slightly exaggerated calmness, 'I think you did. If the difference in the situations of the two sisters didn't strike you as very extraordinary, what did you mean?'

'And isn't it extraordinary?' I demanded.

'It wouldn't be considered so in any reasonable society,' he insisted. 'The fact is, my good sir, you haven't yet quite got rid of Exeter. I do believe this place will do you good. Why, damn it! Colclough didn't marry both sisters. You think he might keep the other sister? Well, he might. But suppose his wife had half-a-dozen sisters, should he keep them all! I can tell you we're just like the rest of the world, we find no difficulty whatever in spending all the money we make. I dare say Colclough would be ready enough to keep his sister-in-law. I've never asked him. But I'm perfectly certain that his sister-in-law wouldn't be kept. Not much! You don't know these women down here, my good sir. She's earned her living at one thing or another all her life, and I reckon she'll keep on earning it till she drops. She is, without exception, the most exasperating female I ever came across, and that's saying something; but I will give her THAT credit: she's mighty independent.'

'How exasperating?' I asked, surprised to hear this from him.

'*I* don't know. But she is. If she was my wife I should kill her one night. Don't you know what I mean?'

'Yes, I quite agree with you,' I said. 'But you seemed to be awfully good friends with her.'

'No use being anything else. No woman that it ever pleased Providence to construct is going to frighten me away from the draught Burton that you can get at the Tiger. Besides, she can't help it. She was born like that.'

'She TALKS quite ordinarily,' I remarked.

'Oh! It isn't what she says, particularly. It's HER. Either you like her or you don't like her. Now Colclough thinks she's all right. In fact, he admires her.'

'There's one thing,' I said, 'she jolly nearly cried tonight.'

'Purely mechanical!' said Mr Brindley with cruel curtness.

What seemed to me singular was that the relations which had existed between Miss Annie Brett and Simon Fuge appeared to have no interest whatever for Mr Brindley. He had not even referred to them.

'You were just beginning to draw her out,' I ventured.

'No,' he replied; 'I thought I'd just see what she'd say. No one ever did draw that woman out.'

I had completely lost my vision of her in the boat, but somehow that declaration of his, 'no one ever did draw that woman out', partially restored the vision to me. It seemed to invest her with agreeable mystery.

'And the other sister—Mrs Colclough?' I questioned.

'I'm taking you to see her as fast as I can,' he answered. His tone implied further: 'I've just humoured one of your whims, now for the other.'

'But tell me something about her.'

'She's the best bridge-player—woman, that is—in Bursley. But she will only play every other night for fear the habit should get hold of her. There you've got her.'

'Younger than Miss Brett?'

'Younger,' said Mr Brindley. 'She isn't the same sort of person, is she?'

'She is not,' said Mr Brindley. And his tone implied: 'Thank God for it!'

Very soon afterwards, at the top of a hill, he drew me into the garden of a large house which stood back from the road.

It was quite a different sort of house from Mr Brindley's. One felt that immediately on entering the hall, which was extensive. There was far more money and considerably less taste at large in that house than in the other. I noticed carved furniture that must have been bought with a coarse and a generous hand; and on the walls a diptych by Marcus Stone portraying the course of true love clingingly draped. It was just like Exeter or Onslow Square. But the middle-aged servant who received us struck at once the same note as had sounded so agreeably at Mr Brindley's. She seemed positively glad to see us; our arrival seemed to afford her a peculiar and violent pleasure, as though the hospitality which we were about to accept was in some degree hers too. She robbed us of our hats with ecstasy.

Then Mr Colclough appeared.

'Delighted you've come, Mr Loring!' he said, shaking my hand again. He said it with fervour. He obviously was delighted. The exercise of hospitality was clearly the chief joy of his life; at least, if he had a greater it must have been something where keenness was excessive beyond the point of pleasure, as some joys are. 'How do, Bob? Your missis has just come.' He was still in his motoring clothes.

Mr Brindley, observing my gaze transiently on the Marcus Stones, said: 'I know what you're looking for; you're looking for "Saul's Soul's Awakening". We don't keep it in the window; you'll see it inside.'

'Bob's always rotting me about my pictures,' Mr Colclough smiled indulgently. He seemed big enough to eat his friend, and his rich, heavy voice rolled like thunder about the hall. 'Come along in, will you?'

'Half-a-second, Ol,' Mr Brindley called in a conspiratorial tone, and, turning to me: Tell him THE Limerick. You know.'

'The one about the hayrick?'

Mr Brindley nodded.

There were three heads close together for a space of twenty seconds or so, and then a fearful explosion happened—the unique, tremendous laughter of Mr Colclough, which went off like a charge of melinite and staggered the furniture.

'Now, now!' a feminine voice protested from an unseen interior.

I was taken to the drawing-room, an immense apartment with an immense piano black as midnight in it. At the further end two women were seated close together in conversation, and I distinctly heard the name 'Fuge'. One of them was Mrs Brindley, in a hat. The other, a very big and stout woman, in an elaborate crimson garment that resembled a teagown, rose and came to meet me with extended hand.

'My wife—Mr Loring,' said Mr Oliver Colclough.

'So glad to meet you,' she said, beaming on me with all her husband's pleasure. 'Come and sit between Mrs Brindley and me, near the window, and keep us in order. Don't you find it very close? There are at least a hundred cats in the garden.'

One instantly perceived that ceremonial stiffness could not exist in the same atmosphere with Mrs Oliver Colclough. During the whole time I spent in her house there was never the slightest pause in the conversation. Mrs Oliver Colclough prevented nobody from talking, but she would gladly use up every odd remnant of time that was not employed by others. No scrap was too small for her.

'So this is the other one!' I said to myself. 'Well, give me this one!'

Certainly there was a resemblance between the two, in the general formation of the face, and the shape of the shoulders; but it is astonishing that two sisters can differ as these did, with a profound and vital difference. In Mrs Colclough there was no coquetterie, no trace of that more-than-half-suspicious challenge to a man that one feels always in the type to which her sister belonged. The notorious battle of the sexes was assuredly carried on by her in a spirit of frank muscular gaiety—she could, I am sure, do her share of fighting. Put her in a boat on the bosom of the lake under starlight, and she would not by a gesture, a tone, a glance, convey mysterious nothings to you, a male. She would not be subtly changed by the sensuous influences of the situation; she would always be the same plump and earthly piece of candour. Even if she were in love with you, she would not convey mysterious nothings in such circumstances. If she were in love with you she would most clearly convey unmysterious and solid somethings. I was convinced that the contributing cause to the presence of the late Simon Fuge in the boat on Ilam Lake on the historic night was Annie the superior barmaid, and not Sally of the automobile. But Mrs Colclough, if not beautiful, was a very agreeable creation. Her amplitude gave at first sight an exaggerated impression of her age; but this departed after more careful inspection. She could not have been more than thirty. She was very dark, with plenteous and untidy black hair, thick eyebrows, and a slight moustache. Her eyes were very vivacious, and her gestures, despite that bulk, quick and graceful. She was happy; her ideals were satisfied; it was probably happiness that had made her stout. Her massiveness was apparently no grief to her; she had fallen into the carelessness which is too often the pitfall of women who, being stout, are content.

'How do, missis?' Mr Brindley greeted her, and to his wife, 'How do, missis? But, look here, bright star, this gadding about is all very well, but what about those precious kids of yours? None of 'em dead yet, I hope.'

'Don't be silly, Bob.'

'I've been over to your house,' Mrs Colclough put in. 'Of course it isn't mumps. The child's as right as rain. So I brought Mary back with me.'

'Well,' said Mr Brindley, 'for a woman who's never had any children your knowledge of children beggars description. What you aren't sure you know about them isn't knowledge. However—'

'Listen,' Mrs Colclough replied, with a delightful throwingdown of the glove. 'I'll bet you a level sovereign that child hasn't got the mumps. So there! And Oliver will guarantee to pay you.'

'Aye!' said Mr Colclough; 'I'll back my wife any day.'

'Don't bet, Bob,' Mrs Brindley enjoined her husband excitedly in her high treble.

'I won't,' said Mr Brindley.

'Now let's sit down.' Mrs Colclough addressed me with particular, confidential grace.

We three exactly filled the sofa. I have often sat between two women, but never with such calm, unreserved, unapprehensive comfortableness as I experienced between Mrs Colclough and Mrs Brindley. It was just as if I had known them for years.

'You'll make a mess of that, Ol,' said Mr Brindley.

The other two men were at some distance, in front of a table, on which were two champagne bottles and five glasses, and a plate of cakes. 'Well,' I said to myself, 'I'm not going to have any champagne, anyhow. Mercurey! Green Chartreuse! Irish whisky! And then champagne! And a morning's hard work tomorrow! No!'

Plop! A cork flew up and bounced against the ceiling.

Mr Colclough carefully emptied the bottle into the glasses, of which Mr Brindley seized two and advanced with one in either hand for the women. It was the host who offered a glass to me.

'No, thanks very much, I really can't,' I said in a very firm tone.

My tone was so firm that it startled them. They glanced at each other with alarmed eyes, like simple people confronted by an inexplicable phenomenon. 'But look here, mister!' said Mr Colclough, pained, 'we've got this out specially for you. You don't suppose this is our usual tipple, do you?'

I yielded. I could do no less than sacrifice myself to their enchanting instinctive kindness of heart. 'I shall be dead tomorrow,' I said to myself; 'but I shall have lived tonight.' They were relieved, but I saw that I had given them a shock from which they could not instantaneously recover. Therefore I began with a long pull, to reassure them.

'Mrs Brindley has been telling me that Simon Fuge is dead,' said Mrs Colclough brightly, as though Mrs Brindley had been telling her that the price of mutton had gone down.

I perceived that those two had been talking over Simon Fuge, after their fashion.

'Oh yes,' I responded.

'Have you got that newspaper in your pocket, Mr Loring?' asked Mrs Brindley.

I had.

'No,' I said, feeling in my pockets; 'I must have left it at your house.'

'Well,' she said, 'that's strange. I looked for it to show it to Mrs Colclough, but I couldn't see it.'

This was not surprising. I did not want Mrs Colclough to read the journalistic obituary until she had given me her own obituary of Fuge.

'It must be somewhere about,' I said; and to Mrs Colclough: 'I suppose you knew him pretty well?'

'Oh, bless you, no! I only met him once.'

'At Ilam?'

'Yes. What are you going to do, Oliver?'

Her husband was opening the piano.

'Bob and I are just going to have another smack at that Brahms.'

'You don't expect us to listen, do you?'

'I expect you to do what pleases you, missis,' said he. 'I should be a bigger fool than I am if I expected anything else.' Then he smiled at me. 'No! Just go on talking. Ol and I'll drown you easy enough. Quite short! Back in five minutes.'

The two men placed each his wine-glass on the space on the piano designed for a candlestick, lighted cigars, and sat down to play.

'Yes,' Mrs Colclough resumed, in a lower, more confidential tone, to the accompaniment of the music. 'You see, there was a whole party of us there, and Mr Fuge was staying at the hotel, and of course he knew several of us.'

'And he took you out in a boat?'

'Me and Annie? Yes. Just as it was getting dusk he came up to us and asked us if we'd go for a row. Eh, I can hear him asking us now! I asked him if he could row, and he was quite angry. So we went, to quieten him.' She paused, and then laughed.

'Sally!' Mrs Brindley protested. 'You know he's dead!'

'Yes.' She admitted the rightness of the protest. 'But I can't help it. I was just thinking how he got his feet wet in pushing the boat off.' She laughed again. 'When we were safely off, someone came down to the shore and shouted to Mr Fuge to bring the boat back. You know his quick way of talking.' (Here she began to imitate Fuge.) '"I've quarrelled with the man this boat belongs to. Awful feud! Fact is, I'm in a hostile country here!" And a lot more like that. It seemed he had quarrelled with everybody in Ilam. He wasn't sure if the landlord of the hotel would let him sleep there again. He told us all about all his quarrels, until he dropped one of the oars. I shall never forget how funny he looked in the moonlight when he dropped the oar. "There, that's your fault!" he said. "You make me talk too much about myself, and I get excited." He kept striking matches to look for the oar, and turning the boat round and round with the other oar. "Last match!" he said. "We shall never see land tonight." Then he found the oar again. He considered we were saved. Then he began to tell us about his aunt. "You know I'd no business to be here. I came down from London for my aunt's funeral, and here I am in a boat at night with two pretty girls!" He said the funeral had taught him one thing, and that was that black neckties were the only possible sort of necktie. He said the greatest worry of his life had always been neckties; but he wouldn't have to worry any more, and so his aunt hadn't died for nothing. I assure you he kept on talking about neckties. I assure you, Mr Loring, I went to sleep—at least I dozed—and when I woke up he was still talking about neckties. But then his feet began to get cold. I suppose it was because they were wet. The way he grumbled about his feet being cold! I remember he turned his coat collar up. He wanted to get on shore and walk, but he'd taken us a long way up the lake by that time, and he saw we were absolutely lost. So he put the oars in the boat and stood up and stamped his feet. It might have upset the boat.'

'How did it end?' I inquired.

'Well, Annie and I caught the train, but only just. You see it was a special train, so they kept it for us, otherwise we should have been in a nice fix.'

'So you have special trains in these parts?'

'Why, of course! It was the annual outing of the teachers of St Luke's Sunday School and their friends, you see. So we had a special train.'

At this point the duettists came to the end of a movement, and Mr Brindley leaned over to us from his stool, glass in hand.

'The railway company practically owns Ilam,' he explained, 'and so they run it for all they're worth. They made the lake, to feed the canals, when they bought the canals from the canal company. It's an artificial lake, and the railway runs alongside it. A very good scheme of the company's. They started out to make Ilam a popular resort, and they've made it a popular resort, what with special trains and things. But try to get a special train to any other place on their rotten system, and you'll soon see!'

'How big is the lake?' I asked.

'How long is it, Ol?' he demanded of Colclough. 'A couple of miles?'

'Not it! About a mile. Adagio!'

They proceeded with Brahms.

'He ran with you all the way to the station, didn't he?' Mrs Brindley suggested to Mrs Colclough.

'I should just say he did!' Mrs Colclough concurred. 'He wanted to get warm, and then he was awfully afraid lest we should miss it.'

'I thought you were on the lake practically all night!' I exclaimed.

'All night! Well, I don't know what you call all night. But I was back in Bursley before eleven o'clock, I'm sure.'

I then contrived to discover the Gazette in an unsearched pocket, and I gave it to Mrs Colclough to read. Mrs Brindley looked over her shoulder.

There was no slightest movement of depreciation on Mrs Colclough's part. She amiably smiled as she perused the GAZETTE'S version of Fuge's version of the lake episode. Here was the attitude of the woman whose soul is like crystal. It seems to me that most women would have blushed, or dissented, or simulated anger, or failed to conceal vanity. But Mrs Coclough might have been reading a fairy tale, for any emotion she displayed.

'Yes,' she said blandly; 'from the things Annie used to tell me about him sometimes, I should say that was just how he WOULD talk. They seem to have thought quite a lot of him in London, then?'

'Oh, rather!' I said. 'I suppose your sister knew him pretty well?'

'Annie? I don't know. She knew him.'

I distinctly observed a certain self-consciousness in Mrs Colclough as she made this reply. Mrs Brindley had risen and with wifely attentiveness was turning over the music page for her husband.

VIII

Soon afterwards, for me, the night began to grow fantastic; it took on the colour of a gigantic adventure. I do not suppose that either Mr Brindley or Mr Colclough, or the other person who presently arrived, regarded it as anything but a pleasant conviviality, but to a man of my constitution and habits it was an almost incredible occurrence. The other person was the book-collecting doctor. He arrived with a discreet tap on the window at midnight, to spend the evening. Mrs Brindley had gone home and Mrs Colclough had gone to bed. The book-collecting doctor refused champagne; he was, in fact, very rude to champagne in general. He had whisky. And those astonishing individuals, Messieurs Brindley and Colclough, secretly convinced of the justice of the attack on champagne, had whisky too. And that still most astonishing individual, Loring of the B.M., joined them. It was the hour of limericks. Limericks were demanded for the diversion of the doctor, and I furnished them. We then listened to the tale of the doctor's experiences that day amid the sturdy, natural-minded population of a muling village not far from Bursley. Seldom have I had such a

303

bath in the pure fluid of human nature. All sense of time was lost. I lived in an eternity. I could not suggest to my host that we should depart. I could, however, decline more whisky. And I could, given the chance, discourse with gay despair concerning the miserable wreck that I should be on the morrow in consequence of this high living. I asked them how I could be expected, in such a state, to judge delicate points of expertise in earthenware. I gave them a brief sketch of my customary evening, and left them to compare it with that evening. The doctor perceived that I was serious. He gazed at me with pity, as if to say: 'Poor frail southern organism! It ought to be in bed, with nothing inside it but tea!' What he did actually say was: 'You come round to my place, I'll soon put you right!' 'Can you stop me from having a headache tomorrow?' I eagerly asked. 'I think so,' he said with calm northern confidence.

At some later hour Mr Brindley and I 'went round'. Mr Colclough would not come. He bade me good-bye, as his wife had done, with the most extraordinary kindness, the most genuine sorrow at quitting me, the most genuine pleasure in the hope of seeing me again.

'There are three thousand books in this room!' I said to myself, as I stood in the doctor's electrically lit library.

'What price this for a dog?' Mr Brindley drew my attention to an aristocratic fox-terrier that lay on the hearth. 'Well, Titus! Is it sleepy? Well, well! How many firsts has he won, doctor?'

'Six,' said the doctor. 'I'll just fix you up, to begin with,' he turned to me.

After I had been duly fixed up ('This'll help you to sleep, and THIS'll placate your "god",' said the doctor), I saw to my intense surprise that another 'evening' was to be instantly superimposed on the 'evening' at Mr Colclough's. The doctor and Mr Brindley carefully and deliberately lighted long cigars, and sank deeply into immense arm-chairs; and so I imitated them as well as I could in my feeble southern way. We talked books. We just simply enumerated books without end, praising or damning them, and arranged authors in neat pews, like cattle in classes at an agricultural show. No pastime is more agreeable to people who have the book disease, and none more quickly fleets the hours, and none is more delightfully futile.

Ages elapsed, and suddenly, like a gun discharging, Mr Brindley said—

'We must go!'

Of all things that happened this was the most astonishing.

We did go.

'By the way, doc.,' said Mr Brindley, in the doctor's wide porch, 'I forgot to tell you that Simon Fuge is dead.'

'Is he?' said the doctor.

'Yes. You've got a couple of his etchings, haven't you?'

'No,' said the doctor. 'I had. But I sold them several months ago.'

'Oh!' said Mr Brindley negligently; 'I didn't know. Well, so long!'

We had a few hundred yards to walk down the silent, wide street, where the gas-lamps were burning with the strange, endless patience that gas-lamps have. The stillness of a provincial town at night is quite different from that of London; we might have been the only persons alive in England.

Except for a feeling of unreality, a feeling that the natural order of things had been disturbed by some necromancer, I was perfectly well the same morning at breakfast, as the doctor had predicted I should be. When I expressed to Mr Brindley my stupefaction at this happy sequel, he showed a polite but careless inability to follow my line of thought. It appeared that he was always well at breakfast, even when he did stay up 'a little later than usual'. It appeared further that he always breakfasted at a quarter to nine, and read the Manchester Guardian during the meal, to which his wife did or did not descend—according to the moods of the nursery; and that he reached his office at a quarter to ten. That morning the mood of the nursery was apparently unpropitious. He and I were alone. I begged him not to pretermit his GUARDIAN, but to examine it and give me the news. He agreed, scarcely unwilling.

'There's a paragraph in the London correspondence about Fuge,' he announced from behind the paper.

'What do they say about him?'

'Nothing particular.'

'Now I want to ask you something,' I said.

I had been thinking a good deal about the sisters and Simon Fuge. And in spite of everything that I had heard—in spite even of the facts that the lake had been dug by a railway company, and that the excursion to the lake had been an excursion of Sunday-school teachers and their friends—I was still haunted by certain notions concerning Simon Fuge and Annie Brett. Annie Brett's flush, her unshed tears; and the self-consciousness shown by Mrs Colclough when I had pointedly mentioned her sister's name in connection

305

with Simon Fuge's: these were surely indications! And then the doctor's recitals of manners in the immediate neighbourhood of Bursley went to support my theory that even in Staffordshire life was very much life.

'What?' demanded Mr Brindley.

'Was Miss Brett ever Simon Fuge's mistress?'

At that moment Mrs Brindley, miraculously fresh and smiling, entered the room.

'Wife,' said Mr Brindley, without giving her time to greet me, 'what do you think he's just asked me?'

'*I* don't know.'

'He's just asked me if Annie Brett was ever Simon Fuge's mistress.'

She sank into a chair.

'Annie BRETT?' She began to laugh gently. 'Oh! Mr Loring, you really are too funny!' She yielded to her emotions. It may be said that she laughed as they can laugh in the Five Towns. She cried. She had to wipe away the tears of laughter.

'What on earth made you think so?' she inquired, after recovery.

'I—had an idea,' I said lamely. 'He always made out that one of those two sisters was so much to him, and I knew it couldn't be Mrs Colclough.'

'Well,' she said, 'ask anybody down here, ANY-body! And see what they'll say.'

'No,' Mr Brindley put in, 'don't go about asking ANY-body. You might get yourself disliked. But you may take it it isn't true.'

'Most certainly,' his wife concurred with seriousness.

'We reckon to know something about Simon Fuge down here,' Mr Brindley added. 'Also about the famous Annie.'

'He must have flirted with her a good bit, anyhow,' I said.

'Oh, FLIRT!' ejaculated Mr Brindley.

I had a sudden dazzling vision of the great truth that the people of the Five Towns have no particular use for half-measures in any department of life. So I accepted the final judgement with meekness.

IX

I returned to London that evening, my work done, and the municipality happily flattered by my judgement of the slip-decorated dishes. Mr Brindley had found time to meet me at the midday meal, and he had left his office earlier than usual in order to help me to drink his wife's afternoon tea. About an hour later he picked up my little bag, and said that he should accompany me to the little station in the midst of the desert of cinders and broken crockery, and even see me as far as Knype, where I had to take the London express. No, there are no half-measures in the Five Towns. Mrs Brindley stood on her doorstep, with her eldest infant on her shoulders, and waved us off. The infant cried, expressing his own and his mother's grief at losing a guest. It seems as if people are born hospitable in the Five Towns.

We had not walked more than a hundred yards up the road when a motor-car thundered down upon us from the opposite direction. It was Mr Colclough's, and Mr Colclough was driving it. Mr Brindley stopped his friend with the authoritative gesture of a policeman.

'Where are you going, Ol?'

'Home, lad. Sorry you're leaving us so soon, Mr Loring.'

'You're mistaken, my boy,' said Mr Brindley. 'You're just going to run us down to Knype station, first.'

'I must look slippy, then,' said Mr Colclough.

'You can look as slippy as you like,' said Mr Brindley.

In another fifteen seconds we were in the car, and it had turned round, and was speeding towards Knype. A feverish journey! We passed electric cars every minute, and for three miles were continually twisting round the tails of ponderous, creaking, and excessively deliberate carts that dropped a trail of small coal, or huge barrels on wheels that dripped something like the finest Devonshire cream, or brewer's drays that left nothing behind them save a luscious odour of malt. It was a breathless slither over unctuous black mud through a long winding canon of brown-red houses and shops, with a glimpse here and there of a grey-green park, a canal, or a football field.

'I daredn't hurry,' said Mr Colclough, setting us down at the station. 'I was afraid of a skid.' He had not spoken during the transit.

'Don't put on side, Ol,' said Mr Brindley. 'What time did you get up this morning?'

'Eight o'clock, lad. I was at th' works at nine.'

He flew off to escape my thanks, and Mr Brindley and I went into the station. Owing to the celerity of the automobile we had half-an-hour to wait. We spent it chiefly at the bookstall. While we were there the extra-special edition of the STAFFORDSHIRE SIGNAL, affectionately termed 'the local rag' by its readers, arrived, and we watched a newsboy affix its poster to a board. The poster ran thus—

HANBRIDGE RATES LIVELY MEETING
—
KNYPE F.C. NEW CENTRE—FORWARD
—
ALL—WINNERS AND S.P.

Now, close by this poster was the poster of the DAILY TELEGRAPH, and among the items offered by the DAILY TELEGRAPH was: 'Death of Simon Fuge'. I could not forbear pointing out to Mr Brindley the difference between the two posters. A conversation ensued; and amid the rumbling of trains and the rough stir of the platform we got back again to Simon Fuge, and Mr Brindley's tone gradually grew, if not acrid, a little impatient.

'After all,' he said, 'rates are rates, especially in Hanbridge. And let me tell you that last season Knype Football Club jolly nearly got thrown out of the First League. The constitution of the team for this next season—why, damn it, it's a question of national importance! You don't understand these things. If Knype Football Club was put into the League Second Division, ten thousand homes would go into mourning. Who the devil was Simon Fuge?'

They joke with such extraordinary seriousness in the Five Towns that one is somehow bound to pretend that they are not joking. So I replied—

'He was a great artist. And this is his native district. Surely you ought to be proud of him!'

'He may have been a great artist,' said Mr Brindley, 'or he may not. But for us he was simply a man who came of a family that had a bad reputation for talking too much and acting the goat!'

'Well,' I said, We shall see—in fifty years.'

'That's just what we shan't,' said he. 'We shall be where Simon Fuge is—dead! However, perhaps we are proud of him. But you don't expect us to show it, do you? That's not our style.'

He performed the quasi-winking phenomenon with his eyes. It was his final exhibition of it to me.

'A strange place!' I reflected, as I ate my dinner in the dining-car, with the pressure of Mr Brindley's steely clasp still affecting my right hand, and the rich, honest cordiality of his au revoir in my heart. 'A place that is passing strange!'

And I thought further: He may have been a boaster, and a chatterer, and a man who suffered from cold feet at the wrong moments! And the Five Towns may have got the better of him, now. But that portrait of the little girl in the Wedgwood Institution is waiting there, right in the middle of the Five Towns. And one day the Five Towns will have to 'give it best'. They can say what they like! ... What eyes the fellow had, when he was in the right company!

IN A NEW BOTTLE

Commercial travellers are rather like bees; they take the seed of a good story from one district and deposit it in another.

Thus several localities, imperfectly righteous, have within recent years appropriated this story to their own annals. I once met an old herbalist from Wigan-Wigan of all places in beautiful England!— who positively asserted that the episode occurred just outside the London and North-Western main line station at Wigan. This old herbalist was no judge of the value of evidence. An undertaker from Hull told me flatly, little knowing who I was and where I came from, that he was the undertaker concerned in the episode. This undertaker was a liar. I use this term because there is no other word in the language which accurately expresses my meaning. Of persons who have taken the trouble to come over from the United States in order to inform me that the affair happened at Harper's Ferry, Poughkeepsie, Syracuse, Allegheny, Indianapolis, Columbus, Charlotte, Tabernacle, Alliance, Wheeling, Lynchburg, and Chicago it would be unbecoming to speak—they are best left to silence themselves by mutual recrimination. The fact is that the authentic scene of the affair was a third-class railway carriage belonging to the North Staffordshire Railway Company, and rolling on that company's loop-line between Longshaw and Hanbridge. The undertaker is now dead—it is a disturbing truth that even undertakers die sometimes—and since his widow has given me permission to mention his name, I shall mention his name. It was Edward Till. Of course everybody in the Five Towns knows who the undertaker was, and if anybody in the Five Towns should ever chance to come across this book, I offer him my excuses for having brought coals to Newcastle.

Mr Till used to be a fairly well-known figure in Hanbridge, which is the centre of undertaking, as it is of everything else, in the Five Towns. He was in a small but a successful way of business, had one leg a trifle shorter than the other (which slightly deteriorated the majesty of his demeanour on solemn occasions), played the fiddle, kept rabbits, and was of a forgetful disposition. It was possibly this forgetful disposition which had prevented him from rising into a large way of business. All admired his personal character and tempered geniality; but there are some things that will not bear forgetting. However, the story touches but lightly that side of his individuality.

One morning Mr Till had to go to Longshaw to fetch a baby's coffin which had been ordered under the mistaken impression that a certain baby was dead. This baby, I may mention, was the hero of the celebrated scare of Longshaw about the danger of being buried alive. The little thing had apparently passed away; and, what is more, an inquest had been held on it and its parents had been censured by the jury for criminal carelessness in overlaying it; and it was within five minutes of being nailed up, when it opened its eyes! You may imagine the enormous sensation that there was in the Five Towns. One doctor lost his reputation, naturally. He emigrated to the Continent, and now, practising at Lucerne in the summer and Mentone in the winter, charges fifteen shillings a visit (instead of three and six at Longshaw) for informing people who have nothing the matter with them that they must take care of themselves. The parents of the astonished baby moved the heaven and earth of the Five Towns to force the coroner to withdraw the stigma of the jury's censure; but they did not succeed, not even with the impassioned aid of two London halfpenny dailies.

To resume, Mr Till had to go to Longshaw. Now, unless you possess a most minute knowledge of your native country, you are probably not aware that in Aynsley Street, Longshaw, there is a provision dealer whose reputation for cheeses would be national and supreme if the whole of England thought as the Five Towns thinks.

'Teddy,' Mrs Till said, as Mr Till was starting, 'you might as well bring back with you a pound of Gorgonzola.' (Be it noted that I had the details of the conversation from the lady herself.)

'Yes,' said he enthusiastically, 'I will.'

'Don't go and forget it,' she enjoined him.

'No,' he said. 'I'll tie a knot in my handkerchief.'

'A lot of good that'll do!' she observed. 'You'd tied a knot in your handkerchief when you forgot that Councillor Barker's wife's funeral was altered from Tuesday to Monday.'

'Ah!' he replied. 'But now I've got a bad cold.'

'So you have!' she agreed, reassured.

He tied the knot in his handkerchief and went.

Thanks to his cold he did not pass the cheesemonger's without entering.

He adored Gorgonzola, and he reckoned that he knew a bit of good Gorgonzola when he met with it. Moreover, he and the cheesemonger were old friends, he having buried three of the cheesemonger's children. He emerged from the cheesemonger's with a pound of the perfectest Gorgonzola that ever greeted the senses.

The abode of the censured parents was close by, and also close to the station. He obtained the coffin without parley, and told the mother, who showed him the remarkable child with pride, that under the circumstances he should make no charge at all. It was a ridiculously small coffin. He was quite accustomed to coffins. Hence he did the natural thing. He tucked the little coffin under one arm, and, dangling the cheese (neat in brown paper and string) from the other hand, he hastened to the station. With his unmatched legs he must have made a somewhat noticeable figure.

A loop-line train was waiting, and he got into it, put the cheese on the rack in a corner, and the coffin next to it, assured himself that he had not mislaid his return ticket, and sat down under his baggage. It was the slackest time of day, and, as the train started at Longshaw, there were very few passengers. He had the compartment to himself.

He was just giving way to one of those moods of vague and pleasant meditation which are perhaps the chief joy of such a temperament, when he suddenly sprang up as if in fear. And fear had in fact seized him. Suppose he forgot those belongings on the rack? Suppose, sublimely careless, he descended from the train and left them there? What a calamity! And similar misadventures had happened to him before. It was the cheese that disquieted him. No one would be sufficiently unprincipled to steal the coffin, and he would ultimately recover it at the lost luggage office, babies' coffins not abounding on the North Staffordshire Railway. But the cheese! He would never see the cheese again! No integrity would be able to withstand the blandishments of that cheese. Moreover, his wife would be saddened. And for her he had a sincere and profound affection.

His act of precaution was to lift the coffin down from the rack, and place it on the seat beside him, and then to put the parcel of cheese on the coffin. He surveyed the cheese on the coffin; he surveyed it with the critical and experienced eye of an undertaker, and he decided that, if anyone else got into the carriage, it would not look quite decent, quite becoming—in a word, quite nice. A coffin is a coffin, and people's feelings have to be considered.

So he whipped off the lid of the coffin, stuck the cheese inside, and popped the lid on again. And he kept his hand on the coffin that he might not forget it. When the train halted at Knype, Mr Till was glad that he had put the cheese inside, for another passenger got into the compartment. And it was a clergyman. He recognized the clergyman, though the clergyman did not recognize him. It was the Reverend Claud ffolliott, famous throughout the Five Towns as the man who begins his name with a small letter, doesn't smoke, of course doesn't drink, but goes to football matches, has an average of eighteen at cricket, and makes a very pretty show with the gloves, in spite of his thirty-eight years; celibate, very High, very natty and learned about vestments, terrific at sick couches and funerals. Mr Till inwardly trembled to think what the Reverend Claud ffolliott might have said had he seen the cheese reposing in the coffin, though the coffin was empty.

The parson, whose mind was apparently occupied, dropped into the nearest corner, which chanced to be the corner farthest away from Mr Till. He then instantly opened a copy of The Church Times and began to read it, and the train went forward. The parson sniffed, absently, as if he had been dozing and a fly had tickled his nose. Shortly afterwards he sniffed again, but without looking up from his perusals. He sniffed a third time, and glanced over the top edge of THE CHURCH TIMES at Mr Till. Calmed by the innocuous aspect of Mr Till, he bent once more to the paper. But after an interval he was sniffing furiously. He glanced at the window; it was open. Finally he lowered The CHURCH TIMES, as who should say: 'I am a long-suffering man, but really this phenomenon which assaults my nostrils must be seriously inquired into.'

Then it was that he caught sight of the coffin, with Mr Till's hand caressing it, and Mr Till all in black and carrying a funereal expression. He straightened himself, pulled himself together on account of his cloth, and said to Mr Till in his most majestic and sympathetic graveside voice—

'Ah! my dear friend, I see that you have suffered a sad, sad bereavement.'

That rich, resonant voice was positively thrilling when it addressed hopeless grief. Mr Till did not know what to say, nor where to look.

'You have, however, one thing to be thankful for, very thankful for,' said the parson after a pause, 'you may be sure the poor thing is not in a trance.'

THE MATADOR
OF THE FIVE TOWNS
AND OTHER STORIES

BY

ARNOLD BENNETT

CONTENTS

TRAGIC
THE MATADOR OF THE FIVE TOWNS
MIMI
THE SUPREME ILLUSION
THE LETTER AND THE LIE
THE GLIMPSE

FROLIC
JOCK-AT-A-VENTURE
THE HEROISM OF THOMAS CHADWICK
UNDER THE CLOCK
THREE EPISODES IN THE LIFE OF MR COWLISHAW, DENTIST
CATCHING THE TRAIN
THE WIDOW OF THE BALCONY
THE CAT AND CUPID
THE FORTUNE-TELLER
THE LONG-LOST UNCLE
THE TIGHT HAND
WHY THE CLOCK STOPPED
HOT POTATOES
HALF-A-SOVEREIGN
THE BLUE SUIT
THE TIGER AND THE BABY
THE REVOLVER
AN UNFAIR ADVANTAGE

THE MATADOR OF THE FIVE TOWNS

I

Mrs Brindeley looked across the lunch-table at her husband with glinting, eager eyes, which showed that there was something unusual in the brain behind them.

"Bob," she said, factitiously calm. "You don't know what I've just remembered!"

"Well?" said he.

"It's only grandma's birthday to-day!"

My friend Robert Brindley, the architect, struck the table with a violent fist, making his little boys blink, and then he said quietly:

"*The* deuce!"

I gathered that grandmamma's birthday had been forgotten and that it was not a festival that could be neglected with impunity. Both Mr and Mrs Brindley had evidently a humorous appreciation of crises, contretemps, and those collisions of circumstances which are usually called "junctures" for short. I could have imagined either of them saying to the other: "Here's a funny thing! The house is on fire!" And then yielding to laughter as they ran for buckets. Mrs Brindley, in particular, laughed now; she gazed at the table-cloth and laughed almost silently to herself; though it appeared that their joint forgetfulness might result in temporary estrangement from a venerable ancestor who was also, birthdays being duly observed, a continual fount of rich presents in specie.

Robert Brindley drew a time-table from his breast-pocket with the rapid gesture of habit. All men of business in the Five Towns seem to carry that time-table in their breast-pockets. Then he examined his watch carefully.

"You'll have time to dress up your progeny and catch the 2.5. It makes the connection at Knype for Axe."

The two little boys, aged perhaps four and six, who had been ladling the messy contents of specially deep plates on to their bibs, dropped their spoons and began to babble about grea'-granny, and one of them insisted several times that he must wear his new gaiters.

"Yes," said Mrs Brindley to her husband, after reflection. "And a fine old crowd there'll be in the train—with this football match!"

"Can't be helped!... Now, you kids, hook it upstairs to nurse."

"And what about you?" asked Mrs Brindley.

"You must tell the old lady I'm kept by business."

"I told her that last year, and you know what happened."

"Well," said Brindley. "Here Loring's just come. You don't expect me to leave him, do you? Or have you had the beautiful idea of taking him over to Axe to pass a pleasant Saturday afternoon with your esteemed grandmother?"

"No," said Mrs Brindley. "Hardly that!"

"Well, then?"

The boys, having first revolved on their axes, slid down from their high chairs as though from horses.

"Look here," I said. "You mustn't mind me. I shall be all right."

"Ha-ha!" shouted Brindley. "I seem to see you turned loose alone in this amusing town on a winter afternoon. I seem to see you!"

"I could stop in and read," I said, eyeing the multitudinous books on every wall of the dining-room. The house was dadoed throughout with books.

"Rot!" said Brindley.

This was only my third visit to his home and to the Five Towns, but he and I had already become curiously intimate. My first two visits had been occasioned by official pilgrimages as a British Museum expert in ceramics. The third was for a purely friendly week-end, and had no pretext. The fact is, I was drawn to the astonishing district and its astonishing inhabitants. The Five Towns, to me, was like the East to those who have smelt the East: it "called."

"I'll tell you what we *could* do," said Mrs Brindley. "We could put him on to Dr Stirling."

"So we could!" Brindley agreed. "Wife, this is one of your bright, intelligent days. We'll put you on to the doctor, Loring. I'll impress on him that he must keep you constantly amused till I get back, which I fear it won't be early. This is what we call manners, you know—to invite a fellow-creature to travel a hundred and fifty miles to spend two days here, and then to turn him out before he's been in the house an hour. It's *us*, that is! But the truth of the matter is, the birthday business might be a bit serious. It might easily cost me fifty quid and no end of diplomacy. If you were a married man you'd know that the ten plagues of Egypt are simply nothing in comparison with your wife's relations. And she's over eighty, the old lady."

"*I'll* give you ten plagues of Egypt!" Mrs Brindley menaced her spouse, as she wafted the boys from the room. "Mr Loring, do take some more of that cheese if you fancy it." She vanished.

Within ten minutes Brindley was conducting me to the doctor's, whose house was on the way to the station. In its spacious porch he explained the circumstances in six words, depositing me like a parcel. The doctor, who had once by mysterious medicaments saved my frail organism from the consequences of one of Brindley's Falstaffian "nights," hospitably protested his readiness to sacrifice patients to my pleasure.

"It'll be a chance for MacIlroy," said he.

"Who's MacIlroy?" I asked.

"MacIlroy is another Scotchman," growled Brindley. "Extraordinary how they stick together! When he wanted an assistant, do you suppose he looked about for some one in the district, some one who understood us and loved us and could take a hand at bridge? Not he! Off he goes to Cupar, or somewhere, and comes back with another stage Scotchman, named MacIlroy. Now listen here, Doc! A charge to keep you have, and mind you keep it, or I'll never pay your confounded bill. We'll knock on the window to-night as we come back. In the meantime you can show Loring your etchings, and pray for me." And to me: "Here's a latchkey." With no further ceremony he hurried away to join his wife and children at Bleakridge Station. In such singular manner was I transferred forcibly from host to host.

II

The doctor and I resembled each other in this: that there was no offensive affability about either of us. Though abounding in good-nature, we could not become intimate by a sudden act of volition. Our conversation was difficult, unnatural, and by gusts falsely familiar. He displayed to me his bachelor house, his etchings, a few specimens of modern *rouge flambé* ware made at Knype, his whisky, his celebrated prize-winning fox-terrier Titus, the largest collection of books in the Five Towns, and photographs of Marischal College, Aberdeen. Then we fell flat, socially prone. Sitting in his study, with Titus between us on the hearthrug, we knew no more what to say or do. I regretted that Brindley's wife's grandmother should have been born on a fifteenth of February.

Brindley was a vivacious talker, he could be trusted to talk. I, too, am a good talker—with another good talker. With a bad talker I am just a little worse than he is. The doctor said abruptly after a nerve-trying silence that he had forgotten a most important call at Hanbridge, and would I care to go with him in the car? I was and still am convinced that he was simply inventing. He wanted to break the sinister spell by getting out of the house, and he had not the face to suggest a sortie into the streets of the Five Towns as a promenade of pleasure.

So we went forth, splashing warily through the rich mud and the dank mist of Trafalgar Road, past all those strange little Indian-red houses, and ragged empty spaces, and poster-hoardings, and rounded kilns, and high, smoking chimneys, up hill, down hill, and up hill again, encountering and overtaking many electric trams that dipped and rose like ships at sea, into Crown Square, the centre of Hanbridge, the metropolis of the Five Towns. And while the doctor paid his mysterious call I stared around me at the large shops and the banks and the gilded hotels. Down the radiating street-vistas I could make out the façades of halls, theatres, chapels. Trams rumbled continually in and out of the square. They seemed to enter casually, to hesitate a few moments as if at a loss, and then to decide with a nonchalant clang of bells that they might as well go off somewhere else in search of something more interesting. They were rather like human beings who are condemned to live for ever in a place of which they are sick beyond the expressiveness of words.

And indeed the influence of Crown Square, with its large effects of terra cotta, plate glass, and gold letters, all under a heavy skyscape of drab smoke, was depressing. A few very seedy men (sharply contrasting with the fine delicacy of costly things behind plate-glass) stood doggedly here and there in the mud, immobilized by the gloomy enchantment of the Square. Two of them turned to look at Stirling's motor-car and me. They gazed fixedly for a long time, and then one said, only his lips moving:

"Has Tommy stood thee that there quart o' beer as he promised thee?"

No reply, no response of any sort, for a further long period! Then the other said, with grim resignation:

"Ay!"

The conversation ceased, having made a little oasis in the dismal desert of their silent scrutiny of the car. Except for an occasional stamp of the foot they never moved. They just doggedly and indifferently stood, blown upon by all the nipping draughts of the square, and as it might be sinking deeper and deeper into its dejection. As for me, instead of desolating, the harsh disconsolateness of the scene seemed to uplift me; I savoured it with joy, as one savours the melancholy of a tragic work of art.

"We might go down to the *Signal* offices and worry Buchanan a bit," said the doctor, cheerfully, when he came back to the car. This was the second of his inspirations.

Buchanan, of whom I had heard, was another Scotchman and the editor of the sole daily organ of the Five Towns, an evening newspaper cried all day in the streets and read by the entire population. Its green sheet appeared to be a permanent waving feature of the main thoroughfares. The offices lay round a corner close by, and as we drew up in front of them a crowd of tattered urchins interrupted their diversions in the sodden road to celebrate our glorious arrival by unanimously yelling at the top of their strident and hoarse voices:

"Hooray! Hoo—bl——dy—ray!"

Abashed, I followed my doctor into the shelter of the building, a new edifice, capacious and considerable, but horribly faced with terra cotta, and quite unimposing, lacking in the spectacular effect; like nearly everything in the Five Towns, carelessly and scornfully ugly! The mean, swinging double-doors returned to the assault when you pushed them, and hit you viciously. In a dark, countered room marked "Enquiries" there was nobody.

"Hi, there!" called the doctor.

A head appeared at a door.

"Mr Buchanan upstairs?"

"Yes," snapped the head, and disappeared.

Up a dark staircase we went, and at the summit were half flung back again by another self-acting door.

In the room to which we next came an old man and a youngish one were bent over a large, littered table, scribbling on and arranging pieces of grey tissue paper and telegrams. Behind the old man stood a boy. Neither of them looked up.

"Mr Buchanan in his—" the doctor began to question. "Oh! There you are!"

The editor was standing in hat and muffler at the window, gazing out. His age was about that of the doctor—forty or so; and like the doctor he was rather stout and clean-shaven. Their Scotch accents mingled in greeting, the doctor's being the more marked. Buchanan shook my hand with a certain courtliness, indicating that he was well accustomed to receive strangers. As an expert in small talk, however, he shone no brighter than his visitors, and the three of us stood there by the window awkwardly in the heaped disorder of the room, while the other two men scratched and fidgeted with bits of paper at the soiled table.

Suddenly and savagely the old man turned on the boy:

"What the hades are you waiting there for?"

"I thought there was something else, sir."

"Sling your hook."

Buchanan winked at Stirling and me as the boy slouched off and the old man blandly resumed his writing.

"Perhaps you'd like to look over the place?" Buchanan suggested politely to me. "I'll come with you. It's all I'm fit for to-day.... 'Flu!" He glanced at Stirling, and yawned.

"Ye ought to be in bed," said Stirling.

"Yes. I know. I've known it for twelve years. I shall go to bed as soon as I get a bit of time to myself. Well, will you come? The half-time results are beginning to come in."

A telephone-bell rang impatiently.

"You might just see what that is, boss," said the old man without looking up.

Buchanan went to the telephone and replied into it: "Yes? What? Oh! Myatt? Yes, he's playing.... Of course I'm sure! Good-bye." He turned to the old man: "It's another of 'em wanting to know if Myatt is playing. Birmingham, this time."

"Ah!" exclaimed the old man, still writing.

"It's because of the betting," Buchanan glanced at me. "The odds are on Knype now—three to two."

"If Myatt is playing Knype have got me to thank for it," said the doctor, surprisingly.

"You?"

"Me! He fetched me to his wife this morning. She's nearing her confinement. False alarm. I guaranteed him at least another twelve hours."

"Oh! So that's it, is it?" Buchanan murmured.

Both the sub-editors raised their heads.

"That's it," said the doctor.

"Some people were saying he'd quarrelled with the trainer again and was shamming," said Buchanan. "But I didn't believe that. There's no hanky-panky about Jos Myatt, anyhow."

I learnt in answer to my questions that a great and terrible football match was at that moment in progress at Knype, a couple of miles away, between the Knype Club and the Manchester Rovers. It was conveyed to me that the importance of this match was almost national, and that the entire district was practically holding its breath till the result should be known. The half-time result was one goal each.

"If Knype lose," said Buchanan, explanatorily, "they'll find themselves pushed out of the First League at the end of the season. That's a cert ... one of the oldest clubs in England! Semi-finalists for the English Cup in '78."

"'79," corrected the elder sub-editor.

I gathered that the crisis was grave.

"And Myatt's the captain, I suppose?" said I.

"No. But he's the finest full-back in the League."

I then had a vision of Myatt as a great man. By an effort of the imagination I perceived that the equivalent of the fate of nations depended upon him. I recollected, now, large yellow posters on the hoardings we had passed, with the names of Knype and of Manchester Rovers in letters a foot high and the legend "League match at Knype" over all. It seemed to me that the heroic name of Jos Myatt, if truly he were the finest full-back in the League, if truly his presence or absence affected the betting as far off as Birmingham, ought also to have been on the posters, together with possibly his portrait. I saw Jos Myatt as a matador, with a long ribbon of scarlet necktie down his breast, and embroidered trousers.

"Why," said Buchanan, "if Knype drop into the Second Division they'll never pay another dividend! It'll be all up with first-class football in the Five Towns!"

The interests involved seemed to grow more complicated. And here I had been in the district nearly four hours without having guessed that the district was quivering in the tense excitement of gigantic issues! And here was this Scotch doctor, at whose word the great Myatt would have declined to play, never saying a syllable about the affair, until a chance remark from Buchanan loosened his tongue. But all doctors are strangely secretive. Secretiveness is one of their chief private pleasures.

327

"Come and see the pigeons, eh?" said Buchanan.

"Pigeons?" I repeated.

"We give the results of over a hundred matches in our Football Edition," said Buchanan, and added: "not counting Rugby."

As we left the room two boys dodged round us into it, bearing telegrams.

In a moment we were, in the most astonishing manner, on a leaden roof of the *Signal* offices. High factory chimneys rose over the horizon of slates on every side, blowing thick smoke into the general murk of the afternoon sky, and crossing the western crimson with long pennons of black. And out of the murk there came from afar a blue-and-white pigeon which circled largely several times over the offices of the *Signal*. At length it descended, and I could hear the whirr of its strong wings. The wings ceased to beat and the pigeon slanted downwards in a curve, its head lower than its wide tail. Then the little head gradually rose and the tail fell; the curve had changed, the pace slackened; the pigeon was calculating with all its brain; eyes, wings, tail and feet were being co-ordinated to the resolution of an intricate mechanical problem. The pinkish claws seemed to grope—and after an instant of hesitation the thing was done, the problem solved; the pigeon, with delicious gracefulness, had established equilibrium on the ridge of a pigeon-cote, and folded its wings, and was peering about with strange motions of its extremely movable head. Presently it flew down to the leads, waddled to and fro with the ungainly gestures of a fat woman of sixty, and disappeared into the cote. At the same moment the boy who had been dismissed from the sub-editor's room ran forward and entered the cote by a wire-screened door.

"Handy things, pigeons!" said the doctor as we approached to examine the cote. Fifty or sixty pigeons were cooing and strutting in it. There was a protest of wings as the boy seized the last arriving messenger.

"Give it here!" Buchanan ordered.

The boy handed over a thin tube of paper which he had unfastened from the bird's leg. Buchanan unrolled it and showed it to me. I read: "Midland Federation. Axe United, Macclesfield Town. Match abandoned after half-hour's play owing to fog. Three forty-five."

"Three forty-five," said Buchanan, looking at his watch. "He's done the ten miles in half an hour, roughly. Not bad. First time we

328

tried pigeons from as far off as Axe. Here, boy!" And he restored the paper to the boy, who gave it to another boy, who departed with it.

"Man," said the doctor, eyeing Buchanan. "Ye'd no business out here. Ye're not precisely a pigeon."

Down we went, one after another, by the ladder, and now we fell into the composing-room, where Buchanan said he felt warmer. An immense, dirty, white-washed apartment crowded with linotypes and other machines, in front of which sat men in white aprons, tapping, tapping—gazing at documents pinned at the level of their eyes—and tapping, tapping. A kind of cavernous retreat in which monstrous iron growths rose out of the floor and were met half-way by electric flowers that had their roots in the ceiling! In this jungle there was scarcely room for us to walk. Buchanan explained the linotypes to me. I watched, as though romantically dreaming, the flashing descent of letter after letter, a rain of letters into the belly of the machine; then, going round to the back, I watched the same letters rising again in a close, slow procession, and sorting themselves by themselves at the top in readiness to answer again to the tapping, tapping of a man in a once-white apron. And while I was watching all that I could somehow, by a faculty which we have, at the same time see pigeons far overhead, arriving and arriving out of the murk from beyond the verge of chimneys.

"Ingenious, isn't it?" said Stirling.

But I imagine that he had not the faculty by which to see the pigeons.

A reverend, bearded, spectacled man, with his shirt-sleeves rolled up and an apron stretched over his hemispherical paunch, strolled slowly along an alley, glancing at a galley-proof with an ingenuous air just as if he had never seen a galley-proof before.

"It's a stick more than a column already," said he confidentially, offering the long paper, and then gravely looking at Buchanan, with head bent forward, not through his spectacles but over them.

The editor negligently accepted the proof, and I read a series of titles: "Knype v. Manchester Rovers. Record Gate. Fifteen thousand spectators. Two goals in twelve minutes. Myatt in form. Special Report."

Buchanan gave the slip back without a word.

"There you are!" said he to me, as another compositor near us attached a piece of tissue paper to his machine. It was the very paper

329

that I had seen come out of the sky, but its contents had been enlarged and amended by the sub-editorial pen. The man began tapping, tapping, and the letters began to flash downwards on their way to tell a quarter of a million people that Axe *v.* Macclesfield had been stopped by fog.

"I suppose that Knype match is over by now?" I said.

"Oh no!" said Buchanan. "The second half has scarcely begun."

"Like to go?" Stirling asked.

"Well," I said, feeling adventurous, "it's a notion, isn't it?"

"You can run Mr Loring down there in five or six minutes," said Buchanan. "And he's probably never seen anything like it before. You might call here as you come home and see the paper on the machines."

III

We went on the Grand Stand, which was packed with men whose eyes were fixed, with an unconscious but intense effort, on a common object. Among the men were a few women in furs and wraps, equally absorbed. Nobody took any notice of us as we insinuated our way up a rickety flight of wooden stairs, but when by misadventure we grazed a human being the elbow of that being shoved itself automatically and fiercely outwards, to repel. I had an impression of hats, caps, and woolly overcoats stretched in long parallel lines, and of grimy raw planks everywhere presenting possibly dangerous splinters, save where use had worn them into smooth shininess. Then gradually I became aware of the vast field, which was more brown than green. Around the field was a wide border of infinitesimal hats and pale faces, rising in tiers, and beyond this border fences, hoardings, chimneys, furnaces, gasometers, telegraph-poles, houses, and dead trees. And here and there, perched in strange perilous places, even high up towards the sombre sky, were more human beings clinging. On the field itself, at one end of it, were a scattered handful of doll-like figures, motionless; some had white bodies, others red; and three were in black; all were so small and so far off that they seemed to be mere unimportant casual incidents in whatever recondite affair it was that was proceeding. Then a whistle shrieked, and all these figures began simultaneously to move, and then I saw a ball in the air. An obscure, uneasy murmuring rose from the immense multitude like an invisible but audible vapour. The next instant the vapour had condensed into a sudden shout. Now I saw the ball rolling solitary in the middle of the field, and a single red doll racing towards it; at one end was a confused group of red and white, and at the other two white dolls, rather lonely in the expanse. The single red doll overtook the ball and scudded along with it at his twinkling toes. A great voice behind me bellowed with an incredible volume of sound:

"Now, Jos!"

And another voice, further away, bellowed:

"Now, Jos!"

And still more distantly the grim warning shot forth from the crowd:

"Now, Jos! Now, Jos!"

The nearer of the white dolls, as the red one approached, sprang forward. I could see a leg. And the ball was flying back in a magnificent curve into the skies; it passed out of my sight, and then I heard a bump on the slates of the roof of the grand stand, and it fell among the crowd in the stand-enclosure. But almost before the flight of the ball had commenced, a terrific roar of relief had rolled formidably round the field, and out of that roar, like rockets out of thick smoke, burst acutely ecstatic cries of adoration:

"Bravo, Jos!"

"Good old Jos!"

The leg had evidently been Jos's leg. The nearer of these two white dolls must be Jos, darling of fifteen thousand frenzied people.

Stirling punched a neighbour in the side to attract his attention.

"What's the score?" he demanded of the neighbour, who scowled and then grinned.

"Two—one—agen uz!" The other growled.

"It'll take our b——s all their time to draw. They're playing a man short."

"Accident?"

"No! Referee ordered him off for rough play."

Several spectators began to explain, passionately, furiously, that the referee's action was utterly bereft of common sense and justice; and I gathered that a less gentlemanly crowd would undoubtedly have lynched the referee. The explanations died down, and everybody except me resumed his fierce watch on the field.

I was recalled from the exercise of a vague curiosity upon the set, anxious faces around me by a crashing, whooping cheer which in volume and sincerity of joy surpassed all noises in my experience. This massive cheer reverberated round the field like the echoes of a battleship's broadside in a fiord. But it was human, and therefore more terrible than guns. I instinctively thought: "If such are the symptoms of pleasure, what must be the symptoms of pain or disappointment?" Simultaneously with the expulsion of the unique noise the expression of the faces changed. Eyes sparkled; teeth became prominent in enormous, uncontrolled smiles. Ferocious satisfaction had to find vent in ferocious gestures, wreaked either upon dead wood or upon the living tissues of fellow-creatures. The gentle, mannerly sound of hand-clapping was a kind of light froth on the surface of the billowy sea of heartfelt applause. The host of the fifteen thousand might have just had their lives saved, or their children snatched from destruction and their wives from dishonour; they might have been preserved from bankruptcy, starvation, prison, torture; they might have been rewarding with their impassioned worship a band of national heroes. But it was not so. All that had happened was that the ball had rolled into the net of the Manchester Rovers' goal. Knype had drawn level. The reputation of the Five Towns before the jury of expert opinion that could distinguish between first-class football and second-class was maintained intact. I could hear specialists around me proving that though Knype had yet five League matches to play, its situation was safe. They pointed excitedly to a huge hoarding at one end of the ground on which appeared names of other clubs with changing figures. These clubs included the clubs which Knype would have to meet before the end of the season, and the figures indicated their fortunes on various grounds similar to this ground all over the country. If a goal was scored in Newcastle, or in Southampton, the very Peru of first-class football, it was registered on that board and its possible effect on the destinies of Knype was instantly assessed. The calculations made were dizzying.

Then a little flock of pigeons flew up and separated, under the illusion that they were free agents and masters of the air, but really wafted away to fixed destinations on the stupendous atmospheric waves of still-continued cheering.

After a minute or two the ball was restarted, and the greater noise had diminished to the sensitive uneasy murmur which responded like a delicate instrument to the fluctuations of the game. Each feat and manoeuvre of Knype drew generous applause in proportion to its intention or its success, and each sleight of the Manchester Rovers, successful or not, provoked a holy disgust. The attitude of the host had passed beyond morality into religion.

Then, again, while my attention had lapsed from the field, a devilish, a barbaric, and a deafening yell broke from those fifteen thousand passionate hearts. It thrilled me; it genuinely frightened me. I involuntarily made the motion of swallowing. After the thunderous crash of anger from the host came the thin sound of a whistle. The game stopped. I heard the same word repeated again and again, in divers tones of exasperated fury:

"Foul!"

I felt that I was hemmed in by potential homicides, whose arms were lifted in the desire of murder and whose features were changed from the likeness of man into the corporeal form of some pure and terrible instinct.

And I saw a long doll rise from the ground and approach a lesser doll with threatening hands.

"Foul! Foul!"

"Go it, Jos! Knock his neck out! Jos! He tripped thee up!"

There was a prolonged gesticulatory altercation between the three black dolls in leather leggings and several of the white and the red dolls. At last one of the mannikins in leggings shrugged his shoulders, made a definite gesture to the other two, and walked away towards the edge of the field nearest the stand. It was the unprincipled referee; he had disallowed the foul. In the protracted duel between the offending Manchester forward and the great, honest Jos Myatt he had given another point to the enemy. As soon as the host realized the infamy it yelled once more in heightened fury. It seemed to surge in masses against the thick iron railings that alone stood between the referee and death. The discreet referee was approaching the grand stand as the least unsafe place. In a second a handful of executioners had somehow got on to the grass. And in the next second several policemen were in front of them, not striking nor striving to intimidate, but heavily pushing them into bounds.

"Get back there!" cried a few abrupt, commanding voices from the stand.

The referee stood with his hands in his pockets and his whistle in his mouth. I think that in that moment of acutest suspense the whole of his earthly career must have flashed before him in a phantasmagoria. And then the crisis was past. The inherent gentlemanliness of the outraged host had triumphed and the referee was spared.

"Served him right if they'd man-handled him!" said a spectator.

"Ay!" said another, gloomily, "ay! And th' Football Association 'ud ha' fined us maybe a hundred quid and disqualified th' ground for the rest o' th' season!"

"D——n th' Football Association!"

"Ay! But you canna'!"

"Now, lads! Play up, Knype! Now, lads! Give 'em hot hell!" Different voices heartily encouraged the home team as the ball was thrown into play.

The fouling Manchester forward immediately resumed possession of the ball. Experience could not teach him. He parted with the ball and got it again, twice. The devil was in him and in the ball. The devil was driving him towards Myatt. They met. And then came a sound quite new: a cracking sound, somewhat like the snapping of a bough, but sharper, more decisive.

"By Jove!" exclaimed Stirling. "That's his bone!"

And instantly he was off down the staircase and I after him. But he was not the first doctor on the field. Nothing had been unforeseen in the wonderful organization of this enterprise. A pigeon sped away and an official doctor and an official stretcher appeared, miraculously, simultaneously. It was tremendous. It inspired awe in me.

"He asked for it!" I heard a man say as I hesitated on the shore of the ocean of mud.

Then I knew that it was Manchester and not Knype that had suffered. The confusion and hubbub were in a high degree disturbing and puzzling. But one emotion emerged clear: pleasure. I felt it myself. I was aware of joy in that the two sides were now levelled to ten men apiece. I was mystically identified with the Five Towns, absorbed into their life. I could discern on every face the conviction that a divine providence was in this affair, that God could not be mocked. I too had this conviction. I could discern also on every face the fear lest the referee might give a foul against the hero Myatt, or even order him off the field, though of course the fracture was a simple accident. I too had this fear. It was soon dispelled by the news which swept across the entire enclosure like a sweet smell, that the referee had adopted the theory of a simple accident. I saw vaguely policemen, a stretcher, streaming crowds, and my ears heard a monstrous universal babbling. And then the figure of Stirling detached itself from the moving disorder and came to me.

"Well, Hyatt's calf was harder than the other chap's, that's all," he said.

"Which *is* Myatt?" I asked, for the red and the white dolls had all vanished at close quarters, and were replaced by unrecognizably gigantic human animals, still clad, however, in dolls' vests and dolls' knickerbockers.

Stirling warningly jerked his head to indicate a man not ten feet away from me. This was Myatt, the hero of the host and the darling of populations. I gazed up at him. His mouth and his left knee were red with blood, and he was piebald with thick patches of mud from his tousled crown to his enormous boot. His blue eyes had a heavy, stupid, honest glance; and of the three qualities stupidity predominated. He seemed to be all feet, knees, hands and elbows. His head was very small—the sole remainder of the doll in him.

A little man approached him, conscious—somewhat too obviously conscious—of his right to approach. Myatt nodded.

"Ye'n settled *him*, seemingly, Jos!" said the little man.

"Well," said Myatt, with slow bitterness. "Hadn't he been blooming well begging and praying for it, aw afternoon? Hadn't he now?"

The little man nodded. Then he said in a lower tone:

"How's missis, like?"

"Her's altogether yet," said Myatt. "Or I'd none ha' played!"

"I've bet Watty half-a-dollar as it inna' a lad!" said the little man.

Myatt seemed angry.

"Wilt bet me half a *quid* as it inna' a lad?" he demanded, bending down and scowling and sticking out his muddy chin.

"Ay!" said the little man, not blenching.

"Evens?"

"Evens."

"I'll take thee, Charlie," said Myatt, resuming his calm.

The whistle sounded. And several orders were given to clear the field. Eight minutes had been lost over a broken leg, but Stirling said that the referee would surely deduct them from the official time, so that after all the game would not be shortened.

"I'll be up yon, to-morra morning," said the little man.

Myatt nodded and departed. Charlie, the little man, turned on his heel and proudly rejoined the crowd. He had been seen of all in converse with supreme greatness.

Stirling and I also retired; and though Jos Myatt had not even done his doctor the honour of seeing him, neither of us, I think, was quite without a consciousness of glory: I cannot imagine why. The rest of the game was flat and tame. Nothing occurred. The match ended in a draw.

IV

We were swept from the football ground on a furious flood of humanity—carried forth and flung down a slope into a large waste space that separated the ground from the nearest streets of little reddish houses. At the bottom of the slope, on my suggestion, we halted for a few moments aside, while the current rushed forward and, spreading out, inundated the whole space in one marvellous minute. The impression of the multitude streaming from that gap in the wooden wall was like nothing more than the impression of a burst main which only the emptying of the reservoir will assuage. Anybody who wanted to commit suicide might have stood in front of that gap and had his wish. He would not have been noticed. The interminable and implacable infantry charge would have passed unheedingly over him. A silent, preoccupied host, bent on something else now, and perhaps teased by the inconvenient thought that after all a draw is not as good as a win! It hurried blindly, instinctively outwards, knees and chins protruding, hands deep in pockets, chilled feet stamping. Occasionally someone stopped or slackened to light a pipe, and on being curtly bunted onward by a blind force from behind, accepted the hint as an atom accepts the law of gravity. The fever and ecstasy were over. What fascinated the Southern in me was the grim taciturnity, the steady stare (vacant or dreaming), and the heavy, muffled, multitudinous tramp shaking the cindery earth. The flood continued to rage through the gap.

Our automobile had been left at the Haycock Hotel; we went to get it, braving the inundation. Nearly opposite the stable-yard the electric trams started for Hanbridge, Bursley and Turnhill, and for Longshaw. Here the crowd was less dangerous, but still very formidable—to my eyes. Each tram as it came up was savagely assaulted, seized, crammed and possessed, with astounding rapidity.

Its steps were the western bank of a Beresina. At a given moment the inured conductor, brandishing his leather-shielded arm with a pitiless gesture, thrust aspirants down into the mud and the tram rolled powerfully away. All this in silence.

After a few minutes a bicyclist swished along through the mud, taking the far side of the road, which was comparatively free. He wore grey trousers, heavy boots, and a dark cut-away coat, up the back of which a line of caked mud had deposited itself. On his head was a bowler hat.

"How do, Jos?" cried a couple of boys, cheekily. And then there were a few adult greetings of respect.

It was the hero, in haste.

"Out of it, there!" he warned impeders, between his teeth, and plugged on with bent head.

"He keeps the Foaming Quart up at Toft End," said the doctor. "It's the highest pub in the Five Towns. He used to be what they call a pot-hunter, a racing bicyclist, you know. But he's got past that and he'll soon be past football. He's thirty-four if he's a day. That's one reason why he's so independent—that and because he's almost the only genuine native in the team."

"Why?" I asked. "Where do they come from, then?"

"Oh!" said Stirling as he gently started the car. "The club buys 'em, up and down the country. Four of 'em are Scots. A few years ago an Oldham club offered Knype £500 for Myatt, a big price— more than he's worth now! But he wouldn't go, though they guaranteed to put him into a first-class pub—a free house. He's never cost Knype anything except his wages and the goodwill of the Foaming Quart."

"What are his wages?"

"Don't know exactly. Not much. The Football Association fix a maximum. I daresay about four pounds a week *Hi there! Are you deaf?*"

"Thee mind what tha'rt about!" responded a stout loiterer in our path. "Or I'll take thy ears home for my tea, mester."

Stirling laughed.

In a few minutes we had arrived at Hanbridge, splashing all the way between two processions that crowded either footpath. And in the middle of the road was a third procession of trams,—tram following tram, each gorged with passengers, frothing at the step with passengers; not the lackadaisical trams that I had seen earlier in the afternoon in Crown Square; a different race of trams, eager and impetuous velocities. We reached the *Signal* offices. No crowd of urchins to salute us this time!

Under the earth was the machine-room of the *Signal*. It reminded me of the bowels of a ship, so full was it of machinery. One huge machine clattered slowly, and a folded green thing dropped strangely on to a little iron table in front of us. Buchanan opened it, and I saw that the broken leg was in it at length, together with a statement that in the *Signal's* opinion the sympathy of every true sportsman would be with the disabled player. I began to say something to Buchanan, when suddenly I could not hear my own voice. The great machine, with another behind us, was working at a fabulous speed and with a fabulous clatter. All that my startled senses could clearly disentangle was that the blue arc-lights above us blinked occasionally, and that folded green papers were snowing down upon the iron table far faster than the eye could follow them. Tall lads in aprons elbowed me away and carried off the green papers in bundles, but not more quickly than the machine shed them. Buchanan put his lips to my ear. But I could hear nothing. I shook my head. He smiled, and led us out from the tumult.

"Come and see the boys take them," he said at the foot of the stairs.

In a sort of hall on the ground floor was a long counter, and beyond the counter a system of steel railings in parallel lines, so arranged that a person entering at the public door could only reach the counter by passing up or down each alley in succession. These steel lanes, which absolutely ensured the triumph of right over might, were packed with boys—the ragged urchins whom we had seen playing in the street. But not urchins now; rather young tigers! Perhaps half a dozen had reached the counter; the rest were massed behind, shouting and quarrelling. Through a hole in the wall, at the level of the counter, bundles of papers shot continuously, and were snatched up by servers, who distributed them in smaller bundles to the hungry boys; who flung down metal discs in exchange and fled, fled madly as though fiends were after them, through a third door, out of the pandemonium into the darkling street. And unceasingly the green papers appeared at the hole in the wall and unceasingly they were plucked away and borne off by those maddened children, whose destination was apparently Aix or Ghent, and whose wings were their tatters.

338

"What are those discs?" I inquired.

"The lads have to come and buy them earlier in the day," said Buchanan. "We haven't time to sell this edition for cash, you see."

"Well," I said as we left, "I'm very much obliged."

"What on earth for?" Buchanan asked.

"Everything," I said.

We returned through the squares of Hanbridge and by Trafalgar Road to Stirling's house at Bleakridge. And everywhere in the deepening twilight I could see the urchins, often hatless and sometimes scarcely shod, scudding over the lamp-reflecting mire with sheets of wavy green, and above the noises of traffic I could hear the shrill outcry: "*Signal*. Football Edition. Football Edition. *Signal*." The world was being informed of the might of Jos Myatt, and of the averting of disaster from Knype, and of the results of over a hundred other matches—not counting Rugby.

V

During the course of the evening, when Stirling had thoroughly accustomed himself to the state of being in sole charge of an expert from the British Museum, London, and the high walls round his more private soul had yielded to my timid but constant attacks, we grew fairly intimate. And in particular the doctor proved to me that his reputation for persuasive raciness with patients was well founded. Yet up to the time of dessert I might have been justified in supposing that that much-praised "manner" in a sick-room was nothing but a provincial legend. Such may be the influence of a quite inoffensive and shy Londoner in the country. At half-past ten, Titus being already asleep for the night in an arm-chair, we sat at ease over the fire in the study telling each other stories. We had dealt with the arts, and with medicine; now we were dealing with life, in those aspects of it which cause men to laugh and women uneasily to wonder. Once or twice we had mentioned the Brindleys. The hour for their arrival was come. But being deeply comfortable and content where I was, I felt no impatience. Then there was a tap on the window.

"That's Bobbie!" said Stirling, rising slowly from his chair. "*He* won't refuse whisky, even if you do. I'd better get another bottle."

The tap was repeated peevishly.

"I'm coming, laddie!" Stirling protested.

He slippered out through the hall and through the surgery to the side door, I following, and Titus sneezing and snuffing in the rear.

"I say, mester," said a heavy voice as the doctor opened the door. It was not Brindley, but Jos Myatt. Unable to locate the bell-push in the dark, he had characteristically attacked the sole illuminated window. He demanded, or he commanded, very curtly, that the doctor should go up instantly to the Foaming Quart at Toft End.

Stirling hesitated a moment.

"All right, my man," said he, calmly.

"Now?" the heavy, suspicious voice on the doorstep insisted.

"I'll be there before ye if ye don't sprint, man. I'll run up in the car." Stirling shut the door. I heard footsteps on the gravel path outside.

"Ye heard?" said he to me. "And what am I to do with ye?"

"I'll go with you, of course," I answered.

"I may be kept up there a while."

"I don't care," I said roisterously. "It's a pub and I'm a traveller."

Stirling's household was in bed and his assistant gone home. While he and Titus got out the car I wrote a line for the Brindleys: "Gone with doctor to see patient at Toft End. Don't wait up.—A.L." This we pushed under Brindley's front door on our way forth. Very soon we were vibrating up a steep street on the first speed of the car, and the yellow reflections of distant furnaces began to shine over house roofs below us. It was exhilaratingly cold, a clear and frosty night, tonic, bracing after the enclosed warmth of the study. I was joyous, but silently. We had quitted the kingdom of the god Pan; we were in Lucina's realm, its consequence, where there is no laughter. We were on a mission.

"I didn't expect this," said Stirling.

"No?" I said. "But seeing that he fetched you this morning—"

"Oh! That was only in order to be sure, for himself. His sister was there, in charge. Seemed very capable. Knew all about everything. Until ye get to the high social status of a clerk or a draper's assistant people seem to manage to have their children without professional assistance."

"Then do you think there's anything wrong?" I asked.

"I'd not be surprised."

He changed to the second speed as the car topped the first bluff. We said no more. The night and the mission solemnized us. And gradually, as we rose towards the purple skies, the Five Towns wrote themselves out in fire on the irregular plain below.

"That's Hanbridge Town Hall," said Stirling, pointing to the right. "And that's Bursley Town Hall," he said, pointing to the left. And there were many other beacons, dominating the jewelled street-lines that faded on the horizon into golden-tinted smoke.

The road was never quite free of houses. After occurring but sparsely for half a mile, they thickened into a village—the suburb of Bursley called Toft End. I saw a moving red light in front of us. It was the reverse of Hyatt's bicycle lantern. The car stopped near the dark façade of the inn, of which two yellow windows gleamed. Stirling, under Myatt's shouted guidance, backed into an obscure yard under cover. The engine ceased to throb.

"Friend of mine," he introduced me to Myatt. "By the way, Loring, pass me my bag, will you? Mustn't forget that." Then he extinguished the acetylene lamps, and there was no light in the yard except the ray of the bicycle lantern which Myatt held in his hand. We groped towards the house. Strange, every step that I take in the Five Towns seems to have the genuine quality of an adventure!

VI

In five minutes I was of no account in the scheme of things at Toft End, and I began to wonder why I had come. Stirling, my sole protector, had vanished up the dark stairs of the house, following a stout, youngish woman in a white apron, who bore a candle. Jos Myatt, behind, said to me: "Happen you'd better go in there, mester," pointing to a half-open door at the foot of the stairs. I went into a little room at the rear of the bar-parlour. A good fire burned in a small old-fashioned grate, but there was no other light. The inn was closed to customers, it being past eleven o'clock. On a bare table I perceived a candle, and ventured to put a match to it. I then saw almost exactly such a room as one would expect to find at the rear of the bar-parlour of an inn on the outskirts of an industrial town. It appeared to serve the double purpose of a living-room and of a retreat for favoured customers. The table was evidently one at which men drank. On a shelf was a row of bottles, more or less empty, bearing names famous in newspaper advertisements and in the House of Lords. The dozen chairs suggested an acute bodily discomfort such as would only be tolerated by a sitter all of whose sensory faculties were centred in his palate. On a broken chair in a corner was an insecure pile of books. A smaller table was covered with a chequered cloth on which were a few plates. Along one wall, under the window, ran a pitch-pine sofa upholstered with a stuff slightly dissimilar from that on the table. The mattress of the sofa was uneven and its surface wrinkled, and old newspapers and pieces of brown paper had been stowed away between it and the framework. The chief article of furniture was an effective walnut bookcase, the glass doors of which were curtained with red cloth. The window, wider than it was high, was also curtained with red cloth. The walls, papered in a saffron tint, bore framed advertisements and a few photographs of self-conscious persons. The ceiling was as obscure as heaven; the floor tiled, with a list rug in front of the steel fender.

I put my overcoat on the sofa, picked up the candle and glanced at the books in the corner: Lavater's indestructible work, a paper-covered *Whitaker*, the *Licensed Victuallers' Almanac, Johnny Ludlow*, the illustrated catalogue of the Exhibition of 1856, *Cruden's Concordance*, and seven or eight volumes of *Knight's Penny Encyclopædia*. While I was poring on these titles I heard movements overhead—previously there had been no sound whatever—and with guilty haste I restored the candle to the table and placed myself negligently in front of the fire.

"Now don't let me see ye up here any more till I fetch ye!" said a woman's distant voice—not crossly, but firmly. And then, crossly: "Be off with ye now!"

Reluctant boots on the stairs! Jos Myatt entered to me. He did not speak at first; nor did I. He avoided my glance. He was still wearing the cut-away coat with the line of mud up the back. I took out my watch, not for the sake of information, but from mere nervousness, and the sight of the watch reminded me that it would be prudent to wind it up.

"Better not forget that," I said, winding it.

"Ay!" said he, gloomily. "It's a tip." And he wound up his watch; a large, thick, golden one.

This watch-winding established a basis of intercourse between us.

"I hope everything is going on all right," I murmured.

"What dun ye say?" he asked.

"I say I hope everything is going on all right," I repeated louder, and jerked my head in the direction of the stairs, to indicate the place from which he had come.

"Oh!" he exclaimed, as if surprised. "Now what'll ye have, mester?" He stood waiting. "It's my call to-night."

I explained to him that I never took alcohol. It was not quite true, but it was as true as most general propositions are.

"Neither me!" he said shortly, after a pause.

"You're a teetotaller too?" I showed a little involuntary astonishment.

He put forward his chin.

"What do *you* think?" he said confidentially and scornfully. It was precisely as if he had said: "Do you think that anybody but a born ass would *not* be a teetotaller, in my position?"

I sat down on a chair.

"Take th' squab, mester," he said, pointing to the sofa. I took it.

He picked up the candle; then dropped it, and lighted a lamp which was on the mantelpiece between his vases of blue glass. His movements were very slow, hesitating and clumsy. Blowing out the candle, which smoked for a long time, he went with the lamp to the bookcase. As the key of the bookcase was in his right pocket and the lamp in his right hand he had to change the lamp, cautiously, from hand to hand. When he opened the cupboard I saw a rich gleam of silver from every shelf of it except the lowest, and I could distinguish the forms of ceremonial cups with pedestals and immense handles.

"I suppose these are your pots?" I said.

"Ay!"

He displayed to me the fruits of his manifold victories. I could see him straining along endless cinder-paths and highroads under hot suns, his great knees going up and down like treadles amid the plaudits and howls of vast populations. And all that now remained of that glory was these debased and vicious shapes, magnificently useless, grossly ugly, with their inscriptions lost in a mess of flourishes.

"Ay!" he said again, when I had fingered the last of them.

"A very fine show indeed!" I said, resuming the sofa.

He took a penny bottle of ink and a pen out of the bookcase, and also, from the lowest shelf, a bag of money and a long narrow account book. Then he sat down at the table and commenced accountancy. It was clear that he regarded his task as formidable and complex. To see him reckoning the coins, manipulating the pen, splashing the ink, scratching the page; to hear him whispering consecutive numbers aloud, and muttering mysterious anathemas against the untamable naughtiness of figures—all this was painful, and with the painfulness of a simple exercise rendered difficult by inaptitude and incompetence. I wanted to jump up and cry to him: "Get out of the way, man, and let me do it for you! I can do it while you are wiping hairs from your pen on your sleeve." I was sorry for him because he was ridiculous—and even more grotesque than ridiculous. I felt, quite acutely, that it was a shame that he could not be for ever the central figure of a field of mud, kicking a ball into long and grandiose parabolas higher than gasometers, or breaking an occasional leg, surrounded by the violent affection of hearts whose melting-point was the exclamation, "Good old Jos!" I felt that if he must repose his existence ought to have been so contrived that he could repose in impassive and senseless dignity, like a mountain watching the flight of time. The conception of him tracing symbols in a ledger, counting shillings and sixpences, descending to arithmetic, and suffering those humiliations which are the invariable preliminaries to legitimate fatherhood, was shocking to a nice taste for harmonious fitness.... What, this precious and terrific organism, this slave with a specialty—whom distant towns had once been anxious to buy at the prodigious figure of five hundred pounds—obliged to sit in a mean chamber and wait silently while the woman of his choice encountered the supreme peril! And he would "soon be past football!" He was "thirty-four if a day!" It was the verge of senility! He was no longer worth five hundred pounds. Perhaps even now this jointed merchandise was only worth two hundred pounds! And "they"—the shadowy directors, who could not kick a ball fifty feet and who would probably turn sick if they broke a leg—"they" paid him four pounds a week for being the hero of a quarter of a million of people! He was the chief magnet to draw fifteen thousand sixpences and shillings of a Saturday afternoon into a company's cash box, and here he sat splitting his head over fewer sixpences and shillings than would fill a half-pint pot! Jos, you ought in justice to have been José, with a thin red necktie down your breast (instead of a line of mud up your back), and embroidered breeches on those miraculous legs, and an income of a quarter of a million pesetas, and the languishing acquiescence of innumerable mantillas. Every moment you were getting older and stiffer; every moment was bringing nearer the moment when young men would reply curtly to their doddering elders: "Jos Myatt—who was '*e?*"

The putting away of the ledger, the ink, the pen and the money was as exasperating as their taking out had been. Then Jos, always too large for the room, crossed the tiled floor and mended the fire. A poker was more suited to his capacity than a pen. He glanced about him, uncertain and anxious, and then crept to the door near the foot of the stairs and listened. There was no sound; and that was curious. The woman who was bringing into the world the hero's child made no cry that reached us below. Once or twice I had heard muffled movements not quite overhead—somewhere above—but naught else. The doctor and Jos's sister seemed to have retired into a sinister and dangerous mystery. I could not dispel from my mind pictures of what they were watching and what they were doing. The vast, cruel, fumbling clumsiness of Nature, her lack of majesty in crises that ought to be majestic, her incurable indignity, disgusted me, aroused my disdain, I wanted, as a philosopher of all the cultures, to feel that the present was indeed a majestic crisis, to be so esteemed by a superior man. I could not. Though the crisis possibly intimidated me somewhat, yet, on behalf of Jos Myatt, I was ashamed of it. This may be reprehensible, but it is true.

He sat down by the fire and looked at the fire. I could not attempt to carry on a conversation with him, and to avoid the necessity for any talk at all, I extended myself on the sofa and averted my face, wondering once again why I had accompanied the doctor to Toft End. The doctor was now in another, an inaccessible world. I dozed, and from my doze I was roused by Jos Myatt going to the door on the stairs.

"Jos," said a voice. "It's a girl."

Then a silence.

I admit there was a flutter in my heart. Another soul, another formed and unchangeable temperament, tumbled into the world! Whence? Whither?... As for the quality of majesty—yes, if silver trumpets had announced the advent, instead of a stout, aproned woman, the moment could not have been more majestic in its sadness. I say "sadness," which is the inevitable and sole effect of these eternal and banal questions, "Whence? Whither?"

"Is her bad?" Jos whispered.

"Her's pretty bad," said the voice, but cheerily. "Bring me up another scuttle o' coal."

When he returned to the parlour, after being again dismissed, I said to him:

"Well, I congratulate you."

"I thank ye!" he said, and sat down. Presently I could hear him muttering to himself, mildly: "Hell! Hell! Hell!"

I thought: "Stirling will not be very long now, and we can depart home." I looked at my watch. It was a quarter to two. But Stirling did not appear, nor was there any message from him or sign. I had to submit to the predicament. As a faint chilliness from the window affected my back I drew my overcoat up to my shoulders as a counterpane. Through a gap between the red curtains of the window I could see a star blazing. It passed behind the curtain with disconcerting rapidity. The universe was swinging and whirling as usual.

VII

Sounds of knocking disturbed me. In the few seconds that elapsed before I could realize just where I was and why I was there, the summoning knocks were repeated. The early sun was shining through the red blind. I sat up and straightened my hair, involuntarily composing my attitude so that nobody who might enter the room should imagine that I had been other than patiently wide-awake all night. The second door of the parlour—that leading to the bar-room of the Foaming Quart—was open, and I could see the bar itself, with shelves rising behind it and the upright handles of a beer-engine at one end. Someone whom I could not see was evidently unbolting and unlocking the principal entrance to the inn. Then I heard the scraping of a creaky portal on the floor.

"Well, Jos lad!"

It was the voice of the little man, Charlie, who had spoken with Myatt on the football field.

"Come in quick, Charlie. It's cowd [cold]," said the voice of Jos Myatt, gloomily.

"Ay! Cowd it is, lad! It's above three mile as I've walked, and thou knows it, Jos. Give us a quartern o' gin."

The door grated again and a bolt was drawn.

346

The two men passed together behind the bar, and so within my vision. Charlie had a grey muffler round his neck; his hands were far in his pockets and seemed to be at strain, as though trying to prevent his upper and his lower garments from flying apart. Jos Myatt was extremely dishevelled. In the little man's demeanour towards the big one there was now none of the self-conscious pride in the mere fact of acquaintance that I had noticed on the field. Clearly the two were intimate friends, perhaps relatives. While Jos was dispensing the gin, Charlie said, in a low tone:

"Well, what luck, Jos?"

This was the first reference, by either of them, to the crisis.

Jos deliberately finished pouring out the gin. Then he said:

"There's two on 'em, Charlie."

"Two on 'em? What mean'st tha', lad?"

"I mean as it's twins."

Charlie and I were equally startled.

"Thou never says!" he murmured, incredulous.

"Ay! One o' both sorts," said Jos.

"Thou never says!" Charlie repeated, holding his glass of gin steady in his hand.

"One come at summat after one o'clock, and th' other between five and six. I had for fetch old woman Eardley to help. It were more than a handful for Susannah and th' doctor."

Astonishing, that I should have slept through these events!

"How is her?" asked Charlie, quietly, as it were casually. I think this appearance of casualness was caused by the stoic suppression of the symptoms of anxiety.

"Her's bad," said Jos, briefly.

"And I am na' surprised," said Charlie. And he lifted the glass. "Well—here's luck." He sipped the gin, savouring it on his tongue like a connoisseur, and gradually making up his mind about its quality. Then he took another sip.

"Hast seen her?"

"I seed her for a minute, but our Susannah wouldna' let me stop i' th' room. Her was raving like."

"Missis?"

"Ay!"

"And th' babbies—hast seen *them*?"

"Ay! But I can make nowt out of 'em. Mrs Eardley says as her's never seen no finer."

347

"Doctor gone?"

"That he has na'! He's bin up there all the blessed night, in his shirt-sleeves. I give him a stiff glass o' whisky at five o'clock and that's all as he's had."

Charlie finished his gin. The pair stood silent.

"Well," said Charlie, striking his leg. "Swelp me bob! It fair beats me! Twins! Who'd ha'thought it? Jos, lad, thou mayst be thankful as it isna' triplets. Never did I think, as I was footing it up here this morning, as it was twins I was coming to!"

"Hast got that half quid in thy pocket?"

"What half quid?" said Charlie, defensively.

"Now then. Chuck us it over!" said Jos, suddenly harsh and overbearing.

"I laid thee half quid as it 'ud be a wench," said Charlie, doggedly.

"Thou'rt a liar, Charlie!" said Jos. "Thou laidst half a quid as it wasna' a boy."

"Nay, nay!" Charlie shook his head.

"And a boy it is!" Jos persisted.

"It being a lad *and* a wench," said Charlie, with a judicial air, "and me 'aving laid as it 'ud be a wench, I wins." In his accents and his gestures I could discern the mean soul, who on principle never paid until he was absolutely forced to pay. I could see also that Jos Myatt knew his man.

"Thou laidst me as it wasna' a lad," Jos almost shouted. "And a lad it is, I tell thee."

"*And* a wench!" said Charlie; then shook his head.

The wrangle proceeded monotonously, each party repeating over and over again the phrases of his own argument. I was very glad that Jos did not know me to be a witness of the making of the bet; otherwise I should assuredly have been summoned to give judgment.

"Let's call it off, then," Charlie suggested at length. "That'll settle it. And it being twins—"

"Nay, thou old devil, I'll none call it off. Thou owes me half a quid, and I'll have it out of thee."

"Look ye here," Charlie said more softly. "I'll tell thee what'll settle it. Which on 'em come first, th' lad or th'wench?"

"Th' wench come first," Jos Myatt admitted, with resentful reluctance, dully aware that defeat was awaiting him.

348

"Well, then! Th' wench is thy eldest child. That's law, that is. And what was us betting about, Jos lad? Us was betting about thy eldest and no other. I'll admit as I laid it wasna' a lad, as thou sayst. And it*wasna'* a lad. First come is eldest, and us was betting about eldest."

Charlie stared at the father in triumph.

Jos Myatt pushed roughly past him in the narrow space behind the bar, and came into the parlour. Nodding to me curtly, he unlocked the bookcase and took two crown pieces from a leathern purse which lay next to the bag. Then he returned to the bar and banged the coins on the counter with fury.

"Take thy brass!" he shouted angrily. "Take thy brass! But thou'rt a damned shark, Charlie, and if anybody 'ud give me a plug o' bacca for doing it, I'd bash thy face in."

The other sniggered contentedly as he picked up his money.

"A bet's a bet," said Charlie.

He was clearly accustomed to an occasional violence of demeanour from Jos Myatt, and felt no fear. But he was wrong in feeling no fear. He had not allowed, in his estimate of the situation, for the exasperated condition of Jos Hyatt's nerves under the unique experiences of the night.

Jos's face twisted into a hundred wrinkles and his hand seized Charlie by the arm whose hand held the coins.

"Drop 'em!" he cried loudly, repenting his naïve honesty. "Drop 'em! Or I'll—"

The stout woman, her apron all soiled, now came swiftly and scarce heard into the parlour, and stood at the door leading to the bar-room.

"What's up, Susannah?" Jos demanded in a new voice.

"Well may ye ask what's up!" said the woman. "Shouting and brangling there, ye sots!"

"What's up?" Jos demanded again, loosing Charlie's arm.

"Her's gone!" the woman feebly whimpered. "Like that!" with a vague movement of the hand indicating suddenness. Then she burst into wild sobs and rushed madly back whence she had come, and the sound of her sobs diminished as she ascended the stairs, and expired altogether in the distant shutting of a door.

The men looked at each other.

Charlie restored the crown-pieces to the counter and pushed them towards Jos.

"Here!" he murmured faintly.

Jos flung them savagely to the ground. Another pause followed.

"As God is my witness," he exclaimed solemnly, his voice saturated with feeling, "as God is my witness," he repeated, "I'll ne'er touch a footba' again!"

Little Charlie gazed up at him sadly, plaintively, for what seemed a long while.

"It's good-bye to th' First League, then, for Knype!" he tragically muttered, at length.

VIII

Dr Stirling drove the car very slowly back to Bursley. We glided gently down into the populous valleys. All the stunted trees were coated with rime, which made the sharpest contrast with their black branches and the black mud under us. The high chimneys sent forth their black smoke calmly and tirelessly into the fresh blue sky. Sunday had descended on the vast landscape like a physical influence. We saw a snake of children winding out of a dark brown Sunday school into a dark brown chapel. And up from the valleys came all the bells of all the temples of all the different gods of the Five Towns, chiming, clanging, ringing, each insisting that it alone invited to the altar of the one God. And priests and acolytes of the various cults hurried occasionally along, in silk hats and bright neckties, and smooth coats with folded handkerchiefs sticking out of the pockets, busy, happy and self-important, the convinced heralds of eternal salvation: no doubt nor hesitation as to any fundamental truth had ever entered their minds. We passed through a long, straight street of new red houses with blue slate roofs, all gated and gardened. Here and there a girl with her hair in pins and a rough brown apron over a gaudy frock was stoning a front step. And half-way down the street a man in a scarlet jersey, supported by two women in blue bonnets, was beating a drum and crying aloud: "My friends, you may die to-night. Where, I ask you, where—?" But he had no friends; not even a boy heeded him. The drum continued to bang in our rear.

I enjoyed all this. All this seemed to me to be fine, seemed to throw off the true, fine, romantic savour of life. I would have altered nothing in it. Mean, harsh, ugly, squalid, crude, barbaric—yes, but what an intoxicating sense in it of the organized vitality of a vast community unconscious of itself! I would have altered nothing even in the events of the night. I thought of the rooms at the top of the staircase of the Foaming Quart—mysterious rooms which I had not seen and never should see, recondite rooms from which a soul had slipped away and into which two had come, scenes of anguish and of frustrated effort! Historical rooms, surely! And yet not a house in the hundreds of houses past which we slid but possessed rooms ennobled and made august by happenings exactly as impressive in their tremendous inexplicableness.

The natural humanity of Jos Myatt and Charlie, their fashion of comporting themselves in a sudden stress, pleased me. How else should they have behaved? I could understand Charlie's prophetic dirge over the ruin of the Knype Football Club. It was not that he did not feel the tragedy in the house. He had felt it, and because he had felt it he had uttered at random, foolishly, the first clear thought that ran into his head.

Stirling was quiet. He appeared to be absorbed in steering, and looked straight in front, yawning now and again. He was much more fatigued than I was. Indeed, I had slept pretty well. He said, as we swerved into Trafalgar Road and overtook the aristocracy on its way to chapel and church:

"Well, ye let yeself in for a night, young man! No mistake!"

He smiled, and I smiled.

"What's going to occur up there?" I asked, indicating Toft End.

"What do you mean?"

"A man like that—left with two babies!"

"Oh!" he said. "They'll manage that all right. His sister's a widow. She'll go and live with him. She's as fond of those infants already as if they were her own."

We drew up at his double gates.

"Be sure ye explain to Brindley," he said, as I left him, "that it isn't my fault ye've had a night out of bed. It was your own doing. I'm going to get a bit of sleep now. See you this evening, Bob's asked me to supper."

A servant was sweeping Bob Brindley's porch and the front door was open. I went in. The sound of the piano guided me to the drawing-room. Brindley, the morning cigarette between his lips, was playing one of Maurice Ravel's "L'heure espagnole." He held his head back so as to keep the smoke out of his eyes. His children in their blue jerseys were building bricks on the carpet.

Without ceasing to play he addressed me calmly:

"You're a nice chap! Where the devil have you been?"

And one of the little boys, glancing up, said, with roguish, imitative innocence, in his high, shrill voice:

"Where the del you been?"

MIMI

I

On a Saturday afternoon in late October Edward Coe, a satisfactory average successful man of thirty-five, was walking slowly along the King's Road, Brighton. A native and inhabitant of the Five Towns in the Midlands, he had the brusque and energetic mien of the Midlands. It could be seen that he was a stranger to the south; and, in fact, he was now viewing for the first time the vast and glittering spectacle of the southern pleasure city in the unique glory of her autumn season. A spectacle to enliven any man by its mere splendour! And yet Edward Coe was gloomy. One reason for his gloom was that he had just left a bicycle, with a deflated back tyre, to be repaired at a shop in Preston Street. Not perhaps an adequate reason for gloom!... Well, that depends. He had been informed by the blue-clad repairer, after due inspection, that the trouble was not a common puncture, but a malady of the valve mysterious.

And the deflation was not the sole cause of his gloom. There was another. He was on his honeymoon. Understand me—not a honeymoon of romance, but a real honeymoon. Who that has ever been on a real honeymoon can look back upon the adventure and faithfully say that it was an unmixed ecstasy of joy? A honeymoon is in its nature and consequences so solemn, so dangerous, and so pitted with startling surprises, that the most irresponsible bridegroom, the most light-hearted, the least in love, must have moments of grave anxiety. And Edward Coe was far from irresponsible. Nor was he only a little in love. Moreover, the circumstances of his marriage were peculiar, and he had married a dark, brooding, passionate girl.

Mrs Coe was the younger of two sisters named Olive Wardle, well known in the most desirable circles in the Five Towns. I mean those circles where intellectual and artistic tastes are united with sound incomes and excellent food delicately served. It will certainly be asked why two sisters should be named Olive. The answer is that though Olive One and Olive Two were treated as sisters, and even treated themselves as sisters, they were not sisters. They were not even half-sisters. They had first met at the age of nine. The father of

Olive One, a widower, had married the mother of Olive Two, a widow. Olive One was the elder by a few months. Olive Two gradually allowed herself to be called Wardle because it saved trouble. They got on with one another very well indeed, especially after the death of both parents, when they became joint mistresses, each with a separate income, of a nice house at Sneyd, the fashionable residential village on the rim of the Five Towns. Like all persons who live long together, they grew in many respects alike. Both were dark, brooding and passionate, and to this deep similarity a superficial similarity of habits and demeanour was added. Only, whereas Olive One was rather more inclined to be the woman of the world, Olive Two was rather more inclined to study and was particularly interested in the theory of music.

They were sought after, naturally. And yet they had reached the age of twenty-five before the world perceived that either of them was not sought after in vain. The fact, obvious enough, that Pierre Emile Vaillac had become an object of profound human interest to Olive One—this fact excited the world, and the world would have been still more excited had it been aware of another fact that was not at all obvious: namely, that Pierre Emile Vaillac was the cause of a secret and terrible breach between the two sisters. Vaillac, a widower with two young children, Mimi and Jean, was a Frenchman, and a great authority on the decoration of egg-shell china, who had settled in the Five Towns as expert partner in one of the classic china firms at Longshaw. He was undoubtedly a very attractive man.

Olive One, when the relations between herself and Vaillac were developing into something unmistakable, had suddenly, and without warning, accused Olive Two of poaching. It was a frightful accusation, and a frightful scene followed it, one of those scenes that are seldom forgiven and never forgotten. It altered their lives; but as they were women of considerable common sense and of good breeding, each did her best to behave afterwards as though nothing had happened.

Olive Two did not convince Olive One of her innocence, because she did not bring forward the supreme proof of it. She was too proud—in her brooding and her mystery—to do so. The supreme proof was that at this time she herself was secretly engaged to be married to Edward Coe, who had conquered her heart with unimaginable swiftness a few weeks before she was about to sit for a musical examination at Manchester. "Let us say nothing till after my exam," she had suggested to her betrothed. "There will be an enormous fuss, and it will put me off, and I shall fail, and I don't want to fail, and you don't want me to fail." He agreed rapturously. Of course she did fail, nevertheless. But being obstinate she said she would go in again, and they continued to make a secret of the engagement. They found the secret delicious. Then followed the devastating episode of Vaillac. Shortly afterwards Olive One and Vaillac were married, and then Olive Two was alone in the nice house. The examination was forgotten, and she hated the house. She wanted to be married; Coe also. But nothing had been said. Difficult to announce her engagement just then! The world would say that she had married out of imitation, and her sister would think that she had married out of pique. Besides, there would be the fuss, which Olive Two hated. Already the fuss of her sister's marriage, and the effort at the wedding of pretending that nothing had happened between them, had fatigued the nerves of Olive Two.

Then Edward Coe had had the brilliant and seductive idea of marrying in secret. To slip away, and then to return, saying, "We are married. That's all!" ... Why not? No fuss! No ceremonial! The accomplished fact, which simplifies everything!

It was, therefore, a secret honeymoon that Edward Coe was on; delightful—but surreptitious, furtive! His mental condition may be best described by stating that, though he was conscious of rectitude, he somehow could not look a policeman in the face. After all, plain people do not usually run off on secret honeymoons. Had he acted wisely? Perhaps this question, presenting itself now and then, was the chief cause of his improper gloom.

II

However, the spectacle of Brighton on a fine Saturday afternoon in October had its effect on Edward Coe—the effect which it has on everybody. Little by little it inspired him with the joy of life, and straightened his back, and put a sparkle into his eyes. And he was filled with the consciousness of the fact that it is a fine thing to be well-dressed and to have loose gold in your pocket, and to eat, drink, and smoke well; and to be among crowds of people who are well-dressed and have loose gold in their pockets, and eat and drink and smoke well; and to know that a magnificent woman will be

355

waiting for you at acertain place at a certain hour, and that upon catching sight of you her dark orbs will take on an enchanting expression reserved for you alone, and that she is utterly yours. In a word, he looked on the bright side of things again. It could not ultimately matter a bilberry whether his marriage was public or private.

He lit a cigarette gaily. He could not guess that untoward destiny was waiting for him close by the newspaper kiosque.

A little girl was leaning against the palisade there, and gazing somewhat restlessly about her. A quite little girl, aged, perhaps, eleven, dressed in blue serge, with a short frock and long legs, and a sailor hat (H.M.S. *Formidable*), and long hair down her back, and a mild, twinkling, trustful glance. Somewhat untidy, but nevertheless the image of grace.

She saw him first. Otherwise he might have fled. But he was right upon her before he saw her. Indeed, he heard her before he saw her.

"Good afternoon, Mr Coe."

"Mimi!"

The Vaillacs were in Brighton! He had chosen practically the other end of the world for his honeymoon, and lo! by some awful clumsiness of fate the Vaillacs were at the same end! The very people from whom he wished to conceal his honeymoon until it was over would know all about it at the very start! Relations between the two Olives would be still more strained and difficult! In brief, from optimism he swung violently back to darkest pessimism. What could be worse than to be caught red-handed in a surreptitious honeymoon?

She noticed his confusion, and he knew that she noticed it. She was a little girl. But she was also a little woman, a little Frenchwoman, who spoke English perfectly—and yet with a difference! They had flirted together, she and Mr Coe. She had a new mother now, but for years she had been without a mother, and she would receive callers at her father's house (if he happened to be out) with a delicious imitation of a practised hostess.

He raised his hat and shook hands and tried to play the game.

"What are you doing here, Mimi?" he asked.

"What are *you* doing here?" she parried, laughing. And then, perceiving his increased trouble, and that she was failing in tact, she went on rapidly, with a screwing up of the childish shoulders and something between a laugh and a grin: "It's my back. It seems it's not strong. And so we've taken an ever so jolly little house for the autumn, because of the air, you know. Didn't you know?"

No, he did not know. That was the worst of strained relations. You were not informed of events in advance.

"Where?" he asked.

"Oh!" she said, pointing. "That way. On the road to Rottingdean. Near the big girls' school. We came in on that lovely electric railway—along the beach. Have you been on it, Mr Coe?"

Terrible! Rottingdean was precisely the scene of his honeymoon. The hazard of fate was truly appalling. He and his wife might have walked one day straight into the arms of her sister! He went hot and cold.

"And where are the others?" he asked nervously.

"Mamma"—she coloured as she used this word, so strange on her lips—"mamma's at home. Father may come to-night. And Ada has brought us here so that Jean can have his hair cut. He didn't want to come without me."

"Ada?"

"Ada's a new servant. She's just gone in there again to see how long the barber will be." Mimi indicated a barber's shop opposite. "And I'm waiting here," she added.

"Mimi," he said, in a confidential tone, "can you keep a secret?"

She grew solemn. "Yes." She smiled seriously. "What?"

"About meeting me. Don't tell anybody you've met me to-day. See?"

"Not Jean?"

"No, not Jean. But later on you can tell—when I give you the tip. I don't want anybody to know just now."

It was a shame. He knew it was a shame. He deliberately flattered her by appealing to her as to a grown woman. He deliberately put a cajoling tone into his voice. He would not have done it if Mimi had not been Mimi—if she had been an ordinary sort of English girl. But she was Mimi. And the temptation was very strong. She promised, gravely. He knew that he could rely on her.

Hurrying away lest Jean and the servant might emerge from the barber's, he remembered with compunction that he had omitted to show any curiosity about Mimi's back.

III

The magnificent woman was to be waiting for him in the lounge of the Royal York Hotel at a quarter to four. She was coming in to Brighton by the Rottingdean omnibus, which function, unless the driver changes his mind, occurs once in every two or three hours. He, being under the necessity of telephoning to London on urgent business, had hired a bicycle and ridden in. Despite the accident to this prehistoric machine, he arrived at the Royal York half a minute before the Rottingdean omnibus passed through the Old Steine and set down the magnificent woman his wife. The sight of her stepping off the omnibus really did thrill him. They entered the hotel together, and, accustomed though the Royal York is to the reception of magnificent women, Olive made a sensation therein. As for him, he could not help feeling just as though he had eloped with her. He could not help fancying that all the brilliant company in the lounge was murmuring under the strains of the band: "That johnny there has certainly eloped with that splendid creature!"

"Ed," she asked, fixing her dark eyes upon him, "is anything the matter?"

They were having tea at a little Moorish table in the huge bay window of the lounge.

"No," he said. This was the first lie of his career as a husband. But truly he could not bring himself to give her the awful shock of telling her that the Vaillacs were close at hand, that their secret was discovered, and that their peace and security depended entirely upon the discretion of little Mimi and upon their not meeting other Vaillacs.

"Then it's having that puncture that has upset you," his wife insisted. You see her feelings towards him were so passionate that she could not leave him alone. She was utterly preoccupied by him.

"No," he said guiltily.

"I'm afraid you don't very much care for this place," she went on, because she knew now that he was not telling her the truth, and that something, indeed, was the matter.

"On the contrary," he replied, "I was informed that the finest tea and the most perfect toast in Brighton were to be had in this lounge, and upon my soul I feel as if I could keep on having tea here for ever and ever amen!"

He was trying to be gay, but not very successfully.

358

"I don't mean just here," she said. "I mean all this south coast."

"Well—" he began judicially.

"Oh! Ed!" she implored him. "*Do* say you don't like it!"

"Why!" he exclaimed. "Don't *you*?"

She shook her head. "I much prefer the north," she remarked.

"Well," he said, "let's go. Say Scarborough."

"You're joking," she murmured. "You adore this south coast."

"Never!" he asserted positively.

"Well, darling," she said, "if you hadn't said first that you didn't care for it, of course I shouldn't have breathed a word—"

"Let's go to-morrow," he suggested.

"Yes." Her eyes shone.

"First train! We should have to leave Rottingdean at six o'clock a.m."

"How lovely!" she exclaimed. She was enchanted by this idea of a capricious change of programme. It gave such a sense of freedom, of irresponsibility, of romance!

"More toast, please," he said to the waiter, joyously.

It cost him no effort to be gay now. He could not have been sad. The world was suddenly transformed into the best of all possible worlds. He was saved! They were saved! Yes, he could trust Mimi. By no chance would they be caught. They would stick in their rooms all the evening, and on the morrow they would be away long before the Vaillacs were up. Papa and "mamma" Vaillac were terrible for late rising. And when he had got his magnificent Olive safe in Scarborough, or wherever their noses might lead them, then he would tell her of the risk they had run.

They both laughed from mere irrational glee, and Edward Coe nearly forgot to pay the bill. However, he did pay it. They departed from the Royal York. He put his Olive into the returning Rottingdean omnibus, and then hurried to get his repaired bicycle. He had momentarily quaked lest Mimi and company might be in the omnibus. But they were not. They must have left earlier, fortunately, or walked.

IV

When he was still about a mile away from Rottingdean, and the hour was dusk, and he was walking up a hill, he caught sight of a girl leaning on a gate that led by a long path to a house near the cliffs. It was Mimi. She gave a cry of recognition. He did not care now—he was at ease now—but really, with that house so close to the road and so close to Rottingdean, he and his Olive had practically begun their honeymoon on the summit of a volcano!

Mimi was pensive. He felt remorse at having bound her to secrecy. She was so pensive, and so wistful, and her eyes were so loyal, that he felt he owed her a more complete confidence.

"I'm on my honeymoon, Mimi," he said. It gave him pleasure to tell her.

"Yes," she said simply, "I saw Auntie Olive go by in the omnibus."

That was all she said. He was thunderstruck, as much by her calm simplicity as by anything else. Children were astounding creatures.

"Did Jean see her, or anyone?" he asked.

Mimi shook her head.

Then he told her they were leaving the next morning at six.

"Shall you be in a carriage?" she inquired.

"Yes."

"Oh! Do let me come out and see you go past," she pleaded. "Nobody else in our house will be up till hours afterwards!... Do!"

He was about to say "No," for it would mean revealing the whole affair to his wife at once. But after an instant he said "Yes." He would not refuse that exquisite, appealing gesture. Besides, why keep anything whatever from Olive, even for a day?

V

At dinner he told his wife, and was glad to learn that she also thought highly of Mimi and had confidence in her.

Mimi lay in bed in the nursery of the hired house on the way to Rottingdean, which, considering that it was not "home," was a fairly comfortable sort of abode. The nursery was immense, though an attic. The white blinds of the two windows were drawn, and a fire burned in the grate, lighting it pleasantly and behaving in a very friendly manner. At the other end of the room, in the deep shadow, was Jean's bed.

The door opened quietly and someone came into the room and pushed the door to without quite shutting it.

"Is that you, mamma?" Jean demanded in his shrill voice, from the distance of the bed in the corner. His age was exactly eight.

"Yes, dear," said the new stepmother.

The menial Ada had arranged the children for the night, and now the stepmother had come up to kiss them and be kind. She was a conscientious young woman, full of a desire to do right, and she had determined not to be like the traditional stepmother.

She kissed Jean, who had taken quite a fancy to her, and tickled him agreeably, and tucked him up anew, and then moved silently across the room to Mimi. Mimi could see her face in the twilight of the fire. A handsome, good-natured face; yet very determined, and perhaps a little too full of common sense. It had a responsible, somewhat grave look. After all, these two young children were a responsibility, especially Mimi with her back; and, moreover, Pierre Emile Vaillac had disappointed both her and her step-children by telegraphing that he could not arrive that night. Olive One, the bride of three months, had put on fine raiment for nothing.

"Well, Mimi," she said in her low, vibrating voice, as she stood over the bed, "I do hope you didn't overtire yourself this afternoon." Then she kissed Mimi.

"Oh no, mamma!" The little girl smiled.

"It seems you waited outside the barber's while Jeannot was having his hair cut."

"Yes, mamma. I didn't like to go in."

"Ada didn't stay with you all the time?"

"No, mamma. First of all she took Jeannot in, and then she came out to me, and then she went in again to see how long he would be."

"I'm sorry she left you alone in the street. She ought not to have done so, and I've told her.... The King's Road, with all kinds of people about!"

Mimi said nothing. The new Madame Vaillac moved a little towards the fire.

"Of course," the latter went on, "I know you're a regular little woman, and perhaps I needn't tell you but you must never speak to anyone in the street."

"No, mamma."

"Particularly in Brighton.... You never do, do you?"

"No, mamma."

"Good-night."

361

The stepmother left the room. Mimi could feel her heart beating. Then Jean called out:

"Mimi."

She made no reply. The fact was she was too disturbed to be able to reply.

Jean called again and then got out of bed and thudded across the room to her bedside.

"I say, Mimi," he screeched in his insistent treble, "who *was* it you were talking to?"

Mimi's heart did not beat, it jumped.

"When? Where?"

"This afternoon, when I was having my hair cut."

"How do you know I was talking to anybody?"

"Ada saw you through the window of the barber's."

"When did she tell you?"

"She didn't. I heard her telling mamma."

There was a silence. Then Mimi hid her face, and Jean could hear sobbing.

"You might tell me!" Jean insisted. He was too absorbed by his own curiosity, and too upset by the full realization of the fact that she had kept something from him, to be touched by her tears.

"It's a secret," she muttered into the pillow.

"You might tell me!"

"Go away, Jeannot!" she burst out hysterically.

He gave an angry lunge against the bed.

"I tell you everything; and it's not fair. *C'est pas juste!*" he said savagely, but there were tears in his voice too. He was a creature at once sensitive and violent, passionately attached to Mimi.

He thudded back to his bed. But even before he had reached his bed Mimi could hear him weeping.

She gradually stilled her own sobs, and after a time Jean's ceased. And then she guessed that Jean had gone to sleep. But Mimi did not go to sleep. She knew that chance, and Mr Coe, and that odious new servant, Ada, had combined to ruin her life. She saw the whole affair clearly. Ada was officious and fussy, also secretive and given to plotting. Ada's leading idea was that children had to be circumvented. Imagine the detestable woman spying on her from the window, and then saying nothing to her, but sneaking off to tell tales to her mamma! Imagine it! Mimi's strict sense of justice could not blame her mamma. She was sure that the new stepmother meant well by her. Her mamma had given her every opportunity to confess, to admit of her own accord that she had been talking to somebody in the street, and she had not confessed. On the contrary, she had lied. Her mamma would probably say nothing more on the matter, for she had a considerable sense of honour with children, and would not take an unfair advantage. Having tried to obtain a confession from Mimi by pretending that she knew nothing, and having failed, she was not the woman to turn round and say, "Now I know all about it. So just confess at once!" Her mamma would accept the situation, would try to behave as if nothing had happened, and would probably even say nothing to her father.

But Mimi knew that she was ruined for ever in her stepmother's esteem.

And she had quarrelled with Jean, which was exceedingly hateful and exceedingly rare. And there was also the private worry of her mysterious back. And there was another thing. The mere fact that her friend, Mr Coe, had gone and married somebody. For long she had had a weakness for Mr Coe. They had been intimate at times. Once, last year, in the stern of a large sailing-boat at Morecambe, while her friends were laughing and shouting at the prow, she and Mr Coe had had a most beautiful quiet conversation about her thoughts on the world in general; she had stroked his hand.... No! She had no dream whatever of growing up into a woman and then marrying Mr Coe! Certainly not. But still, that he should have gone and married, like that ... it was....

The fire died out into blackness, thus ceasing to be a friend. Still she did not sleep. Was it likely that she should sleep, with the tragedy and woe of the entire universe crushing her?

VI

Mr Edward Coe and Olive Two arose from their bed the next morning in great spirits. Mr Coe had told both his wife and Mimi that the hour of departure from Rottingdean would be six o'clock. But this was an exaggeration. So far as his wife was concerned he had already found it well to exaggerate on such matters. A little judicious exaggeration lessened the risk of missing trains and other phenomena which cannot be missed without confusion and disappointment.

363

As a fact it was already six o'clock when Edward Coe looked forth from the bedroom window. He was completely dressed. His wife also was completely dressed. He therefore felt quite safe about the train. The window, which was fairly high up in the world, gave on the south-east, so that he had a view, not only of the vast naked downs billowing away towards Newhaven, but also of the Channel, which was calm, and upon which little parcels of fog rested. The sky was clear overhead, of a greenish sapphire colour, and the autumnal air bit and gnawed on the skin like some friendly domestic animal, and invigorated like an expensive tonic. On the dying foliage of a tree near the window millions of precious stones hung. Cocks were boasting. Cows were expressing a justifiable anxiety. And in the distance a small steamer was making a great deal of smoke about nothing, as it puffed out of Newhaven harbour.

"Olive," he said.

"What is it?"

She was putting hats into the top of her trunk. She had a special hat-box, but the hats were too large for it, and she packed minor trifles in the hat-box, such as skirts. This was one of the details which first indicated to an astounded Edward Coe that a woman is never less like a man than when travelling.

"Come here," he commanded her.

She obeyed.

"Look at that," he commanded her, pointing to the scene of which the window was the frame.

She obeyed. She also looked at him with her dark, passionate, and yet half-mocking eyes.

"Yes," she said, "and who's going to make that trunk lock?"

She snapped her fingers at the sweet morning influences of Nature, to which he was peculiarly sensitive. And yet he was delighted. He found it entirely delicious that she should say, when called upon to admire Nature: "Who's going to make that trunk lock?"

He stroked her hair.

"It's no use trying to keep your hair decent at the seaside," she remarked, pouting exquisitely.

He explained that his hand was offering no criticism of her hair. And then there was a knock at the bedroom door, and Olive Two jumped a little away from her husband.

"Come in," he cried, pretending to be as bold as a lion.

However, he had forgotten that the door was locked, and he had to go and open it.

A tray with coffee and milk and sugar and slices of bread-and-butter was in the doorway, and behind the tray the little parlour-maid of the little hotel. He greeted the girl and instructed her to carry the tray to the table by the window.

"You are prompt," said Olive Two, kindly. She had got up so miraculously early herself that she was startled to see any other woman up quite as early. And also she was a little surprised that the parlour-maid showed no surprise at these very unusual hours.

"Yes'm," replied the parlour-maid, wondering why Olive Two was so excited. The parlour-maid arose at five-thirty every morning of her life, except on special occasions, when she arose at four-thirty to assist in pastoral affairs.

"All right, this coffee, eh?" murmured Edward Coe as he put down the steaming cup after his first sip. They were alone again, seated opposite each other at the small table by the window.

Olive Two nodded.

It must not be supposed that this was the one unique dreamed-of hotel in England where the coffee is good of its own accord. No! In the matter of coffee this hotel was just like all other hotels. Only Olive Two had taken special precautions about that coffee. She had been into the hotel kitchen on the previous evening about that coffee.

"By the way," she asked, "where's the sun?"

"The sun doesn't happen to be up yet," said Edward. He looked at his diary and then at his watch. "Unless something goes wrong, you'll be seeing it inside of three minutes."

"Do you mean to say we shall see the sun rise?" she exclaimed.

He nodded.

"Well!" cried she, absurdly gleeful, "I never heard of such a thing!"

She watched the sunrise like a child who sees for the first time the inside of a watch. And when the sun had risen she glanced anxiously round the disordered room.

"For heaven's sake," she muttered, "don't let's forget these tooth-brushes!"

"You are so ridiculous," said he, "that I must kiss you."

The truth is that they were no better than two children out on an adventure.

It was the same when down in the hotel-yard they got into the small and decrepit victoria which was destined to take them and their luggage to Brighton. It was the same, but more so. They were both so pleased with themselves that their joy was bubbling continually out in manifestations that could only be described as infantile. The mere drive through the village, with the pony whisking his tail round corners, and the driver steadying the perilous hat-box with his left hand, was so funny that somehow they could not help laughing.

Then they had left the village and were climbing the exposed highroad, with the wavy blue-green downs on the right, and the immense glittering flat floor of the Channel on the left. And the mere sensation of being alive almost overwhelmed them.

And further on they passed a house that stood by itself away from the road towards the cliffs. It had a sloping garden and a small greenhouse. The gate leading to the road was ajar, but the blinds of all the windows were drawn, and there was no sign of life anywhere.

"That's the house," said Edward Coe, briefly.

"I might have known it," Olive Two replied. "Olive One is certainly the worst getter-up that I ever had anything to do with, and I believe Pierre Emile isn't much better."

"Well," said Edward, "it's no absolute proof of sluggardliness not to be up and about at six forty-five of a morning, you know."

"I was forgetting how early it was!" said Olive Two, and yawned. The yawn escaped her before she was aware of it. She pulled herself together and kissed her hands mockingly, quizzically, to the house. "Good-bye, house! Good-bye, house!"

They were saved now. They could not be caught now on their surreptitious honeymoon. And their spirits went even higher.

"I thought you said Mimi would be waiting for us?" Olive Two remarked.

Edward Coe shrugged his shoulders. "Probably overslept herself! Or she may have got tired of waiting. I told her six o'clock."

On the whole Olive Two was relieved that Mimi was invisible.

"It wouldn't really matter if she *did* split on us, would it?" said the bride.

"Not a bit," the bridegroom agreed. Now that they had safely left the house behind them, they were both very valiant. It was as if they were both saying: "Who cares?" The bridegroom's mood was entirely different from his sombre apprehensiveness of the previous evening. And the early sunshine on the dew-drops was magnificent.

But a couple of hundred yards further on, at a bend of the road, they saw a little girl shading her eyes with her hand and gazing towards the sun. She wore a short blue serge frock, and she had long restless legs, and the word *Formidable* was on her forehead, and her eyes were all screwed up in the strong sunshine. And in her hand were flowers.

"There she is, after all!" said Edward, quickly.

Olive Two nodded. Olive Two also blushed, for Mimi was the first person acquainted with her to see her after her marriage. She blushed because she was now a married woman.

Mimi, who with much prudence had managed so that the meeting should not occur exactly in front of the house, came towards the carriage. The pony was walking up a slope. She bounded forward with her childish grace and with the awkwardness of her long legs, and her hair loose in the breeze, and she laughed nervously.

"Good morning, good morning," she cried. "Shall I jump on the step? Then the horse won't have to stop."

And she jumped lightly on to the step and giggled, still nervously, looking first at the bridegroom and then at the bride. The bridegroom held her securely by the shoulder.

"Well, Mimi," said Olive Two, whose shyness vanished in an instant before the shyness of the child. "This *is* nice of you."

The two women kissed. But Mimi did not offer her cheek to the bridegroom. He and she simply shook hands as well as they could with a due regard for Mimi's firmness on the step.

"And who woke you up, eh?" Edward Coe demanded.

"Nobody," said Mimi; "I got up by myself, and," turning to Olive Two, "I've made this bouquet for you, auntie. There aren't any flowers in the fields. But I got the chrysanthemum out of the greenhouse, and put some bits of ferns and things round it. You must excuse it being tied up with darning wool."

She offered the bouquet diffidently, and Olive Two accepted it with a warm smile.

"Well," said Mimi, "I don't think I'd better go any further, had I?"

There was another kiss and hand-shaking, and the next moment Mimi was standing in the road and waving a little crumpled handkerchief to the receding victoria, and the bride and bridegroom were cricking their necks to respond. She waved until the carriage was out of sight, and then she stood moveless, a blue and white spot

367

on the green landscape, with the morning sun and the sea behind her.

"Exactly like a little woman, isn't she?" said Edward Coe, enchanted by the vision.

"Exactly!" Olive Two agreed. "Nice little thing! But how tired and unwell she looks! They did well to bring her away."

"Oh!" said Edward Coe, "she probably didn't sleep well because she was afraid of oversleeping herself. She looked perfectly all right yesterday."

THE SUPREME ILLUSION

I

Perhaps it was because I was in a state of excited annoyance that I did not recognize him until he came right across the large hall of the hotel and put his hand on my shoulder.

I had arrived in Paris that afternoon, and driven to that nice, reasonable little hotel which we all know, and whose name we all give in confidence to all our friends; and there was no room in that hotel. Nor in seven other haughtily-managed hotels that I visited! A kind of archduke, who guarded the last of the seven against possible customers, deigned to inform me that the season was at its fullest, half London being as usual in Paris, and that the only central hotels where I had a chance of reception were those monstrosities the Grand and the Hôtel Terminus at the Gare St Lazare. I chose the latter, and was accorded room 973 in the roof.

I thought my exasperations were over. But no! A magnificent porter within the gate had just consented to get my luggage off the cab, and was in the act of beginning to do so, when a savagely-dressed, ugly and ageing woman, followed by a maid, rushed neurotically down the steps and called him away to hold a parcel. He obeyed! At the same instant the barbaric and repulsive creature's automobile, about as large as a railway carriage, drove up and forced my frail cab down the street. I had to wait, humiliated and helpless, the taximeter of my cab industriously adding penny to penny, while that offensive hag installed herself, with the help of the maid, the porter and two page-boys, in her enormous vehicle. I should not have minded had she been young and pretty. If she had been young and pretty she would have had the right to be rude and domineering. But she was neither young nor pretty. Conceivably she had once been young; pretty she could never have been. And her eyes were hard—hard.

Hence my state of excited annoyance.

"Hullo! How goes it?" The perfect colloquial English was gently murmured at me with a French accent as the gentle hand patted my shoulder.

"Why," I said, cast violently out of a disagreeable excitement into an agreeable one, "I do believe you are Boissy Minor!"

369

I had not seen him for nearly twenty years, but I recognized in that soft and melancholy Jewish face, with the soft moustache and the soft beard, the wistful features of the boy of fifteen who had been my companion at an "international" school (a clever invention for inflicting exile upon patriots) with branches at Hastings, Dresden and Versailles.

Soon I was telling him, not without satisfaction, that, being a dramatic critic, and attached to a London daily paper which had decided to flatter its readers by giving special criticisms of the more important new French plays, I had come to Paris for the production of *Notre Dame de la Lune* at the Vaudeville.

And as I told him the idea occurred to me for positively the first time:

"By the way, I suppose you aren't any relation of Octave Boissy?"

I rather hoped he was; for after all, say what you like, there is a certain pleasure in feeling that you have been to school with even a relative of so tremendous a European celebrity as Octave Boissy— the man who made a million and a half francs with his second play, which was nevertheless quite a good play. All the walls of Paris were shouting his name.

"I'm the johnny himself," he replied with timidity, naïvely proud of his Saxon slang.

I did not give an astounded *No*! An astounded *No*! would have been rude. Still, my fear is that I failed to conceal entirely my amazement. I had to fight desperately against the natural human tendency to assume that no boy with whom one has been to school can have developed into a great man.

"Really!" I remarked, as calmly as I could, and added a shocking lie: "Well, I'm not surprised!" And at the same time I could hear myself saying a few days later at the office of my paper: "I met Octave Boissy in Paris. Went to school with him, you know."

"You'd forgotten my Christian name, probably," he said.

"No, I hadn't," I answered. "Your Christian name was Minor. You never had any other!" He smiled kindly. "But what on earth are you doing here?"

Octave Boissy was a very wealthy man. He even looked a very wealthy man. He was one of the darlings of success and of an absurdly luxurious civilization. And he seemed singularly out of place in the vast, banal foyer of the Hôtel Terminus, among the

370

shifting, bustling crowd of utterly ordinary, bourgeois, moderately well-off tourists and travellers and needy touts. He ought at least to have been in a very select private room at the Meurice or the Bristol, if in any hotel at all!

"The fact is, I'm neurasthenic," he said simply, just as if he had been saying, "The fact is, I've got a wooden leg."

"Oh!" I laughed, determined to treat him as Boissy Minor, and not as Octave Boissy.

"I have a morbid horror of walking in the open air. And yet I cannot bear being in a small enclosed space, especially when it's moving. This is extremely inconvenient. *Mais que veux-tu?... Suis comme ça!*"

"*Je te plains*" I put in, so as to return his familiar and flattering "thou" immediately.

"I was strongly advised to go and stay in the country," he went on, with the same serious, wistful simplicity, "and so I ordered a special saloon carriage on the railway, so as to have as much breathing room as possible; and I ventured from my house to this station in an auto. I thought I could surely manage that. But I couldn't! I had a terrible crisis on arriving at the station, and I had to sit on a luggage-truck for four hours. I couldn't have persuaded myself to get into the saloon carriage for a fortune! I couldn't go back home in the auto! I couldn't walk! So I stepped into the hotel. I've been here ever since."

"But when was this?"

"Three months ago. My doctors say that in another six weeks I shall be sufficiently recovered to leave. It is a most distressing malady. *Mais que veux-tu?* I have a suite in the hotel and my own servants. I walk out here into the hall because it's so large. The hotel people do the best they can, but of course—" He threw up his hands. His resigned, gentle smile was at once comic and tragic to me.

"But do you mean to say you couldn't walk out of that door and go home?" I questioned.

"Daren't!" he said, with finality. "Come to my rooms, will you, and have some tea."

II

A little later his own valet served us with tea in a large private drawing-room on the sixth or seventh floor, to reach which we had climbed a thousand and one stairs; it was impossible for Octave Boissy to use the lift, as he was convinced that he would die in it if he took such a liberty with himself. The room was hung with modern pictures, such as had certainly never been seen in any hotel before. Many knick-knacks and embroideries were also obviously foreign to the hotel.

"But how have you managed to attend the rehearsals of the new play?" I demanded.

"Oh!" said he, languidly, "I never attend any rehearsals of my plays. Mademoiselle Lemonnier sees to all that."

"She takes the leading part in this play, doesn't she, according to the posters?"

"She takes the leading part in all my plays," said he.

"A first-class artiste, no doubt? I've never seen her act."

"Neither have I!" said Octave Boissy. And as I now yielded frankly to my astonishment, he added: "You see, I am not interested in the theatre. Not only have I never attended a rehearsal, but I have never seen a performance of any of my plays. Don't you remember that it was engineering, above all else, that attracted me? I have a truly wonderful engineering shop in the basement of my house in the Avenue du Bois. I should very much have liked you to see it; but you comprehend, don't you, that I'm just as much cut off from the Avenue du Bois as I am from Timbuctoo. My malady is the most exasperating of all maladies."

"Well, Boissy Minor," I observed, "I suppose it has occurred to you that your case is calculated to excite wonder in the simple breast of a brutal Englishman."

He laughed, and I was glad that I had had the courage to reduce him definitely to the rank of Boissy Minor.

"And not only in the breast of an Englishman!" he said. "*Mais que veux-tu?* One must live."

"But I should have thought you could have made a comfortable living out of engineering. In England consulting engineers are princes."

"Oh yes!"

"And engineering might have cured your neurasthenia, if you had taken it in sufficiently large quantities."

"It would," he agreed quietly.

"Then why the theatre, seeing that the theatre doesn't interest you?"

"In order to live," he replied. "And when I say 'live,' I mean *live*. It is not a question of money, it is a question of *living*."

"But as you never go near the theatre—"

"I write solely for Blanche Lemonnier," he said. I was at a loss. Perceiving this, he continued intimately: "Surely you know of my admiration for Blanche Lemonnier?"

I shook my head.

"I have never even heard of Blanche Lemonnier, save in connection with your plays," I said.

"She is only known in connection with my plays," he answered. "When I met her, a dozen years ago, she was touring the provinces, playing small parts in third-rate companies. I asked her what was her greatest ambition, and she said that it was to be applauded as a star on the Paris stage. I told her that I would satisfy her ambition, and that when I had done so I hoped she would satisfy mine. That was how I began to write plays. That was my sole reason. It is the sole reason why I keep on writing them. If she had desired to be a figure in Society I should have gone into politics."

"I am getting very anxious to see this lady," I said. "I feel as if I can scarcely wait till to-night."

"She will probably be here in a few minutes," said he.

"But how did you do it?" I asked. "What was your plan of campaign?"

"After the success of my first play I wrote the second specially for her, and I imposed her on the management. I made her a condition. The management kicked, but I was in a position to insist. I insisted."

"It sounds simple." I laughed uneasily.

"If you are a dramatic critic," he said, "you will guess that it was not at first quite so simple as it sounds. Of course it is simple enough now. Blanche Lemonnier is now completely identified with my plays. She is as well known as nearly any actress in Paris. She has the glory she desired." He smiled curiously. "Her ambition is satisfied—so is mine." He stopped.

"Well," I said, "I've never been so interested in any play before. And I shall expect Mademoiselle Lemonnier to be magnificent."

"Don't expect too much," he returned calmly. "Blanche's acting is not admired by everybody. And I cannot answer for her powers, as I've never seen her at work."

"It's that that's so extraordinary!"

"Not a bit! I could not bear to see her on the stage. I hate the idea of her acting in public. But it is her wish. And after all, it is not the actress that concerns me. It is the woman. It is the woman alone who makes my life worth living. So long as she exists and is kind to me my neurasthenia is a matter of indifference, and I do not even trouble about engineering."

He tried to laugh away the seriousness of his tone, but he did not quite succeed. Hitherto I had been amused at his singular plight and his fatalistic acceptance of it. But now I was touched.

"I'm talking very freely to you," he said.

"My dear fellow," I burst out, "do let me see her portrait."

He shook his head.

"Unfortunately her portrait is all over Paris. She likes it so. But I prefer to have no portrait myself. My feeling is—"

At that moment the valet opened the door and we heard vivacious voices in the corridor.

"She is here," said Octave Boissy, in a whisper suddenly dramatic. He stood up; I also. His expression had profoundly changed. He controlled his gestures and his attitude, but he could not control his eye. And when I saw that glance I understood what he meant by "living." I understood that, for him, neither fame nor artistic achievement nor wealth had any value in his life. His life consisted in one thing only.

"*Eh bien, Blanche!*" he murmured amorously.

Blanche Lemonnier invaded the room with arrogance. She was the odious creature whose departure in her automobile had so upset my arrival.

THE LETTER AND THE LIE

I

As he hurried from his brougham through the sombre hall to his study, leaving his secretary far in the rear, he had already composed the first sentence of his address to the United Chambers of Commerce of the Five Towns; his mind was full of it; he sat down at once to his vast desk, impatient to begin dictating. Then it was that he perceived the letter, lodged prominently against the gold and onyx inkstand given to him on his marriage by the Prince and Princess of Wales. The envelope was imperfectly fastened, or not fastened at all, and the flap came apart as he fingered it nervously.

"Dear Cloud,—This is to say good-bye, finally—"

He stopped. Fear took him at the heart, as though he had been suddenly told by a physician that he must submit to an operation endangering his life. And he skipped feverishly over the four pages to the signature, "Yours sincerely, Gertrude."

The secretary entered.

"I must write one or two private letters first," he said to the secretary. "Leave me. I'll ring."

"Yes, sir. Shall I take your overcoat?"

"No, no."

A discreet closing of the door.

"—finally. I can't stand it any longer. Cloud, I'm gone to Italy. I shall use the villa at Florence, and trust you to leave me alone. You must tell our friends. You can start with the Bargraves to-night. I'm sure they'll agree with me it's for the best—"

It seemed to him that this letter was very like the sort of letter that gets read in the Divorce Court and printed in the papers afterwards; and he felt sick.

"—for the best. Everybody will know in a day or two, and then in another day or two the affair will be forgotten. It's difficult to write naturally under the circumstances, so all I'll say is that we aren't suited to each other, Cloud. Ten years of marriage has amply proved that, though I knew it six—seven—years ago. You haven't guessed that you've been killing me all these years; but it is so—"

Killing her! He flushed with anger, with indignation, with innocence, with guilt—with Heaven knew what!

"—it is so. *You've* been living *your* life. But what about me? In five more years I shall be old, and I haven't begun to live. I can't*stand* it any longer. I can't stand this awful Five Towns district—"

Had he not urged her many a time to run up to South Audley Street for a change, and leave him to continue his work? Nobody wanted her to be always in Staffordshire!

"—and I can't stand *you*. That's the brutal truth. You've got on my nerves, my poor boy, with your hurry, and your philanthropy, and your commerce, and your seriousness. My poor nerves! And you've been too busy to notice it. You fancied I should be content if you made love to me absent-mindedly, *en passant*, between a political dinner and a bishop's breakfast."

He flinched. She had stung him.

"I sting you—"

No! And he straightened himself, biting his lips!

"—I sting you! I'm rude! I'm inexcusable! People don't say these things, not even hysterical wives to impeccable husbands, eh? I admit it. But I was bound to tell you. You're a serious person, Cloud, and I'm not. Still, we were both born as we are, and I've just as much right to be unserious as you have to be serious. That's what you've never realized. You aren't better than me; you're only different from me. It is unfortunate that there are some aspects of the truth that you are incapable of grasping. However, after this morning's scene—"

Scene? What scene? He remembered no scene, except that he had asked her not to interrupt him while he was reading his letters, had asked her quite politely, and she had left the breakfast-table. He thought she had left because she had finished. He hadn't a notion—what nonsense!

"—this morning's scene, I decided not to 'interrupt' you any more—"

Yes. There was the word he had used—how childish she was!

"—any more in the contemplation of those aspects of the truth which you*are* capable of grasping. Good-bye! You're an honest man, and a straight man, and very conscientious, and very clever, and I expect you're doing a lot of good in the world. But your responsibilities are too much for you. I relieve you of one, quite a minor one—your wife. You don't want a wife. What you want is a doll that you can wind up once a fortnight to say 'Good-morning, dear,' and 'Good-night, dear.' I think I can manage without a husband for a very long time. I'm not so bitter as you might guess from this letter, Cloud. But I want you thoroughly to comprehend that it's finished between us. You can do what you like. People can say what they like. I've had enough. I'll pay any price for freedom. Good luck. Best wishes. I would write this letter afresh if I thought I could do a better one.—Yours sincerely, Gertrude."

He dropped the letter, picked it up and read it again and then folded it in his accustomed tidy manner and replaced it in the envelope. He sat down and propped the letter against the inkstand and stared at the address in her careless hand: "The Right Honourable Sir Cloud Malpas, Baronet." She had written the address in full like that as a last stroke of sarcasm. And she had not even put "Private."

He was dizzy, nearly stunned; his head rang.

Then he rose and went to the window. The high hill on which stood Malpas Manor—the famous Rat Edge—fell away gradually to the south, and in the distance below him, miles off, the black smoke of the Five Towns loomed above the yellow fires of blast-furnaces. He was the demi-god of the district, a greater landowner than even the Earl of Chell, a model landlord, a model employer of four thousand men, a model proprietor of seven pits and two iron foundries, a philanthropist, a religionist, the ornamental mayor of Knype, chairman of a Board of Guardians, governor of hospitals, president of Football Association—in short, Sir Cloud, son of Sir Cloud and grandson of Sir Cloud.

He stared dreamily at his dominion. Scandal, then, was to touch him with her smirching finger, him the spotless! Gertrude had fled. He had ruined Gertrude's life! Had he? With his heavy and severe conscientiousness he asked himself whether he was to blame in her regard. Yes, he thought he was to blame. It stood to reason that he was to blame. Women, especially such as Gertrude, proud, passionate, reserved, don't do these things for nothing.

With a sigh he passed into his dressing-room and dropped on to a sofa.

She would be inflexible—he knew her. His mind dwelt on the beautiful first days of their marriage, the tenderness and the dream! And now—!

He heard footsteps in the study; the door was opened! It was Gertrude! He could see her in the dusk. She had returned! Why? She tripped to the desk, leaned forward and snatched at the letter. Evidently she did not know that he was in the house and had read it.

The tension was too painful. A sigh broke from him, as it were of physical torture.

"Who's there?" she cried, in a startled voice. "Is that you, Cloud?"

"Yes," he breathed.

"But you're home very early!" Her voice shook.

"I'm not well, Gertrude," he replied. "I'm tired. I came in here to lie down. Can't you do something for my head? I must have a holiday."

He heard her crunch up the letter, and then she hastened to him in the dressing-room.

"My poor Cloud!" she said, bending over him in the mature elegance of her thirty years. He noticed her travelling costume. "Some eau de Cologne?"

He nodded weakly.

"We'll go away for a holiday," he said, later, as she bathed his forehead.

The touch of her hands on his temples reminded him of forgotten caresses. And he did really feel as though, within a quarter of an hour, he had been through a long and dreadful illness and was now convalescent.

II

"Then you think that after starting she thought better of it?" said Lord Bargrave after dinner that night. "And came back?"

Lord Bargrave was Gertrude's cousin, and he and his wife sometimes came over from Shropshire for a week-end. He sat with Sir Cloud in the smoking-room; a man with greying hair and a youngish, equable face.

"Yes, Harry, that was it. You see, I'd just happened to put the letter exactly where I found it. She's no notion that I've seen it."

"She's a thundering good actress!" observed Lord Bargrave, sipping some whisky. "I knew something was up at dinner, but I didn't know it from *her*: I knew it from you."

Sir Cloud smiled sadly.

"Well, you see, I'm supposed to be ill—at least, to be not well."

"You'd best take her away at once," said Lord Bargrave. "And don't do it clumsily. Say you'll go away for a few days, and then gradually lengthen it out. She mentioned Italy, you say. Well, let it be Italy. Clear out for six months."

"But my work here?"

"D—n your work here!" said Lord Bargrave. "Do you suppose you're indispensable here? Do you suppose the Five Towns can't manage without you? Our caste is decayed, my boy, and silly fools like you try to lengthen out the miserable last days of its importance by giving yourselves airs in industrial districts! Your conscience tells you that what the demagogues say is true—we *are* rotters on the face of the earth, we *are* mediæval; and you try to drown your conscience in the noise of philanthropic speeches. There isn't a sensible working-man in the Five Towns who doesn't, at the bottom of his heart, assess you at your true value—as nothing but a man with a hobby, and plenty of time and money to ride it."

"I do not agree with you," Sir Cloud said stiffly.

"Yes, you do," said Lord Bargrave. "At the same time I admire you, Cloud. I'm not built the same way myself, but I admire you— except in the matter of Gertrude. There you've been wrong—of course from the highest motives: which makes it all the worse. A man oughtn't to put hobbies above the wife of his bosom. And, besides, she's one of *us*. So take her away and stay away and make love to her."

"Suppose I do? Suppose I try? I must tell her!"

"Tell her what?"

"That I read the letter. I acted a lie to her this afternoon. I can't let that lie stand between us. It would not be right."

Lord Bargrave sprang up.

"Cloud," he cried. "For heaven's sake, don't be an infernal ass. Here you've escaped a domestic catastrophe of the first magnitude by a miracle. You've made a sort of peace with Gertrude. She's come to her senses. And now you want to mess up the whole show by the act of an idiot! What if you did act a lie to her this afternoon? A very good thing! The most sensible thing you've done for years! Let the lie stand between you. Look at it carefully every morning when you awake. It will help you to avoid repeating in the future the high-minded errors of the past. See?"

III

And in Lady Bargrave's dressing-room that night Gertrude was confiding in Lady Bargrave.

"Yes," she said, "Cloud must have come in within five minutes of my leaving—two hours earlier than he was expected. Fortunately he went straight to his dressing-room. Or was it unfortunately? I was half-way to the station when it occurred to me that I hadn't fastened the envelope! You see, I was naturally in an awfully nervous state, Minnie. So I told Collins to turn back. Fuge, our new butler, is of an extremely curious disposition, and I couldn't bear the idea of him prying about and perhaps reading that letter before Cloud got it. And just as I was picking up the letter to fasten it I heard Cloud in the next room. Oh! I never felt so queer in all my life! The poor boy was quite unwell. I screwed up the letter and went to him. What else could I do? And really he was so tired and white—well, it moved me! It moved me. And when he spoke about going away I suddenly thought: 'Why not try to make a new start with him?' After all ..."

There was a pause.

"What did you say in the letter?" Lady Bargrave demanded. "How did you put it?"

"I'll read it to you," said Gertrude, and she took the letter from her corsage and began to read it. She got as far as "I can't stand this awful Five Towns district," and then she stopped.

"Well, go on," Lady Bargrave encouraged her.

"No," said Gertrude, and she put the letter in the fire. "The fact is," she said, going to Lady Bargrave's chair, "it was too cruel. I hadn't realized.... I must have been very worked-up.... One does work oneself up.... Things seem a little different now...." She glanced at her companion.

"Why, Gertrude, you're crying, dearest!"

"What a chance it was!" murmured Gertrude, in her tears. "What a chance! Because, you know, if he *had* once read it I would never have gone back on it. I'm that sort of woman. But as it is, there's a sort of hope of a sort of happiness, isn't there?"

"Gertrude!" It was Sir Cloud's voice, gentle and tender, outside the door.

"Mercy on us!" exclaimed Lady Bargrave. "It's half-past one. Bargrave will have been asleep long since."

Gertrude kissed her in silence, opened the door, and left her.

380

THE GLIMPSE

I

When I was dying I had no fear. I was simply indifferent, partly, no doubt, through exhaustion caused by my long illness. It was a warm evening in August. We ought to have been at Blackpool, of course, but we were in my house in Trafalgar Road, and the tramcars between Hanley and Bursley were shaking the house just as usual. Perhaps not quite as usual; for during my illness I had noticed that a sort of tiredness, a soft, nice feeling, seems to come over everything at sunset of a hot summer's day. This universal change affected even the tramcars, so that they rolled up and down the hill more gently. Or it may have been merely my imagination. Through the open windows I could see, dimly, the smoke of the Cauldon Bar Iron Works slowly crossing the sky in front of the sunset. Margaret sat in my grandfather's oak chair by the gas-stove. There was only Margaret, besides the servant, in the house; the nurse had been obliged to go back to Pirehill Infirmary for the night. I don't know why. Moreover, it didn't matter.

I began running my extraordinarily white fingers along the edge of the sheet. I was doing this quite mechanically when I noticed a look of alarm in Margaret's face, and I vaguely remembered that playing with the edge of the sheet was supposed to be a trick of the dying. So I stopped, more for Margaret's sake than for anything else. I could not move my head much, in fact scarcely at all; hence it was difficult for me to keep my eyes on objects that were not in my line of vision as I lay straight on my pillows. Thus my eyes soon left Margaret's. I forgot her. I thought about nothing. Then she came over to the bed, and looked at me, and I smiled at her, very feebly. She smiled in return. She appeared to me to be exceedingly strong and healthy. Six weeks before I had been the strong and healthy one—I was in my prime, forty, and had a tremendous appetite for business—and I had always regarded her as fragile and delicate; and now she could have crushed me without effort! I had an unreasonable, instinctive feeling of shame at being so weak compared to her. I knew that I was leaving her badly off; we were both good spenders, and all my spare profits had gone into the manufactory; but I did not trouble about that. I was almost quite

381

callous about that. I thought to myself, in a confused way: "Anyhow, I shan't be here to see it, and she'll worry through somehow!" Nor did I object to dying. It may be imagined that I resented death at so early an age, and being cut off in my career, and prevented from getting the full benefit of the new china-firing oven that I had patented. Not at all! It may be imagined that I was preoccupied with a future life, and thinking that possibly we had given up going to chapel without sufficient reason. No! I just lay there, submitting like a person without will or desires to the nursing of my wife, which was all of it accurately timed by the clock.

I just lay there and watched the gradual changing of the sky, and, faintly, heard clocks striking and the quiet swish of my wife's dress. Once my ear would have caught the ticking of our black marble clock on the mantelpiece; but not now—it was lost to me. I watched the gradual changing of the sky, until the blue of the sky had darkened so that the blackness of the smoke was merged in it. But to the left there appeared a faint reddish glare, which showed where the furnaces were; this glare had been invisible in daylight. I watched all that, and I waited patiently for the last trace of silver to vanish from a high part of the sky above where the sunset had been—and it would not. I would shut my eyes for an age, and then open them again, and the silver was always in the sky. The cars kept rumbling up the hill and bumping down the hill. And there was still that soft, languid feeling over everything. And all the heat of the day remained. Sometimes a waft of hot air moved the white curtains. Margaret ate something off a plate. The servant stole in. Margaret gave a gesture as though to indicate that I was asleep. But I was not asleep. The servant went off. Twice I restrained my thin, moist hands from playing with the edge of the sheet. Then I closed my eyes with a kind of definite closing, as if finally admitting that I was too exhausted to keep them open.

II

Difficult to describe my next conscious sensations, when I found I was not in the bed! I have never described them before. You will understand why I've never described them to my wife. I meant never to describe them to anyone. But as you came all the way from London, Mr Myers, and seem to understand all this sort of thing, I've made up my mind to tell you for what it's worth. Yes, what you say about the difficulty of sticking to the exact truth is quite correct. I feel it. Still, I don't think I over-flatter myself in saying that I am a more than ordinarily truthful man.

Well, I was looking at the bed. I was not in the bed. I can't be precisely sure where I was standing, but I think it was between the two windows, half behind the crimson curtains. Anyhow, I must have been near the windows, or I couldn't have seen the foot of the bed and the couch that is there. I could most distinctly hear Cauldon Church clock, more than two miles away, strike two. I was cold. Margaret was leaning over the bed, and staring at a face that lay on the pillows. At first it did not occur to me that this face on the pillows was my face. I had to reason out that fact. When I had reasoned it out I tried to speak to Margaret and tell her that she was making a mistake, gazing at that thing there on the pillows, and that the real one was standing in the cold by the windows. I could not speak. Then I tried to attract her attention in other ways; but I could do nothing. Once she turned sharply, as if startled, and looked straight at me. I strove more frantically than ever to make signs to her; but no, I could not. Seemingly she did not see.

Then I thought: "I'm dead! This is being dead! I've died!"

Margaret ran to the dressing-table and picked up her hand-mirror. She rubbed it carefully on the counterpane, and then held it to the mouth and nostrils of that face on the pillows, and then examined it under the gas. She was very agitated; the whole of her demeanour had changed; I scarcely recognized her. I could not help thinking that she was mad. She put down the mirror, glanced at the clock, even glanced out of the window (she was much closer to me than I am now to you), and then flew back to the bed. She seized the scissors that were hanging from her girdle, and cut a hole in the top pillow, and drew from it a flock of down, which she carefully placed on the lips of that face. The down did not even tremble. Then she bared the breast of the body on the bed, and laid her ear upon the region of the heart; I could see her eyes blinking as she listened intensely. After she had listened some time she raised her head, with a little sob, and frantically pulled the bell-rope. I could hear the bell; we could both hear it. There was no response; nothing but a fearful silence. Margaret, catching her breath, rushed out of the room. I was sick with the most awful disgust that I could not force her to see where I was. I had been helpless before, when I lay in the bed, but I was far more completely helpless now. Talk about the babe unborn!

She came back with the servant, and the two women stood on either side of the bed, gazing at that body. The servant whispered:

"They do say that if you put a full glass of water on the chest you can tell for sure."

Margaret hesitated. However, the servant began to fill a glass of water on the washstand, and they poised it on the chest of that body. Not the slightest vibration troubled its surface. I was—not angry; no, tremendously disgusted is the only term I can use—at all this flummery with that body on the bed. It was shocking to me that they should confuse that body with me. I thought them silly, wilfully silly. I thought their behaviour monstrously blind. There was I, the master of the house, standing chilled between the windows, and neither Margaret nor the servant would take the least notice of me!

The servant said:

"I'd better run for the doctor, ma'am." And she lifted off the glass.

"What use can the doctor be?" Margaret asked. "Only spoil the poor man's night for nothing. And he's had a lot of bad nights lately. He told me to be—prepared."

The servant said:

"Yes, mum.. But I'd better run for him. That's what doctors is for."

As soon as the front-door banged on the excited servant, my wife fell on that body with a loud cry, and stroked it passionately, and I could see her tears dropping on it. She wept without any restraint. She loved me very much; I knew that. But the fact that she loved me only increased my horror that she should be caressing that body, which was not me at all, which had nothing whatever to do with me, which was loathsome, vile, and as insensible as a log to the expressions of her love. She was not weeping over me. She was weeping over an abomination. She was all wrong, all tragically wrong, and I could not set her right. Her woe desolated me. We had been happy together for sixteen years. Her error desolated me, as a painful farce. But a slow, horrible change in my own consciousness made me forget her grief in my own increasing misery.

III

I do not suppose that the feeling which came over me is capable of being described in human language. It can only be hinted at, not truly conveyed. If I say that I was utterly overcome by the sensation of being *cut off from everything*, I shall perhaps not impress you very much with a notion of my terror. But I do not see how I can better express myself. No one who has not been through what I have been through—it is a pretty awful thought that all who die do probably go through it—can possibly understand the feeling of acute and frightful loneliness that possessed me as I stood near the windows, that wrapped me up and enveloped me, as it were, in an icy sheet. A few people in England are possibly in my case—they have *been*, and they have returned, like me. They will understand, and only they. I was solitary in the universe. I was invisible, and I was forgotten. There was my poor wife lavishing her immense sorrow on that body on the bed, which had ceased to have any connection with me, which was emphatically not me, and to which I felt the strongest repugnance. I was even jealous of that lifeless, unresponsive, decaying mass. You cannot guess how I tried to yell to my wife to come to me and warm me with her companionship and her sympathy—and I could accomplish nothing, not the faintest whisper.

I had no home, no shelter, no place in the world, no share in life. I was cast out. The changeless purposes of nature had ejected me from humanity. It was as though humanity had been a fortified city and the gates had been shut on me, and I was wandering round and round the unscalable smooth walls, and beating against their stone with my hands. That is a good simile, except that I could not move. Of course if I could have moved I should have gone to my wife. But I could not move. To be quite exact, I could move very slightly, perhaps about an inch or two inches, and in any direction, up or down, to left or right, backwards or forwards; this by a great straining, fatiguing effort. I was stuck there on the surface of the world, desolate and undone. It was the most cruel situation that you can imagine; far worse, I think, than any conceivable physical torture. I am perfectly sure that I would have exchanged my state, then, for the state of no matter what human being, the most agonized martyr, the foulest criminal. I would have given anything, made any sacrifice, to be once more within the human pale, to feel once more that human life was not going on without me.

There was a knocking below. My wife left that body on the bed, and came to the window and put her head out into the nocturnal, gas-lit silence of Trafalgar Road. She was within a foot of me—and I could do nothing.

She whispered: "Is that you, Mary?"

The voice of the servant came: "Yes, mum. The doctor's been called away to a case. He's not likely to be back before five o'clock."

My wife said, with sad indifference: "It doesn't matter now. I'll let you in."

She went from the room. I heard the opening and shutting of the door. Then both women returned into the room, and talked in low voices.

My wife said: "As soon as it's light you must ..." She stopped and corrected herself. "No, the nurse will be back at seven o'clock. She said she would. She will attend to all that. Mary, go and get a little rest, if you can."

"Aren't you going to put the pennies on his eyes, mum?" the servant asked.

"Ought I?" said my wife. "I don't know much about these things."

"Oh, yes, mum. And tie his jaw up," the servant said.

His eyes! *His* jaw! I was terribly angry, in my desolation. But it was a futile anger, though it raged through me like a storm. Could they not understand, would they never understand, that they were grotesquely deceived? How much longer would they continue to fuss over that body on the bed while I, *I*, the person whom they were supposed to be sorry for, suffered and trembled in dire need just behind them?

A ridiculous bother over pennies! There was only one penny in the house, they decided, after searching. I knew the exact whereabouts of two shillings worth of copper, rolled in paper in my desk in the dining-room. It had been there for many weeks; I had brought it home one day from the works. But they did not know. I wanted to tell them, so as to end the awful exacerbation of my nerves. But of course I could not. In spite of Mary's superstitious protest, my wife put a penny on one eye and half-a-crown on the other. Mary seemed to regard this as a desecration, or at best as unlucky. Then they bound up the jaw of that body with one of my handkerchiefs. I thought I had never seen anything more wantonly absurd. Their trouble in straightening the arms—the legs were quite straight—infuriated me. I wanted to weep in my tragic vexation. It seemed as though tears would ease me. But I could not weep.

The servant said: "You'd better come away now, mum, and rest on the sofa in the drawing-room."

Margaret, with red-bordered, glittering eyes, answered, staring all the while at that body: "No, Mary. It's no use. I can't leave him. I won't leave him!"

But she wasn't thinking about me at all. There I was, neglected and shivering, near the windows; and she would not look at me!

After an interminable palaver Margaret induced the servant to leave the room. And she sat down on the chair nearest the bed, and began to cry again, not troubling to wipe her eyes. She sobbed, more and more loudly, and kept touching that body. She seized my gold watch, which hung over the bed, and which she wound up every night, and kissed it and put it back. Her sobs continued to increase. Then the door opened quietly, and the servant, half-undressed, crept in, and without saying a word gently led Margaret out of the room. Margaret's last glance was at that body. In a moment the servant returned and extinguished the gas, and departed again, very carefully closing the door. I was now utterly abandoned.

IV

All that had happened to me up to now was strange; but what followed was still more strange and still less capable of being described in human language.

I became aware that I was gradually losing the sensation of being cut off from intercourse, at any-rate that the sensation was losing its painfulness. I didn't seem to care, now, whether I was neglected or not. And to be cast out from humanity grew into a matter of indifference to me. I became aware, too, of the approach of a mysterious freedom. I was not free, I could still move only an inch or so in any direction; but I felt that a process of dissolving of bonds had begun. What manner of bonds? I don't know. I felt—that was all. My indifference slowly passed into a sad and deep pity for the world. The world seemed to me so pathetic, so awry, so obstinate in its honest illusions, so silly in its dishonest pretences. "Have I been content with *that*?" I thought, staggered. And I was sorry for what I had been. I perceived that the ideals of my life were tawdry, that even the best were poor little things. And I perceived that it was the same with everyone, and that even the greatest men, those men that I had so profoundly admired as of another clay than mine, were as like the worst as one sheep was like another sheep. Weep—because nature had ejected me from that petty little world, with its ridiculous and conceited wrongness? What an idea! Why, I said to myself, that world spends nearly the whole of its time in moving physical things from one place to another. Change the position of matter—that is all it does, all it thinks of. I remembered a statesman who had referred to the London and North-Western Railway as being one of the glories of England! Parcels! Parcels! Parcels, human, brute, insensate! Nothing but parcel-moving! I smiled. And then I perceived that I could understand and solve problems which had defied thousands of years of human philosophy, problems which we on earth called fundamental. And lo! They were not in the least fundamental, but were trifles, as simple as Euclid. It was surprising that the solution of them had not presented itself to me before! I thought: With one word, one single word, I could enlighten the human race beyond all that it has ever learned. Feeble-bodied, feeble-minded humanity!

And then I had a glimpse.... I was in the bedroom, near the windows, all the time, but nevertheless I was nowhere, nowhere in space. I could feel the roll of the earth as it turned lumberingly on its axis—a faint shaking which did not affect me. Still, I was in the bedroom, near the windows. And I had a glimpse.... The heralds of a new vitality swept trumpeting through me, and a calm, intense, ineffable joy followed in their train. I had a glimpse.... And my eyes were not dazzled. I yearned and strained towards what I saw, towards the exceeding brightness of undreamt companionships, hopes, perceptions, activities, and sorrows. Yes, sorrows! But what noble sorrows they were that I felt awaited me there! I strained at my mysterious bonds. It seemed that they were about to break and that I should be winged away into other dimensions....

And then, I knew that they were tightening again, and the brightness very slowly faded, and I lost faith in the gift of vision which momentarily had enabled me to see the illusions and the littleness of the world. And I was slowly, slowly drawn away from the window.... And then I felt heavy weights on my eyes, and I could not move my jaw. I shuddered convulsively, and a coin struck the floor and ran till it fell flat. And the door swiftly opened....

V

Yes, my whole character is changed, within; though externally it may seem the same. Externally I may seem to have resumed the affections and the interests which occupied me before my illness and my remarkable recovery. Yet I am different. Certainly I have lost again the strange transcendental knowledge which was mine for a few instants. Certainly I have descended again to the earthly level. All those magic things have slipped away, except hope. In a sure hope, in a positive faith, I am waiting. I am waiting for all that magic to happen to me again. I know that the pain of loneliness, when again I shall see my own body from the outside, will be exquisite, but—the reward! The reward! That is what is always at the back of my mind, the source of the calm joy in which I wait. Externally I am the successful earthenware manufacturer, happily married, getting rich on a china-firing oven, employing a couple of hundred workmen, etcetera, who was once given up for dead. But I am more than that. I have seen God.

JOCK-AT-A-VENTURE

I

All this happened at a Martinmas Fair in Bursley, long ago in the fifties, when everybody throughout the Five Towns pronounced Bursley "Bosley" as a matter of course; in the tedious and tragic old times, before it had been discovered that hell was a myth, and before the invention of pleasure or even of half-holidays. Martinmas was in those days a very important moment in the annual life of the town, for it was at Martinmas that potters' wages were fixed for twelve months ahead, and potters hired themselves out for that term at the best rate they could get. Even to the present day the housewives reckon chronology by Martinmas. They say, "It'll be seven years come Martinmas that Sal's babby died o' convulsions." Or, "It was that year as it rained and hailed all Martinmas." And many of them have no idea why it is Martinmas, and not Midsummer or Whitsun, that is always on the tips of their tongues.

The Fair was one of the two great drunken sprees of the year, the other being the Wakes. And it was meet that it should be so, for intoxication was a powerful aid to the signing of contracts. A sot would put his name to anything, gloriously; and when he had signed he had signed. Thus the beaver-hatted employers smiled at Martinmas drunkenness, and smacked it familiarly on the back; and little boys swilled themselves into the gutter with their elders, and felt intensely proud of the feat. These heroic old times have gone by, never to return.

It was on the Friday before Martinmas, at dusk. In the centre of the town, on the waste ground to the north of the "Shambles" (as the stone-built meat market was called), and in the space between the Shambles and the as yet unfinished new Town Hall, the showmen and the showgirls and the showboys were titivating their booths, and cooking their teas, and watering their horses, and polishing the brass rails of their vans, and brushing their fancy costumes, and hammering fresh tent-pegs into the hard ground, and lighting the first flares of the evening, and yarning, and quarrelling, and washing—all under the sombre purple sky, for the diversion of a small crowd of loafers, big and little, who stood obstinately with

390

their hands in their pockets or in their sleeves, missing naught of the promising spectacle.

Now, in the midst of what in less than twenty-four hours would be the Fair, was to be seen a strange and piquant sight—namely, a group of three white-tied, broad-brimmed dissenting ministers in earnest converse with fat Mr Snaggs, the proprietor of Snaggs's—Snaggs's being the town theatre, a wooden erection, generally called by patrons the "Blood Tub," on account of its sanguinary programmes. On this occasion Mr Snaggs and the dissenting ministers were for once in a way agreed. They all objected to a certain feature of the Fair. It was not the roundabouts, so crude that even an infant of to-day would despise them. It was not the shooting-galleries, nor the cocoanut shies. It was not the arrangements of the beersellers, which were formidably Bacchic. It was not the boxing-booths, where adventurous youths could have teeth knocked out and eyes smashed in free of charge. It was not the monstrosity-booths, where misshapen and maimed creatures of both sexes were displayed all alive and nearly nude to anybody with a penny to spare. What Mr Snaggs and the ministers of religion objected to was the theatre-booths, in which the mirror, more or less cracked and tarnished, was held up to nature.

Mr Snaggs's objection was professional. He considered that he alone was authorized to purvey drama to the town; he considered that among all purveyors of drama he alone was respectable, the rest being upstarts, poachers, and lewd fellows. And as the dissenting ministers gazed at Mr Snaggs's superb moleskin waistcoat, and listened to his positive brazen voice, they were almost convinced that the hated institution of the theatre could be made respectable and that Mr Snaggs had so made it. At any rate, by comparison with these flashy and flimsy booths, the Blood Tub, rooted in the antiquity of thirty years, had a dignified, even a reputable air—and did not Mr Snaggs give frequent performances of Cruickshanks' *The Bottle*, a sermon against intemperance more impressive than any sermon delivered from a pulpit in a chapel? The dissenting ministers listened with deference as Mr Snaggs explained to them exactly what they ought to have done, and what they had failed to do, in order to ensure the success of their campaign against play-acting in the Fair; a campaign which now for several years past had been abortive—largely (it was rumoured) owing to the secret jealousy of the Church of England.

"If ony on ye had had any gumption," Mr Snaggs was saying fearlessly to the parsons, "ye'd ha' gone straight to th' Chief Bailiff and ye'd ha'—Houch!" He made the peculiar exclamatory noise roughly indicated by the last word, and spat in disgust; and without the slightest ceremony of adieu walked ponderously away up the slope, leaving his sentence unfinished.

"It is remarkable how Mr Snaggs flees from before my face," said a neat, alert, pleasant voice from behind the three parsons. "And yet save that in my unregenerate day I once knocked him off a stool in front of his own theayter, I never did him harm nor wished him anything but good.... Gentlemen!"

A rather small, slight man of about forty, with tiny feet and hands, and "very quick on his pins," saluted the three parsons gravely.

"Mr Smith!" one parson stiffly inclined.

"Mr Smith!" from the second.

"Brother Smith!" from the third, who was Jock Smith's own parson, being in charge of the Bethesda in Trafalgar Road where Jock Smith worshipped and where he had recently begun to preach as a local preacher.

Jock Smith, herbalist, shook hands with vivacity but also with self-consciousness. He was self-conscious because he knew himself to be one of the chief characters and attractions of the town, because he was well aware that wherever he went people stared at him and pointed him out to each other. And he was half proud and half ashamed of his notoriety.

Even now a little band of ragged children had wandered after him, and, undeterred by the presence of the parsons, were repeating among themselves, in a low audacious monotone:

"Jock-at-a-Venture! Jock-at-a-Venture!"

II

He was the youngest of fourteen children, and when he was a month old his mother took him to church to be christened. The rector was the celebrated Rappey, sportsman, who (it is said) once pawned the church Bible in order to get up a bear-baiting. Rappey asked the name of the child, and was told by the mother that she had come to the end of her knowledge of names, and would be obliged for a suggestion. Whereupon Rappey began to cite all the most

392

ludicrous names in the Bible, such as Aholibamah, Kenaz, Iram, Baalhanan, Abiasaph, Amram, Mushi, Libni, Nepheg, Abihu. And the mother laughed, shaking her head. And Rappey went on: Shimi, Carmi, Jochebed. And at Jochebed the mother became hysterical with laughter. "Jock-at-a-Venture," she had sniggered, and Rappey, mischievously taking her at her word, christened the infant Jock-at-a-Venture before she could protest; and the infant was stamped for ever as peculiar.

He lived up to his name. He ran away twice, and after having been both a sailor and a soldier, he returned home with the accomplishment of flourishing a razor, and settled in Bursley as a barber. Immediately he became the most notorious barber in the Five Towns, on account of his gab and his fisticuffs. It was he who shaved the left side of the face of an insulting lieutenant of dragoons (after the great riots of '45, which two thousand military had not quelled), and then pitched him out of the shop, soapsuds and all, and fought him to a finish in the Cock Yard and flung him through the archway into the market-place with just half a magnificent beard and moustache. It was he who introduced hair-dyeing into Bursley. Hair-dyeing might have grown popular in the town if one night, owing to some confusion with red ink, the Chairman of the Bursley Burial Board had not emerged from Jock-at-a-Venture's with a vermilion top-knot and been greeted on the pavement by his waiting wife with the bitter words: "Thou foo!"

A little later Jock-at-a-Venture abandoned barbering and took up music, for which he had always shown a mighty gift. He was really musical and performed on both the piano and the cornet, not merely with his hands and mouth, but with the whole of his agile expressive body. He made a good living out of public-houses and tea-meetings, for none could play the piano like Jock, were it hymns or were it jigs. His cornet was employed in a band at Moorthorne, the mining village to the east of Bursley, and on his nocturnal journeys to and from Moorthorne with the beloved instrument he had had many a set-to with the marauding colliers who made the road dangerous for cowards. One result of this connection with Moorthorne was that a boxing club had been formed in Bursley, with Jock as chief, for the upholding of Bursley's honour against visiting Moorthorne colliers in Bursley's market-place.

Then came Jock's conversion to religion, a blazing affair, and his abandonment of public-houses. As tea-meetings alone would not

393

keep him, he had started again in life, for the fifth or sixth time—as a herbalist now. It was a vocation which suited his delicate hands and his enthusiasm for humanity. At last, and quite lately, he had risen to be a local preacher. His first two sermons had impassioned the congregations, though there were critics to accuse him of theatricality. Accidents happened to him sometimes. On this very afternoon of the Friday before Martinmas an accident had happened to him. He had been playing the piano at the rehearsal of the Grand Annual Evening Concert of the Bursley Male Glee-Singers. The Bursley Male Glee-Singers, determined to beat records, had got a soprano with a foreign name down from Manchester. On seeing the shabby perky little man who was to accompany her songs the soprano had had a moment of terrible misgiving. But as soon as Jock, with a careful-careless glance at the music, which he had never seen before, had played the first chords (with a "How's that for time, missis?"), she was reassured. At the end of the song her enthusiasm for the musical gifts of the local artist was such that she had sprung from the platform and simply but cordially kissed him. She was a stout, feverish lady. He liked a lady to be stout; and the kiss was pleasant and the compliment enormous. But what a calamity for a local preacher with a naughty past to be kissed in full rehearsal by a soprano from Manchester! He knew that he had to live that kiss down, and to live down also the charge of theatricality.

Here was a reason, and a very good one, why he deliberately sought the company of parsons in the middle of the Fair-ground. He had to protect himself against tongues.

III

"I don't know," said Jock-at-a-Venture to the parsons, gesturing with his hands and twisting his small, elegant feet, "I don't know as I'm in favour of stopping these play-acting folk from making a living; stopping 'em by force, that is."

He knew that he had said something shocking, something that when he joined the group he had not in the least meant to say. He knew that instead of protecting himself he was exposing himself to danger. But he did not care. When, as now, he was carried away by an idea, he cared for naught. And, moreover, he had the consciousness of being cleverer, acuter, than any of these ministers of religion, than anybody in the town! His sheer skill and resourcefulness in life had always borne him safely through every difficulty—from a prize-fight to a soprano's embrace.

"A strange doctrine, Brother Smith!" said Jock's own pastor.

The other two hummed and hawed, and brought the tips of their fingers together.

"Nay!" said Jock, persuasively smiling. "'Stead o' bringing 'em to starvation, bring 'em to the House o' God! Preach the gospel to 'em, and then when ye've preached the gospel to 'em, happen they'll change their ways o' their own accord. Or happen they'll put their play-acting to the service o' God. If there's plays agen drink, why shouldna' there be plays agen the devil, and *for* Jesus Christ, our Blessed Redeemer?"

"Good day to you, brethren," said one of the parsons, and departed. Thus only could he express his horror of Jock's sentiments.

In those days churches and chapels were not so empty that parsons had to go forth beating up congregations. A pew was a privilege. And those who did not frequent the means of grace had at any rate the grace to be ashamed of not doing so. And, further, strolling players, in spite of John Wesley's exhortations, were not considered salvable. The notion of trying to rescue them from merited perdition was too fantastic to be seriously entertained by serious Christians. Finally, the suggested connection between Jesus Christ and a stage-play was really too appalling! None but Jock-at-a-Venture would have been capable of such an idea.

"I think, my friend—" began the second remaining minister.

"Look at that good woman there!" cried Jock-at-a-Venture, interrupting him with a dramatic out-stretching of the right arm, as he pointed to a very stout but comely dame, who, seated on a three-legged stool, was calmly peeling potatoes in front of one of the more resplendent booths. "Look at that face! Is there no virtue in it? Is there no hope for salvation in it?"

"None," Jock's pastor replied mournfully. "That woman—her name is Clowes—is notorious. She has eight children, and she has brought them all up to her trade. I have made inquiries. The elder daughters are actresses and married to play-actors, and even the youngest child is taught to strut on the boards. Her troupe is the largest in the Midlands."

Jock-at-a-Venture was certainly dashed by this information.

"The more reason," said he, obstinately, "for saving her!... And all hers!"

The two ministers did not want her to be saved. They liked to think of the theatre as being beyond the pale. They remembered the time, before they were ordained, and after, when they had hotly desired to see the inside of a theatre and to rub shoulders with wickedness. And they took pleasure in the knowledge that the theatre was always there, and the wickedness thereof, and the lost souls therein. But Jock-at-a-Venture genuinely longed, in that ecstasy of his, for the total abolition of all forms of sin.

"And what would you do to save her, brother?" Jock's pastor inquired coldly.

"What would I do? I'd go and axe her to come to chapel Sunday, her and hers. I'd axe her kindly, and I'd crack a joke with her. And I'd get round her for the Lord's sake."

Both ministers sighed. The same thought was in their hearts, namely, that brands plucked from the burning (such as Jock) had a disagreeable tendency to carry piety, as they had carried sin, to the most ridiculous and inconvenient lengths.

IV

"Those are bonny potatoes, missis!"

"Ay!" The stout woman, the upper part of whose shabby dress seemed to be subjected to considerable strains, looked at Jock carelessly, and then, attracted perhaps by his eager face, smiled with a certain facile amiability.

"But by th' time they're cooked your supper'll be late, I'm reckoning."

"Them potatoes have naught to do with our supper," said Mrs Clowes. "They're for to-morrow's dinner. There'll be no time for peeling potatoes to-morrow. Kezia!" She shrilled the name.

A slim little girl showed herself between the heavy curtains of the main tent of Mrs Clowes's caravanserai.

"Bring Sapphira, too!"

"Those yours?" asked Jock.

"They're mine," said Mrs Clowes. "And I've six more, not counting grandchildren and sons-in-law like."

"No wonder you want a pailful of potatoes!" said Jock.

Kezia and Sapphira appeared in the gloom. They might have counted sixteen years together. They were dirty, tousled, graceful and lovely.

"Twins," Jock suggested.

Mrs Clowes nodded. "Off with this pail, now! And mind you don't spill the water. Here, Kezia! Take the knife. And bring me the other pail."

The children bore away the heavy pail, staggering, eagerly obedient. Mrs Clowes lifted her mighty form from the stool, shook peelings from the secret places of her endless apron, and calmly sat down again.

"Ye rule 'em with a rod of iron, missis," said Jock.

She smiled good-humouredly and shrugged her vast shoulders— no mean physical feat.

"I keep 'em lively," she said. "There's twelve of 'em in my lot, without th' two babbies. Someone's got to be after 'em all the time."

"And you not thirty-five, I swear!"

"Nay! Ye're wrong."

Sapphira brought the other pail, swinging it. She put it down with a clatter of the falling handle and scurried off.

"Am I now?" Jock murmured, interested; and, as it were out of sheer absent-mindedness, he turned the pail wrong side up, and seated himself on it with a calm that equalled the calm of Mrs Clowes.

It was now nearly dark. The flares of the showmen were answering each other across the Fair-ground; and presently a young man came and hung one out above the railed platform of Mrs Clowes's booth; and Mrs Clowes blinked. From behind the booth floated the sounds of the confused chatter of men, girls and youngsters, together with the complaint of an infant. A few yards away from Mrs Clowes was a truss of hay; a pony sidled from somewhere with false innocence up to this truss, nosed it cautiously, and then began to bite wisps from it. Occasionally a loud but mysterious cry swept across the ground. The sky was full of mystery. Against the sky to the west stood black and clear the silhouette of the new Town Hall spire, a wondrous erection; and sticking out from it at one side was the form of a gigantic angel. It was the gold angel which, from the summit of the spire, has now watched over Bursley for half a century, but which on that particular Friday had been lifted only two-thirds of the way to its final home.

Jock-at-a-Venture felt deeply all the influences of the scene and of the woman. He was one of your romantic creatures; and for him the woman was magnificent. Her magnificence thrilled.

"And what are you going to say?" she quizzed him. "Sitting on my pail!"

Now to quiz Jock was to challenge him.

"Sitting on your pail, missis," he replied, "I'm going for to say that you're much too handsome a woman to go down to hell in eternal damnation."

She was taken aback, but her profession had taught her the art of quick recovery.

"You belong to that Methody lot," she mildly sneered. "I thought I seed you talking to them white-chokers."

"I do," said Jock.

"And I make no doubt you think yourself very clever."

"Well," he vouchsafed, "I can splice a rope, shave a head, cure a wart or a boil, and tell a fine woman with any man in this town. Not to mention boxing, as I've given up on account of my religion."

"I *was* handsome once," said Mrs Clowes, with apparent, but not real, inconsequence. "But I'm all run to fat, like. I've played Portia in my time. But now it's as much as I can do to get through with Maria Martin or Belladonna."

"Fat!" Jock protested. "Fat! I wouldn't have an ounce taken off ye for fifty guineas."

He was so enthusiastic that Mrs Clowes blushed.

"What's this about hell-fire?" she questioned. "I often think of it—I'm a lonely woman, and I often think of it."

"You lonely!" Jock protested again. "With all them childer?"

"Ay!"

There was a silence.

"See thee here, missis!" he exploded, jumping up from the pail. "Ye must come to th' Bethesda down yon, on Sunday morning, and hear the word o' God. It'll be the making on ye."

Mrs Clowes shook her head.

"Nay!"

"And bring yer children," he persisted.

"If it was you as was going to preach like!" she said, looking away.

"It is me as is going to preach," he answered loudly and proudly. "And I'll preach agen any man in this town for a dollar!"

Jock was forgetting himself: an accident which often happened to him.

V

The Bethesda was crowded on Sunday morning; partly because it was Martinmas Sunday, and partly because the preacher was Jock-at-a-Venture. That Jock should have been appointed on the "plan" [rota of preachers] to discourse in the principal local chapel of the Connexion at such an important feast showed what extraordinary progress he had already made in the appreciation of that small public of experts which aided the parson in drawing up the quarterly plan. At the hands of the larger public his reception was sure. Some sixteen hundred of the larger public had crammed themselves into the chapel, and there was not an empty place either on the ground floor or in the galleries. Even the "orchestra" (as the "singing-seat" was then called) had visitors in addition to the choir and the double-bass players. And not a window was open. At that date it had not occurred to people that fresh air was not a menace to existence. The whole congregation was sweltering, and rather enjoying it; for in some strangely subtle manner perspiration seemed to be a help to religious emotion. Scores of women were fanning themselves; and among these was a very stout peony-faced woman of about forty in a gorgeous yellow dress and a red-and-black bonnet, with a large boy and a small girl under one arm, and a large boy and a small girl under the other arm. The splendour of the group appeared somewhat at odds with the penury of the "Free Seats," whither it had been conducted by a steward.

In the pulpit, dominating all, was Jock-at-a-Venture, who sweated like the rest. He presented a rather noble aspect in his broadcloth, so different from his careless, shabby week-day attire. His eye was lighted; his arm raised in a compelling gesture. Pausing effectively, he lifted a glass with his left hand and sipped. It was the signal that he had arrived at his peroration. His perorations were famous. And this morning everybody felt, and he himself knew, that all previous perorations were to be surpassed. His subject was the wrath to come, and the transient quality of human life on earth. "Yea," he announced, in gradually-increasing thunder, "all shall go. And loike the baseless fabric o' a vision, the cloud-capped towers, the gorgeous palaces, the solemn temples, the great globe itself—

Yea, I say, all which it inherit shall dissolve, and, like this insubstantial payjent faded, leave not a rack behind."

His voice had fallen for the last words. After a dramatic silence, he finished, in a whisper almost, and with eyebrows raised and staring gaze directed straight at the vast woman in yellow: "We are such stuff as drames are made on; and our little life is rounded with a sleep. May God have mercy on us. Hymn 442."

The effect was terrific. Men sighed and women wept, in relief that the strain was past. Jock was an orator; he wielded the orator's dominion. Well he knew, and well they all knew, that not a professional preacher in the Five Towns could play on a congregation as he did. For when Jock was roused you could nigh see the waves of emotion sweeping across the upturned faces of his hearers like waves across a wheatfield on a windy day.

And this morning he had been roused.

VI

But in the vestry after the service he met enemies, in the shape and flesh of the chapel-steward and the circuit-steward, Mr Brett and Mr Hanks respectively. Both these important officials were local preachers, but, unfortunately, their godliness did not protect them against the ravages of jealousy. Neither of them could stir a congregation, nor even fill a country chapel.

"Brother Smith," said Jabez Hanks, shutting the door of the vestry. He was a tall man with a long, greyish beard and no moustache. "Brother Smith, it is borne in upon me and my brother here to ask ye a question."

"Ask!" said Jock.

"Were them yer own words—about cloud-capped towers and baseless fabrics and the like? I ask ye civilly."

"And I answer ye civilly, they were," replied Jock.

"Because I have here," said Jabez Hanks, maliciously, "Dod's *Beauties o' Shakspere*, where I find them very same words, taken from a stage-play called *The Tempest*."

Jock went a little pale as Jabez Hanks opened the book.

"They may be Shakspere's words too," said Jock, lightly.

"A fortnight ago, at Moorthorne Chapel, I suspected it," said Jabez.

"Suspected what?"

400

"Suspected ye o' quoting Shakspere in our pulpits."

"And cannot a man quote in a sermon? Why, Jabez Hanks, I've heard ye quote Matthew Henry by the fathom."

"Ye've never heard me quote a stage-play in a pulpit, Brother Smith," said Jabez Hanks, majestically. "And as long as I'm chapel-steward it wunna' be tolerated in this chapel."

"Wunna it?" Jock put in defiantly.

"It's a defiling of the Lord's temple; that's what it is!" Jabez Hanks continued. "Ye make out as ye're against stage-plays at the Fair, and yet ye come here and mouth 'em in a Christian pulpit. *You* agen stage-plays! Weren't ye seen talking by the hour to one o' them trulls, Friday night—? And weren't ye seen peeping through th' canvas last night? And now—"

"Now what?" Jock inquired, approaching Jabez on his springy toes, and looking up at Jabez's great height.

Jabez took breath. "Now ye bring yer fancy women into the House o' God! You—a servant o' Christ, you—"

Jock-at-a-Venture interrupted the sentence with his daring fist, which seemed to lift Jabez from the ground by his chin, and then to let him fall in a heap, as though his clothes had been a sack containing loose bones.

"A good-day to ye, Brother Brett," said Jock, reaching for his hat, and departing with a slam of the vestry door.

He emerged at the back of the chapel and got by "back-entries" into Aboukir Street, up which he strolled with a fine show of tranquillity, as far as the corner of Trafalgar Road, where stood and stands the great Dragon Hotel. The congregations of several chapels were dispersing slowly round about this famous corner, and Jock had to salute several of his own audience. Then suddenly he saw Mrs Clowes and her four children enter the tap-room door of the Dragon.

He hesitated one second and followed the variegated flotilla and its convoy.

The tap-room was fairly full of both sexes. But among them Jock and Mrs Clowes and her children were the only persons who had been to church or chapel.

"Here's preacher, mother!" Kezia whispered, blushing, to Mrs Clowes.

"Eh," said Mrs Clowes, turning very amiably. "It's never you, mester! It was that hot in that chapel we're all on us dying of thirst.... Four gills and a pint, please!" (This to the tapster.)

"And give me a pint," said Jock, desperately.

They all sat down familiarly. That a mother should take her children into a public-house and give them beer, and on a Sunday of all days, and immediately after a sermon! That a local preacher should go direct from the vestry to the gin-palace and there drink ale with a strolling player! These phenomena were simply and totally inconceivable! And yet Jock was in presence of them, assisting at them, positively acting in them! And in spite of her enormities, Mrs Clowes still struck him as a most agreeable, decent, kindly, motherly woman—quite apart from her handsomeness. And her offspring, each hidden to the eyes behind a mug, were a very well-behaved lot of children.

"It does me good," said Mrs Clowes, quaffing. "And ye need summat to keep ye up in these days! We did *Belphegor* and *The Witch* and a harlequinade last night. And not one of these children got to bed before half after midnight. But I was determined to have 'em at chapel this morning. And not sorry I am I went! Eh, mester, what a Virginius you'd ha' made! I never heard preaching like it— not as I've heard much!"

"And you'll never hear anything like it again, missis," said Jock, "for I've preached my last sermon."

"Nay, nay!" Mrs Clowes deprecated.

"I've preached my last sermon," said Jock again. "And if I've saved a soul wi' it, missis...!" He looked at her steadily and then drank.

"I won't say as ye haven't," said Mrs Clowes, lowering her eyes.

VII

Rather less than a week later, on a darkening night, a van left the town of Bursley by the Moorthorne Road on its way to Axe-in-the-Moors, which is the metropolis of the wild wastes that cut off northern Staffordshire from Derbyshire. This van was the last of Mrs Clowes's caravanserai, and almost the last to leave the Fair. Owing to popular interest in the events of Jock-at-a-Venture's public career, in whose meshes Mrs Clowes had somehow got caught, the booth of Mrs Clowes had succeeded beyond any other booth, and had kept open longer and burned more naphtha and taken far more money. The other vans of the stout lady's enterprise (there were three in all) had gone forward in advance, with all her elder children and her children-in-law and her grandchildren, and the heavy wood and canvas of the booth. Mrs Clowes, transacting her own business herself, from habit, invariably brought up the rear of her procession out of a town; and sometimes her leisurely manner of settling with the town authorities for water, ground-space and other necessary com-modities, left her several miles behind her tribe.

The mistress's van, though it would not compare with the glorious vehicles that showmen put upon the road in these days, was a roomy and dignified specimen, and about as good as money could then buy. The front portion consisted of a parlour and kitchen combined, and at the back was a dormitory. In the dormitory Kezia, Sapphira and the youngest of their brothers were sleeping hard. In the parlour and kitchen sat Mrs Clowes, warmly enveloped, holding the reins with her right hand and a shabby, paper-covered book in her left hand. The book was the celebrated play, *The Gamester*, and Mrs Clowes was studying therein the rôle of Dulcibel. Not a rôle for which Mrs Clowes was physically fitted; but her prolific daughter, Hephzibah, to whom it appertained by prescription, could not possibly play it any longer, and would, indeed, be incapacitated from any rôle whatever for at least a month. And the season was not yet over; for folk were hardier in those days.

The reins stretched out from the careless hand of Mrs Clowes and vanished through a slit between the double doors, which had been fixed slightly open. Mrs Clowes's gaze, penetrating now and then the slit, could see the gleam of her lamp's ray on a horse's flank. The only sounds were the hoof-falls of the horse, the crunching of the wheels on the wet road, the occasional rattle of a vessel in the racks when the van happened to descend violently into a rut, and the steady murmur of Mrs Clowes's voice rehearsing the grandiloquence of the part of Dulcibel.

And then there was another sound, which Mrs Clowes did not notice until it had been repeated several times; the cry of a human voice out on the road:

"Missis!"

She opened wide the doors of the van and looked prudently forth. Naturally, inevitably, Jock-at-a-Venture was trudging alongside, level with the horse's tail! He stepped nimbly—he was a fine walker—but none the less his breath came short and quick, for he had been making haste up a steepish hill in order to overtake the van. And he carried a bundle and a stick in his hands, and on his head a superb but heavy beaver hat.

"I'm going your way, missis," said Jock.

"Seemingly," agreed Mrs Clowes, with due caution.

"Canst gi' us a lift?" he asked.

"And welcome," she said, her face changing like a flash to suit the words.

"Nay, ye needna' stop!" shouted Jock.

In an instant he had leapt easily up into the van, and was seated by her side therein on the children's stool.

"That's a hat—to travel in!" observed Mrs Clowes.

Jock removed the hat, examined it lovingly and replaced it.

"I couldn't ha' left it behind," said he, with a sigh, and continued rapidly in another voice: "Missis, we'n seen a pretty good lot o' each other this wik, and yet ye slips off o'this'n, without saying good-bye, nor a word about yer soul!"

Mrs Clowes heaved her enormous breast and shook the reins.

"I've had my share of trouble," she remarked mysteriously.

"Tell me about it, missis!"

And lo! in a moment, lured on by his smile, she was telling him quite familiarly about the ailments of her younger children, the escapades of her unmarried daughter aged fifteen, the surliness of one of her sons-in-law, the budding dishonesty of the other, the perils of infant life, and the need of repainting the big van and getting new pictures for the front of the booth. Indeed, all the worries of a queen of the road!

"And I'm so fat!" she said, "and yet I'm not forty, and shan't be for two year—and me a grandmother!"

"I knowed it!" Jock exclaimed.

"If I wasn't such a heap o' flesh—"

"Ye're the grandest heap o' flesh as I ever set eyes on, and I'm telling ye!" Jock interrupted her.

VIII

Then there were disconcerting sounds out in the world beyond the van. The horse stopped. The double doors were forced open from without, and a black figure, with white eyes in a black face, filled the doorway. The van had passed through the mining village of Moorthorne, and this was one of the marauding colliers on the outskirts thereof. When the colliers had highroad business in the night they did not trouble to wash their faces after work. The coal-dust was a positive aid to them, for it gave them a most useful resemblance to the devil.

Jock-at-a-Venture sprang up as though launched from a catapult.

"Is it thou, Jock?" cried the collier, astounded.

"Ay, lad!" said Jock, briefly.

And caught the collier a blow under the chin that sent him flying into the obscurity of the night. Other voices sounded in the road. Jock rushed to the doorway, taking a pistol from his pocket. And Mrs Clowes, all dithering like a jelly, heard shots. The horse started into a gallop. The reins escaped from the hands of the mistress, but Jock secured them, and lashed the horse to greater speed with the loose ends of them.

"I've saved thee, missis!" he said later. "I give him a regular lifter under the gob, same as I give Jabez, Sunday. But where's the sense of a lone woman wandering about dark roads of a night wi' a pack of childer?... Them childer 'ud ha' slept through th' battle o' Trafalgar," he added.

Mrs Clowes wept.

"Well may you say it!" she murmured. "And it's not the first time as I've been set on!"

"Thou'rt nowt but a girl, for all thy flesh and thy grandchilder!" said Jock. "Dry thy eyes, or I'll dry 'em for thee!"

She smiled in her weeping. It was an invitation to him to carry out his threat.

And while he was drying her eyes for her, she asked:

"How far are ye going? Axe?"

"Ay! And beyond! Can I act, I ask ye? Can I fight, I ask ye? Can ye do without me, I ask ye, you a lone woman? And yer soul, as is mine to save?"

"But that business o' yours at Bursley?"

"Here's my bundle," he said, "and here's my best hat. And I've money and a pistol in my pocket. The only thing I've clean forgot is my cornet; but I'll send for it and I'll play it at my wedding. I'm Jock-at-a-Venture."

And while the van was rumbling in the dark night across the waste and savage moorland, and while the children were sleeping hard at the back of the van, and while the crockery was restlessly clinking in the racks and the lamp swaying, and while he held the

405

reins, the thin, lithe, greying man contrived to take into his arms the vast and amiable creature whom he desired. And the van became a vehicle of high romance.

THE HEROISM OF THOMAS CHADWICK

I

"Have you heard about Tommy Chadwick?" one gossip asked another in Bursley.

"No."

"He's a tram-conductor now."

This information occasioned surprise, as it was meant to do, the expression on the faces of both gossips indicating a pleasant curiosity as to what Tommy Chadwick would be doing next.

Thomas Chadwick was a "character" in the Five Towns, and of a somewhat unusual sort. "Characters" in the Five Towns are generally either very grim or very jolly, either exceptionally shrewd or exceptionally simple; and they nearly always, in their outward aspect, depart from the conventional. Chadwick was not thus. Aged fifty or so, he was a portly and ceremonious man with an official gait. He had been a policeman in his youth, and he never afterwards ceased to look like a policeman in plain clothes. The authoritative mien of the policeman refused to quit his face. Yet, beneath that mien, few men (of his size) were less capable of exerting authority than Chadwick. He was, at bottom, a weak fellow. He knew it himself, and everybody knew it. He had left the police force because he considered that the strain was beyond his strength. He had the constitution of a she-ass, and the calm, terrific appetite of an elephant; but he maintained that night duty in January was too much for him. He was then twenty-seven, with a wife and two small girls. He abandoned the uniform with dignity. He did everything with dignity. He looked for a situation with dignity, saw his wife and children go hungry with dignity, and even went short himself with dignity. He continually got fatter, waxing on misfortune. And—another curious thing—he could always bring out, when advisable, a shining suit of dark blue broadcloth, a clean collar and a fancy necktie. He was not a consistent dandy, but he could be a dandy when he liked.

Of course, he had no trade. The manual skill of a policeman is useless outside the police force. One cannot sell it in other markets. People said that Chadwick was a fool to leave the police force. He was; but he was a sublime and dignified fool in his idle folly. What he wanted was a position of trust, a position where nothing would be required from him but a display of portliness, majesty and incorruptibility. Such positions are not easy to discover. Employers had no particular objection to portliness, majesty and incorruptibility, but as a rule they demanded something else into the bargain. Chadwick's first situation after his defection from the police was that of night watchman in an earthenware manufactory down by the canal at Shawport. He accepted it regretfully, and he firmly declined to see the irony of fate in forcing such a post on a man who conscientiously objected to night duty. He did not maintain this post long, and his reasons for giving it up were kept a dark secret. Some said that Chadwick's natural tendency to sleep at night had been taken amiss by his master.

Thenceforward he went through transformation after transformation, outvying the legendary chameleon. He was a tobacconist, a park-keeper, a rent collector, a commission agent, a clerk, another clerk, still another clerk, a sweetstuff seller, a fried fish merchant, a coal agent, a book agent, a pawnbroker's assistant, a dog-breeder, a door-keeper, a board-school keeper, a chapel-keeper, a turnstile man at football matches, a coachman, a carter, a warehouseman, and a chucker-out at the Empire Music Hall at Hanbridge. But he was nothing long. The explanations of his changes were invariably vague, unseizable. And his dignity remained unimpaired, together with his broadcloth. He not only had dignity for himself, but enough left over to decorate the calling which he happened for the moment to be practising. He was dignified in the sale of rock-balls, and especially so in encounters with his creditors; and his grandeur when out of a place was a model to all unemployed.

Further, he was ever a pillar and aid of the powers. He worshipped order, particularly the old order, and wealth and correctness. He was ever with the strong against the weak, unless the weak happened to be an ancient institution, in which case he would support it with all the valour of his convictions. Needless to say, he was a very active politician. Perhaps the activity of his politics had something to do with the frequency of his transformations—for he would always be his somewhat spectacular self; he would always call his soul his own, and he would quietly accept a snub from no man.

And now he was a tram-conductor. Things had come to that.

In the old days of the steam trams, where there were only about a score of tram-conductors and eight miles of line in all the Five Towns, the profession of tram-conductor had still some individuality in it, and a conductor was something more than a number. But since the British Electric Traction Company had invaded the Five Towns, and formed a subsidiary local company, and constructed dozens of miles of new line, and electrified everything, and raised prices, and abolished season tickets, and quickened services, and built hundreds of cars and engaged hundreds of conductors—since then a tram-conductor had been naught but an unhuman automaton in a vast machine-like organization. And passengers no longer had their favourite conductors.

Gossips did not precisely see Thomas Chadwick as an unhuman automaton for the punching of tickets and the ringing of bells and the ejaculation of street names. He was never meant by nature to be part of a system. Gossips hoped for the best. That Chadwick, at his age and with his girth, had been able, in his extremity, to obtain a conductorship was proof that he could bring influences to bear in high quarters. Moreover, he was made conductor of one of two cars that ran on a little branch line between Bursley and Moorthorne, so that to the village of Moorthorne he was still somebody, and the chances were just one to two that persons who travelled by car from or to Moorthorne did so under the majestic wing of Thomas Chadwick. His manner of starting a car was unique and stupendous. He might have been signalling "full speed ahead" from the bridge of an Atlantic liner.

II

Chadwick's hours aboard his Atlantic liner were so long as to interfere seriously, not only with his leisure, but with his political activities. And this irked him the more for the reason that at that period local politics in the Five Towns were extremely agitated and interesting. People became politicians who had never been politicians before. The question was, whether the Five Towns, being already one town in practice, should not become one town in theory—indeed, the twelfth largest town in the United Kingdom! And the district was divided into Federationists and anti-Federationists. Chadwick was a convinced anti-Federationist.

Chadwick, with many others, pointed to the history of Bursley, "the mother of the Five Towns," a history which spread over a thousand years and more; and he asked whether "old Bursley" was to lose her identity merely because Hanbridge had insolently outgrown her. A poll was soon to be taken on the subject, and feelings were growing hotter every day, and rosettes of different colours flowered thicker and thicker in the streets, until nothing but a strong sense of politeness prevented members of the opposing parties from breaking each other's noses in St Luke's Square.

Now on a certain Tuesday afternoon in spring Tommy Chadwick's car stood waiting, opposite the Conservative Club, to depart to Moorthorne. And Tommy Chadwick stood in all his portliness on the platform. The driver, a mere nobody, was of course at the front of the car. The driver held the power, but he could not use it until Tommy Chadwick gave him permission; and somehow Tommy's imperial attitude seemed to indicate this important fact.

There was not a soul in the car.

Then Mrs Clayton Vernon came hurrying up the slope of Duck Bank and signalled to Chadwick to wait for her. He gave her a wave of the arm, kindly and yet deferential, as if to say, "Be at ease, noble dame! You are in the hands of a man of the world, who knows what is due to your position. This car shall stay here till you reach it, even if Thomas Chadwick loses his situation for failing to keep time."

And Mrs Clayton Vernon puffed into the car. And Thomas Chadwick gave her a helping hand, and raised his official cap to her with a dignified sweep; and his glance seemed to be saying to the world, "There, you see what happens when *I* deign to conduct a car! Even Mrs Clayton Vernon travels by car then." And the whole social level of the electric tramway system was apparently uplifted, and conductors became fine, portly court-chamberlains.

For Mrs Clayton Vernon really was a personage in the town— perhaps, socially, the leading personage. A widow, portly as Tommy himself, wealthy, with a family tradition behind her, and the true grand manner in every gesture! Her entertainments at her house at Hillport were unsurpassed, and those who had been invited to them seldom forgot to mention the fact. Thomas, a person not easily staggered, was nevertheless staggered to see her travelling by car to Moorthorne—even in his car, which to him in some subtle way was not like common cars—for she was seldom seen abroad apart from her carriage. She kept two horses. Assuredly both horses must be laid up together, or her coachman ill. Anyhow, there she was, in Thomas's car, splendidly dressed in a new spring gown of flowered silk.

"Thank you," she said very sweetly to Chadwick, in acknowledgment of his assistance.

Then three men of no particular quality mounted the car.

"How do, Tommy?" one of them carelessly greeted the august conductor. This impertinent youth was Paul Ford, a solicitor's clerk, who often went to Moorthorne because his employer had a branch office there, open twice a week.

Tommy did not respond, but rather showed his displeasure. He hated to be called Tommy, except by a few intimate coevals.

"Now then, hurry up, please!" he said coldly.

"Right oh! your majesty," said another of the men, and they all three laughed.

What was still worse, they all three wore the Federationist rosette, which was red to the bull in Thomas Chadwick. It was part of Tommy's political creed that Federationists were the "rag, tag, and bob-tail" of the town. But as he was a tram-conductor, though not an ordinary tram-conductor, his mouth was sealed, and he could not tell his passengers what he thought of them.

Just as he was about to pull the starting bell, Mrs Clayton Vernon sprang up with a little "Oh, I was quite forgetting!" and almost darted out of the car. It was not quite a dart, for she was of full habit, but the alacrity of her movement was astonishing. She must have forgotten something very important.

An idea in the nature of a political argument suddenly popped into Tommy's head, and it was too much for him. He was obliged to let it out. To the winds with that impartiality which a tram company expects from its conductors!

"Ah!" he remarked, jerking his elbow in the direction of Mrs Clayton Vernon and pointedly addressing his three Federationist passengers, "she's a lady, she is! *She* won't travel with anybody, she won't! *She chooses her company—and quite right too, I say*!"

And then he started the car. He felt himself richly avenged by this sally for the "Tommy" and the "your majesty" and the sneering laughter.

Paul Ford winked very visibly at his companions, but made no answering remark. And Thomas Chadwick entered the interior of the car to collect fares. In his hands this operation became a rite. His

411

gestures seemed to say, "No one ever appreciated the importance of the vocation of tram-conductor until I came. We will do this business solemnly and meticulously. Mind what money you give me, count your change, and don't lose, destroy, or deface this indispensable ticket that I hand to you. Do you hear the ting of my bell? It is a sign of my high office. I am fully authorized."

When he had taken his toll he stood at the door of the car, which was now jolting and climbing past the loop-line railway station, and continued his address to the company about the aristocratic and exclusive excellences of his friend Mrs Clayton Vernon. He proceeded to explain the demerits and wickedness of federation, and to descant on the absurdity of those who publicly wore the rosettes of the Federation party, thus branding themselves as imbeciles and knaves; in fact, his tongue was loosed. Although he stooped to accept the wages of a tram-conductor, he was not going to sacrifice the great political right of absolutely free speech.

"If I wasn't the most good-natured man on earth, Tommy Chadwick," said Paul Ford, "I should write to the tram company to-night, and you'd get the boot to-morrow."

"All I say is," persisted the singular conductor—"all I say is—she's a lady, she is—a regular real lady! She chooses her company—and quite right too! That I do say, and nobody's going to stop my mouth." His manner was the least in the world heated.

"What's that?" asked Paul Ford, with a sudden start, not inquiring what Thomas Chadwick's mouth was, but pointing to an object which was lying on the seat in the corner which Mrs Clayton Vernon had too briefly occupied.

He rose and picked up the object, which had the glitter of gold.

"Give it here," said Thomas Chadwick, commandingly. "It's none of your business to touch findings in my car;" and he snatched the object from Paul Ford's hands.

It was so brilliant and so obviously costly, however, that he was somehow obliged to share the wonder of it with his passengers. The find levelled all distinctions between them. A purse of gold chain-work, it indiscreetly revealed that it was gorged with riches. When you shook it the rustle of banknotes was heard, and the chink of sovereigns, and through the meshes of the purse could be seen the white of valuable paper and the tawny orange discs for which mankind is so ready to commit all sorts of sin. Thomas Chadwick could not forbear to open the contrivance, and having opened it he could not forbear to count its contents. There were, in that purse, seven five-pound notes, fifteen sovereigns, and half a sovereign, and the purse itself was probably worth twelve or fifteen pounds as mere gold.

"There's some that would leave their heads behind 'em if they could!" observed Paul Ford.

Thomas Chadwick glowered at him, as if to warn him that in the presence of Thomas Chadwick noble dames could not be insulted with impunity.

"Didn't I say she was a lady?" said Chadwick, holding up the purse as proof. "It's lucky it's *me* as has laid hands on it!" he added, plainly implying that the other occupants of the car were thieves whenever they had the chance.

"Well," said Paul Ford, "no doubt you'll get your reward all right!"

"It's not—" Chadwick began; but at that moment the driver stopped the car with a jerk, in obedience to a waving umbrella. The conductor, who had not yet got what would have been his sea-legs if he had been captain of an Atlantic liner, lurched forward, and then went out on to the platform to greet a new fare, and his sentence was never finished.

III

That day happened to be the day of Thomas Chadwick's afternoon off; at least, of what the tram company called an afternoon off. That is to say, instead of ceasing work at eleven-thirty p.m. he finished at six-thirty p.m. In the ordinary way the company housed its last Moorthorne car at eleven-thirty (Moorthorne not being a very nocturnal village), and gave the conductors the rest of the evening to spend exactly as they liked; but once a week, in turn, it generously allowed them a complete afternoon beginning at six-thirty.

Now on this afternoon, instead of going home for tea, Thomas Chadwick, having delivered over his insignia and takings to the inspector in Bursley market-place, rushed away towards a car bound for Hillport. A policeman called out to him:

"Hi! Chadwick!"

"What's up?" asked Chadwick, unwillingly stopping.

"Mrs Clayton Vernon's been to the station an hour ago or hardly, about a purse as she says she thinks she must have left in your car. I

413

was just coming across to tell your inspector."

"Tell him, then, my lad," said Chadwick, curtly, and hurried on towards the Hillport car. His manner to policemen always mingled the veteran with the comrade, and most of them indeed regarded him as an initiate of the craft. Still, his behaviour on this occasion did somewhat surprise the young policeman who had accosted him. And undoubtedly Thomas Chadwick was scarcely acting according to the letter of the law. His proper duty was to hand over all articles found in his car instantly to the police—certainly not to keep them concealed on his person with a view to restoring them with his own hands to their owners. But Thomas Chadwick felt that, having once been a policeman, he was at liberty to interpret the law to suit his own convenience. He caught the Hillport car, and nodded the professional nod to its conductor, asking him a technical question, and generally showing to the other passengers on the platform that he was not as they, and that he had important official privileges. Of course, he travelled free; and of course he stopped the car when, its conductor being inside, two ladies signalled to it at the bottom of Oldcastle Street. He had meant to say nothing whatever about his treasure and his errand to the other conductor; but somehow, when fares had been duly collected, and these two stood chatting on the platform, the gold purse got itself into the conversation, and presently the other conductor knew the entire history, and had even had a glimpse of the purse itself.

Opposite the entrance to Mrs Clayton Vernon's grounds at Hillport Thomas Chadwick slipped neatly, for all his vast bulk, off the swiftly-gliding car. (A conductor on a car but not on duty would sooner perish by a heavy fall than have a car stopped in order that he might descend from it.) And Thomas Chadwick heavily crunched the gravel of the drive leading up to Mrs Clayton Vernon's house, and imperiously rang the bell.

"Mrs Clayton Vernon in?" he officially asked the responding servant.

"She's *in*," said the servant. Had Thomas Chadwick been wearing his broadcloth she would probably have added "sir."

"Well, will you please tell her that Mr Chadwick—Thomas Chadwick—wants to speak to her?"

"Is it about the purse?" the servant questioned, suddenly brightening into eager curiosity.

414

"Never you mind what it's about, miss," said Thomas Chadwick, sternly.

At the same moment Mrs Clayton Vernon's grey-curled head appeared behind the white cap of the servant. Probably she had happened to catch some echo of Thomas Chadwick's great rolling voice. The servant retired.

"Good-evening, m'm," said Thomas Chadwick, raising his hat airily. "Good-evening." He beamed.

"So you did find it?" said Mrs Vernon, calmly smiling. "I felt sure it would be all right."

"Oh, yes, m'm." He tried to persuade himself that this sublime confidence was characteristic of great ladies, and a laudable symptom of aristocracy. But he would have preferred her to be a little less confident. After all, in the hands of a conductor less honourable than himself, of a common conductor, the purse might not have been so "all right" as all that! He would have preferred to witness the change on Mrs Vernon's features from desperate anxiety to glad relief. After all, £50, 10s. was money, however rich you were!

"Have you got it with you?" asked Mrs Vernon.

"Yes'm," said he. "I thought I'd just step up with it myself, so as to be sure."

"It's very good of you!"

"Not at all," said he; and he produced the purse. "I think you'll find it as it should be."

Mrs Vernon gave him a courtly smile as she thanked him.

"I'd like ye to count it, ma'am," said Chadwick, as she showed no intention of even opening the purse.

"If you wish it," said she, and counted her wealth and restored it to the purse. "*Quite* right—*quite* right! Fifty pounds and ten shillings," she said pleasantly. "I'm very much obliged to you, Chadwick."

"Not at all, m'm!" He was still standing in the sheltered porch.

An idea seemed to strike Mrs Clayton Vernon.

"Would you like something to drink?" she asked.

"Well, thank ye, m'm," said Thomas.

"Maria," said Mrs Vernon, calling to someone within the house, "bring this man a glass of beer." And she turned again to Chadwick, smitten with another idea. "Let me see. Your eldest daughter has two little boys, hasn't she?"

"Yes'm," said Thomas—"twins."

"I thought so. Her husband is my cook's cousin. Well, here's two threepenny bits—one for each of them." With some trouble she extracted the coins from a rather shabby leather purse—evidently her household purse. She bestowed them upon the honest conductor with another grateful and condescending smile. "I hope you don't *mind* taking them for the chicks," she said. "I *do* like giving things to children. It's so much*nicer*, isn't it?"

"Certainly, m'm."

Then the servant brought the glass of beer, and Mrs Vernon, with yet another winning smile, and yet more thanks, left him to toss it off on the mat, while the servant waited for the empty glass.

IV

On the following Friday afternoon young Paul Ford was again on the Moorthorne car, and subject to the official ministrations of Thomas Chadwick. Paul Ford was a man who never bore malice when the bearing of malice might interfere with the gratification of his sense of humour. Many men—perhaps most men—after being so grossly insulted by a tram-conductor as Paul Ford had been insulted by Chadwick, would at the next meeting have either knocked the insulter down or coldly ignored him. But Paul Ford did neither. (In any case, Thomas Chadwick would have wanted a deal of knocking down.) For some reason, everything that Thomas Chadwick said gave immense amusement to Paul Ford. So the young man commenced the conversation in the usual way:

"How do, Tommy?"

The car on this occasion was coming down from Moorthorne into Bursley, with its usual bump and rattle of windows. As Thomas Chadwick made no reply, Paul Ford continued:

"How much did she give you—the perfect lady, I mean?"

Paul Ford was sitting near the open door. Thomas Chadwick gazed absently at the Town Park, with its terra-cotta fountains and terraces, and beyond the Park, at the smoke rising from the distant furnaces of Red Cow. He might have been lost in deep meditation upon the meanings of life; he might have been prevented from hearing Paul Ford's question by the tremendous noise of the car. He made no sign. Then all of a sudden he turned almost fiercely on Paul Ford and glared at him.

"Ye want to know how much she gave me, do ye?" he demanded hotly.

"Yes," said Paul Ford.

"How much she gave me for taking her that there purse?" Tommy Chadwick temporized.

He was obliged to temporize, because he could not quite resolve to seize the situation and deal with it once for all in a manner favourable to his dignity and to the ideals which he cherished.

"Yes," said Paul Ford.

"Well, I'll tell ye," said Thomas Chadwick—"though I don't know as it's any business of yours. But, as you're so curious!... She didn't give me anything. She asked me to have a little refreshment, like the lady she is. But she knew better than to offer Thomas Chadwick any pecooniary reward for giving her back something as she'd happened to drop. She's a lady, she is!"

"Oh!" said Paul Ford. "It don't cost much, being a lady!"

"But I'll tell ye what she *did* do," Thomas Chadwick went on, anxious, now that he had begun so well, to bring the matter to an artistic conclusion—"I'll tell ye what she did do. She give me a sovereign apiece for my grandsons—my eldest daughter's twins." Then, after an effective pause: "Ye can put that in your pipe and smoke it!... A sovereign apiece!"

"And have you handed it over?" Paul Ford inquired mildly, after a period of soft whistling.

"I've started two post-office savings bank accounts for 'em," said Thomas Chadwick, with ferocity.

The talk stopped, and nothing whatever occurred until the car halted at the railway station to take up passengers. The heart of Thomas Chadwick gave a curious little jump when he saw Mrs Clayton Vernon coming out of the station and towards his car. (Her horses must have been still lame or her coachman still laid aside.) She boarded the car, smiling with a quite particular effulgence upon Thomas Chadwick, and he greeted her with what he imagined to be the true antique chivalry. And she sat down in the corner opposite to Paul Ford, beaming.

When Thomas Chadwick came, with great respect, to demand her fare, she said:

"By the way, Chadwick, it's such a short distance from the station to the town, I think I should have walked and saved a penny. But I wanted to speak to you. I wasn't aware, last Tuesday, that your other

417

daughter got married last year and now has a dear little baby. I gave you threepenny bits each for those dear little twins. Here's another one for the other baby, I think I ought to treat all your grandchildren alike—otherwise your daughters might be jealous of each other"—she smiled archly, to indicate that this passage was humorous—"and there's no knowing what might happen!"

Mrs Clayton Vernon always enunciated her remarks in a loud and clear voice, so that Paul Ford could not have failed to hear every word. A faint but beatific smile concealed itself roguishly about Paul Ford's mouth, and he looked with a rapt expression on an advertisement above Mrs Clayton Vernon's head, which assured him that, with a certain soap, washing-day became a pleasure.

Thomas Chadwick might have flung the threepenny bit into the road. He might have gone off into language unseemly in a tram-conductor and a grandfather. He might have snatched Mrs Clayton Vernon's bonnet off and stamped on it. He might have killed Paul Ford (for it was certainly Paul Ford with whom he was the most angry). But he did none of these things. He said, in his best unctuous voice:

"Thank you, m'm, I'm sure!"

And, at the journey's end, when the passengers descended, he stared a harsh stare, without winking, full in the face of Paul Ford, and he courteously came to the aid of Mrs Clayton Vernon. He had proclaimed Mrs Clayton Vernon to be his ideal of a true lady, and he was heroically loyal to his ideal, a martyr to the cause he had espoused. Such a man was not fitted to be a tram-conductor, and the Five Towns Electric Traction Company soon discovered his unfitness—so that he was again thrown upon the world.

UNDER THE CLOCK

I

It was one of those swift and violent marriages which occur when the interested parties are so severely wounded by the arrow of love that only immediate and constant mutual nursing will save them from a fatal issue. (So they think.) Hence when Annie came from Sneyd to inhabit the house in Birches Street, Hanbridge, which William Henry Brachett had furnished for her, she really knew very little of William Henry save that he was intensely lovable, and that she was intensely in love with him. Their acquaintance extended over three months; And she knew equally little of the manners and customs of the Five Towns. For although Sneyd lies but a few miles from the immense seat of pottery manufacture, it is not as the Five Towns are. It is not feverish, grimy, rude, strenuous, Bacchic, and wicked. It is a model village, presided over by the Countess of Chell. The people of the Five Towns go there on Thursday afternoons (eightpence, third class return), as if they were going to Paradise. Thus, indeed, it was that William Henry had met Annie, daughter of a house over whose door were writ the inviting words, "Tea and Hot Water Provided."

There were a hundred and forty-two residences in Birches Street, Hanbridge, all alike, differing only in the degree of cleanliness of their window-curtains. Two front doors together, and then two bow-windows, and then two front doors again, and so on all up the street and all down the street. Life was monotonous, but on the whole respectable. Annie came of an economical family, and, previous to the wedding, she had been afraid that William Henry's ideal of economy might fall short of her own. In this she was mistaken. In fact, she was startlingly mistaken. It was some slight shock to her to be informed by William Henry that owing to slackness of work the honeymoon ought to be reduced to two days. Still, she agreed to the proposal with joy. (For her life was going to be one long honeymoon.) When they returned from the brief honeymoon, William Henry took eight shillings from her, out of the money he had given her, and hurried off to pay it into the Going Away Club, and there was scarcity for a few days. This happened in March. She had then only a vague idea of what the Going Away Club was. But from William Henry's air, and his fear lest he might be late, she gathered that the Going Away Club must be a very important institution. Brachett, for a living, painted blue Japanese roses on vases at Gimson& Nephews' works. He was nearly thirty years of age, and he had never done anything else but paint blue Japanese roses on vases. When the demand for blue Japanese roses on vases was keen, he could earn what is called "good money"—that is to say, quite fifty shillings a week. But the demand for blue Japanese roses on vases was subject to the caprices of markets—especially Colonial markets—and then William Henry had undesired days of leisure, and brought home less than fifty shillings, sometimes considerably less. Still, the household over which Annie presided was a superiorly respectable household and William Henry's income was, week in, week out, one of the princeliest in the street; and certainly Annie's window-curtains, and her gilt-edged Bible and artificial flowers displayed on a small table between the window-curtains was not to be surpassed. Further, William was "steady," and not quite raving mad about football matches; nor did he bet on horses, dogs or pigeons.

Nevertheless Annie—although, mind you, extraordinarily happy—found that her new existence, besides being monotonous, was somewhat hard, narrow and lacking in spectacular delights. Whenever there was any suggestion of spending more money than usual, William Henry's fierce chin would stick out in a formidable way, and his voice would become harsh, and in the result more money than usual was not spent. His notion of an excursion, of a wild and costly escapade, was a walk in Hanbridge Municipal Park and two shandy-gaffs at the Corporation Refreshment House therein. Now, although the Hanbridge Park is a wonderful triumph of grass-seed and terra-cotta over cinder-heaps and shard-rucks, although it is a famous exemplar to other boroughs, it is not precisely the Vale of Llangollen, nor the Lake District. It is the least bit in the world tedious, and by the sarcastic has been likened to a cemetery. And it seemed to symbolize Annie's life for her, in its cramped and pruned and smoky regularity. She began to look upon the Five Towns as a sort of prison from which she could never, never escape.

I say she was extraordinarily happy; and yet she was unhappy too. In a word, she resembled all the rest of us—she had "somehow expected something different" from what life actually gave her. She was astonished that her William Henry seemed to be so content with things as they were. Far, now, from any apprehension of his extravagance, she wished secretly that he would be a little more dashing. He did not seem to feel the truth that, though prudence is all very well, you can only live your life once, and that when you are dead you are dead. He did not seem to understand the value of pleasure. Few people in the Five Towns did seem to understand the value of pleasure. He had no distractions except his pipe. Existence was a harsh and industrious struggle, a series of undisturbed daily habits. No change, no gaiety, no freak! Grim, changeless monotony!

And once, in July, William Henry abandoned even his pipe for ten days. Work, and therefore pay, had been irregular, but that was not in itself a reason sufficient for cutting off a luxury that cost only a shilling a week. It was the Going Away Club that swallowed up the tobacco money. Nothing would induce William Henry to get into arrears with his payments to that mysterious Club. He would have sacrificed not merely his pipe, but his dinner—nay, he would have sacrificed his wife's dinner—to the greedy maw of that Club. Annie hated the Club nearly as passionately as she loved William Henry.

Then on the first of August (a Tuesday) William Henry came into the house and put down twenty sovereigns in a row on the kitchen table. He did not say much, being (to Annie's mild regret) of a secretive disposition.

Annie had never seen so much money in a row before.

"What's that?" she said weakly.

"That?" said William Henry. "That's th' going away money."

II

A flat barrow at the door, a tin trunk and two bags on the barrow, and a somewhat ragged boy between the handles of the barrow! The curtains removed from the windows, and the blinds drawn! A double turn of the key in the portal! And away they went, the ragged boy having previously spit on his hands in order to get a grip of the barrow. Thus they arrived at Hanbridge Railway Station, which was a tempest of traffic that Saturday before Bank Holiday. The whole of the Five Towns appeared to be going away. The first thing that startled Annie was that William Henry gave the ragged boy a shilling, quite as much as the youth could have earned in a couple of days in a regular occupation. William Henry was also lavish with a porter. When they arrived, after a journey of ten minutes, at Knype, where they had to change for Liverpool, he was again lavish with a porter. And the same thing happened at Crewe, where they had to change once more for Liverpool. They had time at Crewe for an expensive coloured drink. On the long seething platform William Henry gave Annie all his money to keep.

"Here, lass!" he said. "This'll be safer with you than with me."

She was flattered.

When it came in, the Liverpool train was crammed to the doors. And two hundred people pumped themselves into it, as air is forced into a pneumatic tyre. The entire world seemed to be going to Liverpool. It was uncomfortable, but it was magnificent. It was joy, it was life. The chimneys and kilns of the Five Towns were far away. And Annie, though in a cold perspiration lest she might never see her tin trunk again, was feverishly happy. At Liverpool William Henry demanded silver coins from her. She had a glimpse of her trunk. Then they rattled and jolted and whizzed in an omnibus to Prince's Landing Stage. And William Henry demanded more coins from her. A great ship awaited them. Need it be said that Douglas was their destination? The deck of the great ship was like a market-place. Annie had never seen such a thing. They climbed up into the market-place among the shouting, gesticulating crowd. There was a real shop, at which William Henry commanded her to buy a hat-guard. The hat-guard cost sixpence. At home sixpence was sixpence, and would buy seven pounds of fine mealy potatoes; but here sixpence was nothing—certainly it was not more than a halfpenny. They wandered and found other shops. Annie could not believe that all those solid shops and the whole market-place could move. And she was not surprised, a little later, to see Prince's Landing Stage sliding away from the ship, instead of the ship sliding away from Prince's Landing Stage. Then they went underground, beneath the market-place, and Annie found marble halls, colossal staircases, bookshops, trinket shops, highly-decorated restaurants, glittering bars, and cushioned drawing-rooms. They had the most exciting meal in the restaurant that Annie had ever had; also the most expensive; the price of it indeed staggered her; still, William Henry did not appear to mind that one meal should exceed the cost of two days living in Birches Street. Then they went up into the market-place again, and lo! the market-place had somehow of itself got into the middle of the sea!

Before the end of the voyage they had tea at threepence a cup. Annie reflected that the best "Home and Colonial" tea cost eighteenpence a pound, and that a pound would make two hundred and twenty cups. Similarly with the bread and butter which they ate, and the jam! But it was glorious. Not the jam (which Annie could have bettered), but life! Particularly as the sea was smooth! Presently she descried a piece of chalk sticking up against the horizon, and it was Douglas lighthouse.

III

There followed six days of delirium, six days of the largest conceivable existence. The holiday-makers stopped in a superb boarding-house on the promenade, one of about a thousand superb boarding-houses. The day's proceedings began at nine o'clock with a regal breakfast, partaken of at a very long table which ran into a bow window. At nine o'clock, in all the thousand boarding-houses, a crowd of hungry and excited men and women sat down thus to a very long table, and consumed the same dishes, that is to say, Manx herrings, and bacon and eggs, and jams. Everybody ate as much as he could. William Henry was never content with less than two herrings, two eggs, about four ounces of bacon, and as much jam as would render a whole Board school sticky. And in four hours after that he was ready for an enormous dinner, and so was she; and in five hours after that they neither of them had the slightest disinclination for a truly high and complex tea. Of course, the cost was fabulous. Thirty-five shillings per week each. Annie would calculate that, with thirty boarders and extras, the boarding-house was taking in money at the rate of over forty pounds a week. She would also calculate that about a hundred thousand herrings and ten million little bones were swallowed in Douglas each day.

But the cost of the boarding-house was as naught. It was the flowing out of coins between meals that deprived Annie of breath. They were always doing something. Sailing in a boat! Rowing in a boat! Bathing! The Pier! Sand minstrels! Excursions by brake, tram and train to Laxey, Ramsey, Sulby Glen, Port Erin, Snaefell! Morning shows! Afternoon shows! Evening shows! Circuses, music-halls, theatres, concerts! And then the public balls, with those

423

delicious tables in corners, lighted by Chinese lanterns, where you sat down and drew strange liquids up straws. And it all meant money. There were even places in Douglas where you couldn't occupy a common chair for half a minute without paying for it. Each night Annie went to bed exhausted with joy. On the second night she counted the money in her bag, and said to William Henry:

"How much money do you think we've spent already? Just—"

"Don't tell me, lass!" he interrupted her curtly. "When I want to know, I'll ask ye."

And on the fifth evening of this heaven he asked her:

"What'n ye got left?"

She informed him that she had five pounds and twopence left, of which the boarding-house and tips would absorb four pounds.

"H'm!" he replied. "It's going to be a bit close."

On the seventh day they set sail. The dream was not quite over, but it was nearly over. On the ship, when the porter had been discharged, she had two and twopence, and William Henry had the return tickets. Still, this poverty did not prevent William Henry from sitting down and ordering a fine lunch for two (the sea being again smooth). Having ordered it, he calmly told his wife that he had a sovereign in his waistcoat pocket. A sovereign was endless riches. But it came to an end during a long wait for the Five Towns train at Crewe. William Henry had apparently decided to finish the holiday as he had begun it. And the two and twopence also came to an end, as William Henry, suddenly remembering the children of his brother, was determined to buy gifts for them on Crewe platform. At Hanbridge man and wife had sixpence between them. And the boy with the barrow, who had been summoned by a postcard, was not visible. However, a cab was visible. William Henry took that cab.

"But, Will—"

"Shut up, lass!" he stopped her.

They plunged into the smoke and squalor of the Five Towns, and reached Birches Street with pomp, while Annie wondered how William Henry would contrive to get credit from a cabman. The entire street would certainly gather round if there should be a scene.

"Just help us in with this trunk, wilt?" said William Henry to the cabman. This, with sixpence in his pocket!

Then turning to his wife, he whispered:

"Lass, look under th' clock on th' mantelpiece in th' parlour. Ye'll find six bob."

He explained to her later that prudent members of Going Away Clubs always left money concealed behind them, as this was the sole way of providing against a calamitous return. The pair existed on the remainder of the six shillings and on credit for a week. William Henry became his hard self again. The prison life was resumed. But Annie did not mind, for she had lived for a week at the rate of a thousand a year. And in a fortnight William Henry began grimly to pay his subscriptions to the next year's Going Away Club.

THREE EPISODES IN THE LIFE OF
MR COWLISHAW, DENTIST

I

They all happened on the same day. And that day was a Saturday, the red Saturday on which, in the unforgettable football match between Tottenham Hotspur and the Hanbridge F.C. (formed regardless of expense in the matter of professionals to take the place of the bankrupt Knype F.C.), the referee would certainly have been murdered had not a Five Towns crowd observed its usual miraculous self-restraint.

Mr Cowlishaw—aged twenty-four, a fair-haired bachelor with a weak moustache—had bought the practice of the retired Mr Rapper, a dentist of the very old school. He was not a native of the Five Towns. He came from St Albans, and had done the deal through an advertisement in the*Dentists' Guardian*, a weekly journal full of exciting interest to dentists. Save such knowledge as he had gained during two preliminary visits to the centre of the world's earthenware manufacture, he knew nothing of the Five Towns; practically, he had everything to learn. And one may say that the Five Towns is not a subject that can be "got up" in a day.

His place of business—or whatever high-class dentists choose to call it—in Crown Square was quite ready for him when he arrived on the Friday night: specimen "uppers" and "lowers" and odd teeth shining in their glass case, the new black-and-gold door-plate on the door, and the electric filing apparatus which he had purchased, in the operating-room. Nothing lacked there. But his private lodgings were not ready; at least, they were not what he, with his finicking Albanian notions, called ready, and, after a brief altercation with his landlady, he went off with a bag to spend the night at the Turk's Head Hotel. The Turk's Head is the best hotel in Hanbridge, not excepting the new Hotel Metropole (Limited, and German-Swiss waiters). The proof of its excellence is that the proprietor, Mr Simeon Clowes, was then the Mayor of Hanbridge, and Mrs Clowes one of the acknowledged leaders of Hanbridge society.

Mr Cowlishaw went to bed. He was a good sleeper; at least, he was what is deemed a good sleeper in St Albans. He retired about eleven o'clock, and requested one of the barmaids to instruct the boots to arouse him at 7 a.m. She faithfully promised to do so.

He had not been in bed five minutes before he heard and felt an earthquake. This earthquake seemed to have been born towards the north-east, in the direction of Crown Square, and the shock seemed to pass southwards in the direction of Knype. The bed shook; the basin and ewer rattled together like imperfect false teeth in the mouth of an arrant coward; the walls of the hotel shook. Then silence! No cries of alarm, no cries for help, no lamentations of ruin! Doubtless, though earthquakes are rare in England, the whole town had been overthrown and engulfed, and only Mr Cowlishaw's bed left standing. Conquering his terror, Mr Cowlishaw put his head under the clothes and waited.

He had not been in bed ten minutes before he heard and felt another earthquake. This earthquake seemed to have been born towards the north-east, in the direction of Crown Square, and to be travelling southwards; and Mr Cowlishaw noticed that it was accompanied by a strange sound of heavy bumping. He sprang courageously out of bed and rushed to the window. And it so happened that he caught the earthquake in the very act of flight. It was one of the new cars of the Five Towns Electric Traction Company, Limited, guaranteed to carry fifty-two passengers. The bumping was due to the fact that the driver, by a too violent application of the brake, had changed the form of two of its wheels from circular to oval. Such accidents do happen, even to the newest cars, and the inhabitants of the Five Towns laugh when they hear a bumpy car as they laugh at *Charley's Aunt*. The car shot past, flashing sparks from its overhead wire and flaming red and green lights of warning, and vanished down the main thoroughfare. And gradually the ewer and basin ceased their colloquy. The night being the night of the 29th December, and exceedingly cold, Mr Cowlishaw went back to bed.

"Well," he muttered, "this is a bit thick, this is!" (They use such language in cathedral towns.) "However, let's hope it's the last."

It was not the last. Exactly, it was the last but twenty-three. Regularly at intervals of five minutes the Five Towns Electric Traction Company, Limited, sent one of their dreadful engines down the street, apparently with the object of disintegrating all the real property in the neighbourhood into its original bricks. At the seventeenth time Mr Cowlishaw trembled to hear a renewal of the bump-bump-bump. It was the oval-wheeled car, which had been to

427

Longshaw and back. He recognized it as an old friend. He wondered whether he must expect it to pass a third time. However, it did not pass a third time. After several clocks in and out of the hotel had more or less agreed on the fact that it was one o'clock, there was a surcease of earthquakes. Mr Cowlishaw dared not hope that earthquakes were over. He waited in strained attention during quite half an hour, expectant of the next earthquake. But it did not come. Earthquakes were, indeed, done with till the morrow.

It was about two o'clock when his nerves were sufficiently tranquillized to enable him to envisage the possibility of going to sleep. And he was just slipping, gliding, floating off when he was brought back to realities by a terrific explosion of laughter at the head of the stairs outside his bedroom door. The building rang like the inside of a piano when you strike a wire directly. The explosion was followed by low rumblings of laughter and then by a series of jolly, hearty "Good-nights." He recognized the voices as being those of a group of commercial travellers and two actors (of the Hanbridge Theatre Royal's specially selected London Pantomime Company), who had been pointed out to him with awe and joy by the aforesaid barmaid. They were telling each other stories in the private bar, and apparently they had been telling each other stories ever since. And the truth is that the atmosphere of the Turk's Head, where commercial travellers and actors forgather every night except perhaps Sundays, contains more good stories to the cubic inch than any other resort in the county of Staffordshire. A few seconds after the explosion there was a dropping fusillade—the commercial travellers and the actors shutting their doors. And about five minutes later there was another and more complicated dropping fusillade— the commercial travellers and actors opening their doors, depositing their boots (two to each soul), and shutting their doors.

Then silence.

And then out of the silence the terrified Mr Cowlishaw heard arising and arising a vast and fearful breathing, as of some immense prehistoric monster in pain. At first he thought he was asleep and dreaming. But he was not. This gigantic sighing continued regularly, and Mr Cowlishaw had never heard anything like it before. It banished sleep.

After about two hours of its awful uncanniness, Mr Cowlishaw caught the sound of creeping footsteps in the corridor and fumbling noises. He got up again. He was determined, though he should have to interrogate burglars and assassins, to discover the meaning of that horrible sighing. He courageously pulled his door open, and saw an aproned man with a candle marking boots with chalk, and putting them into a box.

"I say!" said Mr Cowlishaw.

"Beg yer pardon, sir," the man whispered. "I'm getting forward with my work so as I can go to th' fut-baw match this afternoon. I hope I didn't wake ye, sir."

"Look here!" said Mr Cowlishaw. "What's that appalling noise that's going on all the time?"

"Noise, sir?" whispered the man, astonished.

"Yes," Mr Cowlishaw insisted. "Like something breathing. Can't you hear it?"

The man cocked his ears attentively. The noise veritably boomed in Mr Cowlishaw's ears.

"Oh! *That*!" said the man at length. "That's th' blast furnaces at Cauldon Bar Ironworks. Never heard that afore, sir? Why, it's like that every night. Now you mention it, I *do* hear it! It's a good couple o' miles off, though, that is!"

Mr Cowlishaw closed his door.

At five o'clock, when he had nearly, but not quite, forgotten the sighing, his lifelong friend, the oval-wheeled electric car, bumped and quaked through the street, and the ewer and basin chattered together busily, and the seismic phenomena definitely recommenced. The night was still black, but the industrial day had dawned in the Five Towns. Long series of carts without springs began to jolt past under the window of Mr Cowlishaw, and then there was a regular multitudinous clacking of clogs and boots on the pavement. A little later the air was rent by first one steam-whistle, and then another, and then another, in divers tones announcing that it was six o'clock, or five minutes past, or half-past, or anything. The periodicity of earthquakes had by this time quickened to five minutes, as at midnight. A motor-car emerged under the archway of the hotel, and remained stationary outside with its engine racing. And amid the earthquakes, the motor-car, the carts, the clogs and boots, and the steam muezzins calling the faithful to work, Mr Cowlishaw could still distinguish the tireless, monstrous sighing of the Cauldon Bar blast furnaces. And, finally, he heard another sound. It came from the room next to his, and, when he heard it, exhausted though he was, exasperated though he was, he burst into laughter, so comically did it strike him.

It was an alarm-clock going off in the next room.

And, further, when he arrived downstairs, the barmaid, sweet, conscientious little thing, came up to him and said, "I'm so sorry, sir. I quite forgot to tell the boots to call you!"

II

That afternoon he sat in his beautiful new surgery and waited for dental sufferers to come to him from all quarters of the Five Towns. It needs not to be said that nobody came. The mere fact that a new dentist has "set up" in a district is enough to cure all the toothache for miles around. The one martyr who might, perhaps, have paid him a visit and a fee did not show herself. This martyr was Mrs Simeon Clowes, the mayoress. By a curious chance, he had observed, during his short sojourn at the Turk's Head, that the landlady thereof was obviously in pain from her teeth, or from a particular tooth. She must certainly have informed herself as to his name and condition, and Mr Cowlishaw thought that it would have been a graceful act on her part to patronize him, as he had patronized the Turk's Head. But no! Mayoresses, even the most tactful, do not always do the right thing at the right moment.

Besides, she had doubtless gone, despite toothache, to the football match with the Mayor, the new club being under the immediate patronage of his Worship. All the potting world had gone to the football match. Mr Cowlishaw would have liked to go, but it would have been madness to quit the surgery on his opening day. So he sat and yawned, and peeped at the crowd crowding to the match at two o'clock, and crowding back in the gloom at four o'clock; and at a quarter past five he was reading a full description of the carnage and the heroism in the football edition of the *Signal*. Though Hanbridge had been defeated, it appeared from the*Signal* that Hanbridge was the better team, and that Rannoch, the new Scotch centre-forward, had fought nobly for the town which had bought him so dear.

Mr Cowlishaw was just dozing over the *Signal* when there happened a ring at his door. He did not precipitate himself upon the door. With beating heart he retained his presence of mind, and said to himself that of course it could not possibly be a client. Even dentists who bought a practice ready-made never had a client on

430

their first day. He heard the attendant answer the ring, and then he heard the attendant saying, "I'll see, sir."

It was, in fact, a patient. The servant, having asked Mr Cowlishaw if Mr Cowlishaw was at liberty, introduced the patient to the Presence, and the Presence trembled.

The patient was a tall, stiff, fair man of about thirty, with a tousled head and inelegant but durable clothing. He had a drooping moustache, which prevented Mr Cowlishaw from adding his teeth up instantly.

"Good afternoon, mister," said the patient, abruptly.

"Good afternoon," said Mr Cowlishaw. "Have you ... Can I ..."

Strange; in the dental hospital and school there had been no course of study in the art of pattering to patients!

"It's like this," said the patient, putting his hand in his waistcoat pocket.

"Will you kindly sit down," said Mr Cowlishaw, turning up the gas, and pointing to the chair of chairs.

"It's like this," repeated the patient, doggedly. "You see these three teeth?"

He displayed three very real teeth in a piece of reddened paper. As aspectacle, they were decidedly not appetizing, but Mr Cowlishaw was hardened.

"Really!" said Mr Cowlishaw, impartially, gazing on them.

"They're my teeth," said the patient. And thereupon he opened his mouth wide, and displayed, not without vanity, a widowed gum. "'Ont 'eeth," he exclaimed, keeping his mouth open and omitting preliminary consonants.

"Yes," said Mr Cowlishaw, with a dry inflection. "I saw that they were upper incisors. How did this come about? An accident, I suppose?"

"Well," said the man, "you may call it an accident; I don't. My name's Rannoch; centre-forward. Ye see? Were ye at the match?"

Mr Cowlishaw understood. He had no need of further explanation; he had read it all in the *Signal*. And so the chief victim of Tottenham Hotspur had come to him, just him! This was luck! For Rannoch was, of course, the most celebrated man in the Five Towns, and the idol of the populace. He might have been M.P. had he chosen.

"Dear me!" Mr Cowlishaw sympathized, and he said again, pointing more firmly to the chair of chairs, "Will you sit down?"

431

"I had 'em all picked up," Mr Rannoch proceeded, ignoring the suggestion. "Because a bit of a scheme came into my head. And that's why I've come to you, as you're just commencing dentist. Supposing you put these teeth on a bit of green velvet in the case in your window, with a big card to say as they're guaranteed to be my genuine teeth, knocked out by that blighter of a Tottenham half-back, you'll have such a crowd as was never seen around your door. All the Five Towns'll come to see 'em. It'll be the biggest advertisement that either you or any other dentist ever had. And you might put a little notice in the *Signal* saying that my teeth are on view at your premises; it would only cost ye a shilling.... I should expect ye to furnish me with new teeth for nothing, ye see."

In his travels throughout England Mr Rannoch had lost most of his Scotch accent, but he had not lost his Scotch skill in the art and craft of trying to pay less than other folks for whatever he might happen to want.

Assuredly the idea was an idea of genius. As an advertisement it would be indeed colossal and unique. Tens of thousands would gaze spellbound for hours at those relics of their idol, and every gazer would inevitably be familiarized with the name and address of Mr Cowlishaw, and with the fact that Mr Cowlishaw was dentist-in-chief to the heroical Rannoch. Unfortunately, in dentistry there is etiquette. And the etiquette of dentistry is as terrible, as unbending, as the etiquette of the Court of Austria.

Mr Cowlishaw knew that he could not do this thing without sinning against etiquette.

"I'm sorry I can't fall in with your scheme," said he, "but I can't."

"But, *man!*" protested the Scotchman, "it's the greatest scheme that ever was."

"Yes," said Mr Cowlishaw, "but it would be unprofessional."

Mr Rannoch was himself a professional. "Oh, well," he said sarcastically, "if you're one of those amateurs—"

"I'll put you the job in as low as possible," said Mr Cowlishaw, persuasively.

But Scotchmen are not to be persuaded like that.

Mr Rannoch wrapped up his teeth and left.

What finally happened to those teeth Mr Cowlishaw never knew. But he satisfied himself that they were not advertised in the *Signal*.

III

Now, just as Mr Cowlishaw was personally conducting to the door the greatest goal-getter that the Five Towns had ever seen there happened another ring, and thus it fell out that Mr Cowlishaw found himself in the double difficulty of speeding his first visitor and welcoming his second all in the same breath. It is true that the second might imagine that the first was a client, but then the aspect of Mr Rannoch's mouth, had it caught the eye of the second, was not reassuring. However, Mr Rannoch's mouth happily did not catch the eye of the second.

The second was a visitor beyond Mr Cowlishaw's hopes, no other than Mrs Simeon Clowes, landlady of the Turk's Head and Mayoress of Hanbridge; a tall and well-built, handsome, downright woman, of something more than fifty and something less than sixty; the mother of five married daughters, the aunt of fourteen nephews and nieces, the grandam of seven, or it might be eight, assorted babies; in short, a lady of vast influence. After all, then, she had come to him! If only he could please her, he regarded his succession to his predecessor as definitely established and his fortune made. No person in Hanbridge with any yearnings for style would dream, he trusted, of going to any other dentist than the dentist patronized by Mrs Clowes.

She eyed him interrogatively and firmly. She probed into his character, and he felt himself pierced.

"You *are* Mr Cowlishaw?" she began.

"Good afternoon, Mrs Clowes," he replied. "Yes, I am. Can I be of service to you?"

"That depends," she said.

He asked her to step in, and in she stepped.

"Have you had any experience in taking teeth out?" she asked in the surgery. Her hand stroked her left cheek.

"Oh yes," he said eagerly. "But, of course, we try to avoid extraction as much as possible."

"If you're going to talk like that," she said coldly, and even bitterly, "I'd better go."

He wondered what she was driving at.

"Naturally," he said, summoning all his latent powers of diplomacy, "there are cases in which extraction is unfortunately necessary."

"How many teeth have you extracted?" she inquired.

"I really couldn't say," he lied. "Very many."

"Because," she said, "you don't look as if you could say 'Bo!' to a goose."

He observed a gleam in her eye.

"I think I can say 'Bo!' to a goose," he said. She laughed.

"Don't fancy, Mr Cowlishaw, that if I laugh I'm not in the most horrible pain. I am. When I tell you I couldn't go with Mr Clowes to the match—"

"Will you take this seat?" he said, indicating the chair of chairs; "then I can examine."

She obeyed. "I do hate the horrid, velvety feeling of these chairs," she said; "it's most creepy."

"I shall have to trouble you to take your bonnet off."

So she removed her bonnet, and he took it as he might have taken his firstborn, and laid it gently to rest on his cabinet. Then he pushed the gas-bracket so that the light came through the large crystal sphere, and made the Mayoress blink.

"Now," he said soothingly, "kindly open your mouth—wide."

Like all women of strong and generous character, Mrs Simeon Clowes had a large mouth. She obediently extended it to dimensions which must be described as august, at the same time pointing with her gloved and chubby finger to a particular part of it.

"Yes, yes," murmured Mr Cowlishaw, assuming a tranquillity which he did not feel. This was the first time that he had ever looked into the mouth of a Mayoress, and the prospect troubled him.

He put his little ivory-handled mirror into that mouth and studied its secrets.

"I see," he said, withdrawing the mirror. "Exposed nerve. Quite simple. Merely wants stopping. When I've done with it the tooth will be as sound as ever it was. All your other teeth are excellent."

Mrs Clowes arose violently out of the chair.

"Now just listen to me, please," she said. "I don't want any stopping; I won't have any stopping; I want that tooth out. I've already quarrelled with one dentist this afternoon because he refused to take it out. I came to you because you're young, and I thought you'd be more reasonable. Surely a body can decide whether she'll have a tooth out or not! It's my tooth. What's a dentist for? In my young days dentists never did anything else but take teeth out. All I wish to know is, will you take it out or will you not?"

"It's really a pity—"

"That's my affair, isn't it?" she stopped him, and moved towards her bonnet.

"If you insist," he said quickly, "I will extract."

"Well," she said, "if you don't call this insisting, what do you call insisting? Let me tell you I didn't have a wink of sleep last night!"

"Neither did I, in your confounded hotel!" he nearly retorted; but thought better of it.

The Mayoress resumed her seat, taking her gloves off.

"It's decided then?" she questioned.

"Certainly," said he. "Is your heart good?"

"Is my heart good?" she repeated. "Young man, what business is that of yours? It's my tooth I want you to deal with, not my heart."

"I must give you gas," said Mr Cowlishaw, faintly.

"Gas!" she exclaimed. "You'll give me no gas, young man. No! My heart is not good. I should die under gas. I couldn't bear the idea of gas. You must take it out without gas, and you mustn't hurt me. I'm a perfect baby, and you mustn't on any account hurt me." The moment was crucial. Supposing that he refused—a promising career might be nipped in the bud; would, undoubtedly, be nipped in the bud. Whereas, if he accepted the task, the patronage of the aristocracy of Hanbridge was within his grasp. But the tooth was colossal, monumental. He estimated the length of its triple root at not less than 0.75 inch.

"Very well, madam," he said, for he was a brave youngster.

But he was in a panic. He felt as though he were about to lead the charge of the Light Brigade. He wanted a stiff drink. (But dentists may not drink.) If he failed to wrench the monument out at the first pull the result would be absolute disaster; in an instant he would have ruined the practice which had cost him so dear. And could he hope not to fail with the first pull? At best he would hurt her indescribably. However, having consented, he was obliged to go through with the affair.

He took every possible precaution. He chose his most vicious instrument. He applied to the vicinity of the tooth the very latest substitute for cocaine; he prepared cotton wool and warm water in a glass. And at length, when he could delay the fatal essay no longer, he said:

"Now, I think we are ready."

"You won't hurt me?" she asked anxiously.

"Not a bit," he replied, with an admirable simulation of gaiety.

"Because if you do—"

He laughed. But it was a hysterical laugh. All his nerves were on end. And he was very conscious of having had no sleep during the previous night. He had a sick feeling. The room swam. He collected himself with a terrific effort.

"When I count one," he said, "I shall take hold; when I count two you must hold very tight to the chair; and when I count three, out it will come."

Then he encircled her head with his left arm—brutally, as dentists always are brutal in the thrilling crisis. "Wider!" he shouted.

And he took possession of that tooth with his fiendish contrivance of steel.

"One—two—"

He didn't know what he was doing.

There was no three. There was a slight shriek and a thud on the floor. Mrs Simeon Clowes jumped up and briskly rang a bell. The attendant rushed in. The attendant saw Mrs Clowes gurgling into a handkerchief, which she pressed to her mouth with one hand, while with the other, in which she held her bonnet, she was fanning the face of Mr Cowlishaw. Mr Cowlishaw had fainted from nervous excitement under fatigue. But his unconscious hand held the forceps; and the forceps, victorious, held the monumental tooth.

"O-o-pen the window," spluttered Mrs Clowes to the attendant. "He's gone off; he'll come to in a minute."

She was flattered. Mr Cowlishaw was for ever endeared to Mrs Clowes by this singular proof of her impressiveness. And a woman like that can make the fortune of half a dozen dentists.

CATCHING THE TRAIN

I

Arthur Cotterill awoke. It was not exactly with a start that he awoke, but rather with a swift premonition of woe and disaster. The strong, bright glare from the patent incandescent street lamp outside, which the lavish Corporation of Bursley kept burning at the full till long after dawn in winter, illuminated the room (through the green blind) almost as well as it illuminated Trafalgar Road. He clearly distinguished every line of the form of his brother Simeon, fast and double-locked in sleep in the next bed. He saw also the open trunk by the dressing-table in front of the window. Then he looked at the clock on the mantelpiece, the silent witness of the hours. And a pair of pincers seemed to clutch his heart, and an anvil to drop on his stomach and rest heavily there, producing an awful nausea. Why had he not looked at the clock before? Was it possible that he had been awake even five seconds without looking at the clock—the clock upon which it seemed that his very life, more than his life, depended? The clock showed ten minutes to seven, and the train went at ten minutes past. And it was quite ten minutes' walk to the station, and he had to dress, and button those new boots, and finish packing—and the porter from the station was late in coming for the trunk! But perhaps the porter had already been; perhaps he had rung and rung, and gone away in despair of making himself heard (for Mrs Hopkins slept at the back of the house).

Something had to be done. Yet what could he do with those hard pincers pinching his soft, yielding heart, and that terrible anvil pressing on his stomach? He might even now, by omitting all but the stern necessities of his toilet, and by abandoning the trunk and his brother, just catch the train, the indispensable train. But somehow he could not move. Yet he was indubitably awake.

"Simeon!" he cried at length, and sat up.

The younger Cotterill did not stir.

"Sim!" he cried again, and, leaning over, shook the bed.

"What's up?" Simeon demanded, broad awake in a second, and, as usual, calm, imperturbable.

"We've missed the train! It's ten—eight—minutes to seven," said Arthur, in a voice which combined reproach and terror. And he sprang out of bed and began with hysteric fury to sort out his garments.

Simeon turned slowly on his side and drew a watch from under his pillow. Putting it close to his face, Simeon could just read the dial.

"It's all right," he said. "Still, you'd better get up. It's eight minutes to six. We've got an hour and eighteen minutes."

"What do you mean? That clock was right last night."

"Yes. But I altered it."

"When?"

"After you got into bed."

"I never saw you."

"No. But I altered it."

"Why?"

"To be on the safe side."

"Why didn't you tell me?"

"If I'd told you, I might just as well have not altered it. The man who puts a clock on and then goes gabbling all over the house about what he has done is an ass; in fact, to call him an ass is to flatter him."

Arthur tried to be angry.

"That's all very well—" he began to grumble.

But he could not be angry. The pincers and the anvil had suddenly ceased their torment. He was free. He was not a disgraced man. He would catch the train easily. All would be well. All would be as the practical Simeon had arranged that it should be. And in advancing the clock Simeon had acted for the best. Of course, it *was* safer to be on the safe side! In an affair such as that in which he was engaged, he felt, and he honestly admitted to himself, that he would have been nowhere without Simeon.

"Light the stove first, man," Simeon enjoined him. "There's been a change in the weather, I bet. It's as cold as the very deuce."

Yes, it was very cold. Arthur now noticed the cold. Strange—or rather not strange—that he had not noticed it before! He lit the gas stove, which exploded with its usual disconcerting *plop*, and a marvellously agreeable warmth began to charm his senses. He continued his dressing as near as possible to the source of this exquisite warmth. Then Simeon, in his leisurely manner, arose out of bed without a word, put his feet into slippers and lit the gas.

"I never thought of that," said Arthur, laughing nervously.

438

"Shows what a state you're in," said Simeon.

Simeon went to the window and peeped out into the silence of Trafalgar Road.

"Slight mist," he observed.

Arthur felt a faint return of the pincers and anvil.

"But it will clear off," Simeon added.

Then Simeon put on a dressing-gown and padded out of the room, and Arthur heard him knock at another door and call:

"Mrs Hopkins, Mrs Hopkins!" And then the sound of a door opening.

"She was dressed and just going downstairs," said Simeon when he returned to their bedroom. "Breakfast ready in ten minutes. She set the table last night. I told her to."

"Good!" Arthur murmured.

At sixteen minutes past six they were both dressed, and Simeon was showing Arthur that Simeon alone knew how to pack a trunk. At twenty minutes past six the trunk was packed, locked and strapped.

"What about getting the confounded thing downstairs?" Arthur asked.

"When the porter comes," said Simeon, "he and I will do that. It's too heavy for you to handle."

At six twenty-one they were having breakfast in the little dining-room, by the heat of another gas-stove. And Arthur felt that all was well, and that in postponing their departure till that morning in order not to upset the immemorial Christmas dinner of their Aunt Sarah, they had done rightly. At half-past six they had, between them, drunk five cups of tea and eaten four eggs, four slices of bacon, and about a pound and a half of bread. Simeon, with what was surely an exaggeration of imperturbability, charged his pipe, and began to smoke. They had forty minutes in which to catch the Loop-Line train, even if it was prompt. There would then be forty minutes to wait at Knype for the London express, which arrived at Euston considerably before noon. After which there would be a clear ninety minutes before the business itself—and less than a quarter of a mile to walk! Yes, there was a rich and generous margin for all conceivable delays and accidents.

"The porter ought to be coming," said Simeon. It was twenty minutes to seven, and he was brushing his hat.

Now such a remark from that personification of calm, that living denial of worry, Simeon, was decidedly unsettling to Arthur. By chance, Mrs Hopkins came into the room just then to assure herself that the young men whose house she kept desired nothing.

"Mrs Hopkins," Simeon asked, "you didn't forget to call at the station last night?"

"Oh no, Mr Simeon," said she; "I saw the second porter, Merrith. He knows me. At least, I know his mother—known her forty year—and he promised me he wouldn't forget. Besides, he never has forgot, has he? I told him particular to bring his barrow."

It was true the porter never had forgotten! And many times had he transported Simeon's luggage to Bleakridge Station. Simeon did a good deal of commercial travelling for the firm of A. & S. Cotterill, teapot makers, Bursley. In many commercial hotels he was familiarly known as Teapot Cotterill.

The brothers were reassured by Mrs Hopkins. There was half an hour to the time of the train—and the station only ten minutes off. Then the chiming clock in the hall struck the third quarter.

"That clock right?" Arthur nervously inquired, assuming his overcoat.

"It's a minute late," said Simeon, assuming *his* overcoat.

And at that word "late," the pincers and the anvil revisited Arthur. Even the confidence of Mrs Hopkins in the porter was shaken. Arthur looked at Simeon, depending on him. It was imperative that they should catch the train, and it was imperative that the trunk should catch the train. Everything depended on a porter. Arthur felt that all his future career, his happiness, his honour, his life depended on a porter. And, after all, even porters at a pound a week are human. Therefore, Arthur looked at Simeon.

Simeon walked through the kitchen into the backyard. In a shed there an old barrow was lying. He drew out the barrow, and ticklishly wheeled it into the house, as far as the foot of the stairs.

"Mrs Hopkins," he called. "And you too!" he glanced at Arthur.

"What are you going to do?" Arthur demanded.

"Wheel the trunk to the station myself, of course," Simeon replied. "If we meet the porter on the way, so much the better for us ... and so much the worse for him!" he added.

It was just as dark as though it had been midnight—dark and excessively cold; not a ray of hope in the sky; not a sign of life in the street. All Bursley, and, indeed, all the Five Towns, were sleeping off the various consequences of Christmas on the human frame. Trafalgar Road, with its double row of lamps, each exactly like that one in front of the house of the Cotterills, stretched downwards into the dead heart of Bursley, and upwards over the brow of the hill into space. And although Arthur Cotterill knew Trafalgar Road as well as Mrs Hopkins knew the hundred and twenty-first Psalm, the effect of the scene on him was most uncanny. He watched Simeon persuade the loaded barrow down the step into the tiny front garden, not daring to help him, because Simeon did not like to be helped by clumsy people in delicate operations. Mrs Hopkins was rapidly pouring all the goodness of her soul into his ear, when Simeon and the barrow reached the pavement, and Simeon staggered and recovered himself.

"Look out, Arthur," Simeon cried. "The road's like glass. It's rained in the night, and now it's freezing. Come along."

Arthur bade adieu to Mrs Hopkins.

"Eh, Mr Arthur," said she. "Things'll be different when ye come back, this time a month."

He said nothing. The pincers and the anvil were at him again. He thought of falls, torn garments, broken legs.

Simeon lifted the arms of the barrow, and then dropped them.

"Have you got it?" he demanded of Arthur.

"Got what?"

"*It.*"

"Yes," said Arthur, comprehending.

"Are you sure? Show it me. Better give it me. It will be safer with me."

Arthur unbuttoned his overcoat, took off his left glove, and drew from one of his pockets a small, bright object, which shone under the street lamp. Simeon took it silently. Then he definitely seized the arms of the barrow, and the procession started up the street.

No time had been lost, for Simeon had an extraordinary gift of celerity. It was eleven minutes to seven. Nevertheless, Arthur felt the pincers, and the feel of the pincers made him look at his watch.

"See here," said Simeon, briefly. "You needn't worry. *We shall catch that train.* We've got twenty minutes, and we shall get to the station in nine." The exertion of wheeling the barrow over what was practically a sheet of rough ice made him speak in short gasps.

Impossible for the pincers and the anvil to remain in face of that assured, almost god-like tone!

"Good!" murmured Arthur. "By Jove, but it's cold though!"

"I've never been hotter in my life," said Simeon, puffing. "Except in my hands."

"Can't I take it for a bit?"

"No, you can't," said Simeon. At the robust finality of the refusal Arthur laughed. Then Simeon laughed. The party became gay. The pincers and the anvil were gone for ever. Simeon turned gingerly into Pollard Street-half-way to the station. They had but to descend Pollard Street and climb the path across the cinder-heaps beyond, and they would be, as it were, in harbour. In Pollard Street Simeon had the happy idea of taking to the roadway. It was rougher, and, therefore, less dangerous, than the pavement. At intervals he shoved the wheel of the barrow by main force over a stone.

"Put my hat straight, will you?" he asked of Arthur, and Arthur obeyed. It was becoming a task under the winter stars.

Then Arthur happened to notice the wheel of the barrow—its sole wheel.

"I say," he said, "what's up with that wheel?"

"It's rocky, that's what that wheel is," replied Simeon. "I hope it will hold out."

Instead of pushing the barrow he was now holding it back, down the slant of Pollard Street. The mist had cleared. And Arthur could see the red gleam of a signal in the neighbourhood of the station. But now the pincers and the anvil were at him again, for Simeon's tone was alarming. It indicated that the wobbling wheel of the barrow might not hold out.

The catastrophe happened when they were climbing the cinder-slope and within two hundred yards of the little station. Simeon was propelling with all his might, and he propelled the wheel against half a brick. The wheel collapsed. There was a splintering even of the main timbers of the vehicle as the immense weight of the trunk crashed to the solid earth.

Simeon fell, and rose with difficulty, standing on one leg, and terribly grimacing.

He said nothing, but consulted his watch by the aid of a fusee.

"We must carry it," Arthur suggested wildly.

"We can't carry it up here. It's much too heavy."

Arthur remembered the tremendous weight of even his share of it as they had slid it down the stairs.

No. It could not be carried.

"Besides," said Simeon, "I've sprained my ankle, I fear." And he sat down on the trunk.

"What are we to do?" Arthur asked tragically.

"Do? Why, it's perfectly simple! You must go without me. Anyhow, run to the station, and try to get the porter down here with another barrow."

Man of infinite calm, of infinite resource. Though the pincers and the anvil were horribly torturing him at that moment, Arthur could not but admire his younger brother's astounding *sangfroid*.

And he set off.

"Here!" Simeon called him peremptorily. "Take this—in case you don't come back."

And he handed him the small bright object.

"But I must come back. I can't possibly go without the trunk. All my things are in it."

"I know that, man. *But perhaps you'll have to go without it.* Hurry!"

Arthur ran. He encountered the senior porter at the gate of the station.

"Where's Merrith?" he began. "He was to have—"

"Merrith's mother is dead—died at five o'clock," said the senior porter. "And I'm here all alone."

Arthur stopped as if shot.

"Well," he recovered himself. "Lend me a barrow."

"I shall lend ye no barrow. It's against the rules. Since they transferred our stationmaster to Clegg there's been an inspector down here welly [well nigh] every day."

"But I must *have* a barrow."

"I shall lend ye no barrow," said the senior porter, a brute.

A signal close to the signal-box clattered down from red to green.

"Her's signalled," said the senior porter. "Are ye travelling by her?"

Arthur had to decide in a moment. Must he or must he not abandon Simeon and the trunk? The train, a procession of lights, could be seen in the distance under the black sky. He gave one glance in the direction of Simeon and the trunk, and then entered the station.

Simeon had been right. He did catch the train.

It was fortunate that there was a wide margin between the advertised time of arrival of the Loop-Line train at Knype and the departure therefrom of the London express. For, beyond Hanbridge, the Loop-Line train came to a standstill, and obstinately remained at a standstill for near upon forty minutes. Dawn began and completed itself while that train reposed there. Things got to such a point that, despite the intense cold, the few passengers stuck their heads out of the windows and kept them there. Arthur suffered unspeakably. He imparted his awful anxiety to an old man in the same compartment. And the old man said:

"They always keep the express waiting for the Loop. Moreover, you've plenty o' time yet."

He knew that the Loop was supposed to catch the express, and that in actual practice it did catch it. He knew that there was yet enough time. Still, he continued to suffer. He continued to believe, at the bottom of his heart, that on this morning, of all mornings, the Loop would not catch the express.

However, he was wrong. The Loop caught the express, though it was a nearish thing. He dashed down into the subterranean passage at Knype Station, reappeared on the up-platform, ran to the fore-part of the express, which was in and waiting, and jumped; a porter banged the door, a guard inspired the driver by a tune on a whistle, and off went the express. Arthur was now safe. Nothing ever happened to a North-Western express. He was safe. He was shorn of his luggage (almost, but not quite, indispensable) and of Simeon; but he was safe. He could not be disgraced in the world's eye. He thought of poor, gallant, imperturbable, sprained Simeon freezing on the trunk in the middle of the cinder-waste.

III

The train stopped momentarily at a station which he thought to be Lichfield. Then (out of his waking dreams) it seemed to him that Lichfield Station had strangely grown in length, and just as the train was drawing out he saw the word "Stafford" in immense white enamelled letters on a blue ground. There was nobody else in the

444

compartment. His heart and stomach in a state of frightful torture, he sprang out of it—not on to the line, but into the corridor (for it was a corridor train) and into the next compartment, where were seated two men.

"Is this the London train?" he demanded, not concealing his terror.

"No, it isn't. It's the Birmingham train," said one of the men fiercely—a sort of a Levite.

"Great heavens!" ejaculated Arthur Cotterill.

"You ought to inquire before you get into a train," said the Levite.

"The fact is," said the other man, who was perhaps a cousin of a Good Samaritan, "the express from Manchester is split up at Knype—one part for London, and the other part for Birmingham."

"I know that," said Arthur Cotterill.

"Ever since I can remember the London part has gone off first."

"Of course," said Arthur; "I've travelled by it lots of times."

"But they altered it only last week."

"I only just caught the train," Arthur breathed.

"Seems to me you didn't catch it," said the Levite.

"*I must be in London before two o'clock*," said Arthur, and he said it so solemnly, he said it with so much of his immortal soul, that even the Levite was startled out of his callous indifference.

"There are expresses from Birmingham to London that do the journey in two hours," said he.

"Let us see," said the cousin of a Good Samaritan, kindly, opening a bag and producing Bradshaw.

And he explained to Arthur that the train reached New Street, Birmingham, at 10.45, and that, by a singular good fortune, a very fast express left New Street at 11.40, and arrived at Euston at 1.45.

Arthur thanked him and retired with his pincers and anvil to his own compartment.

He was a ruined man, a disgraced man. The loss of his trunk was now nothing. At the best he would be over half an hour late, and it was quite probable that he would be too late altogether. He pictured the other people waiting, waiting for him anxiously, as minute after minute passed, until the fatal hour struck. The whole affair was unthinkable. Simeon's fault, of course. Simeon had convinced him that to go up to London on Christmas Day would be absurd, whereas it was now evident that to go up to London on Christmas

445

Day was obviously the only prudent thing to do. Awful!

The train to Birmingham was in an ironical mood, for it ran into New Street to the very minute of the time-table. Thus Arthur had fifty-five futile minutes to pass. At another time New Street, as the largest single station in the British Empire, might have interested him. But now it was no more interesting than Purgatory when you know where you are ultimately going to. He sought out the telegraph-office, and telegraphed to London—despairing, yet a manly telegram. Then he sought out the refreshment-room, and ordered a whisky. He was just putting the whisky to his lips when he remembered that if, after all, he did arrive in time, the whisky would amount to a serious breach of manners. So he put the glass down untasted, and the barmaid justifiably felt herself to have been insulted.

He watched the slow formation of the Birmingham-London express. He also watched the various clocks. For whole hours the fingers of the clocks never budged, and even then they would show an advance of only a minute or two.

"Is this the train for London?" he asked an inspector at 11.35.

"Can't you see?" said the inspector, brightly. As a fact, "Euston" was written all over the train. But Arthur wanted to be sure this time.

The express departed from Birmingham with the nicest exactitude, and covered itself with glory as far as Watford, when it ran into a mist, and lost more than a quarter of an hour, besides ruining Arthur's career.

Arthur arrived in London at one minute past two. He got out of the train with no plan. The one feasible enterprise seemed to be that of suicide.

"Come on, now," said a voice—a voice that staggered Arthur. It was a man with a crutch who spoke. It was Simeon. "Come on, quick, and don't talk too much! To the hotel first." Simeon hobbled forward rapidly, and somehow (he could not explain how) the anvil and pincers had left Arthur.

"I got hold of a milk-cart with a sharpened horse, and drove to Knype. Horse fell once, but he picked himself up again. Cost me a sovereign. Only just caught the train. Shouldn't have caught it if they hadn't sent off the Birmingham part before the London part. I was astonished, I can tell you, not to find you at Euston. Went to the hotel. Found 'em all waiting, of course, and practically weeping over

446

a telegram from you. However, I soon arranged things. Had to buy a crutch.... Here, boy, lift!" They were in the hotel.

On a bed all Arthur's finest clothes were laid out. The famous trunk was at the foot of the bed.

"Quick!"

"But look here!" Arthur remonstrated. "It's after two now."

"Well, if it is? We've got till three. I've arranged with the mandarin chap for a quarter to three."

"I thought these things couldn't occur after two o'clock—by law."

"That's what's the matter with you," said Simeon; "you think too much. The two o'clock law was altered years ago. Had anything to eat?" He was helping Arthur with buttons.

"No."

"I expected not. Here! Swallow this whisky."

"Not I!" Arthur protested in a startled tone.

"Why not?"

"Because I shall have to kiss her after the ceremony."

"Bosh!" said Simeon. "Drink it. Besides, there's no kissing in a Registry Office. You're thinking of a church. I wish you wouldn't think so much. Here! Now the necktie, you cuckoo!"

In three minutes they were driving rapidly through the London mist towards the other sex, and in a quarter of an hour there was one bachelor the less in this vale of tears.

THE WIDOW OF THE BALCONY

I

They stood at the window of her boudoir in the new house which Stephen Cheswardine had recently bought at Sneyd. The stars were pursuing their orbits overhead in a clear dark velvet sky, except to the north, where the industrial fires and smoke of the Five Towns had completely put them out. But even these distant signs of rude labour had a romantic aspect, and did not impair the general romance of the scene. Charlie had loved her; he loved her still; and she gave him odd minutes of herself when she could, just to keep him alive. Moreover, there was the log fire richly crackling in the well-grate of the boudoir; there was the feminineness of the boudoir (dimly lit), and the soft splendour of her gown, and behind all that, pervading the house, the gay rumour of the party. And in front of them the window-panes, and beyond the window-panes the stars in their orbits. Doubtless it was such influences which, despite several degrees of frost outside, gave to Charlie Woodruff's thoughts an Italian, or Spanish, turn. He said:

"Stephen ought to have this window turned into a French window, and build you a balcony. It could easily be done. Just the view for a balcony. You can see Sneyd Lake from here." (You could. People were skating on it.)

He did not add that you could see the Sneyd Golf Links from there, and vice versa. I doubt if the idea occurred to him, but as he was an active member of the Sneyd Golf Club it would certainly have presented itself to him in due season.

"What a lovely scheme!" Vera exclaimed enthusiastically.

It appealed to her. It appealed to all that was romantic in her bird-like soul. She did not see the links; she did not see the lake; she just saw herself in exquisite frocks, lightly lounging on the balcony in high summer, and dreaming of her own beauty.

"And have a striped awning," she said.

"Yes," he said. "Make Stephen do it."

"I will," she said.

At that moment Stephen came in, with his bald head and his forty years.

"I say!" he demanded. "What are you up to?"

448

"We were just watching the skaters," said Vera.

"And the wonders of the night," said Charlie, chuckling characteristically. He always laughed at himself. He was a philosopher. He and Stephen had been fast friends from infancy.

"Well, you'd just better skate downstairs," said Stephen. (No romance in Stephen! He was netting a couple of thousand a year out of the manufacture of toilet-sets, in all that smoke to the north. How could you expect him to be romantic?)

"Charlie was saying how nice it would be for me to have a French window here, and a marble balcony," Vera remarked. It had not taken her long to think of marble. "You must do it for me, Steve."

"Bosh!" said Stephen. "That's just like you, Charlie. What an ass you are!"

"Oh, but you *must*!" said Vera, in that tone which meant business, and which also meant trouble for Stephen.

"*She's* come," Stephen announced curtly, determined to put trouble off.

"Oh, has she?" cried Vera. "I thought you said she wouldn't."

"She hesitated, because she was afraid. But she's come after all," Stephen answered.

"What fun!" Vera murmured.

And ran off downstairs back again into the midst of the black coats and the white toilettes and the holly-clad electricity of her Christmas gathering.

II

The news that *she* had come was all over the noisy house in a minute, and it had the astonishing effect of producing what might roughly be described as a silence. It stopped the reckless waltzing of the piano in the drawing-room; it stopped the cackle incident to cork-pool in the billiard-room; it even stopped a good deal of the whispering under the Chinese lanterns beneath the stairs and in the alcove at the top of the stairs. What it did not stop was the consumption of mince-pies and claret-cup in the small breakfast-room; people mumbled about *her* between munches.

She, having been sustained with turkey and beer in the kitchen, was led by the backstairs up to Vera's very boudoir, that being the only suitable room. And there she waited. She was a woman of about forty-five; fat, unfair (in the physical sense), and untidy. Of her hands the less said the better. She had probably never visited a professional coiffeur in her life. Her form was straitly confined in an atrocious dress of linsey-woolsey, and she wore an apron that was neither white nor black. Her boots were commodious. After her meal she was putting a hat-pin to a purpose which hat-pins do not usually serve. She gained an honest living by painting green leaves on yellow wash-basins in Stephen's renowned earthenware manufactory. She spoke the dialect of the people. She had probably never heard of Christian Science, bridge, Paquin, Panhard, Father Vaughan, the fall of consols, osprey plumes, nor the new theology. Nobody in the house knew her name; even Stephen had forgotten it. And yet the whole house was agog concerning her.

The fact was that in the painting-shops of the various manufactories where she had painted green leaves on yellow wash-basins (for in all her life she had done little else) she possessed a reputation as a prophet, seer, oracle, fortune-teller—what you will. Polite persons would perhaps never have heard of her reputation, the toiling millions of the Five Towns being of a rather secretive nature in such matters, had not the subject of fortune-telling been made prominent in the district by the celebrated incident of the fashionable palmist. The fashionable palmist, having thriven enormously in Bond Street, had undertaken a tour through the provinces and had stopped several days at Hanbridge (our metropolis), where he had an immense vogue until the Hanbridge police hit on the singular idea of prosecuting him for an unlawful vagabond. Stripped of twenty pounds odd in the guise of a fine and costs, and having narrowly missed the rigours of our county jail, that fashionable palmist and soothsayer had returned to Bond Street full of hate and respect for Midland justice, which fears not and has a fist like a navvy's. The attention of the Five Towns had thus been naturally drawn to fortune-telling in general. And it was deemed that in securing a local celebrity (quite an amateur, and therefore, it was uncertainly hoped, on the windy side of the law) for the diversion of his Christmas party Stephen Cheswardine had done a stylish and original thing.

Of course no one in the house believed in fortune-telling. Oh no! But as an amusement it was amusing. As fun, it was fun. She did her business with tea-leaves: so the tale ran. This was not considered to be very distinguished. A crystal, or even cards, or the anatomy of a sacrificed fowl, would have been better than tea-leaves; tea-leaves were decidedly lower class. And yet, despite these drawbacks, when the question arose who should first visit the witch of Endor, there was a certain hesitation.

"You go!"

"No, *you* go."

"Oh! *I'm* not going," (a superior laugh), etc.

At last it was decided that Jack Hall and Cissy Woodruff (Charlie's much younger sister), the pair having been engaged to be married for exactly three days, should make the first call. They ascended, blushing and brave. In a moment Jack Hall descended alone, nervously playing with the silk handkerchief that was lodged in his beautiful white waistcoat. The witch of Endor had informed him that she never received the two sexes together, and had expelled him. This incident greatly enhanced the witch's reputation. Then Stephen happened to mention that he had heard that the woman's mother, and her grandmother before her, had been fortune-tellers. Somehow that statement seemed to strike everybody full in the face; it set a seal on the authority of the witch, made her genuine. And an uncanny feeling seemed to spread through the house as the house waited for Cissy to reappear.

"She's very *good*," said Cissy, on emerging. "She told me all sorts of things."

A group formed at the foot of the stairs.

"What did she tell you?"

"Well, she said I must expect a very important letter in a few days, and much would depend on it, and next year there will be a big removal, and a large lumbering piece of furniture, and I shall go a journey over water. It's quite right, you know. I suppose the letter's from grandma; I hope it is, anyway. And if we go to France—"

Thenceforward the witch without a name held continuous receptions in the boudoir, and the boudoir gradually grew into an abode of mystery and strangeness, hypnotizing the entire house. People went thither; people came back; and those who had not been pictured to themselves something very incantatory, and little by little they made up their minds to go. Some thought the woman excellent, others said it was all rot. But none denied that it was interesting. None could possibly deny that the fortune-telling had killed every other diversion provided by the hospitable Stephen and Vera (except the refreshments). The most scornful scoffers made a

451

concession and kindly consented to go to the boudoir. Stephen went. Charlie went. Even the Mayor of Hanbridge went (not being on the borough Bench that night).

But Vera would not go. A genuine fear was upon her. Christmases had always been unlucky for her peace of mind. And she was highly superstitious. Yet she wanted to go; she was burning to go, all the while assuring her guests that nothing would induce her to go. The party drew to a close, and pair by pair the revellers drove off, or walked, into the romantic night. Then Stephen told Vera to give the woman half-a-sovereign and let her depart, for it was late. And in paying the half-sovereign to the woman Vera was suddenly overcome by temptation and asked for her fortune. The woman's grimy simplicity, her smiling face, the commonness of her teapot, her utter unlikeness to anything in the first act of *Macbeth*, encouraged Vera to believe in her magic powers. Vera's hand trembled as, under instructions, she tipped the tea-leaves into the saucer.

"Ay!" said the witch, in broadest Staffordshire, running her objectionable hand up and down the buttons of her linsey-woolsey bodice, and gently agitating the saucer. "Theer's a widder theer." [There's a widow there.] "Yo'll be havin' a letter, or it mit be a talligram—"

Vera wouldn't hear any more. Her one fear in life was the fear of Stephen's death (though she *did* console Charlie with nice smiles and lots of *tête-à-tête)*, and here was this fiendish witch directly foreseeing the dreadful event.

III

Every day for many days Stephen expected to have to take part in a pitched battle about the proposed balcony. The sweet enemy, however, did not seem to be in fighting form. It is true that she mentioned the balcony, but she mentioned it in quite a reasonable spirit. Astounding as the statement may appear to any personal acquaintance of Vera's, Vera showed a capacity to perceive that there were two sides to the question. When Stephen pointed out that balconies were unsuited to the English climate, she almost agreed. When he said that balconies were dangerous and that to have a safe one would necessitate the strengthening of the wall, she merely replied, with wonderful meekness, that she only weighed seven stone twelve. When he informed her that the breakfast-room, already not too light, was underneath the proposed balcony, which would further darken it, she kept an angelic silence. And when he showed her that the view from the proposed balcony would in any case be marred by the immense pall of Five Towns smoke to the south, she still kept an angelic silence.

Stephen could not understand it.

Nor was this all. She became extraordinarily solicitous for his welfare, especially in the matter of health. She wrapped him up when he went out, and unpacked him when he came in. She cautioned him against draughts, overwork, microbes, and dietary indiscretions. Thanks to regular boxing exercise, his old dyspepsia had almost entirely disappeared, but this did not prevent her from watching every mouthful that vanished under the portals of his moustache. And she superintended his boxing too. She made a point of being present whenever he and Charlie boxed, and she would force Charlie to cease fighting at the oddest moments. She was flat against having a motor-car; she compelled Stephen to drive to the station in the four-wheeler instead of in the high dogcart. Indeed, from the way she guarded him, he might have been the one frail life that stood between England and anarchy.

And she was always so kind, in a rather melancholy, resigned, wistful fashion.

No. Stephen could *not* understand it.

There came a time when Stephen could neither understand it nor stand it. And he tried to worm out of her her secret. But he could not. The fascinating little liar stoutly stuck to it that nothing was the matter with her, and that she had nothing on her mind. Stephen knew differently. He consulted Charlie Woodruff. She had not made a confidant of Charlie. Charlie was exactly as much in the dark as Stephen. Then Stephen (I regret to have to say it) took to swearing. For instance, he swore when she hid all his thin socks and so obliged him to continue with his thick ones. And one day he swore when, in answer to his query why she was pale, she said she didn't know.

He thus, without expecting to do so, achieved a definite climax.

For she broke out. She ceased in half a second to be pale. She gave him with cutting candour all that had been bottled up in her entrancing bosom. She told him that the witch had foreseen her a widow (which was the same thing as prophesying his death), and that she had done, and was doing, all that the ingenuity of a loving heart could suggest to keep him alive in spite of the prediction, but that, in face of his infamous brutality, she should do no more; that if he chose to die and leave her a widow he might die and leave her a widow for all she cared; in brief, that she had done with him.

When she had become relatively calm Stephen addressed her calmly, and even ingratiatingly.

"I'm sorry," he said, and added, "but you know you did say that you were hiding nothing from me."

"Of course," she retorted, "because I *was*." Her arguments were usually on this high plane of logic.

"And you ought not to be so superstitious," Stephen proceeded.

"Well," said she, with truth, "one never knows." And she wiped away a tear and showed the least hint of an inclination to kiss him. "And anyhow my only anxiety was for you."

"Do you really believe what that woman said?" Stephen asked.

"Well," she repeated, "one never knows."

"Because if you do, I'll tell you something."

"What?" Vera demanded.

At this juncture Stephen committed an error of tactics. He might have let her continue in the fear of his death, and thus remained on velvet (subject to occasional outbreaks) for the rest of his life. But he gave himself utterly away.

"She told *me* I should live till I was ninety," said he. "So you can't be a widow for quite half a century, and you'll be eighty yourself then."

IV

Within twenty-four hours she was at him about the balcony.

"The summer will be lovely," she said, in reply to his argument about climate.

"Rubbish," she said, in reply to his argument about safety.

"Who cares for your old breakfast-room?" she said, in reply to his argument about darkness at breakfast.

"We will have trees planted on that side—big elms," she said, in reply to his argument about the smoke of the Five Towns spoiling the view.

Whereupon Stephen definitely and clearly enunciated that he should not build a balcony.

454

"Oh, but you must!" she protested.

"A balcony is quite impossible," said Stephen, with his firmest masculinity.

"You'll see if it's impossible," said she, "*when I'm that widow.*"

The curious may be interested to know that she has already begun to plant trees.

THE CAT AND CUPID

I

The secret history of the Ebag marriage is now printed for the first time. The Ebag family, who prefer their name to be accented on the first syllable, once almost ruled Oldcastle, which is a clean and conceited borough, with long historical traditions, on the very edge of the industrial, democratic and unclean Five Towns. The Ebag family still lives in the grateful memory of Oldcastle, for no family ever did more to preserve the celebrated Oldcastilian superiority in social, moral and religious matters over the vulgar Five Towns. The episodes leading to the Ebag marriage could only have happened in Oldcastle. By which I mean merely that they could not have happened in any of the Five Towns. In the Five Towns that sort of thing does not occur. I don't know why, but it doesn't. The people are too deeply interested in football, starting prices, rates, public parks, sliding scales, excursions to Blackpool, and municipal shindies, to concern themselves with organists as such. In the Five Towns an organist may be a sanitary inspector or an auctioneer on Mondays. In Oldcastle an organist is an organist, recognized as such in the streets. No one ever heard of an organist in the Five Towns being taken up and petted by a couple of old ladies. But this may occur at Oldcastle. It, in fact, did.

The scandalous circumstances which led to the disappearance from the Oldcastle scene of Mr Skerritt, the original organist of St Placid, have no relation to the present narrative, which opens when the ladies Ebag began to seek for a new organist. The new church of St Placid owed its magnificent existence to the Ebag family. The apse had been given entirely by old Caiaphas Ebag (ex-M.P., now a paralytic sufferer) at a cost of twelve thousand pounds; and his was the original idea of building the church. When, owing to the decline of the working man's interest in beer, and one or two other things, Caiaphas lost nearly the whole of his fortune, which had been gained by honest labour in mighty speculations, he rather regretted the church; he would have preferred twelve thousand in cash to a view of the apse from his bedroom window; but he was man enough never to complain. He lived, after his misfortunes, in a comparatively small house with his two daughters, Mrs Ebag and

Miss Ebag. These two ladies are the heroines of the tale.

Mrs Ebag had married her cousin, who had died. She possessed about six hundred a year of her own. She was two years older than her sister, Miss Ebag, a spinster. Miss Ebag was two years younger than Mrs Ebag. No further information as to their respective ages ever leaked out. Miss Ebag had a little money of her own from her deceased mother, and Caiaphas had the wreck of his riches. The total income of the household was not far short of a thousand a year, but of this quite two hundred a year was absorbed by young Edith Ebag, Mrs Ebag's step-daughter (for Mrs Ebag had been her husband's second choice). Edith, who was notorious as a silly chit and spent most of her time in London and other absurd places, formed no part of the household, though she visited it occasionally. The household consisted of old Caiaphas, bedridden, and his two daughters and Goldie. Goldie was the tomcat, so termed by reason of his splendid tawniness. Goldie had more to do with the Ebag marriage than anyone or anything, except the weathercock on the top of the house. This may sound queer, but is as naught to the queerness about to be unfolded.

II

It cannot be considered unnatural that Mrs and Miss Ebag, with the assistance of the vicar, should have managed the affairs of the church. People nicknamed them "the churchwardens," which was not quite nice, having regard to the fact that their sole aim was the truest welfare of the church. They and the vicar, in a friendly and effusive way, hated each other. Sometimes they got the better of the vicar, and, less often, he got the better of them. In the choice of a new organist they won. Their candidate was Mr Carl Ullman, the artistic orphan.

Mr Carl Ullman is the hero of the tale. The son of one of those German designers of earthenware who at intervals come and settle in the Five Towns for the purpose of explaining fully to the inhabitants how inferior England is to Germany, he had an English mother, and he himself was violently English. He spoke English like an Englishman and German like an Englishman. He could paint, model in clay, and play three musical instruments, including the organ. His one failing was that he could never earn enough to live on. It seemed as if he was always being drawn by an invisible string towards the workhouse door. Now and then he made half a sovereign extra by deputizing on the organ. In such manner had he been introduced to the Ebag ladies. His romantic and gloomy appearance had attracted them, with the result that they had asked him to lunch after the service, and he had remained with them till the evening service. During the visit they had learnt that his grandfather had been Court Councillor in the Kingdom of Saxony. Afterwards they often said to each other how ideal it would be if only Mr Skerritt might be removed and Carl Ullman take his place. And when Mr Skerritt actually was removed, by his own wickedness, they regarded it as almost an answer to prayer, and successfully employed their powerful interest on behalf of Carl. The salary was a hundred a year. Not once in his life had Carl earned a hundred pounds in a single year. For him the situation meant opulence. He accepted it, but calmly, gloomily. Romantic gloom was his joy in life. He said with deep melancholy that he was sure he could not find a convenient lodging in Oldcastle. And the ladies Ebag then said that he must really come and spend a few days with them and Goldie and papa until he was "suited." He said that he hated to plant himself on people, and yielded to the request. The ladies Ebag fussed around his dark-eyed and tranquil pessimism, and both of them instantly grew younger—a curious but authentic phenomenon. They adored his playing, and they were enchanted to discover that his notions about hymn tunes agreed with theirs, and by consequence disagreed with the vicar's. In the first week or two they scored off the vicar five times, and the advantage of having your organist in your own house grew very apparent. They were also greatly impressed by his gentleness with Goldie and by his intelligent interest in serious questions.

One day Miss Ebag said timidly to her sister: "It's just six months to-day."

"What do you mean, sister?" asked Mrs Ebag, self-consciously.

"Since Mr Ullman came."

"So it is!" said Mrs Ebag, who was just as well aware of the date as the spinster was aware of it.

They said no more. The position was the least bit delicate. Carl had found no lodging. He did not offer to go. They did not want him to go. He did not offer to pay. And really he cost them nothing except laundry, whisky and fussing. How could they suggest that he should pay? He lived amidst them like a beautiful mystery, and all were seemingly content. Carl was probably saving the whole of his salary, for he never bought clothes and he did not smoke. The ladies Ebag simply did what they liked about hymn-tunes.

III

You would have thought that no outsider would find a word to say, and you would have been mistaken. The fact that Mrs Ebag was two years older than Miss and Miss two years younger than Mrs Ebag; the fact that old Caiaphas was, for strong reasons, always in the house; the fact that the ladies were notorious cat-idolaters; the fact that the reputation of the Ebag family was and had ever been spotless; the fact that the Ebag family had given the apse and practically created the entire church; all these facts added together did not prevent the outsider from finding a word to say.

At first words were not said; but looks were looked, and coughs were coughed. Then someone, strolling into the church of a morning while Carl Ullman was practising, saw Miss Ebag sitting in silent ecstasy in a corner. And a few mornings later the same someone, whose curiosity had been excited, veritably saw Mrs Ebag in the organ-loft with Carl Ullman, but no sign of Miss Ebag. It was at this juncture that words began to be said.

Words! Not complete sentences! The sentences were never finished. "Of course, it's no affair of mine, but—" "I wonder that people like the Ebags should—" "Not that I should ever dream of hinting that—" "First one and then the other—well!" "I'm sure that if either Mrs or Miss Ebag had the slightest idea they'd at once—" And so on. Intangible gossamer criticism, floating in the air!

IV

One evening—it was precisely the first of June—when a thunderstorm was blowing up from the south-west, and scattering the smoke of the Five Towns to the four corners of the world, and making the weathercock of the house of the Ebags creak, the ladies Ebag and Carl Ullman sat together as usual in the drawing-room. The French window was open, but banged to at intervals. Carl Ullman had played the piano and the ladies Ebag—Mrs Ebag, somewhat comfortably stout and Miss Ebag spare—were talking very well and sensibly about the influence of music on character.

They invariably chose such subjects for conversation. Carl was chiefly silent, but now and then, after a sip of whisky, he would say "Yes" with impressiveness and stare gloomily out of the darkening window. The ladies Ebag had a remarkable example of the influence of music on character in the person of Edith Ebag. It appeared that Edith would never play anything but waltzes—Waldteufel's for choice—and that the foolish frivolity of her flyaway character was a direct consequence of this habit. Carl felt sadly glad, after hearing the description of Edith's carryings-on, that Edith had chosen to live far away.

And then the conversation languished and died with the daylight, and a certain self-consciousness obscured the social atmosphere. For a vague rumour of the chatter of the town had penetrated the house, and the ladies Ebag, though they scorned chatter, were affected by it; Carl Ullman, too. It had the customary effect of such chatter; it fixed the thoughts of those chatted about on matters which perhaps would not otherwise have occupied their attention.

The ladies Ebag said to themselves: "We are no longer aged nineteen. We are moreover living with our father. If he is bedridden, what then? This gossip connecting our names with that of Mr Ullman is worse than baseless; it is preposterous. We assert positively that we have no designs of any kind on Mr Ullman."

Nevertheless, by dint of thinking about that gossip, the naked idea of a marriage with Mr Ullman soon ceased to shock them. They could gaze at it without going into hysterics.

As for Carl, he often meditated upon his own age, which might have been anything between thirty and forty-five, and upon the mysterious ages of the ladies, and upon their goodness, their charm, their seriousness, their intelligence and their sympathy with himself.

Hence the self-consciousness in the gloaming.

To create a diversion Miss Ebag walked primly to the window and cried:

"Goldie! Goldie!"

It was Goldie's bedtime. In summer he always strolled into the garden after dinner, and he nearly always sensibly responded to the call when his bed-hour sounded. No one would have dreamed of retiring until Goldie was safely ensconced in his large basket under the stairs.

"Naughty Goldie!" Miss Ebag said, comprehensively, to the garden.

She went into the garden to search, and Mrs Ebag followed her, and Carl Ullman followed Mrs Ebag. And they searched without result, until it was black night and the threatening storm at last fell. The vision of Goldie out in that storm desolated the ladies, and Carl Ullman displayed the nicest feeling. At length the rain drove them in and they stood in the drawing-room with anxious faces, while two servants, under directions from Carl, searched the house for Goldie.

"If you please'm," stammered the housemaid, rushing rather unconventionally into the drawing-room, "cook says she thinks Goldie must be on the roof, in the vane."

"On the roof in the vane?" exclaimed Mrs Ebag, pale. "In the vane?"

"Yes'm."

"Whatever do you mean, Sarah?" asked Miss Ebag, even paler.

The ladies Ebag were utterly convinced that Goldie was not like other cats, that he never went on the roof, that he never had any wish to do anything that was not in the strictest sense gentlemanly and correct. And if by chance he did go on the roof, it was merely to examine the roof itself, or to enjoy the view therefrom out of gentlemanly curiosity. So that this reference to the roof shocked them. The night did not favour the theory of view-gazing.

"Cook says she heard the weather-vane creaking ever since she went upstairs after dinner, and now it's stopped; and she can hear Goldie a-myowling like anything."

"Is cook in her attic?" asked Mrs Ebag.

"Yes'm."

"Ask her to come out. Mr Ullman, will you be so very good as to come upstairs and investigate?"

Cook, enveloped in a cloak, stood out on the second landing, while Mr Ullman and the ladies invaded her chamber. The noise of myowling was terrible. Mr Ullman opened the dormer window, and the rain burst in, together with a fury of myowling. But he did not care. It lightened and thundered. But he did not care. He procured a chair of cook's and put it under the window and stood on it, with his back to the window, and twisted forth his body so that he could spy up the roof. The ladies protested that he would be wet through, but he paid no heed to them.

Then his head, dripping, returned into the room. "I've just seen by a flash of lightning," he said in a voice of emotion. "The poor animal has got his tail fast in the socket of the weather-vane. He

461

must have been whisking it about up there, and the vane turned and caught it. The vane is jammed."

"How dreadful!" said Mrs Ebag. "Whatever can be done?"

"He'll be dead before morning," sobbed Miss Ebag.

"I shall climb up the roof and release him," said Carl Ullman, gravely.

They forbade him to do so. Then they implored him to refrain. But he was adamant. And in their supplications there was a note of insincerity, for their hearts bled for Goldie, and, further, they were not altogether unwilling that Carl should prove himself a hero. And so, amid apprehensive feminine cries of the acuteness of his danger, Carl crawled out of the window and faced the thunder, the lightning, the rain, the slippery roof, and the maddened cat. A group of three servants were huddled outside the attic door.

In the attic the ladies could hear his movements on the roof, moving higher and higher. The suspense was extreme. Then there was silence; even the myowling had ceased. Then a clap of thunder; and then, after that, a terrific clatter on the roof, a bounding downwards as of a great stone, a curse, a horrid pause, and finally a terrific smashing of foliage and cracking of wood.

Mrs Ebag sprang to the window.

"It's all right," came a calm, gloomy voice from below. "I fell into the rhododendrons, and Goldie followed me. I'm not hurt, thank goodness! Just my luck!"

A bell rang imperiously. It was the paralytic's bell. He had been disturbed by these unaccustomed phenomena.

"Sister, do go to father at once," said Mrs Ebag, as they both hastened downstairs in a state of emotion, assuredly unique in their lives.

V

Mrs Ebag met Carl and the cat as they dripped into the gas-lit drawing-room. They presented a surprising spectacle, and they were doing damage to the Persian carpet at the rate of about five shillings a second; but that Carl, and the beloved creature for whom he had dared so much, were equally unhurt appeared to be indubitable. Of course, it was a miracle. It could not be regarded as other than a miracle. Mrs Ebag gave vent to an exclamation in which were mingled pity, pride, admiration and solicitude, and then remained,

462

as it were, spellbound. The cat escaped from those protecting arms and fled away. Instead of following Goldie, Mrs Ebag continued to gaze at the hero.

"How can I thank you!" she whispered.

"What for?" asked Carl, with laconic gloom.

"For having saved my darling!" said Mrs Ebag. And there was passion in her voice.

"Oh!" said Carl. "It was nothing!"

"Nothing?" Mrs Ebag repeated after him, with melting eyes, as if to imply that, instead of being nothing, it was everything; as if to imply that his deed must rank hereafter with the most splendid deeds of antiquity; as if to imply that the whole affair was beyond words to utter or gratitude to repay.

And in fact Carl himself was moved. You cannot fall from the roof of a two-story house into a very high-class rhododendron bush, carrying a prize cat in your arms, without being a bit shaken. And Carl was a bit shaken, not merely physically, but morally and spiritually. He could not deny to himself that he had after all done something rather wondrous, which ought to be celebrated in sounding verse. He felt that he was in an atmosphere far removed from the commonplace.

He dripped steadily on to the carpet.

"You know how dear my cat was to me," proceeded Mrs Ebag. "And you risked your life to spare me the pain of his suffering, perhaps his death. How thankful I am that I insisted on having those rhododendrons planted just where they are—fifteen years ago! I never anticipated—"

She stopped. Tears came into her dowager eyes. It was obvious that she worshipped him. She was so absorbed in his heroism that she had no thought even for his dampness. As Carl's eyes met hers she seemed to him to grow younger. And there came into his mind all the rumour that had vaguely reached him coupling their names together; and also his early dreams of love and passion and a marriage that would be one long honeymoon. And he saw how absurd had been those early dreams. He saw that the best chance of a felicitous marriage lay in a union of mature and serious persons, animated by grave interests and lofty ideals. Yes, she was older than he. But not much, not much! Not more than—how many years? And he remembered surprising her rapt glance that very evening as she watched him playing the piano. What had romance to do with age?

Romance could occur at any age. It was occurring now. Her soft eyes, her portly form, exuded romance. And had not the renowned Beaconsfield espoused a lady appreciably older than himself, and did not those espousals achieve the ideal of bliss? In the act of saving the cat he had not been definitely aware that it was so particularly the cat of the household. But now, influenced by her attitude and her shining reverence, he actually did begin to persuade himself that an uncontrollable instinctive desire to please her and win her for his own had moved him to undertake the perilous passage of the sloping roof.

In short, the idle chatter of the town was about to be justified. In another moment he might have dripped into her generous arms ... had not Miss Ebag swept into the drawing-room!

"Gracious!" gasped Miss Ebag. "The poor dear thing will have pneumonia. Sister, you know his chest is not strong. Dear Mr Ullman, please, please, do go and—er—change."

He did the discreet thing and went to bed, hot whisky following him on a tray carried by the housemaid.

VI

The next morning the slightly unusual happened. It was the custom for Carl Ullman to breakfast alone, while reading *The Staffordshire Signal*. The ladies Ebag breakfasted mysteriously in bed. But on this morning Carl found Miss Ebag before him in the breakfast-room. She prosecuted minute inquiries as to his health and nerves. She went out with him to regard the rhododendron bushes, and shuddered at the sight of the ruin which had saved him. She said, following famous philosophers, that Chance was merely the name we give to the effect of laws which we cannot understand. And, upon this high level of conversation, she poured forth his coffee and passed his toast.

It was a lovely morning after the tempest.

Goldie, all newly combed, and looking as though he had never seen a roof, strolled pompously into the room with tail unfurled. Miss Ebag picked the animal up and kissed it passionately.

"Darling!" she murmured, not exactly to Mr Ullman, nor yet exactly to the cat. Then she glanced effulgently at Carl and said, "When I think that you risked your precious life, in that awful storm, to save my poor Goldie?... You must have guessed how dear

464

he was to me?... No, really, Mr Ullman, I cannot thank you properly! I can't express my—"

Her eyes were moist.

Although not young, she was two years younger. Her age was two years less. The touch of man had never profaned her. No masculine kiss had ever rested on that cheek, that mouth. And Carl felt that he might be the first to cull the flower that had so long waited. He did not see, just then, the hollow beneath her chin, the two lines of sinew that, bounding a depression, disappeared beneath her collarette. He saw only her soul. He guessed that she would be more malleable than the widow, and he was sure that she was not in a position, as the widow was, to make comparisons between husbands. Certainly there appeared to be some confusion as to the proprietorship of this cat. Certainly he could not have saved the cat's life for love of two different persons. But that was beside the point. The essential thing was that he began to be glad that he had decided nothing definite about the widow on the previous evening.

"Darling!" said she again, with a new access of passion, kissing Goldie, but darting a glance at Carl.

He might have put to her the momentous question, between two bites of buttered toast, had not Mrs Ebag, at the precise instant, swum amply into the room.

"Sister! You up!" exclaimed Miss Ebag.

"And you, sister!" retorted Mrs Ebag.

VII

It is impossible to divine what might have occurred for the delectation of the very ancient borough of Oldcastle if that frivolous piece of goods, Edith, had not taken it into her head to run down from London for a few days, on the plea that London was too ridiculously hot. She was a pretty girl, with fluffy honey-coloured hair and about thirty white frocks. And she seemed to be quite as silly as her staid stepmother and her prim step-aunt had said. She transformed the careful order of the house into a wild disorder, and left a novel or so lying on the drawing-room table between her stepmother's *Contemporary Review* and her step-aunt's *History of European Morals*. Her taste in music was candidly and brazenly bad. It was a fact, as her elders had stated, that she played nothing but waltzes. What was worse, she compelled Carl Ullman to

465

perform waltzes. And one day she burst into the drawing-room when Carl was alone there, with a roll under her luscious arm, and said:

"What do you think I've found at Barrowfoot's?"

"I don't know," said Carl, gloomily smiling, and then smiling without gloom.

"Waldteufel's waltzes arranged for four hands. You must play them with me at once."

And he did. It was a sad spectacle to see the organist of St Placid's galloping through a series of dances with the empty-headed Edith.

The worst was, he liked it. He knew that he ought to prefer the high intellectual plane, the severe artistic tastes, of the elderly sisters. But he did not. He was amazed to discover that frivolity appealed more powerfully to his secret soul. He was also amazed to discover that his gloom was leaving him. This vanishing of gloom gave him strange sensations, akin to the sensations of a man who, after having worn gaiters into middle-age, abandons them.

After the Waldteufel she began to tell him all about herself; how she went slumming in the East End, and how jolly it was. And how she helped in the Bloomsbury Settlement, and how jolly that was. And, later, she said:

"You must have thought it very odd of me, Mr Ullman, not thanking you for so bravely rescuing my poor cat; but the truth is I never heard of it till to-day. I can't say how grateful I am. I should have loved to see you doing it."

"Is Goldie your cat?" he feebly inquired.

"Why, of course?" she said. "Didn't you know? Of course you did! Goldie always belonged to me. Grandpa bought him for me. But I couldn't do with him in London, so I always leave him here for them to take care of. He adores me. He never forgets me. He'll come to me before anyone. You must have noticed that. I can't say how grateful I am! It was perfectly marvellous of you! I can't help laughing, though, whenever I think what a state mother and auntie must have been in that night!"

Strictly speaking, they hadn't a cent between them, except his hundred a year. But he married her hair and she married his melancholy eyes; and she was content to settle in Oldcastle, where there are almost no slums. And her stepmother was forced by Edith to make the hundred up to four hundred. This was rather hard on

466

Mrs Ebag. Thus it fell out that Mrs Ebag remained a widow, and that Miss Ebag continues a flower uncalled. However, gossip was stifled.

In his appointed time, and in the fulness of years, Goldie died, and was mourned. And by none was he more sincerely mourned than by the aged bedridden Caiaphas.

"I miss my cat, I can tell ye!" said old Caiaphas pettishly to Carl, who was sitting by his couch. "He knew his master, Goldie did! Edith did her best to steal him from me when you married and set up house. A nice thing considering I bought him and he never belonged to anybody but me! Ay! I shall never have another cat like that cat."

And this is the whole truth of the affair.

THE FORTUNE TELLER

I

The prologue to this somewhat dramatic history was of the simplest. The affair came to a climax, if one may speak metaphorically, in fire and sword and high passion, but it began like the month of March. Mr Bostock (a younger brother of the senior partner in the famous firm of Bostocks, drapers, at Hanbridge) was lounging about the tennis-court attached to his house at Hillport. Hillport has long been known as the fashionable suburb of Bursley, and indeed as the most aristocratic quarter strictly within the Five Towns; there certainly are richer neighbourhoods not far off, but such neighbourhoods cannot boast that they form part of the Five Towns—no more than Hatfield can boast that it is part of London. A man who lives in a detached house at Hillport, with a tennis-court, may be said to have succeeded in life. And Mr Bostock had succeeded. A consulting engineer of marked talent, he had always worked extremely hard and extremely long, and thus he had arrived at luxuries. The chief of his luxuries was his daughter Florence, aged twenty-three, height five feet exactly, as pretty and as neat as a new doll, of expensive and obstinate habits. It was Florence who was the cause of the episode, and I mention her father only to show where Florence stood in the world. She ruled her father during perhaps eleven months of the year. In the twelfth month (which was usually January—after the Christmas bills) there would be an insurrection, conducted by the father with much spirit for a time, but ultimately yielding to the forces of the government. Florence had many admirers; a pretty woman, who habitually rules a rich father, is bound to have many admirers. But she had two in particular; her cousin, Ralph Martin, who had been apprenticed to her father, and Adam Tellwright, a tile manufacturer at Turnhill.

These four—the father and daughter and the rivals—had been playing tennis that Saturday afternoon. Mr Bostock, though touching on fifty, retained a youthful athleticism; he looked and talked younger than his years, and he loved the society of young people. If he wandered solitary and moody about the tennis-court now, it was because he had a great deal on his mind besides business. He had his daughter's future on his mind.

468

A servant with apron-strings waving like flags in the breeze came from the house with a large loaded tea-tray, and deposited it on a wicker table on the small lawn at the end of the ash court. The rivals were reclining in deck chairs close to the table; the Object of Desire, all in starched white, stood over the table and with quick delicious movements dropped sugar and poured milk into tinkling porcelain.

"Now, father," she called briefly, without looking up, as she seized the teapot.

He approached, gazing thoughtfully at the group. Yes, he was worried. And everyone was secretly worried. The situation was exceedingly delicate, fragile, breakable. Mr Bostock looked uneasily first at Adam Tellwright, tall, spick and span, self-confident, clever, shining, with his indubitable virtues mainly on the outside. If ever any man of thirty-two in all this world was eligible, Adam Tellwright was. Decidedly he had a reputation for preternaturally keen smartness in trade, but in trade that cannot be called a defect; on the contrary, if a man has virtues, you cannot precisely quarrel with him because they happen to be on the outside; the principal thing is to have virtues. And then Mr Bostock looked uneasily at Ralph Martin, heavy, short, dark, lowering, untidy, often incomprehensible, and more often rude; with virtues concealed as if they were secret shames. Ralph was capricious. At moments he showed extraordinary talent as an engineer; at others he behaved like a nincompoop. He would be rich one day; but he had a formidable temper. The principal thing in favour of Ralph Martin was that he and Florence had always been "something to each other." Indeed of late years it had been begun to be understood that the match was "as good as arranged." It was taken for granted. Then Adam Tellwright had dropped like a bomb into the Bostock circle. He had fallen heavily and disastrously in love with the slight Florence (whom he could have crushed and eaten). At the start his case was regarded as hopeless, and Ralph Martin had scorned him. But Adam Tellwright soon caused gossip to sing a different tune, and Ralph Martin soon ceased to scorn him. Adam undoubtedly made a profound impression on Florence Bostock. He began by dazzling her, and then, as her eyes grew accustomed to the glare, he gradually showed her his good qualities. Everything that skill and tact could do Tellwright did. The same could not be said of Ralph Martin. Most people had a vague feeling that Ralph had not been treated fairly. Mr Bostock had this feeling. Yet why? Nothing had been settled. Florence's heart was evidently still open to competition, and Adam Tellwright had a perfect right to compete. Still, most people sympathized with Ralph. But Florence did not. Young girls are like that.

Now the rivals stood about equal. No one knew how the battle would go. Adam did not know. Ralph did not know. Florence assuredly did not know. Mr Bostock was quite certain, of a night, that Adam would win, but the next morning he was quite certain that his nephew would win.

No wonder that the tea-party, every member of it tremendously preoccupied by the great battle, was not distinguished by light and natural gaiety. Great battles cannot be talked about till they are over and the last shot fired. And it is not to be expected that people should be bright when each knows the others to be deeply preoccupied by a matter which must not even be mentioned. The tea-party was self-conscious, highly. Therefore, it ate too many cakes and chocolate, and forgot to count its cups of tea. The conversation nearly died of inanition several times, and at last it actually did die, and the quartette gazed in painful silence at its corpse. Anyone who has assisted at this kind of a tea-party will appreciate the situation. Why, Adam Tellwright himself was out of countenance. To his honour, it was he who first revived the corpse. A copy of the previous evening's *Signal* was lying on an empty deck-chair. It had been out all night, and was dampish. Tellwright picked it up, having finished his tea, and threw a careless eye over it. He was determined to talk about something.

"By Jove!" he said. "That Balsamo johnny is coming to Hanbridge!"

"Yes, didn't you know?" said Florence, agreeably bent on resuscitating the corpse.

"What! The palmistry man?" asked Mr Bostock, with a laugh.

"Yes." And Adam Tellwright read: "'Balsamo, the famous palmist and reader of the future, begs to announce that he is making a tour through the principal towns, and will visit Hanbridge on the 22nd inst., remaining three days. Balsamo has thousands of testimonials to the accuracy of his predictions, and he absolutely guarantees not only to read the past correctly, but to foretell the future. Address: 22 Machin Street, Hanbridge. 10 to 10. Appointment advisable in order to avoid delay.' There! He'll find himself in prison one day, that gentleman will!"

"It's astounding what fools people are!" observed Mr Bostock.

"Yes, isn't it!" said Adam Tellwright.

"If he'd been a gipsy," said Ralph Martin, savagely, "the police would have had him long ago." And he spoke with such grimness that he might have been talking of Adam Tellwright.

"They say his uncle and his grandfather before him were both thought-readers, or whatever you call it," said Florence.

"Do they?" exclaimed Mr Bostock, in a different tone.

"Oh!" exclaimed Adam, also in a different tone.

"I wonder whether that's true!" said Ralph Martin.

The rumour that Balsamo's uncle and grandfather had been readers of the past and of the future produced of course quite an impression on the party. But each recognized how foolish it was to allow oneself to be so impressed in such an illogical manner. And therefore all the men burst into violent depreciation of Balsamo and of the gulls who consulted him. And by the time they had done with Balsamo there was very little left of him. Anyhow, Adam Tellwright's discovery in the *Signal* had saved the tea-party from utter fiasco.

II

No. 22 Machin Street, Hanbridge, was next door to Bostock's vast emporium, and exactly opposite the more exclusive, but still mighty, establishment of Ephraim Brunt, the greatest draper in the Five Towns. It was, therefore, in the very heart and centre of retail commerce. No woman who respected herself could buy even a sheet of pins without going past No. 22 Machin Street. The ground-floor was a confectioner's shop, with a back room where tea and Berlin pancakes were served to the *élite* who had caught from London the fashion of drinking tea in public places. By the side of the confectioner's was an open door and a staircase, which led to the first floor and the other floors. A card hung by a cord to a nail indicated that Balsamo had pitched his moving tent for a few days on the first floor, in a suite of offices lately occupied by a solicitor. Considering that the people who visit a palmist are just as anxious to publish their doings as the people who visit a pawnbroker—and no more—it might be thought that Balsamo had ill-chosen his site. But this was not so. Balsamo, a deep student of certain sorts of human nature, was perfectly aware that, just as necessity will force a person

471

to visit a pawnbroker, so will inherited superstition force a person to visit a palmist, no matter what the inconveniences. If he had erected a wigwam in the middle of Crown Square and people had had to decide between not seeing him at all and running the gauntlet of a crowd's jeering curiosity, he would still have had many clients.

Of course when you are in love you are in love. Anything may happen to you then. Most things do happen. For example, Adam Tellwright found himself ascending the stairs of No. 22 Machin Street at an early hour one morning. He was, I need not say, mounting to the third floor to give an order to the potter's modeller, who had a studio up there. Still he stopped at the first floor, knocked at a door labelled "Balsamo," hesitated, and went in. I need not say that this was only fun on his part. I need not say that he had no belief whatever in palmistry, and was not in the least superstitious. A young man was seated at a desk, a stylish young man. Adam Tellwright smiled, as one who expected the stylish young man to join in the joke. But the young man did not smile. So Adam Tellwright suddenly ceased to smile.

"Are you Mr Balsamo?" Adam inquired.

"No. I'm his secretary."

His secretary! Strange how the fact that Balsamo was guarded by a secretary, and so stylish a secretary, affected the sagacious and hard-headed Adam!

"You wish to see him?" the secretary demanded coldly.

"I suppose I may as well," said Adam, sheepishly.

"He is disengaged, I think. But I will make sure. Kindly sit down."

Down sat Adam, playing nervously with his hat, and intensely hoping that no other client would come in and trap him.

"Mr Balsamo will see you," said the secretary, emerging through a double black portière. "The fee is a guinea."

He resumed his chair and drew towards him a book of receipt forms.

A guinea!

However, Adam paid it. The receipt form said: "Received from Mr ——the sum of one guinea for professional assistance.—Per Balsamo, J.H.K.," and a long flourish. The words "one guinea" were written. Idle to deny that this receipt form was impressive. As Adam meekly followed "J.H.K." in to the Presence, he felt exactly as if he was being ushered into a dentist's cabinet. He felt as though he had

472

been caught in the wheels of an unstoppable machine and was in vague but serious danger.

The Presence was a bold man, with a flowing light brown moustache, blue eyes, and a vast forehead. He wore a black velvet coat, and sat at a small table on which was a small black velvet cushion. There were two doors to the rooms, each screened by double black portières, and beyond a second chair and a large transparent ball, such as dentists use, there was no other furniture.

"Better give me your hat," said the secretary, and took it from Adam, who parted from it reluctantly, as if from his last reliable friend. Then the portières swished together, and Adam was alone with Balsamo.

Balsamo stared at him; did not even ask him to sit down.

"Why do you come to me? You don't believe in me," said Balsamo, curtly. "Why waste your money?"

"How can I tell whether I believe in you or not," protested Adam Tellwright, the shrewd man of business, very lamely. "I've come to see what you can do."

Balsamo snapped his fingers.

"Sit down then," said he, "and put your hands on this cushion. No!—palms up!"

Balsamo gaped at them a long time, rubbing his chin. Then he rose, adjusted the transparent glass ball so that the light came through it on to Adam's hands, sat down again and resumed his stare.

"Do you want to know everything?" he asked.

"Yes—of course."

"Everything?"

"Yes." A trace of weakness in this affirmative.

"Well, you mustn't expect to live much after fifty-two. Look at the line of life there." He spoke in such a casual, even antipathetic tone that Adam was startled.

"You've had success. You will have it continuously. But you won't live long."

"What have I to avoid?" Adam demanded.

"Can't avoid your fate. You asked me to tell you everything."

"Tell me about my past," said Adam, feebly, the final remnant of shrewdness in him urging him to get the true measure of Balsamo before matters grew worse.

"Your past?" Balsamo murmured. "Keep your left hand quite still, please. You aren't married. You're in business. You've never thought of marriage—till lately. It's not often I see a hand like yours. Your slate is clean. Till lately you never thought of marriage."

"How lately?"

"Who can say when the idea of marriage first came to you? You couldn't say yourself. Perhaps about three months ago. Yes—three months. I see water—you have crossed the sea. Is all this true?"

"Yes," admitted Adam.

"You're in love, of course. Did you know you have a rival?"

"Yes." Once more Adam was startled.

"Is he fair? No, he's not fair. He's dark. Isn't he?"

"Yes."

"Ah! The woman. Uncertain, uncertain. Mind you I never undertake to foretell anything; all I guarantee is that what I do foretell will happen. Now, you will be married in a year or eighteen months." Balsamo stuck his chin out with the gesture of one who imparts grave news; then paused reflectively.

"Whom to?"

"Ah! There are two women. One fair, one dark. Which one do you prefer?"

"The dark one," Adam replied in spite of himself.

"Perhaps the fair one has not yet come into your life? No. But she will do."

"But which shall I marry?"

"Look at that line. No, here! See how indistinct and confused it is. Your destiny is not yet settled. Frankly, I cannot tell you with certainty. No one can go in advance of destiny. Ah! Young man, I sympathize with you."

"Then, really you can't tell me."

"Listen! I might help you. Yes, I might help you."

"How?"

"The others will come to me."

"What others?"

"Your rival. And the woman you love."

"And then?"

"What is not marked on your hand may be very clearly marked on theirs. Come to me again."

"How do you know they will come? They both said they should not."

"You said you would not. But you are here. Rely on me. They will come. I might do a great deal for you. Of course it will cost you more. One lives in a world of money, and I sell my powers, like the rest of mankind. I am proud to do so."

"How much will it cost?"

"Five pounds. You are free to take it or leave it, naturally."

Adam Tellwright put his hand in his pocket.

"Have the goodness to pay my secretary," Balsamo stopped him icily.

"I beg pardon," said Adam, out of countenance.

"Of course if they do not come the money will be returned. Now, before you go, you might tell me all you know about him, and about her. All. Omit nothing. It is not essential, but it might help me. There is a chance that it might make things clearer than they otherwise could be. The true palmist never refuses any aid."

And Adam thereupon went into an elaborate account of Florence Bostock and Ralph Martin. He left out nothing, not even that Ralph had a wart on his chin, and had once broken a leg; nor that Florence had once been nearly drowned in a swimming-bath in London.

III

It was the same afternoon.

Balsamo stared calmly at a young dark-browed man who had entered his sanctuary with much the same air as a village bumpkin assumes when he is about to be shown the three-card trick on a race-course. Balsamo did not even ask him to sit down.

"Why do you come to me? You don't believe in me," said Balsamo, curtly. "Why waste your half-sovereign?"

Ralph Martin, not being talkative, said nothing.

"However!" Balsamo proceeded. "Sit down, please. Let me look at your hands. Ah! yes! Do you want to know anything?"

"Yes, of course."

"Everything?"

"Certainly."

"Let me advise you, then, to give up all thoughts of that woman."

"What woman?"

"You know what woman. She is a very little woman. Once she was nearly drowned—far from here. You've loved her for a long time. You thought it was a certainty. And upon my soul you were justified in thinking so—almost! Look at that line. But it isn't a certainty. Look at that line!"

Balsamo gazed at him coldly, and Ralph Martin knew not what to do or to say. He was astounded; he was frightened; he was desolated. He perceived at once that palmistry was after all a terrible reality.

"Tell me some more," he murmured.

And so Balsamo told him a great deal more, including full details of a woman far finer than Florence Bostock, whom he was destined to meet in the following year. But Ralph Martin would have none of this new woman. Then Balsamo said suddenly:

"She is coming. I see her coming."

"Who?"

"The little woman. She is dressed in white, with a gold-and-white sunshade, and yellow gloves and boots, and she has a gold reticule in her hand. Is that she?"

Ralph Martin admitted that it was she. On the other hand, Balsamo did not admit that he had seen her an hour earlier and had made an appointment with her.

There was a quiet knock on the door. Ralph started.

"You hear," said Balsamo, quietly, "I fear you will never win her."

"You said just now positively that I shouldn't," Ralph exclaimed.

"I did not," said Balsamo. "I would like to help you. I am very sorry for you. It is not often I see a hand like yours. I might be able to help you; the destiny is not yet settled."

"I'll give you anything to help me," said Ralph.

"It will be a couple of guineas," said Balsamo.

"But what guarantee have I?" Ralph asked rudely, when he had paid the money—to Balsamo, not to the secretary. Such changes of humour were characteristic of him.

"None!" said Balsamo, with dignity, putting the sovereigns on the table. "But I am sorry for you. I will tell you what you can do. You can go behind those curtains there"—he pointed to the inner door—"and listen to all that I say."

A proposal open to moral objections! But when you are in the state that Ralph Martin was in, and have experienced what he had just experienced, your out-look upon morals is apt to be disturbed.

IV

"Young lady," Balsamo was saying. "Rest assured that I have not taken five shillings from you for nothing. Your lover has a wart on his chin."

Daintiness itself sat in front of him, with her little porcelain hands lying on the black cushion. And daintiness was astonished into withdrawing those hands.

"Please keep your hands still," said Balsamo, firmly, and proceeded: "But you have another lover, older, who has recently come into your life. Fair, tall. A successful man who will always be successful. Is it not so?"

"Yes," a little voice muttered.

"You can't make up your mind between them? Answer me."

"No."

"And you wish to learn the future. I will tell you—you will marry the fair man. That is your destiny. And you will be very happy. You will soon perceive the bad qualities of the one with the wart. He is a wicked man. I need not urge you to avoid him. You will do so."

"A bad man!"

"A bad man. You see there are two sovereigns lying here. That man has actually tried to bribe me to influence you in his favour?"

"Ralph?"

"Since you mention his Christian name, I will mention his surname. It is written here. Martin."

"He can't have—possibly—"

Balsamo strode with offended pride to the portière, and pulled it away, revealing Mr Ralph Martin, who for the second time that afternoon knew not what to say or to do.

"I tell you—" Ralph began, as red as fire.

"Silence, sir! Let this teach you not to try to corrupt an honest professional man! Surely I had amply convinced you of my powers! Take your miserable money!" He offered the miserable money to Ralph, who stuck his hands in his pockets, whereupon Balsamo flung the miserable money violently on to the floor.

A deplorable scene followed, in which the presence of Balsamo did not prevent Florence Bostock from conveying clearly to Ralph what she thought of him. They spoke before Balsamo quite freely, as two people will discuss maladies before a doctor. Ralph departed first; then Florence. Then Balsamo gathered up the sovereigns. He had honestly earned Adam's fiver, and since Ralph had refused the two pounds—"I have seen their hands," said Balsamo the next day to Adam Tellwright. "All is clear. In a month you will be engaged to her."

"A month?"

"A month. I regret that I had a painful scene with your rival. But of course professional etiquette prevents me from speaking of that. Let me repeat, in a month you will be engaged to her."

This prophecy came true. Adam Tellwright, however, did not marry Florence Bostock. One evening, in a secluded corner at a dance, Ralph Martin, without warning, threw his arms angrily, brutally, instinctively round Florence's neck and kissed her. It was wrong of him. But he conquered her. Love is like that. It hides for years, and then pops out, and won't be denied. Florence's engagement to Adam was broken. She married Ralph. She knew she was marrying a strange, dark-minded man of uncertain temper, but she married him.

As for the unimpeachable Adam, he was left with nothing but the uneasy fear that he was doomed to die at fifty-two. His wife (for he got one, and a good one) soon cured him of that.

THE LONG-LOST UNCLE

On a recent visit to the Five Towns I was sitting with my old schoolmaster, who, by the way, is much younger than I am after all, in the bow window of a house overlooking that great thoroughfare, Trafalgar Road, Bursley, when a pretty woman of twenty-eight or so passed down the street. Now the Five Towns contains more pretty women to the square mile than any other district in England (and this statement I am prepared to support by either sword or pistol). But do you suppose that the frequency of pretty women in Hanbridge, Bursley, Knype, Longshaw and Turnhill makes them any the less remarked? Not a bit of it. Human nature is such that even if a man should meet forty pretty women in a walk along Trafalgar Road from Bursley to Hanbridge, he will remark them all separately, and feel exactly forty thrills. Consequently my ever-youthful schoolmaster said to me:

"Good-looking woman that, eh, boy? Married three weeks ago," he added.

A piece of information which took the keen edge off my interest in her.

"Really!" I said. "Who is she?"

"Married to a Scotsman named Macintyre, I fancy."

"That tells me nothing," I said. "Who was she?"

"Daughter of a man named Roden."

"Not Herbert Roden?" I demanded.

"Yes. Art director at Jacksons, Limited."

"Well, well!" I exclaimed. "So Herbert Roden's got a daughter married. Well, well! And it seems like a week ago that he and his uncle—you know all about that affair, of course?"

"What affair?"

"Why, the Roden affair!"

"No," said my schoolmaster.

"You don't mean to say you've never—"

Nothing pleases a wandering native of the Five Towns more than to come back and find that he knows things concerning the Five Towns which another man who has lived there all his life doesn't know. In ten seconds I was digging out for my schoolmaster one of those family histories which lie embedded in the general grey soil of the past like lumps of quartz veined and streaked with the precious metal of passion and glittering here and there with the crystallizations of scandal.

"You could make a story out of that," he said, when I had done talking and he had done laughing.

"It is a story," I replied. "It doesn't want any making."

And this is just what I told him. I have added on a few explanations and moral reflections—and changed the names.

I

Silas Roden, commonly called Si Roden—Herbert's uncle—lived in one of those old houses at Paddock Place, at the bottom of the hill where Hanbridge begins. Their front steps are below the level of the street, and their backyards look out on the Granville Third Pit and the works of the Empire Porcelain Company. 11 was Si's own house, a regular bachelor's house, as neat as a pin, and Si was very proud of it and very particular about it. Herbert, being an orphan, lived with his uncle. He would be about twenty-five then, and Si fifty odd. Si had retired from the insurance agency business, and Herbert, after a spell in a lawyer's office, had taken to art and was in the decorating department at Jackson's. They had got on together pretty well, had Si and Herbert, in a grim, taciturn, Five Towns way. The historical scandal began when Herbert wanted to marry Alice Oulsnam, an orphan like himself, employed at a dress-maker's in Crown Square, Hanbridge.

"Thou'lt marry her if thou'st a mind," said Si to Herbert, "but I s'll ne'er speak to thee again."

"But why, uncle?"

"That's why," said Si.

Now if you have been born in the Five Towns and been blessed with the unique Five Towns mixture of sentimentality and solid sense, you don't flare up and stamp out of the house when a well-to-do and childless uncle shatters your life's dream. You dissemble. You piece the dream together again while your uncle is looking another way. You feel that you are capable of out-witting your uncle, and you take the earliest opportunity of "talking it over" with Alice. Alice is sagacity itself.

Si's reasons for objecting so politely to the projected marriage were various. In the first place he had persuaded himself that he hated women. In the second place, though in many respects a most

480

worthy man, he was a selfish man, and he didn't want Herbert to leave him, because he loathed solitude. In the third place—and here is the interesting part—he had once had an affair with Alice's mother and had been cut out: his one deviation into the realms of romance—and a disastrous one. He ought to have been Alice's father, and he wasn't. It angered him, with a cold anger, that Herbert should have chosen just Alice out of the wealth of women in the Five Towns. Herbert was unaware of this reason at the moment.

The youth was being driven to the conclusion that he would be compelled to offend his uncle after all, when Alice came into two thousand two hundred pounds from a deceased relative in Cheshire. The thought of this apt legacy does good to my soul. I love people to come into a bit of stuff unexpected. Herbert instantly advised her to breathe not a word of the legacy to anyone. They were independent now, and he determined that he would teach his uncle a lesson. He had an affection for his uncle, but in the Five Towns you can have an affection for a person, and be extremely and justly savage against that person, and plan cruel revenges on that person, all at the same time.

Herbert felt that the legacy would modify Si's attitude towards the marriage, if Si knew of it. Legacies, for some obscure and illogical cause, do modify attitudes towards marriages. To keep a penniless dressmaker out of one's family may be a righteous act. But to keep a level-headed girl with two thousand odd of her own out of one's family would be the act of an insensate fool. Therefore Herbert settled that Si should not know of the legacy. Si should be defeated without the legacy, or he should be made to suffer the humiliation of yielding after being confronted with the accomplished fact of a secret marriage. Herbert was fairly sure that he would yield, and in any case, with a couple of thousand at his wife's back, Herbert could afford to take the risks of war.

So Herbert, who had something of the devil in him, approached his uncle once more, with a deceitful respect, and he was once more politely rebuffed—as indeed he had half hoped to be. He then began his clandestine measures—measures which culminated in him leaving the house one autumn morning dressed in a rather stylish travelling suit.

The tramcar came down presently from Hanbridge. Not one of the swift thunderous electrical things that now chase each other all over the Five Towns in every direction at intervals of about thirty seconds; but the old horse-car that ran between Hanbridge and Bursley twice an hour and no oftener, announcing its departure by a big bell, and stopping at toll-gates with broad eaves, and climbing hills with the aid of a tip-horse and a boy perched on the back thereof. That was a calm and spacious age.

Herbert boarded the car, and raised his hat rather stiffly to a nice girl sitting in a corner. He then sat down in another corner, far away from her. Such is the capacity of youth for chicane! For that nice girl was exactly Alice, and her presence on the car was part of the plot. When the car arrived at Bursley these monsters of duplicity descended together, and went to a small public building and entered therein, and were directed to an official and inhospitable room which was only saved from absolute nakedness by a desk, four Windsor chairs, some blotting-paper, pens, ink and a copy of Keats's Directory of the Five Towns. An amiable old man received them with a perfunctory gravity, and two acquaintances of Herbert's strolled in, blushing. The old man told everybody to sit down, asked them questions of no spiritual import, abruptly told them to stand up, taught them to say a few phrases, in the tone of a person buying a ha'-porth of tin-tacks, told them to sit down, filled a form or two, took some of Herbert's money, and told them that that was all, and that they could go. So they went, secretly surprised. This was the august ritual, and this the imposing theatre, provided by the State in those far-off days for the solemnizing of the most important act in a citizen's life. It is different now; the copy of Keats's Directory is a much later one.

Herbert thanked his acquaintances, who, begging him not to mention it, departed.

"Well, that's over!" breathed Herbert with a sigh of relief. "It's too soon to go back. Let us walk round by Moorthorne."

"I should love to!" said Alice.

It was a most enjoyable walk. In the heights of Moorthorne they gradually threw off the depressing influence of those four Windsor chairs, and realized their bliss. They reached Paddock Place again at a quarter to one o'clock, which, as they were a very methodical and trustworthy pair, was precisely the moment at which they had meant to reach it. The idea was that they should call on Si and announce to him, respectfully: "Uncle, we think it only right to tell you that we are married. We hope you will not take it ill, we should like to be friends." They would then leave the old man to eat the news with his dinner. A cab was to be at the door at one o'clock to carry them to Knype Station, where they would partake of the wedding breakfast in the first-class refreshment room, and afterwards catch the two-forty to Blackpool, there to spend a honeymoon of six days.

This was the idea.

Herbert was already rehearsing in his mind the exact tone in which he should say to Si: "Uncle, we think it only right—" when, as they approached the house, they both saw a white envelope suspended under the knocker of the door. It was addressed to "Mr Herbert Roden," in the handwriting of Silas. The moment was dramatic. As they had not yet discussed whether correspondence should be absolutely common property, Alice looked discreetly away while Herbert read: "Dear nephew, I've gone on for a week or two on business, and sent Jane Sarah home. Her's in need of a holiday. You must lodge at Bratt's meantime. I've had your things put in there, and they've gotten the keys of the house.—Yours affly, S. Roden." Bratt's was next door but one, and Jane Sarah was the Roden servant, aged fifty or more.

"Well, I'm—!" exclaimed Herbert.

"Well, I never!" exclaimed Alice when she had read the letter. "What's the meaning—?"

"Don't ask me!" Herbert replied.

"Going off like this!" exclaimed Alice.

"Yes, my word!" exclaimed Herbert.

"But what are you to do?" Alice asked.

"Get the key from Bratt's, and get my box, if he hasn't had it carried in to Bratt's already, and then wait for the cab to come."

"Just fancy him shutting you out of the house like that, and no warning!" Alice said, shocked.

"Yes. You see he's very particular about his house. He's afraid I might ruin it, I suppose. He's just like an old maid, you know, only a hundred times worse." Herbert paused, as if suddenly gripped in a tremendous conception. "I have it!" he stated positively. "I have it! I have it!"

"What?" Alice demanded.

"Suppose we spend our honeymoon here?"

"In this house?"

"In this house. It would serve him right."

Alice smiled humorously. "Then the house wouldn't get damp," she said. "And there would be a great saving of expense. We could buy those two easy-chairs with what we saved."

"Exactly," said Herbert. "And after all, seaside lodgings, you know.... And this house isn't so bad either."

"But if he came back and caught us?" Alice suggested.

"Well, he couldn't eat us!" said Herbert.

The clear statement of this truth emboldened Alice. "And he'd no right to turn you out!" she said in wifely indignation.

Without another word Herbert went into Bratt's and got the keys. Then the cab came up with Alice's luggage lashed to the roof, and the driver, astounded, had to assist in carrying it into Si's house. He was then dismissed, and not with a bouncing tip either. We are in the Five Towns. He got a reasonable tip, no more. The Bratts, vastly intrigued, looked inconspicuously on.

Herbert banged the door and faced Alice in the lobby across her chief trunk. The honeymoon had commenced.

"We'd better get this out of the way at once," said Alice the practical.

And between them they carried it upstairs, Alice, in the intervals of tugs, making favourable remarks about the cosiness of the abode.

"This is uncle's bedroom," said Herbert, showing the front bedroom, a really spacious and dignified chamber full of spacious and dignified furniture, and not a pin out of place in it.

"What a funny room!" Alice commented. "But it's very nice."

"And this is mine," said Herbert, showing the back bedroom, much inferior in every way.

When the trunk had been carried into the front bedroom, Herbert descended for the other things, including his own luggage; and Alice took off her hat and jacket and calmly laid them on Silas's ample bed, gazed into all Silas's cupboards and wardrobes that were not locked, patted her hair in front of Silas's looking-glass, and dropped a hairpin on Silas's floor.

She then kneeled down over her chief trunk, and the vision of her rummaging in the trunk in his uncle's bedroom was the most beautiful thing that Herbert had ever seen. Whether it was because the light caught her brown hair, or because she seemed so strange there and yet so deliciously at home, or because—Anyhow, she fished a plain white apron out of the trunk and put it on over her grey dress. And the quick, graceful, enchanting movements with which she put the apron on—well, they made Herbert feel that he had only that moment begun to live. He walked away wondering what was the matter with him. If you imagine that he ran up to her and kissed her you imagine a vain thing; you do not understand that complex and capricious organism, the masculine heart.

The wedding breakfast consisted of part of a leg of mutton that Jane Sarah had told the Bratts they might have, pikelets purchased from a street hawker, coffee, scrambled eggs, biscuits, butter, burgundy out of the cellar, potatoes out of the cellar, cheese, sardines, and a custard that Alice made with custard-powder. Herbert had to go out to buy the bread, the butter, the sardines and some milk; when he returned with these purchases, a portion of the milk being in his breast pocket, Alice checked them, and exhibited a mild surprise that he had not done something foolish, and told him to clear out of "her kitchen."

Her kitchen was really the back kitchen or scullery. The proper kitchen had always been used as a dining-room. But Alice had set the table in the parlour, at the front of the house, where food had never before been eaten. At the first blush this struck Herbert as sacrilege; but Alice said she didn't like the middle room, because it was dark and because there was a china pig on the high mantelpiece; and really Herbert could discover no reason for not eating in the parlour. So they ate in the parlour. Before the marvellous repast was over Alice had rearranged all the ornaments and chairs in that parlour, turned round the carpet, and patted the window curtains into something new and strange. Herbert frequently looked out of the window to see if his uncle was coming.

"Pity there's no dessert," said Herbert. It was three o'clock, and the refection was drawing to a reluctant close.

"There is a dessert," said Alice. She ran upstairs, and came down with her little black hand-bag, out of which she produced three apples and four sponge-cakes, meant for the railway journey. Amazing woman! Yet in resuming her seat she mistook Herbert's knee for her chair. Amazing woman! Intoxicating mixture of sweet confidingness and unfailing resource. And Si had wanted to prevent Herbert from marrying this pearl!

"Now I must wash up!" said she.

"I'll run out and telegraph to Jane Sarah to come back at once. I expect she's gone to her sister's at Rat Edge. It's absurd for you to be doing all the work like this." Thus Herbert.

"I can manage by myself till to-morrow," Alice decided briefly.

Then there was a rousing knock at the door, and Alice sprang up, as it were, guiltily. Recovering herself with characteristic swiftness, she went to the window and spied delicately out.

"It's Mrs Bratt," she whispered. "I'll go."

"Shall I go?" Herbert asked.

"No—I'll go," said Alice.

And she went—apron and all.

Herbert overheard the conversation.

"Oh!" Exclamation of feigned surprise from Mrs Bratt.

"Yes?" In tones of a politeness almost excessive.

"Is Mr Herbert meaning to come to our house to-night? That there bedroom's all ready."

"I don't think so," said Alice. "I don't think so."

"Well, miss—"

"I'm Mrs Herbert Roden," said Alice, primly.

"Oh! I beg pardon, miss—Mrs, that is—I'm sure. I didn't know—"

"No," said Alice. "The wedding was this morning."

"I'm sure I wish you both much happiness, you and Mr Herbert," said Mrs Bratt, heartily. "If I had but known—"

"Thank you," said Alice, "I'll tell my husband."

And she shut the door on the entire world.

II

One evening, after tea, by gaslight, Herbert was reading the newspaper in the parlour at Paddock Place, when he heard a fumbling with keys at the front door. The rain was pouring down heavily outside. He hesitated a moment. He was a brave man, but he hesitated a moment, for he had sins on his soul, and he knew in a flash who was the fumbler at the front door. Then he ran into the lobby, and at the same instant the door opened and his long-lost uncle stood before him, a living shower-bath, of which the tap could not be turned off.

"Well, uncle," he stammered, "how are—"

"Nay, my lad," Si stopped him, refusing his hand. "I'm too wet to touch. Get along into th' back kitchen. If I mun make a pool I'll make it there. So thou's taken possession o' my house!"

"Yes, uncle. You see—"

They were now in the back kitchen, or scullery, where a bright fire was burning in a small range and a great kettle of water singing over it.

"Run and get us a blanket, lad," said Si, stopping Herbert again, and turning up the gas.

"A blanket?"

"Ay, lad! A blanket. Art struck?"

When Herbert returned with the blanket Silas was spilling mustard out of the mustard tin into a large zinc receptacle which he had removed from the slop-stone to a convenient place on the floor in front of the fire. Silas then poured the boiling water from the kettle into the receptacle, and tested the temperature with his finger.

"Blazes!" he exclaimed, shaking his finger. "Fetch us the whisky, lad."

When Herbert returned a second time, Uncle Silas was sitting on a chair wearing merely the immense blanket, which fell gracefully in rich folds around him to the floor. From sundry escaping jets of steam Herbert was able to judge that the zinc bath lay concealed somewhere within the blanket. Si's clothes were piled on the deal table.

"I hanna' gotten my feet in yet," said Si. "They're resting on th' edge. But I'll get 'em in in a minute. Oh! Blazes! Here! Mix us a glass o' that, hot. And then get out that clothes-horse and hang my duds on it nigh th' fire."

Herbert obeyed, as if in a dream.

"I canna do wi' another heavy cowd [cold] at my time o' life, and there's only one way for to stop it. There! That'll do, lad. Let's have a look at thee."

Herbert perched himself on a corner of the table. The vivacity of Silas astounded him.

"Thou looks older, nephew," said Silas, sipping at the whisky, and smacking his lips grimly.

"Do I? Well, you look younger, uncle, anyhow. You've shaved your beard off, for one thing."

"Yes, and a pretty cold it give me, too! I'd carried that beard for twenty year."

"Then why did you cut it off?"

"Because I had to, lad. But never mind that. So thou'st taken possession o' my house?"

"It isn't your house any longer, uncle," said Herbert, determined to get the worst over at once.

"Not my house any longer! Us'll see whether it inna' my house any longer."

"If you go and disappear for a twelvemonth and more, uncle, and leave no address, you must take the consequence. I never knew till after you'd gone that you'd mortgaged this house for four hundred pounds to Callear, the fish-dealer."

"Who towd thee that?"

"Callear told me."

"Callear had no cause to be uneasy. I wrote him twice as his interest 'ud be all right when I come back."

"Yes, I know. But you didn't give any address. And he wanted his money back. So he came to me."

"Wanted his money back!" cried Silas, splashing about in the hidden tub and grimacing. "He had but just lent it me."

"Yes, but Tomkinson, his landlord, died, and he had the chance of buying his premises from the executors. And so he wanted his money back."

"And what didst tell him, lad?"

"I told him I would take a transfer of the mort-gage."

"Thou! Hadst gotten four hundred pounds i' thy pocket, then?"

"Yes. And so I took a transfer."

"Bless us! This comes o'going away! But where didst find th' money?"

"And what's more," Herbert continued, evading the question, "as I couldn't get my interest I gave you notice to repay, uncle, and as you didn't repay—"

"Give me notice to repay! What the dev—? You hadna' got my address."

"I had your legal address—this house, and I left the notice for you in the parlour. And as you didn't repay I—I took possession as mortgagee, and now I'm—I'm foreclosing."

"Thou'rt foreclosing!"

Silas stood up in the tub, staggered, furious, sweating. He would have stepped out of the tub and done something to Herbert had not common prudence and the fear of the blanket falling off restrained his passion. There was left to him only one thing to do, and he did it. He sat down again.

"Bless us!" he repeated feebly.

488

"So you see," said Herbert.

"And thou'st been living here ever since—alone, wi' Jane Sarah?"

"Not exactly," Herbert replied. "With my wife."

Fully emboldened now, he related to his uncle the whole circumstances of his marriage.

Whereupon, to his surprise, Silas laughed hilariously, hysterically, and gulped down the remainder of the whisky.

"Where is her?" Silas demanded.

"Upstairs."

"I' my bedroom, I lay," said Silas.

Herbert nodded. "May be."

"And everything upside down!" proceeded Uncle Silas.

"No!" said Herbert. "We've put all your things in my old room."

"Have ye! Ye're too obliging, lad!" growled Silas. "And if it isn't asking too much, where's that china pig as used to be on the chimney-piece in th' kitchen there? Her's smashed it, eh?"

"No," said Herbert, mildly. "She's put it away in a cupboard. She didn't like it."

"Ah! I was but wondering if ye'd foreclosed on th' pig too."

"Possibly a few things are changed," said Herbert. "But you know when a woman takes into her head—"

"Ay, lad! Ay, lad! I know! It was th' same wi' my beard. It had for go. Thou'st under the domination of a woman, and I can sympathize wi' thee."

Herbert gave a long, high whistle.

"So that's it?" he exclaimed. And he suddenly felt as if his uncle was no longer an uncle but a brother.

"Yes," said Silas. "That's it. I'll tell thee. Pour some more hot water in here. Dost remember when th' Carl Rosa Opera Company was at Theatre Royal last year? I met her then. Her was one o' Venus's maidens i' th' fust act o' *Tannhäuser*, and her was a bridesmaid i' *Lohengrin*, and Siebel i' *Faust*, and a cigarette girl i' summat else. But it was in*Tannhäuser* as I fust saw her on the stage, and her struck me like that." Silas clapped one damp hand violently on the other. "Miss Elsa Venda was her stage name, but her was a widow, Mrs Parfitt, and had bin for ten years. Seemingly her husband was of good family. Finest woman I ever seed, nephew. And you'll say so. Her'd ha' bin a prima donna only for jealousy. Fust time I spoke to her I thought I should ha' fallen down. Steady with that water. Dost want for skin me alive? Yes, I thought I should ha' fallen down. They call'n it love. You can call it what ye'n a mind for call it. I nearly fell down."

"How did you meet her, uncle?" Herbert interposed, aware that his uncle had not been accustomed to move in theatrical circles.

"How did I meet her? I met her by setting about to meet her. I had for t' meet her. I got Harry Burisford, th' manager o' th' theatre thou knowst, for t' introduce us. Then I give a supper, nephew—I give a supper at Turk's Head, but private like."

"Was that the time when you were supposed to be at the Ratepayers' Association every night?" Herbert asked blandly.

"It was, nephew," said Si, with equal blandness.

"Then no doubt those two visits to Manchester, afterwards—"

"Exactly," said Si. "Th' company went to Manchester and stopped there a fortnight. I told her fair and square what I meant and what I was worth. There was no beating about the bush wi' me. All her friends told her she'd be a fool if she wouldn't have me. She said her'd write me yes or no. Her didn't. Her telegraphed me from Sunderland for go and see her at once. It was that morning as I left. I thought to be back in a couple o' days and to tell thee as all was settled. But women! Women! Her had me dangling after her from town to town for a week. I was determined to get her, and get her I did, though it cost me my beard, and the best part o' that four hundred. I married her i' Halifax, lad, and it were the best day's work I ever did. You never seed such a woman. Big and plump— and sing! By——! I never cared for singing afore. And her knows the world, let me tell ye."

"You might have sent us word," said Herbert.

Silas grew reflective. "Ah!" he said. "I might—and I mightn't. I didn't want Hanbridge chattering. I was trapesing wi' her from town to town till her engagement was up—pretty near six months. Then us settled i' rooms at Scarborough, and there was other things to think of. I couldn't leave her. Her wouldna' let me. To-day was the fust free day I've had, and so I run down to fix matters. And nice weather I've chosen! Her aunt's spending the night wi' her."

"Then she's left the stage."

"Of course she's left th' stage. What 'ud be th' sense o' her painting her face and screeching her chest out night after night for a crowd o' blockheads, when I can keep her like a lady. Dost think her's a fool? Her's the only woman wi' any sense as ever I met in all my life."

490

"And you want to come here and live?"

"No, us dunna! At least her dunna. Her says her hates th' Five Towns. Her says Hanbridge is dirty and too religious for her. Says its nowt but chapels and public-houses and pot-banks. So her ladyship wunna' come here. No, nephew, thou shalt buy this house for six hundred, and be d—d to thy foreclosure! And th' furniture for a hundred. It's a dead bargain. Us'll settle at Scarborough, Liz and me. Now this water's getting chilly. I'll nip up to thy room and find some other clothes."

"You can't go up just now," said Herbert.

"But I mun go at once, nephew. Th' water's chilly, and I've had enough on it."

"The fact is we're using my old bedroom for a sort of a nursery, and Alice and Jane Sarah are just giving the baby its bath."

"Babby!" cried Silas. "Shake hands, nephew. Give us thy fist. I may as well out wi' it. I've gotten one mysen. Pour some more hot water in here, then."

THE TIGHT HAND

I

The tight hand was Mrs Garlick's. A miser, she was not the ordinary miser, being exceptional in the fact that her temperament was joyous. She had reached the thirtieth year of her widowhood and the sixtieth of her age, with cheerfulness unimpaired. The people of Bursley, when they met her sometimes of a morning coming down into the town from her singular house up at Toft End, would be conscious of pleasure in her brisk gait, her slightly malicious but broad-minded smile, and her cheerful greeting. She was always in black. She always wore one of those nodding black bonnets which possess neither back nor front, nor any clue of any kind to their ancient mystery. She always wore a mantle which hid her waist and spread forth in curves over her hips; and as her skirts stuck stiffly out, she thus had the appearance of one who had been to sleep since 1870, and who had got up, thoroughly refreshed and bright, into the costume of her original period. She always carried a reticule. It was known that she suffered from dyspepsia, and this gave real value to her reputation for cheerfulness.

Her nearness, closeness, stinginess, close-fistedness—as the quality was variously called—was excused to her, partly because it had been at first caused by a genuine need of severe economy (she having been "left poorly off" by a husband who had lived "in a large way"), partly because it inconvenienced nobody save perhaps her servant Maria, and partly because it was so picturesque and afforded much excellent material for gossip. Mrs Garlick's latest feat of stinginess was invariably a safe card to play in the conversational game. Each successive feat was regarded as funnier than the one before it.

Maria, who had a terrific respect for appearances, never disclosed her mistress's peculiarities. It was Mrs Garlick herself who humorously ventilated and discussed them; Mrs Garlick, being a philosopher, got quite as much amusement as anyone out of her most striking quality.

"Is there anything interesting in the *Signal* to-night?" she had innocently asked one of her sons.

"No," said Sam Garlick, unthinkingly.

492

"Well, then," said she, "suppose I turn out the gas and we talk in the dark?"

Soon afterwards Sam Garlick married; his mother remarked drily that she was not surprised.

It was supposed that this feat of turning out the gas when the *Signal* happened to fail in interest would remain unparalleled in the annals of Five Towns skin-flintry. But in the summer after her son's marriage, Mrs Garlick was discovered in the evening habit of pacing slowly up and down Toft Lane. She said that she hated sitting in the dark alone, that Maria would not have her in the kitchen, and that she saw no objection to making harmless use of the Corporation gas by strolling to and fro under the Corporation gas-lamps on fine nights. Compared to this feat the previous feat was as naught. It made Mrs Garlick celebrated even as far as Longshaw. It made the entire community proud of such an inventive miser.

Once Mrs Garlick, before what she called her dinner, asked Maria, "Will there be enough mutton for to-morrow?" And Maria had gloomily and firmly said, "No." "Will there be enough if I don't have any to-day?" pursued Mrs Garlick. And Maria had said, "Yes." "I won't have any then," said Mrs Garlick. Maria was offended; there are some things that a servant will not stand. She informed Mrs Garlick that if Mrs Garlick meant "to go on going on like that" she should leave; she wouldn't stay in such a house. In vain Mrs Garlick protested that the less she ate the better she felt; in vain she referred to her notorious indigestion. "Either you eats your dinner, mum, or out I clears!" Mrs Garlick offered her a rise of £1 a year to stay. She was already, because she would stop and most servants wouldn't, receiving £18, a high wage. She refused the increment. Pushed by her passion for economy in mutton, Mrs Garlick then offered her a rise of £2 a year. Maria accepted, and Mrs Garlick went without mutton. Persons unacquainted with the psychology of parsimoniousness may hesitate to credit this incident. But more advanced students of humanity will believe it without difficulty. In the Five Towns it is known to be true.

II

The supreme crisis, to which the foregoing is a mere prelude, in the affairs of Mrs Garlick and Maria, was occasioned by the extraordinary performances of the Mayor of Bursley. This particular

493

mayor was invested with the chain almost immediately upon the conclusion of a great series of revival services in which he had conspicuously figured. He had an earthenware manufactory half-way up the hill between Bursley and its loftiest suburb, Toft End, and the smoke of his chimneys and kilns was generally blown by a favourable wind against the windows of Mrs Garlick's house, which stood by itself. Mrs Garlick made nothing of this. In the Five Towns they think no more of smoke than the world at large used to think of small-pox. The smoke plague is exactly as curable as the small-pox plague. It continues to flourish, not because smokiness is cheaper than cleanliness—it is dearer—but because a greater nuisance than smoke is the nuisance of a change, and because human nature in general is rather like Mrs Garlick: its notion of economy is to pay heavily for the privilege of depriving itself of something—mutton or cleanliness.

However, this mayor was different. He had emerged from the revival services with a very tender conscience, and in assuming the chain of office he assumed the duty of setting an example. It was to be no excuse to him that in spite of bye-laws ten thousand other chimneys and kilns were breathing out black filth all over the Five Towns. So far as he could cure it the smoke nuisance had to be cured, or his conscience would know the reason why! So he sat on the borough bench and fined himself for his own smoke, and then he installed gas ovens. The town laughed, of course, and spoke of him alternately as a rash fool, a hypocrite, and a mere pompous ass. In a few months smoke had practically ceased to ascend from the mayoral manufactory. The financial result to the mayor was such as to encourage the tenderness of consciences. But that is not the point. The point is that Mrs Garlick, re-entering her house one autumn morning after a visit to the market, paused to look at the windows, and then said to Maria:

"Maria, what have you to do this afternoon?"

Now Mrs Garlick well knew what Maria had to do.

"I'm going to change the curtains, mum."

"Well, you needn't," said Mrs Garlick. "It's made such a difference up here, there being so much less smoke, that upon my word the curtains will do another three months quite well!"

"Well, mum, I never did!" observed Maria, meaning that so shocking a proposal was unprecedented in her experience. Yet she was thirty-five.

"Quite well!" said Mrs Garlick, gaily.

Maria said no more. But in the afternoon Mrs Garlick, hearing sounds in the drawing-room, went into the drawing-room and discovered Maria balanced on a pair of steps and unhooking lace curtains.

"Maria," said she, "what are you doing?"

Maria answered as busy workers usually do answer unnecessary questions from idlers.

"I should ha' thought you could see, mum," she said tartly, insolently, inexcusably.

One curtain was already down.

"Put that curtain back," Mrs Garlick commanded.

"I shall put no curtain back!" said Maria, grimly; her excited respiration shook the steps. "All to save the washing of four pair o' curtains! And you know you beat the washerwoman down to tenpence a pair last March! Three and fo'pence, that is! For the sake o' three and fo'pence you're willing for all Toft End to point their finger at these 'ere windows."

"Put that curtain back," Mrs Garlick repeated haughtily.

She saw that she had touched Maria in a delicate spot—her worship of appearances. The mutton was simply nothing to these curtains. Nevertheless, as there seemed to be some uncertainty in Maria's mind as to who was the mistress of the house, Mrs Garlick's business was to dispel that uncertainty. It may be said without exaggeration that she succeeded in dispelling it. But she did not succeed in compelling Maria to re-hang the curtain. Maria had as much force of character as Mrs Garlick herself. The end of the scene, whose details are not sufficiently edifying to be recounted, was that Maria went upstairs to pack her box, and Mrs Garlick personally re-hung the curtain. One's dignity is commonly an expensive trifle, and Mrs Garlick's dignity was expensive. To avoid prolonging the scene she paid Maria a month's wages in lieu of notice—£1, 13s, 4d. Then she showed her the door. Doubtless (Mrs Garlick meditated) the girl thought she would get another rise of wages. If so, she was finely mistaken. A nice thing if the servant is to decide when curtains are to go to the wash! She would soon learn, when she went into another situation, what an easy, luxurious place she had lost by her own stupid folly! Three and fourpences might be picked up in the street, eh? And so on.

After Maria's stormy departure Mrs Garlick regained her sense of humour and her cheerfulness; but the inconveniences of being without Maria were important.

III

On the second day following, Mrs Garlick received a letter from "young Lawton," the solicitor. Young Lawton, aged over forty, was not so-called because in the Five Towns youthfulness is supposed to extend to the confines of forty-five, but because he had succeeded his father, known as "old Lawton"; it is true that the latter had been dead many years. The Five Towns, however, is not a country of change. This letter pointed out that Maria's wages were not £1, 13s. 4d. a month, but £1, 13s. 4d. a month plus her board and lodging, and that consequently, in lieu of a month's notice, Maria demanded £1, 13s. 4d. plus the value of a month's keep.

There was more in this letter than met the eye of Mrs Garlick. Young Lawton's offices were cleaned by a certain old woman; this old woman had a nephew; this nephew was a warehouseman at the Mayor's works, and lived up in Toft End, and at least twice every day he passed by Mrs Garlick's house. He was a respectful worshipper of Maria's, and it had been exclusively on his account that Maria had insisted on changing the historic curtains. Nobody else of the slightest importance ever passed in front of the house, for important people have long since ceased to live at Toft End. The subtle flattering of an unspoken love had impelled Maria to leave her situation rather than countenance soiled curtains. She could not bear that the warehouseman should suspect her of tolerating even the semblances of dirt. She had permitted the warehouseman to hear the facts of her departure from Mrs Garlick's. The warehouseman was nobly indignant, advising an action for assault and battery. Through his aunt's legal relations Maria had been brought into contact with the law, and, while putting aside as inadvisable an action for assault and battery, the lawyer had counselled a just demand for more money. Hence the letter.

Mrs Garlick called at Lawton's office, and, Mr Lawton being out, she told an office-boy to tell him with her compliments that she should not pay.

Then the County Court bailiff paid her a visit, and left with her a blue summons for £2, 8s., being four weeks of twelve shillings each.

496

Many house-mistresses in Bursley sympathized with Mrs Garlick when she fought this monstrous claim. She fought it gaily, with the aid of a solicitor. She might have won it, if the County Court Judge had not happened to be in one of his peculiar moods—one of those moods in which he felt himself bound to be original at all costs. He delivered a judgment sympathizing with domestic servants in general, and with Maria in particular. It was a lively trial. That night the *Signal* was very interesting. When Mrs Garlick had finished with the action she had two and threepence change out of a five-pound note.

Moreover, she was forced to employ a charwoman—a charwoman who had made a fine art of breaking china, of losing silver teaspoons down sinks, and of going home of a night with vast pockets full of things that belonged to her by only nine-tenths of the law. The charwoman ended by tumbling through a window, smashing panes to the extent of seventeen and elevenpence, and irreparably ripping one of the historic curtains.

Mrs Garlick then dismissed the charwoman, and sat down to count the cost of small economics. The privilege of half-dirty curtains had involved her in an expense of £9, 19s., (call it £10). It was in the afternoon. The figure of Maria crossed the recently-repaired window. Without a second's thought Mrs Garlick rushed out of the house.

"Maria!" she cried abruptly—with grim humour. "Come here. Come right inside."

Maria stopped, then obeyed.

"Do you know how much you've let me in for, with your wicked, disobedient temper?"

"I'd have you know, mum—" Maria retorted, putting her hands on the hips and forwarding her face.

Their previous scene together was as nothing to this one in sound and fury. But the close was peace. The next day half Bursley knew that Maria had gone back to Mrs Garlick, and there was a facetious note about the episode in the "Day by Day" column of the *Signal*. The truth was that Maria and Mrs Garlick were "made for each other." Maria would not look at the ordinary "place." The curtains, as much as remained, were sent to the wash, but as three months had elapsed the mistress reckoned that she had won. Still, the cleansing of the curtains had run up to appreciably more than a sovereign per curtain.

The warehouseman did not ask for Maria's hand. The stridency of her behaviour in court had frightened him.

Mrs Garlick's chief hobby continues to be the small economy. Happily, owing to a rise in the value of a land and a fortunate investment, she is in fairly well-to-do circumstances.

As she said one day to an acquaintance, "It's a good thing I can afford to keep a tight hand on things."

WHY THE CLOCK STOPPED

I

Mr Morfe and Mary Morfe, his sister, were sitting on either side of their drawing-room fire, on a Friday evening in November, when they heard a ring at the front door. They both started, and showed symptoms of nervous disturbance. They both said aloud that no doubt it was a parcel or something of the kind that had rung at the front door. And they both bent their eyes again on the respective books which they were reading. Then they heard voices in the lobby—the servant's voice and another voice—and a movement of steps over the encaustic tiles towards the door of the drawing-room. And Miss Morfe ejaculated:

"Really!"

As though she was unwilling to believe that somebody on the other side of that drawing-room door contemplated committing a social outrage, she nevertheless began to fear the possibility.

In the ordinary course it is not considered outrageous to enter a drawing-room—even at nine o'clock at night—with the permission and encouragement of the servant in charge of portals. But the case of the Morfes was peculiar. Mr Morfe was a bachelor aged forty-two, and looked older. Mary Morfe was a spinster aged thirty-eight, and looked thirty-seven. Brother and sister had kept house together for twenty years. They were passionately and profoundly attached to each other—and did not know it. They grumbled at each other freely, and practised no more conversation, when they were alone, than the necessities of existence demanded (even at meals they generally read), but still their mutual affection was tremendous. Moreover, they were very firmly fixed in their habits. Now one of these habits was never to entertain company on Friday night. Friday night was their night of solemn privacy. The explanation of this habit offers a proof of the sentimental relations between them.

Mr Morfe was an accountant. Indeed, he was *the* accountant in Bursley, and perhaps he knew more secrets of the ledgers of the principal earthenware manufacturers than some of the manufacturers did themselves. But he did not live for accountancy. At five o'clock every evening he was capable of absolutely forgetting it. He lived for music. He was organist of Saint Luke's

Church (with an industrious understudy—for he did not always rise for breakfast on Sundays) and, more important, he was conductor of the Bursley Orpheus Glee and Madrigal Club. And herein lay the origin of those Friday nights. A glee and madrigal club naturally comprises women as well as men; and the women are apt to be youngish, prettyish, and somewhat fond of music. Further, the conductorship of a choir involves many and various social encounters. Now Mary Morfe was jealous. Though Richard Morfe ruled his choir with whips, though his satiric tongue was a scorpion to the choir, though he never looked twice at any woman, though she was always saying that she wished he would marry, Mary Morfe was jealous. It was Mary Morfe who had created the institution of the Friday night, and she had created it in order to prove, symbolically and spectacularly, to herself, to him, and to the world, that he and she lived for each other alone. All their friends, every member of the choir, in fact the whole of the respectable part of barsley, knew quite well that in the Morfes' house Friday was sacredly Friday.

And yet a caller!

"It's a woman," murmured Mary. Until her ear had assured her of this fact she had seemed to be more disturbed than startled by the stir in the lobby.

And it was a woman. It was Miss Eva Harracles, one of the principal contraltos in the glee and madrigal club. She entered richly blushing, and excusably a little nervous and awkward. She was a tall, agreeable creature of fewer than thirty years, dark, almost handsome, with fine lips and eyes, and an effective large hat and a good muff. In every physical way a marked contrast to the thin, prim, desiccated brother and sister.

Richard Morfe flushed faintly. Mary Morfe grew more pallid.

"I really must apologize for coming in like this," said Eva, as she shook hands cordially with Mary Morfe. She knew Mary very well indeed. For Mary was the "librarian" of the glee and madrigal club; Mary never missed a rehearsal, though she cared no more for music than she cared for the National Debt. She was a perfect librarian, and very good at unofficially prodding indolent members into a more regular attendance too.

"Not at all!" said Mary. "We were only reading; you aren't disturbing us in the least." Which, though polite, was a lie.

And Eva Harracles sat down between them. And brother and sister abandoned their literature.

"I can't stop," said she, glancing at the clock immediately in front of her eyes. "I must catch the last car for Silverhays."

"You've got twenty minutes yet," said Mr Morfe.

"Because," said Eva, "I don't want that walk from Turnhill to Silverhays on a dark night like this."

"No, I should think not, indeed!" said Mary Morfe.

"You've got a full twenty minutes," Mr Morfe repeated. The clock showed three minutes past nine.

The electric cars to and from the town of Turnhill were rumbling past the very door of the Morfes every five minutes, and would continue to do so till midnight. But Silverhays is a mining village a couple of miles beyond Turnhill, and the service between Turnhill and Silverhays ceases before ten o'clock. Eva's father was a colliery manager who lived on the outskirts of Silverhays.

"I've got a piece of news," said Eva.

"Yes?" said Mary Morfe

Mr Morfe was taciturn. He stooped to nourish the fire.

"About Mr Loggerheads," said Eva, and stared straight at Mary Morfe.

"About Mr Loggerheads!" Mary Morfe echoed, and stared back at Eva. And the atmosphere seemed to have been thrown into a strange pulsation.

Here perhaps I ought to explain that it was not the peculiarity of Mr Loggerheads' name that produced the odd effect. Loggerheads is a local term for a harmless plant called the knapweed *(centaurea nigra)*, and it is also the appellation of a place and of quite excellent people, and no one regards it as even the least bit odd.

"I'm told," said Eva, "that he's going into the Hanbridge Choir!"

Mr Loggerheads was the principal tenor of the Bursley Glee and Madrigal Club. And he was reckoned one of the finest "after-dinner tenors" in the Five Towns. The Hanbridge Choir was a rival organization, a vast and powerful affair that fascinated and swallowed promising singers from all the choirs of the vicinity. The Hanbridge Choir had sung at Windsor, and since that event there had been no holding it. All other choirs hated it with a homicidal hatred.

"I'm told," Eva proceeded, "that the Birmingham and Sheffield Bank will promote him to the cashiership of the Hanbridge Branch on the understanding that he joins the Hanbridge Choir. Shows what influence they have! And it shows how badly the Hanbridge Choir wants him."

(Mr Loggerheads was cashier of the Bursley branch of the Birmingham and Sheffield Bank.)

"Who told you?" asked Mary Morfe, curtly.

Richard Morfe said nothing. The machinations of the manager of the Hanbridge Choir always depressed and disgusted him into silence.

"Oh!" said Eva Harracles. "It's all about." (By which she meant that it was in the air.) "Everyone's talking of it."

"And do they say Mr Loggerheads has accepted?" Mary demanded.

"Yes," said Eva.

"Well," said Mary, "it's not true!... A mistake!" she added.

"How do you know it isn't true?" Mr Morfe inquired doubtfully.

"Since you're so curious," said Mary, defiantly, "Mr Loggerheads told me himself."

"When?"

"The other day."

"You never said anything to me," protested Mr Morfe.

"It didn't occur to me," Mary replied.

"Well, I'm very glad!" remarked Eva Harracles. "But I thought I ought to let you know at once what was being said."

Mary Morfe's expression conveyed the fact that in her opinion Eva Harracles' evening call was a vain thing, too lightly undertaken, and conceivably lacking in the nicest discretion. Whereupon Mr Morfe was evidently struck by the advisability of completely changing the subject. And he did change it. He began to talk about certain difficulties in the choral parts of Havergal Brian's *Vision of Cleopatra*, a work which he meant the Bursley Glee and Madrigal Club to perform though it should perish in the attempt. Growing excited, in his dry way, concerning the merits of this composition, he rose from his easy chair and went to search for it. Before doing so he looked at the clock, which indicated twenty minutes past nine.

"Am I all right for time?" asked Eva.

"Yes, you're all right," said he. "If you go when that clock strikes half-past, and take the next car down, you'll make the connection easily at Turnhill. I'll put you into the car."

"Oh, thanks!" said Eva.

Mr Morfe kept his modern choral music beneath a broad seat under the bow window. The music was concealed by a low curtain that ran on a rod—the ingenious device of Mary. He stooped down to find the *Vision of Cleopatra*, and at first he could not find it. Mary walked towards that end of the drawing-room with a vague notion of helping him, and then Eva did the same, and then Mary walked back, and then Mr Morfe happily put his hand on the *Vision of Cleopatra*.

He opened the score for Eva's inspection, and began to hum passages and to point out others, and Eva also began to hum, and they hummed in concert, at intervals exclaiming against the wantonness with which Havergal Brian had invented difficulties. Eva glanced at the clock.

"You're all right," Mr Morfe assured her somewhat impatiently. And he, too, glanced at the clock: "You've still nearly ten minutes."

And proceeded with his critical and explanatory comments on the *Vision of Cleopatra*.

He was capable of becoming almost delirious about music. Mary Morfe had seated herself in silence.

At last Eva and Mr Morfe approached the fire and the mantelpiece again. Mr Morfe shut up the score, dismissed his delirium, and looked at the clock, quite prepared to see it pointing to twenty-nine and a half minutes past nine. Instead, the clock pointed to only twenty-two minutes past nine.

"By Jove!" he exclaimed. He went nearer.

"By Jove!" he exclaimed again rather more loudly. "I do believe that clock's stopped!"

It had. The pendulum hung perpendicular, motionless, dead.

He was astounded. For the clock had never been known to stop. It was a presentation clock, of the highest guaranteed quality, offered to him as a small token of regard and esteem by the members of the Bursley Orpheus Glee and Madrigal Club to celebrate the twelfth anniversary of his felicitous connection with the said society. It had stood on his mantelpiece for four years and had earned an absolutely first-class reputation for itself. He wound it up on the last day of every month, for it was a thirty-odd day clock, specially made by a famous local expert; and he had not known it to vary more than ten minutes a month at the most. And lo! it had stopped in the very middle of the month.

"Did you wind it up last time?" asked Mary.

503

"Of course," he snapped. He had taken out his watch and was gazing at it. He turned to Eva. "It's twenty to ten," he said. "You've missed your connection at Turnhill—that's a certainty. I'm very sorry."

Obviously there was only one course open to a gallant man whose clock was to blame: namely, to accompany Eva Harracles to Turnhill by car, to accompany her on foot to Silverhays, then to walk back to Turnhill and come home again by car. A young woman could not be expected to perform that bleak and perhaps dangerous journey from Turnhill to Silverhays alone after ten o'clock at night in November. Such was the clear course. But he dared scarcely suggest it. He dared scarcely suggest it because of his sister. He was afraid of Mary. The names of Richard Morfe and Eva Harracles had already been coupled in the mouth of gossip. And naturally Eva Harracles herself could not suggest that Richard should sally out and leave his sister alone on this night specially devoted to sisterliness and brotherliness. And of course, Eva thought, Mary will never, never suggest it.

But Eva was wrong there.

To the amazement of both Richard and Eva, Mary calmly said:

"Well, Dick, the least you can do now is to see Miss Harracles home. You'll easily be able to catch the last car back from Turnhill if you start at once. I daresay I shall go to bed."

And in three minutes Richard Morfe and Eva Harracles were being sped into the night by Mary Morfe.

The Morfes' house was at the corner of Trafalgar Road and Beech Street. The cars stopped at that corner in their wild course towards the town and towards Turnhill. A car was just coming. But instead of waiting for it Richard Morfe and Eva Harracles deliberately turned their backs on Trafalgar Road, and hurried side by side down Beech Street. Beech Street is a short street, and ends in a nondescript unlighted waste patch of ground. They arrived in the gloom of this patch, safe from all human inquisitiveness, and then Richard Morfe warmly kissed Eva Harracles in the mathematical centre of those lips of hers. And Eva Harracles showed no resentment of any kind, nor even shame. Yet she had been very carefully brought up. The sight would have interested Bursley immensely; it would have appealed strongly to Bursley's strong sense of the piquant.... That dry old stick Dick Morfe kissing one of his contraltos in the dark at the bottom end of Beech Street.

"Then you hadn't told her!" murmured Eva Harracles.

"No!" said Richard, with a slight hesitation. "I was just going to begin to tell her when you called."

Another woman might have pouted to learn that her lover had exhibited even a little cowardice in informing his family that he was engaged to be married. But Eva did not pout. She comprehended the situation, and the psychology of the relations between brothers and sisters. (She herself possessed both brothers and sisters.) All the courting had been singularly secret and odd.

"I shall tell her to-morrow morning at breakfast," said Richard, firmly. "Unless, after all, she isn't gone to bed when I get back."

By a common impulse they now returned towards Trafalgar Road.

"I say," said Richard, "what made you call?"

"I was passing," said the beloved. "And somehow I couldn't help it. Of course, I knew it wasn't true about Mr Loggerheads. But I had to think of something."

Richard was in ecstasy; had never been in such ecstasy.

"I say," he said again. "I suppose *you* didn't put your finger against the pendulum of that clock?"

"Oh, *no!*" she replied with emphasis.

"Well, I'm jolly glad it did stop, anyway," said Richard. "What a lark, eh?"

She agreed that the lark was ideal. They walked down the road till a car should overtake them.

"Do you think she suspects anything?" Eva asked.

"I'll swear she doesn't," said Richard, positively. "It'll be a bit of a startler for the old girl."

"No doubt you've heard," said Eva, haltingly, "that Mr Loggerheads has cast eyes on Mary."

"And do you think there's anything *in* that?" Richard questioned sharply.

"Well," she said, "I really don't know." Meaning that she decidedly thought that Mary *had* been encouraging advances from Mr Loggerheads.

"Well," said Richard, superiorly, "you may just take it from me that there's nothing in it at all.... Ha!" He laughed shortly. He knew Mary.

Then they got on a car, and tried to behave as though their being together was a mere accident, as though they had not become

505

engaged to one another within the previous twenty-four hours.

II

Immediately after the departure of Richard Morfe and Eva Harracles, his betrothed, from the front door of the former, Mr Simon Loggerheads arrived at the same front door, and rang thereat, and was a little surprised, and also a little unnerved, when the door opened instantly, as if by magic. Mr Simon Loggerheads said to himself, as he saw the door move on its hinges, that Miss Morfe must have discovered a treasure of a servant who, when she had nothing else to do, spent her time on the inner door-mat waiting to admit possible visitors—even on Friday night. Nevertheless, Mr Simon Loggerheads regretted that prompt opening, as one regrets the prompt opening of the door of a dentist.

And it was no servant who stood in front of him, under the flickering beam of the lobby-lamp. It was Mary Morfe herself. The simple explanation was that she had just sped her brother and Eva Harracles, and had remained in the lobby for the purpose of ascertaining by means of her finger whether the servant had, as usual, forgotten to dust the tops of the picture-frames.

"Oh!" said Mr Loggerheads, when he saw Mary Morfe. For the cashier of the Bursley branch of the Birmingham and Sheffield Bank it was not a very able speech, but it was all he could accomplish.

And Miss Mary Morfe said:

"Oh!"

She was thirty-eight, and he was quite that (for the Bank mentioned does not elevate its men to the august situation of cashier under less than twenty years' service), and yet they neither of them had enough worldliness to behave in a reasonable manner. Then Miss Morfe, to whom it did at last occur that something must be done, produced an invitation:

"Do come in!" And she added, "Richard has just gone out."

"Oh!" commented Mr Simon Loggerheads again. (After all, it must be admitted that tenors as a class have never been noted for their conversational powers.) But he was obviously more at ease, and he went in, and Mary Morfe shut the door. At this very instant her brother and Eva were in secret converse at the back end of Beech Street.

"Do take your coat off!" Mary suggested to Simon. Simultaneously the servant appeared at the kitchen extremity of the lobby, and Mary thrust her out of sight again with the cold words: "It's all right, Susan."

Mr Loggerheads took his coat off, and Mary Morfe watched him as he did so.

He made a pretty figure. He was something of a dandy. The lapels of the overcoat would have showed that, not to mention the correctly severe necktie. All his clothes, in fact, had "cut and style," even to his boots. In the Five Towns many a young man is a dandy down to the edge of his trousers, but not down to the ground. Mr Loggerheads looked a young man. The tranquillity of his career and the quietude of his tastes had preserved his youthfulness. And, further, he had the air of a successful, solid, much-respected individual. To be a cashier, though worthy, is not to be a nabob, but a bachelor can save a lot out of over twenty years of regular salary. And Mr Loggerheads had saved quite a lot. And he had had opportunities of advantageously investing his savings. Then everybody knew him, and he knew everybody. He handed out gold at least once a week to nearly half the town, and you cannot help venerating a man who makes a practice of handing out gold to you. And he had thrilled thousands with the wistful beauty of his voice in "The Sands of Dee." In a word, Simon Loggerheads was a personage, if not talkative.

They went into the drawing-room. Mary Morfe closed the door gently. Simon Loggerheads strolled vaguely and self-consciously up to the fireplace, murmuring:

"So he's gone out?"

"Yes," said Mary Morfe, in confirmation of her first statement.

"I'm sorry!" said Simon Loggerheads. A statement which was absolutely contrary to the truth. Simon Loggerheads was deeply relieved and glad that Richard Morfe was out.

The pair, aged slightly under and slightly over forty, seemed to hover for a fraction of a second uncertainly near each other, and then, somehow, mysteriously, Simon Loggerheads had kissed Mary Morfe. She blushed. He blushed. The kiss was repeated. Mary gazed up at him. Mary could scarcely believe that he was hers. She could scarcely believe that on the previous evening he had proposed marriage to her—rather suddenly, so it seemed to her, but delightfully. She could comprehend his conduct no better than her own. They two, staid, settled-down, both of them "old maids," falling in love and behaving like lunatics! Mary, a year ago, would have been ready to prophesy that if ever Simon Loggerheads—at his age!—did marry, he would assuredly marry something young, something ingenuous, something cream-and-rose, and probably something with rich parents. For twenty years Simon Loggerheads had been marked down for capture by the marriageable spinsters and widows, and the mothers with daughters, of Bursley. And he had evaded capture, despite the special temptations to which an after-dinner tenor is necessarily subject. And now Mary Morfe had caught him—caught him, moreover, without having had the slightest intention of catching him. She was one of the most spinsterish spinsters in the Five Towns; and she had often said things about men and marriage of which the recollection now, as an affianced woman, was very disturbing to her. However, she did not care. She did not understand how Simon Loggerheads had had the wit to perceive that she would be an ideal wife. And she did not care. She did not understand how, as a result of Simon Loggerheads falling in love with her, she had fallen in love with him. And she did not care. She did not care a fig for anything. She *was* in love with him, and he with her, and she was idiotically joyous, and so was he. And that was all.

On reflection, I have to admit that she did in fact care for one thing. That one thing was the look on her brother's face when he should learn that she, the faithful sardonic sister, having incomprehensibly become indispensable and all in all to a bank cashier, meant to desert him. She was afraid of that look. She trembled at the fore-vision of it.

Still, Richard had to be informed, and the world had to be informed, for the silken dalliance between Mary and Simon had been conducted with a discretion and a secrecy more than characteristic of their age and dispositions. It had been arranged between the lovers that Simon should call on that Friday evening, when he would be sure to catch Richard in his easy chair, and should, in presence of Mary, bluntly communicate to Richard the blunt fact.

"What's he gone out for? Anything special?" asked Simon.

Mary explained the circumstances.

"The truth is," she finished, "that girl is just throwing herself at Dick's head. There's no doubt of it. I never saw such work!"

"Well," said Simon Loggerheads, "of course, you know, there's been a certain amount of talk about them. Some folks say that your brother—er—began—"

"And do you believe that?" demanded Mary.

"I don't know," said Simon. By which he meant diplomatically to convey that he had had a narrow escape of believing it, at any rate.

"Well," said Mary, with conviction, "you may take it from me that it isn't so. I know Dick. Eva Harracles may throw herself at his head till there's no breath left in her body, and it'll make no difference to Dick. Do *you* see Dick a married man? I don't. I only wish he *would*take it into his head to get married. It would make me much easier in my mind. But all the same I do think it's downright wicked that a girl should fling herself *at* him, right *at* him. Fancy her calling to-night! It's the sort of thing that oughtn't to be encouraged."

"But I understood you to say that you yourself had told him to see her home," Simon Loggerheads put in. "Isn't that encouraging her, as it were?"

"Ah!" said Mary, with a smile. "I only suggested it to him because it came over me all of a sudden how nice it would be to have you here all alone! He can't be back much before twelve."

To such a remark there is but one response. A sofa is, after all, made for two people, and the chance of the servant calling on them was small.

"And so the clock stopped!" observed Simon Loggerheads.

"Yes," said Mary. "If it hadn't been for the sheer accident of that clock stopping, we shouldn't be sitting here on this sofa now, and Dick would be in that chair, and you would just be beginning to tell him that we are engaged." She sighed. "Poor Dick! What on earth will he do?"

"Strange how things happen!" Simon reflected in a low voice. "But I'm really surprised at that clock stopping like that. It's a clock that you ought to be able to depend on, that clock is."

He got up to inspect the timepiece. He knew all about the clock, because he had been chairman of the presentation committee which had gone to Manchester to buy it.

"Why!" he murmured, after he had toyed a little with the pendulum, "it goes all right. Its tick is as right as rain."

"How odd!" responded Mary.

Simon Loggerheads set the clock by his own impeccable watch, and then sat down again. And he drew something from his waistcoat pocket and slid it on to Mary's finger.

Mary regarded her finger in silent ecstasy, and then breathed "How lovely!"—not meaning her finger.

"Shall I stay till he comes back?" asked Simon.

"If I were you I shouldn't do that," said Mary. "But you can safely stay till eleven-thirty. Then I shall go to bed. He'll be tired and short [curt] when he gets back. I'll tell him myself to-morrow morning at breakfast. And you might come to-morrow afternoon early, for tea."

Simon did stay till half-past eleven. He left precisely when the clock, now convalescent, struck the half-hour. At the door Mary said to him:

"I won't have any secrets from you, Simon. It was I who stopped that clock. I stopped it while they were bending down looking for music. I wanted to be as sure as I could of a good excuse for me suggesting that he ought to take her home. I just wanted to get him out of the house."

"But why?" asked Simon.

"I must leave that to you to guess," said Mary, with a hint of tartness, but smiling.

Loggerheads and Richard Morfe met in Trafalgar Road.

"Good-night, Morfe."

"'night, Loggerheads!"

And each passed on, without having stopped.

You can picture for yourself the breakfast of the brother and sister.

HOT POTATOES

I

It was considered by certain people to be a dramatic moment in the history of musical enterprise in the Five Towns when Mrs Swann opened the front door of her house at Bleakridge, in the early darkness of a November evening, and let forth her son Gilbert. Gilbert's age was nineteen, and he was wearing evening dress, a form of raiment that had not hitherto happened to him. Over the elegant suit was his winter overcoat, making him bulky, and round what may be called the rim of the overcoat was a white woollen scarf, and the sleeves of the overcoat were finished off with white woollen gloves. Under one arm he carried a vast inanimate form whose extremity just escaped the ground. This form was his violoncello, fragile as a pretty woman, ungainly as a navvy, and precious as honour. Mrs Swann looked down the street, which ended to the east in darkness and a marl pit, and up the street, which ended to the west in Trafalgar Road and electric cars; and she shivered, though she had a shawl over her independent little shoulders. In the Five Towns, and probably elsewhere, when a woman puts her head out of her front door, she always looks first to right and then to left, like a scouting Iroquois, and if the air nips she shivers—not because she is cold, but merely to express herself.

"For goodness sake, keep your hands warm," Mrs Swann enjoined her son.

"Oh!" said Gilbert, with scornful lightness, as though his playing had never suffered from cold hands, "it's quite warm to-night!" Which it was not.

"And mind what you eat!" added his mother. "There! I can hear the car."

He hurried up the street. The electric tram slid in thunder down Trafalgar Road, and stopped for him with a jar, and he gingerly climbed into it, practising all precautions on behalf of his violoncello. The car slid away again towards Bursley, making blue sparks. Mrs Swann stared mechanically at the flickering gas in her lobby, and then closed her front door. He was gone! The boy was gone!

Now, the people who considered the boy's departure to be a dramatic moment in the history of musical enterprise in the Five Towns were Mrs Swann, chiefly, and the boy, secondarily.

II

And more than the moment—the day, nay, the whole week—was dramatic in the history of local musical enterprise.

It had occurred to somebody in Hanbridge, about a year before, that since York, Norwich, Hereford, Gloucester, Birmingham, and even Blackpool had their musical festivals, the Five Towns, too, ought to have its musical festival. The Five Towns possessed a larger population than any of these centres save Birmingham, and it was notorious for its love of music. Choirs from the Five Towns had gone to all sorts of places—such as Brecknock, Aberystwyth, the Crystal Palace, and even a place called Hull—and had come back with first prizes—cups and banners—for the singing of choruses and part-songs. There were three (or at least two and a half) rival choirs in Hanbridge alone. Then also the brass band contests were famously attended. In the Five Towns the number of cornet players is scarcely exceeded by the number of public-houses. Hence the feeling, born and fanned into lustiness at Hanbridge, that the Five Towns owed it to its self-respect to have a Musical Festival like the rest of the world! Men who had never heard of Wagner, men who could not have told the difference between a sonata and a sonnet to save their souls, men who spent all their lives in manufacturing tea-cups or china door-knobs, were invited to guarantee five pounds a-piece against possible loss on the festival; and they bravely and blindly did so. The conductor of the largest Hanbridge choir, being appointed to conduct the preliminary rehearsals of the Festival Chorus, had an acute attack of self-importance, which, by the way, almost ended fatally a year later.

Double-crown posters appeared magically on all the hoardings announcing that a Festival consisting of three evening and two morning concerts would be held in the Alexandra Hall, at Hanbridge, on the 6th, 7th and 8th November, and that the box-plan could be consulted at the principal stationers. The Alexandra Hall contained no boxes whatever, but "box-plan" was the phrase sacred to the occasion, and had to be used. And the Festival more and more impregnated the air, and took the lion's share of the columns of the

Staffordshire Signal. Every few days the *Signal* reported progress, even to intimate biographical details of the singers engaged, and of the composers to be performed, together with analyses of the latter's works. And at last the week itself had dawned in exhilaration and excitement. And early on the day before the opening day John Merazzi, the renowned conductor, and Herbert Millwain, the renowned leader of the orchestra, and the renowned orchestra itself, all arrived from London. And finally sundry musical critics arrived from the offices of sundry London dailies. The presence of these latter convinced an awed population that its Festival was a real Festival, and not a local make-believe. And it also tranquillized in some degree the exasperating and disconcerting effect of a telegram from the capricious Countess of Chell (who had taken six balcony seats and was the official advertised high patroness of the Festival) announcing at the last moment that she could not attend.

III

Mrs Swann's justification for considering (as she in fact did consider) that her son was either the base or the apex of the splendid pyramid of the Festival lay in the following facts:—

From earliest infancy Gilbert had been a musical prodigy, and the circle of his fame had constantly been extending. He could play the piano with his hands before his legs were long enough for him to play it with his feet. That is to say, before he could use the pedals. A spectacle formerly familiar to the delighted friends of the Swanns was Gilbert, in a pinafore and curls, seated on a high chair topped with a large Bible and a bound volume of the *Graphic*, playing "Home Sweet Home" with Thalberg's variations, while his mother, standing by his side on her right foot, put the loud pedal on or off with her left foot according to the infant's whispered orders. He had been allowed to play from ear—playing from ear being deemed especially marvellous—until some expert told Mrs Swann that playing solely from ear was a practice to be avoided if she wished her son to fulfil the promise of his babyhood. Then he had lessons at Knype, until he began to teach his teacher. Then he said he would learn the fiddle, and he did learn the fiddle; also the viola. He did not pretend to play the flute, though he could. And at school the other boys would bring him their penny or even sixpenny whistles so that he might show them of what wonderful feats a common tin whistle is capable.

Mr Swann was secretary for the Toft End Brickworks and Colliery Company (Limited). Mr Swann had passed the whole of his career in the offices of the prosperous Toft End Company, and his imagination did not move freely beyond the company's premises. He had certainly intended that Gilbert should follow in his steps; perhaps he meant to establish a dynasty of Swanns, in which the secretaryship of the twenty per cent. paying company should descend for ever from father to son. But Gilbert's astounding facility in music had shaken even this resolve, and Gilbert had been allowed at the age of fifteen to enter, as assistant, the shop of Mr James Otkinson, the piano and musical instrument dealer and musicseller, in Crown Square, Hanbridge. Here, of course, he found himself in a musical atmosphere. Here he had at once established a reputation for showing off the merits of a piano, a song, or a waltz, to customers male and female. Here he had thirty pianos, seven harmoniums, and all the new and a lot of classical music to experiment with. He would play any "piece" at sight for the benefit of any lady in search of a nice easy waltz or reverie. Unfortunately ladies would complain that the pieces proved much more difficult at home than they had seemed under the fingers of Gilbert in the shop. Here, too, he began to give lessons on the piano. And here he satisfied his secret ambition to learn the violoncello, Mr Otkinson having in stock a violoncello that had never found a proper customer. His progress with the 'cello had been such that the theatre people offered him an engagement, which his father and his own sense of the enormous respectability of the Swanns compelled him to refuse. But he always played in the band of the Five Towns Amateur Operatic Society, and was beloved by its conductor as being utterly reliable. His connection with choirs started through his merits as a rehearsal accompanist who could keep time and make his bass chords heard against a hundred and fifty voices. He had been appointed (*nem. con.*) rehearsal accompanist to the Festival Chorus. He knew the entire Festival music backwards and upside down. And his modestly-expressed desire to add his 'cello as one of the local reinforcements of the London orchestra had been almost eagerly complied with by the Advisory Committee.

Nor was this all. He had been invited to dinner by Mrs Clayton Vernon, the social leader of Bursley. In the affair of the Festival Mrs

Clayton Vernon loomed larger than even she really was. And this was due to an accident, to a sheer bit of luck on her part. She happened to be a cousin of Mr Herbert Millwain, the leader of the orchestra down from London. Mrs Clayton Vernon knew no more about music than she knew about the North Pole, and cared no more. But she was Mr Millwain's cousin, and Mr Millwain had naturally to stay at her house. And she came in her carriage to fetch him from the band rehearsals; and, in short, anyone might have thought from her self-satisfied demeanour (though she was a decent sort of woman at heart) that she had at least composed "Judas Maccabeus." It was at a band rehearsal that she had graciously commanded Gilbert Swann to come and dine with her and Mr Millwain between the final rehearsal and the opening concert. This invitation was, as it were, the overflowing drop in Mrs Swann's cup. It was proof, to her, that Mr Millwain had instantly pronounced Gilbert to be the equal of London 'cellists, and perhaps their superior. It was proof, to her, that Mr Millwain relied on him particularly to maintain the honour of the band in the Festival.

Gilbert had dashed home from the final rehearsal, and his mother had helped him with the unfamiliarities of evening dress, while he gave her a list of all the places in the music where, as he said, the band was "rocky," and especially the 'cellos, and a further list of all the smart musical things that the players from London had said to him and he had said to them. He simply knew everything from the inside. And not even the great Merazzi, the conductor, was more familiar with the music than he. And the ineffable Mrs Clayton Vernon had asked him to dinner with Mr Millwain! It was indubitable to Mrs Swann that all the Festival rested on her son's shoulders.

IV

"It's freezing, I think," said Mr Swann, when he came home at six o'clock from his day's majestic work at Toft End. This was in the bedroom. Mrs Swann, a comely little thing of thirty-nine, was making herself resplendent for the inaugural solemnity of the Festival, which began at eight. The news of the frost disturbed her.

"How annoying!" she said.

"Annoying?" he questioned blandly. "Why?"

"Now you needn't put on any of your airs, John!" she snapped. She had a curt way with her at critical times. "You know as well as I do that I'm thinking of Gilbert's hands.... No! you must wear your frock-coat, of course!... All that drive from the other end of the town right to Hanbridge in a carriage! Perhaps outside the carriage, because of the 'cello! There'll never be room for two of them and the 'cello and Mrs Clayton Vernon in her carriage! And he can't keep his hands in his pockets because of holding the 'cello. And he's bound to pretend he isn't cold. He's so silly. And yet he knows perfectly well he won't do himself justice if his hands are cold. Don't you remember last year at the Town Hall?"

"Well," said Mr Swann, "we can't do anything; anyway, we must hope for the best."

"That's all very well," said Mrs Swann. And it was.

Shortly afterwards, perfect in most details of her black silk, she left the bedroom, requesting her husband to be quick, as tea was ready. And she came into the little dining-room where the youthful servant was poking up the fire.

"Jane," she said, "put two medium-sized potatoes in the oven to bake."

"Potatoes, mum?"

"Yes, potatoes," said Mrs Swann, tartly.

It was an idea of pure genius that had suddenly struck her; the genius of common sense.

She somewhat hurried the tea; then rang.

"Jane," she inquired, "are those potatoes ready?"

"Potatoes?" exclaimed Mr Swann.

"Yes, hot potatoes," said Mrs Swann, tartly. "I'm going to run up with them by car to Mrs Vernon's. I can slip them quietly over to Gil. They keep your hands warm better than anything. Don't I remember when I was a child! I shall leave Mrs Vernon's immediately, of course, but perhaps you'd better give me my ticket and I will meet you at the hall. Don't you think it's the best plan, John?"

"As you like," said Mr Swann, with the force of habit.

He was supreme in most things, but in the practical details of their son's life and comfort she was supreme. Her decision in such matters had never been questioned. Mr Swann had a profound belief in his wife as a uniquely capable and energetic woman. He was tremendously loyal to her, and he sternly inculcated the same loyalty to her in Gilbert.

V

Just as the car had stopped at the end of the street for Gilbert and his violoncello, so—more than an hour later—it stopped for Mrs Swann and her hot potatoes.

They were hot potatoes—nay, very hot potatoes—of a medium size, because Mrs Swann's recollections of youth had informed her that if a potato is too large one cannot get one's fingers well around it, and if it is too small it cools somewhat rapidly. She had taken two, not in the hope that Gilbert would be able to use two at once, for one cannot properly nurse either a baby or a 'cello with two hands full of potatoes, but rather to provide against accident. Besides, the inventive boy might after all find a way of using both simultaneously, which would be all the better for his playing at the concert, and hence all the better for the success of the Musical Festival.

It never occurred to Mrs Swann that she was doing anything in the least unusual. There she was, in her best boots, and her best dress, and her best hat, and her sealskin mantle (not easily to be surpassed in the town), and her muff to match (nearly), and concealed in the muff were the two very hot potatoes. And it did not strike her that women of fashion like herself, wives of secretaries of flourishing companies, do not commonly go about with hot potatoes concealed on their persons. For she was a self-confident woman, and after a decision she did not reflect, nor did she heed minor consequences. She was always sure that what she was doing was the right and the only thing to do. And, to give her justice, it was; for her direct, abrupt common sense was indeed remarkable. The act of climbing up into the car warned her that she must be skilful in the control of these potatoes; one of them nearly fell out of the right end of her muff as she grasped the car rail with her right hand. She had to let go and save the potato, and begin again, while the car waited. The conductor took her for one of those hesitating, hysterical women who are the bane of car conductors. "Now, missis!" he said. "Up with ye!" But she did not care what manner of woman the conductor took her for.

The car was nearly full of people going home from their work, of people actually going in a direction contrary to the direction of the Musical Festival. She sat down among them, shocked by this indifference to the Musical Festival. At the back of her head had been an idea that all the cars for Hanbridge would be crammed to the step, and all the cars from Hanbridge forlorn and empty. She had vaguely imagined that the thoughts of a quarter of a million of people would that evening be centred on the unique Musical Festival. And she was shocked also by the conversation—not that it was in the slightest degree improper—but because it displayed no interest whatever in the Musical Festival. And yet there were several Festival advertisements adhering to the roof of the car. Travellers were discussing football, soap, the weather, rates, trade; travellers were dozing; travellers were reading about starting prices; but not one seemed to be occupied with the Musical Festival. "Nevertheless," she reflected with consoling pride, "if they knew that our Gilbert was playing 'cello in the orchestra and dining at this very moment with Mr Millwain, some of them would be fine and surprised, that they would!" No one would ever have suspected, from her calm, careless, proud face, that such vain and two-penny thoughts were passing through her head. But the thoughts that do pass through the heads of even the most common-sensed philosophers, men and women, are truly astonishing.

In four minutes she was at Bursley Town Hall, where she changed into another car—full of people equally indifferent to the Musical Festival—for the suburb of Hillport, where Mrs Clayton Vernon lived.

"Put me out opposite Mrs Clayton Vernon's, will you?" she said to the conductor, and added, "you know the house?"

He nodded as if to say disdainfully in response to such a needless question: "Do I know the house? Do I know my pocket?"

As she left the car she did catch two men discussing the Festival, but they appeared to have no intention of attending it. They were earthenware manufacturers. One of them raised his hat to her. And she said to herself: "He at any rate knows how important my Gilbert is in the Festival!"

It was at the instant she pushed open Mrs Clayton Vernon's long and heavy garden gate, and crunched in the frosty darkness up the short winding drive, that the notion of the peculiarity of her errand first presented itself to her. Mrs Clayton Vernon was a relatively great lady, living in a relatively great house; one of the few exalted or peculiar ones who did not dine in the middle of the day like other folk. Mrs Clayton Vernon had the grand manner. Mrs Clayton Vernon instinctively and successfully patronized everybody. Mrs Clayton Vernon was a personage with whom people did not joke. And lo! Mrs Swann was about to invade her courtly and luxurious house, uninvited, unauthorized, with a couple of hot potatoes in her muff. What would Mrs Clayton Vernon think of hot potatoes in a muff? Of course, the Swanns were "as good as anybody." The Swanns knelt before nobody. The Swanns were of the cream of the town, combining commerce with art, and why should not Mrs Swann take practical measures to keep her son's hands warm in Mrs Clayton Vernon's cold carriage? Still, there was only one Mrs Clayton Vernon in Bursley, and it was impossible to deny that she inspired awe, even in the independent soul of Mrs Swann.

Mrs Swann rang the bell, reassuring herself. The next instant an electric light miraculously came into existence outside the door, illuminating her from head to foot. This startled her. But she said to herself that it must be the latest dodge, and that, at any rate, it was a very good dodge, and she began again the process of reassuring herself. The door opened, and a prim creature stiffly starched stood before Mrs Swann. "My word!" reflected Mrs Swann, "she must cost her mistress a pretty penny for getting up aprons!" And she said aloud curtly:

"Will you please tell Mr Gilbert Swann that someone wants to speak to him a minute at the door?"

"Yes," said the servant, with pert civility. "Will you please step in?"

She had not meant to step in. She had decidedly meant not to step in, for she had no wish to encounter Mrs Clayton Vernon; indeed, the reverse. But she immediately perceived that in asking to speak to a guest at the door she had socially erred. At Mrs Clayton Vernon's refined people did not speak to refined people at the door. So she stepped in, and the door was closed, prisoning her and her potatoes in the imposing hall.

"I only want to see Mr Gilbert Swann," she insisted.

"Yes," said the servant. "Will you please step into the breakfast-room? There's no one there. I will tell Mr Swann."

VI

As Mrs Swann was being led like a sheep out of the hall into an apartment on the right, which the servant styled the breakfast-room, another door opened, further up the hall, and Mrs Clayton Vernon appeared. Magnificent though Mrs Swann was, the ample Mrs Clayton Vernon, discreetly *décolletée*, was even more magnificent. Dressed as she meant to show herself at the concert, Mrs Clayton Vernon made a resplendent figure worthy to be the cousin of the leader of the orchestra—and worthy even to take the place of the missing Countess of Chell. Mrs Clayton Vernon had a lorgnon at the end of a shaft of tortoise-shell; otherwise, a pair of eye-glasses on a stick. She had the habit of the lorgnon; the lorgnon seldom left her, and whenever she was in any doubt or difficulty she would raise the lorgnon to her eyes and stare patronizingly. It was a gesture tremendously effective. She employed it now on Mrs Swann, as who should say, "Who is this insignificant and scarcely visible creature that has got into my noble hall?" Mrs Swann stopped, struck into immobility by the basilisk glance. A courageous and even a defiant woman, Mrs Swann was taken aback. She could not possibly tell Mrs Clayton Vernon that she was the bearer of hot potatoes to her son. She scarcely knew Mrs Clayton Vernon, had only met her once at a bazaar! With a convulsive unconscious movement her right hand clenched nervously within her muff and crushed the rich mealy potato it held until the flesh of the potato was forced between the fingers of her glove. A horrible sticky mess! That is the worst of a high-class potato, cooked, as the Five Towns phrase it, "in its jacket." It will burst on the least provocation. There stood Mrs Swann, her right hand glued up with escaped potato, in the sober grandeur of Mrs Clayton Vernon's hall, and Mrs Clayton Vernon bearing down upon her like a Dreadnought.

Steam actually began to emerge from her muff.

"Ah!" said Mrs Clayton Vernon, inspecting Mrs Swann. "It's Mrs Swann! How do you do, Mrs Swann?"

She seemed politely astonished, as well she might be. By a happy chance she did not perceive the wisp of steam. She was not looking for steam. People do not expect steam from the interior of a visitor's muff.

"Oh!" said Mrs Swann, who was really in a pitiable state. "I'm sorry to trouble you, Mrs Clayton Vernon. But I want to speak to Gilbert for one moment."

She then saw that Mrs Clayton Vernon's hand was graciously extended. She could not take it with her right hand, which was fully engaged with the extremely heated sultriness of the ruined potato. She could not refuse it, or ignore it. She therefore offered her left hand, which Mrs Clayton Vernon pressed with a well-bred pretence that people always offered her their left hands.

"Nothing wrong, I do hope!" said she, gravely.

"Oh no," said Mrs Swann. "Only just a little matter which had been forgotten. Only half a minute. I must hurry off at once as I have to meet my husband. If I could just see Gilbert—"

"Certainly," said Mrs Clayton Vernon. "Do come into the breakfast-room, will you? We've just finished dinner. We had it very early, of course, for the concert. Mr Millwain—my cousin—hates to be hurried. Maria, be good enough to ask Mr Swann to come here. Tell him that his mother wishes to speak to him."

In the breakfast-room Mrs Swann was invited, nay commanded by Mrs Clayton Vernon, to loosen her mantle. But she could not loosen her mantle. She could do nothing. In clutching the potato to prevent bits of it from falling out of the muff, she of course effected the precise opposite of her purpose, and bits of the luscious and perfect potato began to descend the front of her mantle. The clock struck seven, and ages elapsed, during which Mrs Swann could not think of anything whatever to say, but the finger of the clock somehow stuck motionless at seven, though the pendulum plainly wagged.

"I'm not too warm," she said at length, feebly but obstinately resisting Mrs Clayton Vernon's command. This, to speak bluntly, was an untruth. She was too warm.

"Are you sure that nothing is the matter?" urged Mrs Clayton Vernon, justifiably alarmed by the expression of her visitor's features. "I beg you to confide in me if—"

"Not at all," said Mrs Swann, trying to laugh. "I'm only sorry to disturb you. I didn't mean to disturb you."

"What on earth is that?" cried Mrs Clayton Vernon.

The other potato, escaping Mrs Swann's vigilance, had run out of the muff and come to the carpet with a dull thud. It rolled half under Mrs Swann's dress. Almost hysterically she put her foot on it, thus making pulp of the second potato.

"What?" she inquired innocently.

"Didn't you hear anything? I trust it isn't a mouse! We have had them once."

Mrs Clayton Vernon thought how brave Mrs Swann was, not to be frightened by the word "mouse."

"I didn't hear anything," said Mrs Swann. Another untruth.

"If you aren't too warm, won't you come a little nearer the fire?"

But not for a thousand pounds would Mrs Swann have exposed the mush of potato on the carpet under her feet. She could not conceive in what ignominy the dreadful affair would end, but she was the kind of woman that nails her colours to the mast.

"Dear me!" Mrs Clayton Vernon murmured. "How delicious those potatoes do smell! I can smell them all over the house."

This was the most staggering remark that Mrs Swann had ever heard.

"Potatoes? very weakly.

"Yes," said Mrs Clayton Vernon, smiling. "I must tell you that Mr Millwain is very nervous about getting his hands cold in driving to Hanbridge. And he has asked me to have hot potatoes prepared. Isn't it amusing? It seems hot potatoes are constantly used for this purpose in winter by the pupils of the Royal College of Music, and even by the professors. My cousin says that even a slight chilliness of the hands interferes with his playing. So I am having potatoes done for your son too. A delightful boy he is!"

"Really!" said Mrs Swann. "How queer! But what a good idea!"

She might have confessed then. But you do not know her if you think she did. Gilbert came in, anxious and alarmed. Mrs Clayton Vernon left them together. The mother explained matters to the son, and in an instant of time the ruin of two magnificent potatoes was at the back of the fire. Then, without saluting Mrs Clayton Vernon, Mrs Swann fled.

HALF-A-SOVEREIGN

The scene was the up-platform of Knype railway station on a summer afternoon, and, more particularly, that part of the platform round about the bookstall. There were three persons in the neighbourhood of the bookstall. The first was the principal bookstall clerk, who was folding with extraordinary rapidity copies of the special edition of the *Staffordshire Signal*; the second was Mr Sandbach, an earthenware manufacturer, famous throughout the Five Towns for his ingenious invention of teapots that will pour the tea into the cup instead of all over the table; and a very shabby man, whom Mr Sandbach did not know. This very shabby man was quite close to the bookstall, while Mr Sandbach stood quite ten yards away. Mr Sandbach gazed steadily at the man, but the man, ignoring Mr Sandbach, allowed dreamy and abstracted eyes to rest on the far distance, where a locomotive or so was impatiently pushing and pulling waggons as an excitable mother will drag and shove an inoffensive child. The platform as a whole was sparsely peopled; the London train had recently departed, and the station was suffering from the usual reaction; only a local train was signalled.

Mr Gale, a friend of Mr Sandbach's, came briskly on to the platform from the booking-office, caught sight of Mr Sandbach, and accosted him.

"Hello, Sandbach!"

"How do, Gale?"

To a slight extent they were rivals in the field of invention. But both had succeeded in life, and both had the alert and prosperous air of success. Born about the same time, they stood nearly equal after forty years of earthly endeavour.

"What are you doing here?" asked Gale, casually.

"I've come to meet someone off the Crewe train."

"And I'm going by it—to Derby," said Mr Gale. "They say it's thirteen minutes late."

"Look here," said Mr Sandbach, taking no notice of this remark, "you see that man there?"

"Which one—by the bookstall?"

"Yes."

"Well, what about him?"

"I bet you you can't make him move from where he is—no physical force, of course."

Mr Gale hesitated an instant, and then his eye glistened with response to the challenge, and he replied:

"I bet you I can."

"Well, try," said Mr Sandbach.

Mr Sandbach and Mr Gale frequently threw down the glove to each other in this agreeable way. Either they asked conundrums, or they set test questions, or they suggested feats. When Mr Sandbach discovered at a Christmas party that you cannot stand with your left side close against a wall and then lift your right leg, his first impulse was to confront Mr Gale with the trick. When Mr Gale read in a facetious paper an article on the lack of accurate observation in the average man, entitled, "Do 'bus horses wear blinkers?" his opening remark to Mr Sandbach at their next meeting was: "I say, Sandbach, do 'bus horses wear blinkers? Answer quick!" And a phrase constantly in their mouths was, "I'll try that on Gale;" or, "I wonder whether Sandbach knows that?" All that was required to make their relations artistically complete was an official referee for counting the scores. Such a basis of friendship may seem bizarre, but it is by no means uncommon in the Five Towns, and perhaps elsewhere.

So that when Mr Sandbach defied Mr Gale to induce the shabby man to move from where he stood, the nostrils of the combatants twitched with the scent of battle.

Mr Gale conceived his tactics instantly and put them into execution. He walked along the platform some little distance, then turned, and taking a handful of silver from his pocket, began to count it. He passed slowly by the shabby man, almost brushing his shoulder; and, just as he passed, he left fall half-a-crown. The half-crown rolled round in a circle and lay down within a yard and a half of the shabby man. The shabby man calmly glanced at the half-crown and then at Mr Gale, who, strolling on, magnificently pretended to be unaware of his loss; and then the shabby man resumed his dreamy stare into the distance.

"Hi!" cried Mr Sandbach after Mr Gale. "You've dropped something."

It was a great triumph for Mr Sandbach.

"I told you you wouldn't get him to move!" said Mr Sandbach, proudly, having rejoined his friend at another part of the platform.

"What's the game?" demanded Mr Gale, frankly acknowledging by tone and gesture that he was defeated.

"Perfectly simple," answered Mr Sandbach, condescendingly, "when you know. I'll tell you—it's really very funny. Just as everyone was rushing to get into the London express I heard a coin drop on the platform, and I saw it rolling. It was half-a-sovereign. I couldn't be sure who dropped it, but I think it was a lady. Anyhow, no one claimed it. I was just going to pick it up when that chap came by. He saw it, and he put his foot on it as quick as lightning, and stood still. He didn't notice that I was after it too. So I drew back. I thought I'd wait and see what happens."

"He looks as if he could do with half-a-sovereign," said Mr Gale.

"Yes; he's only a station loafer."

"Then why doesn't he pick up his half-sovereign and hook it?"

"Can't you see why?" said Mr Sandbach, patronizingly. "He's afraid of the bookstall clerk catching him at it. He's afraid it's the bookstall clerk that has dropped that half-sovereign. You wait till the bookstall clerk finishes those papers and goes inside, and you'll see."

At this point Mr Gale made the happy involuntary movement of a man who has suddenly thought of something really brilliant.

"Look here," said he. "You said you'd bet. But you didn't bet. I'll bet you a level half-crown I get him to shift this time."

"But you mustn't say anything to him."

"No—of course not."

"Very well, I'll bet you."

Mr Gale walked straight up to the shabby man, drew half-a-sovereign from his waistcoat pocket, and held it out. At the same time he pointed to the shabby man's boots, and then in the most unmistakable way he pointed to the exit of the platform. He said nothing, but his gestures were expressive, and what they clearly expressed was: "I know you've got a half-sovereign under your foot; here's another half-sovereign for you to clear off and ask no questions."

Meanwhile the ingenious offerer of the half-sovereign was meditating thus: "I give half-a-sovereign, but I shall gather up the other half-sovereign, and I shall also win my bet. Net result: Half-a-crown to the good."

The shabby man, who could not have been a fool, comprehended at once, accepted the half-sovereign, and moved leisurely away—

not, however, without glancing at the ground which his feet had covered. The result of the scrutiny evidently much surprised him, as it surprised, in a degree equally violent, both Mr Gale and Mr Sandbach. For there was no sign of half-a-sovereign under the feet of the shabby man. There was not even nine and elevenpence there.

Mr Gale looked up very angry and Mr Sandbach looked very foolish.

"This is all very well," Mr Gale exploded in tones low and fierce. "But I call it a swindle." And he walked, with an undecided, longing, shrinking air, in the wake of the shabby man who had pocketed his half-sovereign.

"I'm sure I saw him put his foot on it," said Mr Sandbach in defence of himself (meaning, of course, the other half-sovereign), "and I've never taken my eyes off him."

"Well, then, how do you explain it?"

"I don't explain it," said Mr Sandbach.

"I think some explanation is due to me," said Mr Gale, with a peculiar and dangerous intonation. "If this is your notion of a practical joke."

"There was no practical joke about it at all," Mr Sandbach protested. "If the half-sovereign has disappeared it's not my fault. I made a bet with you, and I've lost it. Here's your half-crown."

He produced two-and-six, which Mr Gale accepted, though he had a strange impulse to decline it with an air of offended pride.

"I'm still seven-and-six out," said Mr Gale.

"And if you are!" snapped Mr Sandbach, "you thought you'd do me down by a trick. Offering the man ten shillings to go wasn't at all a fair way of winning the bet, and you knew it, my boy. However, I've paid up; so that's all right."

"All I say is," Mr Gale obstinately repeated, "if this is your notion of a practical joke—"

"Didn't I tell you—" Mr Sandbach became icily furious.

The friendship hitherto existing between these two excellent individuals might have been ruined and annihilated for a comparative trifle, had not a surprising and indeed almost miraculous thing happened, by some kind of freak of destiny, in the nick of time. Mr Sandbach was sticking close to Mr Gale, and Mr Gale was following in the leisurely footsteps of the very shabby man, possibly debating within himself whether he should boldly demand the return of his half-sovereign, when lo! a golden coin seemed to slip from the boot of the very shabby man. It took the stone-flags of the platform with scarcely a sound, and Mr Sandbach and Mr Gale made a simultaneous, superb and undignified rush for it. Mr Sandbach got it. The very shabby man passed on, passed eternally out of the lives of the other two. It may be said that he was of too oblivious and dreamy a nature for this world. But one must not forget that he had made a solid gain of ten shillings.

"The soles of the fellow's boots must have been all cracks, and it must have got lodged in one of them," cheerfully explained Mr Sandbach as he gazed with pleasure at the coin. "I hope you believe me now. You thought it was a plant. I hope you believe me now."

Mr Gale made no response to this remark. What Mr Gale said was:

"Don't you think that in fairness that half-sovereign belongs to me?"

"Why?" asked Mr Sandbach, bluntly.

"Well," Mr Gale began, searching about for a reason.

"You didn't find it," Mr Sandbach proceeded firmly. "You didn't see it first. You didn't pick it up. Where do you come in?"

"I'm seven and sixpence out," said Mr Gale.

"And if I give you the coin, which I certainly shall not do, I should be half-a-crown out."

Friendship was again jeopardized, when a second interference of fate occurred, in the shape of a young and pretty woman who was coming from the opposite direction and who astonished both men considerably by stepping in front of them and barring their progress.

"Excuse me," said she, in a charming voice, but with a severe air. "But may I ask if you have just picked up that coin?"

Mr Sandbach, after looking vaguely, as if for inspiration, at Mr Gale, was obliged to admit that he had.

"Well," said the young lady, "if it's dated 1898, and if there's an 'A' scratched on it, it's mine. I've lost it off my watch-chain." Mr Sandbach examined the coin, and then handed it to her, raising his hat. Mr Gale also raised his hat. The young lady's grateful smile was enchanting. Both men were bachelors and invariably ready to be interested.

"It was the first money my husband ever earned," the young lady explained, with her thanks.

The interest of the bachelors evaporated.

"Not a profitable afternoon," said Mr Sandbach, as the train came in and they parted.

"I think we ought to share the loss equally," said Mr Gale.

"Do you?" said Mr Sandbach. "That's like you."

THE BLUE SUIT

I was just going into my tailor's in Sackville Street, when who should be coming out of the same establishment but Mrs Ellis! I was startled, as any man might well have been, to see a lady emerging from my tailor's. Of course a lady might have been to a tailor's to order a tailor-made costume. Such an excursion would be perfectly legal and not at all shocking. But then my tailor did not "make" for ladies. And moreover, Mrs Ellis was not what I should call a tailor-made woman. She belonged to the other variety—the fluffy, lacy, flowing variety. I had made her acquaintance on one of my visits to the Five Towns. She was indubitably elegant, but in rather a Midland manner. She was a fine specimen of the provincial woman, and that was one of the reasons why I liked her. Her husband was a successful earthenware manufacturer. Occasionally he had to make long journeys—to Canada, to Australia and New Zealand—in the interests of his business; so that she was sometimes a grass-widow, with plenty of money to spend. Her age was about thirty-five; bright, agreeable, shrewd, downright, energetic; a little short and a little plump. Wherever she was, she was a centre of interest! In default of children of her own she amused herself with the children of her husband's sister, Mrs Carter. Mr Carter was another successful earthenware manufacturer. Her favourite among nephews and nieces was young Ellis Carter, a considerable local dandy and "dog." Such was Mrs Ellis.

"Are you a widow just now?" I asked her, after we had shaken hands.

"Yes," she said. "But my husband touched at Port Said yesterday, thank Heaven."

"Are you ordering clothes for him to wear on his arrival?" I adopted a teasing tone.

"Can you picture Henry in a Sackville Street suit?" she laughed.

I could not. Henry's clothes usually had the appearance of having been picked up at a Jew's.

"Then what *are* you doing here?" I insisted.

"I came here because I remembered you saying once that this was your tailor's," she said, "so I thought it would be a pretty good place."

Now I would not class my tailor with the half-dozen great tailors of the world, but all the same he is indeed a, pretty good tailor.

"That's immensely flattering," I said. "But what have you been doing with him?"

"Business," said she. "And if you want to satisfy your extraordinary inquisitiveness any further, don't you think you'd better come right away now and offer me some tea somewhere?"

"Splendid," I said. "Where?"

"Oh! The Hanover, of course!" she answered.

"Where's that?" I inquired.

"Don't you know the Hanover Tea-rooms in Regent Street?" she exclaimed, staggered.

I have often noticed that metropolitan resorts which are regarded by provincials as the very latest word of London style, are perfectly unknown to Londoners themselves. She led me along Vigo Street to the Hanover. It was a huge white place, with a number of little alcoves and a large band. We installed ourselves in one of the alcoves, with supplies of China tea and multitudinous cakes, and grew piquantly intimate, and then she explained her visit to my tailor's. I propose to give it here as nearly in her own words as I can.

I

I wouldn't tell you anything about it (she said) if I didn't know from the way you talk sometimes that you are interested in *people*. I mean any people, anywhere. Human nature! Everybody that I come across is frightfully interesting to me. Perhaps that's why I've got so many friends—and enemies. I *have*, you know. I just like watching people to see what they do, and then what they'll do next. I don't seem to mind so much whether they're good or naughty—with me it's their interestingness that comes first. Now I suppose you don't know very much about my nephew, Ellis Carter. Just met him once, I think, and that's all. Don't you think he's handsome? Oh! I do. I think he's very handsome. But then a man and a woman never do agree about what being handsome is in a man. Ellis is only twenty, too. He has such nice curly hair, and his eyes—haven't you noticed his eyes? His father says he's idle. But all fathers say that of their sons. I suppose you'll admit anyhow that he's one of the best-dressed youths in the Five Towns. Anyone might think he got his clothes in London, but he doesn't. It seems there's a simply marvellous tailor in

Bursley, and Ellis and all his friends go to him. His father is always grumbling at the bills, so his mother told me. Well, when I was at their house in July, there happened to come for Ellis one of those fiat boxes that men's tailors always pack suits in, and so I thought I might as well show a great deal of curiosity about it, and I did. And Ellis undid it in the breakfast-room (his father wasn't there) and showed me a lovely blue suit. I asked him to go upstairs and put it on. He wouldn't at first, but his sisters and I worried him till he gave way.

He came downstairs again like Solomon in all his glory. It really was a lovely suit. No—seriously, I'm not joking. It was a dream. He was very shy in it. I must say men are funny. Even when they really *like*having new clothes and cutting a figure, they simply hate putting them on for the first time. Ellis is that way. I don't know how many suits that boy hasn't got—sheer dandyism!—and yet he'll keep a new suit in the house a couple of months before wearing it! Now that's the sort of thing that I call "interesting." So curious, isn't it? Ellis wouldn't keep that suit on. No; as soon as we'd done admiring it he disappeared and changed it.

Now I'd gone that day to ask Ellis to escort me to Llandudno the week after. He likes going about with his auntie, and his auntie likes to have him. And of course she sees that it doesn't cost *him*anything. But his father has to be placated first. There's another funny thing! His father is always grumbling that Ellis is absolutely no good at all at the works, but the moment there's any question of Ellis going away for a holiday—even if it's only a week-end—then his father turns right round and wants to make out that Ellis is absolutely indispensable. Well, I got over his father. I always do, naturally. And it was settled that Ellis and I should go on the next Saturday.

I said to Ellis:

"You must be sure to bring that suit with you."

And then—will you believe me?—he stuck to it he wouldn't! Truly I was under the impression that I could argue either Ellis or his father into any mortal thing. But no! I couldn't argue Ellis into agreeing to bring that suit with him to Llandudno. He said he should wear whites. He said it was a September suit. He said that everybody wore blue at Llandudno, and he didn't want to be mistaken for a schoolmaster! Imagine him being mistaken for a schoolmaster! He even said there were some things I didn't understand! I told him there was a very particular reason why I

531

wanted him to take that suit. And there *was*. He said:

"What is the reason?"

But I wouldn't tell him that. I wasn't going to knuckle down to him altogether. So it ended that we didn't either of us budge. However, I didn't mean to be beaten by a mere curly-headed boy. I can do what I please with his mother, though she *is* my eldest sister-in-law. And before he started in the dogcart to meet me at the station on our way to Llandudno she gave Ellis a bonnet-box to hand to me, and told him to take great care of it. He handed it over to me, and I also told him to take great care of it. Of course he became very curious to know what was in it. I said to him:

"You may see it on the pier on Monday. In fact, I believe you will."

He said: "It's heavy for a hat."

So I informed him that hats were both heavy and large this summer.

He said, "Well, I pity you, auntie!"

Naturally it was his blue suit that was in the box. His mother had burgled it after he'd done his packing, while he was having lunch.

I was determined he *should* wear that suit. And I felt pretty sure that when he saw my *reason* for asking him to bring it he'd be glad at the bottom of his heart that I'd brought it in spite of him. There is one good thing about Ellis—he can see a joke against himself.... Have another cake. Well, I will, then.... Yes, I'm coming to the reason.

II

A girl, you say? Well, of course. But you mustn't look so proud of yourself. A body needn't be anything like so clever as you are to be able to guess that there's a girl in it. Do you suppose I should have imagined for a moment that it would interest you if there hadn't been a girl in it? Not exactly! Well, it's a girl from Winnipeg. Came to England in June with her parents. Or rather, perhaps, her parents came with *her*. I'd never seen any of the three before—didn't know them from Adam and Eve. But my husband had made friends with them out there last year—great friends. And they wanted to make the acquaintance of my husband's wife. I'd gathered from Harry that they were quite my sort.... What *is* my sort? You know perfectly well what my sort is. There are only two sorts of people—

the decent sort and the other sort. Well, they were doing England—
you know, like Colonial people do—seriously, leaving nothing out.
By the way, their name was only "Smith," without even a "y" in it or
an "e" at the end. They wished to try a good seaside place, so I
wrote to them and suggested Llandudno as a fair specimen, and it
was arranged that we should meet there and spend at least a week
together, and afterwards they were to come to the Five Towns. I
suggested we should all stay at Hawthornden's ... Hawthornden's?
Don't you know—it's easily the best private hotel in Llandudno. Lift
and a French chef and all kinds of things; but surely you must have
seen all about it in the papers!

Now that was why I took Ellis with me. I hate travelling about
alone, especially when my husband's away. And it was particularly
on account of the girl that I stole the blue suit. But I didn't tell Ellis a
word about the girl, and I only just mentioned the father and
mother—and not even that until we were safely in the train. These
young dandies are really very nervous and timid at bottom, you
know, in spite of their airs. Ellis would walk ten miles sooner than
have to meet a stranger of the older generation. And he's just as shy
about girls too. I believe most men are, if you ask *me*.

The great encounter occurred in the hall, just before dinner. They
were late, and so were we. I tell you, we were completely outshone.
I tell you, we were not *in* it, not anywhere near being in it! For one
thing, they were in evening-dress. Now at Hawthornden's you never
dress for dinner. There isn't a place in Llandudno where it's the
exception not to dress for dinner. They seemed rather surprised; not
put out, not ashamed of themselves for being too swagger, but just
mildly disappointed with Hawthornden's. The fact is, they didn't
think much of Hawthornden's. I learnt all manner of things during
dinner. They'd been in Scotland when I corresponded with them, but
before that they'd stayed at the Ritz in London, and at the Hotel St
Regis in New York, and the something else—I forget the name—at
Chicago. I was expecting to meet "Colonials," but it was Ellis and I
who were "colonial." I could have borne it better if they hadn't been
so polite, and so anxious to hide their opinion of Hawthornden's.
The girl—oh! the girl.... Her name is Nellie. Really very pretty.
Only about eighteen, but as self-possessed as twenty-eight.
Evidently she had always been used to treating her parents as
equals; she talked quite half the time, and contradicted her mother as
flatly as Ellis contradicts me. Mr Smith didn't talk much. And Ellis

didn't at first—he was too timid and awkward—really not at all like himself. However, Miss Nellie soon made him talk, and they got quite friendly and curt with each other. Curious thing—Ellis never notices women's clothes; very interested in his own, and in other men's, but not in women's! So I expect Nellie's didn't make much impression on him. But truly they were stylish. Much too gorgeous for a young girl—oh! you've no idea!—but not vulgar. They'd been bought in London, in Dover Street. Better than mine, and better than her mother's. I will say this for her—she wore them without any self-consciousness, though she came in for a good deal of staring. Heaven knows what they cost! I'd be afraid to guess. But then you see the Smiths had come to England to spend money, and—well— they were spending it. All their ideas were larger than ours.

When dinner was over Nellie wanted to know what we could do to amuse ourselves. Well, it was a showery night, and of course there was nothing. Then Ellis said, in his patronizing way:

"Suppose we go and knock the balls about a bit?"

And Nellie said, "Knock the balls about a bit?"

"Yes," said Master Ellis, "billiards—you know."

All four of us went to the billiard-room. And Ellis began to knock the balls about a bit. His father installed a billiard-table in his own house a few years ago. The idea was to "keep the boy at home." It didn't, of course, not a bit. Ellis is a pretty good player, but he did nearly all his practising at his club. I've often heard his mother regret the eighty pounds odd that that billiard-table cost.... *I* play a bit, you know. Nellie Smith would not try at first, and Papa Smith was smoking a cigar and he said he couldn't do justice to a cigar and a cue at the same time. So Ellis and I had a twenty-five up. He gave me ten and I beat him—probably because he would keep on smoking cigarettes, just to show Papa Smith how well he could keep the smoke out of his eyes. Then he asked Nellie if she'd "try." She said she would if her pa would. And she and her pa put themselves against Ellis and me.

Well, I'll cut it short. That girl, with her pink-and-white complexion—she began right off with a break of twenty-eight. You should have seen Ellis's face. It was the funniest thing I ever saw in my life. I can't remember anything that ever struck me as half so funny. It seems that they have plenty of time for billiards out in Winnipeg, and a very high-class table. After a while Ellis saw the funniness of it too. He made a miss and then he said:

"Will someone kindly take me out and bury me?"

That kind of speech is supposed to be very smart at his club. And the Smiths thought it was very smart too. Nellie and her pa beat us hollow, and then Nellie began to take her pa to task for showing off with too much screw instead of using the natural angle!

Ellis went to bed. He was very struck by Nellie's talents. But he went to bed. Probably he wanted to think things over, and consider how he could be impressive with her. I should like to have broken it to him about his blue suit, because it was Sunday the next day, and Nellie was bound to be gorgeous for chapel and the pier, and I felt sure he'd be really glad to have that suit—whatever he might *say* to me. And I wanted him to wear it too. But there was no chance for me to tell him. He went off to bed like a streak of lightning. And usually, you know, he simply will not go to bed. Nothing will induce him to go to bed, just as nothing will induce him to get up. I said to myself I would send the suit into his room early in the morning with a note. I did want him to look his best.

And then of course there was the fire. The fire was that very night. What?...

III

Do you actually mean to sit there and tell me you never heard about the fire at Hawthornden's Hotel last July? Why, it was the sensation of the season. There was over a column about it in the *Manchester Guardian*. Everybody talked of it for weeks.... And no one ever told you that we were in it? Half the annexe was burnt down. We were in the annexe, all four of us. I fancy the Smiths had chosen it because the rooms in the annexe are larger. Have you ever been in a fire?... Well, thank your stars! We were wakened up at three o'clock. It was getting light, even. Somehow that made it worse. The confusion—you can't imagine it. We got out all right. Oh! there was no special danger to life and limb. But after all we only *did* get out just in time. And with practically nothing but our dressing-gowns—some not even that! It's queer, in a fire, how at first you try to save things, and keep calm, and pretend you *are* calm, until the thing gets hold of you. I actually began to shovel clothes into my trunks. Somebody said we should have time for that. Well—we hadn't. And it was a very good thing there wasn't a lift in the annexe. It seems a lift well acts like a chimney, and half of us might have been burnt alive.

I must say the fire-brigade was pretty good. They got the fire out very well—very quickly in fact. We women, or most of us, had been bundled into private parlours and things in the main part of the hotel, which wasn't threatened, and when we knew that the fire was out we naturally wanted to go back and see whether any of our things could be saved out of the wreck.

Oh! what a sight it was! What a sight it was! You'd never believe that so much damage could be done in an hour or so. Chiefly by water, of course. All the ground floor was swimming in water. In fact there was a river of it running across the promenade into the sea. About five-sixths of Llandudno, dressed nohow, was on the promenade. However, policemen kept the people outside the gates.

The firemen began bringing trunks down the stairs; they wouldn't let us go up at first. It really was a wonderful scene, at the foot of the stairs, lots of us paddling about in that lake, and perfectly lost to all sense of—what shall I say?—well, correctness. I do believe most of us had forgotten all about civilization. We wanted our things. We wanted our things so badly that we even lost our interest in the origin of the fire and in the question whether we should get anything out of the insurance company. By the way, I mustn't omit to tell you that we never saw the proprietors after the fire was out; the proprietors could only be seen by appointment. The German and Swiss waiters had to bear the brunt of us.

I was very lucky. I received both my trunks nearly at once. They came sliding on a plank down those stairs. And most of my things were in them too. I was determined to be energetic then, and to get out of all that crowd. Do you know what I did? I simply called two men in out of the street, and told them to shoulder my trunks into the main building of the hotel. I defied policemen and the superintendent of the fire-brigade. And in the main building I demanded a bedroom, and I was told that everything would be done to accommodate me as quickly as possible. So I went straight upstairs and told the men to follow me, and I began knocking at every door till I found a room that wasn't occupied, and I took possession of it, and gave the men a shilling a piece. They seemed to expect half-a-crown, because I'd been in a fire, I suppose! Curious ideas odd job men have! Then I dressed myself out of what was left of my belongings and went down again.

All the people said how lucky I was, and what presence of mind I had, and how calm and practical I was, and so on and so on. But they didn't know that I'd been stupid enough not to give a thought to Ellis's blue suit. One can't think of everything, and I didn't think of that. I believe if I had thought of it, at the start, I should have taken the bonnet-box with me at any cost.

I came across Ellis; smoking a cigarette, of course, just to show, I suppose, that a fire was a most ordinary event to him. He was completely dressed, like me. He had saved the whole of his belongings. He said the Smiths were fixing themselves up in private rooms somewhere, and would be down soon. So we moved along into the dining-room and had breakfast. The place was full and noisy. Ellis was exceedingly facetious. He said:

"Well, auntie, did you have a pretty good night?"

Also:

"A fire is a very clumsy way of waking you up in the morning. A bell would be much simpler, and cost less," etcetera, etcetera. And then he said:

"A nice thing, auntie, if I'd followed your advice and brought my beauteous new suit! It would have been bound to be burnt to a cinder. One's best suit always is in a fire."

I ought to have told him then the trick I'd played on him, but I didn't. I merely agreed with him in a lame sort of way that it *would*have been a nice thing if he'd brought his beauteous suit. I hoped that I might be able later on to invent some good excuse, something really plausible, for having brought along with me his newest suit unknown to him. But the more I reflected the more I couldn't think of anything clever enough.

Then the three Smiths came in. There was some queer attire in that dining-room, but I think that Mrs Smith won the gold medal for queerness. All her "colonialness" had come suddenly out. They evidently hadn't been very fortunate. But they didn't seem to mind much. They hadn't thought very highly of the hotel before, and they accepted the fire good-humouredly as one of the necessary drawbacks of a hotel that wasn't quite up to their Winnipeg form. Nellie Smith was delightful. I must say she was delightful, and she looked delightful. She was wearing a blue-and-red striped petticoat, rather short, and a white jersey, and over that a man's blue jacket, which fitted her pretty well. She looked indescribably pert and charming, though the jacket was dirty and stained.

I noticed Ellis staring and staring at that jacket....

I needn't tell you. You can see a mile off what had happened.

Ellis said in his casual way:

"Hello! Where did you pick up that affair, Miss Smith?" Meaning the jacket.

She said she had picked it up on one of the landings, and that there was a pair of continuations lying in a broken bonnet-box just close to it, and that the continuations were ruined by too much water.

I could feel myself blushing redder and redder.

"In a bonnet-box, eh?" said Master Ellis.

Then he said: "Would you mind letting me look at the right-hand breast-pocket of that jacket?"

She didn't mind in the least. He looked at the strip of white linen that your men's tailors always stitch into that pocket with your name and address and date, and age and weight, and I don't know what.

He said, "Thank you."

And she asked him if the jacket was his.

"Yes," he said, "but I hope you'll keep it."

Everybody said what a very curious coincidence! Ellis avoided my eyes, and I avoided his.... Will you believe me that when we "had it out" afterwards, he and I, that boy was seriously angry. He suspected me of a plan "to make the best of him" during the stay with the Smiths, and he very strongly objected to being "made the best of." His notion apparently was that even his worst was easily good enough for my Colonial friends, although, as he'd have said, they *had* "simply wiped the floor with him" in the billiard-room. Anyhow, he was furious. He actually used the word "unwarrantable," and it was rather a long word for a mere stripling of a nephew to use to an auntie who was paying all his expenses. However, he's a nice enough boy at the bottom, and soon got down off his high horse. I must tell you that Nellie Smith wore that jacket all day, quite without any concern. These Colonials don't really seem to mind what they wear. At any rate she didn't. She was just as much at ease in that jacket as she had been in her gorgeousness the evening before. And she and Ellis were walking about together all day. The next day of course we all left. We couldn't stay, seeing the state we were in.... Now, don't you think it's a very curious story?

Thus spake Mrs Ellis across the tea-table in an alcove at the Hanover.

"But you've not finished the story!" I explained.

"Yes, I have," she said.

"You haven't explained what you were doing at my tailor's in Sackville Street."

"Oh!" she cried, "I was forgetting that. Well, I promised Ellis a new suit. And as I wanted to show him that after all I had larger ideas about tailoring than he had, I told him I knew a very good tailor's in Sackville Street—a real West End tailor—and that if he liked he could have his presentation suit made there. He pooh-poohed the offer at first, and pretended that his Bursley tailor was just as good as any of your West End tailors. But at last he accepted. You see—it meant an authorized visit to London.... I'd been into the tailor's just now to pay the bill. That's all."

"But even now," I said, "you haven't finished the story."

"Yes, I have," she replied again.

"What about Nellie Smith?" I demanded. "A story about a handsome girl named Nellie, who could make a break of twenty-eight at billiards, and a handsome dog like Ellis Carter, and a fire, and the girl wearing the youth's jacket—it can't break off like that."

"Look here," she said, leaning a little across the table. "Did you expect them to fall in love with each other on the spot and be engaged? What a sentimental old thing you are, after all!"

"But haven't they seen each other since?"

"Oh yes! In London, and in Bursley too."

"And haven't they—"

"Not yet.... They may or they mayn't. You must remember this isn't the reign of Queen Victoria.... If they *do*, I'll let you know."

THE TIGER AND THE BABY

I

George Peel and Mary, his wife, sat down to breakfast. Their only son, Georgie, was already seated. George the younger showed an astounding disregard for the decencies of life, and a frankly gluttonous absorption in food which amounted to cynicism. Evidently he cared for nothing but the satisfaction of bodily desires. Yet he was twenty-two months old, and occupied a commanding situation in a high chair! His father and mother were aged thirty-two and twenty-eight respectively. They both had pale, intellectual faces; they were dressed with elegance, and their gestures were the gestures of people accustomed to be waited upon and to consider luxuries as necessaries. There was silver upon the table, and the room, though small and somewhat disordered, had in it beautiful things which had cost money. Through a doorway half-screened by a portière could be seen a large studio peopled with heroic statuary, plaster casts, and lumps of clay veiled in wet cloths. And on the other side of the great window of the studio green trees waved their foliage. The trees were in Regent's Park. Another detail to show that the Peels had not precisely failed in life: the time was then ten-thirty o'clock! Millions of persons in London had already been at hard work for hours.

And indeed George Peel was not merely a young sculptor of marked talent; he was also a rising young sculptor. For instance, when you mentioned his name in artistic circles the company signified that it knew whom you meant, and those members of the company who had never seen his work had to feel ashamed of themselves. Further, he had lately been awarded the Triennial Gold Medal of the International Society, an honour that no Englishman had previously achieved. His friends and himself had, by the way, celebrated this dazzling event by a noble and joyous gathering in the studio, at which famous personages had been present.

Everybody knew that George Peel, in addition to what he earned, had important "private resources." For even rising young sculptors cannot live luxuriously on what they gain, and you cannot eat gold medals. Nor will gold medals pay a heavy rent or the cost of manual help in marble cutting. All other rising young sculptors envied

George Peel, and he rather condescended to them (in his own mind) because they had to keep up appearances by means of subterfuges, whereas there was no deception about his large and ample existence.

On the table by Mary's plate was a letter, the sole letter. It had come by the second post. The contents of the first post had been perused in bed. While Mary was scraping porridge off the younger George's bib with a spoon, and wiping porridge out of his eyes with a serviette, George the elder gave just a glance at the letter.

"So he has written after all!" said George, in a voice that tried to be nonchalant.

"Who?" asked Mary, although she had already seen the envelope, and knew exactly what George meant. And her voice also was unnatural in its attempted casualness.

"The old cock," said George, beginning to serve bacon.

"Oh!" said Mary, coming to her chair, and beginning to dispense tea.

She was dying to open the letter, yet she poured out the tea with superhuman leisureliness, and then indicated to Georgie exactly where to search for bits of porridge on his big plate, while George with a great appearance of calm unfolded a newspaper. Then at length she did open the letter. Having read it, she put her lips tighter together, nodded, and passed the letter to George. And George read:

"DEAR MARY,—I cannot accede to your request.—Your affectionate uncle, SAMUEL PEEL.

"P.S.—The expenses connected with my County Council election will be terrible. S.P."

George lifted his eyebrows, as if to indicate that in his opinion there was no accounting for the wild stupidity of human nature, and that he as a philosopher refused to be startled by anything whatever.

"Curt!" he muttered coldly.

Mary uneasily laughed.

"What shall you do?" she inquired.

"Without!" replied George, with a curtness that equalled Mary's uncle's.

"And what about the rent?"

"The rent will have to wait."

A brave young man! Nevertheless he saw in that moment chasms at his feet—chasms in which he and his wife and child and his brilliant prospects might be swallowed up. He changed the subject.

"You didn't see this cutting," he said, and passed a slip from a newspaper gummed to a piece of green paper.

George, in his quality of rising young sculptor, received Press cuttings from an agency. This one was from a somewhat vulgar Society journal, and it gave, in two paragraphs, an account of the recent festivity at George's studio. It finished with the words: "Heidsieck flowed freely." He could not guess who had written it. No! It was not in the nicest taste, but it furnished indubitable proof that George was still rising, that he was a figure in the world. "What a rag!" he observed, with an explosion of repugnance. "Read by suburban shop-girls, I suppose."

II

George had arranged his career in a quite exceptional way. It is true that chance had served him; but then he had known how to make use of chance to the highest advantage. The chance that had served him lay in the facts that Mary Peel had fallen gravely in love with him, that her sole surviving relative was a rich uncle, and that George's surname was the same as hers and her uncle's. He had met niece and uncle in Bursley in the Five Towns, where old Samuel Peel was a personage, and, timidly, a patron of the arts. Having regard to his golden hair and affection-compelling appearance, it was not surprising that Mary, accustomed to the monotony of her uncle's house, had surrendered her heart to him. And it was not surprising that old Peel had at once consented to the match, and made a will in favour of Mary and her offspring. What was surprising was that old Peel should have begun to part with his money at once, and in large quantities, for he was not of a very open-handed disposition.

The explanation of old Samuel Peel's generosity was due to his being a cousin of the Peels of Bursley, the great eighteenth-century family of earthenware manufacturers. The main branch had died out, the notorious Carlotta Peel having expired shockingly in Paris, and another young descendant, Matthew, having been forced under a will to alter his name to Peel-Swynnerton. So that only the distant cousin, Samuel Peel, was left, and he was a bachelor with no prospect of ever being anything else. Now Samuel had made a fortune of his own, and he considered that all the honour and all the historical splendours of the Peel family were concentrated in himself. And he tried to be worthy of them. He tried to restore the family traditions. For this he became a benefactor to his native town, a patron of the arts, and a candidate for the Staffordshire County Council. And when Mary set her young mind on a young man of parts and of ambition, and bearing by hazard the very same name of Peel, old Samuel Peel said to himself: "The old family name will not die out. It ought to be more magnificent than ever." He said this also to George Peel.

Whereupon George Peel talked to him persuasively and sensibly about the risks and the prizes of the sculptor's career. He explained just how extremely ambitious he was, and all that he had already done, and all that he intended to do. And he convinced his uncle-in-law that young sculptors were tremendously handicapped in an expensive and difficult profession by poverty or at least narrowness of means. He convinced his uncle-in-law that the best manner of succeeding was to begin at the top, to try for only the highest things, to sell nothing cheaply, to be haughty with dealers and connoisseurs, and to cut a figure in the very centre of the art-world of London. George was a good talker, and all that he said was perfectly true. And his uncle was dazzled by the immediate prospect of new fame for the ancient family of Peel. And in the end old Samuel promised to give George and Mary five hundred a year, so that George, as a sculptor, might begin at the top and "succeed like success." And George went off with his bride to London, whence he had come. And the old man thought he had done a very noble and a very wonderful thing, which, indeed, he had.

This had occurred when George was twenty-five.

Matters fell out rather as George had predicted. The youth almost at once obtained a commission for three hundred pounds' worth of symbolic statues for the front of the central offices of the Order of Rechabites, which particularly pleased his uncle, because Samuel Peel was a strong temperance man. And George got one or two other commissions.

Being extravagant was to George Peel the same thing as "putting all the profits into the business" is to a manufacturer. He was extravagant and ostentatious on principle, and by far-sighted policy—or, at least, he thought that he was.

And thus the world's rumours multiplied his success, and many persons said and believed that he was making quite two thousand a year, and would be an A.R.A. before he was grey-haired. But

George always related the true facts to his uncle-in-law; he even made them out to be much less satisfactory than they really were. His favourite phrase in letters to his uncle was that he was "building," "building"—not houses, but his future reputation and success.

Then commissions fell off or grew intermittent, or were refused as being unworthy of George's dignity. And then young Georgie arrived, with his insatiable appetites and his vociferous need of doctors, nurses, perambulators, nurseries, and lacy garments. And all the time young George's father kept his head high and continued to be extravagant by far-sighted policy. And the five hundred a year kept coming in regularly by quarterly instalments. Many a tight morning George nearly decided that Mary must write to her uncle and ask for a little supplementary estimate. But he never did decide, partly because he was afraid, and partly from sheer pride. (According to his original statements to his uncle-in-law, seven years earlier, he ought at this epoch to have been in an assured position with a genuine income of thousands.)

But the state of trade worsened, and he had a cheque dishonoured. And then he won the Triennial Gold Medal. And then at length he did arrange with Mary that she should write to old Samuel and roundly ask him for an extra couple of hundred. They composed the letter together; and they stated the reasons so well, and convinced themselves so completely of the righteousness of their cause, that for a few moments they looked on the two hundred as already in hand. Hence the Heidsieck night. But on the morrow of the Heidsieck night they thought differently. And George was gloomy. He felt humiliated by the necessity of the application to his uncle—the first he had ever made. And he feared the result.

His fears were justified.

III

They were far more than justified. Three mornings after the first letter, to which she had made no reply, Mary received a second. It ran:

"DEAR MARY,—And what is more, I shall henceforth pay you three hundred instead of five hundred a year. If George has not made a position for himself it is quite time he had. The Gold Medal must make a lot of difference to him. And if necessary you must economize. I am sure there is room for economy in your household. Champagne, for instance.—Your affectionate uncle, SAMUEL PEEL.

"*P.S.*—I am, of course, acting in your best interests.

"S.P."

This letter infuriated George, so much so that George the younger, observing strange symptoms on his father's face, and strange sounds issuing from his father's mouth, stopped eating in order to give the whole of his attention to them.

"Champagne! What's he driving at?" exclaimed George, glaring at Mary as though it was Mary who had written the letter.

"I expect he's been reading that paper," said Mary.

"Do you mean to say," George asked scornfully, "that your uncle reads a rag like that? I thought all *his* lot looked down on worldliness."

"So they do," said Mary. "But somehow they like reading about it. I believe uncle has read it every week for twenty years."

"Well, why didn't you tell me?"

"The other morning?"

"Yes."

"Oh, I didn't want to worry you. What good would it have done?"

"What good would it have done!" George repeated in accents of terrible disdain, as though the good that it would have done was obvious to the lowest intelligence. (Yet he knew quite well that it would have done no good at all.) "Georgie, take that spoon out of your sleeve."

And Georgie, usually disobedient, took the porridge-laden spoon out of his sleeve and glanced at his mother for moral protection. His mother merely wiped him rather roughly. Georgie thought, once more, that he never in this world should understand grown-up people. And the recurring thought made him cry gently.

George lapsed into savage meditation. During all the seven years of his married life he had somehow supposed himself to be superior, as a man, to his struggling rivals. He had regarded them with easy toleration, as from a height. And now he saw himself tumbling down among them, humiliated. Everything seemed unreal to him then. The studio and the breakfast-room were solid; the waving trees in Regent's Park were solid; the rich knick-knacks and beautiful furniture and excellent food and fine clothes were all solid enough; but they seemed most disconcertingly unreal. One letter from old

Samuel had made them tremble, and the second had reduced them to illusions, or delusions. Even George's reputation as a rising sculptor appeared utterly fallacious. What rendered him savage was the awful injustice of Samuel. Samuel had no right whatever to play him such a trick. It was, in a way, worse than if Samuel had cut off the allowance altogether, for in that case he could at any rate have gone majestically to Samuel and said: "Your niece and her child are starving." But with a minimum of three hundred a year for their support three people cannot possibly starve.

"Ring the bell and have this kid taken out," said he.

Whereupon Georgie yelled.

Kate came, a starched white-and-blue young thing of sixteen.

"Kate," said George, autocratically, "take baby."

"Yes, sir," said Kate, with respectful obedience. The girl had no notion that she was not real to her master, or that her master was saying to himself: "I ought not to be ordering human beings about like this. I can't pay their wages. I ought to be starving in a garret."

When George and Mary were alone, George said: "Look here! Does he mean it?"

"You may depend he means it. It's so like him. Me asking for that£200 must have upset him. And then seeing that about Heidsieck in the paper—he'd make up his mind all of a sudden—I know him so well."

"H'm!" snorted George. "I shall make my mind up all of a sudden, too!"

"What shall you do?"

"There's one thing I shan't do," said George.

"And that is, stop here. Do you realize, my girl, that we shall be absolutely up a gum-tree?"

"I should have thought you would be able—"

"Absolute gum-tree!" George interrupted her. "Simply can't keep the shop open! To-morrow, my child, we go down to Bursley."

"Who?"

"You, me, and the infant."

"And what about the servants?"

"Send 'em home."

"But we can't descend on uncle like that without notice, and him full of his election! Besides, he's cross."

"We shan't descend on him."

"Then where shall you go?"

"We shall put up at the Tiger," said George, impressively.

"The Tiger?" gasped Mary.

George had meant to stagger, and he had staggered.

"The Tiger," he iterated.

"With Georgie?"

"With Georgie."

"But what will uncle say? I shouldn't be surprised if uncle has never been in the Tiger in his life. You know his views—"

"I don't care twopence for your uncle," said George, again implicitly blaming Mary for the peculiarities of her uncle's character. "Something's got to be done, and I'm going to do it."

IV

Two days later, at about ten o'clock in the morning, Samuel Peel, J.P., entered the market-place, Bursley, from the top of Oldcastle Street. He had walked down, as usual, from his dignified residence at Hillport. It was his day for the Bench, and he had, moreover, a lot of complicated election business. On a dozen hoardings between Hillport and Bursley market-place blazed the red letters of his posters inviting the faithful to vote for Peel, whose family had been identified with the district for a century and a half. He was pleased with these posters, and with the progress of canvassing. A slight and not a tall man, with a feeble grey beard and a bald head, he was yet a highly-respected figure in the town. He had imposed himself upon the town by regular habits, strict morals, a reasonable philanthropy, and a successful career. He had, despite natural disadvantages, upheld on high the great name of Peel. So that he entered the town on that fine morning with a certain conquering jauntiness. And citizens saluted him with respect and he responded with benignity.

And as, nearly opposite that celebrated hotel, the Tiger, he was about to cross over to the eastern porch of the Town Hall, he saw a golden-haired man approaching him with a perambulator. And the sight made him pause involuntarily. It was a strange sight. Then he recognized his nephew-in-law. And he blanched, partly from excessive astonishment, but partly from fear.

"How do, uncle?" said George, nonchalantly, as though he had parted from him on the previous evening. "Just hang on to this pram a sec., will you?" And, pushing the perambulator towards Samuel Peel, J.P., George swiftly fled, and, for the perfection of his uncle-in-law's amazement, disappeared into the Tiger.

Then the occupant of the perambulator began to weep.

The figure of Samuel Peel, dressed as a Justice of the Peace should be dressed for the Bench, in a frock-coat and a ceremonious necktie, and (of course) spats over his spotless boots; the figure of Samuel Peel, the wrinkled and dry bachelor (who never in his life had held a saucepan of infant's food over a gas-jet in the middle of the night), this figure staring horror-struck through spectacles at the loud contents of the perambulator, soon excited attention in the market-place of Bursley. And Mr Peel perceived the attention.

He guessed that the babe was Mary's babe, though he was quite incapable of recognizing it. And he could not imagine what George was doing with it (and the perambulator) in Bursley, nor why he had vanished so swiftly into the Tiger, nor why he had not come out again. The whole situation was in the acutest degree mysterious. It was also in the acutest degree amazing. Samuel Peel had no facility in baby-talk, so, to tranquillize Georgie, he attempted soothing strokes or pats on such portions of Georgie's skin as were exposed. Whereupon Georgie shrieked, and even dogs stood still and lifted noses inquiringly.

Then Jos Curtenty, very ancient but still a wag, passed by, and said:

"Hello, Mr Peel. Truth will out. And yet who'd ha' suspected you o' being secretly married!"

Samuel Peel could not take offence, because Jos Curtenty, besides being old and an alderman, and an ex-Mayor, was an important member of his election committee. Of course such a friendly joke from an incurable joker like Jos Curtenty was all right; but supposing enemies began to joke on similar lines—how he might be prejudiced at the polls! It was absurd, totally absurd, to conceive Samuel Peel in any other relation than that of an uncle to a baby; yet the more absurd a slander the more eagerly it was believed, and a slander once started could never be overtaken.

What on earth was George Peel doing in Bursley with that baby? Why had he not announced his arrival? Where was the baby's mother? Where was their luggage? Why, in the name of reason, had George vanished so swiftly into the Tiger, and what in the name of decency and sobriety was he doing in the Tiger such a prodigious time?

It occurred to him that possibly George had written to him and the letter had miscarried.

But in that case, where had they slept the previous night? They could not have come down from London that morning; it was too early.

Little Georgie persevered in the production of yells that might have been heard as far as the Wesleyan Chapel, and certainly as far as the Conservative Club.

Then Mr Duncalf, the Town Clerk, went by, from his private office, towards the Town Hall, and saw the singular spectacle of the public man and the perambulator. Mr Duncalf, too, was a bachelor.

"So you've come down to see 'em," said Mr Duncalf, gruffly, pretending that the baby was not there.

"See whom?"

"Well, your niece and her husband, of course."

"Where are they?" asked Mr Peel, without having; sufficiently considered the consequences of his question.

"Aren't they in the Tiger?" said Mr Duncalf. "They put up there yesterday afternoon, anyhow. But naturally you know that."

He departed, nodding. The baby's extraordinary noise incommoded him and seemed somehow to make him blush if he stood near it.

Mr Peel did not gasp. It is at least two centuries since men gasped from astonishment. Nevertheless, Mr Duncalf with those careless words had simply knocked the breath out of him. Never, never would he have guessed, even in the wildest surmise, that Mary and her husband and child would sleep at the Tiger! The thought unmanned him. What! A baby at the Tiger!

Let it not be imagined for a moment that the Tiger is not an utterly respectable hotel. It is, always was, always will be. Not the faintest slur had ever been cast upon its licence. Still, it had a bar and a barmaid, and indubitably people drank at the bar. When a prominent man took to drink (as prominent men sometimes did), people would say, "He's always nipping into the Tiger!" Or, "You'll see him at the Tiger before eleven o'clock in the morning!" Hence to Samuel Peel, total abstainer and temperance reformer, the Tiger, despite its vast respectability and the reputation of its eighteen-penny ordinary, was a place of sin, a place of contamination; briefly, a "gin palace," if not a "gaming-saloon." On principle, Samuel Peel (as his niece suspected) had never set foot in the Tiger. The thought that his great-nephew and his niece had actually slept there horrified him.

And further and worse; what would people say about Samuel Peel's relatives having to stop at the Tiger, while Samuel Peel's large house up at Hillport was practically empty? Would they not deduce family quarrels, feuds, scandals? The situation was appalling.

He glanced about, but he did not look high enough to see that George was watching him from a second-floor window of the Tiger, and he could not hear Mary imploring George: "Do for goodness sake go back to him." Ladies passed along the pavement, stifling their curiosity. At the back of the Town Hall there began to collect the usual crowd of idlers who interest themselves in the sittings of the police-court.

Then Georgie, bored with weeping, dropped off into slumber. Samuel Peel saw that he could not, with dignity, lift the perambulator up the steps into the porch of the Tiger, and so he began to wheel it cautiously down the side-entrance into the Tiger yard. And in the yard he met George, just emerging from the side-door on whose lamp is written the word "Billiards."

"So sorry to have troubled you, uncle. But the wife's unwell, and I'd forgotten something. Asleep, is he?"

George spoke in a matter-of-fact tone, with no hint whatever that he bore ill-will against Samuel Peel for having robbed him of two hundred a year. And Samuel felt as though he had robbed George of two hundred a year.

"But—but," asked Samuel, "what are you doing here?"

"We're stopping here," said George. "I've come down to look out for some work—modelling, or anything I can get hold of. I shall begin a round of the manufacturers this afternoon. We shall stay here till I can find furnished rooms, or a cheap house. It's all up with sculpture now, you know."

"Why! I thought you were doing excellently. That medal—"

"Yes. In reputation. But it was just now that I wanted money for a big job, and—and—well, I couldn't have it. So there you are. Seven years wasted. But, of course, it was better to cut the loss. I never pretend that things aren't what they are. Mind you, I'm not blaming you, uncle. You're no doubt hard up like other people."

"But—but," Samuel began stammering again. "Why didn't you come straight to me—instead of here?"

George put on a confidential look.

550

"The fact is," said he, "Mary wouldn't. She's vexed. You know how women are. They never understand things—especially money."

"Vexed with me?"

"Yes."

"But why?" Again Samuel felt like a culprit.

"I fancy it must be something you said in your letter concerning champagne."

"It was only what I read about you in a paper."

"I suppose so. But she thinks you meant it to insult her. She thinks you must have known perfectly well that we simply asked the reporter to put champagne in because it looks well—seems very flourishing, you know."

"I must see Mary," said Samuel. "Of course the idea of you staying on here is perfectly ridiculous, perfectly ridiculous. What do you suppose people will say?"

"I'd like you-to-see her," said George. "I wish you would. You may be able to do what I can't. You'll find her in Room 14. She's all dressed. But I warn you she's in a fine state."

"You'd better come too," said Samuel.

George lifted Georgie out of the perambulator.

"Here," said George. "Suppose you carry him to her."

Samuel hesitated, and yielded. And the strange procession started upstairs.

In two hours a cab was taking all the Peels to Hillport.

In two days George and his family were returning to London, sure of the continuance of five hundred a year, and with a gift of two hundred supplementary cash.

But it was long before Bursley ceased to talk of George Peel and his family putting up at the Tiger. And it was still longer before the barmaid ceased to describe to her favourite customers the incredible spectacle of Samuel Peel, J.P., stumbling up the stairs of the Tiger with an infant in his arms.

THE REVOLVER

When friends observed his occasional limp, Alderman Keats would say, with an air of false casualness, "Oh, a touch of the gout."

And after a year or two, the limp having increased in frequency and become almost lameness, he would say, "My gout!"

He also acquired the use of the word "twinge." A scowl of torture would pass across his face, and then he would murmur, "Twinge."

He was proud of having the gout, "the rich man's disease." Alderman Keats had begun life in Hanbridge as a grocer's assistant, a very simple person indeed. At forty-eight he was wealthy, and an alderman. It is something to be alderman of a town of sixty thousand inhabitants. It was at the age of forty-five that he had first consulted his doctor as to certain capricious pains, which the doctor had diagnosed as gout. The diagnosis had enchanted him, though he tried to hide his pleasure, pretending to be angry and depressed. It seemed to Alderman Keats a mark of distinction to be afflicted with the gout. Quite against the doctor's orders he purchased a stock of port, and began to drink it steadily. He was determined that there should be no mistake about his gout; he was determined to have the gout properly and fully. Indulgence in port made him somewhat rubicund and "portly,"—he who had once been a pale little counter-jumper; and by means of shooting-coats, tight gaiters, and the right shape of hat he turned himself into a passable imitation of the fine old English gentleman. His tone altered, too, and instead of being uniformly diplomatic, it varied abruptly between a sort of Cheeryble philanthropy and a sort of Wellingtonian ferocity. During an attack of gout he was terrible in the house, and the oaths that he "rapped out" in the drawing-room could be heard in the kitchen and further. Nobody minded, however, for everyone shared in the glory of his gout, and cheerfully understood that a furious temper was inseparable from gout. Alderman Keats succeeded once in being genuinely laid up with gout. He then invited acquaintances to come and solace him in misfortune, and his acquaintances discovered him with one swathed leg horizontal on a chair in front of his arm-chair, and twinging and swearing like anything, in the very manner of an eighteenth-century squire. And even in that plight he would insist on a glass of port, "to cheat the doctor."

He had two boys, aged sixteen and twelve, and he would allow both of them to drink wine in the evening, saying they must learn to "carry their liquor like gentlemen." When the lad of twelve calmly ordered the new parlour-maid to bring him the maraschino, Alderman Keats thought that that was a great joke.

Quickly he developed into the acknowledged champion of all ancient English characteristics, customs, prejudices and ideals.

It was this habit of mind that led to the revolver.

He saw the revolver *prominent* in the window of Stetton's, the pawnbroker in Crown Square, and the notion suddenly occurred to him that a fine old English gentleman could not be considered complete without a revolver. He bought the weapon, which Stetton guaranteed to be first-rate and fatal, and which was, in fact, pretty good. It seemed to the alderman bright, complex and heavy. He had imagined a revolver to be smaller and lighter; but then he had never handled an instrument more dangerous than a razor. He hesitated about going to his cousin's, Joe Keats, the ironmonger; Joe Keats always laughed at him as if he were a farce; Joe would not be ceremonious, and could not be corrected because he was a relative and of equal age with the alderman. But he was obliged to go to Joe Keats, as Joe made a speciality of cartridges. In Hanbridge, people who wanted cartridges went as a matter of course to Joe's. So Alderman Keats strolled with grand casualness into Joe's, and said:

"I say, Joe, I want some cartridges."

"What for?" the thin Joe asked.

"A barker," the alderman replied, pleased with this word, and producing the revolver.

"Well," said Joe, "you don't mean to say you're going about with that thing in your pocket, you?"

"Why not?"

"Oh! No reason why not! But you ought to be preceded by a chap with a red flag, you know, same as a steam-roller."

And the alderman, ignoring this, remarked with curt haughtiness:

"Every man ought to have a revolver."

Then he went to his tailor and had a right-hand hip-pocket put into all his breeches.

Soon afterwards, walking down Slippery Lane, near the Big Pits, notoriously a haunt of mischief, he had an encounter with a collier who was drunk enough to be insulting and sober enough to be dangerous. In relating the affair afterwards Alderman Keats said:

"Fortunately I had my revolver. And I soon whipped it out, I can tell you."

"And are you really never without your revolver?" he was asked.

"Never!"

"And it's always loaded?"

"Always! What's the good of a revolver if it isn't loaded?"

Thus he became known as the man who never went out without a loaded revolver in his pocket. The revolver indubitably impressed people; it seemed to match the gout. People grew to understand that evil-doers had better look out for themselves if they meant to disturb Alderman Keats, with his gout, and his revolver all ready to be whipped out.

One day Brindley, the architect from Bursley, who knew more about music than revolvers, called to advise the alderman concerning some projected alterations to his stabling—alterations not necessitated by the purchase of a motor-car, for motor-cars were not old English. And somehow, while they were in the stable-yard, the revolver got into the conversation, and Brindley said: "I should like to see you hit something. You'll scarcely believe me, but I've never seen a revolver fired—not with shot in it, I mean."

Alderman Keats smiled bluffly.

"I've been told it's difficult enough to hit even a door with a revolver," said Brindley.

"You see that keyhole," said the alderman, startlingly, pointing to a worn rusty keyhole in the middle of the vast double-doors of the carriage-house.

Brindley admitted that he did see it.

The next moment there was an explosion, and the alderman glanced at the smoking revolver, blew on it suspiciously, and put it back into his celebrated hip-pocket.

Brindley, whom the explosion had intimidated, examined the double-doors, and found no mark.

"Where did you hit?" he inquired.

"Through the keyhole," said the alderman, after a pause. He opened the doors, and showed half a load of straw in the dusk behind them.

"The bullet's imbedded in there," said he.

"Well," said Brindley, "that's not so bad, that isn't."

"There aren't five men in the Five Towns who could do that," the alderman said.

554

And as he said it he looked, with his legs spread apart, and his short-tailed coat, and his general bluff sturdiness, almost as old English as he could have desired to look. Except that his face had paled somewhat. Mr Brindley thought that that transient pallor had been caused by legitimate pride in high-class revolver-shooting. But he was wrong. It had been caused by simple fear. The facts of the matter were that Alderman Keats had never before dared to fire the revolver, and that the infernal noise and the jar on his hand (which had held the weapon too loosely) had given him what is known in the Five Towns as a fearful start. He had offered to shoot on the spur of the moment, without due reflection, and he had fired as a woman might have fired. It was a piece of the most heavenly good fortune that he had put the bullet through the keyhole. Indeed, at first he was inclined to believe that marksmanship must be less difficult than it was reported to be, for his aim had been entirely casual. In saying to Brindley, "You see that keyhole," he had merely been boasting in a jocular style. However, when Brindley left, Brindley carried with him the alderman's reputation as a perfect Wild West shot.

The alderman had it in mind to practise revolver-shooting seriously, until the Keats coachman made a discovery later in the day. The coachman slept over the carriage-house, and on going up the ladder to put on his celluloid collar he perceived a hole in his ceiling and some plaster on his bit of carpet. The window had been open all day. The alderman had not only failed to get the keyhole, he had not only failed to get the double-doors, he had failed to hit any part whatever of the ground floor!

And this unsettled the alderman. This proved to the alderman that the active use of a revolver incurred serious perils. It proved to him that nearly anything might happen with a revolver. He might aim at a lamp-post and hit the town hall clock; he might mark down a burglar and destroy the wife of his affections. There were no limits to what could occur. And so he resolved never to shoot any more. He would still carry the revolver; but for his old English gentlemanliness he would rely less on that than on the gout.

But the whole town (by which I mean the councillors and the leading manufacturers and tradesmen and their sons) had now an interest in the revolver, for Brindley, the architect, had spoken of that which he had seen with his own eyes. Some people accepted the alderman without demur as a great and terrible shot; but others talked about a fluke; and a very small minority mentioned that there was such a thing as blank cartridge. It was the monstrous slander of this minority that induced the alderman to stand up morally for his revolver and to continue talking about it. He suppressed the truth about the damaged ceiling; he deliberately allowed the public to go on believing, with Brindley, that he had aimed at the keyhole and really gone through it, and his conscience was not at all disturbed. But that wicked traducers should hint that he had been using blank cartridge made him furiously indignant, and also exacerbated his gout. And he called on his cousin Joe to prove that he had never spent a penny on blank cartridge.

It was a pity that he dragged the sardonic Joe back into the affair. Joe observed to him that for a man in regular revolver practice he was buying precious few cartridges; and so he had to lay in a stock. Now he dared not employ these cartridges; and yet he wished to make a noise with his revolver in order to convince the neighbourhood that he was in steady practice. Nor dare he buy blank cartridges from Joe. It was not safe to buy blank cartridges anywhere in the Five Towns, so easily does news travel there, and so easily are reputations blown. Hence it happened that Alderman Keats went as far as Crewe specially to buy blank cartridge, and he drowned the ball cartridge secretly in the Birches Pond. To such lengths may a timid man be driven in order to preserve and foster the renown of being a dog of the old sort. All kinds of persons used to hear the barking of the alderman's revolver in his stable-yard, and the cumulative effect of these noises wore down calumny and incredulity. And, of course, having once begun to practise, the alderman could not decently cease. The absurd situation endured. And a coral reef of ball cartridges might have appeared on the surface of Birches Pond had it not been for the visit (at enormous expense) of Hagentodt's ten tigers to the Hanbridge Empire.

This visit, epoch-making in the history of music-hall enterprise in the Five Towns, coincided with the annual venison feast of a society known as Ye Ancient Corporation of Hanbridge, which society had no connection whatever with the real rate-levying corporation, but was a piece of elaborate machinery for dinner-eating. Alderman Keats, naturally, was prominent in the affair of the venison feast. Nobody was better fitted than he to be in the chair at such a solemnity, and in the chair he was, and therein did wonderful things. In putting the loyal toasts he spoke for half an hour concerning the

King's diplomacy, with a reference to royal gout; which was at least unusual. And then, when the feast was far advanced, he uprose, ignoring the toast list, and called upon the assembled company to drink to Old England and Old Port for ever, and a fig for gout! And after this, amid a genial informality, the conversation of a knot of cronies at the Chair end of the table deviated to the noble art of self-defence, and so to revolvers. And the alderman, jolly but still aldermanic, produced his revolver, proving that it went even with his dress-suit.

"Look here," said one. "Is it loaded?"

"Of course," said the alderman.

"Ball cartridge?"

"Of course," said the alderman.

"Well, would you mind putting it back in your pocket—with all this wine and whisky about—"

The alderman complied, proud.

He was limping goutily home with the Vice, at something after midnight, when, as they passed the stage-door of the Empire, both men were aware of fearsome sounds within the building. And the stage-door was ajar. Being personages of great importance, they entered into the interior gloom and collided with the watchman, who was rushing out.

"Is that you, Alderman Keats?" exclaimed the watchman. "Thank Heaven!"

The alderman then learnt that two of Hagentodt's Bengal tigers were having an altercation about a lady, and that it looked like a duel to the death. (Yet one would have supposed that after two performances, at eight-thirty and ten-thirty respectively, those tigers would have been too tired and bored to quarrel about anything whatever.) The watchman had already fetched Hagentodt from his hotel, but Hagentodt's revolver was missing—could not be found anywhere, and the rivals were in such a state of fury that even the unique Hagentodt would not enter their cage without a revolver. Meanwhile invaluable tigers were being mutually destructive, and the watchman was just off to the police-station to borrow a revolver.

The roaring grew terrific.

"Have you got your revolver, Alderman Keats?" asked the watchman.

"No," said the alderman, "I haven't."

"Oh!" said the Vice. "I thought I saw you showing it to your cousin and some others."

At the same moment Joe and some others, equally attracted by the roaring, strolled in.

The alderman hesitated.

"Yes, of course; I was forgetting."

"If you'll lend it to the professor a minute or so?" said the watchman.

The alderman pulled it out of his pocket, and hesitatingly handed it to the watchman, and the watchman was turning hurriedly away with it when the alderman said nervously:

"I'm not sure if it's loaded."

"Well, you're a nice chap!" Joe Keats put in.

"I forget," muttered the alderman.

"We'll soon see," said the watchman, who was accustomed to revolvers. And he opened it. "Yes," glancing into it, "it's loaded right enough."

And turned away again towards the sound of the awful roaring.

"I say," the alderman cried, "I'm afraid it's only blank cartridge."

He might have saved his reputation by allowing the unique Hagentodt to risk his life with a useless revolver. But he had a conscience. A clear conscience was his sole compensation as he faced the sardonic laughter which Joe led and which finished off his reputation as a dog of the old sort. The annoying thing was that his noble self-sacrifice was useless, for immediately afterwards the roaring ceased, Hagentodt having separated the combatants by means of a burning newspaper at the end of a stick. And the curious thing was that Alderman Keats never again mentioned his gout.

AN UNFAIR ADVANTAGE

I

James Peake and his wife, and Enoch Lovatt, his wife's half-sister's husband, and Randolph Sneyd, the architect, were just finishing the usual Saturday night game of solo whist in the drawing-room of Peake's large new residence at Hillport, that unique suburb of Bursley. Ella Peake, twenty-year-old daughter of the house, sat reading in an arm-chair by the fire which blazed in the patent radiating grate. Peake himself was banker, and he paid out silver and coppers at the rate of sixpence a dozen for the brass counters handed to him by his wife and Randolph Sneyd.

"I've made summat on you to-night, Lovatt," said Peake, with his broad easy laugh, as he reckoned up Lovatt's counters. Enoch Lovatt's principles and the prominence of his position at the Bursley Wesleyan Chapel, though they did not prevent him from playing cards at his sister-in-law's house, absolutely forbade that he should play for money, and so it was always understood that the banker of the party should be his financier, supplying him with counters and taking the chances of gain or loss. By this kindly and ingenious arrangement Enoch Lovatt was enabled to live at peace with his conscience while gratifying that instinct for worldliness which the weekly visit to Peake's always aroused from its seven-day slumber into a brief activity.

"Six shillings on my own; five and fourpence on you," said Peake. "Lovatt, we've had a good night; no mistake." He laughed again, took out his knife, and cut a fresh cigar.

"You don't think of your poor wife," said Mrs Peake, "who's lost over three shillings," and she nudged Randolph Sneyd.

"Here, Nan," Peake answered quickly. "You shall have the lot." He dropped the eleven and fourpence into the kitty-shell, and pushed it across the table to her.

"Thank you, James," said Mrs Peake. "Ella, your father's given me eleven and fourpence."

"Oh, father!" The long girl by the fire jumped up, suddenly alert. "Do give me half-a-crown. You've no conception how hard up I am."

"You're a grasping little vixen, that's what you are. Come and give me a light." He gazed affectionately at her smiling flushed face and tangled hair.

When she had lighted his cigar, Ella furtively introduced her thin fingers into his waistcoat-pocket, where he usually kept a reserve of money against a possible failure of his trouser-pockets.

"May I?" she questioned, drawing out a coin. It was a four-shilling piece.

"No. Get away."

"I'll give you change."

"Oh! take it," he yielded, "and begone with ye, and ring for something to drink."

"You are a duck, pa!" she said, kissing him. The other two men smiled.

"Let's have a tune now, Ella," said Peake, after she had rung the bell. The girl dutifully sat down to the piano and sang "The Children's Home." It was a song which always touched her father's heart.

Peake was in one of those moods at once gay and serene which are possible only to successful middle-aged men who have consistently worked hard without permitting the faculty for pleasure to deteriorate through disuse. He was devoted to his colliery, and his commercial acuteness was scarcely surpassed in the Five Towns, but he had always found time to amuse himself; and at fifty-two, with a clear eye and a perfect digestion, his appreciation of good food, good wine, a good cigar, a fine horse, and a pretty woman was unimpaired. On this night his happiness was special; he had returned in the afternoon from a week's visit to London, and he was glad to get back again. He loved his wife and adored his daughter, in his own way, and he enjoyed the feminized domestic atmosphere of his fine new house with exactly the same zest as, on another evening, he might have enjoyed the blue haze of the billiard-room at the Conservative Club. The interior of the drawing-room realized very well Peake's ideals. It was large, with two magnificent windows, practicably comfortable, and unpretentious. Peake despised, or rather he ignored, the aesthetic crazes which had run through fashionable Hillport like an infectious fever, ruthlessly decimating its turned and twisted mahogany and its floriferous carpets and wall-papers. That the soft thick pile under his feet would wear for twenty years, and that the Welsbach incandescent mantles on the chandelier saved thirty per cent, in gas-bills while increasing the light by fifty per cent.: it was these and similar facts which were uppermost in his mind as he gazed round that room, in which every object spoke of solid, unassuming luxury and represented the best value to be obtained for money spent. He desired, of a Saturday night, nothing better than such a room, a couple of packs of cards, and the presence of wife and child and his two life-long friends, Sneyd and Lovatt— safe men both. After cards were over—and on Lovatt's account play ceased at ten o'clock—they would discuss Bursley and Bursley folk with a shrewd sagacity and an intimate and complete knowledge of circumstance not to be found in combination anywhere outside a small industrial town. To listen to Sneyd and Mrs Peake, when each sought to distance the other in tracing a genealogy, was to learn the history of a whole community and the secret springs of the actions which constituted its evolution.

"Haven't you any news for me?" asked Peake, during a pause in the talk. At the same moment the door opened and Mrs Lovatt entered. "Eh, Auntie Lovatt," he went on, greeting her, "we'd given ye up." Mrs Lovatt usually visited the Peakes on Saturday evenings, but she came later than her husband.

"Eh, but I was bound to come and see you to-night, Uncle Peake, after your visit to the great city. Well, you're looking bonny." She shook hands with him warmly, her face beaming goodwill, and then she kissed her half-sister and Ella, and told Sneyd that she had seen him that morning in the market-place.

Mrs Peake and Mrs Lovatt differed remarkably in character and appearance, though this did not prevent them from being passionately attached to one another. Mrs Lovatt was small, and rather plain; content to be her husband's wife, she had no activities beyond her own home. Mrs Peake was tall, and strikingly handsome in spite of her fifty years, with a brilliant complexion and hair still raven black; her energy was exhaustless, and her spirit indomitable; she was the moving force of the Wesleyan Sunday School, and there was not a man in England who could have driven her against her will. She had a fortune of her own. Enoch Lovatt treated her with the respect due to an equal who had more than once proved herself capable of insisting on independence and equal rights in the most pugnacious manner.

"Well, auntie," said Peake, "I've won eleven and fourpence to-night, and my wife's collared it all from me." He laughed with glee.

"Eh, you should be ashamed!" said Mrs Lovatt, embracing the company in a glance of reproof which rested last on Enoch Lovatt. She was a Methodist of the strictest, and her husband happened to be chapel steward. "If I had my way with those cards I'd soon play with them; I'd play with them at the back of the fire. Now you were asking for news when I came in, Uncle Peake. Have they told you about the new organ? We're quite full of it at our house."

"No," said Peake, "they haven't."

"What!" she cried reproachfully. "You haven't told him, Enoch—nor you, Nan?"

"Upon my word it never entered my head," said Mrs Peake.

"Well, Uncle Peake," Mrs Lovatt began, "we're going to have a new organ for the Conference."

"Not before it's wanted," said Peake. "I do like a bit of good music at service, and Best himself couldn't make anything of that old wheezer we've got now."

"Is that the reason we see you so seldom at chapel?" Mrs Lovatt asked tartly.

"I was there last Sunday morning."

"And before that, Uncle Peake?" She smiled sweetly on him.

Peake was one of the worldlings who, in a religious sense, existed precariously on the fringe of the Methodist Society. He rented a pew, and he was never remiss in despatching his wife and daughter to occupy it. He imagined that his belief in the faith of his fathers was unshaken, but any reference to souls and salvation made him exceedingly restless and uncomfortable. He could not conceive himself crowned and harping in Paradise, and yet he vaguely surmised that in the last result he would arrive at that place and state, wafted thither by the prayers of his womenkind. Logical in all else, he was utterly illogical in his attitude towards the spiritual—an attitude which amounted to this: "Let a sleeping dog lie, but the animal isn't asleep and means mischief."

He smiled meditatively at Mrs Lovatt's question, and turned it aside with another.

"What about this organ?"

"It's going to cost nine hundred pounds," continued Mrs Lovatt, "and Titus Blackhurst has arranged it all. It was built for a hall in Birmingham, but the manufacturers have somehow got it on their hands. Young Titus the organist has been over to see it, and he says it's a bargain. The affair was all arranged as quick as you please at the Trustees' meeting last Monday. Titus Blackhurst said he would give a hundred pounds if eight others would do the same within a fortnight—it must be settled at once. As Enoch said to me afterwards, it seemed, as soon as Mr Blackhurst had made his speech, that we *must* have that organ. We really couldn't for shame to show up with the old one again at *this* Conference—don't you remember the funny speech the President made about it at the last Conference, eleven years ago? Of course he was very polite and nice with his sarcasm, but I'm sure he meant us to take the hint. Now, would you believe, seven out of those eight subscriptions were promised by Wednesday morning! I think that was just splendid!"

"Well, well!" exclaimed Peake, genuinely amazed at this proof of religious vitality. "Who are the subscribers?"

"I'm one," said Enoch Lovatt, quietly, but with unconcealed pride.

"And I'm another," said Mrs Lovatt. "Bless you, I should have been ashamed of myself if I hadn't responded to such an appeal. You may say what you like about Titus Blackhurst—I know there's a good many that don't like him—but he's a real good sort. I'm sure he's the best Sunday School superintendent we ever had. Then there's Mr Clayton-Vernon, and Alderman Sutton, and young Henry Mynors and—"

"And Eardley Brothers—they're giving a hundred apiece," put in Lovatt, glancing at Randolph Sneyd.

"I wish they'd pay their debts first," said Peake, with sudden savageness.

"They're all right, I suppose?" said Sneyd, interested, and leaning over towards Peake.

"Oh, they're all *right*," Peake said testily. "At least, I hope so," and he gave a short, grim laugh. "But they're uncommon slow payers. I sent 'em in an account for coal only last week—three hundred and fifty pound. Well, auntie, who's the ninth subscriber?"

"Ah, that's the point," said Enoch Lovatt. "The ninth isn't forthcoming."

Mrs Lovatt looked straight at her sister's husband. "We want you to be the ninth," she said.

"Me!" He laughed heartily, perceiving a broad humour in the suggestion.

"Oh, but I mean it," Mrs Lovatt insisted earnestly. "Your name was mentioned at the trustees' meeting, wasn't it, Enoch?"

"Yes," said Lovatt, "it was."

"And dost mean to say as they thought as I 'ud give 'em a hundred pound towards th' new organ?" said Peake, dropping into dialect.

"Why not?" returned Mrs Lovatt, her spirit roused. "I shall. Enoch will. Why not you?"

"Oh, you're different. You're *in* it."

"You can't deny that you're one of the richest pew-holders in the chapel. What's a hundred pound to you? Nothing, is it, Mr Sneyd? When Mr Copinger, our superintendent minister, mentioned it to me yesterday, I told him I was sure you would consent."

"You did?"

"I did," she said boldly.

"Well, I shanna'."

Like many warm-hearted, impulsive and generous men, James Peake did not care that his generosity should be too positively assumed. To take it for granted was the surest way of extinguishing it. The pity was that Mrs Lovatt, in the haste of her zeal for the amelioration of divine worship at Bursley Chapel, had overlooked this fact. Peake's manner was final. His wife threw a swift glance at Ella, who stood behind her father's chair, and received a message back that she too had discerned finality in the tone.

Sneyd got up, and walking slowly to the fireplace emitted the casual remark: "Yes, you will, Peake."

He was a man of considerable education, and though in neither force nor astuteness was he the equal of James Peake, it often pleased him to adopt towards his friend a philosophic pose—the pose of a seer, of one far removed from the trivial disputes in which the colliery-owner was frequently concerned.

"Yes, you will, Peake," he repeated.

"I shanna', Sneyd."

"I can read you like a book, Peake." This was a favourite phrase of Sneyd's, which Peake never heard without a faint secret annoyance. "At the bottom of your mind you mean to give that hundred. It's your duty to do so, and you will. You'll let them persuade you."

"I'll bet thee a shilling I don't."

"Done!"

"Ssh!" murmured Mrs Lovatt, "I'm ashamed of both of you, betting on such a subject—or on any subject," she added. "And Ella here too!"

"It's a bet, Sneyd," said Peake, doggedly, and then turned to Lovatt. "What do you say about this, Enoch?"

But Enoch Lovatt, self-trained to find safety in the middle, kept that neutral and diplomatic silence which invariably marked his demeanour in the presence of an argument.

"Now, Nan, you'll talk to James," said Mrs Lovatt, when they all stood at the front-door bidding good-night.

"Nay, I've nothing to do with it," Mrs Peake replied, as quickly as at dinner she might have set down a very hot plate. In some women profound affection exists side by side with a nervous dread lest that affection should seem to possess the least influence over its object.

II

Peake dismissed from his mind as grotesque the suggestion that he should contribute a hundred pounds to the organ fund; it revolted his sense of the fitness of things; the next morning he had entirely forgotten it. But two days afterwards, when he was finishing his midday dinner with a piece of Cheshire cheese, his wife said:

"James, have you thought anything more about that organ affair?" She gave a timid little laugh.

He looked at her thoughtfully for a moment, holding a morsel of cheese on the end of his knife; then he ate the cheese in silence.

"Nan," he said at length, rather deliberately, "have they been trying to come round you? Because it won't work. Upon my soul I don't know what some people are dreaming of. I tell you I never was more surprised i' my life than when your sister made that suggestion. I'll give 'em a guinea towards their blooming organ if that's any use to 'em. Ella, go and see if the horse is ready."

"Yes, father."

He felt genuinely aggrieved.

"If they'd get a new organist," he remarked, with ferocious satire, five minutes later, as he lit a cigar, "and a new choir—I could see summat in that."

In another minute he was driving at a fine pace towards his colliery at Toft End. The horse, with swift instinct, had understood that to-day its master was not in the mood for badinage.

Half-way down the hill into Shawport he overtook a lady walking very slowly.

"Mrs Sutton!" he shouted in astonishment, and when he had finished with the tense frown which involuntarily accompanied the effort of stopping the horse dead within its own length, his face softened into a beautiful smile. "How's this?" he questioned.

"Our mare's gone lame," Mrs Sutton answered, "and as I'm bound to get about I'm bound to walk."

He descended instantly from the dogcart. "Climb up," he said, "and tell me where you want to go to."

"Nay, nay."

"Climb up," he repeated, and he helped her into the dogcart.

"Well," she said, laughing, "what must be, must. I was trudging home, and I hope it isn't out of your way."

"It isn't," he said; "I'm for Toft End, and I should have driven up Trafalgar Road anyhow."

Mrs Sutton was one of James Peake's ideals. He worshipped this small frail woman of fifty-five, whose soft eyes were the mirror of as candid a soul as was ever prisoned in Staffordshire clay. More than forty years ago he had gone to school with her, and the remembrance of having kissed the pale girl when she was crying over a broken slate was still vivid in his mind. For nearly half a century she had remained to him exactly that same ethereal girl. The sole thing about her that puzzled him was that she should have found anything attractive in the man whom she allowed to marry her—Alderman Sutton. In all else he regarded her as an angel. And to many another, besides James Peake, it seemed that Sarah Sutton wore robes of light. She was a creature born to be the succour of misery, the balm of distress. She would have soothed the two thieves on Calvary. Led on by the bounteous instinct of a divine, all-embracing sympathy, the intrepid spirit within her continually forced its fragile physical mechanism into an activity which appeared almost supernatural. According to every rule of medicine she should have been dead long since; but she lived—by volition. It was to the credit of Bursley that the whole town recognized in Sarah Sutton the treasure it held.

"I wanted to see you," Mrs Sutton said, after they had exchanged various inquiries.

"What about?"

566

"Mrs Lovatt was telling me yesterday you hadn't made up your mind about that organ subscription." They were ascending the steepest part of Oldcastle Street, and Peake lowered the reins and let the horse into awalk.

"Now look here, Mrs Sutton," he began, with passionate frankness, "I can talk to you. You know me; you know I'm not one of their set, as it were. Of course I've got a pew and all that; but you know as well as I do that I don't belong to the chapel lot. Why should they ask me? Why should they come to me? Why should I give all that sum?"

"Why?" she repeated the word, smiling. "You're a generous man; you've felt the pleasure of giving. I always think of you as one of the most generous men in the town. I'm sure you've often realized what a really splendid thing it is to be able to give. D'you know, it comes over me sometimes like a perfect shock that if I couldn't give—something, do—something, I shouldn't be able to live; I would be obliged to go to bed and die right off."

"Ah!" he murmured, and then paused. "We aren't all like you, Mrs Sutton. I wish to God we were. But seriously, I'm not for giving that hundred; it's against my grain, and that's flat—you'll excuse me speaking plain."

"I like it," she said quickly. "Then I know where I am."

"No," he reiterated firmly, "I'm not for giving that hundred."

"Then I'm bound to say I'm sorry," she returned kindly. "The whole scheme will be ruined, for it's one of those schemes that can only be carried out in a particular way—if they aren't done on the inspiration of the moment they're not done at all. Not that I care so much for the organ itself. It's the idea that was so grand. Fancy—nine hundred pounds all in a minute; such a thing was never known in Bursley Chapel before!"

"Well," said Peake, "I guess when it comes to the pinch they'll find someone else instead of me."

"They won't; there isn't another man who could afford it and trade so bad."

Peake was silent; but he was inflexible. Not even Mrs Sutton could make the suggestion of this subscription seem other than grossly unfair to him, an imposition on his good-nature.

"Think it over," she said abruptly, after he had assisted her to alight at the top of Trafalgar Road. "Think it over, to oblige me."

"I'd do anything to oblige you," he replied. "But I'll tell you this"—he put his mouth to her ear and whispered, half-smiling at the confession. "You call me a generous man, but whenever that organ's mentioned I feel just like a miser—yes, as hard as a miser. Goodbye! I'm very glad to have had the pleasure of driving you up." He beamed on her as the horse shot forward.

III

This was on Tuesday. During the next few days Peake went through a novel and very disturbing experience. He gradually became conscious of the power of that mysterious and all-but-irresistible moral force which is called public opinion. His own public of friends and acquaintances connected with the chapel seemed to be, for some inexplicable reason, against him on the question of the organ subscription. They visited him, even to the Rev. Mr Copinger (whom he heartily admired as having "nothing of the parson" about him), and argued quietly, rather severely, and then left him with the assurance that they relied on his sense of what was proper. He was amazed and secretly indignant at this combined attack. He thought it cowardly, unscrupulous; it resembled brigandage. He felt most acutely that no one had any right to demand from him that hundred pounds, and that they who did so transgressed one of those unwritten laws which govern social intercourse. Yet these transgressors were his friends, people who had earned his respect in years long past and kept it through all the intricate situations arising out of daily contact. They could defy him to withdraw his respect now; and, without knowing it, they did. He was left brooding, pained, bewildered. The explanation was simply this: he had failed to perceive that the grandiose idea of the ninefold organ fund had seized, fired, and obsessed the imaginations of the Wesleyan community, and that under the unwonted poetic stimulus they were capable of acting quite differently from their ordinary selves.

Peake was perplexed, he felt that he was weakening; but, being a man of resourceful obstinacy, he was by no means defeated. On Friday morning he told his wife that he should go to see a customer at Blackpool about a contract, and probably remain at the seaside for the week-end. Accustomed to these sudden movements, she packed his bag without questioning, and he set off for Knype station in the dogcart. Once behind the horse he felt safe, he could breathe again. The customer at Blackpool was merely an excuse to enable him to escape from the circle of undue influence. Ardently desiring to be in the train and on the other side of Crewe, he pulled up at his little order-office in the market-place to give some instructions. As he did so his clerk, Vodrey, came rushing out and saw him.

"I have just telephoned to your house, sir," the clerk said excitedly. "They told me you were driving to Knype and so I was coming after you in a cab."

"Why, what's up now?"

"Eardley Brothers have called their creditors together."

"*What?*"

"I've just had a circular-letter from them, sir."

Peake stared at Vodrey, and then took two steps forward, stamping his feet.

"The devil!" he exclaimed, with passionate ferocity. "The devil!"

Other men of business, besides James Peake, made similar exclamations that morning; for the collapse of Eardley Brothers, the great earthenware manufacturers, who were chiefly responsible for the ruinous cutting of prices in the American and Colonial markets, was no ordinary trade fiasco. Bursley was staggered, especially when it learnt that the Bank, the inaccessible and autocratic Bank, was an unsecured creditor for twelve thousand pounds.

Peake abandoned the Blackpool customer and drove off to consult his lawyer at Hanbridge; he stood to lose three hundred and fifty pounds, a matter sufficiently disconcerting. Yet, in another part of his mind, he felt strangely serene and happy, for he was sure now of winning his bet of one shilling with Randolph Sneyd. In the first place, the failure of Eardleys would annihilate the organ scheme, and in the second place no one would have the audacity to ask him for a subscription of a hundred pounds when it was known that he would be a heavy sufferer in the Eardley bankruptcy.

Later in the day he happened to meet one of the Eardleys, and at once launched into a stream of that hot invective of which he was a master. And all the while he was conscious of a certain hypocrisy in his attitude of violence; he could not dismiss the notion that the Eardleys had put him under an obligation by failing precisely at this juncture.

IV

On the Saturday evening only Sneyd and Mrs Lovatt came up to Hillport, Enoch Lovatt being away from home. Therefore there were no cards; they talked of the Eardley affair.

"You'll have to manage with the old organ now," was one of the first things that Peake said to Mrs Lovatt, after he had recited his own woe. He smiled grimly as he said it.

"I don't see why," Sneyd remarked. It was not true; he saw perfectly; but he enjoyed the rousing of Jim Peake into a warm altercation.

"Not at all," said Mrs Lovatt, proudly. "We shall have the organ, I'm sure. There was an urgency committee meeting last night. Titus Blackhurst has most generously given another hundred; he said it would be a shame if the bankruptcy of professed Methodists was allowed to prejudice the interests of the chapel. And the organ-makers have taken fifty pounds off their price. Now, who do you think has given another fifty? Mr Copinger! He stood up last night, Mr Blackhurst told me this morning, and he said, 'Friends, I've only seventy pounds in the world, but I'll give fifty pounds towards this organ.' There! What do you think of that? Isn't he a grand fellow?"

"He is a grand fellow," said Peake, with emphasis, reflecting that the total income of the minister could not exceed three hundred a year.

"So you see you'll *have* to give your hundred," Mrs Lovatt continued. "You can't do otherwise after that."

There was a pause.

"I won't give it," said Peake. "I've said I won't, and I won't."

He could think of no argument. To repeat that Eardley's bankruptcy would cost him dear seemed trivial. Nevertheless, the absence of any plausible argument served only to steel his resolution.

At that moment the servant opened the door.

"Mr Titus Blackhurst, senior, to see you, sir."

Peake and his wife looked at one another in amazement, and Sneyd laughed quietly.

"He told me he should come up," Mrs Lovatt explained.

"Show him into the breakfast-room, Clara," said Mrs Peake to the servant.

570

Peake frowned angrily as he crossed the hall, but as he opened the breakfast-room door he contrived to straighten out his face into a semblance of urbanity. Though he could have enjoyed accelerating the passage of his visitor into the street, there were excellent commercial reasons why he should adopt a less strenuous means towards the end which he had determined to gain.

"Glad to see you, Mr Blackhurst," he began, a little awkwardly.

"You know, I suppose, what I've come for, Mr Peake," said the old man, in that rich, deep, oily voice of which Mrs Lovatt, in one of those graphic phrases that came to her sometimes, had once remarked that it must have been "well basted in the cooking."

"I suppose I do," Peake answered diffidently.

Mr Blackhurst took off a wrinkled black glove, stroked his grey beard, and started on a long account of the inception and progress of the organ scheme. Peake listened and was drawn into an admission that it was a good scheme and deserved to succeed. Mr Blackhurst then went on to make plain that it was in danger of utterly collapsing, that only one man of "our Methodist friends" could save it, and that both Mrs Sutton and Mrs Lovatt had advised him to come and make a personal appeal to that man.

Peake knew of old, and in other affairs, the wily diplomatic skill of this Sunday School superintendent, and when Mr Blackhurst paused he collected himself for an effort which should conclude the episode at a stroke.

"The fact is," he said, "I've decided that I can't help you. It's no good beating about the bush, and so I tell you this at once. Mind you, Mr Blackhurst, if there's anyone in Bursley that I should have liked to oblige, it's you. We've had business dealings, you and me, for many years now, and I fancy we know one another. I've the highest respect for you, and if you'll excuse me saying so, I think you've some respect for me. My rule is always to be candid. I say what I mean and I mean what I say; and so, as I've quite made up my mind, I let you know straight off. I can't do it. I simply *can't* do it."

"Of course if you put it that way, if you *can't*—"

"I do put it that way, Mr Blackhurst," Peake continued quickly, warming himself into eloquence as he perceived the most effective line to pursue. "I admire your open-handedness. It's an example to us all. I wish I could imitate it. But I mustn't. I'm not one o' them as rushes out and promises a hundred pound before they've looked at their profit and loss account. Eardleys, for example. By the way, I'm pleased to hear from Sneyd that you aren't let in there. I'm one of the flats. Three hundred and fifty pound—that's my bit; I'm told they won't pay six shillings in the pound. Isn't that a warning? What right had they to go offering their hundred pound apiece to your organ fund?"

"It was very wrong," said Mr Blackhurst, severely, "and what's more, it brings discredit on the Methodist society."

"True!" agreed Peake, and then, leaning over confidentially, he spoke in a different voice: "If you ask me, I don't mind saying that I think that magnificent subscription o' theirs was a deliberate and fraudulent attempt to inspire pressing creditors with fresh confidence. That's what I think. I call it monstrous."

Mr Blackhurst nodded slowly, as though meditating upon profound truths ably expressed.

"Well," Peake resumed, "I'm not one of that sort. If I can afford to give, I give; but not otherwise. How do I know how I stand? I needn't tell you, Mr Blackhurst, that trade in this district is in a very queer state—a very queer state indeed. Outside yourself, and Lovatt, and one or two more, is there a single manufacturer in Bursley that knows how he stands? Is there one of them that knows whether he's making money or losing it? Look at prices; can they go lower? And secret discounts; can they go higher? And all this affects the colliery-owners. I shouldn't like to tell you the total of my book-debts; I don't even care to think of it. And suppose there's a colliers' strike—as there's bound to be sooner or later—where shall we be then?"

Mr Blackhurst nodded once more, while Peake, intoxicated by his own rhetoric, began actually to imagine that his commercial condition was indeed perilous.

"I've had several very severe losses lately," he went on. "You know I was in that newspaper company; that was a heavy drain; I've done with newspapers for ever more. I was a fool, but calling myself a fool won't bring back what I've lost. It's got to be faced. Then there's that new shaft I sunk last year. What with floodings, and flaws in the seam, that shaft alone is running me into a loss of six pound a week at this very moment, and has been for weeks."

"Dear me!" exclaimed Mr Blackhurst, sympathetically.

"Yes! Six pound a week! And that isn't all"—he had entirely forgotten the immediate object of Mr Blackhurst's visit—"that isn't all. I've got a big lawsuit coming on with the railway company. Goodness knows how that will end! If I lose it ... well!"

"Mr Peake," said the old man, with quiet firmness, "if things are as bad as you say we will have a word of prayer."

He knelt down and forthwith commenced to intercede with God on behalf of this luckless colliery-owner, his business, his family, his soul.

Peake jumped like a shot rabbit, reddening to the neck with stupefaction, excruciating sheepishness and annoyance. Never in the whole course of his life had he been caught in such an ineffable predicament. He strode to and fro in futile speechless rage and shame. The situation was intolerable. He felt that at no matter what cost he must get Titus Blackhurst up from his knees. He approached him, meaning to put a hand on his shoulder, but dared not do so. Inarticulate sounds escaped from his throat, and then at last he burst out:

"Stop that, stop that! I canna stand it. Here, I'll give ye a cheque for a hundred. I'll write it now."

When Mr Blackhurst had departed he rang for a brandy-and-soda, and then, after an interval, returned to the drawing-room.

"Sneyd," he said, trying to laugh, "here's your shilling. I've lost."

"There!" exclaimed Mrs Lovatt. "Didn't I say that Mr Copinger's example would do it? Eh, James! Bless you!"

17876424R00306

Printed in Great Britain
by Amazon